Golden Vampires of Tuscany Series

Books 1–4

S. Hamil

Books by S. Hamil (Sharon Hamilton's twisted sister):

GOLDEN VAMPIRES OF TUSCANY SERIES
Honeymoon Bite Book 1
Mortal Bite Book 2
Christmas Bite Book 3
Midnight Bite Book 4
(New!) Golden Vampires of Tuscany bundle, Books 1-4

THE GUARDIANS
Heavenly Lover Book 1
Underworld Lover Book 2
Underworld Queen Book 3
Redemption Book 4
(Coming soon!) The Guardians bundle, Books 1–4

Immortal Valentines: Paranormal Super Bundle

Gideon: Heavenly Fall

SEAL Of Time Trident Legacy

Books by Sharon Hamilton:

SEAL BROTHERHOOD SERIES
Accidental SEAL Book 1
Fallen SEAL Legacy Book 2
SEAL Under Covers Book 3
SEAL The Deal Book 4
Cruisin' For A SEAL Book 5
SEAL My Destiny Book 6
SEAL of My Heart Book 7
Fredo's Dream Book 8
SEAL My Love Book 9
SEAL Encounter Prequel to Book 1
SEAL Endeavor Prequel to Book 2
Ultimate SEAL Collection Vol. 1 Books 1-4 /2 Prequels
Ultimate SEAL Collection Vol. 2 Books 5-7

BONE FROG BACHELOR SERIES
Bone Frog Bachelor Book 0.5
Unleashed Book 1
Restored Book 2
Revenge Book 3

STAND ALONE BOOKS & SERIES
Love Me Tender, Love You Hard
SEAL's Goal: The Beautiful Game
True Blue SEALS Zak
Nashville SEAL: Jameson

All of the above books are available on Audible, narrated by the talented J.D. Hart.

About the Series

Honeymoon Bite

Anne caught her husband cheating with the maid of honor before their wedding cake was cut. She decided to take her planned and paid for honeymoon in Tuscany, alone. On the evening of what was to be her wedding night, she gets bitten by a female vampire.

Marcus Monteleone has waited three hundred years to find his fated female, only to discover her dying in his arms. He saves Anne's life by turning her, and then works to gain her trust, to cope with being a newly-formed golden vampire.

But when Anne finds out Marcus has not been completely truthful about his past, she vows to live as a human, and shuns the vampire world. Alone and unprotected, she falls prey to the very villainess who took her human soul, and who now takes the only man she's ever loved.

Which lover will have to make the ultimate sacrifice to save the other before they both are lost?

Mortal Bite

Golden Vampire Paolo Monteleone begins raising a son he did not know he fathered, after the murder of the boy's mother. He meets a beautiful human college professor, Carabella Sampson, at a Halloween costume ball. She is an expert on vampire lore, but doesn't believe in their existence. Paolo dresses up as himself: a vampire. Carabella Sampson thinks the attraction she holds for the dark gentleman she meets at the party is due to the fact that the man is a great actor with killer looks and an experienced way with women. He has all the little preternatural signs that she refuses to believe, since vampires are myth and the man she's falling for is real flesh and blood. A dark coven leader has targeted her for elimination, before she can reveal secrets of the Golden Vampire lineage she has obtained from an ancient book. Can there be a happily ever after if either his lover or his young son has to pay the ultimate sacrifice to protect the Golden Vampire race? And will he be able to live with himself if he has to choose between them?

Christmas Bite

He is the eldest brother of three orphaned dark vampire waifs, bound by a lifetime vow of service to protect the offspring of the Golden Vampire Monteleone family. This is a debt that Lionel Jett can never discharge.

Phoebe Monteleone is a nineteen year old virgin, a Golden who has not taken the turning and who appears identical to her ancient great-great-grandmother, Maria Monteleone. Lionel Jett once harbored a secret and platonic love for Maria, who died as a mortal over three centuries ago.

The two vampire races are forbidden to mate, yet Phoebe and Lionel's attraction risks their very souls. In addition, the war brewing between the two species threatens the entire vampire society. When the two worlds collide, who will win out? Will their brief affair be worth an eternity of damnation? Or, can duty and honor leave room for love or the possibility of a happily ever after?

Midnight Bite

He's her husband by convenience…

But their love is real.

They're of two different species in a union they're not allowed to consummate…

But somehow, they'll find their way to a Happily Ever After…

Is being together worth giving up immortality?

Or their very souls?

Under the skies of California Wine Country comes this vampiric tale of a three-hundred-year-old love story like Romeo and Juliet, as two star-crossed lovers break all the rules, while the Dark and Golden Vampire wars loom. Under the burden of a centuries-old prophecy in the newly discovered Book of Spawn, either a miracle or a tragedy will be born.

For Lionel must sacrifice himself to protect her to the bitter end and Phoebe will have her Romeo, no matter the cost.

Table of Contents

Honeymoon Bite

Golden Vampires of Tuscany
Book 1

S. Hamil

Dedication

I want to thank my friend and early critique partner, Tina Folsom, for helping me bring my vampires to life. To my Street Team for adopting this author and helping to spread the word. You guys are the best friends a writer could ever wish for in ten lifetimes.

Thanks to my Tuesday Group: Arletta, Kent, Robin, Ronn, and Shane. And to Marlene Cullen for bringing us together in the first place. To Pam and Rochelle for their critical eyes.

Also to my husband for his immortal support and for putting up with the interference from other family members who said, "She's writing *what?*"

Chapter 1

ANNE LOOKED DOWN on the sleeping form of her new husband and, God help her, he looked like the first man she would murder. Nestled into his arms was the naked body of her maid of honor.

This made the second time today the bride had caught them together. First was at the reception. In the bathroom.

Monika's dress and Robert's tux were trampled and splayed over the chair and floor, along with a spilled bottle of champagne, cream satin shoes, a long taffeta slip, a hot pink push-up bra, and Robert's new black socks.

"Not exactly what a bride wants to see on her wedding day." Anne spoke without emotion. These weren't the soft lilting tones she'd gushed when reciting her wedding vows that afternoon. Her statement caused the reaction she'd hoped for. Monika bolted up, her eyes crossed but wide open. She clutched a sheet to her chest. Robert scrambled to the floor.

"Don't bother to put your pants on," Anne delivered.

"Honey—Anne," Robert said in his I'm-so-sorry-I-got-caught voice. His tanned face used to melt her insides, like when he smiled and it was if the sun had come out from behind the clouds. But today his charm wasn't going to work. The bride had murder on her mind.

"I'm so glad you're all right. We were—" Robert began.

"I'm fine. I can see how worried you are. Touching." Taffeta and satin rustled as Anne reached down to the handle of her wardrobe roller, stuffed to bursting with brand new clothes for her honeymoon, most with tags still on them. She made sure her money, passport, and airline tickets were still zipped into the top pocket.

"Your dress, Anne." Her former best friend pointed to the red stains down the front. "Is that blood?"

"Catsup. Not blood. Not yet." Anne saw them both flinch.

"Now wait just a minute." Robert climbed back into the bed and put his arms around Monika, but he'd tucked his body safely behind hers. "I'm sorry about all this, Anne. I've been a fool."

Monika turned around and looked at him in a drunken gaze. Maybe she was wising up already.

"No. It wasn't going to work, you asshole. Don't you think your timing sucked? Couldn't you have done it before we did all this?" Anne lifted her skirts as if to curtsy. Robert relaxed and hung his head on Monika's bare shoulder.

Anne grabbed a black rain slicker and rolled the bag that contained her trousseau out to the hallway. Whispers came from her bedroom. Unzipping the bag, she extracted the red and black outfit she had planned to wear on the plane—the one with the plunging neckline. She locked herself in the bathroom, then shimmied out of her bridal gown and slipped into her new things. Her feet found a comfortable home in her favorite pair of black Crocs, the ones decorated by her bachelorette buddies with little bride and groom charms surrounded by red hearts.

No way.

She grabbed Robert's toenail nippers from the vanity and snipped off both the bride and groom, but left the red hearts there. Romance wasn't dead. But her marriage sure was.

Robert stood in the hallway, clad only in his shorts. "Where are you going?"

"On my honeymoon. I planned it. I paid for it. I'm going."

She descended to the ground floor of her house, and then realized her wedding gown was still draped over her left arm. A convenient row of black plastic garbage cans out at the curb for an early morning pick up became the gown's final resting place. The nuclear tufts of stained and shredded white organza looked like tissue paper stuffing for a tall wedding present.

The limo driver waited by the opened door and cast her a smirk.

Second leg of Plan B. So far, so good.

Anne dove in the back seat of the limo and allowed herself to be swallowed by the groaning black leather. She hunched down, bent her knees, closed her eyes, and leaned her weary neck against the headrest as the driver sped towards the San Francisco airport. They rushed down the freeway, leaving the bucolic countryside of Sonoma County behind and entering the thickening traffic and congestion of the Peninsula. Her driver kept looking at her even after she'd told him, for the second time, she would still be going on the honeymoon but *without* the groom.

A glance in the mirror fished out from the bottom of her carry-on confirmed most of her mascara was now located on her cheeks and chin, so she squirted a drop of lemon-scented hand cream into her palm and used it to wipe off the black excess. The driver sneezed, then apologized.

Today, she'd rather smell good than look good. She wasn't going to let a man touch her for, well, it would be years. She was sure of it. Maybe never.

A group of high school kids first stared at her behind tinted black windows, then began a quadruple moon, butts pressed to glass. She eyed their suspicious happiness.

Perfect.

She sighed.

Life goes on. Nobody cares. Get used to it.

How could she have been so naïve? She pondered the events of the day. The wedding had been perfect. Even Robert seemed to get into it a little. They had kissed during their first dance, a nice, long, languid kiss that was probably done to impress the ladies, she realized in hindsight. He had that cat-that-ate-a-hundred-dollar-koi look to him, with those baby blue eyes of his that roamed all over her body when she turned and caught his expression. He was saying something to his friends who were also giving her close inspection.

Had he ever loved her? Just a little? The chill in her heart sent an arctic telegram to her eyes and froze her tears in place.

Does it matter?

Later it had been time for the cake cutting, but there was no Robert anywhere. No one could find him. As Anne looked around the guests, she'd noticed Monika was missing as well. That's when she got a bad feeling.

She was on her way to check the downstairs dressing room again when she thought she had heard something. With her ear to a bathroom door, she recognized the familiar grunts of her handsome groom and the heavy breathing from a well-used partner. The smooth glass doorknob rattled as she slowly opened the bathroom door. It had to be done. She had to see it. See the reality of it, that her husband's faithfulness had lasted less than three hours after they had taken their vows.

Robert was banging Monika in her pale blue gown, her cream slipper-clad feet bouncing in the air while he humped her. Her pert little ass was cradled in the shallow lavie. Monika's eyes grew the size of grapefruits when she saw Anne, and she struggled to sit up. But Robert would have none of it. He was far too focused on the home run, pumping with thrusts that sent Monika's body bouncing between tufts of egg white chiffon.

It was not the ending to her wedding day Anne had expected. She closed the door and heard panicked voices on the other side.

She whipped out the hundred-dollar bill her Uncle Osborne had given her earlier in the day, and with her clutch deeply embedded in her armpit, hailed the sleepy limo driver. Robert had hired one of his regulars to take them first to the house and then the airport. The man had been clearly surprised.

Bet he knows more about my husband than I do.

She had time to kill, and that was exactly the right way to put it.

"Just drive, but get me back to the house before five to pick up my things." She gave him the crisp Franklin bill.

"No, ma'am. I'm paid for the whole three hours until your flight. I'll take you anywhere."

Can you find me a new groom? Someone who isn't a serial cheater?

"Then just take the hundred as a tip. Oh, and go inside and get me a bottle of champagne, one that's opened."

While waiting in the purring limo, Anne found her tears were threatening rebellion, but a look to the crowd of happy revelers made her suck it up. The driver appeared with two bottles of champagne, one corked and draped with a freshly starched white napkin. Several family members had spilled out on the steps behind him and stood there gawking, as if watching a traffic accident.

"Thank you," she whispered as she zeroed in on the frosty neck of bubbly. She took a swig that wound up mostly in her nose.

Her driver stifled a laugh, then commanded their ship out onto the highway, speeding through lush green vineyards arranged in rows so unlike her life right now.

Anne fiddled with the wedding band, but it was stuck. She'd have to get it cut off as soon as she got back.

She'd starved herself for days and now she wanted a burger, one with bacon and guacamole, so she had the driver pull into Burger Palace. With her white dress flowing behind her like froth from a waterfall, she ran barefoot into the popular spot, then stumbled on her shimmering skirt, almost doing a face plant at the order counter.

She managed to get out her order, then sat down and waited for her number to be called, layers of the flounce partially covering an older gentleman on her right, who maintained a brittle smile, and a young boy leaning into his mom on her left, who didn't. In fact, his mother quickly shuttled him elsewhere. Anne twirled her dark brown ringlets, still entangled by tiny crystal clips, and studied the faces in the room all turned toward her. Strangers stood, mostly in shocked silence, or whispered among themselves. Someone tittered.

A bride can't have a burger on her wedding day?

Except this scene had been just bizarre. Checking outside, she was relieved to see her limo driver still maneuvering for a parking spot that didn't block the parking lot entrance.

"Number sixty-seven," the loudspeaker squawked.

Yep, that's me. Number sixty-seven. She wondered what it would feel like to be a number one as she paid for her burger and fried zucchini.

Just for a day, or a night of love. To be cherished and maybe even worshiped, just for a day.

For once in her life, she'd like not to have to share a man with another woman, or worse yet, another man. Was that too much for a girl to hope for?

She got back in the limo, where the driver watched her eat in the back seat, the bottle of champagne wedged between her legs. She dripped catsup down her front and ate pickles from her lap after they fell from the oozing burger, then directed the driver to take her back to her husband and former best friend for the showdown.

But the burger had tasted heavenly. Sinful. It was probably the closest thing to being a bad girl she could ever be.

Well, that had brought on a wave of tears. She'd had a good, satisfying cry, in her wedding dress smeared down the front with hamburger sauce, on her wedding day.

"IT SAYS ANNE Balesteiri. You are recently married?" The Homeland Security officer, who looked like he could play for the Forty-Niners, checked over her passport and ticket.

In a cruel twist of fate, Robert's mother, the elder Mrs. Balesteiri, had gifted them the tickets and had used Anne's new married name.

"Just today, as a matter of fact."

He looked around to see if he had missed the other half of the happy couple.

"I'm traveling alone," Anne wheezed and gave a casual cough, batting her eyes at Mr. Homeland Security Charles Atlas. Raising her chin, she added, "My husband will join me soon," she said with emphasis on *husband.*

"You're going to have to get that changed." He fingered her passport.

"First thing when I get back, don't worry."

She was itching for a shower to wipe off all the traces Robert had ever been in her life.

The flight to New York was uneventful, except they upgraded a Realtor to the first class seat her husband was to have. Anne wanted to sleep, but the woman just liked to hear herself talk. The stewardess must have guessed Anne's pain from the state of Anne's makeup and her red eyes, because she kept Anne's wine glass filled. In time, the drone of the Realtor's voice merged with the drone of the plane engines, and Anne gratefully fell asleep.

She woke up when the tires hit the tarmac at JFK with a jolt. Her neck was stiff and drool had dried down her chin. After exiting the plane, she hobbled to a nearby women's restroom and washed her face, reapplying makeup and deodorant. With soapy fingers, she tried removing her wedding band, but it was no use. The detritus of her marriage was going to have to stay for a while.

Her carefully coifed curls were tamed, secured with a red scrunchie. She added red lip-gloss and lots of blush. She was a desperate woman, after all. Who but a truly bad person would leave her five thousand dollar wedding gown in a garbage can on the street? She added more red to her cheeks.

Better.

Her cell phone had practically been glowing with calls and messages. Her brother wasn't someone she could ignore. After texting him, saying she was on her way to Tuscany, *by herself*, she asked him to return all the wedding gifts.

Sam: Sis, u OK?

Anne: *&^&*^*%

Sam: LOL That's my baby sister. Now I'll stop worrying.

Anne: Shred the license.

Sam: ??

Anne: The wedding license from the minister. I didn't sign it.
It goes away.

Sam: It never happened. Consider it gone.

Anne: Tnx. Luv U. ttfn.

She flipped her phone shut and turned it off.

With a pounding headache, she boarded the nonstop to Genoa at midnight. The glittering lights of New York moved beyond her line of sight in the tiny window at her side. She adjusted the air, turned off the reading lamp and, all alone, in the dark, under the skimpy green airplane blanket, began to cry herself to sleep.

THE PINK ITALIAN sun timidly poked its afternoon nose into Anne's heart as she exited the airport in Genoa. She was transported to the Swiss Hotel, and within minutes was standing with her bag in the middle of the bridal suite. She took a shower and fell asleep under the cool sheets and heavy damask comforter.

Anne awoke a couple of hours later to a bright orange and purple sunset that bathed the already warm colors of the ancient village square around the corner from her hotel. She passed by open-air cafes crowded with locals, noticing couples holding hands all around her.

Is the whole world in love except me?

Violin music called to her from a neighborhood gypsy café a block off the square. She was going to wait in line, but flickering candlelight that illuminated a chapel at the end of a cobblestoned street caught her eye. She changed course and entered the sanctuary of light as a heavy bell rang, startling her.

Inside, the lonely violin music echoed off carved stone columns in the narthex. The floor was travertine and heavily veined marble in shades of grey, black and sienna. At the front of the church a couple sat, whispering with a priest, their heads bowed. She dipped her fingers into the cool water of the sacristy and, as if they could hear the droplets coming off her fingers, the trio looked up at her.

Anne moved to the side, where a table was covered in garnet-colored votive candles. She lit a votive, and using a stubby yellow pencil from a basket filled with scraps of paper, she wrote her prayer, folded it once, and slipped it under a votive. Her last view up to the nave as she left the chapel was that of the three figures, now standing, ready to leave.

As she wandered the streets of Genoa, the scent of citrus blossoms filled the night air. The dark streets felt oddly safe and familiar. She turned a corner and slammed into someone. She gasped and looked up to see a woman with jet-black hair, dark eyes, and a muscled and toned body. She wore the strong perfumed scent of a woman, and her lips were neon red.

Anne was about to apologize for her distraction when the woman's lips pulled back in a smile, revealing two large white fangs.

Blood pounded through Anne, through her head. Sound muted. Her vision narrowed to focus on the sharpness and angle of the woman's fangs. Her mind eliminated all other thoughts but the terror and havoc those fangs could cause. Her body refused to move. Blotches appeared before her eyes, as if she were having a cluster migraine.

"Your mistake to cross my path tonight, human. Now you'll pay for it with your life."

The woman's words echoed through the empty night but Anne couldn't make sense of what the woman's words. She couldn't run. Could only struggle to suck in oxygen. The vamp seized her body, then tossed her high in the air to let her fall to the ground. A sharp snap and pop sounded and pain shot through Anne. Her mind struggled to make sense of the attack, but all she knew was that something was broken inside her. Bones. Free will. Both.

Anne's scream was cut off abruptly as fangs lodged deep inside her neck. A sweet delirium engulfed her. She thought she heard fluttering in the background, perhaps voices, but the blotches in her vision started connecting with each other and at last, there was only darkness. She collapsed onto the cobblestone alleyway, into the arms of a dreamy sleep that she knew would surely precede her own death.

At least death didn't cheat, she thought just before she lost consciousness.

Chapter 2

WHEN THE WOMAN had entered the chapel, Marcus had seen her face for the first time. He'd known in his heart that he had found her at last. As she'd disappeared behind a pillar of stone, he'd been thirsty for the sight of her.

This is the fating calling to me.

He heard the chicken scratch sounds as she wrote on a slip of paper, heard the pencil being put back into its basket, and the drop of her coin in the prayer box. The flame that roared to life when she struck a match roared an echo in his heart. Blood pulsed throughout his body, making his hands tingle and his face flush. She was so close to him now. After three hundred years of searching, she had finally arrived in his life. "I've found her at last," he said to his companion and the priest. "My fated female."

He heard the heavy doors at the entrance slam shut, echoing off the ancient stone, as his beloved left the chapel.

Marcus finished his business with the priest, begging off any further entanglements, postponing decisions, duties, and promises, and went in search of her.

As he passed by the bonfire of votives where she had stopped to write, he was compelled to stop. He wove his hands through the air and found the little candle flame that protected her prayer. His fingers were drawn to the stiff cream vellum. He drew it to his nose and drank her scent. He read the words aloud softly:

"Help me find the true love of my life. Help me bring to him all the love that still lives in my soul. Please let me remember the magic and power of this place. Anne."

Could she have been talking about him? As his eyes had moistened and he'd rubbed his forefinger against the words she had delicately crafted in pencil, he'd heard her scream. With horror, he'd realized the fantasy in his heart had put her life in danger. He'd looked around the chapel. Maya was no longer standing beside the priest or anywhere in the building.

He flew through the ancient doors and into the night, tracing the woman's steps, until he came to the dirty alleyway where Maya crouched over his female. In an instant, he was at her side. He pulled the vamp by the hair, turning her face to his. The blood of his female was on Maya's gums, dripping down her fangs and onto her chin. She smiled.

"She is delicious."

How he wanted to end Maya's life right there. The directive not to kill another golden on pain of death was the only thing that stopped him, but he felt the urge to twist her neck and remove her head. Gripping her long black locks at her scalp, he swung her like a hammer toss overhead and threw her as far as he could. She cackled, her voice sending an eerie promise of further evil as she catapulted through the sky, end over end until she landed some distance away. Her ghoulish deed had ruined his life, altered his path forever, and that of the woman he now knew as Anne.

He bent down. His female's body looked pale and fragile. Her dark hair lay across the wet cobblestones, like a matted pillow. The ample mounds of her breasts pushed against her blouse; pert nipples made peaks in the bloodstained fabric. Her waist was small. One knee was bent, with her skirt hitched, to reveal creamy, unblemished flesh that covered her thigh. He cupped his palm under her knee and straightened her leg.

She had sustained a scrape on her forehead, which was bruising, but way too slowly. Her cheek was smeared with grit from the alleyway where she fell. He touched the bite wound on her neck with his fingertips coated in his own saliva. The blood stopped flowing, and she was the color of death. But still beautiful. The sun had set on this human life of hers.

There wasn't any time to consider other options. He opened the blue vein at his wrist, puckered her chalky pink lips, pulled her jaw down to open her mouth, and poured a small stream of his own blood onto her tongue. She would come to life again. If he hadn't been too late.

A minute passed with no reaction. He traced his thumb against her lower lip and blew into her face, whispering the ancient calling. There was always the possibility that the change wouldn't take, that she was incompatible with the vampire blood gene, but he knew she was his fated female, and as such, his blood would heal her as nothing else could. She was getting cold. He rubbed her arms and cradled her against his chest.

All of a sudden, like something out of a fairytale, her body stirred. She arched up, inhaling deeply, but remained unconscious, eyes closed. His Snow White, needing a lover's kiss to awaken her from a deep sleep.

He covered her mouth with his lips and tasted his fated female for the first time. Her coldness sent a shiver down his spine.

I've found you at last.

She would need more blood, and soon, and she would need medical attention. He was sure Maya had damaged Anne's body, possibly gravely. But it was good she was breathing on her own.

Welcome to my world. Our world, my beloved. I didn't want it to happen this way.

She would need undisturbed sleep, away from prying eyes and instruments, and then be given more of his blood. Cloaking them both, he basked in the feel of her head, gently propped against his chest, as he transported her through the night sky to the villa he shared with his sister. The touch of her breasts through the fabric of his silk shirt soothed his soul. She would live, he felt certain. He had given her the only chance she had at another life. As he drew her essence in and allowed it to fill his lungs, her scent coated his insides. Where her body touched him skin on skin, he tingled.

The villa appeared, covered with bright blooming pink bougainvillea that defied the night's darkness. He brushed back her long, dark brown hair from her pale face that remained caked with her own blood. He laid her down in the small anteroom off his bedchamber. The smell of her wasted and violated blood was dangerous perfume. Anger burned a hole in his stomach.

He looked over the body of his beloved. Her full breasts rose and fell with her shallow breathing. His blood had brought a peach blush to her plump cheeks and full lips. Her delicate neck, marred with the wound that still gaped, had re-opened to reveal a faintly throbbing vein under pale flesh. He touched her there, tracing his finger up to her ear, and heard her moan. She must have felt the same delicious tingle he felt that extended up his arm, warming him all the way to his heart. He sifted his fingers through her hair, then positioned her face, rubbed her temples, and watched her arch and take one long, deep breath.

My touch is good for you. Yes, beloved. I will heal you inside and out.

He had hoped someday this little room would be a nursery, had planned it for over a hundred years. How fitting that he'd brought her here. It was her new birth, her new life of forever. She would take her first breaths as vampire here. Close to him, but not yet *in* his bed.

He wanted to lay next to her, naked, to take her in the ancient fating ritual, but he could not risk it until the turning was completed and she gained her preternatural strength. Not until she could look at him with her turned eyes and want him as her mate. He would not force her. But how he needed her!

He summoned his sister, Laurel, who examined his female, then dressed the wound to let it bleed out and purge Anne's body of Maya's poison. Laurel objectively checked the young woman's vitals, something Marcus could not do. He retreated to his bedroom to prepare blood for Anne's next feeding.

Laurel timidly entered his chamber and gave him the news that Anne would live. But Laurel did not smile, and instead told him that the turning had started and taken hold, that Anne was already strong in her new form. But still no smile graced Laurel's lips.

"There's a complication, brother," she said.

Marcus didn't like the dark timbre of her tone.

"Come, and I'll show you."

Laurel opened the door and the two of them approached his female, lying naked under a down comforter. He wished he had been the one to remove her clothes. He was jealous of even his sister's touch upon Anne's fragile skin. But he would not take what she wasn't conscious to give her consent to. His fingers fluttered in the glorious feel of her deep breathing, just above her face, as he bent to touch the lips that would soon give back the flame of their eternal love.

Before his fingertips could caress her mouth, Laurel stopped him, gripping firm bony fingers around his wrist.

He stared at his sister's cool steel blue eyes. Had he overstepped his bounds?

Laurel studied him as she raised the woman's left hand and showed him the wedding ring.

She is married?

Envy and anger shot through his body. How could someone take from him what he'd been waiting for all these years? Who would dare do such a thing?

Laurel lowered Anne's arm and tucked the comforter up around her neck, straightening her brown curls still caked in blood. With a finger to her lips, Laurel guided Marcus through the archway to his bedchamber and closed the door.

"This complicates our position here, Marcus."

The words hung like weights attached to his heart. "Yes. I'll pay the price if I must. No reason for you to suffer. Once she is out of danger, you should leave and not know anything about her."

"No. I mean the marriage. She is not free to be your fated female. She belongs to another, Marcus."

"But the fating . . . I *feel* it, Laurel."

"And I believe you, but she is taken already. You know you will have to ask permission. What if her husband is human?"

Marcus's huge frame collapsed to a sitting position on his bed. He glanced around the room. He had hoped tomorrow or the next night he could begin to spend eternity here with his fated female, at last. He would lovingly guide her, show her their ways. Bring her to life, to a life he hoped she would cherish and make her own. Give her time to feel the fating, and then they would mate, mate forever. He felt trapped in a fantasy of his own making.

His insides felt hollow as he spoke. "Then I will not touch her until I have permission. I will ask them immediately, after she has fully accepted the turning."

"But you gave her life without their permission."

"Yes. I had to protect her." He looked up into the gentle face of his sister, his biggest supporter. A woman who had not yet found her mate, who devoted her life to making him comfortable. Her long face and quietly beautiful features never needed makeup, and she wore none. Her peach skin had a natural glow, framed by a perfectly heart-shaped mouth. Her long shiny light brown hair was tied back in a chignon.

They had spent the last century easing each other's pain with a deep devotion and filial friendship. She had been his constant companion and kept him distracted from the fact that he had not yet met his fated female. If Marcus was right about Anne, Laurel would soon be left alone. He opened his arms to her and she kneeled to his embrace. "We'll figure something out," he whispered to the top of her head. "Maybe I just won't tell the Council everything."

Laurel separated, but remained kneeling in front of him.

"The Council will know what you've done. You can't hide this for more than a day or two."

"Yes, but by then, you'll not be suspected of helping," he said as he stroked her cheek with the backs of his fingers.

"Is this worth the risk to you?"

"It is fated. I wasn't given a choice but to answer the call to save her. Maya forced my hand."

"As she does every time when it comes to you. The woman will claim your soul yet."

"Her time will come," he said. He stood, transferred a catheter to another bag, and resumed draining more blood, handing Laurel two full bags. "I must be protector first. Warrior second." He pumped his forearm up and down. "Thank you, Laurel, from the bottom of my heart."

"I only hope when I find my fated male it doesn't cause me the amount of pain this is going to cause you. And everyone around you."

"And then I will come to your aid, if needed." He patted the top of her head. "Go tend to your patient, sister. Tell me she needs my touch, my blood."

Laurel moved back to where Anne lay, and gave Anne Marcus's blood. As minutes passed and the last drops drained, Anne opened her eyes and became fully conscious, inhaling deeply as if she'd nearly drowned. Marcus watched from the crack in his bedroom doorway.

"Where am I?" Anne whispered, suddenly looking at the plastic blood packet hanging from the stand.

"You're at our clinic," Laurel answered. "A private clinic, dear."

"Where?"

"I think very near where you were . . . attacked." Laurel picked up a chart and began to write in it. "May I have your name?"

"Anne Bal—"

Anne. Marcus whispered it, but noticed both women looked to the crack in the door. Had she heard him?

"Well, Anne, you are very lucky we came upon you when we did. I'm quite sure you would have died in that alleyway tonight."

Anne searched the room, her eyes darting over sterile instruments and a jar of bougainvillea blossoms Lauren had placed on the counter. Marcus knew she would think this odd for a hospital room. Her gaze rested on the stand that held the bag of blood.

"I needed blood?" she asked at last.

"Yes. You were drained to within an ounce of your life. How do you feel?"

Anne clutched the blanket close to her, and then looked under it.

"I'm naked. I guess a little cold."

"You feel well enough for a warm shower? It might do you some good, but only if you feel up to it."

"Oh, yes, I'd like to get clean, get all this . . ." She fingered the long curls matted with dark red blood.

Laurel helped her fragile, naked body up. Damn. She was still wrapped in that damned comforter. He longed to see her naked form. Anne allowed Laurel to escort her to the bathroom so she could wash up. Marcus had to work not to throw himself in there and rip that blanket off.

Anne, I could warm you, warm you in ways you can't comprehend.

"Are you sure you're okay?" Marcus heard his sister whisper.

"Yes, oddly."

"We use lots of lemons here, so I have wonderful smelling lemon soap and blood orange shampoo. But keep the bandage on your neck for overnight."

Laurel closed the bathroom door and shot Marcus a disapproving frown. She scooted him away and closed the door behind her as she whispered her disapproval, "Voyeur! Mind yourself."

She barred the door to his prying eyes and listened, waiting for her patient to finish. He returned to his bedchamber to retire for the evening, alone.

Marcus knew Laurel would make a good sister to Anne, in time. His fated female was going to need a confidant if they were all going to survive together. He heard the loud click of a lock and knew Laurel had intended to keep him away from her tonight.

He smiled at the thought. Nothing could ever keep him away. Not now.

ANNE HAD BEEN convinced she was in an outpatient treatment center and had decided to stay overnight and until mid-morning the next day. She was dosed with another infusion of the blood cocktail she'd received the night before, and the blood seemed to heal her further. Marcus wanted to join them for breakfast, but Laurel insisted he not. Anne didn't finish her eggs, but took three glassfuls of blood-laced orange juice.

"What is this? It's delicious."

"I put a spot of my sweet tomato puree into the orange juice, along with some cranberry juice. Unlikely combination, I know, but our water here doesn't taste very good and this masks it."

"Never had it before. I love it."

Laurel explained they were a neighborhood center run by a charity that tended to victims of street violence, alcoholics, and drug addicts. Marcus overheard her tell Anne they liked to operate outside the jurisdiction of local police, but offered her the chance to file a report, which Anne declined.

"You're going to feel a little different, as you heal. I have given you our 'miracle drug,' formulated for this very purpose. It aids especially in the healing of skin scrapes, and . . . puncture wounds, like those on your neck," Laurel said.

"But she bit me."

"No, I think you hit your neck against a couple of sharp objects, perhaps some glass, as you fell against the curb. In these dark places at night, it is easy for the imagination to fly."

Marcus could tell Anne wouldn't argue, but she didn't believe Laurel one bit.

"You may hear strange sounds—even think your hearing is changed. And you might have more difficulty sleeping. You'll have the desire for more . . . protein, especially meat, which would be good for you right now. But stay indoors at night. And don't wander around alone."

"But I am alone."

"Forgive me, but I see that you are wearing a wedding ring. Surely your husband must be curious where you spent the night last night?"

"No. He's back in California. I am here alone."

"Most unusual for a woman to be traveling alone."

"It wasn't planned that way. It was supposed to be my honeymoon. I was married just two days ago."

"Ah, then perhaps it would be better to go back to him, now that this has happened?"

Marcus's hands balled into fists and he clenched his jaw. The thought of his woman going back to the arms of her husband in California filled him with fury. How could a true and honorable man allow his new bride to travel unaccompanied?

"No. I'm afraid the wedding has been a huge mistake, so I'm going on without him. I planned it, paid for it. I've always wanted to drive the coast of the Mediterranean, and I'm going to do it. All alone."

THEY WATCHED HER walk away from the villa down an uneven street. Marcus wanted to go with her, help with her new life, but knew it was unwise. He hoped Maya didn't know Anne still lived. Watching her disappear around the corner was one of the hardest things he'd ever done.

"She is lovely, Marcus. A perfect match."

"Yes. I felt that the instant our eyes met."

"But I wonder, will it be enough?" Laurel was always the practical one.

"It has to be," he answered, and put his arm around his sister. "It just has to be."

"Then there is hope for me yet, brother."

"Always. There's always hope. I'd almost given up, but now there's a bright future."

"I must pack. You are sure I shouldn't stay behind for a few more days?"

"No, Laurel. It's too dangerous. Best only one of us is exposed to it. I don't want you anywhere around when the summons comes from the Golden Vampire Council. And they *will* summon me."

Bright pink bougainvillea covered the villa. He did think the flowers bloomed brighter this morning. As soon as Laurel was distracted with her packing and left the house, he would find Anne again.

Chapter 3

WHEN ANNE HAD awoken in the hospital that morning, it hadn't taken long for her to learn she was now able to hear through walls and smell things from far away. The cacophony of conversations rolling around in her head made her dizzy.

Her flesh felt firm and smooth, as if stretched over cool marble. Colors were intensified. She could even smell the droplets of water holding fast to the walls of the clinic's stainless steel sink. Even the wind had a woodsy taste.

The nurse had said things would change, and she would need protein. She was absolutely starved for a burger. All meat. No bun.

She made her way back to her hotel, stopping at a kebab vendor on the way and devouring four skewers of hot lamb. With each step she took, her muscles seemed to expand and harden. The smell of jasmine and lemon blossoms created a heady elixir. She let her hair down to fall over her face and neck, enjoying the sensual caress.

And she was horny as hell.

By the time she made it to the hotel room, she felt like showering again. She stripped and stepped inside the marble alcove, luxuriating in the feel of her own hands caressing her skin as she squeezed her breasts and pretended a dark lover was suckling them. She placed her fingers between her legs and stroked herself, causing spasms to twist her body inside out. As if some dark lover pressed himself against her back, she felt addicted to his scent, the smell of his need of her. Looking behind her, all she saw was steam. Anne wanted him.

Who was this dark fantasy man? Where did this image come from?

The new clothes the nurse at the clinic had given her even smelled like him.

Anne had made up her mind not to get involved with any man until she could heal, but now, in her newly aroused state, she was in need of a man as she never had been. She was steeped in dangerous and wicked thoughts of tasting and *mating*. Not sex, but *mating*, needing it like an animal in heat. She felt stronger than any man she met on the street, but ached for the man that would tame her, breed with her. A dark instinct was gaining dominance over her emotions.

I am in season.

MARCUS SHOULD HAVE left her alone, but he couldn't. He was drawn to her body just as if there were tethers connecting them, tethers he would gladly wear. Chains even. He didn't care.

But that was a foolish thought.

Having done his duty by seeing her safe return to her hotel, he could have just walked off into the misty streets like any number of gentlemen coming home from a rendezvous. But he couldn't help himself, and instead stood under the blooming pear tree outside her hotel room. He needed to feed in her arousal, bask in her desire. Her scent worked like a homing beacon, a searchlight over the dark and dusty waters of the last three hundred years. He wrapped himself around the lamppost to keep from *tracing* a path to her. He had to be careful. She was not fully available, though he knew she belonged to him. And though it burned a hole in his soul, he stood strong and drank of this bitter cup.

He heard water. Anne was showering. He saw opportunity.

He traced to her bathroom, and, without showing his form, invisibly watched her naked body for the first time. He then wondered how long he'd be able to contain himself but couldn't bring himself to leave.

She bent over, extending her hand to feel the warmth of the water, and then adjusted the brown fluffy curls of her hair with a clip. He would buy her a diamond-encrusted one, he thought. He would be the only one allowed to lace his fingers through her hair and remove that clip and have her locks fall down over his chest as she released herself to him in every way possible.

Her white body glowed like alabaster, evidence of her recent turning. She had strong legs with ample thighs and a bottom plump enough to fondle, to knead into submission. The juncture between her legs was bare, something he hadn't seen in a hundred years, since that woman in France. The lips of her peach dripped with hunger. He could tell they were swollen, needing release. They needed to be suckled.

He watched her raise one leg up over the tiled lip of the shower and disappear into the steamy warmth. She began rubbing her porcelain skin with the lavender-citrus shower gel provided by the hotel. He found himself in front of her as she backed into the showerhead, water cascading down her neck and shoulders. She smoothed the luxurious gel over her slick breasts. And then she reached between her legs and washed her sex.

If you were mine now, you would lie in my arms, covered with my scent. It would bring you pleasure and you would never want it to wash off. Anne, I can give you this . . .

As if she heard him, she smiled, rinsed off, and turned several times, giving him a full view of all of her. He could have taken her twice or three times in the shower. They'd stand there, locked in ecstasy, until the water ran out. Or until they had to feed. And they could do that too, but that would be for the bedroom on the satin sheets he'd picked for that occasion.

His cock was turning to concrete.

She brought a hand to her core and inserted two fingers there. Her mouth opened and her eyes closed as she pleasured herself. He knelt before her, his face just an inch from her sex, his lips opening as his tongue extended and he invisibly swiped a lick from the slit her fingers had invaded. She shuddered and then moaned. She was *feeling* something.

Remove your hands. Let me do it. As if she heard him, she floated her hands to her sides, fingers splayed, and widened her knees to accept his gift.

It took his breath away. *Can she sense me? Does she know I am here?*

It was impossible. But he knew little about the fating process. Perhaps she did sense him after all. He'd had thousands of sexual partners, and the only time this happened was when he was glamouring a human female, trying to help her adjust to his strong sexual needs and size. But he wasn't using his glamour now on Anne, and yet she'd opened herself to him completely.

He inhaled, taking in the scent of her juices, then let his tongue slip aside her pink lips and tasted her bud.

She jumped.

He extended his tongue behind the knob and slid the length inside her labia to the dark passage, where one day he would plant his seed, where he would send his son to be born. He blessed her with a kiss and a prayer, charming her body to accept the gifts he would bring her. The thick cream she gave him tasted like honey and lemons. In that instant, he almost felt like he could live off it.

"Oh, yes," she sighed. "Oh, my God, yes."

You are mine, Anne. Soon. You will be mine.

His own erection was causing him pain. His thick cock was thrusting against his wet breeches, begging to be released. Marcus knew it would have to wait, but how much longer? His member stiffly disobeyed, and he knew it would be strong enough to rip the fabric of his pants. If the head of his penis came in contact with her opening, there would be nothing he could do but plunge in. And then he would have sacrificed both of them for his own desire.

Abruptly, he pulled away from the shower, turned his back to her, and exited to the hallway, then stood and waited for her. He stared at the closed bathroom door between them like it was a twelve-foot stone fence.

Done with her shower, she walked naked from the bathroom, unconscious of how she delighted him. He was jealous of the thirsty pink towel she tamped all over her skin. He could hear the hairs of her forearms press back as she rubbed and damp dried herself. In the mirror over the dresser, she examined her pert nipples, pinching herself and feeling the weight of each bosom in her palms.

And then she climbed onto the bed. Marcus could still taste her peach, which was now displayed before him as she crawled to a mound of pillows at the headboard. He had to adjust his pants as his erection was near erupting, demanding fulfillment.

Marcus watched her ass rise up and then lower slowly down, as if she was dreaming of riding his shaft and sliding down the length of him, feeling every inch penetrate slowly. She settled on the bed sheets, and, mercifully, fell asleep. Had she not, he might have had violated her, violated their eternity together.

He traced back outside and stood, looking up to the window but still feeling her pink lips on his tongue.

Dangerous. He wondered if he could speed up the process, have her come to him early, but still make it a natural selection. He would have to be careful. Eternity was at stake.

Chapter 4

ANNE COULD NOT believe the changes going on in her body. She could hear things streets away. The conversations blended over each other and confused her. She heard the breath of little birds and the scratch of insects climbing up tree limbs.

But the biggest problem for her was her insatiable appetite for raw meat. Her first purchase, cold calf liver, she ate so quickly she left bloody stains down the front of her shirt and scared passersby. She quickly bought a T-shirt at a local vendor and made it home to the motel room before the stains could bleed through.

The obsession to feed also kept her awake. She couldn't sleep, and when she did, dreams haunted her and made her waken, her body tingling as if remembering the touch of a lover.

She knew she was not human.

But a vampire?

No. She decided the answer was no.

Have I contracted some blood disease?

Perhaps the clinic wasn't what it was supposed to be. Perhaps the drug the nurse had given her didn't work properly and was too weak against the raging disease taking over her body. She decided she would get fully sated, give in to the desire to feed, and then go in search of the clinic and see if she could get some answers.

She heard the heartbeat of every person she passed on the street. Even children. She found herself attracted to men her own age. Her eyes involuntarily flirted with them, made them stop, check her out.

And she found she liked it.

She felt powerful. Unafraid. Unsure what was to come, but stronger than she had ever been in her life, and capable of defending herself against anyone.

She gave up her quest to find the clinic, winding around the narrow streets and seeing building after building that looked familiar, then rounding a bend and finding herself lost again. She looked for the little church, but couldn't locate it.

Resigned to follow her itinerary, she began her trip along the Riviera, traveling the narrow highway and switchbacks, overlooking the blue water of the Mediterranean speckled with boats. She stopped to buy meat every few hours. The more she ate, the clearer her vision became and the easier it was for her to tune out conversations so she could understand what was being said around her.

One morning she woke up next to a man in a strange apartment. One look at his fully clothed body and she knew they had not had sex. But his neck lay at a strange angle, and two dark puncture wounds invaded the flesh above his jugular. She knew.

I have killed. I have become a . . . a . . . vampire.

She was filled with disgust. But as she looked at her face in the bathroom mirror, her skin had taken on a glow unlike one she'd ever seen. Her hair was shiny. Her lips were dark red, her breasts felt full.

She felt satisfied. The urge to feed had lessened. But the urge to mate remained.

MARCUS WAS SUMMONED three days later. He had been discretely watching Anne as she made her way along the Riviera, and wasn't of a mind to leave her side yet. He could smell her attraction for other men and it pained him a little.

At first, he was concerned when she did not feed. He watched as she gulped down several ounces of raw liver at the *boucherie* in Nice in front of a horrified tourist crowd. Anne took no notice of this, which was how he knew she was unsatisfied. She counted sailboats at the harbor, counted pigeons in the church squares. She busied herself with visiting every chapel and church that called to her with bells, like she was summoned. And in a way she was. She was searching.

Is she searching for me?

He was greatly relieved when she finally did take her first feeding just before leaving France. And then the next night she did it again, although she seemed to enjoy feeding from younger, attractive men.

But after her feedings, the nights belonged to him. He waited until sleep overtook her, and then he traced next to her body and pleasured her with fingers and lips and his tongue. He used glam to keep her in an aroused sleep while he satisfied her sexual urges without sex. Marcus paid no mind to the fact that his sexual urges were going unfulfilled; he needed to make sure she was spent. He did not want her doing something she would regret, now that she fed. Now that she was so close to strange men every day.

Marcus felt he could travel now, go back to Italy to face the Council. They had not been forthcoming with their reasons for his summons, but he knew it was not good. And their timing was horrible.

MAYA WAS SEATED in the large chair before the Praetor's desk. A vacant chair next to her was where Marcus had been instructed to sit. Maya's face was beautiful, as always. She maintained a smug smile and cool demeanor. Obviously, she had spoken to the Praetor and had worked something out with him beforehand. This didn't bode well for Marcus.

Praetor Artemis was not in a jovial mood. He was a few years older than Marcus in terms of appearance but was in reality easily three hundred years older. He had strikingly good looks and an impressive countenance, which felled the ladies right and left. He had been wise to steer clear of Maya, but on force of personality, they were a match. He also had never taken a fated female, enjoying every available unattached female, and it was rumored he'd slept with some of the council wives as well. Not that anyone would tell.

"Marcus, Maya has brought something to my attention. Naturally, affairs of the heart are private matters between two people." He attempted a smile. "I try not to get involved in things I am not a direct party to."

"I see." Marcus hoped his eyes showed Maya he was completely cold to her. He masked even his anger.

"The boy is now almost six years old," Praetor Artemis continued, directing his attention to Marcus, "yet you have not publically taken responsibility for him. He has known you, but as a friend of his mother's. He perhaps has some inkling of who you really are."

Maya's face was radiant. Marcus noted how someone else's bad news seemed to be good for her. His bad news. She gave him a devoted, sufficiently demure smile. His stomach churned. He wanted to sink his fingers into her neck and rip her throat out.

"It is time the boy got to know his father. It is time you acknowledged the fate between you two."

"I will not. I am not ready."

"Yes, Maya has told me just a week ago you met with Jacobi and had made arrangements for the ceremony at the Chapel. Why was this not acted upon?"

"Praetor, I do not wish to cause you or the boy or Maya any pain."

This seemed to distress Praetor Artemis. His eyebrows drew down in a frown. "Well then, what is the problem?"

"Maya has told me we are fated, yet I don't feel it."

"But she bled for you, bore you a child."

"I admit to having fondness for Maya and the boy." He lied about his feelings for her, but the boy was sweet and did look just like him. "But I have not felt the fate as she does."

"The bleeding is never wrong."

"I have no explanation for it. But I have found my fated female, and I believe Maya has hidden this fact from you."

Her eyes went red with anger. She stood abruptly. "What the hell is this? How dare you say this to me?"

"Maya, sit. I must hear him out." The Praetor was upset as well. "We will get to the bottom of it immediately." He motioned for Marcus to continue.

"I was preparing to meet or address the fate put upon me, one I did not feel. But, as you have said, much time has gone by and the boy is growing up. I had resigned myself to accepting the responsibility of claiming him into my household, and take Maya as well—"

"You act as if you are taking in a charity case," Maya yelled. "I bore your son! Your son! No one ever forced you to bed me. You bed me several times a day for years. It must not have been too unpleasant. You are a dog, but you will pay for your cowardice."

"It isn't cowardice. I don't feel you and I are fated. I enjoyed our time together, but never thought we were fated lovers. And I never took from you or made the oath."

"Is this true, Maya?" the Praetor asked.

"I told him when I bled. I told him I was pregnant with his child. We were exclusive unto each other, or, at least that's what he told me. I thought in time he would bring the oath and take from me. I thought he was a man of honor. Apparently, I was wrong. But my son is paying the price. Our son, Marcus! How can you be so cruel?"

Marcus did feel for the boy. He could have been a father to him, but now there was Anne. "Maybe there is something wrong with me, but I believe I am fated to another. Maya knows this. She tried to kill her."

"Tried?" Maya's face went white.

"She practically drained her," Marcus said, his voice cracking from the emotion.

"Maya fed on your fated female? How did this occur?" Praetor Artemis looked back and forth between the couple.

"You thought you ended her life. But she lives." Marcus was not happy to reveal this obvious surprise to her. But it had to be done.

"You turned that little trollop? You did it just to avoid your responsibility. Does she now bleed? Were you going to tell the Praetor and me that you made two women bleed for you, Marcus?"

"No. She has not adjusted. She is married to a mortal and I will not interfere with her vow of marriage."

"This complicates things. How was it, Maya, you fed from her?"

"Tell him, Maya." Marcus smiled for the first time. "Tell him what you saw."

"She came into the chapel while we were talking with Jacobi. She must have been lost, and so stupid to go out alone, unprotected." She flashed a hard look at Marcus. "I followed her. I took her in an alleyway. I was hungry." She sent her chin out in a huff.

"Ask Jacobi," Marcus responded. "I saw this woman and I immediately told both of them I felt the fate come over me. I declared it. Maya tried to destroy her. She tried to come between her and me. That carries with it punishment. I ask that I be released from this obligation to Maya and the boy in exchange for this violation. I need to sort out my true feelings for this woman, and her for me."

Praetor Artemis nodded his head and scratched his chin.

"You cannot be serious, Praetor Artemis. This is blasphemy!" Maya spat out.

Marcus tried one more time. "You have my word. If it is not meant to be, I will return to Maya, and, if she will have me, I will accept the oath."

IT HAD BEEN decided after a meeting of the Council that Marcus would have to wait one month after Anne's turning before making himself visible to her. And he would have to verify she intended to be divorced. Affairs of the heart were always given a cooling off period, and one month was a mere flick of the eye to the immortal golden vampires.

Marcus agreed to allow the child to live in his home in a shared custody arrangement but refused to live with Maya. He would begin to father him, train him, as a proper father should. This part would not be difficult to do. He had genuine feelings for the boy.

But more importantly, Maya was permanently bridled, enjoined from doing any harm to Anne on pain of death. She was furious with this decision and Marcus knew she would do everything in her power to bend the rules to suit her liberal interpretation of them. Although not accepted into her new family, Anne was now a golden vampire, one of the rarest breeds in the universe, and had to be protected at all costs since Marcus could not interfere with her life.

HE COULD NOT wait until he could get back to Anne and make sure her habits weren't getting her into trouble. Although vampire, she was still an innocent, and it would be days before he could begin to properly train her. He traced to the Island of Majorca, where Anne had rented a room in a converted monastery, which was now a hotel.

Yet, he still wondered about the boy and Maya's bleeding. No, blood was never wrong. There was no precedent anywhere that Marcus could remember where one man had been fated to two females. Try as he could, he just didn't feel anything for Maya.

He put the worry aside as he anticipated finding his female again. He was counting the minutes until he could appear to her in the flesh. Would she recognize the fating as he had?

So much to look forward to.

Just twenty-one days to go.

Chapter 5

R OBERT BOLTED UP in bed. Something was wrong. Sun streamed in through the windows of the dingy motel room like an unkind nurse had switched the light on for an unwelcomed evaluation. He had no idea where he was. Didn't remember checking into the place. He waited for a minute, listening, waiting for who knows what, and then he realized it. His neck hurt like a son of a bitch.

He rolled out of bed and felt the back of his throbbing neck. His fingers came back bloody.

Now what the fuck happened?

With his left hand, he rubbed just under the hairline and found that area swollen, tender, and probably black and blue. The front of his neck was bulging with little bumps too.

I don't remember a goddamned thing about this.

It was a week after the disastrous wedding. He was beginning to get tired of Monika's constant begging for his time, although at first he'd been thrilled. They'd had a little row, so he and Gary had gone to the topless bar and picked up a couple of girls. He'd spent the night with the dark-haired one. At least, he thought he had. Surprised to see the bed sheets stained with spatters of blood, he mumbled to himself, "Whose blood is that? Mine?"

The girl's side of the bed wasn't even warm. She'd ditched him. He didn't even remember falling asleep. Could he have hurt her? Could the blood be partially hers?

This was way over the top. Things were getting stranger by the minute.

He heard a sound from the bathroom and wondered if perhaps she was still there. He walked on tiptoes, naked, to the bathroom, then stood still. Christ. Even his pecker was sore.

Overuse.

He couldn't remember how many times he came. It was like he'd gone in and out of a drunken stupor. The girl was insatiable, he remembered that. He couldn't remember her name or even what she looked like, except for those red lips and a funny smile. And she liked to lick him . . . in places. If she was in the bathroom, would she look like some of the girls he used to pick up in a dark bar who were uglier than sin the next morning in the light of day?

Robert, you need help.

The bathroom door squeaked open from a gentle touch of his palm and he found the source of the noise. A cotton curtain flapped in the breeze of an open window.

His shoulders dropped as he sighed, scratched his scalp at the back of his head, and endured the dull pain.

If any of the boys heard about this, they'd have thought he had a guardian angel. What any one of them wouldn't give for a woman like his date last night, what's-her-name hot pants. Totally horny, easily turned on by the slightest little thing he did. It really was too much, he thought as he stepped into the bathroom.

And then he looked in the mirror.

The front of his neck was red, scarred with little red bumps. Then he turned to the right and was horrified to see large purple hickies the size of his thumb all around the backside of his neck, extending well down to his shoulders. He knew she'd been extra frisky, but he hadn't felt the pain. She had sucked and almost bit him.

Fuck me! There was something not right about this. And then he wondered, what would Monika say? What about Anne?

But of course, it was too late for Anne.

He'd have to get some Neosporin. The wounds on his neck were getting uglier as the minutes drew by.

I'm in some kind of time warp. So much has changed . . .

Just a week ago, on the night before their wedding, the night of Robert's now-infamous bachelor party, he felt lucky to have gotten Anne to marry him. He'd nailed her on their first date two years before, something of a ritual for him with his sexual partners. But Anne was a keeper. He always knew he would treat his keeper different from his other, former girlfriends. She had a healthy sexual appetite, although still not his equal. But she was innovative, and although inexperienced, willing to learn. He liked that in a woman. In time, she would make a real honest-to-goodness sexual siren, and probably would stay that way even after they had kids. The thought thrilled him.

The years during their courtship and engagement were some of the best of his life. He was halfway convinced he would be able to be faithful to her. This was something that had eluded him before in all his other relationships. But Anne was a better person. He hoped some of her goodness would rub off on him.

Not that he was completely faithful to her during their engagement, which was something he saw as a warm-up to marriage, not necessarily a commitment. He'd tried, he told himself. He really had tried. But he seriously thought it would be impossible to be a one-woman man until his marriage. And then, well, he would see.

He looked in the mirror and was embarrassed to admit his faithfulness had not lasted more than a blink of an eye.

"Too much excess. Got to stop drinking. Need some new friends," he said to his reflection. Gary was pulling him down. Monika too.

Making me do stuff I think twice about later. It was like he was an unruly teenager all over again, now in his late twenties.

Why?

Robert opened a plastic bottle of water on the cheap dresser and took stock of his situation as he swirled down the cool liquid, satisfying his parched throat. He had a strange metallic taste in his mouth for some reason. Images of his bachelor party surfaced. He chuckled and let them flood over him.

He had been showing the guys brochures about their trip planned along the Mediterranean. It had been Anne's lifelong dream. They would pick up a car in Genoa and drive all the way to Spain. They would spend the last week in Majorca at a converted monastery, once owned by a Hollywood couple.

His old girlfriend, Monika, had dropped by the house. Well, she wasn't really his "old" girlfriend, since he'd fucked her the week before and just about every week before that.

The party was just beginning and Monika was game, so she went along with the eight of them. Not before everyone was sworn to secrecy, of course. In exchange, Monika promised to do them all—so everyone would be in trouble together.

Only thing Robert insisted on was that they all wear condoms. No telling where some of his friends had been. No need to tempt fate. That would be just stupid. He was pretty sure Monika was a very bad girl as well. He did not want to bring an unnecessary wrinkle to his new bride's beautiful forehead.

His best man and the other friends at the party were happy for him. He knew they all doubted this marriage would work out. But Anne trusted him. And as long as she didn't find out about his activities, and so far Robert didn't think she did, she would continue to trust him.

After all, he did love her.

Robert was notorious for his dumping scenes, and the makeup sex that could go on sometimes for weeks before the final straw. And that usually happened when the girl found out there had been someone else all along. His friends had warned him about Anne, that she wouldn't be so easy to fool. He was convinced this was "it" and committed to making the rest of his life more meaningful than the first part.

But he didn't see why that night he couldn't have a little fun. After all, he was not yet a married man. Almost, but not quite.

The black limo pulled up and one of his groomsmen shouted out they were ready to leave. Robert had just taken his prearranged place with Monika, which was first. His cock fully sheathed and ready to pump into her. No way he would be denied. He wasn't going to waste a perfectly good cherry flavored condom just because the driver was five minutes early.

When Gary opened the door to make sure Robert heard the call, he found the groom riding her hard. Gary got the finger for his efforts.

"Unless you want to jump in, get the fuck out. Have him drive around the block, twice," was Robert's response. Monika's breasts were bouncing as he pumped her. He loved the way her little soft pillows of flesh rippled with each thrust.

Gary gave the instruction and the room was cleared with a clamoring of hoots and hollers and heavy footsteps down the stairs. Then Gary came back to the room and stripped off his shirt.

"Monika, honey," Gary began, "this cowboy might get you off, but I'm gonna make you sing. You deserve better."

"Oh, that's right Gary," she teased. "Give the groom a little competition. I like him all hot and bothered and trying real hard. Ah . . . I feel him rising to the challenge. Oh. That's nice, baby."

Robert grunted as he stroked her, turning her to her side for deeper access, one of her legs over his shoulder. "You bet your sweet ass. You want more of me? Can you handle more of me?"

"Look what you'll be missing. I'll be fucking all your friends, Robbie. Just think about me every day. I'll be fucking them while you are on your honeymoon. I'll be so sore I can barely walk. We'll compare notes when you're back." She locked lips with Robert, who kept thrusting. Their private conversation was too soft for Gary to hear, so he stepped closer. Monika held out her hand.

Gary presented his cock and she grabbed it, squeezing him hard. She leaned over and put him in her mouth.

"Hey, Robert. Wanna flip her over so I can get a little more action, if you don't mind?"

With a big hand under Monika's belly, Robert flipped her forward and then entered her from behind. He left his hand between her legs to finger her clit. She moaned long and hard.

"Oh, here it comes, sweet cheeks." Robert said to her ear as he pulled her onto him. "I used to call you 'Moana.'" Robert leaned over, "Make that sound for me, baby."

She did.

"Come moan all over me, Moana," Gary said as he thrust his cock into her mouth. The two friends faced each other and grinned.

"Hey, this is the best, man." Gary said.

"Nothing better. If the girl's willing," Robert lowered his face to Monika's ear again, "and Miss Moana is always willing"—which elicited a shriek—"isn't she?"

"Oh, yes. Oh, yes. Oh, God," Monika mumbled through her sucking lips.

"Don't tell me, sweetheart, show me," Gary whined. His blond hair and big white teeth made him look the part of the lifeguard he was. "Oh, man, you have a nice tongue." His fingers were clutching her red hair, which fell long and loose over his thighs.

Robert began to shudder, thrusting to finish.

"There it goes. Your last fuck as a single guy." Gary said to Robert's grimacing face. He lowered the tone of his voice as he addressed her. "Monika, honey, you get off? I want to be sure you got off."

She moaned.

Robert looked at her ass as he pulled out. He would miss that ass. "Yea, I'm pretty sure she got off. She just can't talk on account she's got her mouth full." He went into the bathroom to freshen up.

Gary was getting close.

"You want it in the ass?"

"No!" Monika suddenly rose up to her knees. Gary took the opportunity to grab her breasts.

"You know, honey, no reason you need to get dressed tonight," he said as he squeezed and pinched her nipples. "You got eight guys gonna keep you real warm. I might have you twice, if you're nice. And I think you're real nice."

"Shut up and fuck me."

"Never argue with a lady." Gary muttered. He grabbed the box of condoms and prepared himself. Monika rolled over to her back and he began his vigil. Foreplay wasn't necessary, as the limo was honking downstairs.

Robert came back, towel in hand, rubbing his crotch. He stroked himself a few times, watching Gary and Monika, but he couldn't get hard, so he dropped the towel in the bathroom and got dressed. He watched them the whole time.

"I'm giving pointers, Monika," Gary rasped. "Notice what a difference the size makes?"

"Uh hum," was all she could say. She watched Robert as he dressed. The groom understood from the look in her eyes that she had wanted to be the bride. He saw a tear or two before she managed to wipe them away without Gary seeing them. This private moment touched something in Robert's heart, and surprised him.

"You're a good girl, Monika, honey. Thank you. That was real nice." Robert smiled. He meant every word. He walked out to the living room. "Any century now will do, Gary. I'm waiting down at the limo."

He was greeted with cheers. There was a triple-X DVD playing and the guys had popped some champagne and beer. He crawled in front by the driver.

"Hey, Charles. Thanks for taking us out tonight."

"No problem, Mr. B. Are we all here, then?" The driver had been on assignment for several of their parties.

"No. Gary's coming, and there's the girl."

"Right."

Noise erupted from the back at the sight of Gary, who strode fully clothed from the house but tugging a bare-footed Monika along, who wore only one of Robert's shirts buttoned halfway up the front. Robert looked at her nice legs and pink toes and sighed. The driver chuckled.

"Looks like you're gonna have a little fun too," Robert said to the driver.

"Oh, no, I don't touch the merchandise when I'm on duty."

"But you can look, right? She likes it when you look."

The driver laughed again. "Yeah, I can look. That's my favorite part nowadays. I'm happily married."

"Yup. That'll be me tomorrow. But not tonight." Robert punched the driver in the arm and went to join his friends in the back.

Monika was already on another lap. The sound of a belt buckle clanged as they sped off to the topless bar.

When they pulled back to the house at five AM, Monika was asleep in the back, curled up into a ball. Half the party was asleep too, overcome with alcohol and excesses of the evening. The coke had run out. Time to go to bed for a couple of hours.

Robert picked Monika up and carried her inside. Gary made a space for her on the couch but Robert went right past him to the bedroom and closed the door.

YEAH, HE'D BEEN an idiot, he thought. Anne's brother practically decked him the day of the wedding after the bride left in their limo. Gary got so ripped he knocked over the cake, not that there were many guests left to eat it. The DJ kept playing like the orchestra on the Titanic. The place looked deserted. To make matters worse, he caught Monika in a lip-lock with some dark caveman who liked to dance the bear hug. She'd fainted in his arms and the guys laid her on a settee in the dressing room, in her blue maid of honor dress. Too much champagne, he thought. They'd all nearly left her there passed out.

But he'd gone back and brought her to Anne's house. *That* sexual liaison he remembered. Vividly. Unhurried, like the one earlier in the day in the bathroom, but just as urgent. God, he loved fucking Monika. And in a way, Monika made him a better man too. He didn't feel dirty for loving her, and he knew he truly did. Hell, he loved them both.

And then Anne had walked in. He never wanted to see his lovely Anne look at him like that again. Woke him up from the fantasy that he could just go along without making a choice. Saw the reality of the pain he'd caused everyone.

He thought about her place. He'd always liked it there. Maybe she would give him another chance, although he admitted he didn't deserve one. Anne was looking more attractive the less available she was. He began to think he was budding a conscience.

Something messed up with that.

He'd have to mend his ways. Maybe start going to meetings again.

Fuck that.

He knew he was slipping into an abyss. Now it was getting dangerous, and bloody.

Robert shook his head and swore under his breath, slammed his palm down on the coffee tabletop.

He was forgetting things, too. First, he'd cheated on his wife, and now last night he had cheated on Monika. He was going to have to figure out what exactly he wanted and stick to the plan. Getting Anne back was Plan A. But he knew he had a much better chance with Plan B.

Chapter 6

ANNE OPENED THE heavy wooden door to her room, a converted cell in an old monastery. The Majorcan summer night air was warm and fragrant. Maybe she could float. *Something to try another time.* Just five days into her change and she was still getting used to her new self. Tonight she needed to feed—a need that would not be denied or it could get dangerous. And bloody.

She loved the sounds her feet made as she lightly skipped along the moonlit cobblestoned street. The cool smell of dusty stone houses was pleasant.

She could even smell blooming jasmine and orange blossoms from miles away. She was still adjusting to the sensory overload that was now her daily challenge. Pulling a deep purple satin cape about her neck, she drifted down the cobblestoned streets of the village, high atop the hills. If it weren't two in the morning, she would be able to see the ocean, but she could smell its salty air. The unmistakable rusty scent of blood arrived not thirty yards in front of her.

Men.

A whole group of them. Young. Virile. In their peak of health. Her favorite kind.

Her first few attempts to feed had been pathetic failures, and she'd barely enough to satisfy her needs. She'd ruined clothes until she learned she could get her feeding done as they were showering.

She didn't have the desire to kill, just to feed, but her first few attempts ended in death for the human, sadly. If she took someone expendable, like a street drunk, she could get high from the alcohol, or worse, from the drugs in their system. And she hated eating while the smell of urine, vomit, and weeks-old human sweat filled her nostrils.

She had indeed been cursed those first few days until she learned how to leave the humans alive. Then she discovered several other things she liked about her new form.

For the first time in her life, she wasn't afraid of anything. She was able to process every little detail of a scene, even down to the smallest pebble. She could hear the footsteps of small bugs that lived under rocks and the whir of bee wings, the language of crickets and mating calls of frogs in the rain. Liberated from all her doubts and concerns for her own safety, she felt sexual arousal constantly, especially when she caught a particular scent that lingered near her. She'd been aware of it in her bed, in her shower. She'd feel it curl around her like arms of a lover and she'd basked in the tingly feeling it brought her ultra-sensitive skin.

She had no idea what kind of being she had turned into. One thing she knew for sure, she certainly was not human.

She studied the five handsome twenty-something young men who stood before her, probably out for a night of dancing and drinking. Anne sensed they were looking to satisfy their sexual appetites. That worked.

She picked out the tallest, and handsomest male in the group. The alpha, she thought. He was so sexy the way his confident, loose gait carried his muscular body straight to her. His dark brown bedroom eyes perused her over, and yes, she had to admit, her nipples tightened so hard they hurt, and she felt the delicious wetness in her panties as her sex vibrated to life.

Hands on her hips, she smiled back at him. The others hung slightly back, gawking. This alpha was the stud, the legendary one.

Perfect.

"Hi there," she whispered. The boys were animated. They registered she was an American and spoke among themselves.

Alpha rubbed his palm against his chin, then swiped his fingers across his lips and made no mystery of focusing on her cleavage. Anne flushed at the attention. She was hungry too.

"It is late and you are alone in a dangerous place," he said in English with a thick Spanish accent. She liked the way his Adam's apple bounced up and down his tanned throat as he spoke.

"But I've found you. Will you save me?"

His friends laughed enthusiastically. Alpha was wary. "You do not look like a professional—"

Anne urgently stepped to him, then rubbed her breasts against his clean white shirt opened two buttons too low. She noticed the golden cross tucked in his dark chest hair. "I am not a professional," she said, "but are you?"

The boys roared. Whistles and catcalls laced the air. Alpha searched the smiling faces of his compadres, who encouraged him. At last, he inhaled and took a long, slow look into her eyes, then dropped his gaze down to her chest. His half smile showed a delicious dimple on the right. In a husky voice he answered, "It has been said a time or two."

This was good news. She craved him even more for his bravado. She saw the flush cover his face and the rush of blood heading down to his groin. The scent of his blood was laced with tangerines and red wine. He stood tall, his chest extended, showing her he was all male, that he was capable of pleasuring her in surprising ways. She liked that.

Without taking her eyes off his, she extended her hand. She touched his cheek and watched it deliciously flush his skin again. Then she moved her palm to rest at the side of his neck, underneath his muscled jaw line. His pulse was strong and intoxicating.

"Can you show me around and then take me home? Are you up for that?" She rubbed the length of him with her other hand, ignoring the whoops and hollers of the other boys. He stood before her, caught in the web of her glamour, every delicious drop in his body trying to jump ship. Her effect on him was obvious: he would do anything she wanted him to do to pleasure her.

Anything.

MARCUS STOOD ALONE in the shadows, fully cloaked, and hung back well away from the crowd. He watched Anne lean in and kiss the tall male. As difficult as it was, he couldn't take his eyes off her. His hands fisted as he saw the male place his palms against her backside, and then creep into and under her wrap to find her flesh.

She is mine.

The erection in his pants was getting uncomfortable. He could send an erotic wave toward her and make her so horny she'd ignore the stranger and run up the little hill, straight into his arms, where he could finally claim her.

Anne and the young Spaniard were fully engulfed in a deep kiss, exploring each other's bodies. The young man's group moved away, clearing their throats and making whistling noises, but getting no response from their tall friend. The group evaporated into the streets. Anne and the large male were alone, surrounded by warm night air. Would she remove some of her clothing? Show herself to him before she took his blood? Marcus hoped not, but knew well about the new erotic forces making her do things she wasn't used to.

Either way, he was bound by duty not to interfere. This was to be his curse of the moment. All he could do was watch. She was a married woman, and the possession of another man. A mortal man who didn't deserve the heavenly gift of her body and all its charms, someone incapable of understanding what her needs were or that she was created for a higher, more powerful love. A love only Marcus could give her.

The male nuzzled her breasts. For one brief moment Marcus saw the magic of her flesh exposed to him in the moonlight, saw the beautiful mound, now glistening wet from the stranger's probing tongue.

She lets him have his way with her. Will she open her other parts to him as well? Marcus was filled with unspeakable sadness. He had to do something.

He double-checked his cloaking, then moved to stand behind her and was immediately charmed by her sweet vanilla scent, which brought his groin to life. He reached an invisible hand to her shoulder, to touch her there, or perhaps her neck, to feel the fullness of her soft dark brown curls, to beg her to feed from him instead. Her name stuck in his throat and he whispered what only he could hear, "Anne."

The ache in his chest intensified as he smelled her arousal. He placed his lips to her ear and pretended she could hear him tell her of his need for her. Of his centuries spent waiting, longing for the one woman created for him. His fated female. Marcus needed to pour out his melancholy so he could purge himself forever of this burden.

You are here at last. See me, Anne. See and feel me. Feel how I love you, have always loved you.

He wanted to think her sigh and the sultry smile on her lips came because she somehow knew her fated male stood behind her, ready to open the doors to their love, arousing her need to partake of the ancient ritual for their kind.

The male was expecting sex, and he had shoved her skirts up, seeking her core with his long fingers. This was to be Marcus's right. He felt her swoon as the man's finger traced over her pleasure button. He could smell her wetness, her need for sexual release.

He whispered to himself again. *Anne, it is I you need. Let it be me who pleasures you, makes you moan hour-by-hour, day-by-day. Let it be me you crave more than the blood in any vein. Crave my blood, Anne. Drink of me, and let me fill you with eternal pleasure. It is our fate. Our destiny together.*

Marcus felt the hunger for blood rise in her chest, the smell of the glamour that came on just before the feeding. It would calm the human, would transform the bite into a memory, make the male think he had the best sex of his young life instead of what it really was.

She came at his neck with fierce determination. She was so beautiful. So strong. So demanding. And Marcus knew he could meet every one of her demands. Only he could do it, he thought as she brought her thigh up over the male's hip. They collapsed to the ground. Marcus kneeled at her back, rested his head there and smelled the scent of her flesh, listening to the blood from this male rush in to fill her cavities, bringing her strength, life.

Yes. Make yourself strong. Take the blood and join me forever.

He had waited three hundred years. He could wait just a little more. But just a little.

ANNE FELT AROUSED and unsatisfied, even though her craving to feed had subsided. Something about the dark young man in her arms sparked a tender chord in her heart. She brushed the curly hair from his neck and licked the two puncture wounds there, following it up with a kiss. She'd discovered yesterday if she licked any wound, it would heal immediately. It was a nifty trick.

This young stallion was delicious—in every sense of the word. His chest rose and fell, the golden cross glinting in the moonlight like the delicate twinkle of an angel's kiss. Her fingers scanned his full red lips as she looked into his closed eyes.

He would wake up soon, probably with a hard-on, and, as she confirmed this, he started to stir. She undid his button fly and slid his pants down one hip, then raised her skirts so he would think they had just been intimate. As she felt his hardness against her abdomen, she found she did feel intense desire. But it wasn't for him, exactly. And it wasn't for Robert either.

He awakened. She smiled, giving him the satisfied glamour of a woman who had been pleasured by a skillful lover. "Thank you," she said, and kissed him.

His fingers gripped her skirts, drawing her against his groin. "Uno mas," he whispered, *one more time*. He buried his head between her breasts, which were flaming hot with desire.

"Lover, as much as I want to, I can't. I must go before my husband misses me." She displayed her ring.

It was a lie, but she didn't need entanglements.

Pain registered in his face, sending a frown and a worry line between his eyebrows. His silky lashes glistened as he squeezed her breast and took in his last look at her warm flesh.

"Where are you staying, then? I must see you again," he whispered to her chest. He groaned and pushed his cock against the black lace panties she wore, dangerously tempting her.

She was not going to have sex with this tall, dark Adonis of a man, even though he looked at her in a way that thrilled her. She would need another feeding tomorrow. The timing would work out nicely for her.

"I will meet you tomorrow night, if you like, but not late. I'll meet you here at six, after dinner."

He threw his head back and laughed. "Dinner? I don't eat until nine or ten." He kissed her apple-shaped breast, licked her bottom lip, and then covered her mouth. "But I will meet you here tomorrow night, and take you to dinner afterwards," he whispered between kisses. "We will dance with the gypsies, and then I will take you to my bed, and—"

"Do you have a shower?" she interrupted.

"Of course."

"Good. You will take me to your place, and then I must leave. I go to bed early and leave the next morning. Sorry."

Now it was her time to frown and kiss his right temple. His pulse roared back strong, nearly recovered. She saw visions of feeding on him while he pleasured her with his cock, of her allowing him to feed on her. She was wet all over again as a little orgasm tickled her insides.

So it was arranged and they kissed as he thanked her for the evening of sex he thought he had. He reluctantly let her go, lingering and begging one more time, which Anne sidestepped with a sweet kiss. She was thrilled she could take a wet feeding in the shower tomorrow. No mess that way, but no sex either. The thrill of being naked with him fueled anticipation. It would be the first time she'd feasted on someone for the second time.

He watched her adjust her skirts and re-button her bodice, but at the last minute tore it open to feast on her breasts again. He would have been a wonderful lover, she thought, if that were what she was looking for.

Am I looking for something? Someone?

Yes, she thought. She was certain it wasn't her husband, and it couldn't be this young stranger.

But who?

So many things had changed. She wasn't afraid as she walked through the wet streets all alone. She heard people inside rooms eating food, arguing and making love. She heard children snoring in their beds. Dogs barked as she passed and she found if she sent them a gentle message they would quiet.

Very odd. But not unpleasant.

She found it easy to run up the narrow steps to the room. She used her heavy iron key to unlock the door, which groaned open. In the dark, she undressed. Did she see a figure standing below under a streetlamp, perhaps looking up at her?

She blinked, rubbed her eyes, but this time all she saw was a swirling white steam coming from a grate embedded in the stone sidewalk.

Anne slipped into the sheets naked, loving the sensation of cloth against bare skin. She pinched her nipples and turned her face to the light of the streetlamp. Her sexual need was driving her crazy.

Perhaps I'll let him tomorrow. I'll try feeding and fucking at the same time.

As she scanned the room in the early morning hours, hoping for another erotic dream to overtake her, she suddenly felt sleepy, as if a warm breeze had floated over the back of her neck. She felt protected, as if arms held her warm and secure. She would live forever. She could live and die in his arms. Whoever *he* was.

MARCUS HAD BEEN standing outside the Monastery Hotel under a streetlamp when he saw her figure in the darkened window. His body absorbed the swirling white misty air, hiding him from her sight.

He'd made sure she got home safely, walking behind her as tears streamed down his face with need as he'd smelled her arousal and knew he could satisfy her. As she prepared for bed, he traced to the Spanish lad, her intended meal for tomorrow, and made sure he would not be physically able to keep his appointment with Anne. Then he'd come to her as she lay naked and full of desire. He'd pleasured her until she said those words that haunted him now:

"Take me."

And he very nearly had, too. He'd sucked at her peach and vibrated her core with his tongue, making her come, and beg for more.

Her sexual appetite was growing by the day. He knew it wouldn't take long before he would no longer be able to satisfy her with just oral sex. She wanted *him*.

He would make sure tomorrow's feeding, the last before her trip back to America, would not take place. He had disabled the young Spaniard—not permanently, but enough so that he wouldn't be able to keep his appointment. Anne would have to feed on a stranger.

As he lay invisibly spooned behind her, awash in the scent of her flesh, her hair, her juices, he reminded himself to be careful and not get too carried away, though his animal side was rattling the cage to get out. He sighed and placed a gentle kiss on the back of her neck.

How in the world am I going to last another twenty days?

MARCUS WAS GOOD as his word. Anne returned to California and he continued to check up on her by day and appear, like in a dream, at night.

He purchased an estate property, suitable for royalty, in the countryside north of her, with over a thousand acres of some of the finest grapes in the valley. He brought the boy Lucius with him, and started his instruction by telling him of the ancient stories. About fating. About the blood. About the choice he would take at puberty whether or not to turn vampire or remain human. He treated the boy as his own. It helped to pass the time until he could contact her and appear in person.

And on the thirtieth day from the imposition set by the directive, he stood in line behind Anne at Starbucks, hopeful he could now put an end to a bittersweet chapter in his life and open a new one. A chapter that would bring him joy and all the wishes his heart desired.

He hoped.

Chapter 7

"DOES YOUR HUSBAND know about your appetites?" From behind Anne came a gravelly male voice that sent shivers down her spine. The screams of the Starbuck's espresso machine made her wonder if she'd really heard the voice. But the male scent of him was impossible to miss. The hairs at her neck stood at attention, telegraphing urgency. The sensation extended well beyond her waistline. Time stood still before she could bring herself to turn around and fall under the warm gaze from this tall dark male that covered her.

Not man. Male.

He held her gaze as she stood, transfixed, unable to move or to speak. That was the way it felt. Being held. "I'm sorry?" she blurted out finally.

"Don't be sorry, my dear. It's a simple question." The ends of his lips curled up at the corners. When he inhaled, his chest extended, and he appeared several inches taller. Then he exhaled and she was covered with the same musky scent, incapacitating her, wrapping around her like a warm shroud. It was familiar.

She heard mournful viola music drip with slides and rifts that pulled on her heartstrings. She felt dizzy. Did she hear him murmur a groan? Or maybe it was a small earthquake? Probably an ordinary person wouldn't hear or feel it. But she did.

Anne was on alert; this male took liberties with her feelings.

What a crazy thought. Ridiculous.

He leaned forward, grazing just the edge of her forearm with his warm hand. An electric spark pricked her. He leaned against the counter and looked at the barista, not her. "I'll pay for the lady's drink."

She noticed the strong pulse at his neck. *Healthy. Smells wonderful.*

"And what would *you* like, sir?" The young barista was pert. Anne didn't like her perfect white teeth. That and the fact the girl's shirt was made for a ten-year-old, showcasing her pierced bellybutton.

"I have all I need." The rumbling words sparked shivers again down Anne's spine. He said it just next to her ear, barely touching the small of her back . . . He was facing the barista, but deep inside Anne knew the words were meant for her ears only.

"You didn't have to do that." Anne suddenly found the urge to speak.

"My pleasure." He removed his hand and gave a slight bow.

A bow? No one had ever done that before. Anne had just fed. She wasn't hungry enough to play the game this afternoon, having gorged herself on a salesman who liked to eat garlic fries. His blood was thick with fat globules she could almost see as well as taste. But it went down smooth.

So maybe she would play along. This stranger might be a good candidate for a snack tomorrow. She had never fed twice in one day. She wondered what being too full would feel like in her current state. It would probably make her horny. Well then, maybe she should reconsider. She should do a wet feeding. That way she wouldn't have to be too careful, could gorge herself on him. He'd be wonderful to look at in the shower, and his hands might do something unexpected to her. Something memorable in a string of unmemorable feedings.

His hand gently touched the small of her back again, and she allowed herself to be ushered to a corner table, flanked by two purple velvet overstuffed chairs. They sat, facing at right angles to each other. The counter girl called out Anne's drink. He was up and walking over to pick it up for her before she had a chance to react.

She watched him cross the coffeehouse like a thirsty traveler eyeing a pitcher of water. He was probably six foot six. His dark hair was pulled back in a short ponytail. His black leather bomber jacket showed his nice ass and those long lanky legs that went all the way to Heaven. Even for his size, he appeared graceful. Unassuming. Confident. And the nicest looking male from behind that she had ever seen.

And then he turned, holding the little white paper cup with two fingers, the other ones splayed out, large as antlers. She could see how long his fingers were, how substantial. She envisioned what those hands could do to her. But as sexy as he was, he also made her mouth water to feed.

His prominent jaw line sported blue-black stubble. His strong pulse would be no problem at all, but she would have to bite a little harder to crack the skin. Maybe he would let her take him slowly. Then she could kiss other parts of him in between while his heart pumped more of the blood she craved. His lips were bright red and full. She would enjoy sucking them, licking them. Perhaps biting them.

His eyes found their way to hers, and when she met his gaze, she became self-conscious of her thoughts, as if somehow he could read her mind. Anne told herself it was her craving for blood that caused the almost sexual attraction for this male. After she fed, surely she wouldn't feel this way, she thought.

He delicately deposited the white cup in her hands. One finger touched and almost rubbed against hers. She thought she was imagining the touch, of course. Between her legs, a warm pool had formed. It was a curious place to feel hunger, a hunger of another kind. She blushed at her erotic thoughts.

"You like cappuccino?" He seemed intrigued by the idea. Dancing eyes, all over her upper torso, his breathing steady but deepening.

"Yes. I need the caffeine in the afternoon."

That little hitch in his throat, almost like a moan of surprise. "And here I thought your cheeks were flushed and ripe from a good meal." Those black eyes peered right to her soul. Almost as an afterthought, he smiled, and the dark became brown, ringed with a coppery color that drew her in.

I'll play your game.

"Yes. After a big meal, I get tired sometimes."

He nodded. "I remember that."

Anne looked out the window. This was beginning to feel dangerous. She grabbed her drink and stood. He stopped her by placing one hand on her wrist. His action was soft, but deliberate. *This male won't be denied.*

"Please, sit just a little longer. Then I'll let you go home to your husband."

"Go? You'll let me go? What kind of talk is that? I think . . ." She began to rise again, but his firm grip on her forearm stopped her.

"Hear me out just a bit." He did appear to be begging. Could it be she saw a flash of pain there? *No way.*

"How do you know I'm married?" she snapped out, letting her impatience show.

"You wear a wedding ring." He fingered her ring slowly, sensually. She let him touch her, perhaps a bit too long. She was going to correct his misconception but decided to leave him thinking she was protected by another man. Safer that way.

But was she looking for safe?

There was an obvious physical attraction between them. She had not felt this before, not since before she was made.

"Do I know you?" she asked, ignoring the comment about her marriage.

"No. Ask it another way." The huskiness of his voice made her ears buzz, like he was brushing his lips across them, like they were in bed whispering unmentionable things to each other.

"Do you know me?" Her eyebrows rose at the ridiculous suggestion that seemed to be planted in her brain from somewhere else.

He very lightly nodded, his obsidian eyes flashing. "Oh, yes. I have waited a long, long time for you."

"Okay, that's it. I'm outta here." Anne jumped up, her coffee in her hand. She slung her purse over her right shoulder and stormed off. He followed her outside, keeping pace like they were walking in unison. She stopped suddenly.

"Look. Whoever you are, I will call the police if you don't leave me alone."

"And tell them what?"

"Tell them there is a very strange male following me, bothering me."

He groaned again. The ground beneath her feet rumbled when he did that. "I like that you say male."

She backed up, raising her palms up and out in his direction. "Please, please leave me alone."

"Agree to meet me here tomorrow at this time and I won't follow you." He smiled. "I promise." He held his hand over his heart. Anne felt a small tug at her own, as well as an ache down below.

"Alright," she said, willing herself to say no when her body wanted to say yes. She'd wrestle with her decision if she could just get away from him right now. This coffee house would have to be forever off her list. "Tomorrow at four. But I will call the cops if you don't stop this, this, *way* you are being—"

He grabbed her upper arm and pulled her close to his chest. She struggled, but he held her tighter the more she wiggled, and yet she enjoyed the physical play between them. No matter how hard she fought, he would win. She softened and heard his sharp inhale. The spice on his cheeks was a familiar scent to her and, relaxed her just enough so she wouldn't collapse entirely being so close to him. He leaned down and whispered into her ear, "Go for now, little one. But as for leaving you alone, there isn't a chance in Hell that will ever happen. See you tomorrow."

And then he was gone. Just gone. Nowhere to be found. She turned around and around and there was no trace of him. No car leaving the parking lot. No door being opened. Just the normal day all around her.

She was hungry and scared. She liked feeling both emotions equally.

She knew it was going to be forever until four o'clock tomorrow.

A feeding would take up the next hour. Only twenty-three more to go.

Chapter 8

IN ROBERT'S 1948 Oldsmobile, and with an hour to kill, Anne cruised through the parking lot. Driving the Olds was like gliding on an overstuffed horsehair couch on wheels. She loved the green bomber and how positively ageless and invincible she was. She counted all the cars on her first pass, then did another pass and separated out the sedans and SUVs. On her third run, she counted all the red cars, then 4-wheel drive vehicles. She had a list in her mind of the other things she could count, like the number of whitewall tires, cars with sunroofs, dirty cars, top ten cleanest cars. But then she saw the man she'd met the day before drive in. He was a full five minutes and thirty-seven seconds early.

It was hard to miss his black Ferrari as it roared into the parking lot. She memorized the sleek vehicle's every detail. She noticed things more than ever before, ever since the turning. The change her body created a compulsive need to count things, just for fun, but especially when she was hungry.

And she'd come hungry.

The man parked the low-lying vehicle and somehow extricated himself from the driver's side. Anne thought he must have been almost supine while driving the beast. A nice, classy beast, though. Like the driver. Dark-haired men with nice cars were becoming a lethal combination, usually for the man. She wet her lips as her pelvic muscles tensed.

Anne was weighing how it would feel to feed on him when he spun around and pointed to a parking space beside his and smiled.

Let the games begin.

She aimed her old green bomber three spaces away and parked.

He was there by her door as soon as she had collected her keys and her purse. He opened the door for her. That was kind of a nice touch. There were so few men who knew how to be polite these days. Too bad.

He held her left hand, helping her slide off the light brown fabric of the front seat. The old tank was so high, Anne's small frame had to drop the remaining six inches or so until her feet settled on the ground, barely touching his. Her right knee nudged his left thigh as she slid, initiating a buzz that traveled up her spine. She balanced on his hand like a bird perched on a golden bar. His firm grip kept her steady while he looked over her shoulder and scanned the sleek lines of the vintage car.

"I like your vehicle," he said, still holding her fingers.

"My . . . husb—soon to be ex-husband's, actually. A '48 Olds fast-back."

The man released her, stroked the backside of the forest green metal like he was caressing a lover.

You're in trouble if you don't stop this. Everything he did reminded her of some sexual play.

"Gets terrible gas mileage and it smokes," she added.

"Ah, but makes quite a statement, doesn't it?"

Anne shrugged, but she had to admit, that's one of the reasons she liked driving the Olds.

He was still admiring her Olds. "I like old things. And I love cars." His eyes sparkled as he looked down to her. He completely blocked the sun.

Anne peered around his massive frame and nodded to his black Ferrari. "You like fast cars. How many vintage cars do you have?" she asked, sure he didn't own one like the Olds.

"Fifty-nine." He smirked and added, "but not a single Oldsmobile. You must take me for a ride in it sometime."

She wasn't sure where this was heading, so she shrugged again. It was Robert's legendary car, the one he nailed all his girlfriends in on their first date. Unfortunately, she learned this after she'd been conquest number one hundred and something. But for now, it was hers, since Robert had given the Olds to her as an engagement present. And though Anne knew her relationship with Robert was at an end, she felt she deserved it after what he had put her through. She could understand why a guy would love the roomy back seat. She did too.

His white long-sleeved collared shirt gaped open at his throat. Hard to miss the thick pulsing vein so large she could almost smell it. It was the size of her little finger. He was making it easy for her, showcasing all the highlights of his body. He seemed to enjoy the luscious look she gave his neck. She would have to be careful. Not a good idea to give this guy too many clues as to what turned her on. And she was hungry. Famished. But Anne sensed an exotic, sensual danger lurking between them. She wasn't sure if this was dinner or a date.

After he closed her door, he stood back and gave her the once over. Apparently she'd passed the test, since his gaze fluttered slowly, lingering on parts he liked best, traveling down her whole body and back up again without missing a single detail. He smiled.

"I can buy you coffee, or we can take a drive." Although she doubted he could hurt her in her now powerful state, she thought it unwise to go off with this strange male. And her curiosity about this meeting was taking a close second to her desire to feed.

"Coffee is fine. Just remember what I said yesterday." Her voice didn't sound convincing.

"Oh, yes." He put his massive palm at her lower back again like he had yesterday, and then lead her to the café front doors. "You were telling me you would call the police if I didn't stop . . . being this way." The last part he had said as he leaned over, brushing her ear with his lips.

Damn but it was hard to pull away from him. Everything inside Anne wanted to lean in so she could have a proper kiss. On her ear. Anywhere.

"You invade my space before I give you permission."

"And you don't like it?"

Oh, God. It was hard to lie to him as well.

"No . . . n-no. I don't." Anne could tell he knew what she was thinking.

He held the door open and smiled. "I know what you like," he said as she grazed his chest with her shoulder. "Go find us a seat, okay?" His voice followed behind her.

Anne found the corner with the purple velvet chairs available. She already thought of it as *their spot.* This was not a good sign. To vary the routine, she sat in the other chair this time. Her throat was parched but her pulse quickened with the anticipation of their conversation. Being in the proximity of this man made her feel as if she'd just fed. Her heartbeat so loud she thought anyone in the room would be able to hear it.

He walked across the floor with confidence, the object of every-one's attention. He appeared oblivious he was attractive to both sexes. Anne wondered if he liked both men and women. But when his dark eyes flashed up to meet hers, all was answered. She was convinced he wasn't interested in any other man or woman. He was interested in one woman only.

Me.

Being the object of his attraction was just as exciting as it was scary. She accepted the cardboard cup with its plastic hat, which was dwarfed by his enormous hands. He sat, crossed his long legs, propped his on the arm of the chair, and rested his cheek against the third and forefinger of his right hand.

With difficulty, Anne tore her eyes away. She sipped her cappuccino and looked around the room. She caught furtive glances from other women who tried to look away before they were detected snooping. But his gaze was locked onto her face. At least, when he wasn't looking at her neck.

He leaned forward and put the tips of his fingers and his palms together, elbows resting on his knees. "So, here we are at last."

"Yes. What is it you wanted to talk to me about?"

"I find it funny I am at a loss for words. There is so much I want to say."

"Oh, come on. You don't look like the type who usually gets

scared. You look like the one who does the scaring."

He threw back his head and laughed to the ceiling. She smiled in spite of herself. Watching his lips curl, the dimple at the left side of his mouth and the dark sparkle in his eyes as he focused his attention on her mouth, warmed her whole body.

"True," he said in a soft rumble she could feel deep in her chest. "Very perceptive."

Anne's heart did flip-flops. He was so gorgeous to look at when he smiled. But her need for blood was rising. Now she wished she had fed beforehand so she could concentrate. She was about to count his eyelashes but removed her gaze from his face and instead counted the tufts of carpeting at her feet. It would be impossible to savor him like she'd planned. Her need for his blood was making her ravenous.

And horny as hell.

He held out his hand, palm up.

"Excuse me?" Anne scowled at his impropriety. "I'm not going to sit here and hold your hand. I am still a married woman." She was beginning to convince herself some of what she said was true. There was safety in having him think she was married.

"Give me your hand, Anne. I wouldn't do anything to hurt you, ever. You know this already."

"No. You promised you would behave."

"I am behaving. This is me behaving, believe it or not."

"Then I would hate to see you when you misbehave." Anne knew it was a ridiculous statement. "Don't say a word." She warned.

He chuckled behind a smile.

She looked around the room for help, or for any distraction to the steadfast gaze he was flooding her with, a gaze that made all of her sensitive body parts tingle. She sighed. "Oh, alright. Here." She stuck out her hand.

He took it quickly, held it in both his, warming her cool, sweaty palm. His fingers massaged and kneaded her knuckles. His touch released tension like he knew exactly where she was stiff, like he knew every sinew and muscle of her. His hand was twice the size of hers. She could imagine those fingers working at the tops of her shoulders, down her spine. Other places.

God help her. His touch made her feel wonderful all over.

"Anne, like I said yesterday, I have waited for you a long time. Over three hundred years." He gave a little squeeze to her hand. She took it to mean he knew it was a bit much to take in.

And it was. Anne looked at her fingers, which had become intimately entwined with his. His eyes were pure golden brown now, tethering her to him in some ancient way. Part of her screamed to run for safety. The newer part of her kept her glued to the chair.

"You going to explain this? Don't you think I deserve it?"

"Forgive me. I thought that perhaps . . . well, I wasn't sure how you would take this news." He bent and kissed the backs of her fingers.

"You mean if I believed your story, which I don't?"

"Search your soul." Those three words felt as intimate as if she was standing in front of him naked. Did he know what was inside her soul? How?

She'd been wondering if she indeed had a soul, with all the changes coming at her so fast these days. Maybe he would have some answers. Curiosity was beginning to out-position hunger in the war for her attention.

"So, who am I . . . to you?"

"You are my fated female."

Fated female! What the hell is that? Like I'm born and bred for him? Like I belong to him? No. This isn't happening.

"Why are you so thick-headed? I have told you at least three times, I am married." The more she said those words the more ridiculous they sounded, but her protestations didn't seem to stop him. "And what does this mean, fated female?"

A couple of students reading at the next table looked up. Her voice had carried. Anne pulled back her hand and refused to look at him. But she did want to know what he was dying to tell her. She knew her life would never be the same after this conversation.

"I know what you are, Anne."

And there it was. "I asked you before, how do you know my

name?"

"I told you yesterday, I know you."

"But I don't know you."

"Then I will formally introduce myself. I am Marcus Monteleone." He nodded his head carefully while lowering his eyes.

Something fluttered inside her chest at the sound of his name. "I'm Anne B—um, Morgan. My maiden name is Morgan."

"Yes. Nice to meet you, Anne."

"This doesn't answer any of my questions. What is a fated female?"

"Do you want to continue here, or—"

"Here is fine. Please continue."

"You have undergone a recent change. I know about that."

"And how would you know about that?"

"Because I am the same. The same as you."

A mixture of relief and fear filled her. Finally, she'd met someone she could talk to about the event that occurred in Italy a month ago. She was afraid of finding out the truth about what she was. She knew she was not human. There was a part of her that didn't want to know what that really meant. She would use this chance to ask anyway.

"So what exactly am I?"

"You are one of a golden vampire. Goldens are very rare."

"*Vampire.* Okay." She held out her hand into a ray of sunlight flooding through the coffee shop window. "See? I don't seem to catch fire, and being in the sunlight isn't at all painful."

She saw his eyes dance with something more than humor as she waved her hand around in the sunlight, twisting her fingers and arm in different directions, demonstrating for him.

He raised his fingers to touch the same ray of sunlight, then smiled when he noted her watching his fingers glisten in the bright light, unharmed. "As I said, you are *golden* vampire, like me."

"As opposed to the dark ghouls that run around in rags all the time and sleep in coffins? The ones that can't come out in the sunlight?"

"Exactly. Actually, some of the dark vampires are among my best friends. But each breed usually stays with their own kind."

He was struggling with words. "We are able to live in the sunlight. But we still need to feed. We mate for life. We have children who are born and raised human. They make the choice whether to remain human or turn when they enter puberty."

"And so you chose to become vampire. You were born human?"

"Yes. Just like you. I had a normal human childhood."

"But I *was* human. Neither one of my parents was vampire. My kind *is* human."

"Not any more, Anne."

The truth of his words wounded her. He was right. No longer was she anything close to the same woman she was when she left on her honeymoon. She could pretend. But she could never go back. She was permanently altered. And now would live . . .

Forever?

"But, I prefer to live as a human." Anne knew she had it in her to adjust. No one had to know. And she didn't have to join any weird vampire coven, either.

"You will need help," he said.

"I've adjusted just fine, thank you very much. So far."

He nodded and then smiled back at her with those eyes and she wilted. She felt her will, her control waning. His body sat before her like a magnet, drawing her into some dark, strange journey she hadn't asked for. She'd been made, not born this way. Someone had stolen her human life from her. As much as she didn't want to admit it, she needed information. How had this happened?

"There are things you must be curious about, Anne. Let me help you."

She wasn't sure she trusted him, regardless of the undeniable attraction to his lean body and the way she felt just listening to his voice, feeling his presence, his strength.

"Look. I acknowledge I am no longer human, thanks to that bitch who almost killed me in Italy. Do you know her, as well?"

"Unfortunately, I do. Her name is Maya."

"Well, if she's part of your little group of friends, no thanks. I'm much safer on my own. Your crowd's a little too dangerous for me. I'm better off in the company of my own kind, as you say. My husband and my family . . . of origin."

"He cannot protect you. I can."

She agreed with him. Robert would never be able to protect her, even if she wanted him to. He was a louse and a coward. Always had been.

"You talk about protection. Why wasn't I protected when I was attacked by this woman?"

"She won't hurt you again. She has been enjoined from contacting you personally. She's bridled."

"Bridled, as in a horse?"

"Yes, similar. 'Restrained' may be a better word."

"So then it's up to me to protect my family and friends from her kind?"

"Our kind," Marcus corrected her.

"I don't want anything to happen to Robert just because I had a bit of bad luck."

"I understand. But others might cause him harm as a way to get to you."

"I do care about him." She could see Marcus wasn't convinced.

"Yet you don't live together," he said.

"No. We've had some difficulties." She examined her nails, removed an invisible piece of lint from her skirt.

"Are you truly married to him, Anne?"

"How do you know my name?" She looked up at him and felt his pulse race. She could hear his beating heart. And he felt hers beating in tandem.

"Answer my question and I'll tell you."

"What question?"

"Are you still married?"

Oh, that.

"Technically, probably not." There didn't appear to be any reason to deny what was obvious to him.

"You renounced the ceremony?"

"You mean the wedding? You talk funny."

"Forgive me." He laid his palm against his heart and inclined his head slightly.

"Yes, I renounced the ceremony. But Robert has been a little stubborn about it. He's not quite given up. But legally, I don't believe we are married. And I sure as heck don't feel married."

"Why do you wear his symbol?" Marcus pointed to her ring.

"I can't get it off."

Marcus chuckled, revealing the crease at the side of his mouth that was so damn attractive. "Would you like me to help?" Now he looked like the Cheshire cat.

Anne caught herself gasping for air. Fear mingled with attraction and made her stomach churn. "I'll have a jeweler do it."

Marcus nodded his head slightly. "You put your own husband in jeopardy the longer you are near him. Don't you ever fantasize feeding on him? You could kill him, you know."

I've already had that thought. Every day.

"I think I have more control than you give me credit for. The reason I feed is so I can be strong. I may not want Robert as a husband, but I wouldn't want him to come to harm, would you?"

Marcus gave her one of those confident smiles. "You have no need to worry about me. I will not cause either of you harm." His gaze drilled his words into her head.

"Who then? Why is he in danger?"

"I'll explain it later. Trust me, as long as others think he is your husband, he is in grave danger."

"Then I will protect him. And I am going to live my life as a human. No one but you will know about this. So, you see, you need not worry. I'm all taken care of."

"What will you do when people notice you do not age? What will you tell them, my pet?"

"I'm not your pet. Look, all this is new. I'll figure something out."

"Don't you want children?"

"Yes. Someday."

"What will you do when you don't get pregnant? You can't be

tested or your secret will be revealed."

"I might be able to have children. I don't see why not. I'm healthy, just eccentric in my eating habits." It felt good to say it, even though she knew he didn't believe her.

"Do you bleed?"

"Excuse me? Don't you think that is a little personal?" She couldn't believe he had asked her about this.

"How can you get pregnant if you don't bleed? Do you bleed now?"

Anne waited a minute before she answered. "So what? I've skipped a cycle. I can't be pregnant, but I don't see why I couldn't. Maybe I will when my body gets adjusted."

"If you were with me, you would bleed."

"This is getting to the point where I feel like I should leave."

He covered her hand resting on the arm of the chair. Anne could see the tenderness he was trying to convey.

"I wish you wouldn't. I would like the chance to earn your trust. To become your . . . friend."

"I thought you said I was your fated female."

"Well, that is what I feel. Clearly you do not, yet."

"No. And I'm not going to allow even the hint of that thought in my head." As she said this, she saw his body covering hers on a bed with black sheets in a room lit by candles. She knew she wouldn't have to be careful not to hurt him. She saw him feeding on her neck as she fed on his. Her face flushed. He smiled.

"Are you spying on me? Following me around? At night?" Her cheeks flushed as she recalled her erotic dreams.

"Oh, yes, I admit it. But don't worry about your safety. I'm actually going to help you protect your husband. There are those of our kind who don't think you should be married to a mortal. People are watching you."

"I think it's creepy so many people want to insert themselves into my life. What did I ever do to them? Why me?"

"Because of who you are and what you represent."

"Well, I want to be left alone. To live my life as I see fit. Without all this baggage. I didn't ask for this."

"I believe you. I promise not to interfere. But, Anne, you must accept the fact that you have changed, and you need someone to help you along with this change. I would like to be that person. I will promise not to be inappropriate. You won't do anything you don't want to. You won't be unfaithful to your 'husband,' if that is your choosing. I won't ask that of you."

"I do have questions, but I don't think this is a good idea."

"Let me earn your trust. I won't ask you to compromise your standards. I am discreet."

Like hell you are. You're about as discreet as an ambulance with a screaming siren running through a playground filled with children. The things I think about when I'm with you. I seem to not have a will of my own.

Anne fiddled with a seam on her jacket. She noted Marcus had five buttons on his shirt, all mother of pearl, except that one which was slightly grey in color and didn't match the others. And then there might be another mismatched button, but it was tucked into . . . into . . . wait. There were thirteen people in the coffee shop and they had made twenty-six espresso drinks in the last fifteen minutes, which meant they sold one hundred four espresso drinks an hour, at an average price of three dollars and sixty-five cents, that would mean $379 and thirty . . . no . . . sixty cents per hour just on the espresso . . .

"Please?" His words brought her back to their conversation. "I have nothing but the best of intentions. Honest."

"My better judgment says no."

He leaned forward and collapsed his fingers together, which he then tented on his lap. "Trust your heart, then."

There it was again, the battle between logic and emotion. She looked up. There must be something else that needed to be inventoried. She started scanning the room again.

He placed his hand on hers. "Stop counting."

She stared at him, stunned. How did he know?

"Have just a little trust in me. I will not hurt you in any way, and I won't have you do something you will ever live to regret. Ever."

"You promise?"

"Absolutely."

"I'm still not convinced."

"That's my job."

She knew he would not have any trouble with this. The tough front she was showing was in actuality paper-thin. Her resistance was futile. "This meeting turned out much different than I thought it would. I don't usually talk to strange men."

He chuckled. "Not polite to talk with your mouth full."

"That was awful! Stop that." But she was smiling inside and couldn't help but show him on the outside.

"Well, this was a good start. It's good to see you can find the humor in our . . . our . . . situation." He patted her hand but did not grab it. "But one thing can stay as planned."

"And what is that?" She watched a glow cover his face. His full, deep rose-colored lips curved up at the ends, forming a seductive smile and showing just the tip of one white fang. He had no right to look at her that way, to melt her to the core. Unable to help herself, she focused on those lips as he formed his answer.

"I am still willing to be your meal."

Chapter 9

"AND WHERE WOULD you prefer this feeding to take place, my pet?" He was very close to her, just outside the café entrance.

"Look, Marcus. I know you are trying hard. It bothers me when you call me pet. It feels inappropriate."

"I understand."

They did not touch, but the heat from his body was warm and intimate. Anne would have to say intoxicating. The sound of his voice was velvet. She had the urge to lean closer to him. His breathing was new to her, but becoming familiar the longer she stayed in his presence. She could pick out the unique resonant sounds deep within his chest of his inhalation and exhalation from a crowd of fifty men, at a distance across the parking lot. A group of teenage girls tittered as they scanned his large, looming frame bent over hers. He didn't pay them any attention. A young couple waiting in line inside the store turned and looked back at them several times.

"I will pick a place, then."

He led her to his car. The instant she sat down in the rich black leather upholstery his scent enveloped her. She caught a glimpse of him through the windshield as he made his way around the front of the car. And then he was inside.

The area between her legs throbbed. Her panties felt moist. She was lost in this sensual pleasure, aware of the thin line between the two kinds of hunger, one for blood and one for sex. This male could satisfy both.

His fingers grazed her cheek. His forefinger traced her lips. She parted her lips and let her tongue barely touch the tip of his finger. He moved his hand along her jaw line and turned her head to face him.

He whispered, "Do not be afraid. Please trust me." His eyes had that copper ring at the outsides of the irises, which pulsed to his heartbeat.

She was at the edge of losing her consciousness.

The roar of the car made her jump. The Ferrari was a beast, a living thing, demanding attention. Demanding to be driven. By a strong male. This male. This male who thought she was his female.

Each time the car jerked forward, centrifugal force pressed her body back against the molded seat, and each time her head was jammed into the headrest she felt the thrust of a male inside her. Marcus didn't try to drive carefully. His reflexes were perfect. He drove with confidence and command. Captain of her ship. Keeper of her soul. God help her, he was both.

They drove up the freeway as other cars scrambled to distance themselves from the Ferrari's powerful lunges. About twenty minutes later they had passed a town square surrounded by shops, and then turned left out into the valley floor, which was covered in vineyards, lush and verdant.

"See, Anne, the grapes are still green." He slowed down, leaned across her, and pointed out the window so she could see the clusters glowing in the early July sun. "Some of these will be deep burgundy in color within just a couple of weeks. The change happens fast."

She nodded her head. He pulled back his arm and she felt the airspace in front of her grow cool.

"Everything changes, turns. The leaves turn colors. The grapes. The grasses in the fields. Even the sky turns from blue to gray to black, and then back to blue again."

She continued nodding, accepting the lesson.

Teach me more. Her insides ached for a touch from him. She rested her hand on his as he maneuvered the gearshift lever. She felt the rumble of a groan emanating from his chest.

"You touch me, female. You touch me."

"I couldn't help it."

He pulled over to a gravel trail that led through a rusted gate he clicked open with the touch of a button on the dashboard. They climbed a small hill. He positioned the car so they could see the rows of vineyards stretched before them. The beautiful sight brought tears to her eyes. She was filled with emotion—both confusing and delicious.

"I will kiss you now, my female."

She should resist, but found she couldn't lift a finger to stop him. He leaned toward her face as she parted her lips. "Anne. Just say Anne," she barely got out just before her breath was taken away.

His lips on hers made the ground tremble. He was warm and seeking. There was not an ounce of hesitation in the way his mouth claimed hers, in the way he angled his head to gain more access to her. The suckling between them became more forceful as their tongues danced. He chased her, and she was so willing to be caught. She was aware of the faint smell of his light citrus cologne and the harsh sound of his breath as he tasted her.

They parted for air, then repositioned their bodies to face each other. The car was unforgiving and the leather seats groaned. Her back and thighs were wet with the sweet sweat of arousal. She looked into his dark eyes but could not see the copper there. She studied his lips and mentally willed them to take her again. He must have known because he reached for her again.

After a long moment, Anne put her hand to Marcus's cheek and brushed her thumb over the prominent bone under his eye, then lightly rubbed her three middle fingers over his mouth to feel his breath there. She licked her lips, then touched the sharp tip of her fangs on her tongue. She was desperately hungry for him now and wasn't afraid to show it.

He moved her hand open so he could kiss the inside of her palm. He followed that kiss with others up to her wrist. His tongue traced the blue vein that throbbed there. The question was in his eyes before he said it.

"May I taste you?"

She inhaled and nodded.

He closed his eyes, then very lightly pricked the vein with one sharp fang. He drew upon her. Her palm went limp but then pressed against the side of his face as she offered her wrist to his needy mouth.

He didn't take much. She almost wished he had taken more. Sensing this small snack could be dangerous, she allowed the moment to pass. He kissed the skin and left it slightly red and violated.

"How do you feed?" She wondered why she suddenly wanted to know.

"I have a delivery service bringing me fresh blood daily. I don't like to hunt. I am like you that way."

She watched his tongue lave over the little red marks on her wrist and suddenly wanted the marks to show so she could trace her fingers over her sensitive flesh and see he had been there.

"But Anne, you will feed from me."

"Will I be satisfied feeding only from you? I mean, can we each keep each other satisfied?"

His face broke into a warm smile that lit up the afternoon. "In time, I hope to be able to satisfy your every need. But the answer to your question is we could do this for a short—a few days or maybe a week. However, one of us would need outside blood or else we would begin to get tired and perhaps age. You can feed from me without having to hunt, for the time being." He leaned over and whispered in her ear, "And I hope you will be fully satisfied with my blood."

Anne knew she would be. Her lips were anticipating the taut texture of his skin. Her fangs ached and her throat was thirsty for the rich coppery taste of his life force.

"Come, it's time, my p— . . . Anne." He smiled and got out of the car. It took an eternity for him to walk around the front, to come to her side and to open the door. He gave his hand, gripped hers, and pulled her from the vehicle. The car seemed to shudder as it released her.

When she fully stood, they faced each other but did not touch. She felt the heat from his body as he carefully kept the space between them. She knew he did not want space between them. She understood the sacrifice offered. The gesture made her both grateful and stimulated. He dropped her hand.

He pulled out a quilt from the rear of the car, wrapped it over his arm, and then held his other hand out to her to walk alongside him.

They were at a hillside vineyard, and as they walked among the vines, Anne frequently turned to look at the display of the valley floor below them. Everything was alive and growing. Everything was green and golden, bathed in sunlight, as if she were looking through a tinted windowpane. The view and the moment were perfect. She felt the happiest she had ever been. The setting felt like Tuscany all over again.

Marcus spread the thick quilt down between the vines and sat. She stood above him.

"You may take me, Anne, but except for a little taste you've been permitted, I will not feed from you. I only do that when I make love, and I will not ask that of you today. You won't have to worry about stopping. Come." He held out his hand and she took it, then stooped to her knees. He put her hand on the buttons of his shirt and left it there.

She unbuttoned the first one. He watched her in silence. Then she unbuttoned the second one. She looked into his dark eyes and felt his pulse quicken at the touch of her fingertips on the skin of his chest. She peeled his shirt back to the side and slid her hand up his neck, feeling the strength of the blood flow there. The touch of his skin gave her little jolts of pleasure. His eyes showed her his complete surrender.

"Take me," he begged, his voice husky as if he were barely able to speak. "You will see it won't take much to satisfy."

Anne wished his hands were on her breasts.

MARCUS HEARD HER words of apology, words she didn't need to say. Just the same, he loved hearing them.

"I will try to be gentle. I'm learning." Anne flashed her dark eyes at him. Her eyebrows rose, making shallow creases form above the bridge of her nose. Her silky eyelashes sparkled and fluttered, fanning his cheeks. His desire flamed for her, just as he expected.

"You won't hurt me." *Though I wish you would.* "Don't be afraid to bite deep and"—he got distracted by her pouty lips—"suck hard." His voice trailed off, wavering. He wasn't anxious to hurry the touch of her lips, the feel of her fangs in his flesh. He had waited three hundred years and could wait a few delicious minutes more.

Marcus lay back on the blanket but did not draw her to his chest. She was not yet his to possess. Anne adjusted her body, carefully leaning on him as if she could hurt him. Her long brown curls grazed his bare chest for the first time, sending him into ecstasy. He knew, but she didn't, that in lying down she would have to press her breasts to his chest in order to feed. He could have merely seated himself in a chair and had her come at him from behind.

I am not sorry for this little deception. I am not a gentleman. I am a scheming rake. But he wasn't crossing the line. Not yet.

With his gaze fixed deep into hers, he saw her quick little inhale when she scanned his chest, felt the side of his neck, and then inhaled his scent. He felt her change focus from lover to ravenous female in need of feeding. Her eyes swept up to the side of his neck, taking in his thick pulsating vein. He let his blood hammer hard and course lower, into his groin. Her thigh moved in response.

Swallowing first, she lowered her chin, then took a deep breath. When she placed her right palm against his exposed pectoral muscles, he felt her warmth all over his body. Her fingers lightly dusted his skin. Her breath came over him, timid and demure, belying something deeper inside. She hungered for him. After one last check and his nod of approval, she lowered her upper body onto him, laced her fingers through his hair, and then pulled it aside, giving herself full access to his neck. He got a glimpse of her fangs just before her lips touched him. He grew thirsty. Thirsty for her blood.

And then she bit down on him.

The fating was unmistakable. Her lips pressed against his skin and she suckled, drawing his life force into her body. It left him feeling delirious, invincible, and ageless. He felt the dust from years of loneliness fall away, as if he'd stepped into a warm shower. And then something wonderful happened.

She moaned.

Reflex action made him raise his hand, wanting to press her into him deeper, but he stopped just before he could touch the small of her back.

At last! Worth the three hundred years of waiting. My fated female drinks of me. She tastes me. She needs me.

THE WARM ELIXIR, his life force, moved over Anne's tongue and filled the caverns of her soul. What she drank almost didn't taste like blood, but rather like a fine brandy, laced with something else that was more emotion than taste. She felt every cell of her body plump up with the vitality of his liquid, then scream for more. She felt places that had withered and her body and soul suddenly become alive and supple.

She slowed down the taking to make it last and found that she could savor him. She moved one knee across his lap, which lightly grazed across his bulging pants. His shaft came alive with the stimulation. He groaned and pressed his cheek to hers. She straddled him and very carefully set herself down, placing her sex just above his. She tingled where her mound touched his erection.

She inhaled one more time and took the last bits and found, with relief, she could stop without draining him. This was the first time she had been satisfied without taking life. Nothing had ever felt better.

She kissed the two holes in his skin. A tear came to her eye at the sight of the damage she'd caused him. He pulled her with both his hands to face him, then rubbed the tears from her cheeks. His mouth came over hers. She sighed into his kiss.

"Oh, God. Thank you. That was so wonderful," she whispered, "I never knew about this."

His serious eyes almost looked sad. "It has been a long time since I first had this dream. You have no idea how wonderful it is to have my female love the taste of me."

He put his hands at her hips, then moved her over his crotch, watching her. She let him, and let him slide one hand up under her stretchy top. His fingers brushed across her nipples, which hardened and knotted under the flimsy fabric of her bra. She arched up at his touch. She drew close to an orgasm. Every part of her body was more sensitive than ever before.

He withdrew his hand. "I've made you a promise. I will keep it."

"Yes, thank you." Anne looked down. Somehow, she had become shy.

"With my blood inside you, you will experience strong erotic dreams tonight."

Anne knew exactly what he meant. She was starting to feel the sexual intensity coming already. But there was no desire for anyone but this man before her. Just an empty room. Waiting. Waiting to be filled with the scent and body of this man.

She bent down and kissed him again. He slid a finger up her thigh to the front of her panties, then rubbed her through the thin fabric. He could have dipped a finger or two under the elastic at the leg and felt her sex, but his hand remained still. He started to remove his hand, but she held him there, rubbing his hand against the thin fabric of her panties. But he did not violate the trust, even though he must have understood she would not deny him. He pulled her back from the brink.

"Someday, Anne, you will be mine in every sense of the word. Until then, you can take me as often as you like. Drink only from me. I don't want you in the company of strange men. It is safer this way." His finger continued to rub her sex. "I promise I won't hurt you. I will protect you and the man they call your husband. But drink only from me, promise?" He removed his hand and held her face. "Promise me?"

"I promise."

Chapter 10

MARCUS DRANK HIS best red wine and warmed himself by the fireplace in his study, alone. The flames soothed his nerves. He saw her face coming to him, rising above him as she felt the power of his passion coursing through her veins. He hadn't wanted to take her home, but he'd promised not to interfere until he was given permission.

He felt the red bumps at the side of his neck where Anne had bitten him, noting that the swelling was going down. He almost wished the wound wouldn't heal, but rather stay in all its painful glory, a living legacy, a celebration of the love he felt for this woman. She had tasted him and wanted more. And he had so much more to give her. For the first time in decades, he was filled with joy.

Tonight she would feel the full force of his blood in her body. He had decided to let her experience it without interference. He wished he could go over to her house and share her passion. He thought about what they would do some day when they mated in the ancient way of the goldens, and his hard-on increased to painful proportions.

He pressed the bumps again, a little harder this time, until it hurt. He wanted to relive that moment when her fangs had crossed the threshold and had taken something from him and made it a part of her. A part of his body would now be inside hers forever. Nothing else in the universe compared to the thrill of her feeding. And she had promised to use him as her sole source of sustenance and energy. He now had even more of a reason to live, to serve her. His new purpose would help soothe his anxious libido.

He looked down at his cell phone. He'd given her an identical phone so she could call him when she needed him. He'd programmed only one number into it: his.

She does need me. I bring her life's blood. I will fill her every need in time.

He rubbed his thumb over the plastic face piece as if he could will it to light up and ring with her beckoning. He could always go find her in the meantime. He had been finding her on his own for over a month now. But some time tomorrow, she would call and ask for him, as her vampire hunger overrode what was left of her doubt.

He doubted she would sleep at all tonight. It was risky, knowing her friskiness could put her in harm's way, but she'd promised only to feed from him. She would promise much more when their love came to full bloom, when he could claim her, but for now, this little victory was all he had. He'd wait. Even the genetic pull he felt toward her, his fated female, was delicious, albeit painful. He didn't want to make himself unwelcome. It was important she be the first one to reach out.

ANNE BOUGHT EXTRA pillar candles. She opened the Cabernet. She would put the steaks on later, after she called him. She had dropped by Victoria's Secret on her way back and had bought a new black lace bra and panty set. She'd come home, showered, washed her hair, shaved everything she could, and rubbed her body down with almond butter cream. When putting on makeup, she did her eyes darker than usual and used red lip plumper in a cherry flavor.

She removed her robe and felt the wickedness the black lacy underwear that squeezed her breasts and barely hugged her peach, which was bruised with desire. She wished it wasn't so hot, or she would have built a fire. But there were enough candles around for two fires, since she wanted to spend the evening naked with him, and watch the flicker of light caress his skin.

She lit the row of pillar candles that sat on the window ledge behind the couch. Then she lit the ones on the coffee table, then ones in the guest bathroom. She lit the three candles on the tumbled soapstone vanity top in the master bath, and then moved to the bed. She was bent down, match touching a white ginger pillar wick on her side of the bed, when she noticed the burgundy red glass votive and the scented reddish orange candle contained in it. She had not put it there.

Holding the end of the wick, she raised the little stubby candle from its glass holder and read the foil label on the underside.

Blood Orange.

It shouted, "I am here. I wait by your bed at night."

His blood was in her veins, filling her with a sexual desire she hadn't felt in years. She welcomed the change. She felt it as a gift given by someone who truly cared for her. It was a simple fact. Marcus was a welcome guest, and she was thrilled just thinking about seeing him again.

She set the candle back down in the holder and lit it.

Thank you, Marcus.

There was no answer.

But first, she had one more thing to do before she could lose herself in the evening. She needed to set up a meeting with Robert for tomorrow. She needed to put that chapter of her life behind her so she'd be free to—what? She picked up her cell and dialed Monika's number.

"Hello, Anne? Is that you?" Monika's voice seemed far away.

"Tell Robert I need to meet with him tomorrow, at nine."

"I don't know anything about this," Monika replied.

"I'm sure he'll fill you in. Will you tell him?"

"Yes. Anne, I am so sorry about what has happened. Robert and I—"

"Forget it, Monika. I don't want to hear it."

Anne was grateful for the silence at the other end of the phone.

"Monika?"

"Yes. I understand."

"You need to get ready."

"For what?"

"Robert is going to need a place to stay, to save him from himself."

"Not sure what you're talking about."

"He has a lot of stuff. But I'm keeping the car." Anne hung up.

One thing to tell Robert he would have to find another place to stay, quite another to tell the other woman. She was proud of herself. There wasn't an ounce of regret in her body.

She stripped off the sheets on her bed and threw them in the washing machine. She added the new silk sheets she'd bought this afternoon and had washed in lavender soap. They were still warm and filled the room with fragrance.

Anne closed her eyes. She concentrated on the way Marcus's lips felt on hers as she pushed the number "8," which automatically dialed his number.

He picked up at the first ring. "Anne. Is everything well with you?" There was an edge of concern in his voice.

"Yes, Marcus."

He exhaled in relief. "Good. I'm glad. How do you feel?"

In truth, she felt the best she had ever felt in her life. "I feel fine." It was an understatement, but she didn't want to seem too eager. Would it scare him off?

His rolling chuckle starting a buzzing in her ears, like he was blowing on them. "I had hoped you would feel more than fine . . ."

"Yes. You know how I feel."

"Do I? Tell me. I want to hear you say it."

"I. Feel. Wonderful." There, she'd said it. "Thank you."

"My pleasure."

Anne felt her face flush at his words. Everything in her body attuned to the vibrations coming from his words. "Listen," she began. Why was she so nervous? "I was putting on some dinner and wondered if I could have the pleasure of your company?"

He uttered something she couldn't make out. The happy ripples of his laughter trickled down her spine and warmed her.

"You hungry so soon?" he asked.

"Is it too soon? I'm *starved.*"

"That makes two of us."

"I have a couple of rare steaks I would like to share. You do eat rare meat?"

"Only the rarest."

"You didn't tell me I would feel this way. Positively wicked. Dangerous. Am I dangerous, Marcus?"

"Yes and no. To me, no. To others, like your husband . . ."

"Almost-husband," she corrected.

"To all your human family and friends, you are dangerous."

"As in, I could harm them?" She was enjoying playing with him.

"I promised I'd help you protect your husband. I won't violate that promise."

"So you—the man I've known for less than twenty-four hours—are someone I can trust, and my non-husband, who I have known for three years, I cannot?"

"That's about the size of it," he said into the phone. "But I've searched for you for three hundred years. Don't forget that part."

"I found your candle. I thought you might want to watch it burn with me."

"Next time I'll have to bring a bigger one."

"You've already saved his life, you know."

"Robert? How is that?"

"I admit to having unkind thoughts towards my almost-husband. But it wouldn't have been fair to make you visit me in a jail cell, now would it?"

"Inconvenient is the word I was thinking," he said.

"He actually did me a favor, didn't he?"

"I hope he'll do you one more by releasing you from your vows."

"He already discarded me, Marcus."

He was silent. Then he whispered, "You shouldn't feel . . . discarded."

"I'm needing to feel wanted right now. Can you do this for me?"

The warm breath at the back of her neck carried his words. "I shall devote my whole life to it, I promise."

Chapter 11

MARCUS PUT HIS arms on Anne's bare shoulders as he stood behind her and kissed her neck. She shuddered as if she were cold, yet her body was burning like a torch. He brought his arms around her chest and she leaned back against him. She pressed her cheek next to his, as if seeking his connection. He'd thought she'd be more afraid of him.

Fated. She feels it too. She is mine, after all.

He turned her around, then smoothed a hand down her chest, tracing the space between her breasts with his forefinger. He eased his fingers underneath the satin bra. His fingers grazed over her nipples. She leaned back, making him hold her up with his other arm.

"Are you hungry now?"

"No. Yes." She began to cry. "I'm confused. I feel everything . . . stronger."

It made his heart ache to see this. He pressed her face against his chest, and she sobbed as he stroked her hair.

"It is a lot to take in. That's why I'm here, to guide you, to keep you safe. Ease you into this life of ours. Perhaps you had too much this afternoon. In time, you will adjust."

She looked up at him, her eyes filled with tears. Her lips called to him. "I don't want to adjust."

"You will learn how to deal with the fullness of this passion, in time. It's overwhelming at first." He loved how her tears danced in the candlelight, like the sparkle of diamonds he would buy her.

"I don't want to learn how to deal with it. I want to feel this way forever." She stared at his lips, her tongue coming to the edges, as if seeking to taste his mouth. He gave in to her, covering her quivering lips. Her supple body melted against his frame.

He understood fully the new, confusing emotions she was experiencing and the intensity that grew in her flesh by the hour. He was suddenly grateful for the more than three hundred years he'd had to prepare. He'd always thought the wait as a curse, when in fact it had been a gift. Anne was young in her new life. And just a few hours had passed since her first taste of her fated male. She was in need of a satisfaction he was not prepared to give her tonight. In his world, the fating mark would be followed by a night of beautiful sex. But he was enjoined from this claiming. He wanted to be very careful. There was eternity at stake.

He picked her up and sat down on the couch, with her in his lap. He could smell the heat of her passion. "I like these new clothes," he said, hooking a finger through the ribbon of the black thong at her hip.

"I'm overdressed." She begged him with her eyes.

"Insatiable. I had hoped it would be so."

"You knew." She lightly covered his lips with hers and whispered, "Take them off me. Rip them off me."

"Anne, I cannot . . ."

"Don't tell me what you cannot do," she said between kisses. "Do what you can. Please, I need your hands and mouth on me. *Please.*" She laid her head against his heart. Her hand slid underneath his shirt to fan out over his burning chest. She unbuttoned one button and kissed him there. Her little tongue wickedly played with his nipple.

The fact she was consumed with his nearness and the heat of his body sent him into his basic primal nature. He felt the pain of knowing he would have to stop her, but secretly hoped he did not have the strength to. He could not have asked for a better partner. Anne had taken to her new appetites like she had missed them her whole life. He hoped he could teach her fast enough to keep her from getting bored.

"I am flattered you wish to cook dinner for me . . ."

"But you don't want . . . food," she purred to his chest.

"Perhaps a little wine. But dinners are a bit different for us now." He smiled with his lips closed. He found it amusing she had forgotten she was trying to entertain him as a human man.

"A little taste then, Marcus."

"Yes, of course . . . Anne." This he could give her. He would never deny her the taste of his blood.

Her bite was almost a tickle. She supped his essence but was not greedy. He felt her heartbeat race as his blood hit her system and her passion rose.

"You want me?" She looked at him with those deep eyes. "You want me, Marcus?" His hand had found its way to between her legs. His long forefinger was tracing the mystery of her sex over the panties. The muscles at her lower belly contracted. She arched into him. "More."

He tore the ribbon and her panties went limp. Her pelvis rocked back and forth, calling to his groin.

She turned and raised one knee, giving his fingers access to her. "Do you want me?" she asked again as she guided his hand to close in on her mound.

"Yes. But I cannot take you yet."

"I release you from your vow."

"You're not released from yours. So I must uphold it."

"But he has. He has chosen Monika. I am released."

"He must release your vow, not your body."

She sighed.

It was difficult for him to know that he could satisfy her every need, but was not allowed to do so. He'd not yet been given permission. "Soon, soon, my pet."

She raised her arms up to his neck and pulled his head down, then kissed him. She demanded to know his mouth with her tongue. She found his fangs. Her tongue eased over one sharp point, lightly piercing her own skin, and she moaned. A single drop fell to his tongue and he swirled it, mating with hers. The taste of her blood was sweet, and it heightened his passion.

"Careful, careful, pet."

But she wouldn't be denied. She raised herself up to straddle his lap. Her white breasts shone in the candlelight as she arched and undulated on his crotch. He found himself groaning as his cock rose in response to the feel of her warm body massaging it through his jeans. He touched her nipples and then squeezed them with his hands. She was perfect for him, filling his palms with the flesh he had missed for centuries. He kissed the nipples, and then suckled them, grazing one with a sharp nick. He lapped the single drop of blood from her like it was the last on earth. He could feel his resolve and control vanishing. He wanted her, wanted to fill her with his seed. He could not bear the thought of being without her for even a minute.

"Marcus, take me. Please take me." His heart soared with the words, words he thought he might never hear. His hands moved up and down her back, then he kneaded her buttocks as she leaned into him, arms about his neck, squeezing her breasts together, pressing them into his waiting mouth. She rose up, tilted her pelvis over one of his hands that had drifted down her front side to between her legs, and spread her folds by using his own fingers. He rimmed her opening, stroking gently. He felt the slick muscle of her opening and breached her with his first two fingers, indulging in the warmth and wetness there. She moved her sex back and forth, allowing him to massage her clit with his thumb.

She was fully orgasmic, moving to his ministrations of love. He felt her muscles clamp down on his fingers. A new wetness thickly rewarded his efforts.

He whispered in her hair that covered the side of her face, "I have a place I want to take you. Will you let me trace us there?"

"Trace?"

"May I show you how we can travel together?"

Her large eyes scanned his soul. He felt her trust and the blissful experience of her need. She nodded. He stood and held her thighs around his waist, then moved her so he was holding her sideways, one arm under her knees.

"Hold on. Sometimes it gets cold." He set her down, then brought a throw from the couch and placed it around her shoulders. It was his excuse for touching her while covering her lovely body. She nodded again and, laid her head against his chest.

There was a flapping sound as they instantly transported to the sacred temple pool. He set her down at the top of the stairs that descended into the water. Steam rose. A faint smell of oranges and spice lingered in the air.

He started to take his clothes off. Anne let the blanket fall to the tiled floor, then stood naked before him. His erection throbbed. She finished his undress. Each piece of his body that was revealed to her brought kisses. He had never felt so worshiped. No woman had demonstrated her desire for him in such a manner.

On her knees, she encircled his cock with her fingers and looked up at him. She took him into her mouth, the force of her tongue wrapping around his shaft, calling forth a hardness he had never experienced in his ancient lifetime. It was heaven.

Fated. We are fated. It has to be.

She worked over his skin, sucking and caressing him, making him harder, the blood expanding him still. She dug her nails into his buttocks to push him deeper into her mouth. She gasped, and he felt her need for his seed as she drew him in and out with her wet lips. Her moans nearly made him explode. He was desperate to release into her mouth. She paused, the look of need in her eyes, confirmation of what she wanted from him.

He could not speak. His passion flared as she studied him, let him see her desire. With her mouth all over his throbbing cock, her tiny fangs grazed the flesh. The small wound wasn't painful. She drew him in deeper and sucked again, which drove him over the edge. He spilled his seed deep in her throat. The edges of her lips curled up as she swallowed him again and again. He felt her body temperature rise.

She was hot with lust, and she refused to stop. Her skillful mouth and tongue worked on him again, urging his full member on. She rubbed her sex against his leg. He smiled and motioned for her to rise up.

"I am thrilled beyond belief, my little pet, that you have such an appetite." He smoothed the hair back from her forehead and kissed her there. She claimed his lips, pressing her sex into his thigh and rubbing back and forth.

"Ah, Marcus," she sighed into his open mouth, "I will never be able to get enough of you."

"Well, you have only tasted blood these past weeks. We don't want to upset your delicate stomach."

She shot him a questioning look.

"My semen is an aphrodisiac, as perhaps you have noticed, especially for my fated female."

She flashed him a sinful smile. "Then you must not give me so much."

It truly was a wicked thought. Impossible to accomplish as well. He chuckled at her humor. *Fated. Comfortable with me completely.* He took her hand and they walked down the steps into the pool together. Her face became radiant in the light, the ripples of water casting golden ringlets onto her skin.

"What is this place?" Her eyes were wide, excited.

"It is special to our kind. We call it the Pool of Grace. It's where we go to wash our conscience, our bodies of impurities, where we confess . . . things."

"What things?"

"You will see. Soon, my love." He knew she wouldn't be satisfied for long with this answer, but was grateful she had no more questions.

They dipped to their necks into the warm water. She encircled his waist with her legs and wrapped her arms about his neck. She pulled out the leather string that tied his hair back and let the black curls fall at the sides of his face. She kissed him, showing him her hunger for his body.

"Oh, God, I confess I love this man, this man's body. Forgive me for wanting him so."

"Yes, my pet. I'm yours. I'm yours forever." But he did not take the oath. He stopped just short. He wanted to complete the ceremony, wanted to bind them together for all eternity when he was at liberty to do so, when the words could take hold. When it was real. Oh, God, how he wished for that moment now. But he would have to be patient. Just like he told her. *In time.*

He set her on the steps and watched as the golden waters glowed against her body. He put his hands inside her knees, which parted for him at his slight touch.

"I wish to pleasure you. I wish to do more, but this is all I can to-night. Please enjoy what I can give. I hope it is enough."

"Then take all of me you can, please. Take all you can, Marcus."

Her folds were pink and hot for him. She leaned back on her elbows, watching him approach her, her eyes wide and dancing.

I've waited centuries for my female to need me like this.

He needed to see her desire and abandon for him as much as his cock needed to spill inside her.

He slipped his long forefinger into her dripping sex. She arched back, breasts reaching to the sky. He massaged her with gentleness, rubbing over her button, causing her to jump with each little friction. He was thrilled to see her spot swollen and bright red. She moaned as he took forever to tickle his next finger up inside her. His other hand squeezed her nipples. Her warm pink breast filled his hand with the flesh he craved. She jerked as her pleasure began to build.

Anne sat up onto his fingers, pressing her sex against his palm, squeezing his fingers with her muscles. Marcus felt the need to satisfy her fully as she rocked herself back and forth on his hand, looking into his dark eyes. He smiled, loving the vacant stare she gave him when she began to climax, sweat beads collecting on her forehead and on her fuzzy upper lip. That lip needed to be taken, he thought as he bent down and slanted over her mouth. He tasted the salt of her sweat and his fingers completed their thrusting until she fell backwards, but he caught her with one hand at the small of her back, that place where he had touched her in the coffee shop. Her scream was exquisite.

"Ah, yes, my pet. But I am not done with you."

He seemed to have piqued her attention. She raised her head to look at him, a question written on her face. He smiled. *Good, she was not expecting more.* His insides were roaring in flames. He could not get enough of the sight of her, spread before him under the lights. Water dripped and splashed, and the warm moist fragrance of orange spice and sex floated on the air. He licked his lips to taste the salt of her sweat.

He lowered his mouth to her mound and kissed the bare pink flesh. Her lower lips were soft as a newborn's skin as he teased them apart, running his tongue along the meaty dark pink of her insides.

She was fruit of the gods to him—the elixir of life was the taste of her orgasm. He placed one of her knees, then the other, over his shoulders, then knelt on the steps before her, his head deep between her thighs. She clutched his hair. He knew she was pulsing with pleasure that grew inside her with each lap of his tongue.

"Oh, Marcus, Marcus, please. Please take me." Her voice was soft and more breath than words. He heard her perfectly.

"There is one more thing I can do. Oh, sweet Anne, I wish I could do more." He moved his lips to the side of her sex in the little hollow between her labia and the top of her thigh. He replaced his tongue with his two long fingers inside her, twisting them, causing her to gasp. He first kissed the little hollow area, and then bit her hard, drawing blood.

She went wild. Marcus wondered at that moment whether he might not be able to contain himself. But he forced a stop and kissed the redness he'd left behind while her body still shuddered from her orgasm. He slowly lapped up the juice from her sex, then sucked her with his lips and tongue.

"I could live on your taste alone." In his dialect, he whispered some of the ancient love poems he knew, calling forth the goddess of her womb. He would teach her these words in time. In time, she would say them back to him. In time.

In time.

She dropped her knees, then leaned forward and wrapped herself around his body. He floated with her across the pool. Their lips caressed each other's, their hands explored and rubbed. Marcus wanted to put his shaft inside her, but that would be on another night, when he was given permission to take her in the ancient way of their kind.

They lazily wafted around the pool. She was now looking at the white gazebo structure overhead and the stars in the background.

"Don't count them. I am all you need," he said, smiling.

"I don't think I can. I seemed to have lost the ability." She smiled, as if shy.

"Then you're satisfied, my pet."

Chapter 12

"IT PAINS ME to leave you." Anne could hear the crackling in Marcus's voice and the catch in his throat. Sun had invaded her brightly wallpapered bedroom. She rolled over to entangle their legs again, loving the feel of the hard length of his lean body against hers. They'd stayed up all night. First at the temple, then from the early morning hours until this glorious dawn in her own bed. The satin sheets still smelled of lavender as she moved about. But there was also the scent of their mingling love.

"Then don't. Don't leave me, Marcus." She tried to reach his neck again, so he lifted her small frame and held her by her buttocks as she straddled him. She kissed him, begging him to resume their passionate play.

He cupped her face with his enormous hands. "Even immortals rest sometimes. Last night you wore me out, little one." He placed his hand on his chest. "My heart feels like it is going to burst. But there are some things that have to stay the same for awhile. There is much we need to talk about."

His warm smile made her hot for him all over again. She could see herself spending days in bed with him. "But I have only just started."

"Yes." He chuckled deeply, drawing her body to his. "I can only imagine what you have in store. That's what I'm talking about." He put his forefinger on her nose and tapped it. "You have much to do today." He held his palm up to his eyes, looking at the fancy watch he wore on his wrist. "In fact, you'll start in about three hours. These things you must do on your own. It is a big day for you."

"And for you," she said.

"And for Robert." Marcus did not smile when he said this. She had told him Robert was coming to the house to collect his things. They both knew it was important that he recant his vows.

"He will be safe with me. I'll help him with the packing. I could probably move everything for him!"

They both laughed. "He is lucky you are so strong." Marcus kissed her along the sensitive part of her neck just under her right ear. "So deadly beautiful." They kissed again.

She could tell he wanted to say that she belonged to him. She ached to hear it. Anne traced the pectoral muscles of his chest, circling a nipple. "Marcus, what do I have to do to be . . . released, so we can . . . you know?"

"He must agree to let you go. He has to declare it. I must hear him say it."

"Doesn't the fact that there is no license on file satisfy the requirements? I'm not legally married."

"You swore an oath in front of witnesses. The paper is not significant. The oath has to be taken back."

She slipped her fingers along the bulging muscles of his abdomen. "And you have to hear the renouncement?" She continued counting his ribs, running her fingers up and down his chest.

"Um hum." She kept up her fiddling. "Counting so soon?" he asked.

She nodded and sighed. "I'm a hopeless case, aren't I?" She felt his eyes on her as she reveled in the glory of his tanned chest, kissing his nipple in order to feel his flesh on her lips one more time. "Can a golden vampire want . . ." She looked up at him and saw his warm brown eyes pulling her to him again. Resisting him only made the experience more delicious. "Is it a bad thing to want too much?" She gave him a pout, knowing what it would do to him inside.

She felt his body lurch. His erection, unfulfilled, persistently looked for a way inside her.

He laughed. "I have never heard of a golden vampire dying from exertion in the arms of his fated love, but somehow I think if there was a first, I could claim it."

"And then I could bring you back to life, as you brought me back."

Marcus stiffened. "Anne, listen to me. You must never do that. You must never create new life that way. That is forbidden, you understand?"

This new revelation concerned Anne. There was so much she did not know. Could she accidentally do something that could cost either one of them their lives? She suddenly felt vulnerable.

"Then, Marcus, you must teach me these things. Please, I don't want to make any mistakes."

"Yes. We must begin your training tomorrow." He drew her to him again. "We have a lesson, then we play, okay? It has to be in that order."

"Then I'll look forward to recess." She kissed him again, wrapping her legs around him.

AFTER MARCUS LEFT, Anne stepped into the shower. The water trickling down her body made her think of the temple and her evening with Marcus. Just the thought of him between her legs, hungry for her, tasting and drinking blood there, made her little nub pulse. She rubbed it in slow circular motions, her eyes closed. Willing his mouth there, willing his tongue scraping over her pinkness, perhaps taking a tender bite . . .

The shower curtain abruptly parted, and she was caught in Robert's gaze. He looked angry. He had reason to be. But not for the reasons he knew about. His neck was a solid mass of bruises, some of them very dark purple. He looked like he was wearing a collar of black raspberry jam. Anne almost laughed.

"You called Monika last night and woke her up."

"Robert!" Anne crossed her breasts with her arms and turned away from him to hide her nakedness. He disappeared behind the shower curtain after yanking it closed.

"I still live here," he whined.

"We're fixing that today."

"You called for me, over at her place. You needed me."

"I called her," Anne shouted over the top of the curtain, "before ... dinner ... and told her to confirm you're coming over here today to begin the move. I didn't wake her up, Robert. It was the middle of the afternoon."

"Yeah, well someone called at one A.M. this morning. Someone with heavy breathing."

"Absolutely *not* me. I was ..." She couldn't tell him what she was doing. She felt her cheeks blush. "Maybe it was one of Monika's boyfriends you don't know about."

Robert swore.

"Weren't you there? With Monika last night?"

"No."

"So what happened to you? Who did that to your neck?"

"Long story. Gary and I ..." Robert's voice trailed off. "We went out and met some girls ..."

Terrible timing. Now you decide to be a little honest with me. You dog.

"Ah, so that explains your wounds." The thought pleased her.

"Wounds?"

"Your neck," Anne said as she turned off the water and took the towel Robert offered her through the curtain. "Thanks."

She secured the towel around her and pulled back the plastic curtain. Robert's sad eyes scanned her face and shoulders. "Looks like someone repeatedly stabbed you with a pencil," she added. "You got any vampire girlfriends I don't know about? Not that it makes any difference to me."

He squinted and sucked in air. Then he cursed and left the bathroom, slamming the door shut behind him. Through the wooden slats he yelled, "I'll talk with you when you're out. I'll wait in the living room."

Anne slipped into her bedroom, dropped the towel, and dressed quickly. The cream-colored terrycloth still smelled like Marcus. She straightened the satin sheets on her bed and got another whiff of him. She missed him already. Her heart flipped.

She found Robert sitting on the living room couch, one knee over the arm.

He sipped from a mug of fresh coffee. "Damn, I sure do miss your coffee."

Too late. Way too late, Robert.

"I'll bet. I'll bet you miss it real hard as you bang my former best friend all over our house."

"You don't have to say things like that, Anne. Only makes things worse between us."

"How could it be worse, Robert? There is no *us*."

Robert nodded. "Okay. I get how you feel."

"No, you couldn't possibly know how I feel." She heard his heart skip a beat, saw the vein tense at his neck. She held no attraction for him. Just for his blood.

Got to get this over with quickly.

"Forgive me, Robert, if I indulge in a little resentment, seeing as how my best friend was fucking my husband. My husband who should have been enjoying his wedding day with his wife instead of that bimbo."

He turned and faced her.

"She's not a bimbo."

"So, just what is she? She's your girlfriend, the girlfriend you chose over your own wife?" Anne was getting riled, in spite of her desire for control. Was this anger something she would have to be careful of? She felt the fangs in her mouth extend slightly. *Calm down. He doesn't understand.*

"We decided to end it," Robert said. "We talked about it this morning."

"What?" Anne stood there in shock, listening to the sounds of the shower drip. She also heard the lovemaking going on across the orchard, the dog barking on the back porch three streets over, and the bees talking among themselves as they buzzed and hovered in apple trees. She could hear all this, and yet, her world suddenly seemed so small.

"That's all you can say, 'What?' Not exactly a ringing endorsement for my former role as your husband."

"No, you were never really my husband."

"And you in there feeling yourself up. Who were you thinking about, hmm? You have a new boyfriend? So soon?"

"Soon? You, the one who said 'I do' and then banged my maid of honor? What do you care?"

Anne was confused by Robert's comments. Monika apparently was smarter than Anne thought. The mere idea of Robert moving in probably had sent her former friend into a panic. She would bet almost anything except Marcus's life that Monika broke up with Robert, not the other way around. Her admiration for the slut went up a notch.

"I want to talk it over, see if we can work things out. Maybe go to counseling." Robert's eyes were contrite and pleading.

Oh, God, no. This can't be happening. She realized what she had longed for was now beginning to happen—just when she no longer wanted it.

"Sit down, honey." He patted the area beside him. She sat in the cotton flowered overstuffed chair across the room. Robert shrugged and hung his head. He rubbed his face with both hands, suddenly reached for the ceiling, stretching and letting out a large groan.

How hard could this be, she wondered, finally telling the truth? But she guessed whatever Robert had to say wouldn't be one hundred percent the truth. Not like Marcus.

Marcus.

The pain in her heart, the need to be enveloped by Marcus, brought tears to her eyes. She wished she were sitting on his lap. She wished she had his strong neck and chest to hold on to. Then perhaps Robert could see he didn't have a chance. Perhaps he would no longer delude himself that Anne would take him back.

So this is what he's thinking.

But that wasn't happening. Marcus had left her alone to clean up the mess that was her marriage. And now the worst possible outcome was in front of her. Robert wanted to apologize and come back. She could read it all over him. She had hoped he would say something that really pissed her off so that she could just get him out of her life quickly.

She wanted to add a couple of puncture wounds to those hickies on his neck, but that would mess up everything.

He stood up and came over to where Anne sat. He kneeled and put his hands on her knees. His eyebrows arched in forced sincerity.

She did not soften to him. He probably didn't expect her to cave, either. Anne thought his blackberry collar ridiculous and she stifled a laugh.

"Annie, honey, I have been a real fool," Robert said. "I've had the best thing any guy could want, right under my fingers, and I've not appreciated it. God, I am so sorry, honey. I love you so much."

Anne stayed stoic. She was unprepared for this.

"I want to make it work out between us. I want to make it like it was before we got married. Remember that, honey? Remember how we were so much in love? Remember how we found each other, how we just loved being around each other all the time?"

She reached for her memories. Seemed so long ago when the sound of his voice, his laugh, thrilled her. "Yes, I do, Robert. I felt that way at one time. But no more. Something tells me you never did. I don't think you ever stopped seeing Monika."

"No, I did. When we went skiing in Canada, and other times too."

"Damn it, Robert, she was a whole country away!" Anne got up and went into the bathroom, slamming the door and locking it behind her. She was beginning to get hungry and she didn't want him to see it. She didn't trust herself.

Robert followed her. He leaned against the wooden door and whined, "Anne, honey. I am a complete idiot. You are always the one I loved. Look, if I could cut my pecker off for you, I would."

"Go away. I want you to go away. I want you to move out, today."

"No, honey, I can't do that. I love you too much. You'll change your mind. I'm gonna try real hard. You'll see."

The thought of Robert trying really hard was almost laughable, if it wasn't so sad. She recalled her evening last night with Marcus. She smiled and shook her head. It would be impossible for her ever to forget Marcus.

Help me. Help me out here.

There was no answer.

Chapter 13

ROBERT SAT IN the cab of his pickup, staring at the outside of Anne's little place that had been their love nest. At least, up until the wedding the place had been their love nest. Now it was something else entirely. A fortress. A series of locked doors keeping him from talking to her, smiling at her, reasoning with her.

Anne was so different now. She was unshakable in her resolve. He'd had to work to catch a few shirts and another pair of jeans that she had thrown at him. He had begged her not to throw his cell phone, so she'd lobbed it for the easy save. And when he had asked for the cell phone charger, she'd thrown it, aiming for his head. Her arm was as good as any pitcher he'd ever seen, and he even felt she had held back. God, she was beautiful when she got angry. And so strong, too. Why was it he always loved the girls he could never have? Then when he did get one, like Anne, he'd go and blow it by running around.

His life had gone to shit in just a month. Just over a month ago, he had Miss Monika—and as much of her as he wanted as often as he wanted. And he had the woman who had agreed to be his wife, had agreed to share his life with him, and who made him feel like a better man even though she went on their honeymoon without him and claimed the marriage was null and void.

A minor problem.

He wondered why it was that way, how some women seemed to bring out the best in a man and some others, well, they brought out something else.

When they first met, Anne had been everything he looked for in a woman: smart, sexy, and delighted in making him happy. She was always helping out kids at some teen center or at the home for battered women where she volunteered. He had done a little free work for some of these women, replacing windows and doors destroyed by abusive boyfriends or husbands. He kind of loved being a good guy. He had no trouble staying away from those poor women. After all, he wasn't a complete rat.

It was almost like there were two parts of him, the good part, and then the bad part. Anne always fed the good part of him.

He had to admit, he wasn't ready to give up that part of his life—the good Robert. That's why he hoped Anne would change her mind, would come around, like she had before their wedding. He thought she knew about some of his dalliances. But she had been occupied with planning the wedding those past few weeks before the Big Fiasco, and hadn't seemed to notice anything. So Robert had taken the opportunity to roam. And the more he did it, the more the other side of him seemed to pull him harder. He thought one of these days he would change; he'd wanted to keep to the good side permanently. But he sure as hell wasn't there yet. He really was not to be trusted. He just wished Anne wouldn't dismiss him and would give him a second chance.

In the last thirty-plus days, he had gone from having both women to now having none. And how the hell was he supposed to get female companionship when it looked like his last date had been with a gorilla? A gorilla that liked to bite? His neck hurt like hell, too. He could barely turn his head.

How he wished Anne would open that front door and take him back, wearing something black and sexy, like what that woman had last night. How could he have been so dumb?

And Monika was acting funny too, with all her toys and experimental things she wanted to try all the time. He was beginning to think maybe she didn't like his taste anymore. He always had to put something on that smelled like some tropical fruit.

Am I losing my touch? Am I that boring in bed now?

He started the truck and drove off, but not before checking in his rear view mirror, hoping for the sight of Anne running down the street to stop him from leaving. Damn, she'd looked good, healthy and flushed in the cheeks, bright red lipstick that looked way better on her than Monika.

No, the street was empty. No Anne. No second chances this time. He'd try to call her later. Maybe she would change her mind.

He was not sure where he would be spending the night. He decided to keep trying to call both women. Hopefully, one of them would let him in. And then he could do the grateful sex. He was good at it, had lots of practice.

But more than likely, judging from Monika's demeanor on the phone this morning, he would be bedding down at Gary's. He dialed his best friend. When Gary answered, he wheedled, "Ah, Gary, I might need a place to stay tonight. Neither woman is speaking to me. Can I bunk with you if I can't get through to either of them?"

There was silence.

"Gary, you there?"

"Holy crap, Robert. What the hell happened?"

"I don't want to go into it. It kinda hurts." This was true.

"How'd you manage to get them both mad at you, Rob?"

"Incredibly bad timing. Look, I've got a full day, but I'll buy dinner or drinks if I can stay there tonight."

"You're on. I had no plans, not that I didn't try. Hey Robert, Anne divorcing you?"

Great. Just great.

"Not that I blame her, no offense," Gary added.

"You asshole. Shut up, Gary."

"Look, I'm single. You're the one that went off and got married."

"Her brother says we're not even legally married."

"What's Monika's beef? She never seemed to mind before . . ."

"It's a long story. What do you care?"

"I don't. I was just wondering."

"Gary, you piece of shit. If you touch either of them, I'll come over there and go caveman on you with my baseball bat." Except that his bat was at the house he couldn't go into, but the threat sounded good.

"No worries. Who do you take me for?"

"Gary, let's face it. You're just like me."

ROBERT WALKED INTO his construction office. His doting secretary, Elena, took one look at his neck and dropped her coffee cup.

"Oh, Jesus, Mister Robert." She made the sign of the cross. "You have had a fight. Very unfair. He bite you. Very unfair fight, Mr. Robert."

"No, Elena, there was no fight. Don't worry. I'm fine."

She made the sign of the cross again just for good measure. She waddled down the hall, mumbling, then went into the bathroom and closed the door.

Robert checked himself out in the mirrored Budweiser sign over his desk. The color on his neck was intensifying. *Great.*

On his way to one of his job sites, the local police, stopped him for speeding. He pulled out his license and registration. This was one gargantuan fucked up day, and it was only 10:30 AM.

"Can I see your license and . . . what the hell happened to you? You okay?" The officer bent down to look into Robert's eyes. The policeman was about the same age as Robert, but he looked about as straight arrow as they came. Probably went to church regularly, too. Ex-jarhead. *Just my luck.*

"It's a long story. My date got carried away last night."

"Was she pissed?"

Robert's heart sank. He was hoping it didn't look that way. Like he'd been punished. Rather like wearing a scarlet letter. He cursed himself for being so stupid. All these little lapses in judgment were adding up rapidly and were scaring him. If he wasn't careful, his bad luck could stick around for a while, decide to nest in his life.

"Maybe she was mad." Robert handed over his license and registration. He sat and waited while he got checked out. He wondered what the code sign for hickie was. No doubt some dispatcher was getting a laugh at his expense. Suddenly the bench seat in his truck wasn't very comfortable. Several long minutes later, the officer returned.

"Mr. Balesteiri, your license has expired. Just last month. So, I'm going to write you up for that too. You were doing fifty-seven in a thirty-five zone." The officer seemed to wince before he continued. "Look, fella. None of my business, but I'd keep my mind on my driving, and not whatever else you were into here." He pointed to Robert's neck, then smiled.

"Uh huh." Oh, great, now even the cops were giving him advice.

"Better start paying attention to those little warning signs." He handed Robert back his paperwork and passed over the thick leather pad with the citation on top for him to sign. "That piece of art on your neck doesn't look normal. Did she cost very much? Were there two of them? Bet they used handcuffs too." His face was grim, with just a hint of a smile.

Robert almost choked on his own tongue. "My date, you dumb f— Christ. I said it was my date!" This had gone from bad to worse.

"Uh huh. Okay then, someone might say you'd been abused. You might look into that. Men get abused by women every day."

"Sure, thanks."

"It was a woman, right?"

"Of *course* it was a woman! I've already told you it was my date . . . not my girlfriend or my wife." He was a little embarrassed by the revelation.

The officer started to chuckle, shaking his head. "Yeah, that's what I thought. Two women."

Dumb shit. Keep your opinions to yourself. He handed the officer back the pad, swearing under his breath, and took the pink ticket with a scowl. He hated having his manhood questioned. He'd never had to pay for sex in his life.

He knew the ticket would be a whopper. He needed that like castration with a dull knife, although it might solve some of his problems. Now *that* would really hurt.

He pulled up to the jobsite and his long time employee, Enrique, came out to greet him. They were like brothers, having played on the same baseball team in high school.

"Ah, that's fucked up, man. Look at your neck. What happened?"

"Nothing. I don't want to talk about it."

"Jeez, you try to hang yourself or somethin'?"

Something like that.

"You gotta put some ointment, some cream on it, man."

"Look, Enrique. It's none of your goddamned business. I can take care of myself, thank you very much. Now, can we talk about work?"

"Okay, well, I'm glad you're here. The missus is real unhappy with the windows, Mr. B. She's gonna talk to you. I think she'll be here in 'bout a half hour."

Robert looked at his watch, only to see a bare wrist. His watch was at the house. He cursed for about the fifth time today. "Uh, I gotta go get some material for my other site. I can't wait for her. Can you handle it?"

"Nah, Mr. B., she wanna talk to you, man. She's real unhappy."

"What about?"

"Her son, you know the kid in college? Well, he has some construction experience, you know?"

"Yeah."

"Well, he came by yesterday and told her the windows is in backwards. I wasn't watching the guys too good, I guess. The ones I looked at were okay."

Robert went over to the site of the addition. Everything looked fine in the kitchen, but, sure enough, the windows in the bedroom had been installed in reverse. And now he'd have to pay his crew thirty bucks an hour to correct it. He took out his glass marker and put an X on seven windows.

"Hey, get these changed right away. She's right."

Enrique was already rounding up the guys. A little red Mercedes two-seater drove up before Robert could get into his truck.

"Mr. Balesteiri, Mr. Balesteiri." His client was making a beeline for him. On the other side of her, a lanky teen with hair too long joined her. Mrs. Watson was on a mission. She was a well-put together forty-something MILF. Her breasts were expensive. He couldn't help but stare at them. He got hard, even though he was fairly sure he would be punished for it. *So welcome to my life.*

"Good morning." He gave her the grin and the stance in his blue jeans that had earned him the job. "You look lovely today, Kimberly."

His words had no effect. "You are behind schedule. We wanted to be in this house well before Thanksgiving. I've got to order all my stuff and I can't until the walls are finished. We aren't going to make it."

"Don't worry about it. We've got lots of time. Barring something unforeseen, a supply hang-up or something out of my control..." This usually worked. Anything could be excused and deflected off him if he could blame a subcontractor or supplier. She stopped him.

"Putting in those windows backwards doesn't help our situation." She stepped up closer to him, close enough to remind him that she could be grateful in special ways if he played the game her way, but not too close to alarm her college-age son. Her voice was soft and low. "You know, Robert, you were chosen because we had the most faith in you. You weren't the lowest bidder. But my husband and I liked you the best, thought we could—*work* with you the best." She sighed.

Robert knew it was because *she* liked him the best. He had to admit, he did enjoy a few afternoons getting to know the lady's tastes, not just in design.

Then she leaned forward and stared at his neck.

"Good Lord, what is that?" She pointed and spoke so loud the entire place stopped working to look. He shrugged. A smile of bright recognition crossed her beautiful face. "You are a very naughty boy, Robert."

Actually, he was thinking about the fact that all he had done was to lie there. The woman had been the naughty one. She hadn't let him do a thing. When he tried to get up, she'd pushed him back down on the bed with such force the pressure of her hands almost caved his chest in.

Oh, God, I'm screwed. Will this day never end?

Mrs. Watson had renewed interest in the sight before her. "You know, I have some changes I want to consider. I'm tied up tonight." She fluttered her eyes and smiled, probably so he could get the full import of what that meant. She was a very literal person, as Robert had discovered earlier. "But tomorrow night I'm free. I don't think Charles would mind me going over the changes with you. He has a meeting that will go until late."

"Um, sure, Kimberly." He leaned in and whispered, "What about your son?"

She smiled wickedly. "Sometimes he likes to watch."

ROBERT SAID GOODBYE and drove to his next construction site. He was pleased to find things in much better shape. They were actually ahead of schedule. There was a bonus in the contract to finish early, something he hadn't been able to get in the Watson contract. At the time, however, he didn't care how long the Watson project took, as Mrs. Watson's appetites in the sexual arena were voracious.

Best of all, at this project site, no one gawked at his neck. He was beginning to feel like his old self again. Until lunchtime.

When he walked into the Apple Box Diner, the air took on the weight of a funeral procession. The usual jovial crowd stopped talking and followed his gait with quiet stares. They were somber. Robert felt like someone had given him advanced billing. He felt eyes staring at the back of his head, at his neck. Pissed him off.

He sat in his regular booth. His favorite waitress, Adele, came over with a coffee cup. "You eating alone today?"

"Yeah. Thanks."

"You gonna make me ask?"

"I'll have the regular." Robert always had a BLT with a green salad on the side.

"Dummy, I meant your neck tattoo. Can't say as though I've seen one like it before. And I've seen a lot."

Robert knew this to be true. He had dated Adele in high school, back when he was a star baseball player. Back when his life was normal. Back before two women had rejected him in one day, one of them being his wife.

He shook his head. "I think I'm going to explode if one more person asks me."

"You okay? I mean, that's quite a statement."

"Mind your own god-damned business, Adele." She did, retreating to behind the counter.

He looked around the room in time to see several people turning back around so as not to be accused of staring. He rubbed the back of his neck and felt soreness there too. *Even the back of my neck?* He didn't even remember. Must have happened when he passed out.

Robert ate quickly and then got up to leave.

"Bye, darlin'. Don't do anything I wouldn't do." Adele winked and flashed him an orange-lipped smile. Robert remembered those orange lips. He had dreamed about them almost his entire senior year. He glanced at his receipt and noticed Adele had written her phone number prominently in red pen. He looked back, but she was already reaching for something under the counter and was bent over, her cute little ass displayed for his view. She was wearing a black garter belt that held up her black stockings under her blue uniform.

He liked to think about things in baseball terms. *Two hits, two outs, two errors, nobody left on.* Things always came in threes. He was looking for another hit, not an out. But he would be grateful if this day could end without another major incident. His ego was just as sore as his neck.

When he finished his workday, he picked up his mail at the local post office. He opened a letter from the bank and discovered he'd been overdrawn again and had accrued some $260 in overdraft fees. Damn. He'd forgotten to deposit a check. Another little lapse had cost him some money. This needed to stop.

He got to Gary's about six. He was beat. In his arms, he cradled the few things he had bought. He could hear the loud music about ten doors before he got to Gary's apartment. Gary was in a party mood. He always played country western when he was ready to go out.

Robert had to knock twice before he got an answer.

"Hey, partner. Look at you!" Gary surveyed Robert's neck. "All branded up. You are some sore little puppy."

There was a limit to Robert's patience. He threw his clothes down on the floor and grabbed Gary by the collar. "Quit it. Not another goddamned word, Gary, you hear?"

"Hey, don't get the wrong impression." Gary extricated himself from Robert's grip. "I was just trying to make light of a pretty ugly situation." He pointed to Robert's neck.

"Okay, I'm leaving." Robert bent over to retrieve his precious stash, but Gary stopped him.

"Come on. Take a shower and get some clean clothes. We're going out tonight. I'm not going to make you pay."

"That's good." And it was, he thought. Things were finally starting to look a little brighter.

When he found out where Gary wanted to go, his assessment how things were looking up changed. The Double Eights was a topless bar in the seedy part of town, attached to an adult bookstore. The scene of his bachelor party loomed large in his mind. Robert had done some work for the owner, who looked more like a priest than a person who would own such a place. Robert knew what went on in those little rooms in the back, the "chat rooms" as they called them.

When he had worked on the remodel a couple of years back, he had found an assortment of toys and pieces of underwear or paraphernalia like he'd never seen before. The owner had tried to do a trade for services before paying him, which pissed Robert off. But, eventually he got paid. He would have taken the guy to small claims court, but he didn't want it published in the paper. Anne never knew about this particular job and he wanted it kept that way. He wasn't a fool. With Gary, he entered the dive, which smelled of male sweat and smoke. The girls looked good tonight, no doubt due to his circumstances. He was grateful for the darkness there too. Easier to hide his neck.

They chose a table in the corner, but with a good view of the two lighted boxes with the dancers in them. Robert never could eat up at the counter. It just didn't seem right to have some woman's ass that close to his green salad. Of course, his mouth had done worse. He simply didn't like to confuse his needs. That's why Monika's flavored condoms annoyed him so much.

The salads were passable, prepackaged in cellophane and obviously not made on site. Thank God. The only items of protein were hot dogs, sort of a house specialty. In more ways than one.

He lathered his with mustard and had just taken a huge bite when a black-haired vixen made her way over to their table. She sat on Gary's lap. Robert could tell she really was looking at him and had wanted the vantage point from Gary's side.

"Hello, darling. Ain't you cute?" Gary had no trouble talking to strange women, especially those that would sit on his lap without permission.

"Cute? Wow, it's been a long time since I've been called that. I think the last time was when I was a girl of ten or so." She smiled. She had huge white teeth and the reddest shiny lips Robert had ever seen. She wore black velvet stretch pants with a red satin baby doll top that scooped low, showing her breasts. They were bigger than Mrs. Watson's, but all flesh, no plastic. They were luscious. She caught him staring and didn't seem to mind a bit. Neither did he. He quickly finished his mouthful and wiped his mustard-covered lips.

"I think you're just drop dead gorgeous." It was a cliché, but the tired line seemed to work on her. The girl smiled dreamily as Gary's paw found sport down the front of her blouse. The red satin rippled as Gary massaged and squeezed her substantial breast.

Robert got hard immediately. He shifted in his seat.

Gary bent down, descending into the oblivion of her cleavage. Her eyes got deep and dark as she looked at Robert and licked her lips. She made sure he got the message she liked to be nuzzled. And in public. She was telling him she could do other things too, most likely with expert ability. Robert wanted her more than he thought possible on a day like today. Well, maybe it was because of the day he had that made him want her. But it didn't really matter. He had to have her. She was more than willing. He didn't want to share.

Gary whispered something in her ear while his other hand found a home between her legs, which she kept tightly crossed over his. God help him, but Robert wanted to part those legs. His cock felt like a heat seeking missile and her sex was the target.

Gary made the arrangements. The girl had an apartment nearby. Robert thought that would be best, just in case Anne stopped by Gary's to talk as she sometimes did. He felt bad for about a minute, then realized Anne had kicked him out so he was free to roam. No way was he going to be made a fool of by those two women. He would end the day on top, literally.

She brought them to her apartment. It was clear she was a pro. Her place looked more like a seduction stage than a living space. She offered them the use of her full bar. She didn't ask for money. Robert didn't know what had been agreed on, but Gary was the expert with call girls.

They each took a long necked beer from her refrigerator and popped them open. They sat on her command and watched as she peeled off the layers of her clothing. They were both squirming in their seats, eyes lapping up the scene.

When she stood before them, almost naked, her perfectly formed breasts of double D variety staring straight out them, she undulated her narrow waist and started to slip down a black thong panty, moving her hips from side to side in a figure eight pattern. Robert noticed she looked directly at him. She leaned forward to remove the little article from her ankles, her breasts full and extended towards him. Gary was enjoying the view from the back just as well. He stood, then came behind her and rubbed against her ass through his pants.

She rose up and leaned back against him, but her gaze stayed on Robert. Gary's hands were all over her chest, squeezing her breasts. Her heavy breathing and that dark stabbing stare at his groin told him she was becoming aroused. She licked her red lips with the tip of her tongue, her eyes still pinned to Robert.

Then she turned and kissed Gary. Robert saw Gary's hands on her white bottom, his fingers dimpling her skin. She looked over her shoulder at Robert before she reached down and caressed Gary's member through his pants.

Robert felt drawn into her like a moth to the flame. Something told him he was about to have the greatest sex of his life. He never liked the truly bad girls. This would be his first. He sensed he would never be the same afterwards.

She parted from Gary and reached out her hand, the red fingernail polish shimmering. It matched her toes. It matched the red of her tight nipples. It matched her wet lips. Robert grasped her fingers like they were a lifeline. She walked to the bedroom, hooking Robert behind. They left Gary in the other room. Robert didn't even look up to see if this was okay with him.

Everything in her room was red. She clicked a little black device and some sultry music began to play, laced in with some kind of Gregorian chant. There were candles lit everywhere that seemed to come on with a flick of her fingers. He knew he was about to have a full-on religious experience.

She dropped his hand and leaned against the door. With a click, it locked. "You're the one I wanted," she said.

"Well that suits me just fine." Not sure why it mattered, he asked her, "And what do I call you?"

"Maya."

Robert thought to himself. *Three hits. Thank God it's a hit, not an out.* The girl knew how to treat a guy right. She didn't even ask him about his neck, or look at it once. He realized just before his lips covered hers that at last his day was looking up.

Chapter 14

THE NEXT MORNING, Marcus was out in the vineyard inspecting his grapes when Maya suddenly traced behind him. She leaned against him, then threaded her arms around his chest, squeezing her breasts against his back. At first he startled, then willed himself to relax a bit, not wanting her to see how uneasy he was around her. She had not used the formal protocol of asking if she could visit. She had just appeared.

"Marcus, have you no space in your heart for me? For our son?"

He turned to look at her face, which was beautiful as ever. Her generous bosoms were heaving. They were hard to miss. He unpeeled her arms from around his waist. He was trying to be gentle, calm, but everything about her spelled danger. He remembered their bedding, how he never could lose command of his faculties out of fear of her. Their relationship was intensely sexual, but he couldn't say it was very pleasant. And he couldn't feel love for her, although he had tried, for the sake of the boy.

"How is Lucius?" It was about the only subject he could discuss with her openly.

She sighed, twirling a lock of hair between her fingers. "He's fine. But his mother is hungry. Hungry for a real man's touch on her flesh. Hungry for his love, for his bite. Only one man can do that for me." She flashed her gaze up to meet his.

Maya was about Anne's size, only a darker version of Anne. He had always been attracted to shorter women, but only if they were powerful. This woman was *too* powerful for him. And there would be no other now that Anne had appeared in his life.

"Who tends to him when you are . . . traveling?"

"My mother. And I'm not traveling. I've taken an apartment in town, not that it makes much difference. The month is up and you've not claimed her, so I thought we could explore our way to getting you fated, perhaps experience being a family." She sauntered back up to him.

She was very good, he noticed. He would not deny he was getting aroused. That body would arouse anything living. But he knew he could control any urge she would throw his way. Before she could toss her arms around him and lock onto his lips, something they had done hundreds of times over the years, he stopped her. "I am not comfortable with you here. You didn't announce. You can't just appear. We are not fated, and we never will be."

Maya frowned, twisting her head to the side. She crossed her arms and quickly pulled off her red satin top, revealing a lacy red bra she would never need. He knew it was for him. He had a fondness for fancy underwear on his women and she delighted in showing them to him any chance she got. He stood there looking at her and noticed his arousal did not deepen. This was not love. This was lust. Small compared to the feelings he had for Anne.

"You have no effect on me. Cover yourself up. This is why you are not welcome here." He turned and began walking up to the house. She followed him.

She traced in front of him, her shoulders glowing in the morning sun. "You said you would try. You aren't giving us much of a chance. Come on, Marcus." She walked to him and let the tips of her nipples that showed through the red sheer fabric rub against his shirt. "Can't you try just a little bit for the both of us? For Lucius's sake?" She rubbed her hand against Marcus's pants. "No need to hold yourself back. All can be forgiven." She rubbed her mound against his bulge. "All can be as it was before. Remember, Marcus, how right we were together? Don't you miss those days?" She leaned into him further and raised her lips, but he pushed her away in disgust.

"Get out, or I will tell the council."

"The council will be told you are not even trying to fate me. They will be none too pleased with my report."

"I am pursuing the honorable path, doing what I think is best. You must not interfere. You are bridled."

"Yes, I must keep my distance from the woman. But I can't stay away from you. Would you be able to stay away from her, Marcus? That's how I feel."

"Your decision to move to Healdsburg is a bad sign."

"Yes, it is. I don't like to be turned down. I don't lose gracefully. You know this. I can wreak a lot of havoc. But if you were willing, and a little compliant . . ." She started moving towards him again.

"Then I will ask for an injunction. I'll get it, Maya. They'll let me have this."

"Very well." She walked away, backwards. She waved her fingers, then disappeared.

Marcus was worried for Anne's safety, even though Maya had been bridled. He hoped Maya had enough sense not to go against the council's wishes.

He spent the rest of the morning doing chores. Hard work helped him think. He worked on one of his tractors, then experimented with the sugar content of the fruit at the ridge overlooking his villa. Harvest would be soon, and he was ready. He hoped there wouldn't be a late rain. The conditions this fall had been perfect.

He went into the kitchen refrigerator and drank the procured blood from the blood bank.

He sat on the stone balcony that overlooked the valley floor and thought of Anne. He could see the very spot he had laid the blanket down, where she had drunk from him. He did this on purpose. He wanted to see the site every morning of every day he stayed here. He was going to take the grapes that surrounded the little area and make his own special wine. He wanted to drink from the fruit that had watched their love blossom for each other. That elixir would be priceless.

He entered his bedroom chambers, through ornately carved oak doors. When he had bought the property, he had decorated the house with her in mind. There was a pink marble-topped vanity that was hundreds of years old, probably older than he was. He had bought a gold mirror and brush set and which sat on the top of the vanity, waiting for their mistress to come and use them. He touched the engraved letters AM, for Analise Monteleone, the name he would call her, the name he would use when he claimed her. She would have his family's name and would bear his children here, overlooking the vineyard and the place where she had first tasted her fated love.

He eased himself down in the rose colored high-backed chair in the corner, and with his elbow on the chair arm, he rested his fingers at the side of his cheekbones. Anne hadn't called him last night and he missed her, so he traced to her bed and watched her sleeping.

Like a sentinel, he watched her rest, making sure her sleep was uninterrupted. He watched the reflection of moonlight against the flowers in her bedroom wallpaper. Fog covered the street and blurred the dull light from the corner streetlamp. Her face was smooth as alabaster, a light blush at her cheeks. Her lips formed a smile as he kissed them softly, being careful not to awaken her. Did she sense he was watching over her? Was she having any second thoughts about sending Robert away? Had Maya contacted her at all? Her body was getting used to his blood, to the fating that would surely take place soon. So he waited, certain it would be any time now. As she rose to the bright yellow sunlight, he left her to her morning routine.

ANNE HAD GONE back to bed after the scene with Robert and slept until the next morning. She hadn't slept this deep in months, but suspected the evening before with Marcus and the fight with Robert had something to do with how soundly she had slept. Her dreams had been vivid, sensual. Marcus had been everywhere around her, kissing every inch of her body. They had flown through the night sky to the temple. They had made love over and over again in rooms she had never been in before. Big rooms, with beautiful views of ocean and greenery. Her dreams felt like visions of her future spread out before her.

Only thing stopping that future was Robert. His refusal to release her would delay the mating ritual she so desperately wanted with

Marcus. What a time for Robert to finally come to his senses, even though too late. What would have happened had Robert realized his flaws earlier in the year and had made reparations? She might not have been so attracted to Marcus.

Somehow, that was not a logical thought. Loving him was the most natural thing in the universe. And for once, she was ecstatic to know she would live forever.

Yesterday, she'd almost thrown all Robert's things out on the front porch but had stopped herself. She wanted him out of her life but didn't need to punish him or destroy his possessions. She didn't want to be cruel. Cruelty wouldn't get her the desired result, especially if it made him fight the release she needed.

She stretched, still wrapped in her fuzzy robe, naked underneath. She felt groggy but wonderful. She wished Marcus were here with her. She was hungry. She decided to shower and then give him a call.

As she was rubbing herself dry, she noticed blood left behind on the towel. She looked all over her body for an errant bite she hadn't noticed. Then she felt the dullness in her lower belly. Cramps. She was bleeding.

She looked at the pinkish red stain again. Not a lot of blood, but something she hadn't seen in two months, ever since the rehearsal dinner. She wondered if that meant she was fertile. Thank God nothing was wrong with her. She couldn't possibly be pregnant since she hadn't had sex since before the wedding. But now perhaps she could get pregnant.

She brought her phone to bed with her and pushed the number. Marcus's instant response told her he had been waiting for her call. After he greeted her, she said, "I sent Robert away with some of his things. But he wants to work it out. He wouldn't release me."

"I see."

"I feel sorry for him, but my mind's made up. Can I come stay with you while he moves his things out? I just don't want to be around him."

"I'd rather you asked it another way."

"You and your questions. I can't believe I've only known you for a few days. Can you come over here?"

"Not safe, Anne."

"Why do you say that?" Anne could tell something had shifted. "Is there some kind of bad news?"

"No. I must wait for an appointment with the council. I've requested it, but there are more pressing matters."

"I thought you said . . ."

"Patience. Plus the fact that every time we are together it is all I can do to keep from . . ."

"Why can't I come over there? I need you now. I'm starving. Are you on the other side of the world or something?"

"No, I'm right here."

She looked up to see him standing at the foot of her bed. She threw herself into his arms. The pink robe opened up the front to expose her breasts to his hands, and then his lips. He pressed her down and peeled back the robe as slowly as he could, as if she was some fragile china doll. She watched with greedy eyes, her breasts moving up and down from her heavy breathing. The muscles between her legs twitched. He kissed her hip, her bellybutton. He kissed down her stomach, moving lower and lower until he was at her puffy, hairless lips. She inhaled as he extended his tongue and licked her sex.

He grew tense and sat up. "You bleed."

"Yes, I noticed that this morning. It's the first time in almost two months. She watched him as he thought. "Is this a bad thing, Marcus? I mean, you said . . ."

He was serious now. "Get yourself packed. I think I have a solution to your problem about staying here."

"We're going to your place?"

"No, I have to go somewhere. You are coming with me, if you are willing."

He smiled as she squealed with delight and writhed on the bed. Going on a trip with Marcus, just the two of them? How exciting.

He was next to her in an instant, his mouth covering hers. He rolled to his back, pulling her naked body over him. He tugged his shirt away at the collar, exposing his jugular. "We haven't much time.

Feed. Then pack your things and meet me at Starbucks, as soon as you can, okay?"

She nodded, then popped his buttons off, laid her breasts against his bare skin, and dug her fangs into his neck. They both groaned. She took him fiercely, needing to feel his blood course through her. Marcus laughed until he cried.

SHE SPOTTED MARCUS'S long, lanky form while he leaned against the Ferrari, a cappuccino balanced in one hand. She parked the bomber by itself in a deserted area, not knowing how long they would be gone. She wanted to protect the car.

She wasn't going to kiss Marcus and make a scene, but she saw in his eyes that he expected some display, so she ran headlong into him, causing him to juggle the coffee without spilling it on either of them or the car. He felt warm and hard for her. His dark eyes smiled at the corners all the time now. It was thrilling to see him so happy and to know she was partially the cause.

"You going to teach me how to trace with baggage?" she asked as she sunk into the Ferrari's leather seat. He slammed the door and quickly came around to the driver's side. He got in and leaned over, then planted a quick kiss on her lips.

"No, we're flying this time. I have things I have to bring as well."

The Ferrari kicked in and her head slammed into the headrest, something she was quickly getting used to.

"Don't you ever drive slowly?"

"Why?"

They both laughed. Instead of heading to San Francisco to the big airport there, they drove up 101 to the Sonoma County Airport. They parked the black beast and were greeted by a short man in a pilot's uniform, who gestured for them to follow. He knew Marcus.

"No ticket?" she asked.

"Not when you own the plane."

Anne raised her eyebrows up, impressed.

Marcus leaned into her. "There are things you can do on a jet you can't do when you trace."

"Oh." Another new experience.

All by itself, a sleek white jet stood on the runway. They headed straight for it. A cabin steward who asked if they wanted something to drink greeted them.

"A little red wine, I think, or would you like champagne? I have an excellent Merlot Champagne, gorgeous color." Marcus was waiting for her answer. Anne had always loved champagne. She had not had any since her wedding day.

"Is it okay to have alcohol?"

"Sure, as long as you don't have too much." Marcus took her arm and led her to the back as the steward dispatched to get the glasses and the bubbly. There was a desk with computer console and telephone, a combination printer/fax machine, and swivel lounge chairs done in butter frosting white that had the smoothest grain of leather she had ever felt. He took her hand and showed her a full bathroom with shower and double vanity. Two fluffy white robes with an M emblem on the breast pocket lay at the lip of a substantial tub. Anne's eyes grew wide as she looked over everything.

Marcus grabbed her hand and took her to the very back, which was a bedroom. He pulled her to him with a huge hand around her waist, hungry for her. She always felt he was hungry for her. She wanted to do nothing else but please him and give him back her love in return.

His mouth covered hers. He knelt before her and pulled up her top. He kissed her stomach, his long fingers reaching under her bra. She took her top off and showed him the black piece she had bought at Victoria's Secret.

"This is nice, very nice. I know some places where you will be showered with lovelies in every color. But I like you best like this." He released the clasp of the bra and black silk fell to the ground.

The captain spoke, signaling they were about to take off. The steward had left a chilled bottle on the table in its holder and two poured glasses of the ruby colored drink beside it. Marcus handed one to Anne, then took a seat in the recliner, holding his glass and motioning her to join him. Topless, she sat, leaning her back into his chest as he strapped them in with one long seatbelt, securing them for takeoff. She turned slightly to lay her head against his chest.

"A toast?" he asked. "I am parched." With their arms entwined, the two flutes touched with a ring. "To us, may we love forever."

"Yes, Marcus. To us forever."

The bubbles made her nose feel itchy, and she rubbed it. The sensation of drinking something other than blood was odd. But she had to admit it was pleasant.

"Do we get drunk?"

"Not really. Takes an awful lot of alcohol. We usually get sick before we can get drunk. We are immune to most the effects of alcohol, but we can enjoy the taste. I'm actually going to make some very good wine."

After they were airborne, he unhooked them and brought the bottle over for a refill. "I've always wanted to do this. Indulge me, okay?"

He held the flute up to Anne's breast and pressed it against her nipple to wet it with the red mixture. Her nipples hardened from the cold liquid, but glistened and quivered. He put his mouth over the nipple and sucked the champagne from her body. Anne felt the place between her legs gush.

"Shall I do the other one?" He kissed her, searching for her tongue and pinning it down with his own.

"Yes," she moaned into his mouth. "Please."

He dipped her other breast into his flute, spilling some on her pants. He feigned horror. "Oh, my, you have soiled your pants. You must remove them. Jason will wash them for you." He slipped his fingers along the waistband, unhooked the clasp at the front, and pulled down the zipper one bit at a time, kissing her, wiping her lips with his tongue.

Anne was about ready to pass out. Marcus was the best kisser she had ever known. He was skilled in the art of seduction, doing things she didn't even know existed. She was grateful for his experience, for she would be his last lover.

She stood and let him remove her jeans. There she was, in the black thong with just enough lace to drive him crazy.

"Ah, I like this view very much," he said. He knelt in front of her, kissing her through her panties.

"Marcus, I have always wanted to do something. Indulge me, okay?"

He smiled at her imitation of his play.

She bid him to stand. Then she kneeled and undid his trousers, slipping the zipper down his front, kissing the opening. She smoothed his pants down his legs to his ankles, then prodded him to step out of them. She removed his silk boxers. His erection was throbbing, lurching with each little touch of the back of her hand, her fingers, or her hair. She gripped him in one hand and held her champagne flute in the other, holding it up to him.

"More." He reached for the bottle and emptied the contents into her glass. She guided his cock to the flute, and with delicate fingers, dipped him in the cool red bubbly. He jumped at the cold. Anne's eyes were fixated on his velvet shaft. She wet her lips, set her glass down, and covered his head with her mouth, sucking the champagne from him.

"Mmm. This tastes just wonderful. You taste so good." Marcus was almost overcome. She stroked him, massaging his scrotum with her hands, sometimes kissing and sucking. He slammed his hips upward, thrusting his cock deep into her hungry mouth. The tip of one of her fangs nicked him and she tasted just a drop of him as his bulbous head shoved past. At last he came into her mouth, filling her. She shuddered as she took every drop.

He took her hand and led her to the bathroom, then drew bath water. He held her the full length of him, his cock still hard, pressing against her lower belly.

"How many times can you do this? You don't get soft? Ever?"

"Not with you, pet. I've never had my fated female. Nothing else compares, my love."

He slipped off her thong with one long forefinger, which then found the hot spot between her legs. God she wanted him there, but his finger would have to do for now. He picked her up and set her on the granite vanity surface, her back flat against the mirror, raising her knees to over his shoulders. He stroked her now with two fingers.

"I want your cock inside me, Marcus. Please. Please, can I have it?" She felt him inhale. She almost thought he would ram himself into her at that moment, but he moaned and sank to his knees. He spoke the ancient words. Anne could feel the insides of her body vibrate to the rhythm of his voice. He played her like an instrument. Every part of her sang. She felt the long smooth orgasm send radiations of pleasure all the way to her fingertips.

"Ah, my pet," he said into her ear as he raised and kissed her. "I want to so bad, so bad. Help me be strong. We mustn't."

"Why? You said so yourself we are fated."

"It would be unfair of me. I have to ask permission."

Anne frowned at him. "Permission? You need to have permission to have sex?" That was about the most ridiculous thing she had ever heard.

Chapter 15

LAUREL CUT FRESH flowers from her garden, then wrapped them in newspaper after tying them together with a rubber band. She placed the bouquets on top of an envelope addressed to Paolo, her oldest brother. It would be good to see him. It had been almost seven years. She missed his warm, gentle ways. He always maintained contact with her, in secret. None of the other family members, his two other sisters and three other brothers, had anything to do with him, not even Marcus. But she was able to pass on to Paolo family news. His own news stayed with her alone.

She heard his light tap on the front door of the villa. She eagerly ran to the door, pulled it open, and was greeted with a blast of warm sunshine and Paolo's big grin, full of startlingly white teeth.

"Paolo." She whispered into his shoulder as he hugged her fiercely. "I have missed you so much." He smelled of the woods, his favorite place to be.

"Yes, my favorite sister, I have missed you, as well."

"Can you stay awhile? Marcus comes, and he brings his fated female. He will be here tonight."

"Maya?"

"No, her name is Anne. She was mortal when he met her, but he knew right away."

"She is no longer mortal?"

"No." Laurel felt her face fall. She looked down to avoid eye contact.

"I see," Paolo whispered. Laurel looked up to his thoughtful frown and ushered him in.

How can I explain things? Everything has changed since Marcus met Anne. Laurel fixed her hair, bringing the fine strands that had escaped the tortoise shell clip she wore at the back of her neck back under control. It felt like wiping the cobwebs of doubt from her mind.

Paolo stepped into the hallway, then stopped, scanning the carved ceiling covered in gold leaf. Laurel remembered the balls they had attended here, first as children and then later when her brothers were eligible bachelors. She had watched the beautifully gowned ladies her brothers courted. One by one, each of them had found their fated females. Except for Marcus and Paolo. Two of her other sisters had married over a hundred years ago. Their children were now having great grandchildren. Almost two centuries had passed before Paolo declared he'd had enough. It broke her heart that he left their family to seek his own way, to live among mortals. He never had children, but she knew he had married. Three times.

"How is your wife?"

"She is fading, but free from pain at least. This one is living longer. She's seventy now, but still as beautiful as the day I met her."

"You are a good husband to her, I just know it."

"The best. She is my third, you know. This is the painful time for me." Paolo had lost both his other wives when they were young.

"Perhaps you will find your fated female in our kind, then you won't have to go through the heartache again."

"No. That won't be. I don't believe in the fate. Look at the mess it's made for Marcus and yourself."

"I am patient. Mine will come, and I shall wait for him. Perhaps he is yet human and hasn't undergone the change. In the meantime, I have my bachelor brother I must tend to. Come, I have something for you." She took his hand and led him into the kitchen. She handed him the flowers and then the envelope. He smelled the bouquet while dropping a kiss on the top of her head. Then he went to the thick envelope.

"What's this?"

"A surprise. Open it."

He broke the seal and his eager fingers flushed out several old pieces of paper. They were letters. Paolo looked up at Laurel, a question in his eye.

"Father wrote these about his choice to stay mortal," she said. "I thought you would enjoy them. I found a whole trunk full of many of his writings. I had no idea he had written so much. He had opinions about everything."

"Yes, he did."

"He saw in you a big part of himself. You should read what he wrote, Paolo. In the end, he wished he had chosen differently. But Mother would not be swayed, so he chose to stay with her."

Their parents had lived as mortals, something their kind could choose. Upon puberty, they were given a choice, to remain mortal, or become a golden vampire. The Monteleones had both held off the decision until they were sure, something they encouraged all their seven children to do as well. The parents chose to remain mortal and passed on almost two centuries ago. All seven of their children elected to become vampire when the choice came to them; they were so affected by the devastating loss of their parents after they died within one year of each other.

But Paolo had regretted his decision, almost from the day he had turned, Laurel recalled. He had fought it and had been tormented ever since. Finally, he'd had to leave.

He'd returned for a visit, requested by his mortal wife who wanted him to consider reconciliation with the family at the wedding of his younger brother's granddaughter. And then he'd abruptly left again. It had been at a particularly difficult time in his "mortal" fantasy life.

Her nephew Lucius entered the ballroom. He came to Laurel's side and leaned into her, holding her skirts.

"Don't be shy, Lucius. This is my older brother, Paolo." The boy's eyes were round and large. He had the dark features Marcus had, the unmistakable sensual Monteleone nose and lips. Even his hairline was like all three of the brothers, with a slight widow's peak at the center.

"Maya and Marcus have agreed to let him stay with us for a spell so he can become acquainted with the family, in case—" Laurel stopped, sharing a conspiratorial stare with her brother.

"In case of what, Auntie?" Lucius asked. Even though Marcus had not openly admitted the child was his, Laurel allowed Lucius to call her Auntie. And she loved it.

"In case your mother has to leave for extended periods of time." Laurel sighed and looked again into Paolo's knowing eyes.

Lucius stepped forward and extended his hand to Paolo. He had been trained well. Laurel was proud of him.

"Nice to meet you, sir."

Paolo squatted and looked at the boy. Their eyes were at the same height. He shook his hand. "Nice to meet you too, Lucius." Though Laurel had told her brother about the boy, this was the first time Lucius and Paolo had met. He touched the boy's cheek. Lucius pulled away. He didn't appear comfortable with being touched. Especially by a stranger. Family or not.

Paolo chuckled and stood. He mussed the top of the boy's head and then left him alone.

Laurel studied her brother. "He's a wonderful child. Very smart." Lucius scrunched up his nose upon hearing this. "Good with numbers. He's already gone through all the books I have up to the seventh grade and he is only six."

"Six point two-five."

"See what I mean?" Laurel laughed. Paolo nodded, smiling. "He reads practically day and night, don't you?"

"I've read the Twilight series four times," Lucius said with pride.

Paolo tented his eyebrows and whistled. "Impressive, young man."

The youngster basked in the admiring light between Laurel and Paolo.

"We were just going to do some gardening," Laurel said. "Later I have to run him over to his grandmother's house. Why don't you two go pick some apples? You could take some home to your wife, Paulo. She would love them." The Monteleones gave away most of the fruit they raised, since they had no need. It gave them some good will with the community. Laurel baked berry pies for Lucius every week. It was his favorite food, other than ice cream.

"Show Paolo the orchard, and the berry patch." She knelt before him and poked him in the chest with her forefinger. "Sweet pea, try not to get berry stains on your shirt, okay?"

She touched his cheek. "Your beautiful skin we can wipe off, but the shirt could get ruined."

Lucius took the initiative and shyly grabbed Paolo's hand, then pulled him across the terrazzo floor to the back. Laurel watched her brother run in little steps with the boy, bending down to make himself shorter. They were instantly in conversation, but never out of earshot.

PAOLO OCCASIONALLY LOOKED at Laurel, who waved back at him as she continued to work in the garden. She probably heard all of Lucius's questions. Paolo thought he did a fairly good job of answering them. The two had put up a ladder, and Lucius was at the top, Paolo holding onto him.

"You don't have to hold me, you know. I won't break, and I never fall." Paolo was struck by the boy's confidence. He realized perhaps he was being a little too protective.

"Alright. But I know your mother, and if anything happens to you, well, let's just say my life in this universe would cease."

"Yeah, she's like that." The boy laughed. "How well do you know my mother?"

"Oh, we all grew up together. But she always had her eyes on Marcus. She only danced with me to make him jealous."

"Did it work?"

"I can't even remember. It was a long time ago." Paolo sighed and looked at Laurel, who stood up and massaged her lower back, then looked their way.

"Paolo, can I ask you a question?"

"That's a very grown up way to say it. Good job, young man."

"Marcus told me to ask permission before I ask something someone may not want to answer."

Paolo stood still, searching the boy's face as Lucius poured apples from the basket he had made with his shirt into the bucket Paolo held.

"Okay, shoot. What is it you want to know?" Paolo leaned in and whispered so Laurel would have a harder time hearing him. "You're too young to have the sex talk."

Lucius burst out laughing so hard he almost fell off the ladder. "Sex, sex, sex, everyone's always talking about sex, whatever that means."

Paolo thought how grown up Lucius was. Old and comfortable in his body, at his age. He wished he had some of the inner peace this little-six-year-old had.

"Exactly, my man. People make too much of it. Way too much. Lucius, my friend, we've just found the first point of agreement between us."

"Yes, gentlemen should find more agreement than disagreement."

This sounded just like Marcus. His brother had done well influencing this young lad, Paolo thought. Just when he thought he'd been able to avoid a query he wouldn't be able to field, Lucius remembered his question.

"Is Marcus my father?"

"Ah, why do you ask that? What has he told you?"

"My mother's told me he is. But he never calls me his son. If he were my father, wouldn't he want to do that?"

Paolo was suddenly heartbroken for the boy. This must be a very trying situation for Marcus, being such a responsible person. And he felt the little heart beating in the six-year-old's chest, still a mortal, still trying to figure out his life and where he stood. It touched Paolo. The pain was identical to what he experienced as a mortal child, not knowing where he belonged in the scheme of things. The sense of not belonging only increased after he chose to become vampire, wishing he had made a different decision.

Paolo also knew Maya would use Lucius for her own ends, and this made him angry. She was not a proper mother. He hoped Marcus would just claim him and take him away from her, for the boy's sake. But until that day, Maya would use this boy as her pawn in a giant chess game. *Not vampire. Must be witch.* Her whole family was a thorn in their side, all of them.

"Lucius, I would trust what Marcus tells you. I would believe him. I presume you've asked."

"I'm afraid to."

"Afraid? Why?" Paolo took a few more apples from the boy's small hands.

"I want him to be my father. I really do. He says he loves me. But I'm afraid he's not my real father." Paolo could not help but melt when he saw the lone brave tear fall down the boy's red puffy cheek. He grabbed Lucius off the ladder, almost scaring him, then held him close for several minutes as the child's little feet dangled off the ground. The boy struggled at first, then buried his head in Paolo's shoulder and sobbed.

PAOLO DROVE LUCIUS over to his grandmother's house. He felt better about leaving Lucius with his mother's family after learning Maya was in America, chasing after Marcus. She wasn't expected back any time soon. The shared arrangement meant Lucius was to spend half the time with each family. But now there was talk of sending him to California to live with his mother and be closer to Marcus, who now spent all his time there. Laurel gave Paolo strict instructions not to mention Marcus coming to Italy.

Paolo enjoyed the time he spent with Lucius. They had picked berries, and a warm pie was setting in a box in the back seat floor, something Lucius would have all to himself, as all others in the household had no need, being that they were all vampires.

Maya's mother, Aurora, wasn't particularly happy to see Lucius or Paolo. She was not quite as beautiful as her stunning daughter, but she had the same dark, sultry look. *Witch blood in there, eons ago.* She turned her nose up when Paolo offered her the pie, like he was handing her a dead cat. In fact, Paolo thought she might have preferred a dead cat to a berry pie. She made it quite clear where her tastes lay.

Paolo figured her lack of culture would cause her to drink blood in front of the boy, something considered low cast. Or worse yet, feed on a farm animal or some helpless human. God, he was filled with visions of what this boy's life might be like. He squeezed his fingers so tight he almost drew blood from his own palms.

"So now Marcus has his substitute bringing him over." She looked Paolo up and down. "A poor substitute at that."

"Nice to see you too, Aurora."

She hissed and showed her fangs to him, luckily out of sight of Lucius, who had run into the house with the pie he had snatched from his grandmother's hands.

"May I come in to say goodbye to Lucius?"

"No." She slammed the door.

He hated them, absolutely hated them. He decided to stay a few more days to talk to Marcus. He knew his brother had requested Lucius go back to Maya's, and although she didn't say it, Laurel implied Anne did not know about the boy. He wondered how long Marcus could keep this secret.

So many secrets . . .

So many lives ruined.

Chapter 16

ANNE WAS ANGRY. She sat in an overflowing bubbled bath all alone, at 39,000 feet in a jet that cost twenty-five million dollars or more. And the man who had plopped her into the tub without ceremony, the man who owned this jet and a vineyard in California as well as a villa in Italy, the man who had confessed she was his fated female, the man who had waited three hundred years for her, refused to have sex.

This was beyond unbelievable. No way would she be able to tell her friends. But then, not much of Anne's current life and lifestyle could be believed either.

What was Marcus doing? Why had he abruptly left her panting and wanting? She snuggled under the warm bubbles that smelled of lavender and melted into the scented water. She rubbed a sweet citrus gel over her breasts as she massaged them. She swirled the lavender liquid between her legs. She didn't feel she was bleeding, but some cramping continued.

She hadn't bought any tampons with her. The thought of having to wear one now disgusted her. Draining a human didn't disgust her, but wearing a tampon did. How her life had changed.

The mirrored bathroom door opened and Marcus stepped in, wrapped in a white towel, naked to the waist. The front of the towel pushed out like a tent.

"May I join you?" He didn't wait for her answer, and instead dropped his towel and showed Anne his huge erection. She swore under her breath. *So not fair.*

"Are you going to tease me or please me?" She pouted, but didn't take her eyes off his cock.

"I think a little of both." He stepped over the tub's lip and sat in the bath, facing her. He slid his legs under her thighs to rest along her hips. The look of him, the smell of him and his blood force, so male, so tall, surrounded by light purple bubbles, almost made her laugh. Her chill was thawing.

"I have never done this before." He smiled, his face filled with wonder like a schoolboy. His hulking lower body disappeared under the water—all except his knees, which perched high above the bubbly foam. The tub was obviously too small for him. Anne could somehow believe he'd never shared a bath with a lady, for all his three hundred years.

So much for experience. She liked being his first.

Although she wanted to ravish him, Anne waited for him to advance to her. Her cheeks felt pink, her thoughts scattered—the effects of the delicious red champagne. Anne moved just out of his long reach, leaned against the back of the tub, and squeezed her breasts. She called to Marcus's dark eyes that followed the movements of her hands, which traced up the side of her neck and covered her lips.

By the sight of Marcus's flaring nostrils, she could tell he was barely in control. It was delicious knowing he could handle anything she could give out and she wouldn't have to be careful. She wanted so much to demonstrate to him she could handle anything he wanted to do to her as well. This need burned inside her belly, increasing in intensity the more she was around him.

"Are you hungry?" Marcus stopped before his chest touched hers. She felt his warm breath. He looked so sweet with his concern for her. She felt the last vestiges of her anger evaporate.

"Aren't you worried I'll get fat if I drink too much?" Anne curled her lips up at the sides. She sat up, still facing him, and scooted her slippery body over to rest her sex against his lap, making him touch her entrance with the head of his penis. "There is only one need I have at the present time. Please, Marcus. Let me have it."

He leaned into her, and with an arm around her waist, pulled her higher up to rest on his thighs. She wrapped her legs around him. He kissed her neck as she pressed into his chest. She turned to the side, made her neck long. She craved his bite. "For you," she whispered, then bit the top of his shoulder.

"Anne." He brushed her ear with his lips, then nipped her earlobe without breaking the skin. "I give you all that I can."

She drew back to look at him, then kissed him hard. His tongue worked into her mouth, his urgent pressure causing a little blood and a tiny drizzle of pain. She wrapped her arms around his neck and held as tight as she could. If she could possess his body, she would have done it right then and there.

"Please take me, Marcus. Feed from me."

"Would you give up a lifetime of forever for a few minutes of pleasure?" He looked at her without flinching. The dripping water faucet broke the silence of the room.

Anne shook her head and sighed.

The council would have to decide. Some stupid body that was probably made up of old crones and shriveled ancient-long-black-finger-nailed-vampires she had yet to meet would determine her fate. Would they have to run their gnarled hands over her pure white flesh to inspect her menstrual blood? She knew this was important evidence of their fating. Why was this so important?

"Come, pet. Feed, then take a nap in my arms."

He moved her with ease to switch sides, then lay back against the tub's edge. Anne leaned forward and took from his neck, undulating her body back and forth, maneuvering her clitoris against his marble hard cock. The sensation of his blood in her veins and the heat of his body against hers sent her into an orgasm, and her last drops had to be taken with short quick breaths as her body sizzled. She stroked him while she finished up her feeding. Her breathing was ragged. She was just getting started.

Far from satisfied, she moved to place her mouth over the head of his cock and encircled him, moving up and down in slow rhythm. "Give me what you can give me. I will take all of it," she whispered as she let her lips rub the length of him.

"At this rate, I think I might make you fat. I think you might be the first fated female to gain weight from her male's semen."

MARCUS SECURELY HELD Anne. She was so much shorter than him; her feet were not able to touch the end of the tub. She could have floated except for being bound by his embrace. *My female trusts me completely. She sleeps as I protect her.*

He was thinking about the council meeting scheduled for the next day. First, he would introduce Anne to Laurel and get a tour of the villa. Then he would have to instruct her on what would likely happen at her council interview. He shuddered as he thought about how important this meeting was. He could not bear to think about a life without Anne now. And, if he had to choose between a few stolen hours with her followed by certain death or a life without her, he would have to say he would pick the first. His life was not real without her. He hoped they saw it the same way, that her bleeding would convince them.

But there was the boy. He felt guilty for not telling Anne about Lucius, but he wasn't exactly sure what he should say, not knowing what was truth. He didn't trust Maya. That the boy looked just like Marcus, there was no question. He hoped the council didn't make him choose between the boy and Anne. *Another tough decision and path.* Perhaps a lesser man would choose a course of being on the run from the council and their long reach, constantly living in fear. This would be a stupid choice. No, better to face them, and then deal with the circumstances accordingly.

He pushed it all out of his mind for now as he felt her breathing, smelled the wonderful scent of her hair, its silkiness against his chest. Nothing in the world had made him feel so complete as to have her feed from him, to lie here in his arms. He turned the hot water on with one of his feet, careful to be delicate so as not to awaken her. The little trickle of hot water did its work, warming the lovely womb they lay in together. He sighed.

How he wanted to be able to plunge into her pink nether lips and make her scream his name. And do it over and over again. As a new vampire, her lips would swell, turn rosy red.

As much as he felt their fating, he would only know for sure once they had sex. He had not told her about that. If they weren't fated, they could remain great sexual partners. Some of his vampire friends had chosen to follow this path rather than raise a family with a fated female. But then, eventually, the true fated female would appear, and everything would change. For him, it had taken three hundred years, not the longest duration to wait for a fated female that he had ever heard of, but definitely a rare number. Maya had been a most pleasant sexual partner during the last part of that, and he treated her with the respect that came with it, being exclusive only unto her, considering that perhaps for him, there would be no real fating. In fact, he'd almost resigned himself to it.

He had lots of opportunity to pick a mate, not only in the golden vampire species, but with the darks as well. Mortal women, especially little witches with their secret spells, had even tempted him, but he'd kept to Maya, with the need to keep things uncomplicated. It was curious that he had not felt any form of jealousy when he had learned Maya had been unfaithful to him more than once. He allowed her infidelity, perhaps as proof to himself they were not actually meant for each other.

Maya was known for her scenes, something she inherited from her family. She was wild and exciting, no denying that. But he did not feel the fate. Perhaps she had spelled him, like Laurel said. It was rumored her family had some witch blood in them from some ancient ancestor.

But time for all that later. First order of business was to meet his sister, then prepare Anne for the council interview. Each would have to face the council separately. With any luck, once Robert released her vow, Marcus could have his fated female in every sense of the word. Just thinking of it made his cock rise and push against this woman's buttocks, seeking release. His cock tickled her and roused her from her deep slumber. He chuckled deep in his chest. He had such a selfish cock, a very independently thinking cock. *Soon, my little friend. Behave and you will get a treat.*

ANNE WOKE UP in Marcus's arms, still feeling the luxury of the warm scented water. One of his hands was on her breast, the other rested on her lower belly. She guided his fingers between her raised knees. She moaned and arched her back, rolling her head from side to side, exposing her neck to him again. His fingers entered her and she began to shudder with pleasure. His other hand squeezed her nipples, one at a time. He licked her neck, letting her know he wanted to bite her there. He kissed her with gentleness, as if she was as delicate as a snowflake. It sent her into waves of ecstasy. Soft or hard, everything Marcus did to her was pure pleasure.

Anne knew it would be like this until they got permission. He would never let them go beyond a certain point, and Anne would not get enough of him in the meantime. If only they had a month to themselves. A precious life without interruption. Staying naked. Getting cleaned up, then getting naked again. No having to get up to eat, to prepare dinner. So much more efficient being in love with one's host. This tall vampire could satisfy all her needs. She laughed. She'd probably come back from a month alone with him even more addicted to him than she already was.

THE PLANE TOUCHED down in Genoa at sunset. The pink ring on the horizon looked like a watercolor stain. Marcus admitted to himself he had a fair amount of trepidation. Meetings with the council were sometimes dangerous. The decisions the council made could be arbitrary, and were always final.

The driver met them at the airport. They sped off south towards Naples in a black Mercedes sedan. Anne cuddled against his chest, looking out the blackened window at countryside and village scenes. They traveled on a two-lane freeway, through several roundabouts and then through a town center back out into the country. At the rise of a gentle hill, they turned into a crushed gravel driveway that stretched out behind iron gates, which opened as they neared them. The sign at the gate said Monte Olivio. They drove under large pine trees that stretched almost as wide as they were tall.

Marcus pointed to them. "These are from the oldest trees in the world. They came from trees alive during the time of Christ."

Anne watched how his face turned soft and sported a smile, though she knew he was under some stress. A woman at the entrance to a large stone villa stood waving.

"And that would be my sister, Laurel. You will recognize her." He smiled again and kissed her with tenderness. "Welcome to my country villa in Tuscany, my pet."

Anne's heart ached that he didn't say "our" home. Some of her frustration returned. God, if Robert didn't release her from their spoken vows, she would kill him herself. And then the reality of what she said fell upon her and she was suddenly ashamed. Marcus loved her for who she was. She must always keep her word and be trusted to do the right thing. Always. It was dangerous to be thinking even in jest about taking shortcuts, even if it meant freedom from Robert.

The purring of his chest when Marcus talked to her softly, when he pointed something out, when he brought her along into his world, sharing more of himself, when he held her body in the warm scented bath, when he kissed her and made her body pulse, when the aliveness of his blood inside her veins turned her into some magical creature, gave her one tiny slice of Heaven. And she was not ashamed to say the more of this life she got, the more she craved, could not live without.

The car stopped. She reached up and touched his cheek. "Marcus, I know this is an important time for us. I want to thank you—for everything, even before we do this, I want to thank you for giving us a chance like this. I—" Tears welled up in her eyes. All she could say was, "I am so grateful you found me—whatever happens."

"Yes." He kissed her. "Always remember I love you. You can trust in that. No matter what happens, please know that. Never forget that, Okay, my pet?"

"Yes, Marcus. Even if I find out you spend every waking moment away from me looking like a green lizard, I don't care. I love you and nothing will ever stop me."

"We will be tested." He traced her lips with his forefinger. "Our love must survive no matter what."

Marcus's sister came up to the car and tapped on the rear window.

Anne looked up and gasped. Laurel was the nurse who had treated her after the attack. The attack that had changed her life forever.

Marcus exited the rear door and embraced Laurel, who jumped into his arms. She showered him with kisses and he laughed. "Careful, careful, Laurel. Anne will get jealous of my own sister. How scandalous!" It didn't stop her from kissing him further.

Marcus held a hand out. Anne let him help her out of the back seat. She stood not more than a foot apart from them. Laurel, who surprised her when she reached out and pulled her to her chest. "Welcome, Anne. It's so nice to see you so healthy, so beautiful. You glow with inner love."

"Yes, I think anything Marcus loves blooms." All three were silent for a bit. "I want to thank you for taking such good care of me that day. I have questions maybe you can answer."

"Later." Marcus said into her ear. He wrapped his big arm around her waist and began walking, almost carrying her to the stone structure.

Through large carved doors, they entered an enormous hallway. Ceilings frescoed in colorful paintings in bright colors warmed the room, which looked several hundreds of years old, with a few faded watermarks. Oil paintings of family members, some of them colorful, some of them very dark due to age, surrounded the walls, affixed to thick plaster walls.

"We have a strange ancestor." Marcus pointed to the frescoes on the ceiling. Anne couldn't see what he was pointing to. She saw some monkeys and banana leaves, birds, plants, and people with short pantaloons and shoes with pointed toes and square buckles. She shrugged and looked back at Marcus.

"Look at their chests." Anne looked at the monkeys and sure enough, they all sported large breasts. So did the birds. And the women were bare to the waist and had enormous breasts as well. She laughed, covering her mouth.

"How old are these?" Anne thought it was hysterical.

"I think about four hundred years, give or take a hundred. Maybe more, right, Laurel?" He looked at his sister.

"I think easily four hundred." She shook her head from side to side. "Marcus, of all the things you could show her . . ."

Marcus picked Anne up and whisked her up the stairs. "That's all of a tour you get for now. It's dinnertime!"

Anne waved to Laurel, who returned the wave just before she and Marcus disappeared through a high archway into a bedroom the size of Anne's place. The dark walnut ceiling was carved with monkeys with large breasts. He set her down and cupped her, then bent down to kiss her. "I have never brought a woman here to this room before. I have never bed a woman here. You will be the first, and the last."

It was a simple statement. Anne felt her heart would burst. However important their fating was, especially to Marcus and someday to her, no matter how urgent it was that she be able to have sex as a true partner with him, her life was now complete with these simple words coming from this man's lips. Everything else in her life would pale in comparison. She was certain her life would begin and end here. With Marcus, in his arms, in his bed.

LATER ON, MARCUS explained some of the rules she would need to know. The blood was never wrong. Fating meant that the couple could have children. Otherwise, the sexual union would not produce any offspring.

And not every golden chose this kind of life. He told her his brother had chosen to live with mortal women and would continue to outlive them. He also explained that children born would be born human and were given the choice at puberty whether they wanted to go forward as a human or a vampire. He explained his parents had chosen to stay mortal. But all his brothers and sisters had chosen to eventually become vampire.

A blood relative could only do the turning, so it was critical a teen stay close to the biological family in case a turning was required. It was rare for them to stray away. And any turning had to be approved by the Council.

"So why was I turned?" Anne asked.

"That was a violation."

"I don't understand."

Marcus kissed her. "Enough questions. We need to focus on the interview with the Council. I will answer all your questions later. There is still a lot for you to know."

Chapter 17

ROBERT FINGERED THE note Anne had left. She'd demanded he be out of the house by the weekend. Well, his name was on the lease too. What the hell was she thinking? She couldn't just do that.

And then he read over the part where she said she was asking for him to publically renounce the wedding vows, even though she acknowledged they were technically not married. *What's up with that?* This sounded like something legal. Maybe he should consult Gary.

But he probably wouldn't.

Robert decided he wasn't going to go down that quickly. What was the point? Things weren't really so different than they'd always been. Anne was the one who had changed. *He* hadn't. It was just that he'd gotten caught. Even with her change, things could have remained the same between them. Maybe they could have even stayed married, *if* he hadn't gotten caught.

Damn Monika and her cherry flavored condoms. He'd be the only lonely ex-married man on a condom diet. Lambskin was just fine, thank you very much.

So why would *he* have to go to all the trouble to move out? That wasn't the Anne he married. She had changed ever since she'd come back from Italy. Now she ate like a bird but wasn't getting skinny. She used to be a cautious driver and now she was wicked fast. The neighbors told him she'd taken to gardening in the dark. Said it was so she could see the critters eating her flowers. Now that stuff was just weird. Even Gary thought it was weird, and he should know.

He thought about his friend Gary's taste in women. That one last night with the red bedroom, for instance. He didn't remember a lot of the encounter except for everything being red: her clothes, her bedroom, her bed, and—was there blood too? He tried to focus, but all he saw were her ginormous breasts and the red—that was it—red satin sheets, or deep pink sheets with red stuff.

Fuck me.

This mental fog was starting to piss him off, because he really wanted to get his money's worth. That was one time he wished they'd been in one of those rooms you could put on video. Bet she had some moves. Almost like it was a waste of the hundred bucks. Gary said it was a terrific deal, but not if he couldn't remember anything other than her letting him take a taste of her tits and then giving him that kiss that almost hurt. She really wanted him too, he could tell.

Gary had awoken him on the couch later. The woman had tossed him from her bedroom like sloppy seconds after they were done, and had locked her door. Helluva bedside manner. *Not very fucking professional.* Next time he'd tell her "no, thanks."

They helped themselves to another beer on their way out and compared notes as soon as they were alone in Gary's truck. They had their wallets, and Gary's cross and Robert's wedding ring were still in their possession. They decided they should take a dose of penicillin he had just in case, and a good, hot shower. They both smelled of burnt feathers, and each had figured it was the incense she burned that made their eyes water. He'd heard somewhere smelling burnt feathers was a sign of a brain tumor. Not likely something like that would occur to them both at exactly the same time, so Robert ruled it out.

On the way home, they both discovered their dicks hurt, which prompted a quick trip to a Starbucks bathroom. Screw that little punk with purple hair and the lip piercing for thinking they were gay. But when they both dropped their drawers and examined themselves, they both had two holes in the side of their dicks. They didn't look anything like pimples or a reaction to some cream he'd had in the past. Something very kinky had gone on there. That's when he found out Gary didn't remember screwing her either. They were of a mind to go back there tonight and ask for a goddamned refund at first. And Gary had set this all up. Who can you count on if not your very best friend? *Dickwad.*

He shook his head and realized his neck no longer hurt. He looked at himself in the mirror. There was very little of the purple mark left from the day before. Good riddance. Finally, he'd caught a break. Now if he could just lose the little holes too. He was glad the swelling in his dick didn't interfere with his urine stream.

Thank God for small favors. Now if I can just get my marriage back together.

Robert jumped into the shower as soon as he got home. No way he was going to get an infection and have his cock get all swollen, turn yellow, or drain puss. He'd seen that before, to someone else on his baseball team who had a lost weekend in Mexico. So, try as he might, he could not remember a single one of his hundreds of sexual partners who had ever done this to him. What exactly was it, anyhow? A bite? *Jeez.*

The phone rang just as he stepped out of the shower. Dripping wet, he hobbled over and answered it.

"Meester Robert. You got a lady," Elena was underscoring the word *lady* with emphasis she didn't normally do. This could not be good. "She want to see you right away. Joo close by?"

"Um, who is she?"

He heard muffled voices as Elena asked the woman for her name.

"Mr. Robert, her name is Maya Monteleone. She's looking to talk to you about your wife."

"Anne?"

"Yeah. Dat one. Joo comin' down here right now?"

"I can't get there for at least an hour." There were more muffling sounds, and over Elena's protests, a new voice came on the phone.

"Robert, this is Maya. We met last night, remember?"

No, Robert didn't really remember. But he knew who she was just the same. His dick lurched under his towel. *Fucking traitor.*

"Robert, are you there?"

"Yes, I'm here." He wanted to shout, *and what are those god-damned marks on my pecker?* but he didn't.

"How do you feel this morning?"

"How do you think I feel? Like a lab experiment."

Maya laughed. She didn't sound so dark when she did that. She actually sounded a little like Monika. And then he got worried the holes would make a scar. What would he tell Monika when she had her change of heart? He was sure she would. Maybe Anne wouldn't, but Monika could always be counted on.

"Listen, Robert. I have a business proposition for you, something I think you will be interested in." She lowered her voice to a whisper, no doubt trying to calm Elena's death stare. "I also thought I could make it up to you, if you like."

He didn't like, but his cock did. He felt like slapping it but that would make it worse. "I'm out of money." That was true, after all. Lawyers were expensive.

"You silly. I'm looking to help you *make* a little money. You interested?"

Robert wondered if she had in mind donating blood again through his dick. Maybe he had some rare blood type they would pay thousands of dollars an ounce for or something. Then he thought of Gary and knew this wasn't true.

"What about Gary?"

"He had his fun. This is between you and me." Elena was making lots of noise in the background. "You better tell your secretary it is okay we speak."

"I'll tell her tomorrow. What kind of business thing are you talking about?"

"Can I see you?"

"Um, I'm not coming in today. I've got some things I have to do at home."

"Okay, I will meet you there. What's your address?"

There was a pause. Robert knew it was a mistake to give the address out. Wouldn't be the first mistake he made today. Certainly wouldn't be the last.

SHE WORE RED again. And damn, she must have been a faster driver than Anne, because it only took her about five minutes to get to the door. He didn't even have his clothes on, just his shorts. She noticed. She didn't ask to be invited in, but walked up to him and slid against his chest, right past him into the living room. That was all his traitorous body part needed. It was very clear who its master was.

She scanned the room, even raised her nose as if to smell the air. Robert smelled under his arms. He'd just showered. Was part of the experiment learning what kind of shower gel he used?

"Is your wife at work?" she asked as she stepped to face him, touching her breasts against his chest. She rubbed them from side to side. The traitor under his shorts liked it. He was making a real fuss down below.

Robert stepped back, a little cautious. "She doesn't work. I think she's at the place she volunteers at today."

"Oh." Maya's eyebrows arched. "When will she be home?"

"I'm not sure. What is this about?"

"What is this about? What is this about?" she mimicked as she closed the distance between them. "This is about how much time we have before she comes home."

"Uh huh."

"So, how much time do we have?"

"Ah. I'm not feeling too good right now. Something *bit* me last night, did you know that?"

Maya smiled and looked at the bulge in his shorts. She squeezed it through the cotton fabric with one hand. God, she had strong hands. He didn't dare move. Wasn't anything like Monika, even on one of her "frisky" nights.

"I hope I didn't hurt you."

Robert was thinking that yes, she was hurting him a little bit right now. Traitor hadn't figured it out yet. This wasn't going anywhere good. Besides, how did she know the bite was on his dick?

"So, you admit to biting me?"

"Yes." She massaged his dick, being gentle now. That was more like it. Traitor purred. "Let me see what I've done. I am so sorry. I want to make it up to you." She got on her knees and slid his shorts down to his ankles.

"No biting." Like he could stop her.

"No biting, unless you want to bite me." She slid his cock in and out of her mouth and he lost his shame and fear all at once. "Do you want to bite me, Robert?"

"I don't bite."

"Maybe you should try. To get even with me, hmm?" She licked the length of his shaft. Her dark eyes begged him to come all over her face, but something told him she wanted something else. "Oh, Robert, you taste so nice."

He jerked a bit. Had she told him the very same thing last night? A vague memory surfaced, a memory of hearing the same words from under his jaw line, as she'd been *biting* his neck! Holy cow!

"I'm, I'm not sure what's going on here." He backed away from her. His cock bounced in the air, starved for her stroke, trying to stand up like a drunken sailor. He quickly pulled up his shorts. Maya was still on her knees, watching him. Then she slid the straps of her red top over her shoulders, but stopped before her breasts were completely bare. She lowered her eyes to look at her hands folded in her lap.

"You don't like me. I'm sorry." It was a whisper, so faint, but it was as effective as a shout.

Robert lifted her pure white chin with one hand and looked at the closed eyes and pouting red lips and knew he would get lost in them. He looked at her like how he looked at Monika asleep in the limo on the morning of his bachelor party and felt compelled to be tender, to try to give her back some of the pleasure she gave him, gave all of them.

"No, honey, I like you just fine." He thought she looked sufficiently grateful. He liked grateful sex. He liked feeling like the best lay in the county. Maybe he could surprise her with some moves of his own.

And yes, maybe he would bite her.

What the hell.

Chapter 18

ROBERT WAS ROCK hard again. This was too good to be true. Something about this woman, Maya, brought out all the best in his maleness. He bet he'd showed her a few things. He was so satisfied, lying in his bed feeling like he was eighteen again and horny as hell. He looked around and noticed Maya was no longer next to him.

He got up and slipped on his shorts. He found her in the bathroom. She was sniffing one of Anne's bottles of perfume. She had found Anne's robe hanging on the peg behind the door. Robert wasn't sure he liked this. Even Monika would *never* do that. Not like Maya was anything like Anne. He decided he just attracted strong female types and loved Monika for the wanton variety she was.

"Oh, hello there." She greeted him with a smile. She didn't hide what she had been doing.

Robert leaned over and took the perfume from her hands. "This belongs to my wife."

Maya let the open robe slip to the floor and stood in front of him, naked. "Spray it on me so you can think of her when you fuck me again."

Robert thought this was a strange thing to say. Certainly a twist he hadn't run across before. It irritated him for some reason. He picked up the robe and put it back on the peg.

"If you need clothes, I can give you something else to wear." He turned to walk away, but noticed she had removed the robe and put it on again. He sighed. *Pick your battles carefully.* He had to admit, this one was real different.

"Come on, Robbie, let's talk." She tried to grab his hand but he yanked it free.

"Don't call me Robbie. Call me Robert or Rob."

She sauntered over to him and placed his hands on her breasts. "How about I call you big boy. How about Superfuck?"

Now that was nice of her. But all the same, he could tell she was lying. There would be no outsmarting this one. Better get ready and let her have her way, and then maybe she would leave him alone. But damn, he felt great. Really great.

"You want another taste?" She bared her neck and, sure enough, there were human bite marks there, two rows of them, even spaces for some of the molars he'd had pulled. So he hadn't been dreaming. And it looked like his bite had broken the skin, too.

"I'm so sorry, Maya." He was shocked at his behavior. What in the world was happening to him?

"Oh, don't be. You only gave me a little bite. I think you got maybe one or two drops. You were just having fun punishing me, remember?"

He felt her breasts, then moved his hands down and behind to encircle her waist and pulled her to him. "I wanted to be tender. I didn't mean to hurt you." His statement was genuine. He wasn't some animal, after all. He looked at the mark, rubbed his fingers over it. He could see it almost disappearing right before his eyes. He looked at the end of his finger. Nothing there. Maybe he had a healing touch. Who knew?

"You see, you didn't hurt me." She ground herself into his crotch. "I like it when you taste me."

"Well, I'm not used to tasting my ladies' necks. I prefer other parts." His voice became husky again.

"Oh. That's nice too. Want to try it?"

He nodded as he kissed over the remains of his punishment. She moaned and melted into him.

"But, Robert, one thing. If you taste me, you have to give me just a little bite, okay?"

ROBERT WASN'T SURE whether she liked the sex or the bite better. Just his luck he managed to find someone who he could hurt and would heal so quickly. He was thrilled.

"So, we have to talk now."

God, Maya was beautiful. Seemed to become more and more beautiful every minute he spent with her. Robert loved kissing her everywhere. Her skin was so white, so completely white. But her nipples were deep red, as were her lips. And the nice slit between her legs was blood red when he peeled back the petals and tasted her, bit her. She came when he did it. He thought that was what he liked doing most to her.

"Robert?"

"Yes." He lay next to her, looking up at the ceiling. He couldn't concentrate when he looked at her.

"Do you know where your wife is? You don't seem to be very afraid of having her come home and finding us naked together. What's going on?" She rolled over, then propped her head with her arm.

Robert inhaled and then decided to just tell the truth. "She kicked me out. I have to be out this weekend. We're splitting up."

"What?" Maya sat up straight and looked down at him, a sneer on her face.

"What difference does it make?"

"All the difference in the world." She whirled around and presented her back. Robert rubbed her there. Her skin was so pale, and smooth. Like alabaster. He leaned over and kissed each of her ass cheeks and the base of her spine, moving up.

Maya stood and put on Anne's robe again. She sat in the chair Anne sat in three days ago, when she'd told him it was over. Same robe. Same chair. He hoped the message wasn't the same as well.

"You have to tell me where she is right now."

"How should I know? For all I know she's gone to visit her parents in Portland, or over to a friend's house. I don't think she will be back over here today."

"What makes you say this?"

"Her suitcase is gone."

"Damn."

He could tell Maya was thinking hard about something. "Um,

Maya. Why all this interest in . . . in . . . Anne. I thought you and I . . ."

"Oh, shut up and let me think."

This offended Robert's sense of dignity. He felt like he was the last one in on a dirty little joke. Maybe the joke was on him. "Wait a minute. What the hell is going on? I need to know right now." Robert thought that sounded pretty strong. Manly.

Maya flew off the chair and landed on top of him, pinning him to the bed. She almost knocked the wind out of him. He was suddenly very afraid. She looked down at him with her dark eyes. A golden ring began to form in the middle. Robert squinted as her expression changed from docile kitten to ravenous beast.

No wonder she liked the bites better than the sex.

Bile rose in his stomach. Maya turned her head at an awkward angle and smiled at him. Her mouth looked like she was working hard to keep her lips covering her teeth. She sat still, her eyes closed, and sighed. All of a sudden, she was calm. None of the wolfish face remained. Robert was a little relieved.

"Did she take a big suitcase or small one, dear?" The dear part was added a bit too late. Like she was masking something, feigning affection.

"Big." Robert didn't care if she saw he was shaking. He had the urge to pee.

"Thank you." She traced his lips with her forefinger. "And where, Robert, does she keep her passport?"

Robert couldn't speak. He pointed to the dresser. In an instant she was off him, rummaging through the top drawer. Then through the next one, then the bottom drawer. She wasn't putting things back. Anne would be pissed. He was thinking what he would say to her if she found out. Of course she would find out. He was the one leaving. She was staying.

Robert sat up, making sure to cover his crotch. What did he know about this woman? Nothing! Nothing except she was wicked fast, wicked strong, could light candles faster than anyone he had ever seen, worked in an adult bookstore, and took men home to her red bedroom. And she liked to bite, in strange places, too. And . . . *I bit her!*

His stomach gave up on him. He put his palm over his mouth, bolted for the bathroom, and almost made it. What he threw up on the floor didn't make him happy. His bile was black, and it seemed to burn holes in his brand new linoleum. There was that burnt feathers smell again.

Shit, what have you done, Robert?

Maya stepped behind him as he was wiping up the mess. She didn't look surprised at the damage to the floor. When she bent over to touch his back, he leapt up and pinned himself against the opposite wall, protecting his privates with both hands.

"Don't touch me." He didn't care he was sounding like a first-rate coward. He had gone along with everything, the biting, the blood stuff, but now he was poisoned as well. And this bitch was looking for his wife! His *wife*!

As if she read his mind, Maya held up his cell phone. She extended it out in front of her while spearing him with that look in her eye. Robert flinched. He carefully took the phone, not wanting to touch her skin as he did so.

"Call her."

"Who?" He sounded like a fifth grader. He swore to himself.

"Call your wife. Ask her where she is."

Robert was going to say no, but one look at Maya's face told him that would have dangerous consequences. Not lethal, but more than likely painful. Well, hell, it was *just* a phone call. Not like he was going to set a trap for Anne or something. He had to have time to consult Gary, who would know what to do about this situation. And then maybe they would go to the police, or visit his friend who was a security guard at Wal-Mart. At least his friend owned a gun and knew a lot about law enforcement, although Gary *had* flunked the police exam.

Maya was still wearing Anne's robe. She was not in a sexy mood. "I said call her, or I will make you call her. Do it now, before I get mad." Maya walked up to him very close. He felt trapped, helpless. "You really don't want to get me mad, Robert, do you?"

Chapter 19

PAOLO STEPPED INTO the entryway and perused the bags by the front door. A cell phone chirped in the pocket of a jacket hanging on a hook by the door. The jacket didn't look to be Laurel's, so he took it to be one belonging to his brother's woman. He fished through the pocket, grabbed the phone, and noticed the name "Robert" flashing on the screen. He put it back without answering it.

Laurel joined him.

"Are they upstairs?" He pointed to the ceiling.

She nodded.

A smile graced Paolo's lips as he thought about his brother in love at last, after all this time. Perhaps there was hope for him, after all. He wondered if Marcus ever really loved Maya and guessed not.

"What's she like?"

Laurel looked up for a minute before answering. "Anne is beautiful, but then, Marcus has never been interested in anyone but real beauties."

Paolo nodded. This was true.

"She's small, petite. They look nice together." She stared off into the distance, through kitchen windows to the orchard. "I have never seen him bending over so much. He shows her things and almost kneels down to her eye level. It's very sweet. He's so tender with her."

Both he and his brother had a fondness for small women, made even more is distinctive by the fact that they were both so tall.

"Nice."

"Yes, it is. Nice to have lovers in this house again. You notice how the air smells better, the flowers seem brighter?"

"Yes, we are basking in the glow of their love." Paolo hoped she didn't pick up his sarcasm.

"You will too, some day."

"I love my wife now." He looked at his hands. "But it is different. Not like this."

Laurel hugged him, burying her head in his chest. "Promise me, brother, your next choice won't cause you so much pain. You should choose from your own kind."

"I am not human, but I choose to live and love that way."

"At what cost?"

"She is worth the price. Any price."

"Why not bring her here, let her meet the rest of the family?"

"She's ill now. Cannot travel. Maybe if she gets better I will, but I think this may be the end for her." Paolo sighed and stroked Laurel's hair. "Does he know I'm here?"

"No. There wasn't time."

Paolo smiled. "That anxious to get upstairs, hum?"

"Afraid so." Laurel broke their embrace and looked into his eyes. "We must be happy for him, Paolo. He mustn't see our pain, our loneliness."

"Agreed." He said this as he nodded.

The cell phone in the jacket rang again.

"Who's Robert?" Paolo asked. "He seems to be calling Marcus's woman."

"I don't know. Marcus would. Should we bring it to them?"

They looked in each other's eyes and both shook their heads.

The door to the master opened and Marcus descended the stairs with Anne in tow.

"Paolo! What a surprise." Marcus almost crashed into him as he gave his brother a big hug and slap on the back. They stood at the same height, eye to eye, regarding one another, looking for changes that would never occur on their faces.

"This is Anne," Marcus said, presenting her hand to Paolo's bow.

"Enchanted." Paolo kissed the back of Anne's knuckles and traced a lovely citrus and vanilla fragrance. He instantly wanted to bite her.

Anne giggled.

He dropped her little pink newly turned fingers and noticed her face flushing. She seemed bashful. Paolo could read the sigh of contentment in his brother's demeanor.

Marcus beamed, looking at Anne, obviously proud of his new love. And protective. Then Marcus became serious. "How long are you staying, Paolo?"

"I leave tomorrow. Sorry, but this was just a quick trip. My wife is ill, in her final stages of cancer."

"I'm sorry."

"Where do you live, Paolo?" Anne seemed genuinely interested.

He knew he and Marcus could pass for twins if it weren't for his sandy brown hair compared to Marcus's black locks. Did this female find him attractive as well?

"South of France."

"Beautiful countryside. I was there earlier this summer." She dipped an arm around Marcus's waist, adding a seductive look that Marcus returned along with a caress to her cheek, followed by a little kiss.

How Paolo longed to have a female look at him like that. He was suddenly filled with need. It was difficult to see the flesh of his human wife whither and gray before his eyes. And the pain of watching her age was probably more difficult for him to bear than it was for her. How would it feel to have someone love you who was so young, who would look budding and luscious forever?

"You going to finish the tour, Marcus?" Anne's eyes were bright as she looked up at her man. "Paolo, you want to come?"

The flash in her eyes quickened his pulse. He hoped Marcus didn't notice. This female was indeed intoxicating. He looked at Laurel, who was fanning herself and shaking her head.

Yes, my sister. Some things never do change.

"Actually, Marcus, let's have Laurel give her the tour. I need to speak to you alone, if you don't mind."

Before Marcus could reply, Laurel took Anne by the arm. The two women got into quick conversation, their heads bowing to each other as they walked through the hall to the kitchen and out the back door.

Secrets. Women always had secrets, and whispers. Were they talking about him?

"She's lovely." Paolo said as he watched the women.

"And she's mine."

"Of course." Paolo smiled at the slight verbal slap on the cheek.

The two brothers went into the study.

"Something to drink, Paolo?"

"Two fingers, please."

They retired to the leather chairs in the corner. Marcus handed Paolo the tumbler with the hundred-year-old whisky without ice. "So, what's up?" Marcus asked.

"I met the boy today. He's a handsome one."

Marcus's brow furrowed but he nodded his head and took a sip of the deep amber liquid.

"Does Anne know?"

"No. Not yet."

"What are your plans?"

"First I have to meet with the council, so we can marry. I will ask Maya for permission to adopt Lucius, if Anne will agree. I think she will. I hope she would grow to love him, as I do."

Paolo looked at his glass and nodded, a faint smile toying with his lips. "You're probably right. You are sure, then?"

"What, about the fating? I am sure about being fated to Anne. I have no explanation for the fathering of that child. But I sense he is mine, just as I feel I was meant to wed Anne and not Maya."

"How can you feel for the boy and not for the mother?"

"I don't know, but that's the truth of it. I just hope the council sees it the same way."

"Marcus, I wanted to speak to you because I feel you must decide to raise this child as your own no matter what the council says. He shouldn't be allowed to spend any time with Aurora and the rest of Maya's family. You know they are long suspected of having part witch blood. I cannot think any of them would ever make a proper guardian. All those women are deadly to the boy. I even fear for his life." He looked up at Marcus, feeling the weight of the difficulty of his position. "That boy needs a father. Deserves a father."

"First things first. Once Anne is approved and accepted, anything is possible. I think she will help me do this."

"Yes, I hope so too." Paolo remembered the ringing phone. "By the way, who is Robert?"

"Robert?"

"Yes, Anne's cell phone has gone off twice. I noticed someone named Robert was calling her. Does that name mean anything to you?"

"He's her husband."

"Excuse me?" Paolo wasn't sure he heard correctly. *Marcus has fated to a woman who is married to another?*

"They pledged their vows. That's partly why I need council permission."

"Marcus, you've made a mess of things. For once, you've outdone me!"

"Robert's not worthy of Anne. And he's mortal. She knew that before we became close."

"So, you are not bedding her?"

"And risk separation forever? Hell, no."

"When do you see them?"

"This afternoon. We have an appointment in one hour." He stood up. "I think we should get ready. I need to prepare her for the inspection."

"She bleeds?"

"She does indeed." Marcus looked proud.

They said their goodbyes.

As Marcus walked out to the garden to get Anne, Paolo watched him. Was his brother man enough to do the unthinkable, be fated to two females at the same time? Was that even possible? And what would the council decide?

Chapter 20

O N THE WAY to the council meeting, Marcus took Anne's hand and kissed it. "Your hands are freezing."

Anne had been looking at the countryside as they passed by. The gently sloping vineyard rows and red rocky soil looked familiar. She felt an odd connection to this strange land. The driver behind the clear partition of the big Mercedes limo paid no attention to them.

Marcus always rode in style. She would have enjoyed it except for being so nervous. Who were these people on the council, and what power did they have over Marcus? Over her? Their entire future depended on what this panel of elders decided.

She still bled, but there was hardly a trace. She was slightly concerned it had dried up completely.

"Marcus, I have a bad feeling about this meeting."

"Don't, my pet. You will see. They just need to learn who you are. We have to follow the rules so we can enjoy the *benefits* of our society." By benefits, she took it to mean they could have sex. Unlimited sex. Nothing less than that would do. She'd never had to ask permission for this before.

He nibbled on her fingers. She knew he was trying to get her attention, trying to seduce her again with those dark eyes. All she had to do was look at him, and she would do anything.

God, she loved watching him take command of her body, and of everything else around him. He owned it all. She craved the maleness of him—the way he smelled, how his huge dark form enveloped her, devoured her. She wished they were just going wine tasting or on their way to the jet or going on a road trip. Something fun. Not something she dreaded.

What would she do if she somehow didn't pass muster? Was her life in danger? Was his?

He gazed at her now with that look that said he needed her, that he needed her kiss, the reassurance she was up to the challenge of facing them. She leaned forward and made her lips as soft as she could, then pressed them against his lips, flesh on flesh. He went deeper with his tongue, as if he could not resist. His hands—his wonderful big hands—covered and squeezed her breasts. He was totally hers.

If the council allows it.

"May I, just a little taste?"

She loved it when he begged. "I'm thinking, Marcus."

"About what?"

He explored the valley between her aching tits. His tongue was hot and snaked under the black bra he had bought her for the occasion. The one with the matching panties that had the hole down the length of the crotch. She tingled with the thought of what his tongue would do as he nuzzled and found that opening. *Make him beg a little more.* She wanted to feel the fullness of his need.

"Just a little of you on my tongue."

Yes. She nodded as he bit her breast in the dark fold underneath, so it wouldn't show.

His body shuddered as he supped her precious drop of blood, and whispered, "My sweet, sweet Anne."

How glorious it would be when she could completely surrender to him. Maybe she could get Robert to give her that freedom tonight, if she and Marcus were successful with the council.

A vision popped into her head, forcing a smile. She saw Marcus with her naked, his cock just at the folds of her sex, ready to enter and blast her to heaven and back, and her dialing Robert on the phone. The phone would ring, the anticipation fueling the passion. Just as Robert would be about to say he'd agree to release her, Marcus would thrust inside her. In just that second, she'd be free. No longer than a second. It couldn't come soon enough.

The panties were handy for Marcus's fingers as well. He stroked her. Anne saw the driver's gaze fastened to the road. He was discreet and never looked back at them. The possibility that someone was watching heightened the danger of it, though, made her even hotter. She would have let Marcus do more, but he withdrew his hand.

"What were you thinking about just then, hmm?"

"About how it will be, our first time together. Having sex."

He kissed her. "Me too, pet."

"Taste me again," she whispered with barely a sound.

But Marcus could hear. He watched the words form on her lips, leaned to her neck, and licked her pulsing vein. "Soon, very soon now." His hot breath and one sharp fang slowly slid up her cool flesh, following the vein throbbing underneath.

Their lips claimed each other again, and she nicked her tongue on his elongated canine. He inhaled when her blood dropped onto his tongue, then rubbed the blood all over the insides of their lips. He pulled away and held her gaze without blinking.

"I have not told you something you need to know. They are going to have to inspect you. Inspect your bleeding. Just like at a doctor's office."

"Okay."

"Someone other than I will need to witness, as well."

"Like one of the directors?"

"Yes."

"Perverts." She was not looking forward to this at all.

"You're unbelievable. Wicked and strong. I like this in you." He gave her that smile, all white teeth, just showing the tips of his fangs. Just the look of his fangs could get her wet now. How her life had changed in such a short time.

She offered her wrist to him for another taste.

He took a small nip then said, "Thank you." He licked the wound, blew on it, and rubbed it with his forefinger, accelerating the healing process.

"You should take more. I could live with wounds of your love all over my body."

"In time, my pet." His voice almost purred.

She saw the euphoric effect her blood had on him. His red lips puffed up, full. She knew his manhood was equally swollen. She knew they would do this when they made love. He would become so engorged from drinking of her. And her lips would swell from the drinking of him. Her muscles contracted in waves as she thought about them enjoying each other all night long. Unspeakable pleasure.

"You must feed now."

Anne knew he was right.

He drew her to his chest. She peeled back his unbuttoned shirt and bit him just above his nipple. She resisted the urge to straddle him, her favorite position now when she was feeding, so she could rub him against her sex. That's why they always had to feed in private. It was as intimate as making love.

She pulled away.

Marcus whispered, "Take more, love. You need your strength. I want them to see you fully sated on my blood. I want them to see the effects of our fating. I want them to smell the chemistry, the blood between us."

The car descended to the council compound. Anne noticed Marcus's glow had faded. His eyes squinted, as if in alarm, and his body tensed. He grasped her head between both his hands, and while smoothing over her lips with his thumbs, looked deep into her eyes. "Just answer all their questions truthfully. We have nothing to hide, right? You can tell them about Robert. You can tell them we have not had sexual intercourse. You'll want to tell them what it feels like to be vampire. They need to know these things."

She nodded. She knew there was something he wasn't telling her. Was he worried they wouldn't rule they were fated?

But how could they deny this evidence? She decided perhaps Marcus was just overly cautious.

"I will tell them how much I need you, crave you, Marcus. Surely they will recognize signs that I am fated to you."

He was silent, watching their fingers entwine on her lap. "Whatever you hear, know that I love you. Whatever they ask you to do, you must do it. Please do whatever they ask."

"But, Marcus, what if they ask something of me I cannot do?"

He looked down. She could tell he was thinking about that.

"My pet, I hope that you are able to do anything they ask you to do, please, for us. Then we can be together, forever."

"Yes. I will do it."

"Remember that I love you. I would do anything for you."

"Yes, I will remember. You can't tell me anything more?"

"What we are asking has never been done before."

THEY WERE USHERED into the drawing room where they were instructed to wait on opposite sides, facing each other across the large spans. He was summoned. As he came over to give her another kiss, the messenger hissed at him and he was forced to follow, denied Anne's touch. She did not like this one bit. Her bad feeling grew worse.

And then she was summoned.

The room was dark and had a smell she found disgusting. *Vampire sweat.* Old vampire sweat. All of the seven council members were ancient. Two of them were especially hunched over, looking barely alive, sitting in wheelchairs, which squeaked and echoed off the walls of the enormous hall lined in mirrors.

How can these be immortal? They look like they are dying.

She guessed this large room had been the scene of many great pageants and celebrations over the centuries, but now was covered in cobwebs. There was no music, no laughter. Just cold marble statues and dusty two-story high mirrors in heavy baroque gilt frames.

The two sick council members had IVs of red liquid attached to their arms. All of them wore deep red robes. She could see Marcus nowhere.

"Welcome, child." All but the two infirmed stood as she approached the long raised table. The two who didn't stand grunted and frowned. The vampire in the middle motioned for her to have a seat in the red leather chair in front of them.

Anne's first reaction to all the red and the smell was to be sick to her stomach. How could Marcus abandon her to this group? They appeared disinterested and dangerous.

After she took her place, the leader began the questioning. "So, my dear. You are a conversion, is that correct?"

"Excuse me?"

"You are not a naturally born vampire, right?"

"Right."

"And tell me about that experience." His eyes turned to slits as he leaned forward to hear. "And you must speak up because several of us have hearing problems."

Anne thought one had already fallen asleep. Odd. Very odd. This vampire appeared to be mortal. "Well, I was bitten, by a woman. I was told later it was Maya."

"Who told you this?"

"Marcus."

Two of the members grunted in open disgust, nodding to each other.

"Go on."

Anne wasn't sure what to say next. "Well, she bit me, and then I woke up in a hospital room, or what I thought was a hospital room. I was released the next morning, and they said I was okay, free to leave, and that I hadn't been harmed."

"Who are 'they'?" the robe next to the leader shouted.

"The nurse." She decided to leave off the fact that it had been Laurel. No sense getting her into this mess, though she was probably already involved.

It worked, as the heads bobbed while they conferred in whispers. When they looked back at her, she realized they were expecting her to continue the story.

"I drove from Genoa, along the Mediterranean all the way to Spain, then went by boat to Majorca. I had my first urge to feed four days after the bite. So I did."

"And how was that?"

Anne remembered what Marcus had told her. She decided to appeal to their maleness, if that was still present under their wrinkled skin and somber demeanor. She thought she would use a little helpless charm.

"It went awful. I got blood absolutely everywhere."

Several of the vampires chuckled.

The sleeper woke up. "Is it over?" he blurted out.

Someone reassured him he hadn't missed anything. They stared back at her. She figured she'd continue talking until they asked her to stop. Her time to show what she was made of, perhaps. Maybe this was what Marcus had meant.

"I ruined a perfectly good pair of jeans that cost me $140."

She got no reaction. Maybe they didn't know about jeans.

"I was embarrassed, ashamed at having caused so much of a mess. My intention was not to draw so much interest. And I felt sorry for the man I essentially murdered." She kept her eyes lowered in a sorrowful demonstration. But it was an honest depiction of how she had felt that day.

One of them leaned forward and opened his mouth, about to say something. The man next to him stopped him. "You have fed many times since then, right? No problems?"

"Yes. Until recently, I preferred doing my feeding in the shower so I could wash up afterwards. I'm sorry, but I don't like to walk around with blood all over me. Besides, buying new clothes is expensive."

She saw some faint nods again. Maybe this was working. "One thing I do not like."

"And that is?"

"I really don't like taking lives just to eat."

"But when you were human you sacrificed animals to eat, no doubt."

"But they were raised for food. I don't see the human population as being raised for food. For us."

More nods. "Go on."

"I work at a home for battered women, as a volunteer. I have taken to feasting on some of the awful men I have heard about. I am careful. I try to choose people who have no redeeming qualities. People no one will miss. But do not mistake me, I still believe every life is sacred."

The room was silent, except for the vampire on the end who snored.

"I want to ask you about Marcus," One of the council asked her, leveling a bony finger in her direction. His voice was irritatingly shrill.

"Yes. I love Marcus. He has told me about the fating that goes on between golden vampires mates. I do feel we are meant for each other."

"But I understand you are still married."

"No, not legally. We had a wedding performed, but I am severing all my ties with him. He has never honored our bed. I cannot live a life where I have to worry about where he is, and with whom he is sleeping."

They were nodding again, so Anne added, "He does not honor me. Why should I continue to honor him?"

"Do you want him eliminated? Have you asked Marcus to do this?"

Anne's stomach clenched up. She gripped the arms of her chair, indignant at the insinuation she could ask Marcus to kill off her no-good husband. And how could they think Marcus was capable of such cruelty?

"What?" She squinted her eyes in anger. Had Marcus told them that? "As cruel as Robert is to me, I would never wish my ex-husband harm. Never." She was shaking. She hoped the fervor of her feelings didn't interfere with their decision.

"One more question, if you please." A new visitor came into the room. Handsome, tall, though not as tall as Marcus. He appeared to be the younger vampire. The whole room deferred to him, seemed to center around him.

"Praetor. We are honored with your presence." Most of the council bowed in deference.

With a swagger that told Anne he was used to bedding any woman he wanted and could get away with it, he looked her up and down, resting his eyes on her breasts, then lower to the place between her legs. He licked his lips and sighed. She instantly didn't trust such a powerful, sexy man.

I hope you can do whatever they ask of you. She remembered Marcus's words. What if he asked for . . .?

"I understand you bleed now." His expression was serious.

"Yes, I am bleeding now."

"When was the last time you bled before now?"

"It was before my wedding day, about two months ago."

He smiled and nodded his head, turning to the council. He shrugged.

"Fine." The middle robe stood up. "I have no further questions. I am satisfied. Let's get on with the inspection."

Oh, God, an inspection? With these creeps and this gorgeous male?

Now the reason for her black lacey things with the slit up the middle made sense. Marcus had known. *Damn the man!*

The leader rang a silver bell. Two young girls dressed in harem costumes came into the room to stand by Anne's side. They eased her up from the chair, one on each arm. Anne saw Mr. Handsome peruse all three of them, hand under his chin, stroking his lips like he was studying something. She didn't like being on display. The council members who could, stood up and watched as she was escorted out of the room.

She was taken down a tiled corridor to an exam room. After undressing and putting on the familiar paper dress, she had to suffer through a gynecological exam performed by an elderly doctor as Praetor stood in the room, observing.

Remember that I love you. Marcus had told her to do anything they asked her to do. God damn him. He didn't tell her because he knew she would never agree to it.

The doctor excused himself with the swab, now tinged red at the tip. She sat up and snarled at Praetor. "I find this whole process revolting, sickening. Barbaric, even."

He bowed slightly. Anne could see he perhaps agreed, but did not say anything.

"So, what happens now?"

"He is confirming it is menstrual blood. If that is verified, I'd say you and Marcus could have *a little party.*"

There was something about how he said the last part that made her suddenly catch her breath. *Could we be that close?*

"They've accepted me?"

"They believed your story."

"That's because it's true. All of it."

The doctor returned. "It's confirmed, and now Praetor, you have witnessed it. It is menstrual blood. I will go inform the council." He was almost to the door when he turned. "She is not to be left alone. Bring her back to the chambers once she has dressed."

"Of course."

The physician left. Anne slid off the table, being careful with the placement of the paper wrap and skirt. She glared at Praetor, raising her chin in defiance, aware that although covered, she was naked from the waist down. He broke the silence.

"I see what Marcus has found in you. I only wish I could have seen you first."

"You don't believe in the fate, then?"

He smiled. "It's difficult to believe in something that hasn't happened yet. I, like Marcus, have waited a long time. Let's say I have faith, but I do not believe yet, no." He abruptly turned around to let her finish dressing.

Anne, donned her skirt, muttering to herself about the ridiculous panties. She straightened her hair, making a fuss, harrumphing and gasping, hoping she showed her indignation at the ordeal.

"I have a question," she said.

"Ask me anything."

"What's with the old council members? I thought all vampires are immortal."

"We are not immune to all disease, contrary to folklore. And sometimes there is an errant ancestor of questionable parentage. Some of us age, but age slowly."

"Will this happen to me? Because I started out human?"

"No way to know, my dear. Not a question of your humanity. It's a question of bloodline and breeding."

"The children . . ."

"Can die of normal childhood diseases. Very sad. Very sad indeed."

She stopped. She understood why the children were so important. They were rare. And they were fragile. It was sad.

Anne continued to dress, fiddling with the buttons at the back of her blouse so that she didn't have to ask Praetor's help. It was something she knew he would gladly assist her with.

"Okay. I'm done."

He turned around and looked her up and down, drinking in every curve, every valley. Unashamed to let her see how tantalizing he found her.

"Stop that."

"Stop what?"

"That. That thing you are doing. I don't belong to you."

"My dear, you don't belong to Marcus, either. I don't think you ever will."

He brought her back to the chamber room.

A brief statement was read into the record, verifying all the facts. And then it was over. The directors filed out, including the two sick ones in their wheelchairs. All but Mr. Handsome. Praetor had an expression that was hard to read. She couldn't mistake the tease in his eyes, the invitation to show him some affection if she chose.

She wanted to set him on fire.

He extended his elbow in her direction. "Come, Anne. There is someone dying to see you."

"Where are you taking me?" she asked.

He put his finger to his lips. "It's a surprise."

He waited for her to put her arm through his. She didn't want to do it, so he grabbed it and put it there himself. He patted her hand that rested on his forearm, leaving his hand in place over hers. "Don't worry. Everything will be alright." He hesitated, then turned to face her. His large brown eyes were as beautiful as any woman's eyes Anne had ever seen. And he clearly knew it. "I know my place here, my dear. But, if you ever tire of Marcus the Magnificent, I have some skills that would make your soul tremble. The door to my bedroom is always open to one such as you."

"I'll have to ask Marcus if he thinks that would be such a good idea. He doesn't seem to think I need much instruction. But if I did, Marcus is an excellent teacher."

He was surprised with her boldness, Anne could tell. But she was careful he didn't take it as a slight. That would be a mistake.

They walked through a door to an anteroom, an auxiliary sound-proof chamber. Marcus instantly sprang up, hesitating to come over to her. Stress was written all over his face. And when his eyes fell over Praetor and Anne locked arm in arm, he frowned. She couldn't remember when she had seen his hair so disheveled. The room was littered with chewing gum wrappers and cans of Red Bull. He looked miserable.

"Praetor. How nice to see you." Marcus's speech was measured.

"Marcus, I'm afraid I have some news . . ." Praetor started.

Suddenly Anne was overwhelmed. She disengaged from Praetor and ran to Marcus, burying her head in his chest.

"I passed."

Marcus picked her up with ease, holding her sideways. He nodded to Praetor, then tore off down the hallway, headed to the outside. Anne clung to him, her arms wrapped around his neck, looking over one broad shoulder at the handsome vampire who stood behind them, watching them leave.

Praetor raised his hand up and waved with a couple of his fingers, as if to say, *I'll still be here if you change your mind.*

Chapter 21

ROBERT PICKED HIMSELF up off the floor as soon as he came to. He was covered in blood. His cell phone was shattered. Little pieces of the blue plastic and silver parts littered the bottom of the tub where Maya had thrown it. God, that woman had a temper. For the first time in his life, perhaps he had misjudged a female. Maybe that wasn't quite right. Maybe it was the first time a female *scared* him, like the bullies at school had scared him, like the gangbangers who walked past his job sites scared him.

He'd passed out after she bit him, and, damn, yes, she'd actually drawn blood there. He looked at himself in the half-broken mirror. Sure enough, two puncture wounds stood out on his neck, just like the ones on his dick two days before. No question about it. This one was an animal.

And she was so interested in Anne. Why? Anne had never hurt a fly. All she ever did was work at the women's shelter, helping those ladies get their lives back together. Everyone loved Anne. She was like a mother lion with her cubs. Hard to figure one of her clients would be this angry. No, it must be something else.

He wondered how Anne could meet a woman like Maya. He doubted Anne had ever stepped foot inside the Double Eights. The whole thing just didn't make sense.

He placed the pieces of his phone in the trash and removed his clothing. His dick had healed. Thank God for small miracles. Well, now maybe Monika would take pity on him. He jumped into the shower. The wounds on his neck really hurt.

Afterward, he wet down his shirt and used it to clean up some of the blood on the wall and bathroom floor. He tossed his clothes, including his socks, into the washer, added extra bleach and detergent, then turned it on.

With fresh clothes and a shower, he sure didn't look as bad as he felt. He hurt all over. *All* over. Like he'd been beat up when he was unconscious. Like how he felt the day he had woken up after having his wisdom teeth pulled. That day his cheeks had been so swollen that he could have sworn the dentist had taken aim and punched him just for fun.

First, he would try to call Anne and tell her about this crazy lady, and then he would see about having Monika help him with his stuff. If she'd have him back, that is. And if all else failed, well, he could always promise Gary a night of drinks and a free dinner. Hell, Gary owed him at least a place to stay, after all the trouble he had caused him. If it wasn't for Gary, this bitch wouldn't be stalking Anne, he'd have a cell phone, and he wouldn't feel so tired and drained of energy. He just hoped there wasn't some medical condition that would spring up at an inopportune time. Like that time he and Gary went down to Mexico. That would really suck.

Robert picked up the landline and dialed Anne's phone. All he got was voicemail. Again. He left a message asking her to call him on the house phone, then he called Monica. Monica sounded annoyed, and when he asked where Anne was, she called him a dipshit and hung up. He called Elena and told her he wouldn't be in, then sat down to wait. Surely Anne would call sometime today.

About an hour later, he got a call from Anne.

"God, you sound far away," he said. "Where are you?"

"Umm the connection just isn't very good here. I'm at a friend's house. They live in Healdsburg."

There was a lot of background noise. He could hear someone talking and the peel of church bells. He didn't remember hearing bells before in Healdsburg.

"Well, I've missed you."

"Umm."

Robert knew she wasn't listening to him, or she would have protested his sentiment. There was the sound of something rustling in the background.

"Are you okay, Anne?"

"I'm perfect." More rustling. "Ah, Robert, I need to ask you a very important question."

"Shoot. I'm all ears."

"Will you renounce your marriage vows?"

This was not what he expected. Anne was going to go through with this.

"Please, Robert." She sighed one of her very best, long, sighs. "If you have ever loved me, please say you will fully release me."

Should he set her free? Should he say no? "Could we talk about it? I'm real sorry about everything."

"No, it's over. Let's face it, you love Monika. Go be happy with her. I want you to be . . . happy." She gasped. "Please, please, just tell me you agree to end our marriage. Release me, Robert."

"But in my own way, I love you Anne. I know if we went to counseling, we could revive our marriage. I've learned my lesson."

"Please, Robert."

"I can take anger management classes. I think I'm a sex addict, Anne. There are twelve-step meetings for this. I'm willing to become a changed man."

"I don't want to change you," Anne said. "I want you to let me go. I've released you with my full heart. Please do the same for me. Please, Robert."

It was against his better judgment, but it was the right thing for Anne. He'd messed up things enough, put her through enough. He could do this.

"Okay," he whispered, surprised the word came out of his mouth.

There was a pause. It sounded like she was whispering to someone.

"Okay, what?" Anne said breathlessly.

Had she been running? "Okay I release you! Jeez, that sounds funny. But I still love you."

He was crying, actually crying when he heard her say, "Robert I did love you too, once. Thank you."

He knew Anne thought she had hung up the phone properly, but the line remained open. Robert could hear the passion play going on and could not help but recognize the moans of his young wife being completely sated by someone else. Another man. Someone named Marcus.

It was a fitting end to his short marriage.

After a few minutes, he softly laid the phone back on its cradle. He looked at his crotch and wondered if he ever would feel aroused again.

Then he remembered he had not told her about that strange woman with the oral fixation. Well, if she was with a man, perhaps that guy could protect her. He should at least warn her.

He redialed the phone and got her voicemail.

"Anne, forgot to let you know. There was some woman here who wants to know where you are. She is a real bitch. Uh, honey, I want you to be happy and I'm sorry. I'm gonna need a few days to clear out everything—" Then the line on the other end went dead. He wasn't sure his message was left, after all.

Perfect.

THEY LAY ON the massive four-poster walnut bed. Anne loved the feel of the deep red satin quilting against her bare back and buttocks. She spread her arms to the sides, and Marcus found them. He pinned her fingers with his and then brought them back to his lips. His warm body sheltered and protected her, covering her torso and thighs. She knew he tried to touch her flesh with as much of him as he could, and what he couldn't touch he had kissed over and over again.

She stared up into his coppery eyes, committing to him for all eternity. She was so willing to become the mate he had searched for his whole life. He had pleasured her with his mouth, whispering incantations to her sex, making her quiver as he lapped and sucked her juices. She wondered if the blood was still there. God, she hoped so. She hoped so that she could be fertile for him. That she could be the vessel of his passion, the keeper of his progeny, the holder of his soul.

Her breasts glistened in the late afternoon Italian sun. She barely could remember the events of earlier today. She was in his home, the home of his ancestors. He'd brought her here, flying through the large mullioned windows overlooking the family vineyard, placed her on the bed, and walked around back and forth. She had disrobed button by button, hiking her clothes up here and there. He'd refused to touch her, making her remove each item of clothing until she was writhing on the bed naked with a need between her legs as deep as the Grand Canyon. That's when he'd asked her call Robert.

He was lapping between her creamy thighs when she sat up with a little "Oh" like she did sometimes when the excitement of his tongue was too much for her. But this time she held the little phone out to him and asked Robert to repeat something so he could hear it.

"Okay, I release you! Jeez, that sounds funny, but I still love you." She could have kissed the man. Marcus laved the space between her thighs, then whispered something she felt take hold inside her womb, where it stayed warm and coiled. Some magic glam or spell that waited to receive him and his seed.

With reverence, he stowed the phone on the side table. She felt the muscles at his back move under his tanned flesh, felt his torso press her breasts against him. He wrapped his arms around her and pulled her hair from her neck. He licked the length of her as she moaned and wrapped her legs around his waist, arching up to meet him. His long kiss claimed her again, as they both pricked each other and drank the combined blood, their tongues washing over teeth and gums, covering all the surfaces of their mouths with the elixir of their love.

"Marcus. At last, Marcus."

He groaned and whispered something to her she didn't understand. Words in a dialect she didn't recognize, something ancient. And she heard music between the timbres of his deep voice. Was she dreaming this? She felt him press against her slick opening. She needed to be filled with the strength and power of him.

He looked down, then kissed her eyes, the sides of her face, under her ears, and in the valley under her chin. "Will you fate to me forever?" he breathed. She could smell the blood on his lips. "Will you love me, allow me to give you my seed, protect you? Will you share my bed, my pleasure, my family, my life for all eternity?"

"God, yes." It was everything she'd always wanted. He was everything she'd ever wanted in a mate. She added demands of her own. "Will you love me forever? Will you let me give you children? Never leave me, Marcus. Hold me for all eternity."

"Yes. I claim you for my own, in the ancient way, as you own me. You are ... mine."

He pulled her hair aside, angled his own throat for her hungry access.

"Now," he groaned.

She bit down at the same moment she felt his fangs sink into her neck, at the same moment his cock thrust inside to the hilt. His plunging entrance sent her body into spasms as her insides stretched to receive his huge gift. His blood was sweet, tinged cinnamon. It awoke every cell in her body. His scent warmed her heart, made it flutter as the blood filled all her cavities. She drank without holding back, loving the sound of his ravenous sucking, feeling the strong muscles of his back and shoulders as he took her blood into him, as he ground into her and rhythmically played her sex until she felt a glow below her waist. His deep thrusts demanded she give him all of her. Passion ignited a flame long held low in her belly—something that had been lurking there her whole life. The warmth traveled up her spine, made her thighs and knees tingle, made her press her neck into his hungry mouth. She wanted to be taken, and it wasn't anything like what she'd felt before.

He stopped, brushing thumbs over her cheeks, wiping the tears of joy from her eyes. Awash in the scent of their love, she felt him spasm. Every drop of his seed refreshed and coated her willing womb.

They kissed, barely touching, tenderly speaking a language she didn't realize she spoke, nor did she understand, but when his eyes filled with tears, she knew he heard her ancient message to him, the male of her life. For the rest of eternity. He continued to thrust into her.

"My beloved," she said as she angled her neck. "Take all of me.

Take as much as you can. I give myself to you in every way possible."

He was staying hard inside her and she could sense something was happening. Perhaps he was going to come again. All of a sudden a golden light shone from their joining, enveloping them in a warm electric pulse of energy. Marcus shuddered. Anne's muscles clamped down on him and her whole body began to shake in a wrenching orgasm that left her gasping for air. Their shouts echoed off the paneled ceiling surfaces. The faces of the monkeys overhead smiled down on them.

Marcus rolled over and pulled Anne on top. He held her body at her hips, moving her up and down his shaft as he arched into her, then filled her with more of his seed.

Her thirst for his neck brought her forward, breasts pressing against his chest as she drank at the base of his throat. His fingers urgently clutched at her hair, moving it aside again. His tongue warmed the other side of her neck as his fangs plunged in to mark her again. The twitching his cock made deep inside her forced a series of spasms. She lowered herself onto him, deep and hard. He brought her feet up to his shoulders and held her ankles while she rode his bucking frame. He bit her right wrist and took from her. He licked her ankle and fed from her there.

She wanted him to fill her from behind, something he seemed to understand without her needing to communicate to him. He smoothed over her rear with his large palm, turning her body on her knees so she could present her peach to him. He leaned forward and sunk his fangs into her labia, kissing and sucking, then lapping with his tongue. He placed himself at her violated opening and she felt a delicious pain as she took him in. He rode her, whispering ancient words that made every cell of her flesh tingle with delight.

At last they collapsed into a sweaty pile of arms and legs. She allowed her wet body to be crushed in his embrace. He wouldn't let go, even as she tried to tug the satin coverlet over them so they wouldn't get cold.

"I will do it. I will keep you warm," he said.

And it was true. As he tasted the side of her neck again and rubbed her breasts with his massive hands, she warmed to the touch of his flesh all over her body.

He'd pierced her body and drank her blood from numerous places, but she smiled to think she hadn't counted the wounds he had made.

I am indeed fully satisfied, sated.

A FAINT BEEPING sound interrupted their nap. Marcus grabbed her cell phone that lay on the floor, then raised it to her face so she could see the battery had died. He placed it back on the night table. She felt a twinge of regret that perhaps she had not dealt with Robert properly. There was a part of her that felt sorry for him. She had loved him, once. She was honest with that statement, at least.

She looked up at the man who gazed down at her, the mysterious man who filled her with wonder. Tracing the profile of his face along his hairline, she let her fingers dance across his lips. She rose to meet those lips. His strong hand held her, pulled her to him, and then let her head fall back. He kissed the arch of her neck that she extended for him. He licked the two little holes he had made in the heat of his passion, when he had claimed her, where she would have him claim her again an hour later, where she hoped he would claim her every day for the rest of eternity.

He drew himself to a sitting position, holding her in his lap. She wrapped her arms around his neck, happy to be draped against his body. She inhaled his maleness, the scent of their lovemaking, and the scent of their blood for each other. She kissed his wound, stroking up the sides of his thick neck with her fingers.

His arms enveloped her as he bent his head to rest on the top of hers. "Ah, my pet. You are mine at last. Fully mine."

"Yes. Always, Marcus."

He produced a small black box. Anne was surprised at this, and looked around the bed to see where the box had come from. She searched his smiling eyes, then planted a kiss on his lips as he rubbed a hand along her thigh. He moved two fingers lazily along her flesh to find her wet opening and stroked her there while she popped open the box. His fingers stopped while she took a deep breath.

"Oh, my. Marcus. It's . . . lovely!" A large emerald glittered and glowed in an intricate setting. The ring looked very old. The stone was almost the size of the nail on her little finger, in a deep forest green color, surrounded by a circle of smaller diamonds.

"The stones are new, but the setting belonged to my mother. I think it belongs on your finger, now."

He took the ring and held it as she placed the fourth finger of her left hand into it. A perfect fit.

"I bought this very rare emerald while I was waiting to be able to come to you. It reminds me of your eyes, my love. I slept with it every night." He held his hand over his heart.

Anne looked at the physical evidence of their fating and what it meant to him. He had brought her his past and laid it at her feet. "Oh, Marcus. I am touched beyond belief. I accept this ring, but I have nothing to give you in return."

He didn't speak, but instead put a warm hand on her belly. She could feel his heat radiate up throughout her whole body. She knew she would bear him a child from tonight. The wheels of the future had been irrevocably set in motion.

She righted herself, then straddled him, clasping her arms behind his neck as she leaned her breasts to his bare chest and sought the heat of his mouth on hers. Her tongue tasted the soft breath of a moan coming deep from inside this man. She was overwhelmed with the rising tide of her emotions that were taking over her body in waves. Her heart felt stretched to bursting. She hoped there would never be an end to the way she felt this evening.

Marcus lay back as her hands traveled over the rippled landscape that was his chest. Her sex awakened to the knowledge of the need between her legs again as she rubbed against a growing hardness. She closed her eyes as she felt him move against the little knob that sought attention. His powerful hands lifted her up slightly and she sighed at the brief cold, parting between their bodies. Then he set her down on top of his shaft.

"Oh, yes, Marcus."

Anne's body rocked back and forth as he massaged her breasts, pinched her nipples, squeezed her buttocks, and caressed her thighs. Every inch of her was worshiped, explored, conquered, kissed, and caressed. The penetration of his shaft deep inside set off a long, undulating orgasm. Marcus was a demanding lover, but not easily satiated. He watched her experience the ecstasy that was theirs before he would allow himself to release again.

She was on fire with the touch of his cock inside her, where it needed to be, where it belonged, where it always had belonged. Every drop milked from him as he shot inside left her thinking it still wasn't enough.

They rested, Anne covering him with her body. "Do you have any plans for the next week?" She smiled, holding her hair back with the hand that bore his mother's ring.

"Well, we should announce the Council's decision to the family. I think you should meet my other brothers. And my other sisters. Perhaps we'll have a gathering." His finger outlined her nipple, and he watched as it hardened to his touch. When he stilled, it softened, and he played with it again. "And there is a fating ceremony we should plan after that."

"Is it a wedding?"

"It is an important acknowledgement of our fating, and recognized in the chapel. You know the one. Where I first saw you."

Anne frowned. "You saw me in a chapel? I thought you saw me in town."

"Yes, remember, when you came to the chapel in Genoa? You lit the candle and wrote a prayer? That's our fating chapel."

Anne sat up. "Wait a minute. You were there? The only other people there were—"

"Yes." His fingers laced down her spine. He stopped suddenly.

MARCUS THOUGHT HIMSELF a fool. Things had moved along so rapidly, and in his haste to make sure the Council saw her fating blood, he had forgotten to explain to Anne about Maya and the claims Maya had on him. He had been so confident the Council's decision would have given him the right to pursue Anne in the fating that he had forgotten to tell the one person who did not know about the boy and the history of his relationship with the boy's mother. He could see Anne stiffen. He had made a very grave mistake, one he hoped he would not pay as dearly for as he deserved.

You are a rake. Consumed by your own selfish desires.

He'd told himself to be patient, thought he was, but damn, was she right? Had he used Anne in his haste to end the years of loneliness and lack?

Was it really the fating power, or my own hunger for a woman of my own?

Would a true fated partner not even consider the consequences of his omission? Of his lie? Had he hidden his relationship with the boy's mother from Anne, implying he was free to take her, join with her, just so he could spill his seed and perhaps create another progeny? Or worse yet, was he becoming the type of vampire like his dark brethren? The ones who used women as playthings and pastimes to distract them from an otherwise boring eternal life?

Marcus was beside himself with loathing. He returned his attention to Anne.

She was off the bed, seeking a robe, pacing back and forth in the room. Marcus donned silk pajama bottoms as he continued to watch her. Her head was down and he could tell she was counting the loops of carpet at the foot of the massive bed. This wasn't a good sign.

"Anne, let's talk."

He reached for her arm, but she shook him off.

"If . . . if you were in . . . the . . . chapel . . . you were there next to a woman." She looked up at him with tears in her eyes. "A woman, Marcus. You were *not* the priest. You sat next to a *woman*. You were *participating* in the ceremony with someone *else*."

"No, not actually *doing* the ceremony. We were planning—" He couldn't bring himself to say more. Panic seized him. Why had he been so stupid not to think about this? "Please, Anne, let's sit while I explain this all to you."

"You will goddamn explain it to me right now!" Anne's face was contorted in a nasty sneer he'd never seen before. Her cheeks were flushed and red. Red with the passion his blood gave to her as it circulated inside her body, giving her life. But her body had been taken over by a rage he didn't know she was capable of. Her eyes were murderous. Accusatory. Devoid of the soft surrender he had just witnessed.

She squinted. "What have you done?" She walked to within a foot away from him. He could smell sex and the revulsion—a painful elixir of dashed hopes and dreams. "You have bedded me for your own pleasure. But you are already taken? You have done the ceremony with someone else! How could you?"

Anne flew to her clothes and began putting them on.

"Don't. Don't do this, Anne. You have to let me explain this to you. You don't understand anything. Oh, it's my entire fault. I should have told you sooner. I am not married or taken. Please believe me." He came over to Anne's seated frame. She was pulling on her boots. In kneeling position, he begged, "Anne, I love only you, and I can explain everything so you understand."

She looked down at Marcus with the coldness of death in her eyes. "Do you deny you were there? With a woman? You intended to be fated to another?"

"No, I don't deny it, but I can explain." He reached up for her hand and she slapped him across the face.

"Don't you touch me."

He ran over to the door, blocking her passage.

Anne pulled back and took a deep breath. Her face became red and splotchy. "Now you're going to force me, keep me captive? I am not sure how ugly you want to make this."

"I need to explain. Please let me do this."

"Move. I want out of this room now. I need to get away from your smell. I will come back later to get my things and perhaps you will explain, but not now."

Marcus moved to the side, heartbroken. Tears streamed down his face, covering his chest. He couldn't get enough breath to satisfy his parched throat. Everything inside him felt constricted, like he was dying. Everything but his heart, which was racing wildly, ready to burst from his chest.

She ran down the curved stairs into the foyer below, Marcus right on her heels. She yanked open the front door just as someone else burst into the room, almost toppling her.

Maya.

Oh, God, no. Not now.

The dark vixen stood her ground, seemingly pleased with her sense of timing. Her eyes flashed to Marcus. She raised her nose to the air.

"Ah, I smell puppy love. An afternoon of passion. And such a lovely little pup. You've created for yourself quite a little fuck buddy, Marcus. An enjoyable love puppet who will live forever. Was she as good as you'd planned? Hmm?"

Anne spoke. "You are the filthy bitch who turned me."

The vehemence in Anne's voice put Marcus on alert. In a direct attack, Maya would be able to defend herself, and she'd fight to the death. Anne's death.

Maya laughed with a cackle that must have been a throwback to her ancient ancestor. The echo reached all corners of the carved living room and made the monkeys smile. "Oh, this is too rich."

"Maya, I order you to leave this house immediately." Marcus was on his way to forcibly remove her from the foyer.

Maya hid behind Anne and whined into her ear, "So he has not told you, little one. *He* is your creator, not I. He lusted for your body, gave you immortal life so he could screw you forever. You are Marcus's eternal whore." Her laughter rumbled the glass windows of the whole house.

Anne's expression showed Marcus she was dead to him, as dead as she had been the evening he'd found her in the alleyway, after Maya had drained her of her mortal life. He watched as Maya's words settled all over his fated female like acid.

"Marcus and I have shared over one hundred years of passion.

Did you know that? And, has he told you I bore him a child?"

Anne whirled around, venom spewing from her eyes. Her lips were pale and parched. He could hear the bile collecting in her stomach. Maya eluded her and ran into the middle of the ballroom. "Marcus and I danced together in this room almost two hundred years ago. Has he told you this? He held me tight and we danced and danced. We fucked everywhere we could find. Ravenous. He was ravenous for me . . ."

As Maya sang some tune and twirled, her arms outstretched, Anne turned to Marcus, obviously unafraid to show him the hatred in her soul. In a calm voice, she asked him the question he had not wanted to answer. "So, you have a child as well. Why am I not surprised?" Her sad face repeated the words.

Marcus came as close to her as he dared. He suspected she wanted to do him real harm, and he didn't blame her.

"I am not sure the child is mine," he whispered.

"I thought you said the blood never lies." She eyed him with steely conviction, and yes, some hatred.

"I never felt the . . . the . . . fating with Maya," he begged.

"Well she bled. She bore you a child. What else is there? I find the fact that you never told me any of this to be all too convenient. You are a liar, Marcus Monteleone. No doubt your night of passion with her felt equally as . . . as . . . stirring." Her eyes filled with tears.

He reached out to grab hold of her, to reassure her, to ease the pain he knew she was feeling in her soul, but she drew away. He cursed himself. With the backdrop of Maya's swirling and cackling, Anne barely spoke, but Marcus could hear every word.

"I will be returning to California. The only thing I ask of you is to help me get there. I do not want you to follow me. I do not want to ever see you again."

ANNE CRIED ALL the way into town as the limo driver brought her to a country inn and paid for a room. She thanked him, unable to tip him because she had no money. He informed her arrangements were being made and that in the morning some clothes and money would be delivered.

"And I do not want Marcus here. You must come, not him."

"Understood."

"And I won't take the jet back. I don't ever want to set foot on anything he owns again."

"Pardon me, ma'am. Just to be completely honest with you, he owns this inn, but he has told me in case I had to reveal this, not to worry. He will not come to you again. You can feel safe in that, at least."

She nodded.

"So sorry, ma'am. We all are."

Alone in the room, without audience, she collapsed. Suddenly she didn't want to live any longer. And then it hit her.

She was immortal.

ALL THE WAY back on her first class flight to New York, Anne tried to sleep. Every time she woke up, she started to cry. She began to wonder if she would have to start feeding on the plane because she had cried so much. She had cried herself to sleep on her first trip to Italy, on her honeymoon, and now she was bawling again on her way back to California.

She was exhausted. She tried to watch the movie. She adjusted her sleeping chair, closed the window, and put the eye patch on. She drank more whisky than she ever had before, thinking maybe she could get good and drunk and then be able to sleep off the horrible pain in her chest. There was a hole where her heart should be.

She hadn't figured Marcus for the cad type. But, judging from her past taste in men, she shouldn't be too surprised. She hadn't seen anything but innocent randiness on the part of Robert. But his appetites clearly stretched long and deep in several very dark directions.

No, what she needed was something else in her life. A new start. And she needed to be alone, away from anything that reminded her of the wine country, Italy, or from her former life with either Robert or Marcus. She would need to get a job, an apartment, and a new passion for life. And in that order, too.

In the JFK airport, waiting for the flight to San Francisco, she walked down the halls between the shops, noticing the families. People were going to or from vacation destinations all over the world, or were like her, waiting for their next flight, carefully marking time until the next adventure. She saw the faces and happy chatter of children and the mothers and fathers who loved them.

Something I'll never have.

Once again, she was grateful for her first class ticket to San Francisco. She noticed no one had a seat next to her and deduced two seats had probably been booked for her so she would be left alone or not risk the chance she would meet some millionaire or handsome prince that would sweep her off her feet. Funny, how in such a short period she had begun to know how Marcus thought, how he orchestrated everything in his life. Even as she was leaving him forever, he was controlling her every move.

She sighed. He would be hard to forget. But she would. After all, she had spent the last three years of her life letting someone use her. Nothing could be more difficult than facing that again. And, if she were with Marcus, she would have to turn a blind eye to the fact that she had been used. While Robert had stolen her trust, Marcus had stolen her mortal life, and that could never be recovered. A broken heart then was something that could be fixed. No way was she going to be human again.

Marcus could go back to Maya, his true mate, just as Robert was to go back to Monika. Good riddance to both of them.

A car waited for her at the airport. She hadn't planned on that. The sign had properly read, "Anne Balesteiri." She looked down at her hand and saw the emerald she had forgotten to return. No doubt Marcus thought this to be a hopeful sign. But it wasn't.

The ring was a reminder of what could never be.

Her eyes filled with tears. Perhaps she was mourning the woman who used to own this setting, the woman who had decided to remain human and die a human death with her husband. Anne also mourned the woman who had accepted the gift and thought her life would be perfect forever. That woman was dead as well.

Casualties of life. Casualties of love.

The two beautiful Italian leather suitcases were deposited by the front door of her old house. Robert's truck was not in the driveway, but his green bomber was. She smiled in spite of her misery. She had missed that car. Anne tipped the driver from the wad of hundred dollar bills she had been handed in a perfumed envelope with her name written in Marcus's distinctive script. She was at last home. Alone.

Marcus had put her keys in the matching carry-on bag, along with a few things she had at the villa in Genoa, including a small bottle of her favorite hand cream that couldn't be bought in the US, and the sample bottle of the Carpathian perfume she loved from Capri. He was funny about the details. Of course, everything was thought out with Marcus. Which was further evidence he had planned her seduction, the making of her new life. If she had stayed with him, she too would have become a jealous vampire female consumed with hate as he found another, and then another and another new bride to add to his collection.

She could almost sympathize with Maya. Anne just wasn't going to stay around for that chapter. The humiliation of being discarded. She wouldn't be able to take that. Again.

Her house was strangely comforting to her. Everything as it was before. Robert had taken a few things. She decided to let him have it. Sort of her present to him and his new life, too. Everyone would go on with their lives. Everyone would find their way. She had to be optimistic.

Her top dresser drawer moved smoothly, revealing her favorite nightie. After drawing a bath and removing her clothes, she added lavender bath salts, remembering the bubble bath on the jet. With Marcus. And then came the tears again. But they didn't last as long this time. The pain was getting easier to bear.

The warm water soothed her bones and washed away the travel

grime. The steam caused her face to sweat. She felt a delayed reaction to the whiskey she had on the two plane rides. Maybe this was how it works. As a vampire, she still would feel the effects of the alcohol, but perhaps it took longer to arrive in her system. So much she still didn't know. She and Marcus had gotten so caught up in their "fating" that he'd forgotten to show her how to live as a vampire. Typical. He'd figured he would always be there to take care of her, show her everything. Arrogance. Total arrogance.

She fell back into a warm, deep sleep.

Anne awoke when the water was cold. She dried off and slipped on the white satin nightgown with the soft lining. She liked the way it hugged her body. She went to light candles in the bedroom, but omitted lighting the garnet red votive with the blood orange candle in it. Instead, she moved it to her dresser. She would throw it out tomorrow. Tonight, she just wanted to rejuvenate her body.

No decisions tonight. Just get a little sleep. Maybe get up early and feed. Back to that again. One thing had not changed, at least. There were still probably plenty of bad guys out there who deserved to die. Perhaps some of her revenge could taste sweet after all.

Her cell phone rang. She picked it up. Monika. That meant Robert. Good for him. Glad at least he has someone to share his life with.

"Hello?"

"Oh, hey, I thought I was just going to leave a message for you. You sound not so far away. You back from Healdsburg?"

This actually caused Anne to smile. Her first genuine smile. She surprised herself.

"Yes, I'm in the house tonight."

"Uh, Anne, I kind of know you have a new guy. Can't say as I blame you. So, I was wondering, would it be okay if Monika and I move into the house?"

"Sure, Robert." So he had heard, after all. Well, thank God for small favors. She wasn't upset. No reason to tell him "the guy" was in Robert's league. No sense giving him that satisfaction.

"Gee, Anne. You're being really great about this. Monika says thanks. And she's really sorry too about how all this went down."

"Yeah, Robert, I bet she is." Anne shook her head. She partly blamed herself. Her own twisted logic created a world where Robert never belonged. So now he was reverting to the person he was meant to be, with the person he was meant to spend his life with. Things were going to work out just the way they should.

"Well, honey. You have a good rest. We'll talk more about it to-morrow. You don't have to rush on moving things out. Just get to it when you can. She still has three weeks left on her rent here at the apartment, and we're fine here until, until, until you're ready, okay?"

"Have a nice evening, Robert, and you too, Monika." She knew her ex-maid of honor was listening to every word.

Anne set the phone down on the dresser, next to the burgundy candle. She brought the votive to her nose. Why did she think it wouldn't smell so sweet?

She decided to unpack and then finally return to bed.

When she unzipped the larger bag, there was a letter with her name on it in Marcus's handwriting, lying on top of the neatly folded clothes. She sucked in breath at the sight of it, then quickly rezipped up the bag. No way was she going to read that until she had some decent sleep and a good feeding. Wouldn't be fair to her.

She set the leather bag on the floor, next to the smaller bag. She pulled back her comforter, pouring herself into the creamy linens that smelled of lavender. Finally surrounded by her own environment she fell asleep, with the faint acknowledgement she would have to wash the sheets tomorrow to remove the traces of his scent.

She never wanted to smell it again.

FIRST THING SHE saw when she woke up in the morning was the dark form of another vampire standing at the foot of her bed.

Praetor.

Chapter 22

ANNE WASN'T ABOUT to let Praetor make the first move. He'd already let himself into her house, *into her bedroom,* without permission. That in itself was crossing an invisible line. Although numb from the long plane ride and the fretful night of sobbing herself to sleep, a tiny ounce of self-preservation remained.

At least she still felt *something.*

Fear.

Pulling the covers to her neck, she wondered how long he had been there. What had he witnessed?

She knew Marcus could trace, and had half expected he would come to check on her from time to time, though she had asked him not to. Perhaps he had sent Praetor in his place.

Was the handsome golden vampire standing at the foot of her bed here to protect her, or help her forget? He was a completely unknown element in an already complicated life. The reality of finding a new place to live, a job, and some means of going on without Marcus suddenly hit her, bringing tears to her eyes. Did he see?

He smiled.

Can he read my mind? His eyes said no. She needed to figure out Praetor's intentions. Could she trust him? But if Marcus had not sent him, what was he here for? What would the rules of engagement be?

But still the most important question of the morning was the one hardest to figure out. What did *she* want? Did she want another friend, someone to take her mind off Marcus? Or did she want to be left alone to figure out everything on her own? Exhausted from the emotional pain she'd been suffering, she didn't have an answer. That put her at a distinct disadvantage with this handsome, sexual being who clearly had given her signals before he was interested in doing more than escorting her into the arms of her then love, or watching her eyes in an exam room.

Careful. Must be very, very careful.

She was not about to make the same mistake she made the first time she'd met a large alpha male vampire.

"Under the circumstances, I'm not sure if I should say good morning to you, or throw something at you. I've given you neither permission, nor encouragement to just show up when you feel like it." Anne tried to sound disinterested and strong, but she heard the waver of her words as they crashed together.

This struck him, and he yielded a crooked grin and gave a slight nod of his head. "Then *I* will say it. Good morning, Anne."

"What made you think I would welcome you here without asking?"

"Your need."

He said it like he had whispered the words into her ear as she rested on a pillow in a soft bed after a night of lovemaking.

"I think you are mistaken." Although her pulse had quickened, she understood part of it was plain fear. She did not want to be hurt, and right now she was vulnerable.

"Oh? I believe you need to feed, my dear. Why, what were you thinking?" He smiled again. This time, she felt her cheeks flush.

Far too confident. Her stomach pitched and growled, feisty and temperamental. Her mouth was parched. She swallowed and watched his dark form as he stood motionless, awaiting her instructions. His total focus was on her eyes, except for one glance down to a space underneath the covers where her breasts lay covered. Had he been able to see them?

Or could he?

Or worse yet, did he?

"If you came to offer yourself as a meal, you could have picked up a phone and called me. Or slipped a note under my door."

"True. I prefer to do it *this* way."

"Well, I don't. You are acting like you got an invitation I did not extend. Am I clear?"

"Quite. Now, would you like to feed?" He began unbuttoning his shirt.

Anne found herself inhaling, her eyes wide with shock at the sight of him baring his neck and upper chest to her. She could not help but lick her lips at the sight of his large pulsing vein. She got the impression he would be tempting her with it all morning, until she partook. He waited again, his dark eyes boring into her flesh, bringing out a warmth in her chest that caused her to perspire. She could smell him, the muskiness the younger males had. He didn't smell of lemons, like Marcus. He smelled like the wind.

"I will not ravish you. You may feed without worry. Come, I think your lack of nourishment is clouding your judgment." He held his hand out to her.

She found herself reaching out to take his fingers. He pulled her toward him. She walked on her knees as he guided her to the end of the bed. With a slip of his hand around the small of her back, he brought her to stand. He stepped back, took an appraisal of her body beneath her gown, then grabbed her fingers and led her to the living room. He did not let her go as he sat in her leather couch. His eyes asked her to join him there, while his fingers entwined in hers. He was not going to pull, but he did not release her hand, either.

She sat crossways on his lap, suddenly conscious of the closeness of his mouth, his strong jaw, and his chest open and waiting. Her hair touched him just underneath his chin on her way to his neck and he groaned, tensing slightly. His hands lay on the couch, palms up. He did not try to touch her as she bit into his neck and took the sweet elixir he offered.

She stopped, just to make sure she could. He exhaled, and then inhaled deeply when she reapplied her lips and drew more of him. One hand came up to her back involuntarily, and after grazing the satin fabric of her nightgown lightly, fell back to the couch.

She withdrew, leaning forward as her tongue finished the remnants of his blood on her lips, her eyes closed.

It did not feel the same.

Then she realized she was not fated to him. A huge sense of relief came over her. The immediate sexual energy she received from Marcus's blood was not present now. She was sated, but she was not hungry for sex with Praetor.

He brushed her hair from her eyes, untangling it behind her neck. He left his long probing fingers there, rubbing the muscles at the top of her shoulders, which felt wonderful. She had been so tense. She turned to look at his face, finally. He spoke first.

"So beautiful, so delicate. Do you feel better now?"

She had to admit, she did feel vital, full of life suddenly. "Praetor Artemis . . ."

"Just Praetor, please. And I desire to call you Anne."

He touched her chin, raising it a bit, but he did not kiss her. She was not sure she liked the possessiveness of his actions. Was every unattached vampire female his for the taking? She supposed this was something to do with his status.

"I'm sure you would not have appeared here, were it not for the fact that Marcus and I, Marcus and . . ." Anne could not bring herself to say it. She found her eyes welling up with tears.

He pulled her head to his chest, then patted her shoulder as she sobbed into the smooth flesh of his chest. She could not help it. The well of sadness opened in her soul and she just could not stop.

"I know, Anne. I know how you love him."

She sat up and looked at his eyes. They were still smiling down at her. He traced a forefinger across her lips.

"Yes, my dear. I know of your pain. I have felt the same."

"You do?" This did surprise Anne, after all.

"I have experienced loss, although not quite the same circumstance. My pain is in never having met my fated female. I grieve for a love I have yet to feel. So you see, you are much more experienced than I." He smiled as he stroked the sides of her cheek with the back of his fingers.

Anne felt she could trust him. She lay her head against his chest again and let him hold her, this time without her tears. His arm rubbed hers up and down through the fabric of the white gown. She was struck with his sense of tenderness and concern.

"Maybe we can help each other fill the loneliness, the void in our lives, just for a time."

Anne thought about that. A little warning bell went off in the back of her mind. But try as she could to honor her doubts, she was beginning to trust him. Within reason.

"Praetor, I have to tell you something."

"Go on." His voice was smooth as velvet. His hand movements did not change.

"When I fed from you, I didn't feel anything. I didn't feel anything for you sexually." She drew back to look at his full face, looking deep into his dark eyes.

"Nor did I," he whispered. "Although I was hoping I would. I really thought I would."

SO IT WAS decided. Praetor would help her get situated. He would be a loyal and true friend, help her with money and teach her things about tracing and what the capabilities and limitations of her new life were, things Marcus was unable to do because of the distraction of their fating.

She took a job at Starbucks. Praetor had insisted he pay for the rent on the new apartment she found. It was brand new. Marcus had never been there. Nothing about the place reminded her of either Robert or Marcus. It was hers and hers alone.

Praetor spent the night half the time. He never asked for her intimacy. They went to movies together. He learned to drive the green bomber, something he seemed to delight in.

"You never learned to drive a car?" she asked one day as they rode through the countryside on their way to St. Helena.

"Why drive when you can fly?" he asked. "And now you can too."

"Barely," she said. She was getting better. She had traced herself once into a treetop and had gotten stuck in the branches. He'd arrived shortly to release her from her bondage. But he teased her about her broom handle being bent.

"So you think you will ever find your fated female?"

"Perhaps she was born and died before I ever got to meet her. It happens. Some never find their true mates."

"Do some people marry without the fating."

"Pretend? Play house?"

"Yes."

"When the sexual chemistry is strong enough. Sure." He wiggled his eyebrows. "Tell me you'd like to try this, my dear."

Anne delighted in his joy. But she didn't want to ruin their friendship by sleeping with him. "If I change my mind, you'll be the first to know."

Two weeks into their arrangement, she finally began to feel settled. The pain in her heart was dulling by the day. She was grateful nothing in her life reminded her of Marcus or Italy. Praetor was sometimes gone for days at a time, but he never brought up any family business, never mentioned his communications with Marcus, if he had any.

When he returned, she welcomed him like a brother.

They laughed in private when Robert thought Praetor was her new beau. It was just easier to let him think that. No way would he understand.

Never was there the hint of sex between the two of them, though they took long walks down by the water, holding hands. The strong arm he frequently slipped over her shoulder or around her waist was comforting. Anne loved the fresh man-scent of him and the timbre of his voice as she listened to him speak—even when he was whispering. His presence made her tingle all over, but not in a sexual way. She was healing.

Anne could see herself being his sexual partner, though unfated. But he never offered himself to her again or suggested it, even in jest. Her life was beginning to return to a satisfying normalcy.

She helped the women at the shelter and chose candidates for "educational sessions," Praetor even helping her from time to time with suggestions. Nothing was more satisfying than terrorizing a wicked husband or boyfriend, then glamming him with the suggestion he should move away and stop causing problems. Some were harder cases than others, but she was careful not to eliminate the predators, though she felt they deserved it. Though she scared these men half to death, she justified she was doing a good thing for the women in her charge.

One day, a bloody towel appeared in her wastebasket. She didn't recognize the scent and made sure it wound up in the alleyway garbage cans. Then bloody T-shirts and rags started appearing in her trash. Careful to dispose of them, she wondered why someone who had a chronic nosebleed problem would use her wastebasket at work. She didn't like to walk into her office and have the smell of blood hit her between the eyes. Even though no one else could smell it like she could, she couldn't help thinking perhaps someone was trying to plant evidence at her expense.

She enjoyed being a barista, working in the public view, surrounded by the smell of coffee. Her one cappuccino a day fulfilled her in some magical way, as glimpses of a life she could lead formed. Life appeared to be perfect again.

Until one day Maya showed up, filled with murderous rage.

THE VAMPIRE, DRESSED in red, as usual, was standing by Robert's old green bomber. Because Anne had been rushing, late for her volunteer shift at the Center, she almost ran into the woman. The vampire was flushed from a recent kill, red lips plumped and full, and fresh blood under her fingernails. Anne wondered why Maya hadn't bothered to clean up.

The look in Maya's eyes had something else. A glow. Sadly, Anne could only attribute this to the Marcus effect.

Though she tried, Anne could not stop dreaming about Marcus occasionally. His kisses felt as real in her dreams as if he were constantly there beside her. She knew a tiny part of her would always be his.

Praetor hadn't wanted to get very specific, but had told her Lucius had moved in with Marcus. He told her too, just so she would be mentally prepared, that sometimes Maya stayed over. She assumed there was going to be a fast tracking of their vows at the chapel, now that all the pieces had fallen into place.

So Anne was more than a little curious why the vamp chose to appear to her today. Anne could not be considered to be a threat any longer. So, why was the vamp here? Perhaps to gloat. Show off her wedding ring, or tell her how happy Marcus was in her bed.

"I am not in the mood, Maya." The gaze she got back from the vixen was predatory. She was watching every movement Anne made.

Maya's dark hair framed her face like a bonnet and her eyes were dark with a tinge of fire at their center that burned deep red. It matched her lips, her red form-fitting dress with the low bust line, and highlighted her tiny waist and ample bosom. It was showtime, and Maya was playing some deadly part in a diabolical play. Anne stiffened for the worst.

"No, I guess not. I can see you aren't especially happy to see me," the seductress answered.

"And you expected what?"

Maya nodded her head and studied her. "Does Marcus know Praetor spends so much time with you here?"

"Oh, you mean, like how you stay over at Marcus's?"

Her eyebrows rose. "You have your little spies. Very good." She leaned into Anne, letting their perfumes mingle as they studied one another. It took everything Anne had to keep from running. She wasn't going to call for backup. Yet.

"Actually, Maya, I could care less. What Marcus does is none of my concern."

"Oh, really? Are you sure?"

"Completely. I've moved on. I thought both of you had as well." Anne studied her face. "You two are well suited to each other." She wasn't sure why the vampire had an issue with her. Perhaps she was here to rub her nose in the fact that she and Marcus were together. There was something else on the tip of Maya's tongue. Anne didn't want to know.

"May I ride with you? I don't want to interfere with your daily routine—or your life."

Anne glowered in response. Her insides were boiling. "No. Say what you came to say and then get away from me. I think the order still stands. You are not supposed to contact me. And now I'm late for work."

It did seem like a slap across Maya's pretty face. For a brief second, her witch nature, the ugly side of a long line of dominating female predators, came to Anne's view.

There it is. That's what Marcus saw, too. She understood his unease.

Maya composed herself. "Not when I have to defend my fated male from someone coming between us."

Interesting.

"Worried about keeping your man? I hear that's a problem for the women in your family."

Maya's eyes sparked with flame and she bit her own lip, sending a trickle of blood to the side of her mouth. She swiped it aside with her tongue and inhaled. "You wish," she hissed.

Anne forced a smile in return. "I don't come between you. I am no longer interested in Marcus. He has told you the same, I'm sure. I have not spoken to him or seen him since the last day I saw you."

"I don't believe you."

"Not a requirement. You can rot in hell, for all I care." Anne liked her control and composure. She felt strong, powerful, and whole. The anger she felt towards Maya only strengthened her experience. She added, "Maya, you and I both know Marcus uses women. What makes you think he has not found another innocent mortal he can turn into—what was that you said?—his eternal whore? Maybe you should be looking elsewhere for the female coming between you and Marcus in his bed. It isn't me."

"Oh, really? I have seen him over here before."

Anne's pulse increased. This surprised her. Then she discounted the truth of it. "Impossible. I have not seen him anywhere."

But what about the dreams?

She added, "Look, would you two just leave me alone? I don't want to have anything to do with either one of you."

"My God, I actually believe you, Anne."

Anne opened the car door to get in. Maya stopped her from closing it. "He doesn't know he has lost you to Praetor. I can keep that a secret, if you like."

"Ah, so he hasn't traced here and seen Praetor leave my house in the morning. So he hasn't seen how he makes me feel in bed."

"But you aren't fated."

"No. Sadly, no. But we're working on it." Anne liked the effect this lie had on Maya's face.

"He has not bed you. I would know."

"My God, Maya. Now you want the *other* man in my life? You're bored with Marcus and now you want Praetor?" Anne removed Maya's arm from the car door. "That's out of my hands. He'd never be a pleasure partner of yours. And we all know you're fated to Marcus, right? So how come the roaming eyes, hmmm?" It was working. Maya's eyes were darting about. She developed a twitch at the side of her nose. Anne saw a red blotch form on her chest.

She's nervous about something. Maybe she was after Praetor, after all.

"I can keep your secret—your relationship with Praetor—from Marcus. I have no designs on Praetor. But if Marcus asked him to keep his distance from you, he would. You know this."

"You really think it's a secret?"

"I do."

"Why would it matter to me? There are others I can be with. I've learned to adjust."

"Perhaps you are thinking Marcus will come back to you?" The smile Maya followed her words with wasn't pretty. More like a grimace.

"Like I said," Anne began, "I think you should be looking elsewhere for the temptress who bulges his pants. I assure you, it isn't me. If you do catch up to her, tell her I wish her luck. I am done with this."

Anne stepped inside the cab and closed the door after Maya stepped away. She watched the dark-haired beauty from the tiny rear view mirror of the bomber. She knew it wasn't likely Maya would give up this easily and wondered what event had occurred to bring her back to California.

It was a busy day at the Center. The new director, Peter, had invited Anne to an early dinner, but she'd wanted to decline. Eating meals with mortals was tricky, at best, since she had to feign being sick to explain for her lack of partaking, or eat and then get rid of her stomach contents right away, which she detested. She saved those occasions for events she absolutely could not get out of, like a society gala dinner or private sit down party. She reluctantly said yes, then drank mineral water with lemon, citing she was on a special diet.

"They've done an investigation on some missing persons," Peter said. "These are people associated with some of our clients at the center. I thought I should share these details with you."

Anne's blood pressure went up. She scanned the face of her friend.

"What details?" Her interest was avid, but tried not to show it.

"They all are related to women you've counseled, Anne." He leafed through the spinach salad with his fork.

"I wasn't aware of that."

"Anne, they are looking for people who would want to see these guys dead."

"I would imagine that could be a pretty long list. Can't see why they are spending the time."

"Well, they wouldn't. Except it has come to their attention we've lost eight relatives of women at the Center during the past four months or so. That was as of yesterday. Today, they found another two."

She was filled with dread. Her perfect life was beginning to unpeel like the veneer on a dresser left out in the rain.

How could this be? She would need to ask Praetor. The timing of Maya's appearance and the deaths of relatives at the center were too much of a coincidence.

"Two more? Who?" Anne asked.

Peter handed her a list of names, the last two circled. All of them were boyfriends or husbands of her clients, just as he'd told her.

"All these men have died?"

"Yes. And these all have occurred since you came back from your trip to Italy." He looked back at Anne with sad eyes. "All of them stabbed."

Anne shuddered. "How awful."

"I'm afraid the police want to talk to you. I just thought I would give you a head's up."

Anne went instantly into high alert. She wondered if Praetor was lending a helpful hand—too helpful. He'd been good at his word, supplying her with his own blood, and told her he didn't hunt any longer. Did he have a sudden lapse in judgment? An urge he couldn't control?

She could see Peter noticed her concern. "Anne, I am one hundred percent positive you had nothing to do with any of these. I mean, how could you?"

She didn't want to look him in the eyes. She didn't want him to see that she had a theory, and that theory involved Maya.

This could be something Maya could do. And it would be something impossible for Anne to explain, even if they believed her about vampires being real. She needed to speak to Praetor. Surely he would be able to help figure something out.

But how could he control the local authorities if they came after her?

PRAETOR WAS GRIM when Anne told him of the finding. He said he would investigate who the victims were and what evidence they had. He was most disturbed by Maya's recent appearance.

"So, she says Marcus traces here occasionally?" he asked.

"Yes. Why can't I detect him?"

"Maybe it's a bluff. She could be paranoid, you know. Or, maybe he does and just doesn't want you to know. Maybe my presence here has alarmed him." Praetor was thoughtful. He tapped his fingers on the table as he mulled something over in his mind.

"He couldn't be responsible for the killings, could he?"

"No, impossible, Anne. He would never do that." Praetor tried to smile, but failed. Anne hadn't seen him worry like this before.

"Then who? Maya?"

"This is someone who is making it look like you are the culprit. That would never be Marcus. My bet is on Maya." He leaned forward and took Anne's hands in his. "I need to speak to Marcus in person, make sure we have not started a war between us."

"Perhaps Maya is right. What if he doesn't know you have been here?"

"And what likelihood do you think Maya will keep this information to herself?"

"Yes, I see your point."

"With Maya on the scene, I will need to send someone else to watch over you. I think . . ."

"No. I will be fine. She is bridled from hurting me."

"But not from hurting your situation or those you care about."

"Make your peace with Marcus, if you must. I will be fine here. She's mistaken if she thinks Marcus has shown himself around here." She chose not to tell him about her erotic dreams. "Once she learns I am truly not with Marcus, I have to think she will leave me alone. How could they accuse me of these murders? Surely there's no proof."

Then she thought about the bloody traces in her wastebasket at the office.

"I think you are too optimistic, Anne."

"She has a child to raise. Surely she has a life to live."

"You don't understand. Marcus was her life. You took that away from her. It sounds like that has not returned to her. Regardless if he finds another, you are still the one who stopped their fating ceremony from taking place."

Anne worried as Praetor's words echoed over and over. Her *perfect* new life was now unraveling. Even though she'd told him she would be safe, being without the protection of this kind friend was making her nervous.

Someone wanted her to be blamed for these murders, and she had a pretty good idea who that was. And now she would be completely alone.

Chapter 23

ROBERT AND GARY left the Double Eights about eleven o'clock. Gary had too much to drink, so Robert drove his own pickup in order to drop Gary off at his apartment. He helped his friend get out of the truck and pushed him in the direction of the walkway. Robert thought he saw a shadow under the stairwell leading up to Gary's unit. His friend was babbling something about how unfriendly the girls had been tonight at the bar, and didn't notice the shadow.

"Not like I don't tip them. They're conspiring. Holding out on us," Gary said to the clear night air.

"Maybe they're tired of us, Gary," Robert said.

"Tired of this?" His friend brought his arms out to his sides and immediately was jolted by the blade of a knife that passed through his torso from behind. Gary tried to scream, his eyes bugging out with the shocked realization of his own death.

Robert saw Gary's mouth open one last time to let out a gurgling sound as he threw up blood and sank to his knees. Fingers clutched under his jaw and ripped a hole several inches long, nearly from ear to ear.

The movements were so quick, Robert couldn't make out who was the attacker. But he knew he had to get out of there as fast as he could. It was clearly too late for Gary.

Robert ran to the truck and nearly made it. The attacker had just smashed the driver's side window and had reached around to tear at his neck like he'd just done to Gary, when Robert's car horn went off. Momentarily stunned, the attacker hesitated, which gave him time to push the onCall button above the rear view mirror. He could hear the emergency phone ringing.

Then he couldn't answer the pert operator who wanted to know what the nature of Robert's emergency was because someone with black hair and boobs the size of cantaloupes was sucking at his neck.

With the squawk of the operator in the background, Robert felt a dark coldness descend on him. He was yanked from the cab of the truck and thrown. He landed on his knees, in excruciating pain. One leg had twisted and was under his torso at an odd angle. He'd also landed with his left arm tucked underneath him and he felt pain at his wrist and elbow.

He was aware blood from the neck wound was rapidly spreading over the asphalt.

And then mercifully, he passed out.

ANNE WAS BEING questioned on a daily basis, and instead of it taking a few minutes, the interviews had lasted for over an hour. She lost her job at Starbucks. She was exhausted without Praetor's blood. She had to travel farther away to find victims to feed on.

Occasionally she saw a police tail. Her tracing abilities were not yet perfected and she couldn't trust doing it without winding up in some boiling cauldron or fire pit somewhere, ending her life. So she waited until she absolutely had to feed, and then ventured out.

Where is he?

She was weary of the box that was beginning to close in around her as the days turned into nearly a week of hell.

Six days later, she was greatly relieved to find Praetor back in her living room when she returned late from a feeding in San Francisco. She ran to him and gave him a hug, genuinely happy to see him.

"I am sorry it has taken so long to get back to you. Council business has been neglected while I have been here with you. And I needed time with Marcus."

"So he knows?"

"Yes. I got to him just before Maya did. But he already knew. He was not happy."

Anne understood this reaction. But she felt Marcus had brought it on himself. He had caused the whole problem by lying to her in the first place.

"I have some news you are not going to like to hear, Anne." Praetor hugged her again. Anne felt tears well up in her eyes as she steeled herself. She had some faint idea it was going to cause more pain than anything she had felt previously. Worse than her leaving Italy without Marcus. Worse than Robert's infidelity. She sighed.

"Go ahead. I'm ready," she said to Praetor's' shirt.

"Marcus has announced he and Maya will be fated. The ceremony is being rushed. I will have to return tomorrow for the preparation. By the weekend they will be formally recognized, and the ceremony makes it final."

Anne's knees gave out. Praetor held her as she lay limp in his arms, unable to move. She felt as dead inside as that night in Italy. She had no will to live. She couldn't even cry. Everything was gone.

He laid her gently on the living room couch. She still couldn't move. But she could cry.

"Anne, there is something else, though." Praetor kneeled in front of her. "He has done this so that Maya will stop preying on you. I know about your ex-husband and his friend. Word traveled to Tuscany and the council is concerned. I have spoken to Laurel. She thinks Marcus sacrifices himself. She begged me to handle Maya myself."

She looked into his eyes, which firmly said the obvious.

"She doesn't want him to spend eternity in a loveless union," he said. He underscored the predicament they were in with his words. "As much as I would like to, if I did that, it would mean the end of me, and possibly you. I cannot interfere."

Marcus could do this, she thought. He could fate to Maya. Bind himself forever to the Queen of Hell herself.

She had not dreamed about him for several nights, which probably meant he was staying away from her, and spending time with Maya. He could bring himself to do this for her, he would try to appease Maya first, and then if that didn't work . . .

What an ironic twist of fate. She understood now just how deeply he had loved her, and what he would do to keep her safe. And now she knew how much she had loved him.

The reality of her barren life of forever without him loomed large. She inhaled and beheld her new reality, like she was walking up the steps to a hangman's noose.

Except that would have been merciful compared to what she was going to have to endure.

ANNE WAS ARRESTED the day after Praetor left to negotiate and arrange the fating ceremony. Another man had been found with his throat slashed, draped over the fence of his house, where a group of children found him on their way to elementary school the next morning. They were fourth graders, and because of their age, there had been an outcry from the community, causing the Chief to make a quick arrest of the most likely suspect.

Anne.

For the first time in her life, her picture was on the front page of the local paper.

As she sat in the cell awaiting her appointed legal counsel, she got the impression none of the guards or even the arresting officer believed she was the real killer. But too many things had pointed in her direction. The man who had been killed and left for the children to view had been the ex-husband of one of her clients, a man who witnesses had seen Anne argue with on more than one occasion. The circumstances were too compelling to ignore. Anne had to give it to Maya. That woman knew how to be diabolical.

Anne was glad Marcus would be in the boy's life now more than ever, so that the boy wouldn't fall prey to her family.

Anne's feelings were so raw and ragged she wasn't sure she could respond to anything. She was resigned to just let herself be the cog in the system. Let them take her away. After all, they couldn't kill her. She would be able to trace at night, so even if she was confined to a jail cell, she would be able to spend the night in a comfortable bed away from the dangers of prison life. She just needed a little more training.

Surely Praetor would have the time to do this. The wheels of the human criminal justice system moved so slowly, she probably had years before she would have to think about it.

Her biggest concern, other than trying to repair the hole in her heart, was what the vampire coven would do to her as punishment. There wasn't much a human judge and jury could do to her, but the council was another story. If the human world thought she was guilty, why wouldn't the vampire world?

And perhaps this had been worked out with the council. Perhaps Marcus's capitulation to Maya included the agreement that Anne would be left untouched and perhaps banished by the coven, or at best, left alive in her vampire body.

Her eyes filled with tears as she realized this was perhaps the last thing he could ever do for her. She knew his fating would mean Maya would be placed before any other female in his past, present, or future. She would forever be his queen, someone he would defend to his own death, if need be. He would go on to father other children. One happy family, as if the day she came to the chapel never existed.

She spent the night crying her eyes out for the last time. Praetor traced her to his own bed. He held her all night long, stroking her hair, and when she closed her eyes, she pretended it was Marcus bidding her farewell. That somehow made it better.

She had come to see Praetor as her only friend in the world. Perhaps, if he would have her, if the scandal could be overcome in the coven, he would be allowed, would be willing to take her as his partner. She knew they would never be true mates. But not having the hundreds of years of experience, as well as a family unit in place to help, she was left at such a disadvantage that for the first time in her life, she felt she could not face eternity alone.

She asked him about it as they sat in bed and watched the peachy stain on the morning sky grow, and then fade into the bustle of the day. He'd have to return her to her cell before the guards checked morning rounds.

"I am honored, Anne. But then what would happen if I find my female? You would be discarded again, for the third time."

"Is there any precedent for people to grow into a fating? Marcus is truly going to try. He must believe something like that is possible."

"My honest opinion? The answer is no, regardless of what Marcus tells himself." He continued to stroke her hair and the side of her arm. "You should not make any decisions now. Wait until after the ceremony. Wait until you hit bottom completely." He kissed the top of her head and whispered, "And then you start to build back up. If you are mending, perhaps we can talk about it. But not now." He leaned her head back examining her lips, which she parted for him.

Anne could fall in love with him, maybe. Her eyes drew him to her and he softly complied. His tongue tasted her bottom lip but did not pry its way into hers. When she began to push into his mouth, he closed his teeth and drew his lips together, sealing her out.

"You don't feel anything for me, Praetor?" Anne asked.

"I love you like a sweet friend. As a most precious sister, or a long lost childhood crush. I think if you examine yourself, you will see it is the same." He traced her lips with his forefinger and smiled. "You are a wonder, Anne. Those hours you shared with Marcus I'm sure made him feel like master of the universe, to have someone such as you love him."

"And I think he did love me back. He did."

"Yes, I think you are right. But now we have to accept another reality. Not healthy to dwell on the past. Time to return you to your cell."

SHE WAS OUT on bail later that afternoon and came home to her apartment that had obviously been searched. She straightened up, cleaned some of the litter of multiple strangers who did not care about her or her things.

She went to the hospital to visit Robert.

He had a cast on each leg and on one of his arms. Bandages were wound around the top of his head. Someone had played a cruel joke on him and had tied the bandage around his neck with a big gauze bow right under his chin. Anne was most concerned about that wound, as she smelled fresh blood. She looked at him for signs Maya gave him vampire life, like Marcus had done for her. She decided he was healing as a human, not an immortal. Even a recent turn would have shown up.

She gave him a kiss on his lips, which were swollen and deep purple. "Are you in pain, Robert?"

"Uh huh. But I'm letting them blast me full of anything they'll give me. I might fall asleep. They have me pretty much wacked out."

"You go ahead and fall asleep if you need to. I'm just paying respects."

"I'm not dead yet."

That got her thinking. Had Maya intended on killing him or hurting him? Anne believed the attacks would stop, and, if she could survive the investigation, maybe she was finally at the turning point. The fating was scheduled for tomorrow morning. How nice it would be to just leave this all behind, have all the drama be finally over.

"You hear they are looking for a female who did this?"

"I'm not surprised. They have been questioning me non-stop. My contempt for some of these men was pretty well documented," Anne replied. "And people knew I thought Gary was a scumbag."

"Oh, no." Robert tried to sit up but let out a sharp groan as something hurt and he stopped. "Anne, I told them it wasn't you. I told them I met her, in a bar before."

Anne looked at him with what she hoped wasn't too much pity in her eyes. He was in enough pain.

"She's a weird one. We met her that next day after you kicked me out."

Anne remembered the jet plane ride, the lavender bubble bath. Robert could have told her he had screwed fifty women that night and she could have cared less.

"What did she say? Did she give a reason?"

"She told me she killed Gary. But she told me that she'd come after me over and over again until I jumped off the Golden Gate Bridge."

Anne looked out the window. Surely that was before Marcus gave

Maya the news he was going to give in to her demands.

"Robert, I don't think you have to worry about her anymore. I think she has moved on to someone else. She's in Italy, getting ready for her . . . wedding . . . tomorrow."

"Hell she is. She came here not more than an hour ago. She untied this bandage and sucked more blood from me. I couldn't do a thing. Hurt like hell."

Anne looked at Robert's white bow tie.

So THAT WAS how it was going to be. Anne understood now that Maya would never give up. She was going to needle her for the rest of her life, and everyone around her. She would make Marcus miserable. She would ruin his life, ruin the life of the boy. She would turn everything upside down for all eternity.

But maybe Anne could stop it. Maybe it was up to her, after all. Everyone would get what they wanted, or close to what they wanted. Marcus would be free. The boy would have a father. Laurel would live to find her fated love and comfort her brother. Robert would survive to go on his eternal search or find in himself the good part Anne had seen in the beginning, and, at last make a good husband to Monika, perhaps have that family he wanted.

And everything would revert to where it had been when she lay in the cobblestone street in Genoa, drained of blood. That was the night she *should* have died.

But she had been given the miracle of finding love, or she would have died without it. She was never born to be vampire. But, God help her, she loved one with all her heart. And she had to feel grateful for having received this gift, precious and so limited as it was.

And if she couldn't have him, she could remove the devil in his life.

She was going to pick a fight with Maya, and she hoped the element of surprise would give her the edge.

Protecting Marcus might become her dying wish.

Chapter 24

ANNE SAT IN the apartment reading a book, *A Hunger Like No Other*. She sensed movement downstairs. One quick glance to the street revealed the strikingly beautiful female in her best red, eyeing the car. She wondered if Maya coveted the beast because it belonged to her or because it would be a trophy she could bring back to Italy and make Marcus ride in it, proving once and for all her dominance over Anne. What a wedding present that would make Marcus, if Maya could figure out how to transport it before tomorrow. Anne smiled because she knew she was thinking about it. Could almost hear her thinking about getting her trophy, for her trophy husband.

Robert made sure the trap was set. He played the part perfectly. God bless his little cheating heart, Anne thought. For once, he got something right.

Anne couldn't really read Maya's mind, but people like her were not hard to figure out. She wouldn't be able to resist gloating over her victory. It was simply not in her nature. Win or lose, she'd be nasty to the end. Anne was counting on that nasty side to keep her distracted.

It was nice that Maya knocked on Anne's door, even though she had the ability to trace right through it. This indicated the element of surprise was still with Anne. If Maya sensed danger, she would spring into action and go for Anne's throat. But apparently, she thought she'd already won. Maya had decided to behave, for once.

Good.

Anne knew Maya didn't want to do anything to anger Marcus. After all, he had given in to her desire to mate for life. She'd gotten what she wanted, even though everyone knew he would have made a different choice. At least this is what Anne told herself.

But who cares, now?

When she opened her front door, Maya gave her a smile that had probably aroused Marcus the first and probably hundredth time he saw it. Anne thought about Marcus's large cock riding this woman who stood before her. About how he would kiss her. How Maya would ride him and writhe, squeezing her own breasts. How he would kiss her nipples until they hurt. Did he bite her next to her sex like he had Anne? Did he enjoy Maya's blood?

These images helped Anne feel the conviction in her soul. No one could resist Maya. And no one ever would. It would have to be a woman to bring her down, a woman who came at Maya from her blind side. A woman so desperate she had nothing to lose.

A woman like me.

Maya had made the miscalculation of her life.

"I see you got my message. Thanks for coming."

"The least I could do," Maya responded. Her grin was defiant. She was searching Anne's face for evidence she had caused her pain.

"Thank you for sparing the life of my ex—my almost husband," Anne said, allowing her lower lip to quiver sufficiently.

"On our tastes in men we agree. He is quite worthless. Untrustworthy. So unlike Marcus." Her eyes flared with the tiny red flames Anne had seen before.

"I trust he will be left alone now."

"Of course. You are free to have him. I give him back to you. I, on the other hand, take Marcus. Or rather, he takes me." Maya looked Anne up and down, and then added, "I will make sure his days are filled with every fantasy he desires."

Another evil challenge. Anne was sure she was doing the right thing.

"Come in." Anne said, turning her back on the vamp. She hoped Maya didn't see it as a test of her dominion. "I thought we could bury the hatchet between us." Anne led Maya into the hallway.

"Very civilized of you. I didn't expect this."

"And so good of you to come, so close to your wedding day. I'm sure you have a million things to attend to."

"I've been planning this fating ceremony for a hundred years." Maya frowned. "Under the circumstances, I felt it prudent not to invite you."

"No thanks. Weddings are a painful reminder of what we cannot truly have." Anne inhaled and began her prepared speech. "You won, Maya. I hope you and Marcus are filled with centuries of love and many brilliant children."

"Thanks." Maya slid beyond Anne into the living room, looking unmoved. She glanced around the room as if looking for someone.

"Still trying to rub salt into the wound? Didn't you hear me? I said you won. Marcus isn't here. Neither is Praetor. Come, look at your trophy. Can you see it in my face?"

Maya turned and gave Anne a sultry smile again after looking her up and down. "So, Robert said you had a wedding present for us. A car. That one?" She pointed outside to the bomber, which stood silent, innocent as a green frog. Deadly bait. Anne loved that car on so many levels. Now more than ever before.

"Yes, my car."

"Really? I am surprised."

"I can't drive it anymore, truth be told. Marcus and I made love in it several times. I realized yesterday, it brings back too many memories, unhappy memories. Marcus's smell is all over the seats." Anne hesitated and leaned into Maya to whisper, "And a little on the ceiling, if you know what I mean."

Maya's smile was long and deep, and wicked. Anne knew she was thinking about taking him for a ride in it, and the things they could do made Anne blush.

"See, that's why he has made the right decision. None of my memories of being with Marcus are unhappy." Maya walked over to Anne. "My body aches for him. And when I next bed him, he will belong to me forever."

"Yes. But I thought you would appreciate my telling you I have found the fating with Praetor even more wonderful. See, you will be taking Marcus away from me just as I am opening another thrilling chapter in my life. Have you ever had Praetor, Maya? He is centuries older. He hasn't been so prudish or exclusive as Marcus. His conquests number in the thousands. He has forgotten more than Marcus ever knew about sexual pleasure." Anne smiled for the effect she hoped it would have on the woman.

There was a split second where Maya's eyes got wide, then she looked into Anne's eyes with pure hatred.

That's when Anne struck. She reached out and grabbed Maya by the hair, and, with her other hand, grabbed her shoulders. She wrenched Maya's head from the top of her body like breaking a twig. She was surprised at her own strength.

Had Anne wanted to get even, she would have made it a fight so she could enjoy the conquest. But this was no conquest she would enjoy. It was an execution. Maya's headless torso almost danced, pirouetted in the room from the force of the twisting motion, spewing blood on the ceiling and walls as her arms flailed helplessly at her sides.'

Anne held the head up to her face and let the blood drip down her front. It stared back at her, lifeless. Anne liked the change in Maya's expression, and for the first time felt truly rid of the evil vampire.

Her front door burst open. Praetor and Marcus entered. Marcus shrieked, "No, No, No!"

Even Praetor was white with shock. His lips had turned purple, his forehead creased as he stared between the lifeless head of Maya and Anne, very much alive.

Anne wouldn't look at either of them. She dropped Maya's head with a dull thud and went into the bathroom to take a shower.

She took her clothes off behind the curtain, listening to the men shout and argue in the other room as they dealt with the reality of what she had done. Anne's insides were dead. She was washed of Maya's blood, but she had no desire to touch Marcus, to get any of the taint on him. Her only thought was that she hoped it would be all over soon. She hoped the council would act faster than their human counterparts were known to.

She stepped out and wrapped herself in the towel, her bloody clothes remaining in the shower. The man she once loved was bent over Maya's headless body, sobbing, no doubt grieving for his lost bride.

"You are free. You gave me life. Now I give you the same. We are even," Anne felt the chill in her soul as she spoke these words.

"No, Anne. We are *not* even." He rose up and stood, his hands and shirt covered in blood. He did not smile. Anne felt like she had put her own stake through his heart.

Praetor ushered her into the bedroom, instructing her to dress. "We are going to Genoa to secure your fate immediately. You must pack some clothes."

Anne dressed quickly. She got out the Italian leather suitcase, remembering she had never unpacked the bag Marcus had sent her home with two weeks ago. The one with the letter in it she had never read. She added her makeup kit to it, brushed her hair, and told him she was ready.

"I'm going to trace us there. We have little time left."

"I don't want to travel with Marcus."

"He'll come later, after he makes the arrangements for Maya. Her family will be all over this."

"Yes." Anne could only imagine the retaliation they'd want to foist upon her. Their darling child, dead.

Praetor added, "He needs to stay away from you, for obvious reasons. Come." He held out his hand. Anne reached out and he pulled her to him. She wrapped her arms around his body as they transported through the afternoon sky.

ANNE FELT DEAD inside. Praetor paced back and forth in the foyer of the great hall, jotting down notes. He was muttering to himself. She wasn't even counting the small nail holes in the wooden paneling on the walls.

At last they were summoned.

They stood in the exact spot where Anne had faced the inspection interrogation. The council sat, stoic, both infirmed members wide awake, and only one was on a blood IV. They looked disheveled, like they had been summoned in haste. They wore nightshirts under their crimson robes.

Praetor began his prepared speech. He brought out the piece of paper he'd written his notes on earlier.

"Most respected Council, I come to you today with distressing news you have no doubt heard. Our sister, Maya, has been murdered. She was savagely beheaded. The transgressor has done this deed, it is said, because of love. We in the coven know this cannot be the case. Only in cases of self-preservation can this be a justified crime. I find no such justification in this case. The person responsible for this unspeakable crime is one Marcus Monteleone."

"What?" Anne whipped her head around to face Praetor.

"Council, you need to know he has warned me that Anne would try to take the blame for him, but I saw it with my own eyes, saw the blood wash over his body and can attest to the fact that he is the murderer."

Anne was livid. "That is not what happened. They have conspired to lie to you. Your Praetor lies!"

"Silence!" The middle vampire held up his hand. "You are a conversion. You have caused us nothing but problems since you came here. I will not take your filthy word over that of Praetor Artemis, who has served the Council faithfully for centuries."

One of the other Council members spoke up. "It is well known Marcus was only fating Maya as a means to protect you. I would expect more gratitude towards him. Calling Praetor and Marcus both liars makes a mockery of their station."

And so it was decided. Marcus had been arrested, left in a cell underneath the great hall. Anne wanted to meet with him, but Praetor said Marcus did not wish her company.

The trial lasted only one day. Marcus was found guilty, by his own admission. Anne was not allowed to attend. She was desperate for the opportunity to speak with him.

But she was promised a night with him before his sentencing. The hearing being set for tomorrow, Anne would spend her last night with Marcus tonight.

MARCUS SAT IN the room given him for his last night. It was not large, but boasted a large bed with fresh linen sheets and opulent satin pillows. He had been given warm blood after being given the choice for a human whore, which was something he flatly turned down. He was reading, strangely calm, and looking forward to his one night with Anne. Should his sentencing determine he would be given the death penalty, it was always carried out within an hour of pronouncement. He was encouraged to set his affairs in order, which he had.

He met with Lucius, who was beside himself with grief. Laurel promised she would be both father and mother to the boy, at least until she found her fating. Lucius was already sleeping in Laurel's bed, crying himself to sleep every night. Laurel said it actually helped her to have him there. It truly broke everyone's heart. Lucius's pain had been an ancillary casualty of the war between Marcus and his two women.

Marcus knew everyone wished he had taken Lucius into account before acting. But, Laurel would make a righteous mother to him and had let Marcus know she would tell him stories of his father and what a wonderful man he was, and how his honor in the end had been his undoing. And Marcus told her he was going to ask that Paolo help out as well. Laurel agreed. Paolo had been conspicuously absent during the trial and pre-trial ordeal, called to the side of his dying wife.

Marcus was visited by his other brothers and sisters on this eve as well. The women cried. The men were angry. He made them promise to accept Anne as part of the family that he would never share in. Reluctantly, they agreed, but none of them came away with anything but contempt for her.

Paolo finally came on his own after the rest of them had left.

"You look well, Paolo. How is your wife?"

"She has passed on. She is no longer in pain. I am sorry, I was attending to the affairs of her household and could not leave before now."

"No worries. I'm sorry for your loss."

Paolo shrugged. "Nothing compared to yours. I knew this would be the outcome for me. You, on the other hand, had a life of eternal love snatched away from you. It's not fair."

"It's entirely fair. We are only as good as the rules we have crafted for the benefit of us all. I will not have my family mock the Council's decision."

"You know they have no choice but to sentence you to death."

"I am hoping they do. I can't live with myself. I've murdered someone who was to be my fated female."

"You can't be serious."

"I am. Paolo." Marcus stood up, walking to the one tiny window, with bars on it, overlooking the front entrance of the compound. "I have thought about this many times. You have now lost your wife. I was going to ask you something, one last request before I slip away and am no more."

"Ask me then. It will be granted before you even finish."

"I want you to take Anne. Love her, as I would have. She doesn't understand our ways. She feels for Praetor Artemis, but they know they are not fated. I ask you to pretend you feel something for her, that you feel a fating. I don't think she would question you."

"Marcus, this is insanity. Are you of right mind?"

"I am entirely."

"I can't do this."

"Too late. You already said my wish was granted before you heard of it. It is done. I need to hear it from your lips."

"Marcus."

"Say it, damn you!" Marcus stood and boomed so loud it shook the building.

Tears streamed down Paolo's face. "Brother, you cannot ask me to watch you die, then take that miracle that brought you such joy after years of loneliness. Take Anne for myself?"

"With one exception."

"Anything, Marcus. Tell me you were joking, playing some kind of morbid hangman's game."

"I will bed her one last time. Tonight."

"Of course. I'll bring her within the hour."

"I do miss that woman. I do miss her touch. I'll not tell her of our agreement. You must make it appear completely natural. Do I have your vow?"

"My heart is breaking."

"Do I have your vow?" Marcus said, raising his voice.

"Yes. Yes, brother." Paolo answered with a whisper.

"And you will raise the boy. All three of you will see to it he is showered with love, yes?"

"Marcus, I wish I could speak longer with you about this."

"No, brother. I miss my female. You must bring her to me now. If she won't come, tie her up and bring her. I will not die without bedding her one more time. It's for her I die tomorrow. Do not refuse me."

PAOLO DIDN'T HAVE to tie Anne up. She fell at Marcus's feet when the door to the bedroom chamber was opened. He instantly kneeled before her, holding her head between his hands, which shook slightly. She noted the binding bracelets on both his wrists, their coppery dull glint catching in the late afternoon sun, clinking as they touched their counterpart on the other wrist. She held one of his wrists with the band in both hers, tracing the ancient symbols embedded in the metal with her fingers. She bent and kissed his wrist, kissed the band, then drew it to her heart and pressed like she could absorb it there. As if she could dissolve the restraints and set his soul free forever. She turned her face up to his.

"Love, you cannot do this. I never took this on expecting you to pay the price for my indiscretion."

"Anne, it's my indiscretion. I never should have agreed to the fating with Maya. I killed you just as if I had dismembered you the night I promised to fate her. I knew it almost instantly, but tried to make her feel I would honor my word."

He covered her mouth with his, then drew her to him with strong hands that pressed her chest to his. "I just couldn't sleep with her, even kiss her. She knew she would never have my heart. Only you have that. Only you ever will."

He kissed her again. Anne melted into him, leaning her body against his torso. Her arms came up around his neck. She had been crying so long it seemed like the natural state to her.

"Come, love. Let's take what we have left."

Anne knew the difference between this embrace and the embrace Praetor had given her. The kiss was different, too. Marcus prepared her mouth, bringing his tongue to her lips, over her teeth. He let her hook her tongue over his fang. A huge drop of blood fell squarely into his mouth, causing him to shudder. He was urgent with his need to taste her, nibbling on her lips and pulling them into his. She felt he consumed her.

Anne then opened her dress to him, to let him taste the rosy tips denied him for too long. He was brave. He did not cry, but shuddered as she kissed his forehead, his ear, his neck, as he played with her nipples. She came as she straddled his thigh, rocking on him with urgency and burning need. Marcus thoroughly enjoyed her breasts. She whispered into the soft curly hairs at his temple, "These were to be yours for eternity. They will always be, even . . ." Her voice broke.

She could tell he was pushing out the visions of tomorrow. For right now, his head would stay connected to his torso, long enough to feel the texture of her white skin, the salty taste of the flesh that needed his tongue and his lips. He would take from her all her moans and sighs. He would secret them away to a place deep inside his heart, and would take them with him forever.

His lips on her bud caused her to burst into tears. "I will not be able to live without this." He whispered how he regretted his decision to join with Maya. He should have stolen Anne away to some island somewhere they could love until the Council found them. He would have stolen her away forever, would have willingly taken on the pressure to watch out for Council guards coming after them so she could sleep in the pink tenderness of the morning, in his arms. He whispered how he loved her, had always loved her, and would always love her, somehow.

"How many days could we have had? Maybe one or two more? It

would have been worth it." His sigh made her tingle. "We could have had a few days, until they found us. Maybe we should have."

Marcus spoke the ancient words to Anne's womb. Her body constricted and she took in air, involuntarily reacting to his mysterious words that celebrated the life force that would grow there. He spoke as he gently kissed and sucked the juiciness of her fruit of life. His body knew hers and how to make her insides come alive. He would remain, a part of him would, inside her forever. Anne knew that she carried his child, created from the first time they made love.

FOR NOW, THE most beautiful love in the universe would have to end come morning. Marcus hoped as he placed his cock inside her warm folds, that Paolo would learn to worship this holy place as he had, that he would feel something like he did as he thrust inside her, stroking and fueling her passion, and covering her insides with his seed over and over again. Perhaps, on the eve of his death, he could give her a child. If there was a God, and he never had believed in one before, this God would find it in his heart to give her a child she could love and remember him by. Just one more miracle. He needed just one more.

Anne could not be sated. She drank from him in long feedings that nearly caused his vision to disappear. Blackness came upon him. He saw how she felt the energy and the golden fating come over them both. More tears. He drank liberally from her, biting her as the claiming ritual demanded, on her neck. The holy elixir filled his body with a glow that numbed the reality of their short time left.

Anne convulsed, then silently wept as he claimed her neck.

"Not now. You must not cry now. Love me, Anne. Love me enough for the centuries we will be apart. Maybe there will be a time we will be together. Humans have this, maybe there is a place for us, for our love."

She was trying to be very brave. But it was difficult to look at her eyes and not see the utter sadness there. "Bear me a child, my love. Bring a child into the world for me. Can you do this for me? Just one more thing I ask of your body? Bring to the world something made from us both, together."

She nodded. "You will have your wish. I will get big with a healthy child. I will watch him grow up and marry. I will watch our grandchildren. You must understand I will make this happen, Marcus. This will happen, love. They will know and love you as I have. They will know of the wonderful lineage from which they came."

He nodded his head. "I give . . . you . . . life. . . . I leave my love with your womb."

There were no more tears to cry by morning. They had fed from each other, made love more times than even Anne could count. They watched the orange tint fade, and with it, their time together.

"No tears. I go a happy man that I have loved you."

"I am fulfilled, Marcus. Anything else is bonus."

They parted as Marcus prepared for the sentencing.

Chapter 25

THE GREAT HALL was filled to capacity. Half the audience, those from Maya's family side, were hostile, huffing and flouncing in obvious disapproval of the entire proceedings. They aimed nasty stares at anyone related to Marcus, the coven's admitted Golden Boy, the man who was the object of desire for any unattached lady, vampire or otherwise. Young females grew up hoping, in fact, that they would come to puberty and discover their fate was tied to Marcus.

Maya's family didn't appreciate the show of relief coming from other goldens that Maya was gone. She had caused trouble with the group for decades. Her demands were loud, her decisions arbitrary. She got her way most of the time, like her mother, Aurora, because fighting either of the two women was more distasteful than just agreeing to their terms. And it was rumored they cast spells and were more witch than they openly admitted.

Now Marcus would pay for Maya's death with his own life.

Aurora gathered her family members like a mother hen. Her sorrow was very public and loud. Maya's father was still alive somewhere, but even Aurora's fated male could not stand to be in her company and had sought the arms of other women far away from Genoa and rarely came home. He did not do so today, either. Not that any of the coven blamed him.

In contrast, Marcus's side was reserved, except for their quiet sniffling. In mourning already, many of them wished the ordeal over and felt guilty for those thoughts. At Marcus's request, Lucius was allowed to come to the hearing, something Marcus had promised the boy on his final visit. At six years of age, Lucius was going to have to understand quickly his part in this passion play. And running from it, at any age, was never Marcus's style.

But the sight of Lucius was difficult for all of Marcus's family. In their final show of support for their favorite son, they stood by his decision, and each braced him, hugged him, told him how brave he was and said, though they denied it on the inside, they were glad he was there.

Anne sat between Praetor Artemis and Laurel. Paolo sat next to Lucius, who insisted on sitting behind the seat Marcus would take when he was led in, a spot traditionally saved for the mate. It was obviously the right choice, under the circumstances.

MARCUS ENTERED THROUGH a side door just ahead of the council in their red robes. Young female attendants, who, thankfully, were more respectfully dressed in robes, wheeled in the two infirmed ones. Anne looked up at Praetor and he managed a smile.

Marcus found his seat, but first leaned in to kiss the boy then shake Paolo's hand. His eyes connected with Anne's and she tried to look satisfied, but at last it was impossible. She broke from the row and ran to his arms as Maya's side of the aisle let out gasps of outrage.

"We agreed. You need your strength. Don't trouble yourself." Marcus leaned in to her ear. "I can feel the life I started in your belly. Bring him up with love, not hate. Don't let him avenge me, Anne. Raise him to be strong, but raise him to love as I have loved you."

She nodded before they were asked to separate. Marcus gave a bow to his family in a general greeting, and sat down. This last action caused the side of the room behind him to stir. Several were sobbing. Anne sat up as straight as she could, staring at the back of the man she might only be able to see for a few more minutes.

Looking old beyond his time, the Council leader rose. "We are gathered here this day to pronounce sentence on the convicted murderer of one Maya D'Alessandro. Will the condemned please rise and hear sentence?"

Marcus rose, his white silk shirt billowing out behind the tail tucked into his dark pants. He wore his tall leather boots. Anne realized, with sudden horror, that Marcus wore the same outfit he'd worn that day she had met him in at the Starbucks, not so long ago. She remembered his tall lanky frame in those boots as he got her coffee. She swallowed the salty tears, choking on a sob. Praetor stretched his arm around her and brought her head to his chest. Laurel clasped Anne's fingers and laid her cheek against the hand on Anne's shoulder. Anne was grateful for the support, feeling like an old book carefully placed between two substantial bookends.

"Marcus Monteleone—"

"Excuse me, Head Council." Paolo stood up. "I have something you must hear."

Maya's side of the room burst into shouts and catcalls. Anne knew they took this as an offense, so eager were they for Marcus's blood. They didn't want to be denied one more chance to show their indignation and outrage.

"This is highly irregular." Several of the Council conferred in whispers and nods. "This has to do with the sentencing?"

"I believe it does." Paolo hadn't waited for an invitation. He made his way up to a lectern at the middle of the center aisle, with Lucius in tow, who looked just as confused as Marcus. Laurel squeezed Anne's hand. When Anne looked at Laurel, she saw Laurel give a faint smile to Paolo.

The audience gasped when Paolo raised Lucius up and set him on the top shelf of the lectern. He held the tiny hands in his large ones. Paolo's face was lined with tears. Lucius began to cry openly, his lower lip quivering. The poor boy was scared silly. Marcus moved, as if about to come to his aid, but Paolo gave him a glance and a gesture with the palm of his hand, telling him to stop.

The Council members were stunned into inaction.

"Lucius," Paolo began, taking a deep breath and releasing it. "I am your father."

Both sides of the room erupted. One of Maya's male relatives grabbed Paolo and tried to wrestle him to the ground. He was restrained, but not after ripping the sleeve from Paolo's dark coat. Paolo recovered, soothed his sleeveless jacket, and then resumed his conversation with Lucius as if the two of them were alone in a room some-where.

"Your mother and I were fated lovers, for a short couple of days. I ran away afterwards, not knowing you had been conceived during our mating. I was married at the time to a human woman who needed me and whom I loved, although not in the same fating way. She was a good woman and didn't deserve my indiscretion. It was confusing for me. I am truly sorry."

The audience had hushed. Paolo hugged the boy on the lectern. The whole room could see the boy did not hesitate to hug Paolo back. Lucius closed his eyes. Paolo pulled away and put his hands on the sides of Lucius's face. "I am ashamed of my actions, Lucius. I have caused pain and death. I have robbed you of a home and a father who loves you dearly. I ask your forgiveness. You are the only one I live for now, my son."

Aurora stood up. "This changes nothing. How touching. This only goes to prove what a depraved family we have here before us. You will pronounce sentence now and wipe this man off the face of the earth. And as contributory, you should take the scum Paolo as well!" She pointed a red tipped long forefinger at Paolo.

The Council was clearly in disarray. It was obvious they did not know what to do. Praetor Artemis stood and addressed them, his hand remaining on Anne's shoulder.

"Council, it appears we have two crimes here, but only one trial." He leveled a glassy stare at Paolo. "And we have one crime of un-speakable cowardice, which will have its own punishment."

At this, Paolo sadly nodded. He hugged Lucius again, who tried to steal a look at Marcus.

"Praetor. Explain," Council Chairman requested.

"Is it not a crime to come between two fated mates?"

"It is," Council Chairman replied.

"And I have been told Maya fed on this female as a mortal, drain-ing her, actually set off to kill her after she heard from Marcus's lips she was his fated female. This is part of the record. I wrote it so several months ago."

"You are correct."

"Maya knew the boy was not Marcus's. She had felt the fating with Paolo. But, faced with a life of raising a child by herself and spending the rest of her life with a mate who refused her, she did only what she was trained to do." Praetor gave a harsh look to Aurora, who stood immediately.

"He disrespects me and my family. The Council has spoken already and convicted this man by his own admission."

"Silence," the Chairman boomed.

Paolo looked at Laurel and Anne noted the two shared a nod and a smile. She wondered if this was true, and, if so, had Laurel known?

"I think we will have to adjourn so the Council can take this new finding under advisement," the Chairman declared.

"Excuse me, Chairman," Praetor began, "if I may perhaps speak for the entire Council in recommending Marcus Monteleone be exonerated, under the circumstances. I think these families have suffered enough."

"Outrage!" Aurora screamed so loud it made Lucius jump and grab hold of Paolo.

Amid catcalls and shouts from the family members beside her, the Chairman raised his voice and commanded, "Have this woman removed from these halls!" Immediately, guards by the door forcibly picked her up, restraining her as she tried to scratch their eyes and kick them. Seeing Aurora contained seemed to calm Maya's other family members. Before she was ushered out the door, Chairman stopped them.

"And, madam," he said as he stood. "Let me declare to you that you are bridled from causing any harm to this man or this woman." He pointed to Marcus and Anne. "Nor any member of their family." He rubbed his fingers through the air in a sweeping gesture, addressing the general side of Marcus's family.

"And if any member of *your* family, madame, is responsible for causing any harm to any member of this family, I will hold you, Aurora, responsible for it one hundred percent. Do I make myself clear?"

Everyone in the room looked at the red face of the Chairman.

"Do I make myself clear, ladies and gentlemen?" he shouted again.

At last, several of Maya's family turned down their heads and nodded. Aurora's chin stood upright in quiet defiance.

The Chairman pointed a finger at Aurora. "I can hold you until you agree. Your freedom is contingent on your vow."

Aurora tore her arms from the guards. On her own, she nodded and whispered, "I agree."

"Now, remove her." The guards picked up the wild-eyed woman, who still spewed hatred towards the Chairman. But, she was led outside without further incident.

Marcus at last turned to look at Anne. Her heart was racing, the pulse in her veins quickening, unafraid to show her need of him. She saw him call to her in the ancient way her fated male would call to her, through his dark eyes that looked into her soul. From afar, he kissed her there.

The Chairman again addressed the crowd. "I thank you for your words, Praetor. And you, young son, your bravery is noted. Paolo, you have much to answer for, but I see your course is tracked. I wish I could physically punish you, if I could do it without hurting the boy. Your punishment is of a different nature, and I hope you pay the price forever. Please be seated." As Paolo and the boy made their way back to their seats, Marcus stopped Lucius and gave him a hug the boy returned. Then Lucius kissed Marcus on the cheek, and smiled.

The Chairman looked at the other Council members, many of whom nodded in a silent agreement. "Marcus, please rise."

He did. Anne wanted to run to his side, but held her spot between Laurel and Praetor. She leaned forward, placing her hands on the back of the seat in front of her, next to Paolo. She patted his back.

"Although I regret we cannot take back the pain that has been caused by this proceeding, I find that, in light of the fact that you did everything in your power to protect your fated female from her attacker, this homicide is justified." When the shouts from the opposite side of the room died down, he continued. "I want to say we do not condone violence. This is never the solution to any problem, as

I'm sure this illustrates. We should always seek to find another way. I am not sure in this case, though, it could be avoided. Marcus Monteleone, you are exonerated and are free to go."

Shouts of joy rang through the room. Marcus's family descended upon him. He was wet with tears, covered in lipstick, jostled with hugs and slaps on the back. His hair came untied and hung loose around his face. Anne stood back, but could see his eyes scanned above the crowd.

"Anne? Anne? I want to see Anne."

Anne pushed her way through the crowd, who took no notice of her. She wedged herself between body after body until at last she broke through to the front of the circle of well-wishers surrounding him, and ran into his arms.

"At last. Forever and forever. We have forever now."

She had no words and no tears left. She collapsed into the chest of the man who loved her with the intensity she loved him.

Chapter 26

THEY WALKED DOWN the rows of green fruit that hung below slender vines. Anne looked out the Dry Creek Valley to the vineyards on the flats below, Marcus's warm hand in hers. The verdant view took her breath away. She watched the vines grow in front of her eyes, the liquid from their fruit like the blood she and Marcus lived on. This place was her sanctuary. Her mortal life had ended on a cobblestone street so far away, but her new life had begun right here, at the place where Marcus had laid the blanket down when she tasted him for the first time. The time she'd felt the fating. And here again, her new life was starting over as she watched Marcus lay down the same blanket, stretch out the long lean length of his body, and call to her with his eyes.

Anne wore a peasant skirt and white top she had seen once on a gypsy dancer in Spain. It was comfortable in her present condition. Her enlarged belly needed room. She gave herself many lacy petticoats for Marcus to get lost in on his quest for her opening. They mussed his hair as he explored. He took his time, though, catching on the rhythm of the game, peeling back one layer at a time, as he brought her closer and closer to the familiar core of her passion.

She had decided not to make him work too hard and had not worn panties. When he found this, he dipped his tongue into the pool of her sex and, looking up to her eyes, whispered, "Thank you."

Licking the sensitive fold next to the lips of her sex, he whispered a question he didn't need to ask. The way she was splayed out for him should have told him the answer, but she loved hearing him beg for her anyway. She loved that he respected her body. Though he had the keys to every door in her heart and soul, he would always ask permission, never take what was not freely given.

"May I taste?"

"Please. You can have any part of me you wish to devour. Every part but the child I am carrying."

He licked her again with a warm tongue, his touch, vibrating over her white skin as if to calm her flesh and prepare it for the bite. The punctures through her skin stung and then dulled into a sensual glow that radiated out from it, making the lips of her sex quiver and release its juice. Marcus suckled her blood, and then suckled the juice of her passion.

He was whispering secrets again to his child, to the womb inside her, making the child strong. He could hear his son's strong heartbeat. The sound of his father's voice quickened it, along with his mother's.

Marcus raised himself up to take Anne's lips that she parted for him. He moaned and gave her his hot breath.

"I am yours. Forever." Marcus bit her earlobe.

"Yes, my love. And every cell in my body belongs to you."

Long male fingers inched their way under her blouse, stopping only to squeeze the taut nipples and warm flesh of her breasts. He delicately raised the white blouse off her and sighed at the new red satin and lace bra he'd bought her. She knew he liked it when she dressed inappropriately for him. She even liked doing it in public, making his pants tent in front of lots of people, making him nail her in his mind against any available wall. She wanted to always have this effect on him, and she knew she would.

"Are you going to punish me for not wearing the matching panties you bought me?"

"Under the circumstances, this is a violation that deserves punishment, don't you think?" He kissed her neck, then followed his lips with exploring fingers up and down her pulsing vein.

"I am truly sorry for my sins. But I fear the punishment will bring me too much pleasure." She liked that he smiled and showed his white teeth, the tips of his fangs.

"Then you have no choice but to bring the executioner of this punishment into your body and show him. To be truly punished, he needs to know all things about you to exact his measure."

"I hope his measure is lost inside me and never wants to return to his body again."

"Ah, but only for the delicious bridle of it until it is free to exact its punishment again. The yearning is delicious."

Anne loved the whispers they gave each other. She looked at the vines surrounding them. They knew. The grapes knew. They were indeed witnesses to their love for each other. Marcus's maleness was so strong he could exact juice from the grapes at her sides. Everything in the world deferred to him.

She sat up, then helped him off with his shirt. She kissed his chest, working her tongue over his nipples. She bit him gently and took a drop. Her tongue wanted more. Her mouth ached for him as her sex dripped for him.

She unbuckled his jeans and helped slide them down his long legs. His erection was fully red and glistened in its velvet goodness in the afternoon sun. Anne covered him with her wet lips, working her tongue over his head, letting the warm shaft bulge further and throb for her.

One knee grazed his thigh. She dipped her sex and rubbed herself up and down on his flesh as she leaned into his chest and sucked on a nipple. Her round belly pressed against him and she watched his pleasure as she rubbed their offspring against his tanned abdomen. Then her knee reached over his other thigh so that her wet sex hung over his balls, his erection pressed against her and lost in her petti- coats. She raised the lacy fabric so his cock could find its home, then looked at his dark eyes as she raised herself up. She set herself down upon his shaft in one long motion as his hands gently massaged her belly.

"Ah, this is how it is done, my son. This is how your fated female will make you feel," Marcus whispered, and then looked at his wife.

There were no words for how Anne felt. His shaft thrust from be- low into her belly, reaching to touch all of her insides, seeking to create pleasure wherever it pressed. His cock was demanding and hard. She would remember this mating for centuries, this sunny summer day when she was large with his male child. Full circle in a life that started out mortal and became immortal, and in time, legendary.

Anne's muscles began to twitch as she lowered herself down to his neck and claimed him in her orgasm. He did the same, claiming her with a new strength and urgency to shoot his seed she had not felt before. They were life force for each other as their bodies tangled in the mating where there wouldn't be satisfaction, but a growing need for each other and the love they shared. They would bloom together. Not grow old. They would just grow.

And they would drink the wine of their love forever.

Mortal Bite

Golden Vampires of Tuscany
Book 2

S. Hamil

Chapter 1

PAOLO MONTELEONE SWIRLED the black cape around his body as he checked the guest chamber's full-length mirror. The fabric arrived at his knees and calves well after he stopped spinning, and then draped back away to sway a few inches from the floor. He could see his face in the polished sheen of his shoes. The tux and red cummerbund, an elegant presentation, belonged to his brother, Marcus, but it fit him perfectly. Marcus's man had done well. The costume was a fitting outfit for any good vampire gentleman.

It had been a year since he'd returned to Italy, repairing the damage he'd caused his brother and his new wife. A year of learning to be a father to his son, making amends to the other Monteleone family members who at first didn't trust that he wouldn't run off again and try to live as the mortal he wasn't.

When Marcus and Anne graciously invited him to join them in California wine country, Paolo immediately agreed. The change of scenery was doing him good. Tonight he was going to attend his first party without a member of his family.

The door burst open and Lucius, all four feet of him, raced straight for Paolo. The boy wore his Superman cape and red boots—rain boots, to be exact—with all the pride of the superheroes he loved to emulate.

Paolo bent over and lifted his son, pressed the flesh of this little superhero to his chest and nuzzled just under the boy's right ear. The fresh smell of his mortality was the most satisfying moment of Paolo's day. Eventually, Lucius would have to make the choice whether to remain mortal or become golden vampire. But not yet. Not until he was of age.

"And just where are you heading out to? Anne taking you trick-or-treating? It's not Halloween yet," he murmured affectionately into the side of the boy's face.

Lucius drew back and his dark eyes flashed at his father, which always managed to melt Paolo's heart.

"I'm going with you to the party, father." His coppery brown eyes and pink cheeks made him look sweet despite the heavy, jagged, and uneven eye makeup he must have applied himself.

"Lucius, you could hurt yourself putting all that kohl around your eyes. You should have asked your aunt for help."

"Well, Anne and Marcus..." the boy paused and blushed. "They're busy all the time."

"Ahhhhh," Paolo said. He envied his brother and his long-awaited fated female and their new baby. The fact that Marcus found Anne after three hundred years of searching meant there might still be hope for him. Not a fated female, but someone to love and be loved in return.

A shadow suddenly covered his heart, and gave him a chill. He composed himself and addressed his son.

"Lucius, time enough for parties when you're older. This one is for grownups only. Not for..."

"Kids," Lucius finished with resignation. "But I *want* to go. You will protect me, father."

Indeed he could. Not an hour went by when Paolo wasn't fearful of the fact that Lucius, still mortal, could die, and Paolo, vampire, would be left to grieve for all eternity.

"I'm sure cook will find you something sweet in the kitchen. I think she made a berry pie." He winked as he set his son down, while he savored the change in the boy's face.

"Berry pie? Whoopee!" Lucius zipped out of the room and down the hall, down the massive wooden staircase yelling "Berry Pie!" at the top of his lungs. It echoed throughout the whole mansion, brightening a home that hadn't held the sound of a child's voice in over a century.

Then Paolo heard the carved wooden doors to Marcus and Anne's suite open. Marcus, dressed in a long paisley velvet robe, ambled across the landing to stand at his door. He was barefoot.

"That should get you the attention you deserve," he said as he sauntered into the room. "You'll be fighting the ladies off you tonight, brother. A real feeding frenzy."

Marcus was in a jolly mood, and comfortable, even though he was probably naked beneath his robe. At seven o'clock in the evening. After, no doubt, making love to his beautiful wife for most of the day—between the infant's feedings, of course.

Paolo forced his mind out of his brother's private bedroom activities "Your hair." He touched the back of his head, indicating Marcus's bed head.

Marcus patted down the errant strands and rocked back and forth in his bare feet. "We didn't get much sleep. The baby was up half the night last night, and today, well…"

"No doubt harkening back to our dark vampire ancestors."

Marcus smiled and looked at the floor like he actually believed his lie had worked.

Paolo leaned into Marcus and whispered, "If I had a beauty like Anne, I'd never leave my bed either. Your secret is safe with me, although I've heard the staff gossip."

"Gossip? About what?" The look of concern darkened Marcus's eyes.

"Your prowess. They have to have heard the screams and moans. You even wake the baby sometimes, or were you not paying attention?"

Paolo said this without an ounce of jealousy, even though his life had been one lonely death after another, with the marriage and death of all three of his mortal wives. Paolo never begrudged his brother's happiness, or his choice to mate with a vampire female. On the contrary. Hope kindled a little bonfire in his soul.

Marcus seemed pleased that the staff had wondered about his stamina. Because he and Anne could go out in the sunlight, their family being the Golden of the vampire lineage, it required they have two sets of staff. One for day. One for night. Though he complained of the infant, Marcus rarely was in bed for sleep.

"Well, I'd say it's time for you to enjoy some of the comforts of the flesh, Paolo. And I believe you have created a most interesting net to catch them in. Rather like bees to honey." Marcus winked and padded back to his room.

On the way to the ball, Paolo allowed his mind to wander over recent changes in his life. He enjoyed staying with Marcus and Anne in California, in the legendary Sonoma County. Living in his native Italy the past year had made him feel morose and brooding. He had often wandered the dark, cobblestoned streets looking for something to warm his heart. But now there was Lucius to provide warmth. His son.

During one of his brooding walks through Tuscany seven years ago, he'd committed the ultimate sin, creating a debt for which he was now trying to repay. Paolo remembered that night all too vividly, like it was yesterday.

In a cruel twist of fate, Anne killed Maya, a fate punishable by death. His brother had nearly been executed by the High Council, since Marcus attempted to take the blame and was tried and found guilty of it. Paolo managed to save his brother's life by admitting publically he was the boy's father and Maya's fated mate. Marcus was forgiven.

But Paolo still had much to answer for. If there were a god that watched over vampires, would he find it in his heart to grant him peace, forgiveness? Give him a chance to make up for the mistakes he had made all those years ago?

He hoped so.

Like a dark whisper, the limo slid to the sidewalk in front of the grand ballroom. Marcus's driver got out, opening the rear door for Paolo. The night was crisp and without rain. People flocked to the doors looking like actors waiting to go onstage for a performance of *Midsummer Night's Dream*. The grand old hotel, steeped in history from trysts of the San Francisco elite over the past two centuries, sat stoically with its secrets amongst the bevy of faeries, butterflies and princesses. There were stewardesses and nurses so scantily clad they appeared to have costume malfunctions. Several dark vamp women clung to men dressed as pirates or gentlemen, astronauts and, yes, more than a few vampires. A group of blue unisex Smurfs arrived and crowded in behind him, giggling.

Paolo was surprised that tonight, for the first time, he enjoyed appearing as who he really was. Somehow, he was glad he had chosen to become vampire instead of remaining mortal. He'd spent nearly three hundred years regretting the decision to change which was made in haste when he'd seen his mortal parents die.

He didn't really understand why tonight was oddly different. He only knew that his vampire skin felt like his elegant, comfortable cape. Appropriate, dashing and fatally attractive.

Blaring music echoed through the hallway as soon as he stepped out of the metal cage elevator. Warm brown, heavily marbled stone marked his path to the ballroom. His pumps tapped down the stone corridor to the beat of the drums. Music throbbed in rhythms so strong that they tickled and thudded in his chest. His limbs felt the vibration of the beat, and his pulse quickened.

Excitement. It had been centuries since he'd felt this way.

He walked under blue and silver twinkle lights covering two tall tree boughs which framed the ballroom entrance. The photographer's flash blinded him momentarily, but he smiled and nodded his head as he accepted a chit allowing him to purchase the photo later. Perhaps he would. It gave him another thing to smile about.

The heavily gilt walls and ornately carved walnut paneling of the ceiling reminded him of some of the ballrooms in Vienna and Paris he'd seen as a youth, when he and Marcus had danced their way through the lovelies of Europe during the 18th and 19th centuries.

I feel at home.

His instinct was to find a dark table in a secluded corner away from everyone else so he could scope out the crowd. Homing in on the perfect spot, a table with only one shimmering gauze scarf next to a top hat, and the rest of the place settings unoccupied, Paolo selected a chair several spaces over from the party of two, brushed his cape to the side, carefully adjusted his tails, and sat, prepared to enjoy the revelers.

Sparkle dust was in the air, tickling his nose. The amber-colored candle on the table filled the air with the fragrance of blood oranges, Anne's favorite scent. He should know, he chuckled to himself, since Marcus had placed hundreds of them throughout his villa for her.

Paolo watched faeries dance with trolls, and idly ran his gaze over a scantily clad woman in black with huge breasts as she undulated and massaged her body over her partner's. There were werewolves, storm troopers, kings and queens. Some men and women danced with partners of their own sex, some cavorted in groups.

He removed his cape and left it dangling over his chair as he went in search for a good glass of port. He preferred to have the enticing sweetness of port on his breath, should he meet a lady he wanted to speak with. His fangs craved the flesh of a mortal woman tonight.

The scent of jasmine was strong as he edged his way between the dancers and a table filled with donuts of every size, color and confection. The pastries were resting on a bed of candy corn and caramel popcorn. Paolo's teeth ached at the thought of tasting the over-sweet treats.

Lucius would have loved this. Paolo smiled as he mused how sick the boy would have been the next day.

Something soft bumped into his backside. Something that smelled wonderful.

He turned and brushed intimately against a beautiful, auburn-haired woman with green eyes, whose curves made the most of a white Renaissance gown with a plunging neckline. Feathered wings were sewn on the back of the dress, and her long, draping sleeves almost touched the floor when her hands were down. Everything he'd lectured himself about not getting involved with mortal women flew away with the blink of his eye.

Upon seeing Paolo, she raised her palms to her face and hitched her breath, as if startled.

"Oh, my. What have we here?" she said.

To a mortal, the loud music would have made it impossible to hear what her voice. Paolo could hear every breath, every syllable rolling off her pink tongue as clearly as if she'd whispered it in his ear. Something silky slid down his spine as a door within him opened.

"I am a vampire, madam, at your service." Paolo bowed and kissed her extended fingers.

Did I make her offer her hand, or did she volunteer it?

"But your lips are warm. That means you are an imposter." She smiled and the world lit up.

"I assure you, madam, I am no imposter." He felt his groin go rigid. He noted the blue pulsing vein at her neck quicken as her heart fluttered, sending her scent to his waiting nostrils.

She turned and gazed over her shoulder at a young man dancing madly into oblivion. Her partner did not notice his date had been distracted by the charms a new dark visitor. Someone who could be dangerous to her health.

Modern men. So naïve. They let their women wander way too much, allowing them to be gobbled up by straycatchers...

She turned and looked up at him, as though she was expecting Paolo to say something.

"Would you like some refreshment?" he finally asked her. His insides began to flutter in tandem with the beating of her heart.

Her eyes took on a momentary sparkle that thrilled Paolo. She turned and regarded her young dancing partner without much interest. Putting her hands aside her mouth, she shouted to him, "Johnny!"

The blond dancer jerked, then broke out in a toothy grin, raising his palms and undulating his torso in tune with the grinding music. Paolo didn't like the sexual sway and suggestive jest aimed at his new interest.

"I'm getting something to drink," the woman mouthed her words silently and followed it by drinking from an imaginary glass in her right hand.

Johnny gave her the thumbs up and started to go back to his wild gyrations, but hesitated as he looked at Paolo. A frown of worry marred his sunny countenance.

She shook her head and waved him away from across the dance floor. Paolo heard her say, "No problem. You have fun," but doubted Johnny had heard a thing.

A glittery faerie dancer came up behind Johnny and slid under his knees, pressing into his backside that drew a whoop from him. The young man was instantly distracted by the way the little one rubbed herself all over his trousers.

Paolo's new friend leaned back and laughed, her neck and shoulders sparkling with glitter. He could smell how good she would taste. He saw as well as felt what she liked sexually and knew he could satisfy her—do things, make her feel things, she had never dreamed possible. He stole glances while she was distracted by the bodies writhing on the dance floor and the sparkle of the costumes.

Then she turned. Paolo and his mortal beauty and her red lips faced each other fully at last. Her reddish-brown curls called to his fingers as his mouth anticipated kissing her, tasting her, making her shudder in his arms.

The woman was waiting for him to lead the way. Paolo held his breath. He wanted to be sure she was coming of her own accord. He refrained from glamoring her.

Does it matter?

He decided that tonight it did.

Paolo tucked his arm under hers and led her to the open bar, and away from the loud music. There was a fireplace and a deserted table nearby.

"I'll get us something to drink. Why don't you claim that table over there?"

"Claim?" she asked. Her green eyes reflected tiny fires from the twinkle lights in a canopy of stars overhead. She bit her lower lip, but obviously couldn't keep the ends from upturning into a smile. Her fluttering eyelids danced, flashing fireballs at his heart, allowing himself to be seduced by her mortal charms.

"I figured we'd start on some port. Something deep and red." He waggled his eyebrows, and she giggled, leaning against him. He could feel the firmness of her breasts against his upper torso. He swung his arm around her waist and pulled her even closer with a gentle tug. She arched back and examined his face, while he brushed the laces at the back of her dress, fingering every eyelet and silken strand.

He couldn't resist touching her, and spoke, releasing his dark power as he covered her with glam.

"I'm entranced by your scent. Do you taste as good?"

She was still for a second while she considered his question. Could she feel the threshold they were stepping through like he did? Caught in each other's gaze, he heard a throat being cleared behind him and turned to face the red-haired bartender.

"Something to drink?" the man asked. The bartender's bulbous, deep purple nose seemed to fill his entire face. He held a wet towel in his chubby right hand while he tapped fingers on the bar countertop with his left.

"Two ports. The oldest and rarest you have." Paolo turned and whispered as he stroked the length of his Renaissance angel's cheek and let his finger trail over her red lips, "Rare as the lady at my side." Her eyelids fluttered under the weight of his control. He loved how she was so susceptible to his power, seemed to crave it.

He almost leaned in to kiss her, but couldn't bring himself to take advantage of her vulnerability. He cursed himself for his lack of manners. He held onto her with both hands at her waist, righted her firmly on her feet, separating her warm body from his and waited for her to regain sense of herself.

She shook her head. "Whew, don't know what came over me. I got dizzy there for a second."

"Why don't you sit down, then, and I'll come along with our drinks? Maybe the fire will warm you." He pointed to the corner again.

"Yes. That's a good idea." She shuffled with tiny steps, holding her palm to her forehead and mumbled to herself.

He watched her body move under the silken gown, her hips, her small waist, and the small of her back outlined by a row of lacings that stretched all the way up to her shoulders. He wanted to see her naked. Wanted to rub his hands all over her flesh and kiss every inch of it.

If she'll let me of her own free will.

And if that didn't work—well, he could always use his vampire powers of charm and confusion. He could make her see him for the first time all night long. He could conquer her over and over again.

And no one would be the wiser.

He suddenly didn't want the evening to end.

Chapter 2

CARA SAT IN the corner and thought about how the evening was progressing. Her heart was pounding, a tympanic rhythm she felt all the way to her fingertips. She wasn't here to meet someone. She already had a date—Johnny, the sexy research assistant all her professor girlfriends lusted after. That's why she'd asked him. She wanted to be the talk of the department. What she was doing right now? She was waiting for a handsome, very tall, masculine creature to bring her some refreshment and indulge her senses. It wasn't something she wanted her girlfriends to find out about.

I'll worry about my coworkers and all the rumors tomorrow. Tonight she felt soft, compliant. *Sexy.*

Her friends used to speculate that Johnny must be gay, he was so good looking. When she asked him to accompany her to the ball, he enthusiastically agreed, and then had enticingly curled a strand of her hair around his tanned finger, letting her know non-verbally that he was definitely interested in more. In the past they'd shared dinners, and accompanied each other to University functions, but never to a costume ball.

And then, as soon as he'd accepted her invitation, he blew his bubblegum into a huge, pink bubble, and then grinned mischievously. Johnny was like that. Still a kid at twenty-five.

Cara hadn't been looking for a sexual liaison. At least, not with Johnny. He was five years her junior. Tall and athletic. Well-defined abs she'd seen beneath t-shirts while they studied together at the library. Earlier, she'd watched him show off his dance moves. He was attracting great attention under the strobing lights and heavy beat. Ordinarily, she'd be right there, by his side. They'd have been backup for each other.

But not this time. Cara was being led to a dimly lit corner by a dark gentleman with a whole set of mysterious intentions. Johnny was daytime to this man's night. And right now, she was lingering in his shadowed influence, in a lustful, confused state.

I love the way he makes me feel.

How could that be? She was focused on her career and hadn't found time for a lovelife. Was something else looming on the horizon? A new adventure, perhaps?

God, yes!

She asked herself for permission to follow her hormones several times and came up with the same answer every time: Johnny could take care of himself, and she needed to learn more about this man she'd just—met? *Is that the right word for it?* She felt herself melting into his sphere, somehow being enveloped into his sexy, Continental aura. She felt starved for his affection for some strange reason.

The gentleman was coming back to the corner table she had *claimed.* He made a perfect vampire, tall and brooding, with a devilish smile that made her knees wobble even while sitting. She smiled, enjoying the play-along.

His body had seemed muscular and firm when he drew her close at the bar. He smelled of spice, and something else, an exotic mixture of lemon, nutmeg and cinnamon, like an incense from an ancient land. She remembered reading about exotic fragrances and their pheromone-like effect on the human body.

His breath had been cold, but his lips warm as they'd nibbled on fingers she couldn't help offering up to him, as though she wanted him to taste her. Had she felt the slight touch of his tongue on the knuckle of her third finger? Had he tasted the flesh between her third and fourth fingers? He'd studied her afterward, the clear black eyes searching her face, seeming to search for traces of a reaction, as if he was asking permission. His slow, sexy smile and fluttering of his long lashes, seemed to request approval to advance. To walk through her doorway.

Yes, she felt her heart whisper.

She decided to allow herself to be explored. Her soul tingled with each gentle nod of his head as he looked at her hair, her earlobes, and the soft tissue beneath her jaw, his eyes wandering down to her throat when she couldn't help swallowing. His almost old world charm encouraged her to trust him. A door she usually kept closed and locked had opened.

Normally, she'd be afraid. *But not tonight.*

Tonight she felt positively immortal.

He leaned forward, his shadow falling over her face and shoulders. Their fingers touched as he handed her the little blood-red short-stemmed glass of glittering port.

"To us," he said as he clinked their glasses together and bowed to her.

Please sit with me, she said to herself.

As if he heard her thoughts, he sat, not across the table, but next to her on the burgundy plush cushion, then leaned against her. When he lifted the glass to his lips, she felt compelled to do the same. His eyes drew her to hm. The dark brown edges were tinged with a ring of golden fire at the outsides. His lips tasted the sweet liquid as hers did. He licked his lower lip and she did the same, from right to left. Just as he was doing. If he leaned into her, she knew she would let him…

"Do you like the port?" he asked. Did she see a tiny effort, as though he tried to bridle himself? Tiny creases at the sides of his eyes gave him away.

"Yes. I do." She was rewarded with his smile. She saw the tips of his…*fangs?* Her eyes fluttered again as her pulse quickened. "Your costume is quite realistic."

"Yes?" He raised his eyebrows and hid the fangs.

"Those. Do they come off easily?" She pointed to his mouth.

He smiled, and there were no fangs. "Whatever do you mean?"

"You can make them go up and down like that? I've never seen fangs that can do that."

"Indeed." He smiled again and they were back.

"You must show me how they work."

He leaned into her. The lemon spice flooded her head with erotic images of bonfires and soft music. His lips were close, but not touching. Her flesh craved a caress, and, as if on cue, his fingers wandered to her cheek and stroked her there. "I can show you many things, my dear."

Yes, I want you to—whatever am I doing?

Abruptly, she sat up and pulled away from him. *What is going on?*

She found her glass and took a sip, not wanting to stare into his eyes. An alarm was going off somewhere in the back of her mind. It had broken the moment.

He crossed his legs and moved slightly away from her. The left side of her body noticed the lack of warmth immediately. When she ventured a look back up to his face, he was smiling, his obsidian eyes twinkling in the shadows, as he stared not at her, but into the fire just over her shoulder.

"I'm Carabella Sampson," she said as she extended her hand.

"Paolo Monteleone," he said. His fingers slid into hers, entangling her, making her heart sputter. The touch was intimate.

She withdrew her fingers from his and took another sip of the delicious red port. "I like this. I don't usually drink sweet drinks."

"But you should. Contrary to popular fiction, sweet wine is good for your blood."

She had to chuckle at that one, working not to burst out in a full belly laugh. "You are a method actor. You play the part of a vamp very well."

"Ah. And you are experienced with vamps, no doubt?"

"Very," she said.

At this he started, and his dark sparkly eyes widened. The edges of his full red lips curled up like a thin moustache. "Do tell. I want to hear all about it."

Her face warmed as she looked down at her port. She could tell he was smiling as he watched her. She toyed with him. She wanted to make him wait. She heard something deep and low in his throat. Was there a rumble, a small earthquake?

One of his fingers touched the top of her shoulder and drew a line down her upper arm. "Has another vampire touched your flesh before?"

She shivered, loving the game Her body scooted away from him, yet craved to be chased. He waited. She experienced the distance between them he must have also felt, and she could tell he was having difficulty with that. She was suddenly aware of his heavy breathing.

"I'm an expert on vampire mythology." Cara spoke to her nearly empty glass. "I teach legends and mythology at Sonoma State."

"Really?"

"Yes." She looked back up at him. "Vampire mythology dates back to pre-biblical times. We've had vampires as long as we've had angels. Did you know that?"

"How very interesting." He blinked and she thought he made an effort to keep his smile pasted to his face.

"They are a symbol of something that can never be. Of people's desire to delve into the unknown, the dangerous. Does that make sense?"

"Entirely."

"We want to believe in things that we can't see. Religion is all about believing in things we can't prove, either."

"Like angels, for instance."

"Oh, yes, people have seen angels and lived to tell about it."

"As opposed to vampires."

"Good point. So there you have it. Because they aren't real. Just myth." She threw her head back, downing the rest of her port. Cara loved being in the presence of this man, a man who didn't run away, or scoff, when she told him of her interest in the vampire myths. "I think that's why you find pictures of angels in churches, but not vampires."

"So there's a vampire religion, too?"

Now he *was* toying with her. "Somehow I think not." She smiled at her empty glass.

"You would like more?"

"Yes...no. I—I'm not sure what I want at the present time," she said.

He took her glass in his long fingers and stood. "I know exactly what you want," he said. He was at the bar in seconds.

She sat back and relaxed into the velvet seat cushions, feeling the warmth of the fire on her face, her upper arms and her thighs under the tapestry fabric of her dress. As he stepped onto the brass boot rail of the bar with one long leg, she noticed the shape of his ass and the straightness of his spine. His long, elegant neck and broad shoulders made him a giant specimen of devastating masculinity she'd have noticed anywhere. The fact that he was now coming right towards her, with that crooked smile revealing one fang, thrilled her. Something about their play was natural.

But it defied logic.

He slid in to sit close, one long thigh against hers. He extended his arm over her shoulder in a possessive gesture she didn't fight.

"Let's drink again to us," he said.

"Why not?" She took the first sip, but he did not, seemingly caught in watching her swallow. He looked mesmerized.

"Something wrong?" she asked.

"Not at all." He sipped and then set his glass down on the black tabletop. "So, tell me about your vampires."

"Really?"

"I'm completely serious" he replied.

Cara slipped comfortably into professorial mode. "Vampires throughout history have been used to describe pure evil. To describe things too horrible to consider any other way. Like missing children. Vampires were said to steal them from their beds."

He nodded. "But you don't think they ate children, do you?"

"Of course not." She looked at him. "Vampires aren't real, you know."

"Of course not." His answer triggered a flood of visions of her lying in a huge bed by a raging fireplace as he looked down on her body, with exactly the same expression as now.

She cleared her throat.

"Children were much more likely to become prey to wild animals, or evil members of their own population. But this was a way to blame horrible things on despicable creatures, not members of one's family."

"Despicable?"

"Totally. It's really been in the past few decades that vampires have been thought of as sexy or even desirable, in a crude, repulsive way." She looked at his blank face. His eyes had gone somewhere else.

Had he lost interest? She continued anyway. "Who would want to fall in love with one of the undead? A cold corpse who sucks the life blood from your body? When you think of it, someone who entertains those kinds of thoughts is probably filled with self-loathing. A truly flawed person. Someone whole and sane would never desire it."

"I see." His flat monotone concerned her.

"But we *can* pretend. That's what's so fun about dressing up. For one night of the year we can be anything we want. Halloween is when we dare to be what we would otherwise be repulsed by."

He had truly gone away, mentally. Well, he was probably tired of the subject. She'd done it again. Bored yet another handsome man to distraction. The charming fellow at her side was suddenly interested in anything or anyone but her.

"Are you feeling okay?" she asked.

"Yes. Why?"

"Well, you seem so, well—so different. Have I said something that offended you?"

"I didn't realize you knew so much about—I guess I had a tiny bit of regret at having chosen this costume, now I know how you feel about vampires."

"But we're just play acting. You don't repulse me like the vamps I study do."

It wasn't working. Something was off kilter. His eyes were still dull, like he was forcing himself to smile but didn't want to. She decided perhaps she had picked a scab and didn't want to wait around for the blood and gore. Her common sense returned as she realized she shouldn't have been so trusting.

"You know, I'm sorry—what was your name again?"

"Monteleone. Paolo Monteleone."

"Mr. Monteleone then. I should be returning to my date. I feel like I've ignored him, been impolite." What had she been thinking? She wrinkled up her nose and patted his hand. She felt a faint jolt of electricity at the touch of his flesh. And she heard him hitch his breath.

They both stood. She wasn't sure what was happening, except that she suddenly needed to create distance between them. She needed to think. "Thank you for the port. It was delicious," she said.

"Made even more so by your presence," he said, and bowed.

"Oh, now that was the perfect touch," she said, pointing to him. "You really have it down. You must be an actor. Are you?"

"How did you guess?"

"I can tell. I read people very well. It's a gift."

"Indeed."

"There you are!" Johnny's flushed face appeared before her at the perfect moment. His hairline was dripping with sweat, and he was fanning himself with a cardboard coaster and grinning like the devil. "You've got to come out on the dance floor with me. This band rocks! Please save me, dear, sweet angel, from these women who want to leave their men behind and take me home to have their way with me." His straight white teeth and dimples made him look entirely kissable.

She disliked that she'd been so caught up in conversation with this stranger that she'd let her good friend down. A friend she would normally love to flirt and tease with, perhaps a little more.

But not tonight.

She turned and said a polite goodbye to Paolo, then allowed Johnny to lead her away by the hand. She lost herself in the crush of bodies, the heat, sweat and flashing lights. But just before the crowd filled in behind her, she felt the mysterious dark eyes of the gentleman she'd just met. A gentleman who made her pulse quicken just by being near him.

Chapter 3

PAOLO WAS STUNNED. The blow Cara had delivered had felled him as quickly as a sword. Of course any sane woman would be repulsed by the thought of being with him. The only things in this world that craved him were half-witch vampires who wanted to suck him dry.

I am truly lost.

His glamour had worked on her. She might have been warming to him on her own as well. Things had been going along so beautifully. Then he had to go ask her about what she did and learned that she studied *vampires* and had decided they were *despicable beings.*

Am I despicable? Am I a cold, blood-sucking monster who preys on little children?

With horror, he realized perhaps the answer to his question was…

Yes.

He'd fathered a child. Was he now leading that child to a life of loathing? Could he bear to hear Lucius tell him that some future woman had found him repulsive? How could he be honest with his son, or would he simply not tell Lucius how much he regretted his own decision to become vampire? How could he counsel Lucius when the time came for the boy to make his own irrevocable, permanent, life-altering decision?

What would he say if Lucius asked about how he was created? It hadn't been with love, an act of love. Paolo's cock had lurched, and his balls had constricted and spewed forth the seed that would become Lucius. That's all. It had been a loveless, animal act, a betrayal, he'd believed, of his brother. He'd used Maya, the woman he'd believed was his brother's *fated* mate countless times with abandon over a lost weekend in an animal mating he was powerless to stop.

He'd copulated frantically and repeatedly, despite his revulsion for the object of his animal desire, with the woman who proved to be his—not his brother's—one and only fated female, because only a fated mate could have borne his child. And he still hated the mother of the child he loved so deeply, even now, after her death.

Despicable? Yes. He would shoot his seed into anything. His *fating* had completely owned him, taken over completely during those fateful days. He had been nothing more than a set of balls wanting to heave. Afterwards, when the urge finally released its grip on his soul, he fled back to America and into the arms of his dying mortal wife. He regretted ever having come over to Tuscany for the wedding.

Still mortally shamed by his long-ago decision to turn, there wasn't a day of the centuries that had gone by when he didn't feel the sharp pain of regret. God in Heaven, he wished he'd made the other choice, to remain mortal. He would have died in the 1700's like his parents. He'd be buried right next to them on the plot of land bordered by the family vineyard.

Paolo would be dust and not a danger to anyone else. Not able to feast on the blood of innocents, ruin mortal life.

Lucius would never have existed.

It is what I deserve.

He made his way back to the ballroom. The party was ramping up to full rave Even the windows were foggy with the detritus of frenzied exhalations and hot human sweat. The dull dance beat dispensed like candy from the mobile D.J. made his chest rumble in a not unpleasant way. Paolo felt the pain and anguish pouring out of the partygoers as they danced off their fears, exorcised their demons. Could they feel that death was stalking them? Walking amongst them?

He turned around in the center of the dance floor. Had they made a circle around him? Were they mocking him as they undulated, showed him their flesh, the dark patches usually left in shadow for a lover? Did they wiggle and send their pheromones blasting out to allure him or torture him? Who was master and who was slave here?

Three pixie-like women dressed in butterfly princess costumes flew around him and surrounded his body with the luscious softness of their flesh. They touched him places he never let women touch him in public. His groin tightened and in spite of the debasement he felt, he got rock hard. Two of the ladies sandwiched him and he dry-humped one sweet little faerie, holding her by her tiny glistening waist as she writhed on his hardened member and let him feel the heat of her sex through her flimsy costume. His erection became so strong he feared it would rip through his trousers and take her through the silvery gauze that did little to protect her core from a thrust of his kind.

I could do it. I could show them what I am.

The scent of her body juices made him want to bite the little nymph. He could hold her while she experienced the euphoria of his tongue as he coaxed out her sweet red elixir until it filled the empty spaces inside him. He'd seal off the little holes in her neck, then re-bite her and partake again, then heal her, over and over again, until he was sated.

He could feel what she would taste like, how her sweet scent could fill his nostrils as he explored the penetrations he made, dominating her, and sending his thanks to God that he could immerse himself in the life force of this beautiful creature.

As he readied himself to bite down, he caught sight of Carabella Sampson, watching him from across the room. She stood in partial shadow, but Paolo could see her just as clearly as if she'd been standing in full sun. The dancers almost parted so that he could look upon the wonder of her full, luscious body. It made him stop gyrating his hips. He released the faerie and she tumbled to the floor like a rag doll, glamoured, but otherwise unharmed.

Cara stood to him, unwavering across the expanse of the large room, letting him feast on her beauty, letting his eyes roam in places she should have been shy about revealing to him. She didn't turn, or cover herself up, or fold her arms across her ample chest. Her red lips were moist, and he could hear her breathing across the huge hall. He could smell the tiny beads of sweat condensed on her upper lip, which quivered so very slightly. He drank of her in every way but with his fangs.

The faeries were all over him again, one hugging his thigh between hers, another rubbing her breasts into his chest, raising his shirt, seeking a flesh-to-flesh connection. He continued to stare into the eyes of Carabella. His rod was red hot, but it was Carabella who was touching him, working on the zipper, trying to obtain purchase.

Stop it, he mentally told them. He could not let them do this. He wasn't that far gone yet. He would not subject Carabella to this sort of decadence or the darkness in his lonely heart. He tore his eyes from hers and danced with the nymphs, teasing them, staying just out of reach. He sent glam out to the crowd. More women, and a few men came and joined their circle. He paraded around the perimeter, touching faces and tickling their souls. They were starving. Starving for the passion he could unleash upon them.

He turned and she was still there, watching him. He raised his arms to the ceiling and she did the same. One of the faeries unbuttoned his shirt. Carabella could see his chest, see the muscles that wanted to hold her shuddering body.

Let me love you. There. He'd said it, finally.

Her eyes got wide. Her hands came down over her own chest as she kneaded her breasts together. She searched the floor and then raised her eyes to his. Clear across the room from each other they danced together. Through the space of thin air he kissed her neck and watched as she moaned and rolled her head, exposing the blue vein for him.

Paolo licked his lips. He undulated his lower torso as he barely managed to keep from exploding.

I'm coming into you, lovely Carabella. I will make your flesh sing.

She nodded softly as she lowered her chin and pouted her lips. One hand did what Paolo wished he could do, it laced down from her left breast to the juncture between her legs. Then she grabbed her skirts and raised the hem just enough so he could see a well-developed and tanned thigh. He wanted to bite the soft flesh on the inside, up by her core.

Let me see it.

He fell to his knees. The crowd parted and he was able to again see the lovely angel writhing in tandem with him half way across the room.

I will bring you unspeakable pleasure, Carabella. Use me. I am the instrument of your pleasure. If I cannot be your love, use me—even if you must throw me away.

One of the faeries broke his line of sight, lowering herself onto his lap, dancing on his hardness, driving him crazy by kissing his neck and exposing hers. His natural vampire instincts almost got the better of him. Control was slipping away.

"Take me," the glittery faery whispered. She leaned back and he watched as first one, then the other breast found freedom from her small, restrictive costume as she arched back, planted her palms on the dance floor and bent back. Ruffles and her scratchy fabric filled his face.

It brought him to his senses. He righted the faerie and whispered an apology with a kiss to her neck.

"I am claimed already, little one."

"Take me anyway," she begged.

"Not tonight."

As he helped get her to her feet, the crowd applauded and the music ended. He searched the room, looking for the angel, but she was gone. He surreptitiously adjusted his pants, took another bow, and then released the faeries to the crowd. As he wandered toward the outer edge of the crowd of dancers, arms and lips grazed him, sought his attention, but his focus was elsewhere.

Where did she go?

Every spark of white caught his eye…and disappointed him when it was not the angel he sought. He searched the bar, hoping to find her tucked in the corner again by the fireplace, revisiting a glass of port, waiting for him. But no luck.

The vision of her lying across his massive bed, all her lovely flesh exposed to the night air, nipples taut and knotted, her heavy breathing as she anticipated his mouth on her sex, his tongue inside her, making her rise and burn. He would take her every way he knew. He would love her until she craved no other. He would work out of her the loathing she felt for his kind, and he would convince her he was alive and everything she needed.

Because he knew he was.

That's when he saw her, over by the table where he had placed his cape. Johnny had grabbed the top hat and she swung the silver scarf around her neck, protecting her lifeblood, demurely covering up what he longed passionately to see, touch and taste.

When she looked up at him, he softened. He would have run to her, but he was unsure.

On a night filled with miracles another one dropped down upon him. The God of vampires touched him when she smiled. It was a sweet smile. No seduction. No play. Just acceptance. He had not sent glamour to her. She smiled of her own free will, so delicious, so innocent.

The world of the possible opened in front of him. It caused him to step softly toward her as she stood straight and tall, awaiting his arrival. One hand fingered her gauzy scarf, the other was tucked into the crook of Johnny's arm as he attempted to draw her away. But she appeared to resist.

She's waiting for me.

When he arrived at her side, she reached into her scarf and pulled out something. It was a business card she held between the tips of two fingers.

"Call me." Her flushed face was moist with a thin layer of her own excitement. Her eyes held his. Unafraid, but needy.

It was all she said. His heart hung on every strand of her bountiful, beautiful hair as he watched her turn her head and follow Johnny from the ballroom.

Chapter 4

CARA WAS SILENT as Johnny drove her car, taking them both to her house, where he would catch a late bus to his own place across town. They'd only done this twice, gone Dutch and spent the time watching others. Theirs was not the dating relationship they hoped to find in the crowds they scanned. Instead, they worked "cover" for each other.

Cara checked the mirror. Her cheeks were definitely flushed, mirroring the excitement coursing through her veins. She'd never felt so alive, so sexy, and so irresistible. She halfway wished they were on their way to another party. She could dance all night.

She flipped the mirror up and looked across the console at Johnny. He was a *beautiful* man. Even features, smooth tanned skin and white teeth. His vibrantly healthy tanned skin, warm eyes and long lashes made him the perfect cover model or poster man for a milk commercial.

He should be her type, she thought. Though he was younger, he could be a wonderful distraction. But no matter how hard she thought about it, no matter how lusty she felt this evening, to the point that she almost felt immortal, she never could quite see him as a sexual partner. And this made her a little sad.

"I'm sorry I didn't dance with you more." She was feeling melancholy, a little sorry about her lack of attention.

Why? Was she feeling guilty, perhaps?

"That's all right," he flashed her one of his legendary fresh smiles. Johnny could turn on the charm, look just as tempting as any soap opera hunk, but unaffected. He was refreshingly natural, apparently unaffected by his good looks. "I had a good time. But you almost hooked up with that old guy," he said as he winked at her.

"Old guy?" *Was the mystery man old? Hardly!*

"The vampire."

Maybe it was his costume, his makeup. He looked like he was around thirty, not much older than she. However, thinking about him brought a smile to her lips and revved up her engine a couple of notches. She felt in the mood to play with Johnny a bit. "You jealous now?"

"*I'm* the one who's taking you home." He gave her The Bedroom Look. The one that said he meant business.

Cara frowned. Was this getting complicated all of a sudden? Though she was feeling like a free spirit, her affections weren't aimed in Johnny's direction.

He kept his serious tone. "Would you sleep with me some time—one of these evenings?"

Cara was surprised this didn't turn her on. There was absolutely nothing wrong with Johnny or his hunky body. It was something else. "Do you think of me *that* way, Johnny?"

He looked at her as if she had a third eye in the middle of her forehead. "Are you nuts? I'm crazy about you."

"Wouldn't that make me a cougar? Preying on a younger guy?"

"Hardly. You're only five years older. I think you'd have to be ten or twenty years my senior to qualify. Besides," he grabbed her hand and kissed it tenderly, "you're one hot lady. Don't know why, but I saw a different side of you tonight." He dropped her hand after giving her a squeeze. "I kind of like it."

It was true. She was a different person this evening. Some switch had been turned to "on" position, and she was enjoying every minute of it.

She knew he was discreet, so a quick, passionate liaison was possible, and no one need know. But they *worked* together. They had to spend hours in close proximity in her tiny office at the college. They ate Chinese food over research projects and hashing over lecture notes. He was the brother she never had. She needed a true friend. But a lover?

No.

There was only one man on her radar. And for him she'd do just about anything. Even something inappropriate…

"So, what about it?"

"What about what?"

"You gonna make me a lucky man tonight?" He frowned after searching her face, obviously realizing the answer was no. She didn't have to say a word.

"It isn't wise," was all she could think to say as she looked through the windshield at the passing lights. Wet streets and colorful signs twinkled between droplets of rain that diffused and refracted the view. What was she looking for?

"Wasn't asking for wise," Johnny said, his voice deepening. "Was asking for totally hot freaking sex."

She felt the giggle erupt from deep inside her. She loved the way it rippled and fluttered throughout her chest. She was filled with mirth, and it had been years since she'd felt this good.

"You think sex is funny?" he asked. "Or is it just me?" He scowled. "What about you and gramps?"

"Why do you say *gramps?* He doesn't seem old to me," she said. She wasn't going to let anything ruin her evening.

"Because he has something old and sinister on his agenda. Something he's hiding. I don't trust him. It's creepy."

Cara threw her head back onto the headrest and laughed. "Oh, Johnny. I don't get that at all." She scrunched her nose.

"Whatever," he whispered and then sighed.

They remained silent until he pulled into her condo complex. In the underground garage they both got out and he handed her the keys.

"Last chance." His little smile was infectious, but didn't win her over.

"Thanks, but no thanks. I had a really nice time, though."

"Cara, you're a big girl, and a smart one, too. Please, please, for my sake, be careful. I don't like that guy, and it isn't because he's better at mesmerizing the room. There is something really off about him." Johnny hesitated, then stepped closer to Cara, and she moved back to avoid an embrace, in case one was on the way.

"Okay, I get it. But I just don't want to see you get hurt. Aren't you in the least bit concerned?"

Cara had to admit there was some worry there, but it was covered over by something exciting growing inside her soul.

"I can handle myself." She immediately realized she'd hurt him. The flicker of a frown glanced off his face. "But Johnny, it's sweet that you care. Thank you so much for that." Cara moved into his arms and allowed him to encircle her. He was safe.

Am I crazy? What could it hurt?

But the answer was still no. She held him at arm's length. "Thank you. For being my date tonight. For understanding. For being my friend. You don't know how valuable that is to me," she said.

"Me, too," he sighed with a bit of a pout on his brooding face.

He gave her a safe peck on the cheek, backed away, waved, and walked toward the gated door. Carabella headed for the elevator and waved back just as the doors began to close. None of her friends would ever understand how she could just leave him standing there when he'd made himself so totally available to her.

The elevator groaned slowly to the third floor. Inside her condo she turned on her bath and stripped, leaving the angel costume in a heap on the tiled floor. The fuzzy white wings perched in the middle of the pile, stubbornly standing guard over the mounds of white satin. She was grateful to be done with the scratchy protuberances.

Cara swiveled the big screen TV arm so it would angle over her while she soaked. She slipped into the warm, sudsy water and sank up to her neck in lavender-scented bubbles. She flipped on the remote and watched an old Bella Lugosi film. The closeup of his eyes reminded her of the intense way Paolo had looked at her when he whispered, "I can show you many things, my dear." She felt her legs quiver under the warm water.

She sighed and allowed herself to relax against the back of the tub. As her eyes closed, she imagined dancing with him. He spun her around the floor of a grand ballroom filled with candlelight. The hall was empty except for the two of them, but somewhere a string quartet played a waltz as she twirled and leaned back, held by his powerful arms. First they swayed one way, then the other. She wore a golden gown like she'd seen in movies, and felt the taffeta swishing along her hips, the color matching satin dancing slippers encrusted in pearls.

His palm pressed to the small of her back when he stopped her in the middle of the music, as they stood motionless on the polished wooden floor. His finger traced down the side of her face, rubbing over her lower lip as she opened her mouth to him and she tasted his full lips. She heard his inhale, like he was holding back, trying to be gentle with her.

Then she saw herself on a large bed with cream satin sheets, naked, waiting. He covered her body and watched her face, her body as she moaned her pleasure, as he pumped inside her and made her come again and again, each time leaving her craving more.

The visions continued as she lingered in the state of half dream half erotic trance, surrounded by the foaming bubble bath. Organ music leaked from the TV's low volume control, sounding tinny but somehow fitting. At last she opened her eyes and the visions released her. She was left with the delicious lingering effect of her pulsing orgasm.

Panting, she was still not sated, and she gripped the sides of the tub until her body returned to its relaxed state.

What is this feeling that's come over me? She could almost say she'd been bewitched. The powerful ache she felt for this man defied anything she'd experienced before. It was almost as if he were standing beside her, making her feel what she had felt when he touched her hand, or barely brushed her arm at the party.

It had been a sudden impulse to give him her card tonight. It was his move now, not hers. She was not going to chase him.

She wanted to be pursued. Hunted. She knew she needed to run from him.

So he could claim her for his own.

Chapter 5

D AG NIELSEN, SUPREME Dark Vampire Coven Leader hoped that the virgin sex would calm his nerves. His specialty was deflowering young girls with his fangs and then drinking from them until the urge grew so great he had to ram himself deep inside them. Being careful wasn't in his dictionary. He refused to alter his behavior to become acceptable. He rather liked that people ran for the hills or screamed until they passed out when he showed up.

His black Harley was waiting outside. Two members of his coven had parked next to the Harley, trying to look disinterested, but he could tell they had their ears tuned to the little closed window at the cheap motel, listening for the kill bite, after the moans and eventual screams of passion from the blonde waif.

She'd made the mistake of asking him for a little spare change in front of Starbucks. He asked her some questions after putting her into an altered, glamoured state, confirming that she was indeed a virgin, which surprised him. But she told him telepathically she knew how to give good head, which was exciting. Dag offered her a drink and a meal, and glamoured her a bit more so all she could say was, "Please."

"Please," she said again as he licked her nether lips. He could still taste the soap she'd used. He'd required she take a good, hot shower before he would insert his tongue in any of her orifices. He licked her again. She jolted, and then he tasted blood.

Calm down. He was hungry for her, but he needed a meal, not just a snack. And he was pissed off today, so wouldn't be leaving anything around for his bodyguards in the way of sloppy seconds.

He inserted his forefinger in her anus and her eyes flew open.

"Oh, yes, you'll like this. Just relax and feel my finger, Sheila."

"Shirley. My name's—ahhhhhh—Shirley."

He pulled his finger out. "Makes no difference whether your asshole is called Shirley or Shelly. My thumb wants a taste."

He inserted his fat thumb and she gripped the tops of his shoulders, digging her nails into his vampiric flesh.

"Now we're talking, Baby. Go ahead, try to hurt me."

"I don't want to hurt you. I want you to—"

He stretched her enough to insert two fingers into her sweet little ass.

"To what? Fuck you? That what you wanted?" He leaned over her, breathed into her face and saw her eyelids flutter. "Sweet little Susie. You have a lovely pink peach of a twat and a tight little ass. Please, my dear, can I ravage your ass first?"

She was struggling with the answer. He could tell that her real self wanted to say no, but her glamoured self couldn't help but say yes. She bit down on her lip. Hard.

"That's my job," Dag barked. He bent over and bit her lip, drawing just a little blood as his fang moved over her rosy plumpness. His tongue had to work to coax hers out of the black hole that was her upper palate where it was trying to hide. He sucked hard, mumbling, "Mine." She didn't resist him.

They never did.

"Ahh," she moaned. Dag noticed it got one of his guards' attention as the sudden head movement gave him away. The guard licked his lips.

Not today, lover boy. She's all mine.

He tried to send that message telepathically, but Dag was positive the thickheaded dark vampire didn't get it.

He refocused on his meal.

Taking his fingers out of her ass he set himself on her pussy. It was swollen already and bright pink. "Lovely color, my dear Sarah." He said as he admired it.

She opened her eyes and released her grip on his shoulders.

"Did I say to stop that?"

"No, I just, I just like you licking me better than—than—the other—"

Dag inserted his finger back inside her ass. "Than that?" He twisted it.

"Well, okay, but only one, just one, please?"

"Fair enough, my sweet. Fair enough." He kissed her again, leaving her tongue alone. "Only if you scratch me."

She looked at him as if he were crazy. He knew he was, of course.

"Scratch you?" she asked.

"That's right. Grab onto my shoulders and squeeze. Draw blood. I like it rough," he said.

"But—" she couldn't finish because he had laved her clit so hard he tasted her lovely blood again.

"You want it in the butt?"

Her eyes flew open in terror. "No!"

"Then scratch me. Make me hurt. I promise, I won't get angry. I'll get gentler the more you hurt me. It helps me come."

She slowly nodded, disturbing her blonde hair where splayed all over the white pillow, beckoning him like a mermaid under water. He willed her to look deep into his eyes so she could see the danger there. She'd be delicious as she feared for her life.

At first she frowned, but then, as the flames tickled her insides and she appeared to share his passion for the dark side, her eyes became fixed, and she grabbed his right butt cheek and scraped hard enough to actually drag a layer of his skin under her nails.

Dag became hard as granite. He was impressed. He'd figured she didn't have it in her. But this new, sweet gesture on her part to cross the great fiery chasm touched him. Perhaps she was worth saving, like the farmer who ate his fabled pig one limb at a time, as the joke went.

But this was no joke. It was a reveal that someone mortal might be able to share in his pleasure and live to tell the story. And she was virgin. No one else had had her. How wonderful it would be that he would be the only creature to have her. And he could do it again and again and again. Perhaps give her the surgery, make her virgin again so he could rip that from her all over again.

She brought her bloody fingers to her mouth, and, staring hard into his eyes, licked them. Her eyelids fluttered with the new energy his blood gave her.

"Yes, my lovely. That's it. Do you feel the blood on your tongue?"

"Your name."

"Huh?" Dag wasn't sure what she was asking.

"You have a name. I want to speak it to you with your blood on my tongue. I want to kiss you while I moan your name."

He arched back and looked down on her, cocking his head to the side. He quickly surveyed the room, half thinking perhaps she was speaking to someone else. He felt her heartbeat double-tapping his chest in a most unusual rhythm.

Her tongue swiped a pinkish swath across her upper lip. He could see his blood covering her teeth and gums. She did not blink. Her deep blue eyes seemed to go midnight on him. Her lips began to form a word.

"More."

Dag felt his erection falter and then wither completely. She was not afraid of him. Perhaps it had been a mistake to let her taste him.

"More," she whispered again. She scratched across his buttock again. The right side of her lip twitched up in an involuntary reflex. She dug deeper. He found himself sighing into the pain. His dick responded, pressing against her thigh, begging to claim her.

Her fingertips, covered in blood, painted her own lips, then reached up and touched his. She pulled his head down to her and moaned as their flesh touched. Her tongue found one of his fangs and impaled itself. He felt drops of her blood cover his tongue. Her little core arched up against his cock. She whimpered, and he found he loved the sound of her submission. Her total submission.

He was used to the fear, the certainty of death in their eyes just before he took their lives away from them forever. Their violent, terrified thoughts fed his need not only for their blood, but also for the depth of their despair, their fear. This little one was giving herself to him, *willingly*.

He brought his hand up to her face, expecting it to feel plastic, or porcelain, or something not real. She had wispy strands of hair at her temples where the golden curls were unruly. She bowed her forehead into his palm as if she needed the blessing of his touch. She rolled her head to the side and exposed for him her strong jugular vein.

You are virgin. Are you virgin to the bite?

I am yours. He tensed as he heard her reply in his own head. *Take me. Taste me. Master.*

His fingers smoothed over her soft, creamy neck. He licked her on the vein that rose up to the surface. She sighed. *Take me.*

His shaft was thick and pulsing. He had never wanted to be inside anyone this bad during his miserable hundred years of vampiric life. He reached under him and drew her right leg up and over his shoulder. He angled himself at her opening, forcing the head of his cock just inside. She struggled to accept him.

She was so tight he had to force himself deep inside her. He felt the skin protecting her virginity give way. Her eyes glazed over and she rolled her head back, raising her neck to his mouth. He penetrated all the way to the hilt, splitting her insides as he forced his way into her narrow channel. And then he bit down on her neck.

The sweet elixir that was her life's blood covered his tongue and continued down his throat. He brought his fingers up and entangled them in her golden locks, pulling her head up and over. He sucked as he dug himself deeply in her trench.

Dag. Say it. My name is Dag.

"Dag. Fuck me, Dag. Come inside me. Take me."

He had never heard a woman say his name before. He'd been called devil, other names that thrilled him. But never before had he felt pleasure hearing his own name spoken by the bloody lips of his sexual conquest.

She began to shake. He had drained much of her. Her skin was cool. She was at the point where, if he continued, she would be dead to him. Truly dead. Her lifeless body was the vessel he wanted to spew his seed into. His guttural moans shook the windows.

After several minutes, she lay there with her eyes staring off to the side, with practically no pulse or signs of breathing. Her skin was turning a light shade of blue. Bloody saliva dripped from the corner of her mouth.

Her sacrifice had moved him. Suddenly, he didn't want to be done with her. In a totally selfish mood, he used his fang to slit his own wrist and placed it to her lips. She did not respond. Her blue skin was turning purple.

Drink. Drink my blood.

He first felt the tip of her tongue trace the gash he'd made in his wrist. Then her lips puckered and formed a seal around his wound and she sucked. Immediately her color changed. Her breathing started in a rattled rhythm, then dark and deep. She rolled her head back on the pillow and stared into his eyes. Her fingers, still covered in his blood, laced behind his ear. His shaft shuddered inside her and she closed her eyes, then opened them again as she moved against him.

For the first time in his life, he wanted to give a woman pleasure. This woman, who had given herself to him freely. Of her own will.

She was putty for his soul. To do with whatever he wanted.

She suddenly became the most important thing in his world.

Chapter 6

Dag told his men the little panhandler was dead and that he'd been interrupted by a cell phone call. It was partly the truth, anyway. He was going back inside to tidy up, and then they'd go run their errand, he told them.

"You want us to clean up?" The one with the thicker brow and thinner forehead asked as he drooled over himself. Dag knew the cretin liked fresh kill, as it would be the closest thing he would ever get to a warm-blooded human female lover. And the dark vamp was cursed with more than the Neanderthal forehead; he also exuded the mind-numbing smell. Some said it was like fermented cabbage, or some shit humans liked to eat with their tofu.

On the phone, his watcher had reported a possible lead from a bookseller in Prague. He had work he needed tonight to prepare for a possible trip.

Dag looked into the bathroom mirror just before he stepped into the shower for a quick one. The towels were rough and cheap, and he made a mental note to bring some of his own next time. Cheap motels were great for anonymity, but not so good for the accommodations. But it had always been too risky, especially since the purge was nearly upon them, to bring mortals to his own inner sanctum and his own bed. Maybe it was time to change that.

He left his phone number for the blonde. He figured that once her head cleared and she stopped her vomiting—something he didn't like to watch but which always occurred when he created a new vamp—she'd decide to try out her new powers. Dag hoped she'd use him as her guinea pig. Was looking forward to it. If he was right about her, she'd know that no one else would do. She'd find him like a homing beacon on a drone.

The drapes were shuttered tight. The door scraped on the ageing step sill. One last look at the lovely, sleeping lady, who had begun to pink up quite nicely, lying with her legs spread, a sexy little trickle of blood coming from her upper thigh. Her breasts heaved, covered in his blood, or hers, when he'd devoured them, sucked them and covered them with his scent to claim her. He could make her come with just one finger, placed anywhere now. And that electrified him.

He sighed and closed the door behind him. Forcing his fangs back up into his gums, he licked his lips one last time, and felt the lurch in his trousers.

It took a minute before he could look at his two dark cohorts. He didn't want them to see the satisfied lust in his eyes, or that he wasn't nearly done with her. It was God's cruel joke, this miracle that made it so she would regenerate herself, mixing the best of both worlds: her human side, which was retreating in surrender, and her new vamp side, which was commanding her body to change. In this half-changed state, the lady would be an absolutely stunning meal, and the fuck of a lifetime.

In the old days, before the responsibility of Coven Leader had be-fallen him—well, being totally honest, before he'd murdered his boss and maker—he'd had long evenings of sex and orgies. Now duty called. It was the one thing he regretted and hadn't considered before he took that momentous step.

He thought about *The Book of Spawn*, the "Bat Book," his mentor had called it. There were things in that book that could end his race forever, and give dominance to the Golden Vampires he was hunting down and killing daily. Since he had no intention of giving up his existence without a fight, that book had to be found and eliminated. Much as he wished he could spend time exploring the blonde's beautiful body, scoring it, mutilating it and watching the miracle as she regenerated, the future of his power and dominion over the world for all eternity was at stake.

Even a world-class piece of ass like hers wasn't worth that. If he succeeded, he'd have centuries to enjoy himself later.

After he got rid of all the Goldens and their offspring. After he completed his mission.

Chapter 7

CARA AWOKE TO the sound of a car horn blaring. Checking the clock, she realized she had overslept and missed church. Her head ached, as if she'd been drugged. Had someone slipped her something in her drink last night?

She felt as if she was exhausted from staying up all night making love. The feel of a new relationship burned in her belly. As though she'd been intimate with him. As though he'd seen her naked, seen her full of the hot pleasure that was her vivid dreams. And he wanted more.

No. I slept alone. Though she looked around her bedroom, she found no evidence that he had been there last night. She discovered her sex was swollen and sensitive when she stroked herself and discovered she was wet with her own desire. But no man had penetrated her last night. She'd been alone with her naked fantasies.

Cara ripped herself free from the bed and showered. She put her hair in a clip and wore her tightest pair of jeans with a small, pink long-sleeved top. She applied her makeup fast, adding some sparkles to her eyelids and pink cherry lip-gloss.

Just in case, she thought as she smacked her lips together to spread the creamy glitter lip gel.

She was starving and parched for some orange juice and decided to visit a popular bistro she knew was open for Sunday brunch. She found a corner table in the shadows, ordered eggs and French press coffee and settled in to listen to Brazilian love songs and read one of her vampire romance novels.

The hair at the back of her neck and forearms tingled as she read a steamy scene of blood and sex. The vampire hero became the man she met last night. He was the one biting her own neck as she writhed under him.

"Cara?" a female voice interrupted.

Cara had been staring into her coffee, leaning on her book, but not reading, dwelling instead in her own fantasies. She recognized the voice, and looked up with a smile.

"Valerie. Sorry. I was pretty engrossed in this book." Cara held it up to show her friend.

"Hmmm. Let me see that," the redhead demanded as she pulled it out of Cara's hands and began reading where she had left off:

"His thick cock thrust upwards, impaling her with his will to possess every inch of her body. At last she felt the bite on her neck, as he took from her what she had never given before. Her blood. And with it, he took her heart. Completely." Val fanned her face but remained standing in front of Cara's table. "You'll have to lend me this book when you're done."

Cara searched the room, making sure they hadn't attracted the wrong kind of attention, and smiled. "At this rate, that's liable to be tonight. There's sex in every chapter."

"My kind of book," Val answered. "You sure you won't give your friend a little priority claim? I promise to return him in the morning."

Val meant the hero in the book, but Cara felt possessive of the arms and eyes of the man she met last night.

"He's mine," she said and grabbed her book, placing it in her backpack. "Come, sit with me. I'm buying." She motioned to the chair and Val eagerly accepted.

"Thanks." Her friend leaned her chin onto her laced fingers and searched Cara's face. "You have glitter on your forehead. You went to that party last night with Johnny."

"Yes," Cara said as she blushed and searched the tabletop. A waiter took Val's order and afterwards Cara continued. "It was a blast."

"You and Johnny?" Val's face revealed a mock frown as she tilted her head to the side, watching Cara's reaction.

"No. He's all yours, if you want him. We're just friends. You know that, Val."

"I've seen the way he looks at you."

"Not gonna happen." Cara decided not to reveal what Johnny had offered last night. She just couldn't picture the two of them together. With Paolo, she had no problem conjuring up the fantasy of a sexual liaison.

"So what else happened?" Val was her most persistent and, at times, invasive friend. Nothing was off limits, taboo.

"Just beautiful costumes. Great music. My feet are sore from the dancing."

"You wore sparklies. What did you go as, a Fairy Princess?"

Cara remembered the three faeries swarming over Paolo's large frame in sensual abandon. How his face had twisted in lust as she tried to follow him, get his attention and become part of his sexual dance…

"…and they didn't have anything, but—Cara, are you listening?"

Cara realized she had gone back to her fantasy evening. She shook her head and rubbed her temples. "Sorry, Val. Sensory overload. Something you said made me think of one of the dances. There was this guy…"

"You thought about a hunky guy when I mentioned the feed store? You're worse off than I thought. How long has it been?"

Cara sipped her coffee, embarrassed. "Hmmm?"

"Since you've been with a man." Val was all military now. No way Cara was going to escape the interrogation.

"A year. Two perhaps."

"Perhaps? Are you insane?"

Am I? Am I filled with need and lust?

The answer deep down in her soul, which felt positively ancient this morning, was…

Yes.

Chapter 8

MARCUS WAS UP uncharacteristically early. He'd whistled his way past Paolo's door, heading down to the kitchen, his boots thumping on the carpeted staircase.

Paolo thought again that his brother was a happily married man. And very satisfied. He had a child to raise and a beauty in his bed.

Paolo hadn't slept much, and had spent the hours since dawn half hypnotized by the shadow patterns from the old oak tree outside his window, as they danced across his ceiling in the early morning sunlight.

Every fresh, sparkling morning reminded him how grateful he was that his family heritage was Golden vampire and not that of the dark covens. He felt sorry for the dark cousins and friends of his who were destined to go wandering during moonlight hours and could never experience the taste of sunlight he called Heaven. If he had been a dark, he'd have ended his life a couple of centuries ago.

His restless thoughts got him out of bed to dress and head downstairs to catch up with his brother. He could smell pancakes and heard Lucius's voice prattling along, making idle conversation with their sensational cook. The woman was a seventh generation servant to his family. Paolo remembered every one of her ancestors. They were good as gold to the young vampire children they were employed to attend. Part nursemaid, part teacher, they all were excellent cooks and doted on their charges as if they were their own flesh and blood. The Monteleones had been generous with their kind in return. The relationship between the human and vampire families was cheerfully symbiotic.

"Papa!" Lucius called out. "Look at the mouse ears." He held up his plate as the cook laughed. The pancakes had been made in the face of the famous cartoon mouse, and chocolate chips made eyes, nose and the smiling mouth.

"Perfect," said Paolo. "You spoil the boy," he said to the short, round woman whose salt and pepper braid formed a crown atop her head.

"As is your wish, Signore Monteleone." She nodded to him. "It's been a long time since we've had a child in this house. And now we have two."

"Dad, did you know the baby drinks milk from Anne? She has bottles built right into her chest, right here." He pointed to his own flat chest on the right and then the left. "Do human women do the same?"

Lucius's question reawakened all Paolo's conflicts about the realities of his existence, and his son's. What kind of a boyhood was this for his son, who knew about vampires and humans, and that he was of one kind, for now, and his father belonged to another?

"Of course," he said, as he mussed the top of Lucius's head. "But you must never talk about this in front of non-family, you understand?"

The boy looked up at him. "I know." He was pensive. "But I can talk about it with cook."

"Francesca is like family," Paolo agreed. The little woman quivered with delight at the comment.

Paolo looked outside to find Marcus working on a piece of equipment near an old wooden barn off in the distance. "I'm going to give Marcus a hand, if he'll let me."

"Careful, sir. Your brother has just bought a used tiller. You remember last time he tried to pull it behind his tractor?"

"That's because he forgot to take off the brake on the blasted thing," Paolo said as he made his way out the back.

Stepping out onto the patio overlooking their vineyard revealed one of the most glorious sights of the modern world, he decided. He loved looking at living things. Most the leaves were gone. The grapes were harvested, but the leaves had turned from golden or red to brown with flashes of orange as if they were mourning their loss of fruit, and bled from the wound that took their offspring away to a crusher.

Marcus looked up and wiped his hands on a rag as he addressed his brother.

"I didn't expect you'd be home last night. Rather thought you'd be enjoying the company of a nubile young mortal." Marcus's smile was as wide as the valley before them.

"I enjoyed myself. Nearly had myself a foursome. Lovely little green and silver faeries who worked wonders." He blushed.

"That's a twist, for you."

"Things change," he said as he shrugged his shoulders. "The one I wanted was with another man."

"I imagine you could fix that."

"I have a plan. Going to call her later."

He thought about the card she offered him. She was telling him to find her. She was interested. He adjusted his tight pants.

AFTER THEY WORKED in the vineyard and spoke with two winery field hands, the brothers went back up to the house. Before returning to Lucius, they drank stored blood Marcus had delivered to his wine cellar on a regular basis. Anne had joined Lucius and cook in the kitchen. She was holding Ian, their pink baby boy, who had been named after Anne's father. She cooed at the little face, blew into his eyes and held the pink fist that made a handle of her little finger.

"He's so strong," she said as Marcus came to her side and kissed her neck. "I think he will be stubborn, too."

Marcus nodded. "Going to pay you back, my dear." He threw a glance to Paolo. "We sure gave our folks hell, didn't we, brother?"

"Absolutely," Paolo agreed. "Ian must learn from his cousin here. Lucius has learned to get his way without being stubborn or petulant."

"Wouldn't go that far," cook muttered.

"Hey, what's petulant?" Lucius asked.

"Means you act like a man inside a boy's body."

"No, it means you're spoiled," Anne amended. "But then, you're supposed to be."

Everyone laughed. Lucius remembered something. "Dad, you taking me trick-or-treating tonight?"

Paolo had started to say no, but then changed his mind. "Yes, sir. We'll go out as soon as the sun sets."

Marcus and Paolo shared a look of concern. One of their nephews in Scotland had recently been abducted and murdered by a black vampire coven leader. The man had demanded ransom, and then as the family was formulating plans for the boy's rescue, his body was discovered. The ransom demand had only been a stalling tactic to allow the killers to get away.

Protecting their mortal children was an all-consuming task. The world was getting more and more dangerous for their kind each day. Fewer children were being born to their lineage. The elders were contracting diseases previously believed impossible, and some began to experience aging for the first time in their history. Tainted blood was showing up in their food supply. And vampire blood began showing up in human blood banks, causing a string of mental cases and near zombie-like creatures that had to be eliminated. The balance of power was shifting, and it was becoming obvious the Goldens were in danger of extinction.

All the more reason to protect Lucius tonight. He didn't want his son to become another statistic.

"Do you mind if I use the Jett boys?" Paolo asked, referring to the four brothers of dark vampire lineage who had sworn allegiance to Marcus and his family, and had protected them for generations. They dedicated their lives, foregoing their own families, to remain single and loyal. In exchange for their sacrifice, the Monteleone family bestowed on them great wealth and property holdings all over the world, which the brothers used to support their other siblings' families and their parents.

Three of the brothers were currently residing in California, now that Marcus had an heir.

"I'll have them drop by. You want them costumed?" Marcus had a twinkle in his eye. "Perhaps dressed up as green faeries?"

Paolo shot him a look and mumbled a curse under his breath. "You'd have to watch your own neck if you asked them to do that."

"And I'd deserve it all." He slapped Paolo on the back. "You going as yourself, like you did last night?"

"No. I'll let the Jett brothers be the scary ones. Tonight I'm just going to play the part of Lucius's father."

Chapter 9

CARA WENT TO the college and worked on her lecture for Monday. She scanned her bookshelf filled with novels and books on symbolism and mythology. As she ran her finger along the spines, she stopped at the first edition she'd purchased a month ago and hadn't had time to read.

Pulling it out, she flipped open the pages, carefully peeling over an onionskin that protected a black and white etching of a vampire biting the neck of a buxom young maiden in harem costume. Her expression as she stared back from the page of the old text into Cara's eyes was filled with euphoria. The vampire held her by the waist, two of his long fingers pressing into her right breast. His other arm was entwined with hers as she reached towards heaven.

The book had intrigued her. Printed in 1865, it chronicled the travels of a renowned Scottish theologian who went to India on a pilgrimage to study ancient Hindu texts. Cara had read that this scholar was fascinated with the theory of Divine Coupling he'd discovered through his studies. Before Chapter One of his travels, there was a photograph of the clergyman and scholar. Handsome. Full lips and dark eyes. His curly hair barely submitted to being plastered to his head and brought under control. There was a wild look about him.

Cara turned back to the etching this man had done. The vampire looked just like him.

Self-portrait?

Her fingers idly moved over the leafy parchment-colored page edges. She opened the book to a random spot and began to read.

It was Tuesday when I got to the temple site. Although I had planned on arriving in the morning, I had transportation difficulties and was left stranded for several hours in the heat and morass of the train station. Beggars accosted me everywhere. But with all the filth and death around me in that crowded place, there was a spicy scent to the air, especially as the Sultan's harem literally floated past me as if on a magic carpet. Several sets of dark eyes undressed me from behind veils that covered their entire bodies. One set of blue eyes, heavily lined in black charcoal and accented by three light turquoise stones affixed to her forehead and bridge of her nose, haunted me. I saw those eyes all evening as I lay in my lumpy bed at the hotel, and dreamed of possessing her.

Cara caught her breath.

Possessing her...

That was exactly how she felt. He was possessing her with his eyes, his every action. She wasn't going to go to him. She'd let him come. Willingly, she'd let him come and...

What am I doing?

Angry with herself for wasting her free time, she collected her notes for class, and with the book under her arm, turned out the lights and locked the door to her office.

THE EVENING WAS beginning to go dusk as she finished her dinner and cleaned up the kitchen, turning on the dishwasher. The neighbor directly below her was having a Halloween party, so Cara resigned herself to the likelihood that she wouldn't be able to turn in early. Only residents and their guests were allowed behind the metal gates of her complex, which meant there would be no trick-or-treaters. Accompanied by the whir of dishwasher water jets, she sat at the kitchen table and opened her old book again.

She'd been thrilled when she received the alert that this text was available. There had been several other first editions that sold for thousands of dollars, and which were, on her salary, totally out of the question. But this one came to her for less than a month's pay. Someone from Prague had sent it, wrapped in green plastic bubble wrap. Parts of the leather cover had flaked off in her hands as she'd eagerly unwrapped and fondled the old tome.

Pieces of that leather cover now lay on her table as she opened the book once more and looked for the passage where the author visited the Shastra Temples.

These temple ruins had pictographs of couples engaging in every kind of sexual liaison possible, and several that were anatomically impossible. Cara's studies had turned up pictures like these for years. In fact, she had been quite stunned that some of the earliest temples erected in this region—which was renowned for its ancient vampire stories—were filled with such erotic and practically pornographic reliefs and statues. It was almost like they were built to honor sex. *All kinds* of sex.

Locals had visited the temples to pray for fertility and long life. Children were conceived here until the government passed decency laws that forbade the sacred coupling that had gone on for generations. It was a portion of Queen Victoria's plan to clean up the heathens of India.

Cara read his words.

As I arrived at the first temple, I was struck with the total lack of sound. All along the way I had heard monkeys screaming and birds calling to one another, yet, when I took the stone steps to stand beneath the twenty-foot statue of Jamal making love to his queen, there wasn't a sound. Not even the chirping insects that had serenaded me on my short hike. It was like the world held its breath in reverence for these sacred sculptures, entwined in each other, pleasure filling the faces of the God and his bride.

The relief was quite good, depicting her sexual cave. Jamal's member was fully embedded in her, but a portion of his shaft was exposed and had been touched by countless pilgrims over the years. The granite was as smooth as a woman's breast.

Cara closed the book at the end of the chapter. She discovered her breathing had become labored. She fingered the spine with the gold letters, *Temples of the Vampire, by Alasdair Fraser.*

She jumped as the phone rang.

The caller ID showed it was a local number, but she didn't recognize it. She picked up the phone anyway. "Hello?"

"Carabella?" The sultry Italian accent was unmistakable.

"Paolo." Her heart was racing. Would he be able to hear it?

Stop this, Cara. You are reading too much into his voice, the sound of his Italian accent and your need for companionship.

"I decided I'd take you up on your offer."

"My offer?"

"Yes. To call you. Invite you to lunch. Isn't that usually what happens when a woman gives a man her telephone number?"

He was right, of course, but she hadn't thought it out that far.

As she dithered, she tapped her fingers on the book, and then picked it up, startled to see a yellowed letter fall out. She was having a hard time reading the flowing script. The red wax seal had been broken, indicating the letter had been previously read.

"Cara, are you still there?" he asked.

She put the letter back inside the book and set it down again, pushing it away.

"Sorry. I just ordered this old book and had been reading some passages. I apologize."

"I could call at another time," he offered.

"No. No, this is fine. Again, I apologize."

"No apology needed, but you can make it up to me by agreeing to have lunch with me tomorrow. Are you free?"

Am I free? Am I able to say no?

"I have class that lets out at noon. I could meet you somewhere near the college. I have office hours in the afternoon, two until five."

"Then I shall have you between noon and two?"

She chuckled. "Yes, I supposed you will."

"Excellent. Shall I meet you at your classroom, then?"

"No." Her radar clicked on. Status: elevated. She didn't want him to know where her office was. Yet. "Meet me at the Chowder Grill on Harrison, okay? That's one of my favorites for lunch."

"The Chowder Grill it shall be. Looking forward to it. Good-bye." He hung up.

Chapter 10

"SIDNEY. GOOD TO hear from you at last. You found the book?" Dag spoke into his black cell phone while waving away the cigar smoke coming from two of the three seats occupied by the hulking dark vampires in front of him. He made an effort not to cough. The squeal of their leathers as they crossed and uncrossed their gangly arms and legs annoyed him. His eyes were irritated but he couldn't let on. That would have shown weakness.

"No, sir. I did not," came the voice on the other end of the line.

Dag sat up and immediately the front row did as well. All three sets of size eighteen shoes slammed onto the concrete floor in unison. It felt like a small earthquake. Dag's eyes were unwillingly drawn to the hole the size of a silver dollar that had been cut from one shoe belonging to the vamp in the middle, revealing a battered big toe with a black curling toenail extending out from the flesh like the horn on a ram.

"So where the hell is it?" Dag demanded.

"He says he sold it."

"Well, ask him again, and this time, make sure he understands he'll lose a body part."

There was silence. Dag knew he wasn't going to like the answer.

"I…I already did that, sir."

"Well then kill his wife, in front of him."

"Did that, too."

"His child then!"

"Yes, and their pet dog before the boy."

"Fuck me." Dag wanted to kill someone. He eyed all three of his comrades, very slowly. They stared back at him, and only the one with the toe problem squirmed, moving back and forth and scratching his ankle. Dag took a deep breath and then let it out. No sense getting upset over a lowly bookstore owner and his family.

"Sir?" Sidney squawked on the line.

"I'm thinking, damn you. This will cost you, Sidney."

Dag could hear water running and realized it was the sound of someone peeing in his pants. No doubt Sidney had been smart enough to call his paramour first, telling her to disappear before he made this call. Dag would find her, if he had to.

"Sir, I think I have a way to find out who bought the book. He uses a book selling service online. I'll have to get the information from the company who actually deposited the funds in his account. Take me, oh, maybe a couple of days, tops." Sidney's words were wavering. Dag heard the heart pounding in the man's mortal chest.

"*One* day. You have only one, then I come and eat you, and everyone you know." Dag flipped his phone shut with a snap of the wrist.

Two of the onlookers stared into the eyes of the third dark vampire. Did they think he was so stupid he didn't know that the third dark vamp was Sidney's halfling son? A vampire/human son of the man he'd just threatened to torture and destroy? They scooted their chairs away from the young vamp, and Dag smiled.

There would be time enough for killing, getting even. He had an errand he wanted them to run first.

Chapter II

PAULO WATCHED LUCIUS climb the wooden steps to the white gingerbread house on Johnson Street. At least that's what Lucius had called it. Paolo agreed that the ornate Victorian trim did look like frosting on a wedding cake. In San Francisco they called them Painted Ladies. Here in Healdsburg they were sparkling jewels of a bygone era. Summerhouses for the San Francisco elite during the latter part of the 1800's.

A young, beautiful witch with long flaxen curls, about Lucius's age, greeted him at the door with a plastic jack-o-lantern and deposited a healthy handful of candy into the brown shopping bag he had colored at school on Friday. And she gave him a smile that Paolo knew Lucius could not appreciate just yet.

Paolo saw the Jett brothers leaning against a Jeep, whispering to each other. He nodded to them, but didn't get a response. He knew they preferred a racier detail than watching a lone mortal child trick-or-treating with his vampire father. It wasn't personal. It was just boring.

He thought he might release them early to go do whatever it was that they did at night. They weren't celibate, and were known to love women, yet he wondered how much sex, blood, beer and pool they could consume in one evening if they had the night off.

Or, maybe they never had the night off. Paolo had never asked Marcus what the arrangement was.

Lucius had squeezed through an overgrown hedge in front of a dark house next door.

"Hey there, Lucius. Light's not on. That means…"

The front door swung open and a tall, dark female vamp stood in the candlelight of her front room. Heavy blackout curtains were draped over the windows, which had made it appear that no one was home, or that they didn't wish to be disturbed.

Paolo watched the Jett brothers whip to attention and trace right up on the porch to stand guard next to the boy.

She looked them over like they were two enormous pieces of black licorice. Their leather pants showed bulging muscles, and no doubt they had a wild man-scent that charmed her in that dark way. Paolo didn't like the animalistic behavior and hair trigger of the darks. There wasn't anything human or soft or familiar about any of them. It was all force and instinct. It was the part of him as a vamp, although a Golden one, that he despised the most.

"Well, I got me a little boy and his friends. I'll give the boy some candy, but you three can come in for a while, if you'll trust your little charge to the night," She said it as she began to unbutton her black dress.

Lucius was staring at her chest with his mouth open. Lionel Jett grabbed her arm and twisted it behind her, which released her left breast to full visibility. Even Paolo had to admit it was a thing of beauty. But the Jett boys were unmoved.

"Save it, Drucilla. We're correcting the boy's mistake."

"You hear that, young prince?" she said to Lucius, as she wiggled against the Jett bodyguard. "He dares to call you a mistake. I sense a bit of Maya flowing in your veins. Where, pray tell, is your delicious father?"

Lucius started to turn and point to Paolo, but the brothers shoved the vamp inside and picked the boy up, instantly transporting him halfway down the block.

Paolo walked quietly down the sidewalk toward them, but when he looked up, Drucilla stood at the doorjamb and smiled in that way Maya used to, like she had all the secrets and would use them to destroy you. He was relieved to discover his dick did not respond. She toodled with her fingers. He could feel her eyes follow him down the street.

It bothered him for the rest of the evening, how the presence of fearless dark vamps here in California was infringing on the idyllic life they used to have. Encounters like these were more frequent. Everyone in their family had noticed. The darks appeared to be picking a fight, or preparing for war.

He wasn't afraid of war, since it took a lot to cause his death. But war always took its toll on the innocent, as it had claimed the lives of the entire older generation of Monteleones. The mortal women who loved Goldens risked their lives every day by doing so.

And so did Golden children.

MARCUS WAS IN the study when Paolo got home with Lucius. The Jett boys took off on their Harleys.

"Straight to your room. Go shower, and I'll come in to read you a story in a bit," he said to his son. With the sound of little footsteps attacking the wooden staircase, Paolo strolled to the open door of the study to consult with his brother. He closed the door behind him.

"Something wrong, brother?" Marcus said as he frowned and looked up from his ledger.

"How well do you know the Jett brothers?"

"Almost as well as you. We spent a lot of time together while you were off in the New World getting yourself serially married."

A flash of anger overtook Paolo and he let his brother see it.

Marcus got up and embraced him. Paolo held his arms straight at his sides. "Those were unkind words, and I apologize. I never understood your decisions, but then, I never spent any time trying to. That's my fault. Not yours."

"It's not anyone's fault. I merely sought a different path." Paolo stepped back and out of the embrace. He twisted the heavy Monteleone ring he wore on his right hand, a ring identical to the one his brother wore. "I should be more used to it. Of course you wouldn't understand."

"Not until I saw Anne that night as a mortal female could I fathom how you could fall for a human woman. But I felt the fating with her that night, even though I didn't smell vampiric blood. Even though I hadn't tasted her, yet."

Paolo nodded at the small acknowledgement from Marcus, and turned to examine the extensive collection of rare books. He thrummed his fingers along the bulging and withering spines. "The woman I met last night studies vampires, can you believe that?"

"Well then, good for you. Although I would warn you to be cautious. She is mortal?"

Paolo nodded. "She thinks they are abominations."

"Ah. I suppose you'll go about changing her opinion, then?"

"I'm thinking I won't tell her anything."

"Well, that's your choice. Probably best. No need to breathe a word to have a pleasurable accommodation, is there?"

Paolo's nostrils flared. Fire burned in his gut. He normally would have been overcome with anger, but the thought of seeing her tomorrow kept him thinking about what she would look like, smell like, taste like. If he had to lie to have that opportunity over and over again, he knew he would.

I am a wretch. Not worthy of this noble family's name.

Marcus came over and stood squarely in front of him. "What in the devil's gotten into you, Paolo? You are not yourself."

Paolo fingered a frayed burgundy book with gold lettering. How many of these books had his mortal father read? How many times had he read them, looking for answers? Looking for a path?

"I feel a swelling in the dark vampire covens. They are everywhere now. We even saw them tonight when Lucius was trick-or-treating. I was most grateful for the Jett brothers."

"Where was this?"

"Johnson Street. You know the house next to the one Lucius calls the Gingerbread House?"

"No. I do not know it."

"There was a dark vamp there who knew Maya, or at least said she did."

"I can see how this would distress you."

"Not sure what would have happened if the brothers hadn't been there. Is the world changing so fast we cannot stroll down a dark street without worrying about them using the opportunity to prey on the most vulnerable of our kind?"

Marcus was deep in thought.

"You obviously trust them—the brothers, I mean," Paolo added. "What if they aren't enough?"

They looked at each other the way they used to when they were reaching their age of decision. Marcus had always been sure he wanted to turn. Paolo waited until the last minute, and had been looking for a sign their other siblings convinced him was never going to come.

In the end, Marcus had waited for Paolo, both brothers taking the step the same day. They spent the sunlight hours watching their skin turn, watching the changes take hold. By nightfall they were completely turned and starved for blood, and for sex. They set out together to satisfy both urges until morning of the next day.

Paolo had spent the next day alone, in bed, in complete despair, sure he would spend eternity in hell.

They heard a soft knock on the door. Marcus opened it to see Lucius standing there in his Batman pajamas with a book under one arm.

"What are you reading, young prince?" Marcus didn't notice Paolo's gasp, but did see Lucius' eyes expand. "Did I say something wrong?" He glanced between Paolo and his son.

"That mean lady called me a prince, too," Lucius blurted. "I could tell she doesn't like children, and she showed me her fangs. Nice ladies don't do that."

"She's the one I was telling you about," Paulo whispered to Marcus.

Marcus knelt in front of the boy. "Well, we have very good security here. You are under my protection. And your father is one of the strongest men I know, Lucius."

The boy nodded and collapsed into Paolo's embrace. Marcus stood and again the brothers shared a look.

It was time for bed and the story Paolo had promised. He set his sights on making sure the rest of the evening went off without a hitch, that Lucius could fall safely asleep in his bed without a care in the world.

He knew he and his brother would be up half the night talking about the dark days and the even darker ones arriving very soon.

Chapter 12

CARA POINTED TO the eastern bulge on the map of India. The overhead projector purred. Heat from the lamp wafted up to her face, making her perfume bloom. She'd worn a low-cut, fuzzy sweater and had added some cologne between her breasts.

I'm way too young for a hot flash. But that's exactly what it felt like. And the experience was pleasurable, not embarrassing. No mistaking the signs of what she recognized as pure lust, unadulterated animal attraction. She couldn't wait to see the dark man she was meeting today at lunch.

"It was here that Fraser did extensive studies on the temples in the Sind. Being a man, he was fascinated with the harem women there, especially one blue-eyed beauty whose name we do not know." She looked up as her class chuckled. She couldn't see their faces, but noticed the projector light reflecting off the glasses of some of her students.

This was always part of the story classes loved the most. She removed the map of India and replaced it with a cellophane page of text, adjusting the focus so the class could read along with her on the white screen.

"I had heard stories about British officers marrying Indian women and fathering children. Often these daughters came to no good end, as they stood between the thresholds of two cultures. They were dark-skinned beauties with blue eyes. They were not considered British, although they were British subjects without rights. Their mothers could find no place for them in India, and unless they married a Halfling, one of their own caste, they were reduced to becoming the pleasure things of the Sultans and wealthy families. But Indian society hated them. They

were a scourge, a reminder of a failed policy of colonialization, hypocrisy."

The room was silent. Carabella continued. "I was introduced and allowed access to one harem of the great Sultan scholar, Martam Vishnu, who had been tutored in the classics by a teacher from my birthplace in Scotland.

I was allowed to study at will. I read scrolls that were nearly 1500 years old. I began reading about the vampires of the Sind for the first time, in documents dating back to some 300 years A.D. The temples at Shastra were conceived at that time. A whole village was planned, and may have flourished there. Very little of that civilization remains, except for some of the precious writings, and the temples.

I found the writings to be fascinating, sensual, and certainly erotic. I was taken aback that they worshiped a blood lord who ruled over their kin. It was rumored that he could raise the dead. He could also cure any number of sexual problems, especially lack of desire on the part of the woman."

Carabella looked up and switched on the lights. There was a groan from the class.

"Have to save something for you to look forward to in Wednesday's class. Until then, write a five- to ten-page essay as though you were this explorer Alasdair Fraser. Go on your own private journey. What would you find? What would you write about?"

"Are we supposed to do research?" a student asked.

"You should probably ask a girl out for the first time, Kevin," someone chimed in and the class burst into laughter.

"Only into your own psyche. That's all the research I want you to do," Cara told her class with a smile.

"That's going to be a scary place, Ms. Sampson," one student shouted out.

"Well, do your best, then. Borrow someone else's fantasy," Cara answered. "Remember, this isn't real. Vampires aren't real. But just pretend, if they were, how would you go about doing your own research. What could you find?"

The class spilled out, one by one. Cara collected her things and slung her computer case over her shoulder, heading to the parking lot.

HE WAS SEATED at a table near the rear of the restaurant, in a corner. The Monday lunch crowd was never a large one. She'd forgotten how tall he was, so when he rose to his feet when she approached, it startled her. Her shortness of breath made the room seem to spin. He wore a citrus and spice combination cologne she didn't recognize, but instantly loved, almost as though it was laced with pheromones.

"Thank you for coming," he said without touching her. Her hand had started to wander out in front of her, so she diverted it to remove her jacket.

"It's self-service. Everything is very good here," she said trying to calm her nerves.

"What can I get for you, then?" He moved along the wall and brushed past her on his way to the counter. The glancing touch warmed her skin and she felt her cheeks flush.

"Chicken Caesar salad. I'm afraid that's what I order every time."

"And to drink?"

"What are you having?"

"I was having a glass of red wine. They have a very good Merlot."

"Um…too soon for me. I'll have an iced tea."

He motioned to the chair in front of her. "Please. I will be right back."

She felt him looking at her while she heard him ordering her food. Though she was facing the back wall, she had the sensation that his gaze covered her in a thin, sensual veil. It felt like she was protected as well as being held in a golden cage. She closed her eyes and wet her lips. She remembered the moment at the ball when he had run his finger down her cheek and over her lower lip. She could feel it all over again right now.

"Your food, Carabella," he said as he leaned very close and whispered in her ear. The feel of his warm breath on the side of her face brought her gently out of her trance. One hand rested on her shoulder, and the other offered a plate of crisp romaine covered in slices of chicken breast and grated Romano cheese.

He sat across from her and raised his wineglass. She raised her iced tea and sipped, dropping her eyes. But he did not.

"You aren't eating?" she said.

"My schedule's been hectic. I ate something earlier. Sorry."

She shrugged her shoulders and breathed in deeply to gather herself. She picked up her fork and began to dig into the salad. He was leaning back, tipping the wooden chair, and smiling right at her.

"Have we met before?" she asked between bites.

Whatever are you doing? Where did that come from?

"No. I think I would have remembered." After a brief pause, he added, "Why do you ask?"

"It's just the way you…I don't know. You act like you know me. Like there's some joke I'm not privy to."

His face dropped the smile and he adopted a serious tone. "I'm not joking with you. And I'm sorry if I make you feel…uncomfortable."

"No, it's just me. I spook easily."

"No doubt due to the dark creatures you study all the time."

Cara had to agree he was right. "My friends say I find conspiracies behind every corner, mysteries everywhere. Drives them crazy sometimes."

"But it's what you love."

It was a strange thing to say, but again he was right.

He leaned forward, resting his elbow on the table, and continued. "Studying mythology and symbolism makes you seek out and notice the unexpected, and things that can't be explained easily. Like vampires."

"Exactly."

"But you don't believe they exist."

"God, no." Her hunger evaporated. "I'm going to take this home and have it for dinner." She got up and requested a take-home box. After the server left she transferred most of her salad to the cardboard carton. "I'm more thirsty than hungry right now for some reason."

He nodded.

Cara drank some of her iced tea and crunched on the ice chips. Placing the box and her plate to the side, she leaned onto the table and asked him, "So, what did you think of the ball?"

"It was wonderful. The first one I've been to in many years. I've missed them. The costumes were...over the top."

Cara laughed, thinking about some of the outfits. "I'd say you have a fondness for little green faeries."

"I admit to it," he said with his hand to his heart. He leaned toward her. "But my fondness for angels is unequaled."

Cara could feel the blush coming on, and suspected the top of her chest was covered with blotchy red marks. The centers of his eyes took on an iridescent coppery glow, as if small bonfires resided there. He dropped his eyes to her heaving chest and she allowed herself to be admired. When their eyes connected again, something was understood between them.

What is this?

"I'd like to hear about your studies, Cara. May I call you Cara?"

"Please. Well, I became interested in the myth of the vampire because of the symbolism. They represent the ultimate alpha male figure. Strong. All-powerful. Dominant and controlling. Immortal. The ultimate bad boy you wouldn't want to bring home to meet your mother."

"Interesting. Go on."

"Women read romance novels today because they are looking for the hero in their fantasy life they would never find in real life."

"And you think that's wrong?"

"Of course not. I read romance novels all the time, especially paranormal romance, with vampire heroes."

"For pleasure?"

"Yes."

"And so you began studying them?"

"Well, no. I am new to reading romance. Probably a good thing, too, or I would have never made it through college. Hard to tear me away from my favorites."

"You like your alpha males."

"Love them."

"And do you have alpha males in your real life?"

It was a very personal question and it brought her up short. She grabbed for her iced tea, swallowed heavily and averted her eyes. With her forefinger, she traced the beads of vapor on the outside of her glass of tea. He was very still, awaiting an answer.

"I think the answer to that would be no," she said to the top of her glass.

He squirmed in his chair, recrossing his long legs, tilting slightly back again. "Tell me more."

"About my studies or about alpha males?"

"Whatever you want to tell me. Tell me something I wouldn't think to ask you."

Another strange question. His proximity made it so she couldn't respond to the alarm bell sounding somewhere. It was like her body wanted to, but couldn't for some reason.

"I've recently discovered some books by a 19th century Scottish theologian and scholar. He claims to have located the first written recordings of vampire myth. He found evidence of stories of raising the dead, giving life. Sort of like what we read about in novels about a turning."

"Vampires turning humans. Into vampires."

"Yes. Only this clergyman claims there was a group of people who worshiped and studied these myths shortly after the time of Christ. He wrote that there were people who practiced these black arts, but also practiced what he calls the *Divine Coupling*. Like there's some blood mating ritual."

The smile had erased from Paolo's face. Cara knew she'd lost him again.

"I'm sorry. You asked me to tell you something I wouldn't have normally, and I can see this was a mistake."

He was watching her fingers move up and down her iced tea tumbler. "Couldn't these texts be explained away as just a healthy curiosity in sex? It has been something men and women have worshiped and studied for centuries," he finished.

"No. Well, maybe for others, but that's not why I'm interested in it. If it's true, he may have stumbled on the secret to immortality. I don't think it was about the sex. It was about living forever, and dealing with living forever. What does one do when one lives forever?"

"He drinks port?"

She smiled, glad he wasn't taking her seriously. It didn't hurt her feelings in the slightest. "I keep wondering what sex would be like after having a thousand years of it. Maybe the temples were built, the religion of the divine coupling was created, to fill the needs of a bored society. Maybe some of them didn't want to live forever, and that was a problem for them."

"Why do you say that?"

"Because I think they lost their immortality. On purpose. Chose to be mortal. That's why they and most of the evidence of their civilization disappeared."

Chapter 13

PAOLO HAD NEVER been curious about the origins of his species, which was odd, since he loved mysteries. Perhaps he was unsure what he'd find if he dug too deeply. He assumed vampires, both dark and golden, had always co-existed with the human population. But many of his kin had lived centuries, longer than his three hundred years, and could see changes occurring in their vampiric DNA. New children were born with special powers. Certainly there were breeding oddities forming when a dark and a golden vampire mated. Exceptions were occurring at an alarming rate.

He searched what he had been taught. He'd been a gentleman scholar, in the classical sense, almost three hundred years ago, growing up in Tuscany. But what fascinated him for most of his life was *human* nature. Paolo knew he wanted to be mortal—be and live life as a human—even with its brevity. It was these mortals he befriended, drawn like a moth to the flame. Once he had accepted the turning, he never could really *be* human again, even though he walked amongst them as much as was possible.

To idle the time away, he focused on amassing wealth, something he did very successfully, and tried to live as "normal" a life as possible. He guarded the secret of his vampire genes, and was a dedicated husband to his mortal wives. In the end, though he tried very hard, he failed miserably.

Could someone have discovered the apex? When their immortality began? He also wondered if these early vampires were dark or golden.

Or was there a difference at the beginning?

He was fascinated.

"Where have you gone?" she asked him, and he realized he'd been daydreaming.

"I'm enchanted with your story, Cara. I've never heard it before." It was the truth.

"Well, at this point that is all it is, a good story. But I just feel like there's something to it. My classes are the way I pay my bills. But what I'd rather do is research full time. I haunt libraries like some haunt bars."

They both laughed. It felt good to see her smile. It seemed to bring out the sun in the room.

"So this is what you do with your free time?" he asked.

"Pretty much. I have to force myself to get out and do something decadent, like going to that costume ball."

"Where you meet a mysterious gentlemen dressed as the creature you study."

"Exactly. Like it was fated."

She was smiling, shaking her head from side to side and looking down at the table. Paolo wanted to take her in his arms and cover her body with kisses. He consciously toned down the glamour, releasing her reluctantly. But then he couldn't help it. His soul needed warming.

Come to me, Carabella. Show me you have interest and I will fulfill your wildest fantasies.

She was making figure eights with her forefinger in the water spot from her iced tea. The design was flowing, sensual. Curved, and that point she seemed to linger on where the two rings touched and crossed over one another. Unexpectedly, she looked up into his face and he felt her need. It wasn't a glamoured attraction. It was coming purely from her.

"Tell me about yourself, Paolo."

He sat up straight and laid his forearms on the wooden table, sliding them over so that his palms rested on her fingers. "Gladly," he said as he gently squeezed her hands. He waited to feel any hesitation on her part. There was none.

"I'm from an old family in Tuscany. Generations of Monteleones have lived all over the Mediterranean, but mostly in Italy." He searched the warmth of her cheeks, down her neck, examining the length of it, and the curve as it connected to her shoulders.

"And?" she asked.

"You must forgive me, but I find you so beautiful, it is distracting."

That brought a flush of blood to her face. She jerked her fingers slightly, but did not remove them from under his large hands. He rubbed the side of her palm with his thumb. Slowly, he brought her hand to his mouth and kissed the delicate flesh of the backs of her fingers, which smelled of jasmine and lavender. He felt her pulse quicken.

"Thank you," he whispered.

"For what?" She smiled through a sudden realization that she'd been blushing, embarrassed.

"For not running away."

She slipped her hands free and dropped them in her lap. He resisted the temptation to glam her as she straightened her spine and averted her eyes. But then she came back to him, her lips slightly open, moist. And she looked at his mouth.

You come to me of your own free will, Carabella. I will not hurt you.

"I, too, am a bit of a loner," he began. "I like dark corners in large rooms, stay to the outside. Don't like to attract attention. I don't have any alpha females in my life, either."

Her face lit up at that.

"You certainly looked like you enjoyed being the center of attention at the ball," she said.

"Faeries. Faeries are always beta. Angels are alpha." He tilted his head to see how these words affected her. She leaned in, putting her chin in her palm, not seeming to notice that she'd planted her elbow in the small puddle of condensation on the table. She finally shrugged, as if unable to give him a comment, her eyes wandering all over his face, down the front of his chest.

"Sometimes I get carried away." He said as he looked directly at her and was rewarded when he saw the blue vein at her neck pop up, as if greeting his hungry fangs. He was filled with desire to taste her, and to mate with this charming mortal woman.

"So tell me something about you I wouldn't ask," she whispered.

"I am staying with my brother and his wife in Healdsburg. They have a small winery there. But I have a home in Tuscany."

"That wasn't a very daring reveal. Surely you can do better than that." Her eyes sparkled with the taunt.

He hesitated, and then answered, "I have never found the love of my life. I am the only one of my brothers who has not found that special someone."

She raised her eyebrows, and waited for more.

"I have tasted wines from all over the world. You might call me a professional taster, but I have no degrees."

"A professional taster of women, too, it seems. Never been close to taking the plunge?"

"Close, yes. Several times. I do enjoy mortal women." His slip-up earned him a frown from across the table. He quickly recovered with a smile, indicating it was a joke, "I identify playing the part of your vampires. The dark loner, brooding type, occasionally bored with my life. I don't attract women who last very long."

It was the truth, and seemed to satisfy her.

"What do you do to them to send them away?"

That was a good question. "Every good fantasy has an untimely death, right? You believed in Santa Claus and the Tooth Fairy…"

"You really believe a fantasy love can't last forever?" she asked, dismissing the childhood references.

"As in immortal?" he asked. He was coming closer to the dangerous edge of a reveal, and he knew she'd rein herself in very soon.

"I mean a love that can last a lifetime," she spoke the innocent words which captured him. He could see this was important to her.

"With all my heart. Yes." He placed one palm on his chest as his other hand wanted to hold hers. But Cara was primly sitting, hiding her hands under the table. He could feel her resolve, a combination of control and desire.

Let me unleash your inner fantasies, Carabella. Let me teach you the pleasures of...

Cara's cell phone blurted out the sound of a car horn. She fished for it from her computer case and answered, "Hello Johnny. What's up?"

Paolo listened to the squawking on the other end of the line. He looked out the window as he heard her assistant's tinny words. "You wanted me to go down to Berkeley to speak to that researcher. Can I bail on the office time if I promise to do it for you this afternoon?"

"Anyone signed up?" Cara asked.

"Well, I'd blocked out the afternoon for our discussion time, so I don't think anyone will be here. I can't go to Berkeley tomorrow, so thought I'd take advantage of the time today. You okay with that?"

Cara looked at Paolo, who was pretending he had no idea the lovely woman in front of him was now free for the entire afternoon.

"I'm fine with that. Leave it marked off. I'll see you Wednesday. Thanks for calling." She ended the call and placed her phone on the table.

Cara's screen saver was a picture of Frank Langella dressed as Dracula.

"Good news?" he asked. He tried not to stare at the actor's picture.

"It seems my office hours have been cancelled."

Paolo took her hands in his. "I've got some excellent thoughts on how we might spend the afternoon. If you're willing."

She stared at their entwined fingers as she allowed her forefinger to rub along his flesh. Her touch sent him into a trance of desire.

"I think I might like that."

And that was all she had to say.

Chapter 14

THE DRIVER TOOK them the back way, up through vineyards in Alexander Valley. Paolo leaned back into the leather seat so he could get a side view of Cara, who was fascinated with the dark limo's interior and sparkling lights. She looked like she was on her first chauffeur-driven ride for her high school prom. She turned and caught him staring at her, but he didn't care. If it concerned her, she didn't show it.

"I like all the colors this time of year," she said, looking out the window at the richness of vineyards bursting with gold and burgundy.

It was true, but the color he liked best was the red of her lips, and her flushed cheeks, and her light pink fingernail polish. He wanted to feel those pink fingers on his flesh, feel the sharpness of her nails digging into his back as he plundered her deeply, claimed her for his own over and over again.

Even though he didn't use glamour, she leaned into him, as he pulled an arm around her shoulder. She sighed and seemed to melt into his frame. Her hot flesh sent warmth to every cell of his body. "I feel absolutely decadent," she whispered. "Have never done this in the middle of a school day."

"Ah. And here I thought it was perhaps the company you're keeping."

She grinned. "That, too."

"Come. We shall celebrate." He leaned forward and opened a glass of port, pouring one for each of them.

"You come prepared."

"Always." He did not tell her he traveled with a case at all times.

"So you had a feeling this would happen?"

"Eventually, yes." It was difficult not to give her the gloating grin he knew would turn her off.

"Eventually? What's that supposed to mean?"

"Like you, I'm a fairly good judge of people."

"People, or women?"

"Women too." *Like I can tell what you are feeling.* He didn't think he would have the gift of mindspeech with Cara, but perhaps could develop it in time. If he was given the time, that is. Paolo could sense her emotions.

He felt her pulse quicken slightly. Her eyes widened and he could hear the little breath she sucked in and tried to hide.

"Bella—may I call you Bella?"

"Yes."

"Bella, you are safe with me. And," he pointed to the chauffer, "we have a witness."

"Behind glass," she said.

"Absolutely, so even your words are safe with me." She was lovely the way her eyes danced in the afternoon sunlight. *For my eyes only. Words for my ears only.*

"This rather reminds me of one of those novels I read. The vampire seducing a mortal woman."

"Hmmm…I thought I was being subtle," he whispered to the top of her head. He was going to say more, but the giggle she gave him as she squeezed herself against his chest sent a spark traveling straight down to his groin.

Was it always going to be like this around her? Her lightness of spirit thrilled him. His fondness for mortal women was driving his delight higher than it ever had been before. So uncomplicated, simple, and with a lack of the darkness he found in vamp women, who liked to dominate and push their power. Sex with them was a tug of war and a near fight to the death. When he was younger, he used to love it. But especially since Maya, he'd lost all desire to bed women with fangs. In between his wives, he'd usually sought the arms of mortal women.

With Bella, he *wanted* to be gentle. He liked the feeling of being bridled.

"Is there anything you want?" he asked as he played with curls falling at the base of her neck. He lightly touched her skin with the tips of his fingers. She jumped like this gesture scared her at first.

Relax.

"Did you just ask me to relax?" She leaned forward and looked back at him with a frown.

Incredible. She'd heard his thoughts.

"As a matter of fact, *I did.* That's very strange. We must have an extra connection." He was barely able to hold back his desire to ravish her with kisses.

"And why did you say that?"

"I felt you were nervous, perhaps." He laughed at how trusting she was. "No, Bella, I'm just making it all up. I had no idea."

That seemed to settle her.

He knocked on the glass as they pulled up to the popular Jim Town Store, a Healdsburg icon. The chauffer opened their door, Paolo helped her alight, and she held his hand as they climbed the old wooden steps of the roadside café and eclectic general store.

"Coffee?" he asked. "You want a cappuccino?"

"Sure."

Overlooking the two-lane highway with the occasional car driving past, she sipped her cappuccino, her gaze far away. He tried not to look, but it was hard keeping his eyes off her face, the soft lips leaving a pink semicircle on the edge of the white paper cup. He wanted everything about her, even the paper cup she would eventually discard.

Enchanting. She is enchanting.

"So tell me," she said.

He didn't know what she meant. "Tell you what?"

"Where are we going? Didn't you expect me to ask you?"

"My brother has a home in Healdsburg. I thought I would show it to you. He and his wife have recently had a baby."

"You're visiting from Italy. For how long?"

"Haven't decided." He fingered the back of her hand as it clutched the cup. "When I'm ready."

She nodded. "What are you here for?"

Very good question. Perhaps to fall in love. To forget. To learn to be a father. To start to live again. "I came here so my son could spend some time in California with my brother and his wife."

"He has been raised in Italy, then?"

"Actually, no. But we do travel a lot.

"I see," she said.

Do you see, my Bella? Do you feel the urgency between us? As if she could feel what he said, she sat up straight. She smiled. Did she hear him?

"So what do you do for a living?" she asked.

"I study human nature."

"A psychologist?"

"No."

"A psychiatrist, a doctor?"

"No. I read. I live. I have the luxury of being a gentleman of means, free to do what I wish, to pursue my interests as I will."

"You sound positively ancient. Johnny warned me about you." Her eyes twinkled as she tilted her head.

He stopped smiling. Some of his mirth was bottled. The pause was pregnant, on purpose. He wanted to see how she would answer herself.

She had blushed. "I don't mean to suggest you're way older than I am. Perhaps a couple of years…"

I like that guess, Bella.

"But I haven't heard anyone calling themselves a gentleman other than in a movie, or in one of my romance novels." She took another sip of her cappuccino. "You have a funny way of speaking sometimes. Like you've traveled here from another time."

He was nailed by her warm brown eyes, caught, as if staked through the heart. He willingly allowed himself to squirm, if it meant she was looking at him. Anything to have her look at him.

"It is my family, my old family roots you are sensing." *That and the way my fangs ache to taste you, to throw up your skirts and take the blood from your upper thigh, to satisfy myself by plunging in and looking at the rapture of your sweet, peach-colored face. I could bring you to heaven and back, if you will allow me...allow me in...*

The glamour had taken hold. Her eyes slightly crossed and she became stiff, motionless and staring straight at him, as if tethered. He was sorry for this lapse, but couldn't help himself. He slipped to a chair next to her, placed his palm under her chin, turned her face toward his as she fell against him. Without knowing if it was right or wrong, he covered her mouth with his. Her soft lips welcomed him.

She turned her body into his chest, her right arm coming up over his shoulder to play with the hair at the back of his neck. She drew her fingers under his ear and along the bone of his jaw, and touched his lips, as if needing to feel the kisses between them.

He whispered words he used to hear in his dreams as a young man. Words of love passed down to him from others who spoke a tongue that was long dead. The incantation sent her pulse soaring. His followed along right behind.

"Bella I need..."

"Yes. I need this, too," she said. Her eyes told him he could have his way with her right here on the table in the Jim Town Store, if he wanted. But he wanted her all to himself.

"I know a place," he said.

"Your brother's home?"

"No. Some place we can be alone."

"Yes." She held his head in her palms and kissed him of her own free will. He could hear the pulsing of the veins underneath the delicate white flesh at her wrists, which were positioned right over his ears. His mouth went to one wrist as he kissed her there, and felt the lifeblood inside her rise up to meet his tongue.

He held back. This would have to be just sex. He couldn't bite her. Not yet. Perhaps not ever. But God in Heaven, the sex would be glorious, and that would have to be enough for now.

Almost lifting her out of the chair, he took her back to the waiting limo. The driver had been asleep in the front, and came round to open the door for them.

"Is she all right, sir?" he asked as he frowned at Cara's flushed face and half-opened eyes.

"She's tired. I'm going to take her to the Stone Creek Inn. You know it?"

"Sure. You need me to call ahead?"

"Please."

"No problem," the driver said as he closed the door. In the privacy of the darkened limo interior, he had her all to himself, for a few seconds.

"Bella, are you okay going with me some place where we can…"

"Yes," she said breathlessly. "Please. I would like that."

He covered her mouth again, his hand finding the thrill of the feel of her nipples budding through her bra. He couldn't wait to have her naked.

The car purred along the curved country road and up a noisy crushed granite driveway to a stone structure with a water wheel turning slowly to the side.

"I will call for you when she feels more like traveling," he said to the driver, who grinned back at him in response.

"Of course, sir. I'll return to Marcus' home, then."

"Perfect."

Inside the reception area he secured a room on the upper floor, one with a view of the vineyards below. Cara was leaning against him, her hands untucking his shirt, her palms finding his chest as she slid them up and rubbed herself against his back.

The clerk was efficient, seeming to take no notice.

"Would you have a bottle of your best port delivered to our room?"

By the time they were at the top of the stairs and had passed the water wheel, Cara had his shirt completely unbuttoned. He was glad there wasn't much of a crowd on a Monday afternoon. They didn't pass a soul.

He unlocked the heavy carved door and stepped inside an over-sized room with a roaring fireplace and huge four-poster bed covered in silk pillows. He turned to see her expression, and was hit with her flying body as she slammed into him and they toppled to the bed.

Chapter 15

CARA WAS BEYOND shame. The need she had for this man—he had called it *urgency* and that certainly was a great way to put it—consumed her like she was a piece of tissue paper that had hit water. She was melting, floating into his rock hard body as he laughed and allowed her to overcome him, not because she was in any way stronger than he, but because he seemed to love watching her have her way with him.

Him.

Who was this man? She knew practically nothing about him, yet she was going to let him see her naked, let him kiss her in places where she ached to be kissed. Like her life depended on it to feed her soul.

She had read about animal attraction between a man and a woman, like an ancient hormonal rule of nature passed down through generations, but she hadn't been close to feeling it. This was…

What? She heard him say something in a language she didn't understand. Some internal memory. She saw torches, and a campfire. She saw the stars over a village lit by candlelight. Not a trace of an incandescent bulb or neon sign anywhere.

"*Amore,*" he was saying over and over again in his mind. He was thinking of that word over and over again.

She loved the feel of his hands as they slid under her skirt, as they smoothed over her bottom. She raised her fuzzy shirt so the tops of her breasts could brush against his hard chest. She held the back of his neck and leaned in to his ear and whispered, "Amore."

He flinched as he heard her speak it. With eyes wide open and full of wonder, he held her face between his long fingers.

"Amore," he said. "Love me, Carabella."

But she heard something else, too.

"Heal me. Make me believe."

He was saying other things as well, but she didn't understand. His thumbs were rubbing against her lips as he held her just an inch from his face. He studied her, with his dark eyes and rich brown hair. Her fingers sifted through the hair at his temples, smooth as silk. She saw the delicious movement of his Adam's apple as it bobbed when he swallowed. She kissed him there, under his chin. Then along his neck, under his ear. Again, she whispered to him,

"Yes, amore."

His groin arched up and she felt his erection—so large she was certain it hurt as she ground herself down on him, rubbing the length of him against her pubic bone.

She removed her fuzzy top and bra in one smooth move, and drank in the look on his face. He was hungry for her. Her breasts overflowed in his hands as he squeezed them. As she gave her flesh to him.

She peeled his shirt over his massive shoulders and stared down at the wonder of his well-defined chest and trim waist. Beautiful. A sculpture of Adonis himself couldn't have appeared more masculine, more luscious. He watched as she partook of the vision that was this man's wonderful body.

She reached for his belt buckle and found he had none. He was wearing old-fashioned pants with filigreed silver hooks and eyes. One by one, she undid them, and slid her cool hands into the darkness to find his sex. She removed his pants and his arousal sprang forth. She could hardly close her hand around it, as its girth was nearly as large as her own wrist.

"Too large, Bella?" she heard him think.

She shook her head from side to side and slowly climbed down his torso, and, while looking up at his face, put her red lips on the tip of his cock. His head fell back into the pillow as he arched to her touch, as the stiffness of his sex grew even further, as she sheathed him with her lips, her tongue, and tasted him.

A flash of golden light blinded her, as if his precum had a psychedelic quality to it. Her body shuddered, convulsed with need. She moaned as he sunk himself deep into her mouth.

"Carabella, mi amore. Carabella, mi amore," he rasped repeatedly as his hands played in her hair, as he pulled her to him, pulled her up so he could plunge his tongue deep down her throat. The musty, spicy taste of his arousal, the warm heat arising from his chest and from the moist warm places in his hair drove her to new heights with every inhaled breath. His taste, his scent—everything was an elixir. The lips of her sex were quivering with desire.

In one smooth move he had flipped her over onto the bed.

"*Your turn,*" he thought.

She smiled her complete compliance. "Yes," she whispered as she followed the arc of her fingers as they traced the shape of his ear. They listened to each other's breathing. She watched his eyes grow darker to almost black.

He lifted her skirt very slowly, slid his long fingers up her thighs to her panties covering her swollen sex. He took forever to slip down the lacy black underwear she'd had the good fortune to wear today. He let it trail along her thighs until he bent one of her knees, slipped the panty over it, extricating her leg. Then he drew the panties down the other leg, watching her face as she waited, her heart pounding in her chest with lust for him.

He deftly slid a hand under her and unzipped her skirt, removing it. She was naked to him now as he watched her breathing, watched the juncture between her thighs and watched the rise and fall of her breasts. Gently he parted her knees and gazed upon her, and sighed.

Let me see your desire, Carabella, he said to her in thought.

She guided his long fingers to her opening, and pressed two of them inside her, arching her back up, bracing herself up so he could penetrate fully. He manipulated his hand, pressing in and out. She heard how wet and hot and swollen she was. He tasted his forefinger, closing his eyes, and when he opened them again, his eyes were jet black, with small flames in the center. His nostrils flared as she saw him press his teeth with his tongue, pushing against his own canines.

He had pressed so hard, a small drop of blood formed at his mouth on one side, as if his teeth had been so sharp he had cut himself. She licked her lips, and looked at the blood. She wanted…

What am I doing? She felt her arms pull him down to her mouth, and she sucked the blood from his cut tongue. Another golden flash overtook her. Every cell in her body sparked with need for the taste of this man.

His eyes were wide. He looked surprised. Had she gone too far? Was this something he didn't like?

But then she was rewarded with a red, closed-lip smile. He kissed her under her right ear and she pressed her neck into him. Just like the mortal women did with their vampire lovers. She wanted him to taste her, bite her neck.

What would it feel like, if?

But then he was down on her chest, kissing first one, and then the other nipple, sucking them, making noises as he played with them and flicked them about with his agile tongue. That tongue that left the promise of things to come.

No man had tasted her sex before. She wanted him to be the first. He kissed her belly button, nipping a sharp pinch that made her jump. He followed this with the laving of his tongue that stimulated her as well as took away the pain of the sting. Inch by inch, he kissed from her belly button to the top of her hairless mound.

"I love hairless women," she heard his thought. She felt her mound swell.

She was grateful she had thought to shave closely this morning. His lip crinkled as he kissed the top of her slit, as he slid his tongue into the cavern there, over her nub on its way to her opening. She was shuddering with pleasure. The room was spinning. He made noise, slurping her sweet moisture, drinking from her, letting her feel his eagerness feeding her own.

She was beginning a slow orgasm that was sure to explode soon. His slow and steady ministrations played her body like an instrument, demanded she feel the intensity of his desire for her.

She didn't want him to stop. She could have spent the afternoon with his mouth on her sex, but at last she felt the cooler room air on her and felt him climb atop her. She noticed he had sheathed himself in a light pink condom, but the burgundy red from his blood-bulging cock still shone through. It looked like he would burst it if he got any bigger. He settled himself between her legs and pressed just the head of his cock into her opening and stopped.

She took in a breath. He was already stretching her. She drew her hands to his buttocks and pressed his groin into her. He resisted, making her pull hard to get him firmly planted all the way to his root, watching her struggle to accept his full girth.

And then he began a gentle, rhythmic in and out movement. He looked down upon her. His face faded and came back into focus as she moaned, closing and opening her eyes. Those dark eyes spoke to her.

"Need this."

Yes. She needed it too. She hoped it would be the first of many, as he pumped her deeply. In between he would stop, she would feel the thrill of how he filled her. He'd kiss her tenderly, licking and sucking at her neck, arching back to watch her face. Just holding him inside her was delicious. Her core began to vibrate as if the flesh of his member gave her flashes of passion. The crescendo of their mating was intensely increasing. She'd never felt so sated, and left so vacant between his powerful thrusts. His voice, deep and low inside his chest, rumbled, making her nipples taught. He was whispering things in a foreign tongue she understood as ancient, a sad litany of need and desire, something overcoming him and consuming him.

She arched back and groaned, and felt him seek her mouth, cover it possessively and take her breath, holding her chest underneath with his huge hands, pressing her breasts into him while pressing his thumbs into her waist at her hips. He rooted deep again and again, setting up a rhythmic tantra as he adjusted his hips to angle with his thrusts, sending her new scitters of pleasure, making her shudder with delight. Their skin made slapping sounds as his movements picked up, as she was sent into higher and higher orbit with every deep stroke into her. She was on the edge of something...

The orgasm hit her hard as he pressed against her cervix, almost causing her pain. The soft folds of her pussy separated and violated as he trembled, whispering her name in raspy tones. She recognized the jerking movements as he was spending into the condom, but it went on for long luscious minutes. The low satisfying rumble in his chest as he spent his last drop made her want him all over again.

At last he collapsed on top of her. She stroked his back, his backside and explored the nape of his neck with her fingers. His scent was like oranges. His skin was sweet and salty on her tongue. She could still taste the remnants of his small tongue injury in her mouth, giving her another little spark as she licked her lips.

What is this? Who is this man?

Most of her sexual partners had not lived up to her expectations, and she found herself actually grateful when the sexual act was over. She cared more about the closeness than the flesh on flesh experience.

But with this man, she wondered if she would ever be able to get enough. She hoped he would recover soon, because she could hardly wait to be penetrated again.

And then maybe again.

In fact, she hoped they could stay naked and stay in this room all night.

No one had ever made her feel this way before. She knew she wouldn't be able to say no to him.

Ever.

Chapter 16

IN THE LAZY afternoon sun she awoke to the sound of the door to the room opening. She smelled the fresh pine logs in the fireplace, and heard them sputter and crack. Paolo walked back to the bed, naked, holding a tray with a bottle of Port and two glasses.

"Time for fortification." He set it down on the bedside table and sat next to her. "Are you hungry, Carabella?" he asked as he stroked the side of her face, and then down her neck to her breast.

His touch ignited the flame that had been burning inside her, pulsing in the erotic dreams over the past few minutes she had slept. Or was it a lifetime she slept?

"Yes and no," she answered as she scanned his massive shoulders, his flat abdomen and powerful thighs dusted with light brown hair. She rubbed her palm over him, seeking the spot between his legs.

She would gladly burn in the look he gave her in return. The longing he held for her almost made her levitate.

"What is this?" she asked.

"This?" he raised one eyebrow.

"This…attraction. I've always thought authors who wrote about this feeling were making it up. I feel wonderful. Alive for the first time in my life. And I don't even know you." She frowned, but continued rubbing over the muscles in his forearm, up his elbow to his biceps. "It's like the more I touch you the more I want you."

He broke eye contact and looked to the side, outside the room to the orange glow of the late afternoon vineyard view. She followed his line of sight.

"Oh, my God," she giggled, putting a hand over her mouth.

He turned, clearly alarmed.

They hadn't closed the drapes. The person delivering the Port had surely seen them.

"Hotel workers learn to be discreet," he said with a smile. He leaned down and with his soft lips barely touching hers, he whispered, "And I wouldn't care anyway. I'd make love to you at a baseball stadium if I had to."

His long, penetrating kiss put her into a dreamy trance. She saw torches again, roaring fireplaces and stone floors. Her breasts needed his hands, and he obliged. Her thighs needed to be kissed by his, and he obliged, sliding his long body into the warm bed.

His hands were everywhere. He kissed her neck, her breasts. He pressed himself against her as he held the small of her back, stroking down her backside along the cleft between her buttocks. In gentle movements he felt her warm sex and, peering into her eyes, he inserted his fingers.

"I love feeling, touching your arousal. Seeing how you come to me so willingly," he said.

It was an odd thing to say, but she found herself liking it. As if he had the power to *make* her want him, but wasn't exercising it.

"It's where I belong," she said in return. "In your bed, your hands on me, your cock deep inside me."

"Yes," he said as he angled his head, slid his knees between her legs, opening them, replacing his fingers with his shaft, rubbing against her swollen lips. He stopped until she quit looking at the headboard. She had arched back to accept him. With their eyes locked in a dream-like gaze she never wanted to awaken from, he entered her.

She could hear her own heart beating in time with his slow, persistent pushing, rubbing against the sides of her sex, filling her, melting her. She raised her knees and placed them over his shoulders, allowing him to fill her deeper. He moaned and pumped her fully, back and forth, like rocking a cradle, closing and then opening his eyes.

"Need this."

"Yes, I need this too," she said. "Mi amore," she said between his strokes, noticing that his eyes had started to water. "I do belong here, with you."

He crossed one of her knees in front of him and stroked her from the side. She continued to roll over to her stomach while he continued his rhythmic movements, pulling her hips up to elevate her bottom, holding and fondling her nub with the hand he held underneath her. He pressed her there. She brought her hands to his and entwined his fingers, felt the root of his powerful cock as it stretched and then buried deep within her peach. She squeezed the veined surface of his shaft when he withdrew, and cupped his balls as he dove in to the hilt.

Deep inside her she began the spasms that took her breath away. She raised herself up on her knees, pressing against him, her head buried in the soft down pillows. She moaned into the cotton fabric, tore with her fingers the soft feathers beneath. Her chest was on fire, her breasts had become engorged. Her peach sucked at him, begging for more.

"Yes. Please. Oh yes, *please*," she shouted to the pillow.

He leaned in and something sharp nicked her neck, which gave her a start. But then his tongue and his lips were there, heightening the delicious feel, turning the stinging pain into something she craved. His lips were sucking her neck, drinking from her.

Like a vampire.

Chapter 17

SHE LOOKED INTO the mirror in the bathroom, alone at last. Raising the glittering glass of port to her lips, she stared hard into her own eyes. She wasn't sure if she wanted to know what was real and what wasn't. Or if it was important. Her imagination had been working overtime.

She angled her neck to dare look at the place where she had felt his lips on her, the sharp stinging sensation, but, other than a reddened area from a deep kiss, there was no wound there. Her forefinger laced up and down the smooth surface of her skin, feeling for a bump, a callus, a…

Bite?

But there wasn't one. Nothing marred the cool surface of her skin. Her cheeks hadn't stopped their flush; her lips were swollen from the claiming kisses he gave and from her pressing against him almost to the point of pain. She pulled up the hair at the nape of her neck and looked at herself again. Her curls fell about her face as she pouted her lips. She felt positively ancient, wicked, and desired as never before.

A gentle knock on the door stopped her daydream.

"Cara, are you okay?" he murmured through the painted wooden door.

"Of course. You can come in," she answered.

He leaned into the doorframe, his dark curls shiny and tousled. His dark eyes wandered from her face, to the pink mounds of her breasts, and down to the juncture between her legs. Just the way he looked at her made her feel like molten chocolate.

He watched as she let go of her curls and they fell about her shoulders.

"Your hair. I love your hair," he said as he stepped in, standing behind her. He kissed her neck as she watched him through the mirror, as she felt him linger on her neck, breathe into her ear and whisper something to her that made her shiver.

"What is it you are saying to me? You put me under some spell with your incantations?"

He raised his face and placed his chin at the top of her head, with the Cheshire cat smile she'd already gotten used to. But not really.

"Guilty," he sighed.

She tilted her head. "Is your brother going to feed us? I am starved."

"We have two choices." He busied himself kissing the back of her neck, and each vertebra down her back. "We can stay here tonight and order room service, or, go to Healdsburg and visit with the family."

The choice was so unfair. She wasn't sure any other afternoon for the rest of her life would ever equal this one. She was hesitant to give it up, or end it with polite conversation of a non-sexual kind.

"I will do whatever you ask of me. Especially if you continue doing that," she whispered as he squeezed her breasts and rubbed his erection up and down the cleft in her behind.

"So willing. So beautiful."

"Can we do both?"

He leaned back and laughed. She turned and faced him, her thighs against his, her mound pressing into his lower belly.

"My dear Carabella. You have school tomorrow, yes?"

"Yes. And I don't require much sleep. I promise."

THEY SHOWERED, SHARING her glass of port. She enjoyed the kisses he scattered all over her, the way his tongue probed her, the way his fingers played in her hair, between her legs, massaged her neck and shoulders. He carefully dried her off like a marble statue of Venus. He would say, "I like this," and kiss her there. He made no mystery of his favorite places on her body.

The driver arrived just at sunset and whisked them by moonlight up the narrow winding road until they arrived at a large house built at the side of a hill overlooking rows of vines.

"All this belongs to Marcus," he said as he spread his hand, illustrating the wide expanse without another house in sight. The stone manor house at the top of the hill was lit with torches that crackled and sputtered up into the night sky.

"Torches. I've been seeing them all afternoon," she said.

"Interesting. I love a big fire."

"It was like I could read your mind. I saw old cobblestones and torches in darkened curved hallways."

"I might have been dreaming of Italy," he said absent-mindedly as he stroked her upper arm. "But you are thinking about our family. I told you we have a very old family, although none of the older ones are alive today."

"Must be what I was dreaming. In any case, I don't want it to end, if it is a dream."

He adjusted her against him again and gave her upper body a squeeze.

At the front door, a young boy waited. Warm yellow light spilled out onto him and the stoop as he stood, holding a very tall man's hand.

The man was a darker version of Paolo, but perhaps a little taller.

"Welcome to Villa Monteleone, Cara," Paolo whispered to the top of her head. The driver opened the door and she allowed him to get out first, then allowed him to pull her hand and present her to the man and the boy.

"Carabella Sampson, this is my brother Marcus Monteleone and my son, Lucius."

The boy was as handsome as his father. He stepped forward with a stiff bow and extended his hand. "Lucius Monteleone," he said, as if there might be some question.

"Nice to meet you, Lucius," she said as she grasped his little hand in both of hers. "Please call me Cara." She stepped toward Marcus and extended her hand, which he quickly took and kissed, just as his brother had done two nights ago at the ball. The way they behaved was identical. She felt herself blush, as if Paolo had touched her himself. "Wonderful to meet you as well, Mr. Monteleone."

"Marcus."

She saw the darker brother give a tiny wink to Paolo and show them the way inside.

The foyer was done in deep red tones. Old tattered and faded flags and oil paintings of long-ago ancestors graced all four of the wallpapered surfaces in the entryway. Paintings depicting hunting trips, exotic animals and castles were scattered here and there. "These are some of your ancestors. No one current, I see?"

"They've been gone a long time."

In the doorway to the kitchen, a beautiful auburn-haired woman carrying a blanket-wrapped baby suddenly appeared. "Welcome to our home. I'm Anne," she said as she reached out and shook Cara's hand firmly.

Cara had never seen such a strikingly handsome family. She was at a loss for words.

"Thank you for allowing us to just pop in on you without notice," Cara said.

"Oh no, the driver told us you would be coming as soon as you were done at the Inn." Lucius piped up. This surprised a chuckle from Marcus, though he worked to stifle it. Cara saw he'd earned a reproachful look from his wife.

Cara felt her cheeks flush. Paolo placed his arm around her waist and squeezed her. The nearness and electricity of his body touching hers was intoxicating and her knees wobbled. She heard a low rumble inside Paolo's chest.

"Lucius was anxious to see his father, and when the driver returned, he naturally ran out to greet him, and was told you two had decided to stay in town *for a while*," Anne's quick explanation was adequate, but Cara felt there was something else she wasn't privy to. "Are you hungry, Cara?" Anne asked as she handed the baby to her husband.

"Yes. Starved," Cara said and stepped closer to the baby. "What a beautiful little girl."

Lucius laughed out loud. Marcus spoke up first, "I'm not going to tell him you said that" He smiled down on her with the same commanding presence Paolo had. "His name is Ian."

She needed to change the subject. "Anne, may I help with anything?"

"Oh, I'm not fussing. We're going very casual and simple tonight" She looked at Paolo, "Paolo, are you hungry this evening?"

"Of course. Haven't eaten in hours." His words were stiff, but he winked at Cara.

"I know, silly question." She motioned for Cara to follow her into the kitchen.

Cara had never seen such a beautiful, grand room. Ornately carved crown molding hovered in the tall shadows above the kitchen cabinets. The ceiling was at least twelve feet above them. Old Italian tile covered the countertops, but the floor was a light hardwood. One end of the kitchen was open to an intimate room with leather couch and a floor-to-ceiling brick fireplace. A two-foot tree trunk was burning on ornate iron grates with dragon's heads on them. Fire flickered in the cut out eyes of the fierce beasts of burden.

Anne was setting out some hand-painted square plates. With the crackling sounds and smoky scent of the fireplace as background, she started to ask the questions Cara knew were coming.

"How long have you and Paolo known each other?" Her nimble fingers were adjusting light green lettuce leaves on the plates, placing one leaf on the small plate Cara knew must be for Lucius. She didn't look up, but when Cara didn't answer right away, she stopped and waited.

"Well, let's see, since day before yesterday."

Anne's face beamed with a warm smile.

"I completely understand," she said.

How could you? "He is rather handsome. I find he has quite an effect on me," Cara answered.

"Yes..." Anne drifted off into a reverie all her own. "The brothers are like that. Women falling all over them, yet, they are discreet, and they choose wisely." She smiled again, and licked her lips.

"How long have you and Marcus been married?"

"About a year, a little longer."

"Was it sudden. Did you—"

"Yes." The look Anne gave her said she was done talking about it. Some divide had opened up a chasm, and nothing Cara knew would be able to bridge it.

Anne took a hot casserole out of the oven with red oven mitts. Smells of bubbling cheeses warmed Cara's spirits. She bent over to look at it carefully, her eyebrows coming to a point on her forehead.

"Macaroni and cheese?"

"Yes. It's Lucius' favorite. He asks for it every night. We humor him when we have guests. Keeps him at the table a little longer." With a spatula, she scooped a square onto each plate. She then added tomatoes and sliced peppers to the lettuce, poured a hand-shaken dressing mix over the top and garnished them with crumbled blue cheese.

"You guys eat a lot of cheese, I see."

"We always have tons of it around. Goes with the wine. And actually, I think it is our biggest source of protein."

Cara looked at Anne's beautiful figure and wondered how she could stay so slim on a diet of cheese. "No fish, other meats?"

"Very little. We're practically vegetarians, although we love fresh eggs and our cheeses. We make many of our own here at the winery".

"I'd have a hard time not devouring a good steak now and then. Don't think I could ever be a vegetarian."

Anne gave her a thoughtful look. "I had an unfortunate experience with some beef liver, got very ill. Ever since then, I cannot stomach meat from animal flesh."

"Ah." It was certainly an odd thing, Cara thought.

"Although, sometimes the boys do enjoy a good barbeque, maybe a couple of times a year, and usually when we're entertaining."

Anne handed Cara two plates. "This one is for you and this is for Paolo. If you would serve them and take your seat, I'd be so grateful. I'm going to check on Ian first, and then I'll join you."

"No problem."

Cara presented Paolo with his plate, and just after she seated herself, he leaned over and gave her a sweet kiss on her cheek that tingled all the way to her sex.

Anne returned to the table. "He's sleeping like a log, which means he will keep us up all night."

Marcus looked brightly at his wife as she seated herself and motioned for everyone to begin.

"No worries, pet. I'll take one shift so you can sleep," Marcus told her.

"He has an appetite like his father," Anne said, and then blushed. "We'll figure it out."

Paolo leaned an arm over the back of Cara's chair, letting his fingers make little circles in the top of her arm. She'd remembered those circles he'd made this afternoon around her nipples, those same fingers.

Her panties were sopping wet already. She thought perhaps she could even smell her own arousal. Turning to face Paolo, with his beautiful tanned face framed with dark curly hair, with his high cheekbones and full lips, his stormy dark eyes, his nostrils flaring—she saw that he understood. He leaned into her as his warm breath drifted over her ear, making her shiver. Then her body began to hum to some frequency. It was something she'd never felt before.

"I feel the same way every time I look at you, Bella," he said.

Again the hair at the back of her neck prickled. Paolo's warm hand clamped down on it and he massaged the top of her spine with his long fingers.

Those fingers that have been all over my body.

She closed her eyes and fell into his rhythm. When she opened her eyes, both Marcus and Anne diverted their gazes quickly. But they had been watching.

Marcus made a grand gesture of opening up one of his favorite red wines and pouring them each a handsome goblet. A coat of arms was etched into the crystal of each glass, along with a design around the letter M.

Monteleone.

The four grownups listened to Lucius tell them about school and his day. Cara helped Anne clear the table, but as she leaned over Paolo, she felt his hand slip along her backside, felt the heat through the fabric of her pants. She gave him a nudge with her hip.

"Not at the table," she whispered in his ear.

He grabbed her onto his lap as she glanced at Marcus with embarrassment, and then he whispered in her ear, "On the table, under the table, anywhere. Anytime."

She stood up and lurched away, cheeks flushed. "You have an impossible brother, Mr. Monteleone."

"Not impossible. A very healthy alpha male vamp—" Concern flashed all over Marcus' face as he corrected himself. "A very healthy alpha male vagabond from Tuscany—a land legendary for men who mess with women before they have a right to."

She wondered if he was going to say vampire. No doubt, Paolo had told him of her studies.

"I do study vampires, Mr. Monteleone. In fact, I gave my favorite lecture today."

"Yes, Paolo has told me."

Cara had removed all the dishes. "To be continued," she said as she exited to the kitchen.

Anne had dished up a piece of berry pie and a scoop of ice cream for each of them. She handed two to Cara. "Give the big one to Lucius. The other one is for Paolo. I'll bring the rest."

Lucius inhaled the berry pie and didn't say a word. He politely asked to be excused, and Paolo gave him permission, instructing him to go upstairs to study.

First, the boy came around the table and shook Cara's hand again.

"Nice to meet you. I'd like to show you my room some time, if you come back again. I have a big collection of vampire books as well."

"You do?" Cara was momentarily distracted from the tension she'd caused. "I used to read about them too, when I was your age, until I discovered romance novels. Somehow romance and vampires didn't mix very well for a young girl." She smiled, expecting a smile on the faces of her hosts, but not one of them did so.

Lucius withdrew his hand and turned, giving his father a hug, burying his face in his father's neck.

Paolo said something to Lucius in a foreign tongue and the young boy nodded, leaving the room without looking back.

The pie was delicious, but neither of the brothers touched theirs. She saw Marcus lift his fork and then stop before cutting himself a bite, as if he was trying to decide whether he wanted it. Anne nibbled on the tip of her slice, and after having only a few bites, lay her fork down beside the unfinished piece, and sighed.

Cara decided to bring up the verbal slip from Marcus' earlier in the conversation. "So, I got the impression you were going to say male alpha vampire, were you not?"

"You reading my mind now?" Marcus asked with a mock frown. Ann sat up, wary.

"I'm afraid I may have told him too much of our encounter at the ball, Bella. Forgive me." It looked like an honest apology.

"But I want to know why he said it. Was it because of the costume? You guys play vampire around here or something?"

No one said a word, which Cara thought was extremely strange. She felt like she'd just said the seven forbidden words on a live radio program.

Paolo took her left hand in his and squeezed it on top of the table. "Bella, dear. Our family comes from Italy, where they have a healthy respect for the legends of the past. You probably know about the little superstitions in the Black Sea countries about vampires. We trace some of our roots to that ancient land."

"So, you grew up hearing the old stories."

"Exactly," Marcus said.

She looked at Anne.

"Don't look at me. My upbringing was totally Northern California. No vamps in my past, except for some of the guys I used to date. And my ex-hus—my almost husband." Anne said, holding her palms out to the group. Marcus looked pained.

"So, sometime could I interview the both of you, ask you some questions, for my research? I've recently discovered some really interesting things."

"Certainly. We can arrange that," Marcus said as he eyed his brother carefully and winked at his wife. "Start with Paolo, though. He knows everything I know."

"Fair enough." Cara squeezed Paolo's hand. Her gaze traveled to his lips. "Let me ask you both one thing first. Have you ever heard of a historian named Alasdair Fraser?"

Marcus dropped his wine glass onto his pie plate.

Chapter 18

CARA FELT LIKE she'd committed a sin in front of the pope. In the dangerous silence that ticked past like the mechanisms of several ornately carved clocks in the living room, she looked up at Paolo, asking him in her mind what was wrong.

"Nothing, mi amore," came the non-verbal reply.

"These dark stories, Paolo? Did I do wrong to bring them up?"

Paolo picked up her hand, turned it palm side up and kissed her there with more tenderness than she'd ever felt. He seemed to devour her in his lingering kiss, inhaling every bit, as if his life depended on it.

"Our family has secrets, Cara," Marcus began. "These things must remain secrets until such time as, as—" he looked over at Paolo before completing his sentence. Anne had a frown line between her lovely brows. Marcus continued, "When Paolo selects a life mate, there are things that must be discussed."

"Don't you think someone would want to know about the family secrets beforehand? How would they know they wanted to join the family?" Cara's back was erect as she reacted to the fact that she wasn't going to be told any of those secrets. And yet she desperately wanted to know.

She searched Paolo's eyes, which had grown dark and dangerous.

"You fucked me, Paolo. You kissed parts of my body no man has ever touched—"

Paolo nodded. His huge body rose. He threw the damask napkin down on top of the pie and stomped off into the hallway.

"What did you say to him?" Marcus asked as he stood to go after his brother.

Cara was alarmed that Marcus knew they had telepathic communication. "How did you know that?"

"Because I told him," Paolo said. He had silently arrived and was leaning into the doorframe at the other end of the dining hall. She'd not heard him take a single step. "Sit, Marcus. Since I made a muck of this, I'll straighten it out. If I can. I'm going to need help explaining a few things to Bella."

Anne began to rise, but Cara stopped her. "No. Stay, Anne. Please." Anne assumed her position at the other head of the table and leaned over, placing her elbows on the tablecloth and weaving her fingers together.

Cara tried to pick up a faint conversation in a foreign tongue between the two brothers. Paolo nodded and began to speak.

"I've told you we are an old family. Unfortunately, not all of our family history is pleasant. We have some family members who have done things—" he glanced up to Marcus, who added,

"Been outlaws. There are some family members who engaged in activities that got them and the family into trouble."

"Okay. Every family has these people."

"It is perhaps difficult to understand here in the States, where families can be traced back maybe a hundred years, and of course, some longer. But in Europe, family dynasties can last for centuries. Wars fought. Kingdoms claimed." Marcus began to pace back and forth.

The way he gestured, the way he turned and took those long strides, reminded Cara of Paolo. She remembered his naked frame coming towards her as she lay on the bed full of ripe anticipation. She blushed and looked at her lap, ashamed that her lover might be able to discern her transference onto his brother.

"No shame, mi amore. You are mine, and it is me you are thinking about."

Cara began to well up inside. At last, the floodgates opened and she burst into tears. In a flash, Paolo was next to her, on his knees, his long arm wrapped around her shoulder.

"I'm sorry, but this is beginning to get to me. I've just—" The sexual glow had worn off, and she was staring down into the dark cavern of what she'd just done. She'd met a strange man who made her feel excited sexually as never before in her life, a man she had made love to half a dozen times. And she knew nothing about him. He could be a serial axe murderer, for all she knew.

And now, sitting here, with his family around her, she felt literally *sucked* in to their stories, like she was beginning to lose control over her own life's course. There was something dangerous and predatory about them all, even Paolo.

As if he felt her change of heart, he rose, and stood a healthy few feet from her. Her mind cleared. She was grateful for the space.

What is this power?

She could feel that he stood inside her mind, ready with an answer. But she didn't have the nerve to ask the question. She felt his unease. Out of the corner of her eye saw him grip his hands and squeeze his fists down by his sides.

"I think it would be best if you took her home, Paolo," Marcus said with finality.

"Of course," Paolo's reply was barely audible. He didn't tell her anything telepathically, but she could feel something hurting him.

It's your secret, Paolo. Cara sent him the message but was dying to ask him more. Then she realized with certainty that his secret was going to be something she didn't want to know.

And that was what was causing him the pain.

Chapter 19

CARA WAS GRATEFUL Paolo allowed her to be driven home alone. She knew he'd be monitoring her thoughts, and that drove her deeper into despair. On the one hand, this man had awakened something inside her soul that gave her more happiness and pure pleasure than she'd ever experienced.

And on the other hand, she wasn't ready to give up her own free will. She'd never before felt tempted to sink into some dark abyss, do risky things with someone she barely knew, someone who demanded everything from her.

She decided it wasn't good for her, no matter how wonderful she felt when he kissed her, when he whispered incantations that heightened her sexual arousal, even when he just stood next to her. It wouldn't be long before she'd need him too much. She just couldn't allow that to happen.

The leather seats of his brother's limo felt like the cool flesh of a giant serpent against her warm skin. She leaned back and closed her eyes. She recalled him standing by the front door to the villa, his white shirt billowing out from his trim black, old-fashioned pants with the silver clasps. He was such an odd combination of sensual softness and almost a predator's thirst. As the prey, she longed to be captured again and again. She knew she would be safe. Somehow she knew this.

But that didn't make it wise.

Mi amore. She heard him say this as the driver drove down the crushed granite driveway, away to the safety of her own apartment. Paolo hadn't been afraid to let her feel his pain at their separation. She refused to reassure him. She needed space and time.

When they arrived in Santa Rosa, Cara thanked the driver, who waited until she was inside her gated entrance before driving off. She wondered what Marcus' servant thought about taking his master's brother and his new lover to a bed and breakfast for the obvious purpose of having an afternoon of sex. Was this a common occurrence? Did their wealth allow them almost unlimited freedom to explore their sexual appetites with abandon, without drawing attention to the activity? Anne had said that the brothers were discreet. Just what did that mean?

She thought about Marcus' wife, the beautiful Anne, and the little one. She was a California girl, not from an ancient lineage like the rest of the Monteleones she'd married into. Cara thought perhaps someday she could have a frank discussion with Anne, if—

If what? If I let him touch me again?

Cara wondered how she would ever be able to feel another man's touch on her flesh and not remember Paolo. Somehow, he'd claimed her.

"You are mine," he'd told her. The thrill of those words sent a shiver down her spine again as she dropped her purse and keys on the kitchen counter. She thought about them as she pulled off her clothes and left them in a heap in the bathroom. She started the shower but was hit with the warm cloud of Paolo's scent that ricocheted off her own moist skin. She closed her eyes and felt her sex clench. The obvious truth was, she ached for him.

Cara decided against the shower at the last minute. Picking up her clothing, she walked back to her bedroom, hung up her things and slipped naked into the huge bed she'd tossed and turned in last night. The cool sheets warmed quickly. His scent was all over her. As she began to drift off to sleep, she wondered if he could hear her dreams, too.

PAOLO HELD THE little glass of port up, looking through it to the flames of the fire as he sat in a winged back chair next to his brother. He was working to push his emotions back. He'd felt her distance growing, like blood draining from his veins, as he'd watched the limo escort his love home to where she thought she was safe. She would be safe from his thoughts, at least, since she was mortal. If she were vampire, she'd be able to feel him across the ocean.

He forced himself to find solace in the ruby color of the port, which was stunning. The sharp sweetness bit down on his palate and filled his nostrils with a heady bouquet. He was grateful for the distraction.

"This is outstanding port, Marcus."

"Yes. Can you imagine how it will be ten or twenty years from now? This is barely two years bottled."

"You must save some for Ian's wedding day."

"That I must. Won't that be a day?" Marcus was admiring the color in his glass just the same way his brother did. Without looking at him, he added, "The girl is lovely, Paolo."

"Carabella. Her name is Carabella."

"Yes. You speak of her in a haunted, almost fated manner. Is there some evidence you could be fated?"

"I feel something like it, yes." Paolo didn't want to think about the brief few days of savage sex he spent with his son's mother, the way he couldn't stay away from her. Maya hadn't loved Paolo any more than he loved her. But their species instincts pulled them together in a tangle of arms and legs, resulting in her bearing him a son.

With Cara, it was an animal attraction, but not without reason. If they were truly fated, he never would have been able to send her home in the limo by herself. He'd have fucked her several times, with or without the audience of the driver in the front seat.

He had been a good husband to his three mortal wives, who, one by one, died in his arms. He hated himself for the fating that had taken over his body, forcing him to break his marriage vows.

Being married to mortal women was pleasant, but they were childless years as he watched them age, watched as each of them grew to realize he wasn't aging like they were. He never minded the wrinkles and sags of older flesh. He loved and was devoted to his wives. His love wasn't about the flesh, it was about the heart.

Cara, even if he could convince her to be with him, would someday want a family and children of her own. A marriage or long-term relationship with her would therefore be out of the question. He might even be prohibited by the Vampire Council from contacting her further, based on tonight's events. Perhaps the God of vampires had been kind to him by removing the distraction of her scent, her body, before he became too involved. The lady was going to talk herself out of anything that could have happened, and if he resisted the urge to glamour her, she could successfully escape his influence.

Pain was a constant companion to Paolo, who had learned to hold it inside, tuck it away in a satin drawer inside his heart and move on. Three hundred years of practice made him good at it. He knew some day he'd become brittle, perhaps sarcastic, as he watched others of his clan raise their children, love their wives forever and live an eternity wrapped in love and family. This would not be his fate.

As bad as this was, it would have been worse had the half witch-half Golden vampire Maya survived the war she'd started. Paolo would have forever been tethered to a loveless bed of obligation, doing so only to protect his son.

What kind of a father would he be to Lucius, who would have to make the choice some day to either remain mortal or become a Golden vampire? Paolo felt he was a bad role model for the young boy. It might have been better had Marcus married Maya, as she demanded, and raised the boy as his own. Marcus was a better man, Paolo thought. He doubted he could have done it himself.

And then beautiful Anne, so sweet and lovely, Anne, with the force of all the goddesses his ancestors had worshiped centuries ago, herself a new vampire, brought to life by Marcus' blood, sacrificed herself by committing an act punishable by death.

Paolo felt weak when compared to his other family members. His turmoil about becoming vampire at first, added to his pain that the decision could not be undone. He longed for the simple human emotions of loving with a full heart, free of glamour and manipulation, in a measured lifespan of some eighty to one hundred years and no more. It wasn't the living forever that bothered him. It was the feeling that he wanted to love and be loved as a mortal.

He finished his port and pretended to be settled inside. He would be grateful to be alone tonight. Cara would have certainly sensed his scathing pain. Marcus would have to guess.

"Your plans for her?" Marcus asked.

"Why, brother? You doubting my prowess?"

"You know what I mean. Don't joke about that. There is an attraction there. No denying that. You continue seeing her and she will find out things on her own that I'd rather she learned from us."

"Us? Or you? Can't you trust I will do the right thing?"

"That's just it, Paolo, I don't know what that is anymore. Do you?"

The two brothers fixed gazes on each other without moving a muscle. They used to do this when they were boys in a stare-down contest to see who could show emotion first. It was the same now.

Paolo flinched and looked at the fire.

"I am lost, brother. I want what I cannot have. What I could have I didn't want."

"And your son will pay the price," Marcus whispered. Paolo could tell he was a bit angry.

"Without my son, I wouldn't be here." Paolo looked back at Marcus. "I'd be gone."

"Don't say such things. You are a member of this family. Just because you will never have a fated female doesn't mean your life is over, without meaning. You have a legacy to pass on to Lucius. You know this should be your prime directive."

Paolo nodded.

"And with this war coming on, you owe your best efforts to defeat the dark forces descending upon us. In short, we need you. Too many of our kind are disappearing. Something evil is happening."

"The apex." Paolo whispered into the fire.

"Yes, I feel it, brother. Something has shifted. I feel like this is the last stand of our species. We are under open attack."

"I pledge to protect the family. Protect my flesh and blood." He extended his hand to Marcus. "You have my solemn vow, brother. No harm will come to you or your family, *our* family, as long as I'm alive."

Chapter 20

D AG TRANSPORTED HIMSELF to his flat in San Francisco so he could pick up his Harley Road King. He liked to scare the mortals as he fired up the beast and drove at midnight over to the little coven library his uncle ran in the heart of the Tenderloin. His black leather spiked saddlebags were full of mayhem, but he also kept a spare change of clothes in case his encounters got messy.

The storefront said *Mystical Books*, but everyone in the coven knew it was just a ploy to bring in young unsuspecting college-age coeds who wanted to dabble in the black arts. It was a storefront even the homeless didn't dare sleep under.

They'd had séances in the library. But after the séances, there were some mighty fine orgies, which usually left half the attendees dead. For those who survived, unless they were special, and it was getting difficult to find special ones, their memories would be wiped and they'd never return.

No one ever commented about the fact that the store was only open at night. Daylight hours were spent recovering from the roaming nights of sex and death. Although most the dark vampire hordes didn't sleep in coffins as the old myths described, they did have to stay out of the sunlight. Even a pinhole in a shade or drape could cause burning and pain.

It was another reason Dag never brought any mortal to his own bed. And he detested other dark vampire women, mostly because they were not easily scared. Therefore, he would be heirless, since darks could only successfully breed with other dark vampires. And unlike Goldens, darks became blood-sucking babies and toddlers prone to feasting on their nannies and housekeepers.

So be it. Dag didn't want the little shits running around his household causing chaos, anyway. Besides, it could be something someone could hold over on him. He made a point of not having anyone around him he couldn't do without. The little blonde was already becoming a problem, messing up his focus as his anticipation heightened for their next encounter, but he knew it was way too early to tell how that would turn out.

Colin was sorting a box of books that had come in the mail. He was "made" later in life, so he looked more than twice Dag's age, more like Dag's grandfather than uncle, despite the fact that they would both live forever. The older vamp had been despondent over the theft of his younger wife's life. She'd been turned by a warring coven that used her as a pleasure doll for nearly a year before she was found. The fact that she had strange desires and needs after the turning made their reunion pure hell, so Colin begged the Supreme Leader to be allowed to join her in vampiric form, and was granted the request. It was Dag's last turning before he himself became Supreme.

And then Dag and his cohorts took care of the coven, eliminating its members one by one in a slow and excruciatingly painful death, as an example to other covens. No one ever questioned their power again, until the Supreme Leader began to make nice with Golden vamps, which was something Dag and his family could not tolerate, so they eliminated him as well.

And now there would be a satisfying, blood-spewing purge to take the final solution to its last stages. It had been foretold in the book. The book Dag needed to find in order to complete his plans.

"Uncle Colin, what have you found for me today?" Dag knew his uncle didn't necessarily like him, but he respected his power and authority. Colin had no taste for the vampire wars or politics.

"'Fraid nothing, Dag. Everyone's into eBooks these days, and we haven't had any large scale invasions lately, so no looted libraries, sorry to say."

"What have you got here?" Dag pawed through the opened brown box with the Priority Mail sticker on it.

"Not much you'd like." Colin took a leather-bound book from

Dag's fingers, "*King Arthur's Witch*—somehow I think that wouldn't interest you."

"Pictures?" Dag smiled. "Even black and white ones? Naked mortals?"

Colin flipped through the gold edged tome and shook his head. "Not a one. Sorry."

"You know we've heard the Bat Book has surfaced?"

This got Colin's attention. "Yes, I know. Where is it?" Dag wondered if Colin was keeping something from him.

"A bookseller in Prague has sold it to someone. We're trying to locate it now. Can't believe it was there practically under our noses all this time."

"Was beginning to think it was another urban legend. You really think this book exists? Sure it's not a hoax?" Colin asked.

"Not many mortal men can withstand the kind of pain we dispensed to find out."

Colin frowned and mumbled something to the armful of books he took back to his desk. It didn't bother Dag in the slightest that Uncle Colin was afraid of him. He liked it that way.

"So you will let me know if you hear of this book, or anything about it, won't you, Colin?"

"Of course," Colin said to the desk.

"How's dark Vicky?" Dag was referring to Colin's young vampire wife, who had been spared death by the competing coven because of what she could do in the bedroom. Whispers still surrounded her whenever there was a gathering.

"She's shopping."

"At midnight?" Dag noticed Colin's expression was pained and suspected that his aunt, who had expressed an interest in her own nephew, was not exactly faithful to her dumpy librarian of a husband.

The front door opened with a tinkling bell. Two very thin male vamps in their twenties with spikes in their ears and lips entered. Dag regarded them carefully. There was something a bit off about their appearance, and he didn't recognize them. They also had the smell of Vicky on them.

"Hey pops, we found a couple books at a garage sale and thought perhaps they might be worth something," the slightly taller one of the two said. He nodded to Dag, obviously not realizing he was the Coven Supreme Leader.

Dag considered a punishment, but decided to table it. If these two were Vicky's new playthings, then perhaps Colin might enjoy the sport at a later time. He doubted it, but stored it away in his memory just in case.

"Boys, first I'd like you to meet the Supreme Leader, Dag Nielsen," Colin blurted out before the young vamp could hand him the book. "You'd be wise to address him with respect," he continued. To Dag, he added, "They're Vicky's progeny." His uncle's bloodshot eyes shifted from side to side. Dag could tell Colin was nervous as hell. "Just babes, really."

Colin shrugged and started to examine the first of two large books he'd been handed.

The young vamps bowed and left their heads cowed, avoiding eye contact.

That's way more like it.

"Sir, we mean you no disrespect," the other vamp whispered. "New to this fiefdom."

Dag inhaled briskly, like he'd been slapped. The younglings darted quick glances at him. "That smacks of attitude." Dag pounced in front of the taller boy. "You like fucking Vicky? What's she like?"

"S-s-sir. I'm sure I don't know." The boy was trying to get Colin's attention and help.

"Liar." Dag grabbed him by the collar and shook him until the boy's head rocked back, exposing bite marks under his jaw line and purple hickeys like a collar of blueberry jam around his neck. "She's a mean bitch, isn't she?"

Dag heard the sound of water running and realized the youngling had peed his pants, and all over Dag's shoes. The boy's friend stepped away, out of Dag's reach and separating himself from the whimpering vamp. Dag took a bite from the boy's neck and only drew a mouthful before he released him and spit the blood out.

"You filthy, dope-smoking, pieces of shit. What'd she do, offer you free sex for the rest of your miserable lives? Tell you to bring her husband books to keep him happy and occupied while you fucked her brains out?"

"Dag—" the librarian pleaded.

"Why do you let her humiliate you so, uncle? Wouldn't you love to watch your wife's lover have his dick torn off?"

Colin looked horrified. Dag wasn't sure if it was the retribution Vicky would bring down upon him if the boy were harmed, or whether he was really averse to the violence. In an uncharacteristic act of mercy, Dag released the young vamp, sending him to the floor. The two scrambled out the door.

"This is getting out of control, Colin. You have to teach your woman how to respect you."

"I know. I am just not her type. Ever since—"

"First you begged us to turn her so she wouldn't die. Then you begged the Supreme, which really pissed him off, to turn you so you weren't such a disappointment to her, with her new appetites. Now what? I can't undo what is already done. You're gonna have to man up, Colin. Or, do you want me to show you how it's done?"

"Dag, she's your *aunt!*"

"By marriage only. But believe me, I'd have to hold my nose if I fucked her. No telling where that twat's been. Most men, especially vamps, would love a woman who wants to have sex 24/7. And you're complaining?"

"Not when she's—"

"You think I'm stupid, Uncle Colin? I know she doesn't fuck when she sleeps. But I've done it. Left my cock inside them while we slept and resumed screwing at sunset when we awoke at night again" Dag picked up one of the books and fingered the spine. "Of course, now I only fuck mortals. I have no taste for vamp whores. You should try young human flesh again. Perhaps give you good practice for Queen Vicky."

"Dag, it's no use. She doesn't fancy me."

"Then glamour her."

"I don't have the gift."

"Then get a potion."

"Where?"

"Damn it, man. You've got books all over the place here. Do a little research."

"I suppose—"

"Tie her up, make her submit to you. I think she'd actually like that. You're too easy with her. She liked it rough before, am I right?"

"Yes. A little."

"And that's what you liked, too."

"She got rough with *me*. I didn't—"

"She was trying to egg you on, get you to be a man. Don't you get it?"

"I just want to love her. I don't want to cause her pain. I don't care if she hurts me. If that's what she likes, I can take it, especially now that I am vampire. I heal within 24 hours. I just don't want her to leave me."

Dag spat on the wooden floor. "I can't believe we are even blood related. You are a fuckin' disgrace."

For the second time today he took pity on someone. Dag hoped it wasn't going to be an annoying trend. Looking at the shaking form of his uncle, his hair disheveled, shirt barely tucked into his banana slug yellow-brown corduroy pants, his jiggling pot belly taking up all the extra slack and making it impossible for him to wear a belt, Dag felt sorry for him. He knew Colin to be a gentle soul. Not many vamps had any real family, so they would have eternity to work out their relationship.

He gripped Colin's shoulder and stared back at him across the length of his outstretched arm. "Let's talk about books, shall we? That's a more pleasant topic."

Colin's eyes lit up. "Yes."

"How can I get a track on that book? Where it got shipped to?" Dag asked.

"If it was a credit card order, they would have the record. If you get me that detail, I can perhaps have an answer within a few hours.

Will the bookseller cooperate?"

"Not now." Dag said with a scowl.

Colin backed up just a hair. "I see. Well, then, perhaps someone else who manages the shop can find it. He has a family?"

Dag cleared his throat. "That's a problem, too."

"Ah. Well then, take his computer. It would all be done online. He have an Amazon account? It would be easier if it were through eBay or Craigslist. But the credit card company would be best."

"I'll get the computer and see what we find and have it emailed to you."

"No problem. I'll drop everything and devote my day to it. I promise, Dag."

"Thank you, Colin. You've been a great help already." Dag slapped his uncle on the back. "We'll work on that other problem, too. I think I can help you there in exchange."

"No. Not necessary, but thanks anyway." Colin was in visible distress again.

"No? Well then, I want you to promise me one thing."

Colin hung his head, clearly afraid to hear what kind of an order Dag was going to deliver.

"I want you to try tying up your wife when she's asleep. Bind her hands and feet to the bedpost. Let her squirm. Use silver if you have to. You have some silver chain?"

"I do. I know Vicky has some in her underwear drawer."

"Your wife's a fuckin' freak, Colin."

"I know this, but I love her."

"Well, tie her up with the silver—her own silver for fuck's sake—and make it really secure. Don't worry yourself about the wounds; you know she'll heal. But she'll think twice before hurting your heart again, believe me. Let her stay there for a day. Careful not to let any light in while you are taking your sleep. Ask her first to be more docile and tell her you'll let her go if she can act convincingly. She's going to be mad as hell, but she'll like the game I think. See if she's interested in playing along. Can you do that for me and report to me in a day?"

Colin appeared to hesitate.

"Colin. You know you are required to master her. Otherwise, she's a loose cannon. I cannot afford to have someone out of control so close to me. You understand how it would look?"

"Yes."

"Try it. You might discover a part of yourself you never knew existed."

DAG CHUCKLED AS he rode his Harley back to his rented flat. There was going to be one of two outcomes in the next twenty-four hours. Either the problem of wild Vicky would be solved, or Colin would wind up with a hatchet between his eyes.

Either solution worked for Dag. Now that he was close to finding the book, the need for a coven librarian was soon going to be redundant.

Chapter 21

LIONEL JETT SEARCHED the sparkling lights of the City of Healdsburg from his loft apartment overlooking the square. A trio of young men laughed sharply, and it drew his attention to the sidewalk below, where fall tourists had descended upon the little wine country town to feast at one of the two hundred wineries nearby. There weren't many days he wished he was mortal. He didn't often wish he was Golden vampire, instead of the dark vamp of his ancestors. But today, he definitely wished he possessed the powers the Goldens enjoyed.

His weariness was beginning to creep into his everyday consciousness, almost like a kind of aging process. Of course, he would never age. He'd seen changes in the world, especially with the explosion of the mortal population over the past four hundred years since his birth. The Golden population had remained about the same, or perhaps decreased slightly recently. But that was just something he sensed, rather than knew. He wasn't privy to all the inner workings of the Golden society, which was as it should be.

He'd been hired on roughly four hundred years ago to help Marcus and Paolo's father establish his little estate in Tuscany and raise his eight children, and sadly, watched both Sr. Monteleone, a lion of a mortal man, as was his namesake, and his beautiful wife, who was Lionel's contemporary in school, die as mortals, without taking the change. He wondered if the brothers he now served understood the depth of his feeling for their mother. His service was the least he could do for a kind lady who took pity on him as a young, struggling waif trying to raise two orphaned brothers after the death of their parents.

Serving the Monteleones had given his life purpose, and the routine hadn't bothered him one bit. He served at night, unless he was given an unusual night off, like tonight. During the day, he was dead to the mortal world, locked in a special bedroom that might be impenetrable to anything but a direct RPG attack. It would withstand a 9.0 earthquake.

No, the vulnerabilities were happening within. Something was brewing inside him. A sense of loneliness and perhaps a little despair. He'd scented down dark coven lords who wanted to do injury to the Monteleones, and "liquidated" their blood, as he was fond of saying.

Sending them back to the source.

That part of his life wasn't what was causing the problem. It was the living forever, alone, that began to eat a small hole, like a pinhole in a curtain during daylight.

This war felt different from all the other attacks he'd survived and protected the Goldens from. More than about power, this war almost seemed like a planned annihilation of the Goldens and their progeny. And for what purpose? He didn't like fighting a mission he knew nothing about.

So, though it was his night off, he decided to do a little R&R, check out some haunts some of his dark brethren frequented on the fringes of mortal society, where it was dangerous, but sometimes delicious. He was in need of information, but a sexual liaison wouldn't be half bad, either. It might even release the tension dwelling in his loins.

He decided to connect with his brothers, Jeb and Hugh. He picked up his black cell phone and pushed number two. Jeb's voice came on the line immediately.

"Hola."

"Hello, brother. You available?" Lionel asked.

"You need me tonight? Thought we had the night off." Jeb's husky voice was somehow reassuring to him.

"Yes. But I'm going to go mingle, see if I can pick up some information on the currents I'm feeling."

"You too, huh?"

"Yes."

"You talk with Marcus and Paolo tonight?" Jeb asked.

"You mean, do they feel it?" Lionel wished he'd brought it up when Marcus called him at dusk to tell him he could have the evening off. "I'm sure they do. But no, I haven't discussed it with them. He's been pretty focused on Paolo and the girl."

"She's a stunner. Mortal, though, isn't that right?"

"Very much so."

"Paolo's playing with fire. That one will get the whole family in trouble if he doesn't decide which side of the gene pool he belongs to."

It was true. It could get more than the Monteleone family in trouble. It could cost him on a more personal basis. Lionel was not only protector to the Goldens, he would do anything to keep his two brothers safe, being the elder of the three.

Though they'd never discussed it, Lionel knew Marcus was worried about his brother, and the little one Paolo was learning to raise. That was the hard part, he thought. The innocents who were in danger. The Goldens didn't worry about defending themselves, but it was their children who were vulnerable. Hard to live forever with the loss of a mortal child, and he knew that was part of the strategy of the dark covens encroaching upon the Golden vamps and their community.

"I wonder how smart it is for Marcus to be set up here in California. Much safer, I would think, back in Tuscany, where there is a certain safety in numbers," Lionel said.

"But I kind of dig it here. From what I can see of it."

Both the brothers laughed. They lived in one of the most picturesque places in the whole world, except they couldn't enjoy it because they only came out at dark.

"You want to go out?" Lionel asked at last.

"If you need me. Sure. But I had plans."

"That would be that little red-headed witch you fancy, brother?"

"The very same. She's been experimenting with some herbs, and I rather like the effect, if you know what I mean."

"Be careful."

"Always. You going to call Huge?"

The nickname was an apt description of the youngest of the three

Jett brothers. Hugh Jett was the tallest by nearly five inches, and stood a whopping 6'7", a tad taller than his employer, Marcus Monteleone. His size also made him a favorite of women of all species. It was with some regret that Lionel watched his youngest brother's life roll out before him. The vamp would have made a good family man. But that wasn't their fate.

No sense arguing with the gods.

"Right after you tell me you'll not do something foolish. Like fall asleep in the sun. Remember, Jeb, to indulge in a little play, but keep your wits about you."

"Most definitely."

"In service, then," Lionel said.

"In service, brother," Jeb echoed.

Lionel pushed number three on his cell. He heard dead air space at first, then a lot of static as it sounded like the phone had been dropped right after it had been answered.

"Hugh here."

"You all right, brother?" Lionel asked. Huge's heavy breathing was a little disconcerting.

"Working out before they close. Why do they call it 24 Hour Abs when they close at nine o'clock?" Hugh exhaled and Lionel could hear the sound of a barbell either being dropped or thrown onto a rubber mat.

"You up for a little downtown time?" Lionel asked.

"Sure. I need a few to get cleaned up. Almost done. Got one more rep. Then I'll shower."

"Why do you go to all that work? You're going to return to your natural state tomorrow, you know."

"But what a glorious twelve hours I get, and it makes me feel double-immortal, if you can wrap your head around that. Totally awesome."

"Okay, meet me at PRESS in half an hour?"

"Sure. This official, or recreational?"

"Kinda little bit of both. Just doing some digging around, but who knows, perhaps we could share a little sweet thing, if the right one comes along?"

"Hell yes. Didn't get pumped up for nothing. I'm going to infect the whole square with my pheromones."

"So I'll have to keep careful watch over you. You feel the dark forces?" Lionel asked.

"Like a rash. All over the place. Wish they'd just come out and meet us directly. If it's going to be a fuckin' war, wish they'd just get on with it."

"Could be part of the plan," Lionel added.

"Or calm before the storm. Maybe they don't have their ducks in line yet."

Lionel laughed, thinking he heard it wrong. "You say dicks?"

"Those, too."

They shared another throaty laugh.

"That's why I gotta go rooting around, investigate. Things just aren't adding up, Huge. Something major is brewing."

"You know they have a new dark coven leader, this Dag fellow?" Hugh said.

"I've met him a time or two. Newcomer."

"Like one of their dark toddlers. Hosted off the hands that created him. Not a good dude. Definitely someone to watch, if we can catch him."

"Okay, well laters, and Huge—"

"Yeah?"

"Go light on the cologne, 'kay? I was sneezing blood last time we made the rounds."

Hugh's chuckle was deep and rich like chocolate. Like what he'd tasted of chocolate, anyhow.

"Au naturel, but fresh soap. They won't be able to keep their hands off me."

"Let's be discreet, though."

"Always."

"In service."

"In service."

Chapter 22

DOWNTOWN HEALDSBURG WAS balmy at night this time of year, though it was tickling winter on this particular late fall evening. Scores of tourists came too late for crush, when the newly picked fruit was placed in it's first fermentation. But they were just in time for some early barrel tasting. Outsiders liked to demonstrate their ignorance, he thought. While they were imbibing wine and getting high, the dark coven hordes were feasting off the lifeblood of the tourist population, then glamouring them to forget their night of wild decadence The result was that the strangers would go back home and say they had a great time, but would remember little of it.

It was the same anywhere in the world where the innocent would gather and the dark creatures would come to host off them in their altered and unsuspecting state. Lionel had never before asked a man if he could sleep with his new young wife, but his brother had on numerous occasions. Hugh said he liked to watch the anger of the husband for a few seconds before he sent out the glam and put him in a most agreeable state.

"Sure, show her a good time," they would say. Hugh would promise to do his best. He would promise the husband he'd send his wife back well trained to be a most avid sexual partner. And that is usually what happened. So, Hugh never thought he was doing anything wrong. He was, in fact, enhancing the human sexual experience, in his opinion.

But it gave Lionel problems. "Just because they don't remember doesn't mean it's right," he'd argued with his brother. It was the old tree-in-the-forest-with-no-one-to-hear-it-fall-argument. In Lionel's mind, the tree fell whether or not anyone was around to hear it. If a woman was violated and forced to go outside of her marriage vows, it mattered little that she didn't remember it afterwards. It was never right. Lionel would never take a woman who didn't fully consent and wasn't free to choose.

Young Maria Monteleone, Marcus and Paolo's mother, had gotten dangerously close to Lionel on several occasions in their young adult years, after he'd been recently turned. He used to watch her close the drapes and ask him if he was comfortable on the few occasions he'd had to be alone with her, as her security detail. She knew he had to sleep during long sunny days, and had tried to make him feel at ease with her. But there was a dark side that had wanted to reach up and take hold of this woman and claim her for himself.

Thoughts. Just thoughts. He hoped his actions never revealed his inner feelings, but somehow he knew she did suspect his loyalty was more than just duty and honor. It was as close to a love as he'd ever experienced, though one-sided. That was more than three hundred years ago, and nothing had tarnished the bright memory of that lady since, even as he watched her age and wither, as he tended to her physical needs in the end, after the death of her husband, carrying her to the garden pools at midnight or pushing her around in the wheelchair by starlight. They'd watch the moon set together. She used to love the stars, and it was on one starry night that she died of natural causes, as a human. He'd made a solemn vow to protect her children throughout eternity. He intended to keep that promise.

Unlike the Goldens, dark vampires had no Council that ruled on disputes. Dark covens were created by leaders who risked their immortal lives to grow in power and stature, and their culture became, in a strange Darwinian fashion, a survivor of the fittest society, ruled by the darkest covens and the wars they could generate. Outside of a coven supreme leader, there wasn't anyone in authority, unlike the Golden vampire community with its Council.

So where, exactly, did that leave him and his brothers?

Employed. They had nearly unlimited funds, but nowhere to spend it. Sexual powers and desires that would rival the Goldens, but no time to use them. They existed to protect the families of what

Lionel had begun to believe was the master race of vampires. He'd never thought about whether or not it was a fair tradeoff. He'd never considered any other line of work.

Lionel was relaxed but wary as he strode down the wet streets of the little winery town. The heels of his scuffed Doc Martens pounded along the sidewalk, causing storefront glass to wobble. He made a point to go lighter, so as not to draw attention to his preternatural powers. He wanted to spend the evening without drawing undue attention, if he could.

His standard uniform was black leather jacket with the myriad of zippered pockets, his tight black Levis with more pockets, and the lace-up boots with the steel toes he wore everywhere except for a tuxedo affair. Since those only came along a couple of times a century, he still had a pair of pumps he'd bought back in the 1800's made from pressed alligator—an illegal substance in today's world—which were perfect and drew little attention.

PRESS was full of people tonight. The first thing that struck him was the giddy laughter coming from the bar and dark corners of the place, even though the lighting was darker than usual. It wasn't the romantic quiet he usually found at a hook-up place. There were groups of people everywhere. Things were being said indiscreetly. Boundaries were being pushed. He was hit with glamour from all directions, indicating the dark forces were very present.

Perfect. Just what you wanted, right?

He felt his brother's words coming from his right and he turned to find Hugh toasting him with a dark red glass of what was probably Meritage, his favorite blend of three wines, which matched his sexual tastes to a T.

That it is, brother. "You are eager tonight, Huge," Lionel said as he took his seat in front of him and watched his brother's features by light of the little votive candle on the shiny laminate tabletop.

"As ever." Hugh nodded to a couple of new lovelies who had just walked into the den of sins, eyes as wide and blue-green as the ocean. Lionel knew they had no idea what was in store for them. They were expensively dressed, and obviously not aware of what a rough crowd they'd walked in on.

Hugh apologized to him, and stood, then walked over to the two mortal girls and invited them to their table. They had to crane their necks to look up into their host's face, and then pulled a look around him to see Lionel sitting at the table. He nodded to them, and the redhead smiled and started walking right toward him. That left Hugh with the brunette, and Lionel knew that would be just fine.

The redhead's light pink skin and fresh scent pounded a flush to Lionel's groin area and his pants became unbearably tight. Then she touched his shoulder, balancing herself on him while she tried to sit down gracefully in spite of an impossibly short skirt and four-inch heels with laces that came to her knees. The dark shadow between her thighs made Lionel's fangs ache, but he pressed them back up and swallowed. He'd surely bite himself if he couldn't have her, and very soon.

But then he remembered himself and his mission. He needed to gather information about the dark hordes lounging here this evening, looking for recreation and perhaps willing to slip their guard a bit. He chuckled as the redhead removed her jacket to reveal an exquisite set of breasts that all but shouted his name, and this time his fangs dropped properly low and would not behave.

Did she see?

He send a little glam her way just as Hugh and the other girl slid past her shoulders and took a place next to each other on the bench seat across from him.

Hugh was having great fun watching him, Lionel could tell. Not that his brother hadn't taken the time to adequately appreciate the redhead's mammary glands.

Would be a shame to have a dark toddler suck those beautiful orbs and deform them, brother. Not that you were thinking along those lines, Hugh sent out to him.

Not possible, Huge. You know that.

No? With the powerful cum you're going to lay inside her, who knows what could happen? I know you can see what she'd look like.

Keep your eyes on your own plate, brother, Lionel answered.

You suggested sharing...

Lionel squinted a dark glare at Hugh, who sat back, and draped his arm around the brunette. Her impossibly red lips parted and a whole new set of visions flooded Lionel's head.

Hugh chuckled, raised his glass to his brother, and then motioned for a cocktail waitress. The redhead touched her bare thigh against Lionel's, and through the jeans he felt the intentional caress of a mortal woman who had come to the bar to find sex. Well, he'd have to oblige, but not until his need for information was satisfied. Then he could satisfy himself with the knowledge of what she had barely covered up so with her panties. The knowledge of what it would feel like to slip in and out of her, what the taste of her blood would be as she moaned his name. He didn't need to drink wine to get high. He'd get it from her.

The cocktail waitress went off in search of a very expensive bottle of Ravenswood Meritage, mumbling something about having to go downstairs to the cave storage to look for it. Lionel could tell Hugh had glamoured her too. Hugh had a fondness for taking his mortal conquests in wine caves and cool refrigerated private collections.

Lionel adjusted his jacket and the blue-green-eyed beauty on his right smiled as she appraised the leather and what lay underneath. "Can I help you with your jacket? You look hot."

Her scent came to him like a blast furnace, along with the double meaning. It was good to be coveted, he thought. Nice that it happened without him having to expend an ounce of glam on her, too. Totally willing.

"Sure," he said, adjusting his fangs before breaking a smile. She'd probably think he was trying not to smile, but he didn't want to scare her, until it was time to do so. Just a little scare before the bite. Before the rapture of what it would feel like as he breathed into her ear, whispered incantations and took her. "But mind your hands. I have vera vera sensitive skin," he added in a mock accent.

"Oh, I hope so," she gushed. Her tiny pink fingers traveled quickly over his pecs, and tugged at the thick collar of the jacket, pulling it off his shoulders. He leaned forward, his face close to hers, allowing his dark hair to brush against her cheek, and felt her body shudder in response. She finished removing the heavy jacket and let it drape behind him on the chair. "Sorry, it's very heavy, and a little too heavy for me. I'm afraid I've made a bit of a mess."

You have no idea. He had practically come in his pants, but willed himself some control. He nodded, slowly perusing her chest while she watched him do it. "I don't mind. I'm enjoying whatever your hands can do, and I can see you are skilled."

The girl blushed. Had he glammed her? If she caught a little breath from him, it wasn't intentional. He loved that his proximity made her tingle, blush, feel self-conscious. It's what he loved most about mortal women. He never liked women that threw themselves at him. Her combination of subtlety and grace charmed him, and he allowed it to be so. Even fantasized she could glamour him.

Lionel broke the tension by looking over at his brother. Hugh had his tongue down the brunette's throat and had already a hand under the table, snaking up her red knit dress. He would be no use tonight, Lionel thought. He could feel his brother sending sexual fantasies into the lady's consciousness, and could hear her slight moan in response.

So far so good. Lionel scanned the room just before the waitress returned with the bottle of wine Hugh had selected. She frowned when Hugh didn't acknowledge it, being otherwise occupied.

"Thank you," Lionel said to the waitress as he pressed a one hundred dollar bill into her palm. This got her attention.

"Oh, thank you so much. Let me know if you need anything else?" Her smile was brave, but Lionel could see she fancied his brother, as most mortal women did.

Lionel removed the cork and slowly poured the wine while tipping the glass, so that the deep burgundy substance rolled back in a wave that resembled thick blood. The aroma was excellent, but he put the glass to his nose anyway the way humans did when savoring a nice bouquet. He closed his eyes as he swirled the liquid over his palate, wishing it were the feel and taste of the redhead's lovely life force.

There will be time enough for that.

"You like?" He said to her. She had been watching his Adam's apple, almost like a vamp female. But her scent told him she clearly wasn't.

"Yes, I like." She looked him straight in the eyes. He could feel her saying words, although unclear, like there was a filter between them, but part of the telepathy was working. *Take me,* she was saying.

"Good." He tipped the glass to her lips. She closed her eyes and mirrored his tasting actions, swirling the liquid over her tongue. She licked her lips and coated them with the fermented elixir.

It was totally spontaneous. With her eyes still closed, he covered her mouth with his and she parted quickly and allowed him access. She sucked at his lips as he did the same. She was lovely, and just what he needed. He brought his hand to the back of her head and sifted through her long locks. She was intoxicating to him.

"More wine?" he asked as they parted and stared into each other's eyes.

"Please." It meant more than the wine.

"Your wish is my command." They both smiled.

He was suddenly aware of motion coming from his left. The room had taken on an agitated air. He heard a chair crash and something very large hit the floor.

Lionel saw that his brother had surfaced from his erotic reverie and had noticed the same thing. A large enforcer for one of the dark coven lords had been thrown on the floor. He was the lord's executioner, and Lionel had always thought the man had been brought to modern times from the sixteen hundreds, where he no doubt worked as an executioner in a dungeon before turning. He was legendary for his torture methods. The fact that he was in obvious pain concerned Lionel.

Both brothers stood, as did most the non-mortal males in the bar. Several couples made it discreetly out the entrance into the night air. A wall of males began to form in a circle around the two fighting vamps.

The challenging vamp was Rory Monteleone, Marcus and Paolo's young nephew, who had just undergone the change. The struggle on the floor was between a Golden and dark vamp. Last Lionel knew,

Rory was attending school in France, but his family lived in Tuscany. He wasn't sure Marcus or Paolo even knew he was in California.

Lionel was in a quandary. Hugh was ready to jump in, though it might cost him his night of sex.

Hold it, brother. Not now. Observe first. Lionel was satisfied to see that although Hugh had made fists with his hands, his giant brother inhaled and slumped his shoulders in resignation. He knew it was hard for his brother to control his urge for a good, hot fight.

The large dark vamp hit the back wall this time. Rory appeared to have gotten the better of him, having used some new moves he must have learned recently. He acted without hesitation, and anticipated the large giant's moves. No doubt the Executioner wasn't used to working out, nor felt any need to.

Both girls had scooted their chairs together and were clearly distressed. Lionel let his fingers lace through the redhead's hair and patted her head to reassure her.

Lionel watched the two sparring vamps who were making the whole block rumble, until the dark one suddenly straightened up to attention and turned at the arrival of another dark vamp, dressed all in black. Lionel remembered hearing a motorcycle revving up outside when the door had opened, and he knew this was probably Dag Nielsen, the new Coven Supreme Leader, though he couldn't see his face.

He wanted to ask Hugh mentally what Dag was doing here, but he didn't want to risk the uncloaking that could create. If he focused on it, Dag would realize who he was.

"Rory, my friend," Dag said as he grabbed the young Golden's shoulder and wrenched him around and back into the crowd of his friends. "You'd do well to leave California to our kind. We don't need you stirring up trouble."

Rory spat out blood and glared back at Dag. He looked from face to face, and Lionel could tell the Golden vamp was assessing who would be for him and who would be against him. The executioner was clearly taking directions from Dag. Hugh hung a worried look back as Lionel sought to ask a question without raising it mentally. What in the hell was happening? Had Dag been consolidating his ranks by eliminating another coven leader and adopting his Executioner?

The two brothers were careful, but Lionel could see Hugh gently nodding, biting his lip.

Rory took a swig of beer, straightening himself to address Dag. "I hold him personally responsible for the death of my little brother," he said.

This was news to Lionel. Had Morgan, Rory's ten-year-old mortal brother, been killed at the hands of this dark vamp? It made his stomach seethe, and he could feel Hugh wanting to step closer and get right in the middle of the fray. Loyalty and honor made Hugh spread his chest and take a deep breath.

Not now, Lionel quickly blurted out with mental energy. Dag immediately turned and looked over the faces in the crowd. The Jett brothers focused on Rory and turned off their minds. Their training was to go into focus on some detail of someone or something they hadn't noticed before, and that would mask them.

Through their peripheral vision, they saw that Dag appeared to stop searching for the thought source and returned to the two enemies before him.

"Rory, that has yet to be proven. But I think you need to understand you are way outnumbered here in California. And it's getting more so. You run home to mama, and tell her I send my love," Dag snickered in triumph.

Rory started to bolt toward the dark coven leader at the insult to his beautiful mother, Daria, but was held back by a cadre of dark security forces, who hauled him out of the bar.

Dag breathed in the agitation and smiled. It was like he got energy from the strife and Lionel could feel the power surging in the other man's veins. But that masked a probe he could feel like barbs in a wire fence. He wasn't going to fall for it. He resisted nothing, allowed the barbs to mentally scrape his flesh and did not flinch. He hoped his brother did the same, as they both sat down.

The one thing he would not do was look directly at Dag; otherwise the safety of their anonymity would be shattered. He pulled the redhead to his lap and laid down a kiss so intense she nearly fainted. Her arms were wrapped around his neck, her fingers making luscious circles through the dark curls of his scalp. He wished she would pull his hair a little, and she did.

He drew his head back and looked at the dizzy expression she wore. The woman was a walking, talking sex doll, and he planned to take his time learning every inch of her. He felt the dark coven leader swish by him on his way outside. The executioner was on his heels.

A few stilted minutes later the room returned to its party atmosphere. The music resumed, but the laughter was careful. The reckless abandon of the last hour was clearly altered. Lionel felt a grip on his upper arm.

"Let's get out of here, brother," Hugh said.

"Brothers? You two are brothers?" the redhead said.

Lionel smiled and nodded, focused on her lips. He'd caused a tiny cut and there was a drop of blood near the corner of her mouth he wanted to suck dry.

"We're sisters!" she said, her breasts giggling like they were bursting to break out in song.

"Perfect."

It was all he could think to say.

Chapter 23

CARA WAS ANXIOUS to return to poring over the old book she'd recently acquired from the bookseller in Prague. As she pried open the thick green leather, the letter she'd seen before but never read fell from the interior. The cream-colored envelope had a distinctive letter "M" embossed on the upper left corner. As she noted before, it did appear to be addressed to an A. Fraser of Edinburgh.

Her fingers smoothed over the ripped surface of the flap on the back where a red seal had been broken. The relief pattern in the fragile sealing wax was that of a Medusa-like face with lips that drew together as if mouthing the letter "O". Cara held it closer to her and detected a faint lemony-camphor wax scent as she examined the puffy checks of the image, and realized the face was caught in the act of blowing something in the reader's direction.

Strange.

Her fingers shook with anticipation as she removed the single sheet from the envelope and began reading the old black script.

Dear Brother Ignatius,

I fear I must warn you of something that has come to light recently. I believe you have purchased a book, specifically The Book of Spawn, as it is known. This book has been illegally sold from our family library, and is of great personal value to us, and is the final book of a series of volumes. My wife and I are worried sick about it, fearing it might have fallen into black hands.

My dear Brother, your calling to God on high has no doubt acquainted you with the black arts and those who practice them. They would use these sacred texts which have been handed down from generation to generation amongst clergy trained to contain and dampen the effects of these black arts. In the wrong hands, the book could prove to be lethal, not only to the possessor, but to those who would cause our society harm.

I must implore you to return the tome to my estate in Tuscany immediately. You will be compensated handsomely, and will be free from prosecution, I assure you.

As a further warning, I need to inform you that the person who sold you the book has met a most disagreeable end, and not by my hand, or that of any of my family. I believe there are other dark forces at work who will stop at nothing to make sure they have full possession of this book.

You will be doing your race and the future of mankind a great service by returning the book to me as soon as humanly possible. I would be happy to entertain you at my estate as well as make a sizeable donation to the church, or to any one person or organization you choose.

Again, this is not a matter of money. It is a matter of life and death. And you, my dear Brother, are in grave danger until you divest yourself of this book.

Ever yours,
The—

Cara couldn't make out the signature, except for the fact that it was heavily inscribed in an artistic scrawl. The black letters bounced across the page in front of her, appearing to be breathing. Under the signature line was scripted the date *14 February 1710.*

She closed the letter in half again and slipped it inside the envelope. She was going to put it back into the book, but thought better of it. She added the book to the false bottom compartment of the old desk in her living room. The letter she slipped under the floral drawer liner of the underwear compartment in her bedroom dresser.

She was distressed by this new bit of information, and had a twinge of regret that she'd been so preoccupied with the party and meeting the mysterious Paolo that she hadn't taken time to study the Fraser book. She would have found the letter much sooner, in time to reconsider Johnny's field trip to Berkeley on her behalf. She became concerned for his safety and decided she needed to hear from him. She called his cell phone.

"And here I thought you'd perhaps had second thoughts about spending the night with me," Johnny said with a chuckle.

"You're persistent. I'll give you that."

"Well, I'll take whatever I can get." He turned down his radio and continued. "I was given the name of an occult bookstore owner in San Francisco, although it was too late to call. Will do so tomorrow."

"What did the research assistant say about the book?" Cara asked.

"Said the book you're looking for is called *The Book of Spawn*, but he doubted it really exists. Like pieces of the true cross. Urban legend."

"Ah." Cara hesitated to tell Johnny about the letter she'd found. "When did this book last appear, or did the assistant know?"

"There is some notation of it being recovered in the charred remains of an abbey that burned to the ground in early 1700's in a little village in Tuscany. The brothers there poured over it, tried to restore it, and spend some time cataloguing it. In the end, it seemed to have disappeared until your friend Alasdair Fraser started digging around. Cara, he may have found it."

"Interesting. Is that what the assistant said?"

"He said Fraser was known for his braggadocio. Lots of exaggeration, and who knows what. Up until his death. It was pegged a suicide, but we know the guy just disappeared, along with much of his research."

"Yes, and we know there was a big book burning after he was declared legally dead."

"True."

"Anything else?"

"The assistant seemed to think the bookseller in Prague would be your link, unless the San Francisco bookstore owner, who he says specializes in witchcraft and vampire books, and has one of the most extensive collection of rare books in the world, knows where it is. He thought it even possible the bookstore owner himself might have it, or know where it is."

"Good. That's a great lead, Johnny. Maybe you and I will have to go there sometime soon."

"It would be fun. I'd like that."

"Good. Well, we'll plan it, then."

"Can I ask you something?" Johnny's voice had lowered an octave.

"Sure."

"You talk to your mystery man?"

Cara quivered at the thought of *her* mystery man, and what they had done this afternoon. The way his kisses scorched her flesh. The way his tongue had its way with her private parts...

"Cara? You still there?"

She wondered what she should say. What was wise? Paolo Monteleone was her own private dream, a fantasy she wasn't sure she should even be having. He was dangerous, but his presence demanded consort with her psyche.

She sighed and resigned herself to the fact that she would never be able to keep the secret she hoped she could. Just containing the ripeness of the facts would send her into frenzy. "I had lunch with him today. Right when you called, as a matter of fact."

"I see. I thought about you. For some reason, I was worried. Are you all right? Are you with him now?" The last question he whispered as if he'd been seated next to her, instead of on the other end of the phone. As if Paolo could hear him ask the words.

That was a good question. She somehow felt *with* Paolo Monteleone, even though she had requested, and been granted, her leave. She did not expect to see him again. Not if she could help herself.

"We had lunch. He showed me a little of his family estate in Healdsburg. I had supper with his brother and sister-in-law and his son."

"Son? He's married?"

"No. His wife has passed."

"Ah, dark widower, then. Mysterious. Did he kill her?"

"Johnny, I'm going to stop talking about this if you don't behave."

"Couldn't help it."

"Yes, you can. You can do a lot better. We had a nice supper and then he returned me quite safely to my home, where I am right now, Johnny. No worries. I'm quite safe, and alone."

"And in need of company?"

She paused long enough to briefly think about what she would have considered just a couple of days ago. But not now.

"No. I'm sorry, Johnny. We are not going to have that kind of relationship. We work together. And right now, my work comes first."

She was so close to uncovering the mystery and the myth of the sacred joining, she felt as excited as she had on her first day of school when she was five. She knew her theory of the union between the God of Love, Jamal, and his queen consort had something to do with sexual liaisons, and the mixture of bloodlines.

"I get it. But if I find you the book, you will be sufficiently grateful, right?" he asked.

Cara let a tiny laugh bubble up "Very. But don't pin your hopes on it meaning a night of sex. The book might turn out to be the directions for collecting data on birth control in the third century instead of some divine coupling treatise."

"Yes, boss. I will be your lackey. Your yard dog. But I'm going to exact a price if I find it."

"I'm sure you will. But let's not worry until we find it, okay, Johnny?"

"Yes, ma'am. I'm nearly home. See you in the morning, teach?"

"Most definitely." She was about to sign off when she had another thought. "Johnny, why don't you leave a message for the bookstore owner tonight? Then perhaps he'll call you tomorrow while we're in class, or early before he opens."

"Good idea."

Johnny hung up.

It had been an exhausting day. Cara wanted another hot bath, but hesitated. She'd been enjoying the faint scent of his flesh on her skin. Even the backs of her hands where he had kissed her smelled of him.

The side of her neck, where she could swear he had bitten her, was sensitive to touch. Laying her fingers there, she could feel her pulse flow strong and steady. The vein in her neck seemed to press against the fingers she held lightly in place.

She felt something cold at her neck and turned around. No one was there. She walked to the bathroom and tuned on the bath water, sprinkling lavender salts and bubble bath generously into the swirling hot water. With steam rising beside her, she examined her face in the mirror. She closed her eyes and removed her top. She removed her bra and felt her hardened nipples under the tips of her fingers as they squeezed and kneaded the soft skin of her breasts. She thought perhaps there was a second set of hands helping her along in the process, helping her slip down her skirt and panties until she stood naked.

Something warm between her legs seemed to vibrate, a gentle sensation and she began to orgasm, imagining him tasting her there, lapping and nibbling on the lips of her labia. But when she opened her eyes, there was no one near her, no one appeared behind her in the mirror. Swinging her arms out, she turned and could neither feel nor see anyone standing in her bathroom.

The water continued to pour into the lavender scented bubbles, calling her.

She stepped into the tub and then sat, keeping her knees to her chest until she got used to the heat. She shut off the water and relaxed, leaning back into the tub and closing her eyes.

That's when she heard his words faintly caressing her face as if he was suspended above her.

"Mi amore."

Her eyes flashed open, but no one was there. Cutting across the light purple bubbles and pungent floral scent was the smell of fresh-picked lemons.

The same scent she'd found on the sealing wax.

PAOLO HAD BEEN surprised his whisper traveled to her. Although he was clear across the valley from Cara's home, he could see her in his mind. He saw the beautiful flesh he had tasted, the tapered ends of her fingers as he felt what she felt, those rich pillows of flesh that were her ample bosom. He knew what it tasted like to be between her legs, and his mouth watered as his fangs dropped. He'd been heartbroken when she slipped into the water where her scent would be buried in the lavender.

He'd conjured her, rubbing her vision all over the erection he felt in his pants and he'd said it—"Mi amore,"—more as a need than a prayer. And he saw her react in his dream. She'd *heard* him. He could see it on her face.

"Can you love me, Carabella?" he whispered. He watched as she turned around in the tub and checked the wall behind her. She was looking for him. She rose to her knees. The delicious shape of her shoulders, narrowing at her waist, and the soap bubbles slipping down her back to the upper reaches of her bottom. He was tantalized. With her hair up atop her head she turned again and looked right at him, except he knew she really didn't see him. But she felt him spying on her.

And the lovely object of his desire wasn't afraid.

Thank the God of vampires.

Still on her knees, she inserted a finger between her legs, arching backwards.

"Give me your pleasure, Carabella," he whispered, as he stroked himself. His cock had gotten rock hard and was seeking freedom. He felt her shudder just as if he was deep inside her. "You feel me? You feel my hardness? You feel my seed wanting to find solace in your folds?

He heard her moan, "Yes. Mi amore."

Could it be? Could she hear him, feel him when he wasn't there? What was this connection?

"Deeper, I want you deeper," she said.

Paolo grasped the arms of the chair in his bedroom, then hastily unfastened his pants, peeling them off his thighs and letting his penis leap out unbridled. "Need to be inside you, Bella. Invite me in, please let me come inside you," he whispered.

And then he heard it.

"Yes. Come to me."

The summons took only a second and he had traced to her bedroom. He was in the tub with her, his shirt wet and clinging to his skin, but his cock had found her opening and he raised her knees up over his shoulders and, pulling her buttocks toward him with both his hands, forced her over him, sending him deep inside her.

She opened her eyes wide and saw him. Really saw him.

In a flash of energy, water was splashing everywhere as Cara struggled to get herself out of the tub, knocking bottles of bubble bath and crystals all around the granite ledge, some breaking on the floor. She then stepped on the broken glass and cried out as she began to hop, holding one bloody foot behind her as she ran for a pile of clothes on her bed.

Paolo stood up, at first unaware of how ridiculous he must look, with a wet white cotton shirt and nothing else, his cock drooping, his limbs covered in bubbles.

"Bella, please, love. Let me explain."

"Don't you fucking get near me you animal!" she screamed. She held a knitting needle in her right hand like a dagger.

"I can explain this to you. Please, let me do so."

"I don't want to hear anything from your mouth except the apology you'll give me after I've had you arrested."

"Don't you want to know what happened? Don't you want to know how I got here?"

She looked at him for a second, and he thought perhaps there was a chance she would allow herself a glimpse of the truth. But sadly, she was full of anger and fear. Her naked body shivered, but she seemed not to notice. There was no place where logic could take hold, he realized.

"You get out of my house this instant. I'm still calling the cops. I'll let you explain yourself to them."

"Cara, it isn't what you think. Honestly. Please."

"No? You sneak in and fuck me when I'm taking a bath. Violate me when I'm daydreaming. Did you slip something into my wine or something? I'll bet your creepy brother is on his way over here, too, and you'll both do me and laugh about it all the way home. That the way you rich playboys operate? Can't get girls the right way, so you have to drug them to get your jollies. Well, not with me, you cretin."

"Bel—"

"Get the hell out of here."

"Bella, you called me."

"I did nothing of the sort."

"Yes, you called me. I *traced* here. But you called me. I couldn't help but come."

"You lying son of a bitch. Get out!" she screamed. Paolo was worried someone would come inquiring, she was so loud. Soon her phone began to ring.

"I hope this is the cops that someone in my building called. If I had a gun I'd shoot out both your kneecaps."

"I'll go. But you need to know one thing."

"Just go."

"You need to know I am vampire."

"Just—what? What did you say?"

"I am a Golden vampire. An old race. Yes, Carabella, vampires do exist. There are many of us—"

The phone stopped ringing abruptly, like someone had ripped it out of the wall. Paolo wondered if his powers had done this.

"Shut up with your lies," she said.

"It's the truth. Think about it. One moment you were daydreaming, then you called my name, asked me to come, and I did. You wanted me inside you. I obliged, I am sorry to say." Paolo noticed his member had begun to arch up again at the talk about coming and obliging. In a horrible twist of fate, Cara glanced back at his groin. Her frown and look of utter disgust broke his heart.

"Who do you think I am, some bimbo you have to give some fantastical explanation to so you can get laid? I'm not falling for it. Or, are you one of those who get off on violence. Well, if you want violence—"

She stepped towards him, holding the knitting needle high above her head, ready to strike. He traced to her side so fast she looked everywhere in front but didn't suspect he'd made it all the way around her. He grabbed the knitting needle and tossed it out of the bedroom and down the hallway. His arms encircled hers as he held her in place, covering her back with his chest, making her immobile. He whispered into her ear, with a trace of glamour.

"I love you. I would never hurt you, mi amore."

He could feel the softness of her limbs, the warmth in her heart he had touched, but then her natural human instincts kicked in and she went rigid with fear again. It was no use, he realized.

"You are an animal. Get your filthy hands off me or I'll scream and alert the whole building."

Paolo traced back in front of her, standing now longer than an arm's length away. "Enough," he said. "In time, you will have questions. When you do, I would be happy to answer them."

Cara started to shake. Paolo reached for a large bath towel and threw it toward her so she could cover up, which she quickly did. He found another towel for himself and wrapped it around his waist. He felt completely ridiculous in his sopping shirt, wrapped in a light yellow-colored bath sheet, dripping wet, naked and barefoot.

"I'll return the towel tomorrow," he mumbled, staring at the wet bedroom floor.

"Keep it. I never want to see you again."

Paolo loved the stern fixture of her jaw, lips slammed shut together, the determined stare as she tried to be brave. He knew she'd have a problem with this next part, but he couldn't help himself. He broke a wide grin, and before she could react, he traced home.

Chapter 24

NO WAY THIS *happened in my bedroom. No fucking way.*

Cara was still shaking as she looked at the bamboo floor where he'd just been standing. A puddle of bubbly water quivered and began to fill in two small dry patches where his feet had been. Just five seconds ago. He'd been standing there, wrapped in her bath sheet with that smirk, that satisfied smile on his face.

Is it evil that I am still attracted to this—man?

But he wasn't a man, was he? She walked over to the puddles he'd left behind, as if they held some clue. She dropped to her knees and hesitated before she wiped it up with her towel. His towel's mate. The towel he said he'd return and she said, "don't bother." She didn't care about the damned thing. She cared about the male she'd spent the afternoon and early evening with, shared a bubble bath with. The male she allowed to violate her again.

'I am vampire,' he'd said. *'Vampires exist. There are lots of them.'*

He was completely delusional. Or was she? It didn't make any sense. None of it. She lassoed her mind to focus on him, searching to see if the connection was still intact.

Are you there? No! Don't answer that. Don't contact me unless I call you.

A tiny flame inside her belly made her insides glow, and she had her answer. Yes, he was still there, and he could hear her.

Now what do I do? Don't answer that, she said to him across time and space. *It's a question I have to answer for myself.*

She waited. No answer. This was a good sign. She told herself it was a good sign.

Thank you, she told him mentally.

Always, mi amore, came the reply.

"No!" she screamed. "You can't do this to me," she said out loud to the room. She checked the ceiling, behind furniture, and in the closet. She let out the water in her tub and checked under the bed.

I am right here. At Marcus and Anne's home. In the guest bedroom.

Stop it, she answered. *Get out of my head. Go away and don't come back unless I call you. No exceptions. My rules. We go by my rules.*

There was no response.

Reassured he wouldn't interfere unless called, Cara began to focus on her own body. The shaking began again, like she was going through some kind of withdrawal. The stress and roller coaster of her emotions had made her very tired. She knew she needed sleep.

Cara put on a white satin nightie with a fuzzy lining to take the chill off her skin. She did have the fleeting thought about one way she could instantly warm up; she could have him in her bed and immediately the shaking would stop. But the craving would continue. Her memory of his hot kisses, the feel of his limbs against hers, his chest pressing against hers, the incantations he liked to whisper to her belly were becoming hard to ignore.

She turned off all the lights, but lit a lemony votive candle beside her bed.

Why?

Well, she knew why. She slipped between the smooth cotton sheets, lay back watching the fluttering circle of light from the candle as it projected onto the ceiling, and began to smell its scent filling the room. With heavy eyes, she drifted off to sleep, but not before she saw bonfires, old stone buildings, some of them ruined. Wet cobblestoned streets glowed in the moonlight. She could hear the clop clop of horses. She heard weeping; she saw the tear-streaked faces of beautiful women. Some were modern women, some in older dress, like a parade of characters throughout time. She saw Lucius picking apples on the top of a ladder in a sunny orchard, being steadied by strong masculine hands around the little boy's waist. Paolo's hands. She felt the trembling body of the boy as if she'd hugged him herself.

She sank into oblivion, grateful for her life.

And feeling oddly protected.

PAOLO GAZED OUT the opened window in his bedroom and watched over the nearly bare, leafless vineyard by moonlight. A spitting, raging fire in the fireplace had not sufficiently warmed him. His bones were cold, as if they'd been made of iron. He felt brooding, heavy.

He was both delighted and annoyed that she could still communicate with him. His emotions balanced on the edge of a sabre's blade. While it meant she wasn't dead to him, psychically, he also knew that there was no way he could predict her choice in outcome. If she chose to stay away—and she was strong-willed for a human woman, stronger than his wives had been—perhaps she could physically will herself to stay away from him forever. In time, perhaps she could learn this. They were not fated, after all. That horrible fact felt like the stake in his chest that the dark vamps dreaded.

He was losing her. He'd shown her his horrible, animal side when she summoned him and he had no choice but to obey that summons. Fuck her in a bathtub when all she wanted to do was have an erotic fantasy about him. He had no control. He felt despicable, like a dark vampire animal. Like his enemies. Was he becoming his enemy?

When Cara's natural human psyche took over, she would be dead to him, just as his three wives were. Perhaps that's what had made him think of them, and the pain of watching them age, and their eventual passing. He did not want to bury a fourth. Cara had a human life to live and Paolo refused to take that away from her.

He had been just as addicted to Maya and the fates of their kind as Cara was feeling about him. But Cara had a chance at freedom, whereas Paolo had none. He'd be forever caught between the mortal world he missed and the Golden vampire world he couldn't fully embrace. Which meant no happy household filled with lots of brothers and sisters for Lucius.

Lucius. The little boy would need a father who could wisely counsel him.

He'd made his wives comfortable, showering them with riches, with travel, with things to make them forget their empty wombs. But the emptiness, the grief was still there, after all the gifts and fantastic excursions to all the corners of the earth. And while he could heal many of their physical ailments, but he could not cheat death, all passed into the afterlife mortals go while he held them. While he prayed for their souls. While he grieved, again and again.

Paolo had begun to think it was his purpose in life to grieve. The God of vampires had put him on the planet to demonstrate to Golden vamps everywhere what not to do with their lives. Should he have tried to make a life with that half-witch mother of Lucius? Could that have been the right action he'd missed along the way?

The answer he came up with was always the same.

No.

With the coming war brewing, romantic love, at least for now, would have to take a back seat to the safety of his son, his brother's family, and the future of the Golden vampire race.

He sighed and hoped Cara would find restoration from her much-needed sleep. Sleep that would not come to him tonight. Though he tried to hold the tears back, he found himself weeping silently, looking at the stars exploding in the night sky, wishing for something he could never have. He wondered if the God of man was capable of taking pity on him as well.

He said his prayer for healing Cara's confusion and hurt. He said his prayer for the safety of his son. He asked for courage to do the right thing, and for peace to come flooding into his soul as he prepared for battle and for the uncertain future that awaited them all.

Chapter 25

D AG RETURNED TO his rented two-story flat, and found the little blonde waif waiting for him just the way he'd dreamt he would. She was naked, spread-eagled, and handcuffed by wrists and ankles to his iron bed frame. He had a burning desire to hurt and maim something, and it was the first time he was sorry he was about to fuck his brains out and perhaps kill the mortal woman. This, and this time only, it would have been nice to screw a female vamp so that she could heal and he could do it again later on. Fuck her to death again and again. After all, his needs came first, before that of any other living being, human, Golden or dark.

"Who did this to you?" he asked. Her eyes were dark, and he realized she had taken some drug.

"You did, master." Her throaty voice made him want to shove his cock into her mouth and make her choke on it. He traced next to her and felt the delicious ripple of fear that went like a lightning rod through her tender pink flesh. He liked surprising, scaring her.

"You altered yourself." He sniffed her, then licked one armpit, feeling the elixir of her sweat turn his dick hard as steel. It hung cold and heavy between his legs. He wanted her to feel how ripe he was for her.

"I asked permission of your houseboy."

"Houseboy? I don't have a houseboy."

"The one who opens your front door? I assumed he was your male pleasure partner."

"Can it," He barked and took another lick, this time running his tongue down and over her left breast, over the knot of her nipple that went purple and welted under the sandpaper of his tongue. He could eat that breast, but the pain would distract her from coming, and he so much wanted her to come for him. "I don't fuck boys."

She smiled in that sweet innocent way that had hooked him the first time he'd seen her panhandling in front of Starbuck's.

"Not even their—"

"So you decided you liked it in the ass after all? Is that why you're back?"

"No. I'm back for your cock. I need to be filled with your will." Her eyes were having trouble focusing. She moved her head back on the pillow, jutted out her chin, which arched her back and put her breasts very close.

"Take me, if I am worthy, master."

"Did the 'houseboy' fuck you?"

"What if he did?"

"I would have to wash you. Or kill you. And then I'd kill him."

"If you wish me cleaner than I would otherwise make myself for you, you may wash me. But I have not had another man's cock inside me since the last time you gave me your blessing. I have fingered myself, though. Many times. Remembering—"She groaned into the pillow, exposing her lovely long neck. He could smell her arousal since her legs were wide apart for him.

He wanted to ram himself inside her so bad he felt like shredding his clothes and getting to it. But his phone rang. He swore and looked at the display.

Uncle Colin.

He stood, adjusting himself. She had focused on his package, which pulsed and ached inside his leather pants.

"Uncle?"

"I have good news about the book."

Hope began to grow in Dag's black heart and he momentarily forgot about the girl, until he began to smell her again. "I'm all ears," he said as he watched her struggle against the handcuffs. The pink folds of her labia made his fangs drop and his mouth water. His tongue slid across one sharp point and he tasted his own blood, sending him an erotic jolt.

"The bookseller's transaction records just came through. I told American Express I was his only surviving relative, explained the tragedy of his whole family, you know." Colin's voice trailed off. He continued, after taking a deep gulp of air. "The transaction paperwork and his seller ID you gave me helped."

"Let's not fuck with each other Uncle Colin. Tell me what you know.

"Well, the book was shipped to a post office box in Sonoma County, just north of here." Colin sounded pleased with himself.

"Ah. Very good. And to whom was it shipped?"

"Ah, let me see," Dag could hear the rustle of the slips of notes Colin had pasted all over the wall behind his desk. "Here it is. Carabella Sampson in Santa Rosa."

"They shipped a rare book to a post office box?"

"I suppose so. That way it requires a signature, I believe. Here is the box number. Perhaps you can get more information from the postal authorities."

Dag smirked at the thought. "Not likely. But I think a night visit is in order, and their customer service desk will be closed."

"Well, I wish you luck. Let me know if you need anything else."

"I appreciate that, Colin."

"If that is all, then—"

"Wait a minute. Did you tie up dark Vicky?"

Dag felt the pregnant pause on the other end of the phone. He could barely hear the response. "No."

"You're a lamb playing with a coyote. She'll scratch your eyes out and leave you for dead if you don't control her." Dag glanced at the blonde and gave her a wolfish grin, showing his fangs. Her eyes momentarily got huge and he felt his cock lurch. God, he wanted to fuck her till dawn, but now the book was calling to him.

"Please, Dag, she hasn't been home in a day. Over a day now. I had no opportunity."

Dag knew it was a lie. "Then I suppose I'll have to do it and show you how. You will bring her to me in a few nights, understood?"

"Dag, I don't think that is necessary—"

"Of course it's necessary. I'm going to show you how to control a woman. Make her come until she wishes for death." His upper lip twitched, as the blonde understood the meaning of his words. Tears began to stream down her cheeks as she gave him that soft, pitiful, waif-like look. It tore a hole in his heart, for some reason. And it made him damned mad at the same time. He didn't like anyone to show weakness. He wanted her to defy him so he could break her. So he could scare her to death. Then he'd decide if she could live. Her life was putty in his hands, and he wanted her to know it. Wait for it. Not know what the outcome would be.

"Uncle Colin?" he asked as he licked his lips and crawled onto the bed.

"Yes?"

"Bring her by Friday night around eight. This will be a life-changing event. For both of you." Dag flipped the phone closed and tossed it onto the bear rug on the floor. "Where were we?"

She said nothing. Her tears did not stop in defiance. She bore her fear and pain like a mantle of gold. Her pride made her breasts swell. He sniffed the air, filled with the scent of her. "Shall I ravish you now? Or later?"

"You are going to kill me. What difference does it make?" Her tears had stopped. Her lower lip quivered as her moist lips framed the words.

Dag bent down and kissed her hard, forcing his tongue down her throat until she gagged. "Would you swallow my cock this way?"

"Please."

Dag was filled with the power of his dark passions. His phone rang again. "Fuck!" he shouted and was going to throw it against the wall until he noticed the display. His first lieutenant was trying to reach him.

"Rhys? This had better be important or I'm going to cut off your left big toe, which I understand might not seem like much of a punishment, considering the state of your toenail."

Rhys had a chuckle, and Dag found himself suddenly lighthearted as well. The delay in sexual satisfaction had become pleasurable all of a sudden.

"Supreme, we wanted to be sure we did the right thing by letting the girl into your chambers. She is no longer mortal. But she insisted you'd made her for your own pleasure, and had summoned her."

"Yes, I thought you rather would. You didn't mind sneaking a little something while you cuffed her to my bed?"

"We thought it best she be restrained so she wouldn't get into things. And we figured you wouldn't want us to wait by her side, watching her."

"You did well. Except for the drugs."

"Not my idea. It was hers."

Dag swiveled around and stared at her eyes looking back at him innocently. *She is such a liar. I'm going to be extra rough until she tells me more lies.*

Rhys chuckled again. The blonde raised her sex as high as she could. Her buttocks hung beneath her and quivered. He could hear the slick moisture between her legs.

"Hurry it up or I'm going to come in my pants. Anything else?"

"You sending us out on a mission tonight? I can get Rubin and we can go back and do Rory. Thought you might like that."

"Rory's mine. But you can get the executioner and call on the Librarian. He has a name and a post office box to look up in Santa Rosa. You could go do that. See if you can find the person who has the book. Colin will give you all the details."

"The Post Office will be closed, sir."

"Then open it. You do know how to do that, don't you?"

"Yessir. Will do."

"And Rhys, what did she take?"

"Don't know, sir. She brought it with her."

Dag signed off and turned off his phone. The next person to interrupt him would pay for it with his life. He'd come out when he was good and ready. He hoped to get drunk with lust, and the girl's blood. If she was lucky, and very good, he'd let her live.

Chapter 26

CARA AWOKE WITH a start and then realized she'd slept so soundly, probably in the same position all night long, that her body ached. Daylight had produced a pink blush on the blue-grey sky. Checking the time, she decided to get up early and prepare for a long day of classes and meeting with Johnny.

She smiled as she thought about her research assistant and his proposal the night before. Could she consider him a welcome distraction? Someone she could pass some pleasurable time with as she tried to rid herself of the vision of Paolo? And how awkward would it be if she experienced a wonderful evening of sex with someone else, knowing Paolo would also feel every ripple, shudder and her body's inner explosion?

Would she be able to let herself go, feel the joy of sex with any other man? Ever? Could she beg that he stay away, stay out of her head?

"I am vampire," he'd said. Incredible as that idea was, she could not trust herself right now to believe him. Even though all the evidence pointed to that undeniable fact. Maybe he could be some kind of psychic who could control her thoughts. Maybe he'd convinced himself he was a vampire and she was falling under his mental spell. That she might be able to wrap her mind around and believe.

She lathered herself with shower gel, enjoying the silky feeling of her own skin, letting her fingers slide over areas he'd kissed. Her nipples were taught and tender, her pulse boomed throughout her body as she remembered him beside her, inside her. He was, after all, the man of her dreams, but a vampire? *No way.*

Cara pushed the visions of him in the shower with her out of her head and concentrated on getting clean.

She hardly thought Paolo could be the sort to suck the lifeblood from unsuspecting females in the night, she decided as she toweled off. Besides, she'd been with him in the day, in the sunny afternoon. There were no ill effects, other than the craving she felt for him and his lovemaking, how he satisfied every sexual desire she'd ever had and a lot she'd never imagined by herself. Something just yesterday she'd have thought was heaven-sent.

She hung up her damp towel and looked at herself in the mirror.

I've had sex with a vampire? No. It wasn't true. There must be some other explanation for the things happening around her.

But how could she explain the sudden disappearance, right before her eyes, she wondered as she slipped on her black lace panties and matching bra. She brushed her hair, staring again into the mirror. Would he like the way she looked right now?

Stop this, she scolded herself. Cara tried to focus on the facts, the details of his disappearance. There had to be something she was missing.

Must be some trick. Some sleight of hand. But, she'd checked her room last night, and he simply hadn't been there. And yet she still heard him respond to her, telling her where he was after she questioned it. She knew if she asked him right now, he'd answer her. Should she try it again?

This is crazy.

Cara finished dressing. She had chosen a little black dress and patterned stockings with black pumps. She scrunched her hair up with a crystal-embedded black clip, and wore bright red lipstick.

My version of Elvira, she thought. Yes. He would love the way she looked. Only things missing were red fingernails, and she wouldn't go that far.

PAOLO HAD WATCHED the sun rise, sitting at the kitchen table by himself. He was filled with loneliness and regret. She hadn't called to him, although he'd stayed awake most of the night. He wished she had needed him in her bed. Maybe she *was* going to be able to live without him. He knew he was going to have to prepare himself to live without her. Question was, who would be stronger?

But then he felt her hands smooth down the black wool dress, over her breasts, her hips and her flat tummy. He closed his eyes and could feel the heat of her body as he imagined her standing in front of him, as he bent to kiss her lovely neck so nicely exposed for him. He imagined his palm sliding up under the black fabric to feel—no—to need to feel the softness of her flesh encased in black panties. She wore black for him today. His groin became granite.

Would he be able to concentrate on anything today except the thought of her? He decided he'd better learn to.

Marcus entered the kitchen in his boxers, bare-chested.

"Morning, brother," he said to Paolo.

"It is a beautiful morning. I watched it being born." Paolo tried to sound cheerful.

Marcus went to the coffee maker and poured himself a fresh cup Paolo had brewed. The smells of the Mocha Java blend swirled around the room as Paolo sensed his brother was hesitating to speak of something. Marcus joined him at the table and sipped the hot, black liquid.

"Got a disturbing call from Lionel Jett last night."

Paolo felt alarm spread up and down his spine as he sat up straight and focused on the handsome face of his older brother and the worry lines between his eyebrows.

"Oh? How so?"

"You know Rubin, the executioner?"

"I can hardly say I know him, but, yes, I've seen his despicable work. Don't tell me Lionel had to experience one of Rubin's trophies."

"Rubin was emasculated in front of a whole crowd of onlookers at Press. Not physically emasculated, mind you, but it appears he has a new master," Marcus' dark eyes focused on Paolo's coffee cup, avoiding his brother's questioning gaze.

"Who might that be?" Paolo knew it before his brother answered.

"Dag Nielsen."

Paolo looked out the kitchen window to the garden and bare-limbed orchard that spread down the hill. This was definitely not a good sign.

"Rory Monteleone confronted him about the death of young Thomas. Dag stopped the fight."

"What happened to his protection team?" Paolo wanted to know.

"They were there, but outnumbered by Rubin's men and some new dark vamps Lionel had never seen before. I think they were hoping the fight would just die on its own, but when Dag showed up, Lionel decided to stand down. He was with his brother, Huge."

Paolo nodded. "You sent him out?"

"Not exactly. Took it on his own."

"Where are they now?"

"I'm assuming they're sleeping, hopefully alone."

Paolo found light amusement in the fact that the Jett brothers were extremely attractive to human females and had never had trouble finding fleeting companionship without strings over the decades. Something he was unable to do.

Good for them.

"I have to tell you Lionel is worried. Very worried," Marcus continued. "It appears the numbers of darks are increasing at an alarming rate, almost like an army is being assembled here in California."

"Why here?" Paolo asked.

"Good question."

"So the executioner is now Dag's man. Hard to imagine Trevor Farnsworth would relinquish him," Paolo said.

"Which means Trevor Farnsworth is dead. As is Dag's former Coven Supreme Leader."

Paolo wondered how the other dark coven leaders were handling this turn of events. He suspected there could be an ally or two amongst them, but wasn't sure who he could trust.

"In case you're thinking of getting further involved, I forbid it, brother," Marcus said over the top of his coffee cup.

"I already am, Marcus. As long as I'm in your household here in California, if you are a target, I am certainly the secondary."

"Not true."

"Excuse me?" Paolo knew he wouldn't like what Marcus was going to say next.

"Brother, search your heart. Look at what they have been doing, picking a fight, luring out the younger Goldens. You know as well as I do that the real target is Lucius."

Paolo didn't want to agree, but he had to.

"Leave the research and covert stuff to us. I think Lionel was born for this kind of caper. Your primary responsibility is to your son, to see to it that nothing happens to him. Mine is to Anne and little Ian. I've asked Lionel to find us some human ex-special forces guards he can trust. We may need the protection both day and night now."

"So living in idyllic Sonoma County with heavily armed guards—will this be the kind of lifestyle you wanted, brother?" Paolo asked.

"I have no choice. Not until they come out in the open. I think this will become an all-out assault soon. Don't think we have much time. I've already notified the Council, and they are sending an ambassador.

Paolo knew this had not happened in more than a hundred years. Their species had enjoyed a relative peace with the mortal as well as the dark vampire world, allowing the Goldens to blend into human society and amass great wealth and power. But he knew nothing human could stop the dark forces looming in the distance.

Best keep my wits about me. Humans have gods they can pray to. Right now I can't be bothered with such drivel.

CARA PARKED HER car in the employee lot. She was a half hour early for class, so decided to stop by her office to see if Johnny had thought to do the same. Oddly, she felt happy to get back into the routine of teaching, being of service to her students. It would give her delicious moments away from thoughts of—

The moment she opened the glass door to Montgomery Hall, she noticed that a small group of people had formed a semicircle outside her office door. Her pumps clacked down the shiny vinyl tiles of the otherwise deserted, wide hallway.

The circle parted and left just enough room for Cara to insert herself. She looked down at the floor, where everyone's eyes were focused. Seeping from under the locked door to her personal office was a puddle of thick, red blood. It was getting larger.

She dug into her coat pocket for her keys, setting down her computer. As she reached for the door handle, ready to insert a brass key into the lock she heard a shout from the opposite entrance to the hallway.

"Stop! Wait. Don't touch anything." Two uniformed policemen were running down the vinyl hallway, their equipment jangling on their leather utility belts. "I must ask you to step away—all of you," the heavyset older officer said, scanning the crowd and finally landing on Cara with a scowl. "You have the key to this office?" he said to her.

"Yes. It's my office."

"Any idea what's gone on in there? Who I might find on the other side of this door?" the officer said.

"The only other person who has a key, other than someone in Admin, is my research assistant, Johnny Davis." Cara stared at the blood and for a brief moment, thought she would lose her breakfast all over the policeman's shoes. She inhaled sharply and added, "I was to meet him here, or in the classroom this morning."

"He acting funny or out of sorts?" the officer asked.

"No. I talked to him last night. He seemed fine."

"Let's see your key," the other officer held out his hand. It was clad in a plastic glove. Cara deposited the keys in his palm, isolating the office key. The officer stepped wide to avoid the puddle of blood and knocked on the door while the other officer dispersed the crowd. Sirens were shrieking in the background. When there was no answer, he tried the handle and found it locked.

Cara felt strangely disconnected, and numb as the officer inserted the key into the lock and turned the handle. She watched the other officer with his gun drawn, holding it with both hands with mild detachment. As the door creaked open, the limp body of Johnny fell out into the hallway. His face was caught in a grimace, lips beginning to turn blue, his face ghastly white and not the tanned, healthy look Cara was used to. His head rolled at a weird angle, barely connected to his neck.

Someone had practically ripped Johnny's head from his torso. Cara's blood went ice cold. She couldn't stop herself from staring into the glassy blue-grey eyes of her once fun-loving assistant. It was as if she expected him to sit up and tell her he was playing a prank.

But this was no prank. Death stared back at her and for the first time in her life she was terrified, frozen in place, unable to do a thing about it.

A woman onlooker fainted and another started to scream. People began retching and racing through the hallway doors to the outside. More uniformed officers arrived and took control of the crowd. Cara remained transfixed. She slowly began to wonder if the person who had laid in wait for Johnny had intended her to be the target. She wondered how someone managed to get out of the office without leaving the door unlocked, since the door could only be locked from the inside without a key, almost as if someone could walk through walls.

Or transport.

"That's—that's Johnny, my assistant…" Cara heard her voice waver. Tears had started to collect in her eyes. The sickly smell of fresh blood singed her nostrils. She turned her face to the side and examined the inside of her office door.

"What is it?" one of the officers asked her.

"Someone must have a key. You can't walk out and have it lock behind you automatically. I had the locks changed because I was locking myself out all the time."

"Found a key here," one of the officers said as he searched Johnny's pockets.

"So I gotta ask you one more time, who else has a key?"

"The admin staff, and probably the college janitorial service. They have a whole crew."

The second officer stepped aside and spoke quietly into his shoulder microphone. Cara looked into the office after the light was turned on. Papers and books were scattered everywhere, some with their edges soaking up Johnny's lifeblood. Every drawer in her desk had been upended. All her shelves were wiped clean, the books nearly covering the entire floor of her tiny office. The telephone receiver was left off the hook. Even her trash appeared to have been searched and dumped on the desktop.

"Can you tell if anything obvious is missing?" one of the uniforms asked Cara.

She shook her head. "Impossible to tell. Who would do this?"

"Not a robbery, because it doesn't look like his wallet has been removed," one of the officers said from his kneeling position next to the body.

"I'd say, from the looks of it, someone was looking for something stored in a book or file somewhere. You got anything, a valuable document maybe, that someone would want?"

Chapter 27

PAOLO FELT THE terror in Cara's heart. He saw the body in front of her just as if he was standing there. He had to work on himself not to trace to her side for protection. But he had given his word.

He'd gone back to the guest wing and was planning to take Lucius to school personally when he received the vision of Cara's office. The to-do list he had created was crumpled in his right hand.

"Father, I'm ready." Lucius ran into the room and gave him a hug. The boy's fresh mortal scent always made him feel lucky, and incredibly happy. But today, knowing there was probably a dark vamp on a killing spree, his need to protect his son weighed on him. It was suddenly urgent he talk with the Jett boys to make sure the daytime detail was in place. He wanted to personally interview every one of them.

"You've had your breakfast?" he said to Lucius' dark brown eyes. The boy's freckled nose scrunched up, and Paolo saw he'd forgotten to have anything to eat. "You want a hamburger and French fries and a strawberry shake on the way?"

"Could we?"

"Well, you could. But you know I don't care for the taste."

"I know." Lucius' palms lay flat against Paolo's cheeks. "You are what you are, and I am what I am."

It was one of those moments when Paolo was convinced the boy could not have been of his issue. The roles at this particular moment had been reversed, and suddenly he was student to his son, who was wise way beyond his years. His need to protect his son was paramount. He knew that if he had to sacrifice himself to save Lucius, he would be doing his race a tremendous service. Paolo saw in the boy the future of the whole Golden vampire clan. He could feel the boy's destiny as surely as he could smell the blood of mortals.

Paolo felt ridiculous going through the fast food drive-through while driving Marcus's black Maserati, something Laurel and the other siblings back home in Tuscany would find odd. But this was Lucius's world, and it included drive-through, text messaging and cell phone games. He wanted the boy to have a normal upbringing, not living the gilded princeling days of the superrich, which might distort his warm heart and avid mind. Lucius would be required to do great things in the future, Paolo thought. Time for being a king among Golden vampires would come soon enough. Now it was time to be a normal human boy.

They sat in the car while Lucius finished off his meal and wiped his hands and face with the moist towelettes he carried in his backpack. This also surprised Paolo.

"Where did you get these?" he asked as he held up the foil packet.

"Cook. She said using these would keep me from getting the flu."

"Ah." Paolo made a mental note to thank the cook, who was more a grandmother to the boy than his real grandmother, Aurora, that half-witch bitch mother of his fated female. Paolo found the reminder of the boy's mortal vulnerabilities touching.

He got out of the car and gave Lucius a brief hug so as not to embarrass him, and then watched him join several other friends. The cheerful gang of normal human boys ran together to their classroom just as the bell was ringing.

As he sat in his car, he felt another wave of Bella's despair. He'd seen Johnny's face and felt her mourn for him. It didn't make Paolo jealous. But he wished she would summon him. He could reach out and touch her with a message, but he'd given his word.

As he drove back to the Monteleone estate through downtown Healdsburg, he was struck with how normal the little town looked. Since it was a tourist Mecca, several large white busses were parked near the square. He pulled into a parking spot and went inside to get a cappuccino and hope he would feel Bella reaching out to him soon.

The screaming of the milk foaming machine was harsh, but not as harsh as the sound of sirens whizzing by. Perhaps there had been an accident on the freeway. Paolo's cell phone rang. It was Marcus.

"They've found Rory dead in an alleyway. Ripped the poor boy's head clean off."

Paolo knew Marcus was beside himself with grief. Since Rory was in California, and under Marcus' protection, this would be counted as a failure on their part, but would fall mostly on Marcus.

"I think the time for you to remain in California is limited, brother. You have to ask yourself if it is worth it."

"I'm not running from them. They won't defeat us."

"Maybe not us. Maybe we'll live for eternity, but what about our children, Marcus? Surely they don't have to pay the price."

"I'm taking measures."

"Simple when Ian is little, but I just dropped Lucius off at school. He'll be unprotected until I pick him up. I'm going daft with worry just thinking about it. As much as I hate to, I think I should bring him back to Tuscany, where we have the majority."

"That's your choice. What about the girl?"

"Sacrifice, brother. My primary goal is to keep you, your family and my son safe."

"She knows more than she should, Paolo. You perhaps should wipe her memory."

"That I can do." Paolo flinched inwardly about the difficulty of this task. He wasn't sure he could bear the look on her face when she saw him for what she would think was the first time. But it would be for her own protection. "There is other bad news, Marcus."

"Oh?"

"The girl's assistant was found dead this morning in her office at the University."

"Found dead?"

"From the sight of the face, I'm guessing he was drained. Neck ripped open and head ripped mostly off, though. Brutal. A dark executioner did this, I am positive."

"What's the scene like?"

"I haven't been over. Just what she saw, and she was scared brother. Almost catatonic. The office was ransacked." Paolo paused, and then said in a whisper, "We still have that gift, brother. I can feel her emotions, and hear her thoughts. Like a fating. And it's getting stronger."

"Is it a fating?"

"Sadly, it is not. Definitely not a fating. Although I have tried to tell myself it is. Wouldn't it be incredible if there was the possibility I could have two fated females?"

"Unbelievably lucky. But you say no."

"The physical attraction is there, no question. But not the animalistic, all-encompassing—"

"I get it."

Paolo had always felt guilty for bedding Marcus's long-time paramour. "This is different. The feelings I have for this mortal woman are growing. And with those feelings, the gifts are getting clearer and clearer."

"Interesting."

"And I have control, not that I don't want to be by her side, but I still have some control, not like with—"

"There has to be something of substance there. I'll consult with the Council next I am in contact. In the meantime, why don't you trace to her? Investigate the murder?"

"She hasn't summoned me, and I gave her my word."

CARA SAT ALONE in the lecture hall, where her now-cancelled classes would have taken place, her head resting in her hands elbows dug into the black desk top. She gently rubbed her temples, and remembered how Paolo had done this, to ease her mind. She imagined his long fingers atop hers, imagined hearing his steady breathing and drawing in his spicy, lemony scent. She knew she could call him and he would be right there, in front of her. She knew she wasn't hiding anything from him by refusing to summon him because he knew what she was feeling. The ache she felt for him was growing.

You are still an addiction to me.

She was relieved that he left her alone. But was this smart? Somehow, she knew he had answers she needed.

The coroner and forensics team were done with the office, the body, and their questions for everyone who had been standing around the door, as well as the janitor, the school administration officials and several of her students who knew Johnny better than most. They stuck their heads into the amphitheater door and said their goodbyes. She had a tiny stack of their business cards in case she remembered or found something of interest.

She could not warm up, and a dull ache pounded in her thighs. Cara's bones were stone cold and she felt old. She wanted to be home in bed in her flannel pajamas, wrapped in the comforter her grandmother had made, with a cup of hot tea and a lemon slice on the side.

Lemons. Will I ever be able to smell lemons without—don't answer that.

The shock of the last few hours gave way as she finally allowed herself to grieve for Johnny. Warm tears streamed down her cheeks as she raised her head and stared at the sea of empty lecture chairs.

Why? Why Johnny? Had something happened at the dance she didn't notice? Did Johnny have some kind of secret life that she knew nothing about? Or, was it a random act?

'They're looking for something in a book, perhaps a book itself.' Perhaps it was time to show Paolo the book.

Should I be afraid of him? Who can I trust? He seemed like the only option available to her. Johnny's death left her feeling alone and unprotected in a world that suddenly felt very dangerous.

"Paolo?" She said to the room. "Are you there?"

I am.

I'm afraid. Johnny—

I have seen it through your eyes. You are in danger. Let me come to you.

I have a book I think you need to see.

Book?

Yes, I have located a book by Alasdair Fraser. And there is a letter in it. I think you should see it.

Yes. Cara, do not think about the book right now. Make no mention of it in your mind, either. Summon me so I can protect you. You are in danger, mi amore.

There it was again, that doorway to the unknown. He was asking her to believe in the fact that he was vampire and could be summoned. That perhaps someone else could read her thoughts. Did she really want proof of this?

Nothing can harm you if I am by your side. Alone you are vulnerable. He did sound urgent.

Okay. She remembered what she'd said in the bathtub, *Come to me, Paolo.*

And there he was, standing on the other side of the desk, all six foot something of him. Handsome, eyes ardent and studying her face, her neck, her upper torso, making her tingle and blush. He smiled as if he could feel what she felt inside.

Of course I can. It brings me unspeakable pleasure to do so.

Tears began to well up as her emotions exploded. It was too much for her to comprehend. Johnny was dead. Killed by some sinister person, probably a vampire, perhaps a vampire Paolo knew, which made it even worse. And there was an undeniable attraction to this tall male who could transport himself immediately from here to there, had fangs, and who had made her feel wonderful just yesterday afternoon—all afternoon, making her feel more alive than she had ever felt in her life. It was a strange combination of death and new beginnings.

I am at a crossroads.

You are, mi amore.

I am afraid.

You should be. There is a war brewing.

"Can you help me? Help me understand?" she asked him out loud.

I can, if you will trust me. He held his arms out to the sides, beckoning her to come to him. She had no choice but run to him, nestling her face in his chest, reveling in the feeling of his arms wrapped around her. Protecting her. Perhaps—something else too.

He held her face between his large palms. "Let me teach you about me and my kind. There isn't nearly enough time, and this isn't how I wanted to do it. But if you understand, I can teach you what I believe are some opportunities possible. Things neither of us ever dreamed could happen."

She placed her hands over his wrists and studied the strong face of the man she knew she had fallen deeply in love with. A man she had been searching for her whole life. Cara decided in that moment to embrace the new adventure like her life depended on it.

Because perhaps it did.

Chapter 28

THE FLUTTERING OF warm wind all around Cara made her feel like she was floating in a cloud of butterflies. Pressed against Paolo's chest, as he held her there, she laid her head to the side and listened to a heartbeat she hadn't known he had. In a handful of seconds, the sensation stopped, the tracing was complete, and she was standing in her bedroom, her arms up and about his neck.

She tipped her head back and willed him to bend his full red lips to cover hers. It was delicious to moan into him, and feel the deep rumble of his chest in response. He took everything she could give in the kiss, but she still needed to give him more.

His fingers laced through the hair at the back of her head. He pulled, arching her face away from his, kissing the side of her neck. She pressed her lower torso into his groin and felt his desire.

She needed him too. *Please,* she mentally sent him between kisses, now becoming ravenously needy. She was starved for his ministrations.

Cara began to remove her blouse, watching as his eyes went to fire while she removed her bra. He came to his knees and kissed each nipple tenderly. She held his head, clutching at the loose curls, loving the feel of his mouth on her sensitive flesh.

"You are a wonder, mi Carabella."

You awaken me.

He groaned and lifted her up, laying her tenderly on the bed. He removed his clothes and then shimmied her skirt down her hips like tissue paper. Slowly hooking her black lace panties with one long forefinger he slipped them easily down, the backs of his fingers smoothing over her thigh all the way to her ankles, and then off.

He parted her knees, tenderly easing two fingers inside her folds. She arched with the pleasure of his penetration, of the reassurance of what was going to happen between them in the coming moments.

"I've missed this," Cara said between sighs. She wanted to lose herself in the feel and scent of this man and forget the ugly scene from earlier this morning.

He twisted his head to the side, and with the lopsided smile curling up the corners of his smooth, full lips, said to her, "Bella, mi amore. It has only been one day. Already one day is too much for you?"

There it was, the honesty between them, though there was still so much she did not know about him. She was unafraid to show him how much she needed him to make love to her. "Yes. Already one day is too long without this." It was difficult to get the words out.

He covered her body with his, sliding his thighs beneath hers, lifting her bottom up off the bed with his hands and pausing at her opening. "It is the same for me, Carabella. I dream of this almost every waking moment."

He began to slide inside her, slowly. She lost herself in the dark pools of his eyes, the faint lemony scent of his chest covering her, making her feel safe and protected. Without speaking she was telling him how it felt, how her body ached to be possessed by him. He nodded and gently filled her to his hilt. Then he began to pump and drill deep inside her, pulling her chest up flat against him, pressing her breasts into the warmth of his hard body. She drew her arms up over his neck and he grabbed her underside, moving her up and down on his enormous shaft. His long, fluid strokes rocking her body back and forth on him made her insides explode.

She squeezed down on his girth until at last his spasms overtook him. He lunged deep inside her and held her buttocks in place so hard she thought perhaps she'd have welts.

I will kiss the pain away, if I've left a mark, he told her.

"I'll wear your mark with pride," she whispered. "I didn't want you to let me go."

I never will he said to her. "Mi amore," he whispered into her ear, kissing down the right side of her neck.

She knew he wanted to bite her. He was looking down, at the place where their bodies joined as their breathing hitched in tandem, as she admired his flat abdomen and the shadow that was their joining. She lifted his head, placing her palms under his jaw, and placed his forehead against hers. She relished the feeling of him between her legs, the rhythm of his breathing. His mouth was just out of reach, so she turned her head and mated his lips to hers, and then searched for the fangs inside with her tongue.

She allowed a pinprick from his sharp canine, and presented the drop of blood on her tongue to him, spreading it over his own. His breath became ragged, and labored like a runner. His cock inside her sprang to life and began to lurch. He rocked her body over his groin, burrowing deeper, in a circular motion.

"Take me, Paolo. Take me *your* way. I want to do this for you," she said.

At first he shook his head, but she held his face in her hands again and with firm resolve, nodded back, "Yes, I want you to take me in your way. Your custom."

"There is no custom for this. You are human and I am vampire."

"Please?" she begged.

"This is not wise, Carabella." He groaned as she clamped down on him again with her muscles.

"I need this. I need you to mate with me, Paolo, in the old way, the ancient way." She kissed the side of his neck and under his jawline. "The way of your ancestors," she whispered in his ear.

His eyes held questions. She was searching for some indication as to what he was thinking, but he had blocked his thoughts.

"Let me in, Paolo. Let me see what you don't want me to see."

He smiled. She could feel his will dissolving, and images started coming on strong. She saw herself naked across his big oak carved bed with the cream satin sheets. Torches lit the room and shadows on the heavy stone walls danced in the erotic rhythm of his heartbeat. Her arms were pinned above her head as he held her wrists with one hand.

You would take me to your bedroom?

That is my room in Tuscany. If I took you there, I would never let you go. Never, Carabella. He closed his eyes and the image was gone.

She traced his hairline with her forefinger, marveling at the tanned, smooth skin, the shiny dark hair and the dark, chocolate-brown eyes with lashes that made him look dangerous and demure at the same time. He'd told her he was naturally shy.

Do you blush when you recall what we've done? She asked as she kept her legs wrapped around his thighs, holding on with arms wrapped around his neck.

His warm smile told her everything she needed to know.

Take me now, Paolo. Here, on my bed. Take me and mark me and make me your own.

He bent to give her a brief kiss, then followed below her chin and then laid down a moist trail with his tongue, tracing over the vein pounding in her neck. He held her back with two strong palms beneath her shoulder blades. His eyes scanned her chest, paying close attention to her nipples as they hardened under his gaze.

Relax, he said to her, and immediately she was flooded with waves of pleasure. The touch of his skin against hers, inside her body, warmed her and she began to glow.

She relaxed her weight, trusting that his powerful arms would fully support her. His neck was exposed to her as well. She leaned forward and let her tongue wander and taste the salty goodness of his skin as he had done earlier.

He kissed her again, sucking and nibbling on her lower lip, making little liquid noises, and then inhaled.

Are you sure?

I am sure, Paolo. I want you to take me now.

The sound of her skin being breached was surprisingly loud. Like a bee sting, there was one moment of pain, and then euphoria traveled all over her body. His cock inside her began to swell while the muscles in his arms and shoulders tensed. He was trying to be gentle, but she could feel that urge to turn their lovemaking into a blood feast. He squeezed her flesh with his fingers, rubbing his thumbs over her afterwards to soothe the reddened skin. To his hardness she remained soft and giving. As he squeezed, she gave even more.

Take me. All of me.

She began to get light headed and saw large black spots in front of her eyes. The spots began to join. She lost her grip in his hair, and, without effort, fell back amongst her pillows, her arms raised above her head. Paolo followed her down, lapping the puncture wounds like he had done before, and then pulled away.

She could barely see him through the slits in her eyes, which were hard to keep open. Paolo gave her his wrist. "Drink, Bella."

"No, I don't want to hurt you."

"You can't hurt me. Drink. Drink for me."

"I don't want to bite you."

He smiled. "Very well." He placed two fingers inside her mouth and she tried to suck on them. "Open your mouth," he said as he pressed his lips against hers. "Open," he whispered.

Cara obeyed. Paolo's tongue slid over hers, and presented a few drops of his coppery goodness, blood that sent her ears buzzing. With his fingers, he rimmed her lips with his blood. She licked her lips and he suckled them. He repeated this process several times until her light-headedness subsided.

She suddenly felt like she could jump over the Golden Gate Bridge just using her own energy. A glow emanated from her insides out.

"What is this? Is this the fating I've read about?" she asked him thrilled with the way her body tingled.

"No, Carabella," he said as he traced a finger down her chest, between her breasts and then down to between her legs where he touched her lips and ringed their joining spot. A trace of a smile lit up his face.

"This, Carabella, is love."

Chapter 29

THE BITE AND the rejuvenating droplets of Paolo's blood led to another tussle between the sheets, and a long orgasm that lasted several minutes, leaving her feeling wrung out and totally limp. She heard things happening outside in the park next to her complex—details she'd never heard before, like conversations between people and the tapping of a runner's feet along the garden pathways.

Her ceiling looked the same; however, the reflective light from car bumpers and shimmering leaves cast light and dark shadows on the smooth surface in greater detail. Light patterns seemed to dance all around her. Her entire world had shifted. She was in love, no, she was *consumed* by the love of a vampire.

They lay side by side, their thighs touching. Even her sense of smell was enhanced as she recognized the scent of their joint arousal. The droplet of cum she'd tasted from him during their lovemaking had sent curious jolts of electricity down her spine, jarring her and making her sex hungry again. She knew it was not going to be possible to get enough of him in the days and weeks to come.

I willingly am your addiction. I will host off your pleasure, Carabella.

His words send a shudder of pleasure through her body again. Everything he did sent her into a euphoric state. She turned, leaned onto her side, propped up on her elbow, and looked down at him. Her fingers traveled the smooth tanned surface of his muscular chest, up under his stubbled chin. She wondered if he had to shave. How often did he get his hair cut? There were so many questions she had now.

He'd blocked something from her. She knew he wanted it to be a private thought.

"Why keep certain thoughts from me?" She asked as she kissed his chest and toyed with his left nipple with her teeth.

"I don't want to scare you away."

"What would scare me?"

"The future."

That's when she realized that she was looking forward to her future with all her heart, and he was looking toward it with dread.

THEY DRESSED AND made arrangements to get her car, which had been left at the University. Cara brought the book and the letter inside it, secreting it beneath some changes of clothes in a duffel bag.

"Does this mean you've invited yourself to what you call a 'sleepover'?" he said, his fingers caught in his belt loop. His hips were slung at an angle, and he was mind-numbingly bare chested. Cara couldn't decide whether she liked him in jeans and no shirt, or just plain naked. The effect on her body was the same.

"Hardly," she said as she turned and continued to stuff things into the bag. He moved to sit on the bed, watching her. "I didn't pack any pajamas," she said.

"I don't like pajamas. I like sleepovers without pajamas."

"Good to know. So, am I invited?"

"You are commanded."

She raised her eyebrows and formed an "O" with her lips. "Really? Commanded?"

He blocked another set of visions, but not before she definitely saw her own hands bound with black silk ties, and felt him filling her from behind. "Aha! You weren't quick enough."

He, blushed, and then smiled. A noise outside the window drew his attention. "Cara, we have to go. It isn't safe."

She was worried, so went to look out the window, but he grabbed her, pulling her back into the hallway. "You have the book?"

"Yes, right here." She held up her case.

"Then we are off. Hang on."

Again the fluttering of butterflies mixed with his scent carried her on a sensual cloud until she was standing in the grand room of the Monteleone estate in Healdsburg. An older woman was polishing an antique curio cabinet and jumped, startled, when they arrived.

"Oh, good Lord, Paolo. You nearly scared me to death," she said, clutching her heart.

"I am sorry. I needed the safety of the house perimeter and didn't have time to trace to the front door."

"Paolo, you're back," Marcus shouted out as he appeared from the study. "Cara? Does this mean you'll be joining us again this evening?" he said as he pointed to her duffel bag.

Cara looked back up at Paolo for the proper answer.

"Brother, I believe Cara is in danger, especially with the death of her assistant."

"A real tragedy, in more ways than one," Marcus said.

Cara stepped toward the older brother. "I've scarcely been able to get my breath," she said until she realized what she'd implied. Blushing, she continued bravely, "Do you know who has done this and why? I for one think it has to do with this book." She held up her bag.

Marcus squinted and tilted his head to the side, obviously thinking. Cara wasn't sure he wanted to have anything to do with the book, but Paolo took her bag in one hand, her elbow in the other, and lead her to Marcus' study. "Quickly. We need to act quickly."

Marcus stood at the doorway while Paolo zipped open the bag, which sat on Marcus' paper-strewn desk. "I'm not sure this is wise, Paolo." Marcus's long limbs carried him to beside Paolo in long fluid movements, just like Paolo's gait. The brothers looked remarkably alike, except for the slight difference in height. Marcus placed his hand over the unzipped bag. Paolo took a step back and clasped Cara about the waist from behind, waiting.

"This unlocks doors that, once opened, cannot be closed," Marcus said. "We are investigating something greater than the health and safety of this great family." Marcus's words of warning made her heart pound and her hands sweat.

What does he mean, Paolo? Help me.

Paolo gave her waist a squeeze. "Brother, perhaps you are saying

Cara has to be brought up to date. It may be time for her to learn about our family and what she has unwittingly become involved in."

Marcus examined his knee-high black boots, his legs crossed in front of him as he balanced himself against the front of the desk. "My brother makes it difficult for me, Cara. I must tell you things he has not been able to, due to—"

"I know what he is," she said. "What you all are. I know you are a vampire coven."

Marcus winced. "No, not coven. We are a dynasty. A family. We protect and stand for one another. We don't feed off one another. Our family does not perform the hosting the coven families do. If you can even call them families."

"They are animals," Paolo whispered.

"No, not all. We have some who can be loyal, Paolo. Never forget that. Without them, we would have little information on what is happening in the dark world."

The shiver down Cara's spine forced her to move to the side, away from Paolo. "Dark world?" Cara crossed her arms across her chest and stepped away again when Paolo tried to encircle her shoulders with his arm. "I'm needing some interpretation here. I need some answers and I want them right now."

Marcus motioned to a red velvet settee and asked Cara to take a seat. Paolo wisely sat in an ornately carved chair beside her. At the tall windows of the study, Marcus stared out onto the vineyards below. Mists still burning off the remnants of morning fog sent tendrils of white swirling through the air, framing the handsome Monteleone brother's profile. "Paolo, this is yours to handle. You have to make a decision here, brother."

Paolo stood. The two brothers looked into each other's eyes before Marcus broke it off and placed himself behind the huge desk and collapsed into a wooden chair that groaned under his size. Paolo slowly faced Cara and leaned against the windowsill. He had the same impossibly long, lean legs as his brother, but his face that always looked like it had been kissed by sunshine was slightly fairer than that of his older, brooding brother. No matter what happened this grey morning, she would always love Paolo's face. It would be the face she would see in her dreams the rest of her life.

She hoped it wouldn't turn out to be a nightmare.

I can do this. Was she saying this to convince herself or Paolo?

"I know you can, Carabella. But there is much to share." Paolo stalked across the office from bookshelf to bookshelf, each burdened with more books than Cara had ever seen in a private library. These old books had been dusted and cared for. Some were wrapped in plastic covering. A couple of rolled-up scrolls lay on a reading desk built into the bookshelf, next to a white pair of gloves.

"This is but a fraction of the books we own. The library in Tuscany is second to none. It would probably keep scholars busy for centuries. It rivals some of the great libraries in Paris, the U.K. and the U.S."

Cara noticed Marcus had picked up a book and was letting his fingers filter through the pages, but she knew he was paying close attention.

"The library chronicles the works of our kind, the history, our genealogy, things Marcus and I haven't even had time to learn about. Cara, both Marcus and I are over three hundred years old."

He raised his eyes to watch her reaction. Marcus stopped perusing the book to look up as well.

Cara knew he was telling the truth. "How does that work?" she asked. She felt immediately it was a stupid question.

No, none of your questions are stupid. "We are Golden vampires, which are a different species than the dark vampire covens. We are able to live in the sunlight. We can appear human, just as any other mortal. We are not. Our children are human, and, at the age of puberty or some time beyond, each child is given the choice, one time only. Our choice is to whether remain mortal, human, or become Golden vampire. We can only mate," he blushed, and Cara loved him for it. "We can only produce offspring with our fated mates. Only then is the blood passed down."

"So you have had a fated mate, then," Cara felt the weight of her words falling into the pit of her stomach.

"Yes. Unfortunately, yes." Paolo's steady chocolate gaze poured into her chest, but it didn't lessen the burden.

She told herself it wasn't important. She'd not considered being a mother. She hadn't planned to consider it until she met the right man. And then she knew what had caused the pain in her stomach, what she was unwilling to believe about herself. She was staring right into the eyes of that man whose children she would gladly bear. She decided not to hide her disappointment, instead letting the sadness flow.

Paolo had frowned, furrowing his brow, and brought himself back the task of completing the story. "Our children are especially vulnerable, and, since they are very rare, cherished almost above all life."

As it should be, Paolo. You have a son and he will always be your primary responsibility. I understand this.

Paolo nodded, appearing glad she understood this. "So, until that time of choice, our children can be easily killed, just like any mortal child. It is for that reason we are so protective of our secrets, the secrets of the family."

Cara understood she was now the keeper of information few mortals knew. He trusted her, even if Marcus didn't.

"The fact that this is coming close to you means there is even greater danger than we thought, and certainly a lot less time than we thought we had."

"Time? Time for what?"

"Time to ready for the battle," Marcus added. "There's a war brewing between the dark covens and our kind. It will be a war of annihilation. Only one coven can survive."

"It appears they have chosen to embroil you in this war," Paolo whispered. "Cara, I didn't realize this until this morning. They are coming after you next. You are in grave danger."

"Is it because of us?" she asked.

"No, Carabella. I believe it is because of the book, and your knowledge of its existence. But the relationship we share will certainly complicate things," Paolo answered. "I did not want you involved in this. And now we have two choices, if they can be called that. We can either go forward and enlist your mortal support in this fight, or we can erase your memories and send you elsewhere."

"Elsewhere? You mean—"

"You would essentially become a different person. You could not study vampires. You would not be known as an expert. You could do and be nothing that would attract them to your scent. You understand?"

"You are joking."

"Wish I was. It is a valid alternative," Paolo replied. He walked fluidly over to where she sat on the settee and knelt in front of her. He took both her hands in one of his. "I would do nearly anything to keep you safe. The safest course for you in your life might be to stay completely away from me and my family."

"I couldn't—" she started.

"You could. It could be done. You could be made to forget we ever met."

Forget we ever met? Are you asking me to make that choice? I cannot.

"You remember when I told you, with the proper information, we might be able to do things we never thought possible before? This is one of the choices, Cara. But it would require you to move, to remove yourself from anything you ever knew of your past. Your life would start somewhere else. And trust me, you wouldn't be looking into vampires or the vampire culture, either. We can do that."

Cara felt sick to her stomach. What had she been thinking? She knew Paolo was concerned for her safety. He'd been blocking his thoughts ever since they left her place. The controlled, measured communication he'd just delivered hung over her like an axe. Any way she thought about it, her life, as she knew it, was over.

How could I have been so stupid?

It is my fault, my fault alone. I knew better, Bella. I should never have taken another mortal lover.

"Mortal lover? Am I that to you?" She felt like she'd been slapped. "Am I your pleasure partner for randy afternoons at the Inn, or early morning sex when danger is lurking around the corner? When those that are close to me are dying? Who's next? My students?"

She dropped his hands and pushed him back so she could stand up.

"Bella, I am truly sorry."

"Sorry? Sorry would have meant you wouldn't have involved me. For all I know, they are only interested in me because of you. You knew this—both of you knew this," she pointed to Marcus who was not smiling.

"You bed me, made me—do things," Cara frowned and shook off the sensual images of their sexual encounters. "I don't take risks. I like adventure, but I don't have a death wish, in case you—either of you— were wondering. I'd like to have my life back. I expect you will give that to me. No. I *demand* it."

"It isn't that easy, Cara," Marcus said through his teeth. The muscles in his jaw flexed as he spoke in monotone, choosing his words carefully. "I disagree with your conclusion. You involved yourself because you found something they want. If it weren't for us, you'd be dead already. But, make no mistake, you will have your life back, but you'll have to decide which life it is. Up to you how we handle this. We have limited options, but we will do what is best for our kind, there's no question about that. And Paolo will do whatever it takes to protect his son. Barring that, you can have it any way you want."

"Except I can't be Carabella Sampson, college professor, expert on the myths and mythology of vampires. No. I can't have that back."

Marcus traced over to her so fast it scared her. She could feel the anger boiling in his chest. "Why on earth would you want that if it meant you'd be dead in a day, maybe less? You just stood there and told us you didn't have a death wish, and now are pining like a sniveling child for a life that will mean certain death."

"Marcus!" Paolo inserted himself between his brother and Cara.

Marcus stomped away, then abruptly turned and faced Paolo. "You see now why having a mortal girlfriend is not a good idea? Now you have to make the decision for her, since she's incapable of deciding herself."

"How dare you—" She was going to run over to Marcus and

scratch his eyes out, but Paolo held her back. "Let go of me. I want nothing to do with you. Either of you. You are keeping me here against my will."

"Bella, please. Listen to me," Paolo said while defending himself against her blows.

"I'm done listening to you. I'm—"

Marcus had traced behind Cara, placing his fingers at her temples before she could react. Spots appeared before her eyes as she sank to the ground. Suddenly the whole world turned black.

"WHAT HAVE YOU done?" Paolo said to his brother.

"I've erased part of her recent memory. I gave her what she wanted. Not that she will live long to appreciate it."

"Marcus, you fool."

"No, Paolo. You are the fool. Trying to live in both the mortal and Golden vampire worlds. Your indecision has nearly cost her the only life she has. It still may. You should have left her alone. I told you this would be a problem. She is too strong-willed, and now she knows too much. This is the only way. If she won't choose it, we will make the choice for her, for her own best interest. You will bring her back to her own place and she will not know anything of what has transpired today."

"But what about Johnny, and the book?"

"I'll want you to report on what she remembers. This isn't an exact science. We have to erase any of her memory of you, Paolo, and certainly the book. You understand this is only for her own protection."

Paolo's sadness eclipsed his need for her safety. For a brief moment, he thought about arguing with his brother. But he knew it was no use.

Paolo bent and picked Cara up with one arm under her shoulders and the other under her knees. One arm hung down and Marcus placed it gently on her stomach. Paolo looked down on the face of the woman he knew he loved and sighed. "I will take care of this. I'll take her back to her apartment and stay with her while she revives."

"And say what? She may not know you."

"I'll think of a pretense."

"And you have to be careful. You could be tracing into a battle zone."

"I'll stay to the outside first, then I'll enter. She will need to be somewhere where she feels safe and comfortable. Her office is not the right place."

"Good. Make it quick. I need you back here."

Paolo took a deep breath in and traced to outside the door of her apartment. A door down the hallway closed, but otherwise the floor seemed deserted. He opened her door, which was still unlocked, just as they had left it. He brought her to the bedroom. The smell of their tangled sheets was still in the air. But something else was there as well.

Dag.

He set Cara on the bed and strode into the living room to find the curtains drawn and Dag sitting on the lemon yellow leather chair in the darkened corner. It was the first time Paolo had seen a dark vamp in daylight hours, alive.

"Greetings, cousin. Are you quite done with her? If you don't mind, I might enjoy the leftovers." Dag smiled. It was the first time Paolo recognized the scar that carried from Dag's left brow down his cheek to the flair of his nose. Paolo's beautiful sister had created the same sort of injury to a mortal would-be attacker one dark evening in the alleyway by a theater in New York City. He and Marcus had arrived just in time to trace her away with her two children.

Even as a mortal, Dag had been a devil.

Chapter 30

PAOLO CURSED HIMSELF for not being more prepared, but he hadn't expected any dark coven interference, since it was still daytime. Of course the dark Supreme Leader would show up himself. Which also meant he knew about the Paolo's relationship with Cara. All the more reason he hoped his brother's erasure worked. He also hoped it erred on the side of erasing too much information, rather than too little.

He was careful to guard his thoughts from the clever coven leader.

"Tell me how it is you are out and about in daylight hours?"

"I've been feasting on Golden blood, cousin. You do know what happens when I drain a Golden?"

Paolo tensed, waiting for the identification he knew Dag would be only too pleased to provide.

"Young Rory was quite tasty, Paolo." Dag strummed his fingers on the arm of the leather chair, which sounded like drumsticks across a skin with Paolo's preternatural hearing. "He died badly. But he was quite generous with his blood, although he had not much of a choice. I promised to spare his sisters for a year."

Paolo felt his blood boil. The rage inside him was so strong he felt he could almost explode the whole building, killing them all. "You are an animal. You have no business feasting off innocents."

"Oh, Rory wasn't innocent. He'd have killed my new execution-er—me too, if your thugs hadn't interfered. By the way, where is your protection detail?"

"Where is yours?" Paolo asked.

"Touché. So you can see I want to conduct business, since I have given you the advantage of showing up here alone."

"Her memory has been erased," Paolo informed him, hoping that would make the leader lose interest.

"Hmm. We shall see," Dag shrugged. He suddenly stood. "May I see her?" His dazzling blue eyes, which were a rare occurrence amongst dark coven vamps, contained swirls of deep navy smoke. Paolo knew that was the anger brewing.

"As if I could stop you. But be warned, she will not remember me or anything of what has transpired this morning."

"So she might not understand that she has been your lover, either. How sad for you."

"You assume too much."

"I'm giving you deference, just out of respect to your family, Paolo. Now, let me pass so I can check things out for myself."

Paolo knew Dag's Achilles' heel was his impatience. He decided to string things along a bit, to irritate the dark vamp.

"I will not let any harm come to her, even if she doesn't remember me. She is an innocent. Surely you would rather pester someone who is more important—a bishop, or female knight. Why go after a pawn when you can have a queen?"

"You mean Anne?"

"I didn't mean anyone. Just that this girl is unimportant now."

"Except that you will defend her to the death. I know you Monteleones. Very possessive of your women. Even if she doesn't remember you, I'm willing to bet a thousand mortal souls you'll remember every detail, every inch of her lovely body. And I'm also willing to bet you would protect her from me enjoying the same pleasures. Am I right, Cousin?"

"I abhor unnecessary involvement of mortals."

"Which is why you should never fuck them, Paolo. You see, you are more like me than your pompous brother would like to admit. I thoroughly enjoy fucking mortal women. I drain them, and let them die, too. You should try it. Very exhilarating."

"Isn't that sort of like killing or torturing your pets?" Paolo smelled Dag's foul mood oozing from the dark vamp's sweat. He wrinkled his nose. "Besides, if you smelled like that, how could anyone want to do anything but die after having you violate them?"

"It's the smell of my flesh rotting under the daytime sun. I don't smell at night," Dag said casually and appeared to be turning away. Without warning, he was on Paolo in a flash, hands clasped around Paolo's neck, scratching to tear at his jugular.

Paolo retaliated by tracing them both to the street corner in the center of downtown Santa Rosa, next to the park where the drunks and homeless camped out. Their fight would attract attention of onlookers who would never be questioned afterwards. Dag's flesh would start to burn and the fight wouldn't last long.

The dark vamp howled like a wolf as his skin sizzled and bubbled, turning black.

"You think you will win?" Paolo had pinned Dag's arms behind him, and had reopened the scar on his cheek under his eye. "I'm going to let you go. But she will be protected, and you will give the order, Dag. Or you will have the wrath of the Monteleone family come down hard on your twisted little coven. You prepared to start the war today? Over someone who cannot help you in any way?"

Dag yanked himself from Paolo's grip. He traced to a dark over-hang between two tall office buildings, licking his wounds, cursing. Paolo watched him touch the open wound with fingers covered in his own spittle. The deep gash was healing, but left blood on his collar. Dag would need fresh blood to satisfy the healing requirements of his sun scorch. Paolo entered the alleyway and held his nose at the stench.

"Just be glad you didn't do that in front of my men," Dag hissed. "Your day will come, young Monteleone. Your family will mourn you, as they have all the children I have taken." He looked up at Paolo, who stood several inches taller than the dark vamp. "Your children. Remember your children. Is she worth that?"

Paolo wanted to grab the leader and tear off his head, but he didn't have the permission he needed. Once Dag's deeds could be verified, there would be time for a trial and his ending. Of that, Paolo was sure.

"Slither off to your cave, snake. I will see you in battle. Until then, pick on people who are able to fight you one on one. Not an innocent.

Or, are you going to further prove dark vamps have no honor?"

"We don't live for honor. We live for revenge." Dag spat out. "Remember that when I take everything from you. It is revenge I fight for, and my rightful place above all the creatures of the world."

Dag disappeared, leaving Paolo in the darkened alleyway in front of a semicircle of homeless gentlemen and their shopping carts and puppies. Even the homeless, Paolo noted, didn't mistreat their pets. There were some things mortals did better than vamps, or at least dark vamps.

Paolo slowly began the walk back to Cara's apartment, rather than tracing, in case someone was tracking him. He wished it were nighttime, so he could have the benefit of the Jett brothers entourage. He didn't like the idea that he would have to be Cara's daytime protector, even if Marcus allowed it. He knew Marcus had plans.

The morning had started out so blissfully satisfying. It seemed as though the God of vampires gave him one last gift of her body, before he would have to give her up forever. What was he thinking? Why had he not been able to stop from acting on the attraction to her at that dance? He was stronger than she was, and yet he couldn't leave her alone. She'd called him her addiction. Wasn't it really the other way around?

Marcus was right, of course. But it didn't mean he had to like it. Paolo could barely hope there was a solution to this mess that didn't involve one or all of them perishing.

Other walkers passed by him, on their way to meetings, work, or to a late breakfast or early lunch. He couldn't hear their thoughts, and he was grateful he didn't have those powers. But then, he wondered if he would be able to speak to Cara and she back to him now that her memory had been erased? Would that power disappear?

He walked a little faster, turning the corner onto her street. He was anxious to see her revived, to assess the damage, if any, and where he might have to fix things Marcus had done. It wouldn't be fair not to orient her properly so she wouldn't walk right back into the same situation. He'd have to help Marcus with this, deciding how much to erase and what to leave intact.

Perhaps she could still be a professor, studying myth and lore. Just not an expert on vampires. He wondered if this could be done. He wondered if he could enroll in one of her classes just to be near her. Would it pain his heart to have her answer a question he would pose in class, and have him think about how beautifully their bodies had mingled while she merely answered the question with no such knowledge?

He decided that, if it were required, he could do it.

But, Marcus, don't ask me to stay away.

He heard Marcus' booming thoughts. *Wake her up. We have little time, brother. I need you back here, not wandering around the streets worrying about someone you should not think about. Please be quick. There is news.*

Paolo did as he was told and traced to her door, knocking softly on the frame. He heard shuffling inside, and then heard a chain pulled across the door he knew was still unlocked. She opened it a crack, her hair disheveled, sleep still blurring her eyes. Her full red lips were beautiful and called to him.

"Yes?"

"Sorry, miss. I'm with campus security at the University. You are professor Cara Sampson?" He hoped she remembered who she was.

She looked puzzled for a moment. "Wow. I had one whopper of a dream and just woke up. But yes, I'm Cara Sampson. Is something wrong?"

Paolo decided to try a little glamour. He sighed, sending some of his breath her way. Right on cue, she reeled backward, her eyes crossing.

"I'm sorry. Feeling light-headed right now. Can you come back later?"

"Are you all right?" he asked. He wanted to touch her. He could steady her if he could touch any portion of her skin. He sent a suggestion she release the metal chain. She drew her brows down over the top of her nose as she concentrated on the chain, and then allowed her fingers to slip it loose.

She turned and walked down the hall away from him, which gave

Paolo the opportunity to check out the empty hallway and close her door behind him.

"Here, please sit down. Let me get you a drink of water," he said as he took hold of her wrist. He could feel his calming powers spreading through her body. God, how he wished he could light a flame under her flesh again. He stuffed down the feeling.

Cara sat on the leather chair where Dag had sat no more than an hour before. She brushed the hair from her forehead and leaned back, revealing her long creamy neck. Paolo dashed to the kitchen, pouring a glass of water and coming back to present it to her. Their fingers touched as she took the glass. She jumped.

"Wow. Static electricity," she said as she took a long swallow. Paolo watched the delicate muscles in her neck move. He could still smell the remnants of sex in the room. He was getting hard, and he said a private curse to his errant body part. But it didn't listen.

"So, what does campus security want with me?"

Paolo didn't know whether or not to tell her about Johnny. She didn't appear to recognize him, so perhaps she didn't remember the dance. He decided to take a chance.

"When was the last time you saw your Research Assistant, Johnny Merrill?"

She took another sip of the water and set the glass on the coffee table. "Let's see, would be yesterday—no wait, maybe the day before. I'm supposed to meet him later tonight for a Halloween party."

"Halloween was two nights ago. Someone is having a party after the fact?" he asked, amused she didn't remember the party or spending intimate time with him at the bar.

"Something fuzzy is going on inside my head, like I've been sleeping for a week. Is everything okay? Is Johnny okay?"

"I'm afraid he's been found dead."

Her eyes got large and shimmered with tears. "What?"

"This morning, as a matter of fact. Forgive me if I impose, but you were there. You don't remember?"

She arched up and sat straight. "Don't you think I'd remember if I saw my best friend die? Where did he die, anyway?"

"Your office. He'd been murdered."

"Murdered! This morning?"

"We aren't sure. But you found him. You've already talked to the police. You don't remember any of this?"

She shook her head from side to side. "None of this." She held her head between her palms and began of cry. "What's happening to me?"

Paolo wanted in the worst way to take her in his arms. "I am so sorry, miss. I have seen this happen before. Sometimes graphic events do this to people and their memories. I'm glad I was here to give you the news. Wouldn't want you to find out on the news, or in class."

"My class! I am late for my class," she said as she stood and checked the large clock in the kitchen.

"No miss, your classes, actually all the classes on campus, have been cancelled, pending the investigation. The police I believe will have many more questions for you. So sorry." He tried to look at her with as little emotion as possible. But he couldn't help himself.

Do you feel me? He threw out the little thought, not sure what he would get back in return.

Cara stiffened, looking around the apartment, indicating she heard Paolo.

"Anything wrong?" he asked.

"I just think I heard Johnny's voice. He—he talked to me!"

Paolo was warmed by her misinterpretation. It thrilled him that she was still so available to him. He took his time to savor the moment, knowing it would be the longest time he could be in her presence, for now.

"You are a college professor, Ms. Sampson. Surely you don't mean to say that you believe in ghosts, or people coming back to life after death?" He tried not to use any of his glam, just to see if she would respond to him all of her own.

It worked. She looked at her lap. "No. Sorry. That sounds stupid, doesn't it?" She laughed in that off-handed, unaffected way Paolo loved. She brushed her hair from her shoulders and cleared her forehead. Then she leveled a gaze at him that sent a jolt straight to his heart. Her wide green eyes were luminous; no doubt her body was feeling the effects of his presence, even if her mind knew nothing of it. He felt the same way.

"So you want to tell me why you are here? I never did see a badge or anything. How do I know I shouldn't be afraid of you?"

"Good. It is smart for you to be thinking that way." He produced a card he used on occasion to explain his presence. "This is my card. We don't have badges, or uniforms. We never carry guns. We are merely here, trying to look like everyone else, not stand out, to keep an eye on things. It's not every day that we have a murder on campus. In fact, I don't think we ever have since the founding of the University. You will be contacted again by all the authorities, and we want you to fully cooperate." He stood and she did the same. "I do not mean to scare you. Just checking up to make sure you are not being harassed here at your home."

"Thank you. I appreciate it." Her warm smile hit him in the middle of his chest. Her eyes traced there, as if it were a familiar place, a place where she had lay her head at one time. Or, as if she wanted to be comforted there.

Then she brushed past him, the electricity of their closeness sparking another current he tried to ignore. But he could see she felt it too. At the door, she opened it. "I appreciate your concern. Unlike earlier, I must remember to keep my door locked at all times. This little chain," she said as she touched it with her forefinger, "wouldn't really stop a bad guy, would it?"

"No, indeed." He moved past her, brushing her skin one more time. Her breath hitched. "Call me if anything comes up. Anything at all. I also have some psychic friends who could help you with the other thing, too," he said with a smirk.

She crossed her arms and aimed her glare at him. "No. Thank you very much, but I think I misunderstood something. Remnants of a dream I was having perhaps. No doubt something the police told me I had forgotten until you mentioned it."

"Well, anything at all. Anything I can do, just call me." He turned and walked down the hallway, feeling her eyes on his back.

"You never told me your name. Well, I guess I could look it up on your card," she called out, her voice vibrating down the vacant hallway.

He looked at her one last time. Would this be it, he wondered? The last time he would see her? Would he be able to keep her safe from Dag and his forces? It was everything he could do to simply speak to her. What he wanted to do was rush to her arms, and glamour her until she wanted him again. His heart was breaking.

"I am Paolo Monteleone, at your service, miss." He found himself bowing, as he had done for the past three hundred years.

"I've met you before. You're not from around here, are you? Originally? I can detect an accent."

"Tuscany. Our family is from Tuscany, and some are in Prague."

"Ah! The vampires I study are from those two areas as well."

"Really? I didn't know." Paolo became hyper aware of the vacant hallway, not wanting to be seen there talking to her. "But as far as meeting you before, I'm sure I would have remembered such a beauty." He looked down to allow her blush to be private. "Perhaps you'll have to tell me about your vamps some time."

"Perhaps. Thank you for your concern, Paolo Monteleone." Her voice wobbled a tiny bit from the thudding of her pulse. Paolo loved feeling how he affected her.

She turned and closed the door behind her.

Paulo's heart was ready to leap out of his chest. This mental bond with her, his need to focus on her well-being to the exclusion of the rest of the outside world felt like a form of fating. No way this attraction was ordinary, for human or vampire. It was something else entirely.

He didn't have time to figure it out. The God of vampires was giving him another gift. Just being close to her was going to have to be enough for now. The war was looming and Marcus was screaming in his ear.

"Yes, I'm coming. I'm ready to do battle, Marcus," he said out loud but sent the mental message as well.

Chapter 31

Paolo traced to Marcus' study, where his older brother was perusing the book from Cara's things. He looked up. "Good. I was beginning to wonder if I'd have to come get you."

"I thought it important to make sure she didn't suspect me in any of the morning's events."

"Good. And how is her memory?" Marcus asked.

"Spotty." He smiled, remembering his delight that she'd heard his mental question. "But all in the right places."

"Excellent."

"But brother, there is another problem. When I dropped her off, Dag was in her apartment."

"Bastard. And he knew you brought her back?"

"What else could he have deduced? I told him her mind had been erased."

"Under the circumstances, I would have done the same. Good."

"She hadn't come to. I took Dag for a little discussion downtown Santa Rosa. He won't stay away from her, that much is clear. Not sure he buys she has no memory of her research, or the book either, Marcus."

"I will get the security detail deployed. Waiting to speak to Lionel tonight." Marcus looked back at the book on his desk. "This is fascinating. Pull up a chair and let me show you a few things."

Paolo brought a nearly black lacquered chair around and sat down next to Marcus at the desk. The book was opened to an interior page. There was an image of a horned man carved into a large door. Paolo read the inscription underneath:

This horned man is one of a series of three, which adorn the front of the Banqueting House. The three men represent the emotions of Hatred, Malice and Envy. The Banqueting House was said to be built for the eating of desserts, but others have suspected its use as a place for human hosts to be fed upon by vampires who invite them to dinner. It was a reminder to humans and vampires alike, of their symbiotic relationship.

"Symbiotic relationship?" Paolo asked. "Vampires have always feasted off humans. I don't understand."

"He's talking about some grand legend of a joining between the vampire and human races."

"Vampires have had many pleasure partners amongst mortal men and women. What's so fascinating about these?"

"These Banqueting Houses appeared to be places where more than just blood was exchanged."

"Again, no surprise there, Marcus. I just don't understand."

"New vampires were born there, too. It is referred later as the *Place of Beginning.*"

"Someone took themselves a mortal bride, drained her, and turned her to be his forever. She was born there. That's all he's talking about, brother."

"Alasdair Fraser has uncovered the fact that there are halflings, Paolo. Half vampire, half human. They are another race, brother."

"That cannot be. The fating. It makes it impossible to have children unless there is fating. There is no fating except between species. Even dark vamps—"

Paolo's eyes grew wide as he looked into his brother's stern face. Marcus was nodding when he said, "Yes, Paolo. Darks are Halflings. Half human, half vampire. Some experiment gone horribly wrong. A mixing of the blood that was never intended to be mixed."

Paolo leaned back and stared at the carved walnut ceiling of the study. He'd spent decades studying the reliefs and the stories they told. He wondered what the person who carved the reliefs had been trying to tell them. Suddenly there were more questions than there were answers.

"*The Book of Spawn* this letter references here," Marcus took out the letter that had been embedded in the text, "was once a part of our library, Paolo. It passes on the studies of this transformation, this experiment. I believe Alasdair Fraser found that book."

"This is the book Cara had?"

"No. She found and purchased Alasdair Fraser's book, with this letter in it. But I think the clues to where *The Book of Spawn* is located are in this book. I believe this is a map, a key."

"So the darks are looking for it because it contains the history of their origins as well," Paolo said.

"Exactly."

"Then they do not know about this book. They have no idea this book exists," Paolo guessed.

"I believe you are correct. They are after *The Book of Spawn*. They think that's the book she had. They wouldn't even recognize this one." Marcus was smiling as he stood, closed the book, walked over to the bookcase and placed it between two other older books. "It will be safely hidden in plain sight. If Cara doesn't remember the book, I'm not sure Dag and his dark coven hordes can find it. And I don't think she knows where *The Book of Spawn* is, either."

"Which doesn't ensure her safety, but means she is useless to them."

"That's right."

Paolo looked at the letter on his brother's desk. "What about this?"

"I'm going to take it to the Council. I've booked an audience with Praetor and the council for Wednesday. You want to join me? A little time in Tuscany could do you some good. Perhaps take Lucius where he would be safer?"

"I think he would like that. Would be good to see Laurel again, too," Paolo said, referring to their only unmarried sister.

"I'm going to make arrangements and break the news to Anne," Marcus started.

"You better take her, too. It isn't safe around here without your presence."

"I will be doing that. But you know how stubborn she can be."

They chuckled. After all, Anne was the one who had decapitated Marcus's witch/vampire lover and Lucius' mother within weeks of her turning. They learned never to underestimate her.

"I'll get with Lionel as soon as his sleep is over and make the arrangements for Cara's security detail," Paolo said.

"Good. Take Lionel's advice one hundred percent. He would never let us down. I consider him almost kin," Marcus replied.

"Wonder what the Jett brothers will do when they find out about all this."

"We'd just better hope we are the ones to tell them, Paolo. Be well. I'm off." Marcus took the folded letter, placed it back in the envelope and left the study, leaving Paolo to ponder the future he had not expected.

It was good that Cara should stay away completely, and they could achieve this. It was unfortunate today's findings made the impending war more likely. He thought about Dag and his belly full of hatred and resentment, and saw the dark vamp as if he was standing outside the heavily carved wooden door, not allowed to join the party.

Maybe the dark coven leader knew more than he let on. Maybe he was far more dangerous than any of them had thought.

Chapter 32

DAG TRACED TO his bedchamber in San Francisco. Someone had left a sliver open between his blackout drapes, so his skin burned until he could reposition the fabric and find comfort. He cursed his staff. He'd kill someone for that lapse in judgment.

He ripped off his clothes, sniffing them. He was aware of the fact that dark vamps smelled when they were burning up. Who wouldn't? Burning human flesh was even worse. Had he not had a good dose of Rory's blood, pushing aside his coven cohorts like a pack of dogs, he could have been dead. His hatred of the Golden Monteleones and their powers boiled and burned the insides of his stomach to match the festering blisters on his skin.

He opened his bedroom doors. The house was quiet.

"I need blood," he screamed.

There was no answer. Of course there would be no answer. His daytime staff was worthless, and now he knew they weren't doing their jobs. They were probably out gambling or telling secrets. Well, they'd pay. And any who were unlucky enough to be loyal today would have to be his hosts. No one, not even someone who was grossly overpaid, would willingly share his bed and die for him. Fear him, yes, but sacrifice themselves for him like those ridiculous traitors, the Jett Brothers and their kin? No, none of his paid staff would do such a thing. "No one fuckin' cares."

"I care."

He smelled her before he saw her. The blonde from Starbucks and the cheap motel. His teeth ached as his groin went to granite. He was drooling on himself.

He lurched and grabbed her by the back of her head, forcing her lips up to his, plunging his tongue down her throat, sucking her tongue and then tasting one puncture wound he placed there. His surrounding saliva would heal the wound quickly. These were little love nibbles. But he desperately needed a whole meal, and fast.

"Need you," he heard himself say. *What the fuck is this?* He'd never said this to anyone in his life before.

"Dag take me. Take all of me if you wish. I am totally yours to do with whatever you want."

"Holy fucking nuns without panties. I don't need sex right now. Not until I can have blood, and I'd drain you."

"Then that is what I want."

He couldn't believe it. The woman would fucking die for him. Right here. How the fuck did she get inside his home, anyway? Was this a trap?

"Who let you in?" he whispered as he licked her neck. He pricked the surface of her impossibly smooth skin and lapped a trickle before he would waste a single drop. He began to shake and shudder as her delicious elixir coated his insides. His dick stayed just as hard as it always did. A brief thought flew through his brain. If he ever did die in the sun, his dick would be the last thing standing.

"Someone in an apron and little white cap."

"Why did she let you in?"

"I told her I was to be your sacrifice for this afternoon. When she started to send me away—" the blonde gasped as Dag had gone to his knees and had bitten her on her upper thigh, going for the femoral artery right through her jeans.

"Tell me, damn it." He insisted, licking his lips, growling at the growing red stain on her jeans. "And take these fucking things off."

"Thought you didn't want sex."

"The femoral artery. Bigger than the jugular. I need blood. Fast. Need. Your. Blood."

He allowed her to step back. The blood he'd ingested gave him the strength to wait until she slithered her jeans down to her ankles. Her white cotton top was all she wore. Her panties lay in the pile at her ankles.

"Off," he pointed to her top.

"Yes, Master."

"Quick. Make it quick."

"Yes." She ripped open the shirt, popping the buttons. Like depositing a tissue in the wastebasket she let her cotton top drop to the floor. All that remained was her bra. He liked the look of her bulging bosom all trussed and confined.

"Leave it on."

Her sweet smile drove him insane. He wrapped his naked peeling thigh around her perfect cool flesh. "Do I repulse you, with my burning skin?"

"Yes."

At first he wasn't so sure he liked that answer.

"I repulse you?" he said as he sunk his fangs into her thigh and slurped, blood squirting and spraying over the top of the stairway and cascading to the marble floor below.

"It is all I deserve. I would eat your scaling flesh if you commanded it."

This caught him off guard. He withdrew his fangs and looked at the little waif. "Eeewwww," he said as he scrunched up his eyebrows and wrinkled his nose. "Disgusting."

She did what no mortal or vamp woman had ever done to him before. She touched his flaking member, letting her fingertips travel over the lumpy, charred surface. She placed her palm under his ball sack and squeezed him while he stood there in shock.

She knelt and had him in her mouth so fast he didn't have time to respond. It felt incredible. She rubbed her bitten tongue all over his member and immediately it became smooth, albeit coated in blood. A trickle escaped down the right side of her mouth.

"Holy shit, Sheela,"

"Shirley," she said between sucks. "My name is Shirley."

"Shir—agh—"

She allowed her canine to drag along his shaft, scraping a tiny layer of skin with it. She must have gotten a minute taste of blood because she inhaled and almost swallowed him whole.

Dag traced backwards, looking with incredulity at the little vixen. "What are you?"

"Excuse me," she said, standing. She used her jeans to dab the blood draining from her thigh wound.

"Someone. Someone sent you. Who was it?"

"I believe it was yourself, sire."

"Don't fuckin' bullshit me. Who the fuck sent you?"

"Fate."

Chapter 33

L IONEL JETT AWOKE to the sounds of someone else in his bedroom. Paolo had traced there, melding over the protection he'd placed around the perimeter.

"How'd you do that?" he asked his employer's brother.

"Marcus had the manuals at the study. I read them."

Lionel made a mental note to be more careful with the security literature. He stretched and began to stand, but realized he'd slept naked again. It was becoming a habit, as was the fact that he was making love to his sheets every night, regardless of whether or not he'd had sex with a date the night before. The visions in his head of the sweet green-eyed, red-haired hottie he'd screwed several times the night before, right next to his brother Huge, who had been screwing her sister, came flashing back and his dick boinked to attention. He immediately bent over to cover it up.

Paolo was laughing. It was not funny to Lionel.

"You guys had some fun last night, apparently"

"Still managed to call your brother first."

"And for your loyalty, we thank you. We are indebted to you."

"Thanks." Lionel grabbed a long-sleeved tee from the floor and covered up his groin as he shuffled to a dresser to retrieve some clothes. The evening sky had turned pitch black.

"So what do I owe the pleasure of your visit?" Lionel asked with his back to Paolo. He turned and caught Paolo eyeing his butt cheeks. "Fuck off, Paolo. I don't do guys. You know that. You go both ways now?"

Paolo was still in a good mood, and laughed it off. Lionel could remember a time when it would have cost him another humiliating fight that he was required to lose. Didn't mind the pain, which would heal relatively quickly. It had been about his pride, knowing he could kick young Paolo's ass and still had to take the fall, "for the good of the family." Still, it was his job, and he did it regardless of how he felt. He was glad Paolo had learned to temper his reactions. And he did seem happier these days.

"That's what I want to talk to you about."

"Going both ways. You honestly think you can have a conversation with me about going both ways." Lionel was close to tracing himself anywhere else, even though he was still naked.

"No, about protecting the love of my life."

"Love of your life or love of her—it is hope to God's hangnail a girl, right?"

"Well, yes, and she's mortal."

"A blinding flash of the obvious. How come you don't like female Goldens?"

"You forget what Lucius's mother did to me."

"Half my guys lusted after her too. Hell, you couldn't help yourself, everyone knows that. And most of the guys would have loved to have her abuse them like she did you. Paolo, time for you to grow up and be a man."

"So I've been told." Paolo's smile was getting thin.

"Marcus handled her for almost a hundred years."

Paolo wasn't jealous since he had no feelings for Maya. "But Maya loved Marcus. She barely tolerated me."

It was the truth. Everyone knew it. Sadly, though they were fated, Maya and Paolo would never have survived as a couple. They had enough animal attraction to produce an offspring, but as far as spending eternity together, it had been completely out of the question. It was fortunate her death saved him from the agony.

"Okay, man. Sorry. Tell me what you're here for, and I'll do whatever it is you want me to do." He started to step into a pair of boxers. "Within reason, of course," he added in a mumble.

"Of course."

Lionel put on his dark black jeans, a form-fitting t-shirt that made his muscles look twice a normal man's size, and thick black socks. He sat at the edge of the bed and pulled on his knee-high boots with the steel toe, stowing a KA-BAR on the side of one. Next he donned his shoulder holster, checked his Ultra Crimson Carry II with the 3-inch barrel, stowing it safely under his arm. His black jacket was fitted so no one would ever suspect he was packing. Which is the way he liked it. But one look into his eyes and they would know they were dealing with Dr. Death himself.

He liked that too.

Paolo grinned, glad he could call upon this lethal combination of brains, brawn and equipment sure to keep Cara safe.

"So where are we off to? And don't tell me it's a fuckin' hot tub party."

"Hardly. Call your brothers. We'll meet at that bistro by the square in downtown Santa Rosa. Tell them to be there in less than a half hour."

"I'll have them ready. Meet you there."

THE THREE JETT brothers wore sunglasses, their eyes being extra sensitive, even to the votive candles on the little table they shared. The space was so small their knees almost touched, which meant that when one of them crossed or uncrossed his massive legs, the others had to do the same in tandem. Though it annoyed Lionel from time to time, it was a necessary evil, since they needed to be close together to discuss their plans so they wouldn't be overheard.

"Huge, you bring those magazines?" Jeb asked. He was referring to the fact that Hugh had a well-worn collection of girlie magazines they enjoyed looking at during long stakeouts. Sort of took the edge off their testosterone level for a bit. It never really helped Lionel at all. He found it extremely childish.

"Jeb, you have more money than God. Anything wrong with you buying your own smut?"

"Nah."

"Oh, I get it," Hugh continued. "You just like it free."

"Well, if you are offering and everything. Why not?"

Lionel pointed to Paolo, who was returning from the bar with four glasses of red wine. "Casanova here is on his way to Tuscany. Why don't you ask him to bring back some of those Eastern European magazines?"

"Those girls look young. Really young."

"Some of them are," Paolo interjected. "Big money these days in smuggling little girls into prostitution. You don't want to support them by buying their stuff."

Jeb looked up at the ceiling. Lionel could tell this was one of those times he felt impatient with their Golden vamp employer.

"Marcus over there, too?" Hugh asked.

"Yes. That's why we need your services," Paolo said, holding up his glass. "Cheers, gents."

They clinked glasses. Paolo sipped his wine, savoring it, while the brothers threw theirs back like it was a shot of whisky.

"They got absinthe here?" Huge asked Lionel.

"It's a French bistro. I'd say yes," Lionel answered him. "But let's stay off the green crazy stuff until we find out what's in store for us."

The brothers recrossed their legs in tandem again, Huge and Jeb crossing their arms as well.

"We have reason to believe the new dark coven Supreme Leader, Dag Nielsen, has his eye on a friend of mine, a college professor named Carabella Sampson," Paolo started. "I would be personally taking care of her, except I'm accompanying Marcus to Tuscany, where we have pressing business."

"We get to take care of her the same way, too?" Jeb grinned, demonstrating he had lost a tooth. One of his canines. Paolo frowned.

"What happened to your tooth?" he asked.

"Had it pulled. Was giving me some fits. I got an implant coming."

"How they going to do that?"

"Well Dr. Gervais—you know him, Paolo—done some work for Anne. He says he can give me an implant, but it will have to stay down all the time. The hollow point will be towards the back of the tooth so no one would be able to see it up close."

"Still, Jeb, gotta be kinda awkward walking around with a fuckin' straw sticking out of your lips all the time," Hugh added as he punched his younger brother. The ensuing tussle almost sent them all sprawling. They got temporarily entangled in the canvas curtain of the outside seating area, hitting the aluminum frame and alerting other customers to their presence.

"Would you guys stop with the horseplay?" Lionel whispered to them. "Some pair of covert ops you guys make."

Paolo finished off his wine and leaned into the table. "For the record, my brother doesn't approve of my involvement with the beautiful Cara, so he has erased her memory of me."

The Jett brothers looked like they were responding to a bad smell.

"For her own safety, she has to be kept in the dark. And that's where you come in. We need a detail on her 24/7. Marcus told me you have some brothers in arms you can trust during the day?"

Lionel nodded. "Retired SEALs. Bad ass dudes, for mortals."

"They available for hire?"

"Depends. They evaluate the situation first before they decide."

"No can do. This has to be kept strictly between us. No one outside the family and your family can know all the facts."

"Which are?" Lionel asked. The cat and mouse game was tiring him.

"This lady is a professor at SSU, an authority on myths and mythology, with a special emphasis on vampire lore. She had located evidence that a very rare book on our kind had surfaced again after centuries."

"Had? As in past tense?" Hugh asked.

"That's primarily why we erased her memory. But the other side doesn't know this—well, to be perfectly honest, they've been told, but they don't believe it. We believe this book was part of my grandfather's collection. It disappeared before I was born."

"And you have the book now?" Lionel asked.

"No. We have a book, a book Cara found and had shipped here to California, a sort of cryptic map written in journal form by a man who did find it almost two hundred years ago. That book is in safekeeping. We believe it will tell us where the missing tome can be found."

"And so what's the problem?"

"Dag Nielsen and his dark coven want that book, and they've been killing to get it. You know they killed young Rory Monteleone last night?" Paolo said.

Each brother silently nodded.

"And they got his little brother two weeks ago. They've been killing the Golden children like crazy. We're not sure why they've stepped up this genocide against our race," Paolo continued, "but Dag has something up his sleeve, and he desperately wants what's in the book."

"Makes me wonder too, Paolo. You got any ideas?" Lionel felt like his employer was hiding something, but he couldn't quite make out what.

"I'll give you specifics after I get them. Right now, we're going to Tuscany to get permission for a mission here. We're asking you just keep an eye on things until we return."

"You mean keep an eye on her?"

"Well, yes. We also have staff, loyal, trusted mortals who have served our family for generations. We cannot leave them unprotected."

"But you primarily care about her," Lionel dug deeper.

"I'm not lying when I say she matters a great deal to me, but her importance in this scheme is far greater than just my feelings alone. You've all felt the rumblings of war, right?"

The brothers nodded solemnly. Even Lionel couldn't look into Paolo's eyes. The smell of war and impending death was all around the little wine country community full of innocents who had no idea what was about to befall them.

"We are getting close to understanding what this grudge is all about. And looking for ways to stop the planned attack on us all."

"Why not round them up and take care of it that way?" Lionel wanted to know. He wondered why they were being so careful. "They aren't loyal even to themselves. Should be easy to get the information we need."

"Because we aren't sure they haven't discovered some weapon to use against us. And we don't know where their information is coming from." Paolo leaned back in his chair. "Brothers, we are trying to stop innocent lives from being lost."

The two younger Jett brothers looked at Lionel, who was stewing about a problem he suddenly had to express. "Just what am I supposed to tell the SEAL team? They don't even know we're vamps."

"Lionel, under the circumstances, I think you'll have to level with them."

"Suuuureeee. You fuckin' gotta be nuts, Paolo! They'll never believe it. What am I supposed to do? You ever try to convince someone about vampires? Someone who is absolutely an unbeliever?"

Paolo smiled. "Do what I did once."

"What's that?" Lionel asked.

"Disappear or trace them somewhere."

Chapter 34

CARA CALLED THE University and confirmed what Mr. Monteleone had told her. Classes had indeed been cancelled. It was all over the news about her assistant's murder. She spent the day in and out of bed, with long crying bouts in between.

It was odd how she had lost three whole days, just forgotten what she had taught, who she had talked to, what she had done. Though she tried to retrieve her memories, it was as if they were gone from her forever, not locked behind an iron wall. Just evaporated.

Something had been pressing on her, she could tell that much as she looked over the papers covering her desk. For some reason, just from the way her normally neat papers were splayed across the wooden surface of her home office, she got the feeling she had been looking for something. She started to organize the mess, hoping it would bring back at least a sliver of her memory.

She began to examine every slip of paper she could find, sorting them into piles on the floor. Bills, receipts for payments made, checkbook statements, professional magazines, and correspondence. She even had a couple of early Christmas cards from educational companies wanting her to purchase their teaching aids. There were several requests for donations to charity events coming up.

She'd made a decision to skip any more faculty charity functions until next year. Although she made a decent income as a college professor, she was planning some trips—*what was that? Where had that come from?*

A trip? She'd been planning a trip?

She quickly scanned the travel brochures that she'd tossed on the pile of clothing and bedding catalogues she had planned to recycle.

She found a brochure with a post-it note inside describing a city tour and map of Prague. She read the note, which was not in her handwriting.

If you are in need of lodging, this hotel is very nice and not as expensive as some. My family and I live in a small flat above the bookstore and cannot accommodate you, although we would if we could. My store is quite close, within walking distance.

I am due to receive another crate from a monastery in Scotland in early November. If there is anything of interest there, I shall message you. Until then, please use my travel agent as a resource. She can find you some great airfare that could save you hundreds of dollars, if the tickets are purchased here.

Regards,
Tomas Novotny

Cara put the note down and stared out into the darkening sky. She hadn't even noticed she'd missed her lunch, and now was hungry for dinner.

As she prepared a salad, she thought about the note. For some reason, the name Tomas Novotny was familiar to her. Then she remembered where she had seen the name before. It appeared on her credit card statement as Novotny something. Novotny Travel?

Novotny Books.

She dropped everything in the kitchen and rummaged through her desktop piles and found the one for her credit card statement from two months ago. The single line item for August 15 read: Novotny Books. The charge was for $2450, which meant it was a valuable book, or research material. She just couldn't remember what it was. Sitting behind the desk, placing her forehead to her palm, she concentrated.

What was this book? What was the book about?

She knew it must have been about vampires. And her upcoming trip to Prague was further indication of the connection she had with this particular bookseller. But why couldn't she remember the purchase?

She kept a stack of cards in her center desk drawer. Flipping through them, she came upon the card for a Tomas Novotny, rare bookseller. And there was a telephone number.

Before she thought about what time it was in Prague, she dialed the number but got no answer. The phone rang and rang. She hung up and retried the number. On the third try, an answering machine picked up with a man's voice speaking in broken English.

'This is Thomas Novotny. I am currently unavailable but will return your call if you speak slowly and leave your telephone number. Please also state the nature of your business, and what book or periodical you are interested in. Thank you and have a good day.'

The beep made Cara jump before she collected herself in order to leave a message. "Mr. Novotny, my name is Professor Cara Sampson and I am calling from California. I believe you sold me a book in August, and I would like to discuss this with you. You also mentioned you were receiving another shipment. I'd be most interested in what you have found, if anything. Thank you." Cara left her phone number and hung up.

PAOLO WAS STRUCK with a perplexing feeling. Something was worrying him. He concentrated on it as he rode with Lucius in the family limo to the airport. They were flying to his brother's home just outside Florence.

The persistent, perplexing sensation seemed to be generated from outside himself.

He leaned back into the leather seat, resting his head and closing his eyes.

"Father, are you okay?" Lucius asked.

"Yes, son. I have a bit of a headache. I was trying to see if I could make it go away." He smiled down at his son, who grinned back, and snuggled closer to him. Paolo loved how just being with Lucius made him happy, and vowed he'd spend all his non-working time with the boy. "You excited to be going back in Italy?" he asked Lucius.

"Yes. I like the sunlight there. More yellow. Not as bright as California, more golden."

Paolo had never thought about that before, but Lucius was right. The sunlight in California did seem very harsh and often hurt his eyes.

The pain in his forehead came back. He could just barely make out a statement: *What was this book. What was this book about?*

Paolo gripped the leather armrest and sat forward, which nearly toppled Lucius. It was Cara's thoughts he was hearing. And she was thinking about a book. Looking for a book.

The limo driver was a newer employee, so Paolo dared not risk a cell phone call in front of him. He motioned to have the man pull the vehicle over. He got out of the driver's seat and opened up the rear door.

"Sir? You want something?"

"I just remembered. I forgot something at the house."

"But you will miss your flight if we return there now."

"But I have to go back."

"Sir, should I call the airline and see if you can take a later flight? I am quite sure you will miss your flight."

Paolo wished he'd taken his brother up on the offer to take a private charter, where he could show up late and they'd wait for him. Paolo had insisted on paying for his own way, taking a first class commercial flight.

The driver was waiting for an answer.

"Let's stop at Starbuck's. I need to use the rest room. I'll see if I can get hold of someone at the house. Perhaps they can mail it to me," Paolo lied.

"Very well, sir." The driver resumed his duties, pulling up to a Starbuck's within minutes.

Paolo didn't want to leave Lucius in the car, so he instructed him to accompany him inside. "Can I get you anything?" he asked the driver.

"No thanks. We come stocked. I don't drink coffee, affects my nerves, not to mention my driving."

"Nasty habit. Lucius and I will be right back." He helped his son inside the shop and heard the familiar scream of the espresso machines. "You go first, Lucius. I'll get you, what, a hot chocolate?"

"Oh, yes. Thanks, Father," Lucius called over his shoulder as he skipped toward the men's room. He waited until he saw his son close the door behind him before he made the call to Marcus. His brother picked up on the first ring.

"Problem? You should be on your way by now."

"I just got an image, a feeling from Cara. She's looking for a book. Searching her memory, and she's a little frustrated with it, too. She's investigating it, brother."

"Damn." Marcus was not pleased. "You got the Jett brothers squared away?"

"All set. They should be all around the house. Marcus, what if they learn about the book?"

Paolo could almost feel the wheels turning slowly in his brother's head. "It's a risk we're going to have to take. I need you to get Lucius to safety. I need your help with the Council."

"But if she's beginning to put things together, won't she perhaps begin to regain her memories?"

"That I don't know. There is still only one course for you. You must get you and your son to Italy without any further delay. Let's have the Jett boys earn their salary. Is there a detail for the day?"

"Yes. Marcus, they are mortal."

"Who are they?"

"Friends of Lionel. Retired SEALs."

Marcus chuckled. "They'll do. If they believe in the cause, they're every bit as good as your ordinary black vamp."

Paolo reluctantly agreed to continue with his flight plans. He dialed Lionel just in case and was reassured that Cara had stayed home this evening, and was going through paperwork on her desk. No visitors. Nothing out of the ordinary. Nothing scented or sensed that caused them to worry. Lionel assured Paolo they were vigilant.

"And you wouldn't believe what my buds think of me now that they know I can disappear at will. They all want to learn the trick."

Paolo was glad for Lionel, who seemed to be able to fit into the human world as well as his own dark family, yet still maintain his loyalty to the Monteleone clan. He was indeed a rare warrior.

"They with you tonight?"

"We're training a few at a time. But yes. I've traced them to Murder Burger three times already tonight. They think it's pretty cool. I know it's not the hamburgers. It's the ride they love."

This brought a smile to Paolo's face, just as Lucius was coming from the bathroom.

Damn. He'd been so engrossed in the phone calls that he'd forgotten to order the hot chocolate.

They waited in line to order, holding hands. Then Lucius sat on his lap on the couch while they awaited their order. Paolo was glad he'd decided not to tell his brother the SEALs were going to be told about their Golden Vampire lineage.

He could see that the years of peaceful coexistence with the dark covens and the human world had left their family without their own protective forces made up of Golden vampires wishing to serve and perhaps lay down their lives for their families. That was a tremendous error in judgment. Relying on other species to protect the Golden families had left the dark covens with a distinct advantage. Just by their very nature, the dark covens had never ceased to maintain a fighting stance. And their numbers had been growing exponentially. Paolo intended to inform the Council of this.

The limo continued to the airport, where they got aboard the plane for Florence without a moment to spare. Paolo encouraged Lucius to sleep, but his son was avidly playing with all the gadgets available in first class seating. No doubt the boy would be halfway disappointed when they landed.

Paolo listened for another thought from Cara, but felt nothing. He smiled back at the attendant, who seemed determined to give him extra attention, leaning over him to serve his boy, making it hard for him not to get a whiff of the perfumed flesh between her breasts. It only made him long for Cara.

Paolo thought of Cara and wished that someday he'd get one more day with her. He'd even take a day where she didn't know him. He'd even agree not to glam her if he had to. Anything to be in proximity to her.

The attendant's breast brushed over Paolo's shoulder in an unmistakable gesture. Her peacock-blue eyes were lovely, he thought. Full pink lips that could no doubt do lovely things. But he sighed, careful not to sigh in her direction or she'd orgasm on the spot in front of the entire first class cabin. Perhaps he'd have to get used to this. But he would never forget Cara, or the wonderful music her body played for him. Her voice, her touch, the feel of her skin, were all something he needed, craved. And, unlike a true addiction, she was good for him. She granted him life and spirit. Strength and purpose.

For now, the need to protect his son and his family had to come first. He hoped the Jett brothers and their buddies would do their jobs like they had done for centuries. He prayed there would be time for love later.

Chapter 35

DAG AWOKE ON his bed, but it was different. For one thing, he was spread-eagled. His wrists and ankles were bound with silver, making movement painful. Made not a bit of difference to his dick, however. It stood to attention like a telephone pole.

He was going to yell "fuck you" at himself, but decided his dick would take it as encouragement. The body part was so useful in so many ways, and so completely abnormal in others, and only a bit of that was fun for him. He liked control, and his dick always had a mind of its own.

There was someone else in the room. Suddenly the fact that he was restrained bothered him. "Hey. Who's there?" he said to the half-closed door to his private bathroom. The seconds ticked by and there was no answer. "I fuckin' said who is there? Come here right now and untie me."

Shirley, the little blonde waif, stood in the doorway to the bathroom, stark staring naked but covered with blood.

"What the fuck?"

"Look at your skin, master," She whispered. "While you were sleeping, I repaired you."

Sure enough, Dag looked at his formerly blistered and blackened skin and saw that most of the flakiness was gone. What remained was reddish and blotchy. Rather like blood marble.

"What did you do? And get me out of these cuffs. They're hurting me."

She smiled sweetly again. Something behind that smile alarmed him. Was the girl some species he'd not encountered before? A tiny shiver of fear coursed down his spine and, right on cue, made his dick lurch. She giggled. It pissed Dag off.

Shirley came over to the bed. Her wrists had been cut. She'd used her own blood to wash him, heal him. As soon as he got out of the restraints, he'd properly thank her. Or kill her. He'd decide later. Right now he was focusing on the juncture between her legs. He needed to feed, and that spot would work just fine.

"You want me?" she said as she outlined her left areola with her right forefinger. She held the finger up; there was blood covering the tip.

"Yes. Yes I do. Very much."

"That's not a very sexy way to get a girl to fuck you, Dag."

"Come here and I'll show you."

"You have enough energy? You sure?"

"Look at my fuckin' dick. That should tell you everything you need to know. I'm ready as hell. Come here."

"I want you to beg."

"What?" Dag pulled at his bindings but the burning from the silver chains made him stop. He considered severing his own wrist, since he'd regenerate in a day anyway, but he didn't want to experience the pain. But if he had to, he could do that.

"I said beg me. Be sweet to me."

"Please. Get me the fuck outta these restraints or I'll fuckin' nail your hide to the wall."

"That's not what I meant at all." She turned around, bent over and gave him a good look at her sex from behind. And her anus. "If you ever want to see these again, you're going to have to learn to speak nicely to me. Understood?"

"Whoa! Wait a minute. Nobody talks to me that way."

"I'm the one that talks to you that way. Until you talk nice." She began dancing, gyrating, smoothing the syrupy blood over her body. "You could lick all this off me, wash me. Then you could fuck me until I pass out. How does that sound?"

"Sounds nice."

"Just nice?"

"Okay, sounds like fun."

"Just fun?"

"What the fuck do you want me to say? Tell me what to say and I'll do it. Just get me out of these restraints. This is really beginning to piss me off."

"Tell me you need me. Like you did yesterday."

Did I do that? Holy shit, I did.

"I liked it when you talked to me like that. It made me come almost the instant I heard it."

"Look, Shirley, I have some very important things to do and I'm on a tight schedule. We can have a little fun, but you gotta get me out of these. There are people waiting on me."

"No one has come by the house. The phone hasn't rung. Your phone—where is your phone?"

Dag realized that in his blackened and painful après sunscorched state he had forgotten to look for his cell phone when he peeled off his clothes. "I think it's over there, in that pile of rags."

"What pile of rags? You mean the rags I took out and had burned?"

"You fuckin' did *what*?"

"I burned them. In your fireplace downstairs. Let me go see if the cell phone fell out."

She turned to go.

"No! Wait. Look, honey, this is real fun and all, but could you just undo me, please? I promise to be real sweet."

"I'll go check on the phone and *then* you can be sweet to me." She left.

Dag was livid. He'd never felt like he could have a heart attack before, but he was fairly sure he was on the way to having one now. It wasn't a whole lot of fun being restrained on the bloody sheets with his dick winking at him, taunting him in that unnatural way.

What the fuck is going on? Had everyone gone completely bonkers?

He heard screams coming from downstairs. That would be his staff, heading for the hills at the sight of the little twisted, bloody sister scraping through ashes in the fireplace. What a scene that must have been. He regretted missing it.

Dag searched for another solution. Severing his wrist was beginning to make perfect sense. Except he'd have to bite the damn thing off, and that would take too much time. If he had a knife, easy pezy. But no, that blade had been in his pants pocket, probably in the fireplace too, along with the phone numbers of his entire organization.

Whatever gave her the idea she had to burn his fuckin' clothes anyway? Some ritual sacrifice?

Uh, oh. He'd heard about some tribes who burned the possessions of their enemy before they ate them. Holy shit, maybe she was some freak from another world he knew nothing about. Were her people trying to get control of his coven by destroying him?

He was beginning to regret ever having met the little panhandler that evening in front of the coffee bar. No question about it. She'd been a plant. And boy, did he fall right for it. He'd underestimated them. Well, he wouldn't do that again. As soon as he got rid of his wrist, he'd show them how ruthless he could be with their vessel, their messenger of death and doom. No one was going to put that over on him.

Dag tried to take a bite up by his wrist and realized, to his horror, that he couldn't reach it and would have to eat through his elbow to obtain freedom. That presented a whole new set of circumstances. Big bones. Big arteries and lots of blood. He wondered if he should bite above or below the elbow joint. The skin above looked more tender, and didn't the lower extremity have two bones, not one? Or, was it the other way around?

Fuck! Where is my biology knowledge when I need it? He'd always hated that class. Served him right. He felt like murdering his old teacher just because he hadn't inspired him to learn better. He'd do it, once he got out of these restraints.

What the fuck was taking her so long? Dag sighed. Time to start biting.

The first bite hurt like hell. He'd nailed the soft tissue below his bicep. The skin tore off in ribbons and he spit it out.

This is disgusting.

He was about to take another bite when he heard heavy footsteps coming up the stairs, and the clanging of keys and metallic things.

My boys. Thank the devil himself!

Rhys and another of his men stood by the opened door and stared at the scene before them, appearing to be in shock.

"Don't you fuckin' stand there holding your dicks. Get me out of these things."

"Sorry, boss." Kevin, the one who was Sidney's nephew, hurried to one side of the bed and took out a pair of wire cutters from the toolkit he always wore on his belt. Dag had made fun of him, calling him "the gardener" all the time. Now he was grateful the dark vamp was so handy with his tools.

The silver stung poor Kevin, who whimpered at the blister for a long moment before completing the task on the other side.

"Would you hurry the fuck up?"

"Yessir."

While Kevin was undoing his ankle Dag asked about the girl.

"What girl?" the man asked.

"The one that did this to me. The little vamp slut I turned."

"There was no girl downstairs. Your housemaid called us, but she was hysterical. You don't think she did it, do you?"

"Of course not. But maybe she knows where the little twat went."

"They're all gone, sir."

Free at last, Dag leapt to his feet and ran for the bathroom to take a shower. Except he misjudged the smooth marble floor, slipped on the blood coated all over him and the floor and fell on his butt. He didn't even yell at the two guards who were having difficulty keeping in their laughter. He would have lots of time to get even, after he found the girl and made her pay for her crime.

But that would come after he got his hands on Paolo's girl, extracted the book information from her, and left her for dead. He had to kill something that meant something to someone else. That was the only way to soothe the pain inside him. He needed to even the score. It didn't matter who paid the price, but it made it more likely he'd be satisfied if it was someone who mattered to Paolo Monteleone.

LIONEL JETT SAT in a nest of yellow and white hamburger wrappers. Andrew, the SEAL he'd been training, had fallen asleep, probably due to the large globules of fat coursing through his veins from all the fast food he'd consumed this evening. Boy, those guys could pack it away, he thought. Almost funny.

He decided to let his buddy sleep, knowing that if he needed the man he'd be ready instantly, as ready as any creature on the planet could be. Since Lionel was always awake during the night, it was no problem for him. But he was bored.

He'd watched Paolo's woman sorting through all her stuff like they were sheets of delicate old books she was trying to preserve. Why was it women liked all this paperwork shit, he wondered? They liked to take care of little details that just didn't matter in Lionel's world. He dealt with the big things: life, death. That was about it. Honor was in there somewhere. Love was supposed to be there, too, but it was all lust right now, no chance for love.

Young Maria Monteleone had been like this lady, he thought. She liked to work on her needlepoint, sit quietly by the fireplace and listen. She'd hear things. Like the night she commented on his heart-beat. It happened every time he looked at her. He was grateful his member didn't make a sound or she would have picked up on that, too. Or, maybe she stole little glances at his groin when he wasn't looking.

She didn't belong to him, but it didn't stop him from having the kind of dreams any healthy dark vamp would have. Maria was sophisticated and kind. She didn't have to try to be nice, she was nice all the way through her core. But though his feelings for her ran deep, the fact that they were two distinct species meant that a mating could never occur without the punishment by death. The Council had made examples of other dark vamps who had been entrusted with the safekeeping of the Monteleone family, especially the women and children. Those who strayed and found themselves in an illicit affair with a Golden—and it happened only rarely—were swiftly tried and their lives ended. So sad that love should cause the death of a person. Lionel had always thought this should not be.

But the Council was everything. It controlled everything the Goldens did. It was the gatekeeper of their history, their rituals, the stories passed down from generation to generation. Unlike the dark covens, who were like wild rogue armies that came and went, leaving wreckage in their wake, Goldens enhanced the communities they lived in. And they cared for everyone who was loyal to them. They never sought out recognition, working silently for the good of the community of man as a whole, both vampire and mortal.

Lionel saw she was getting tired. She'd had coffee, and that kept her awake for a couple of hours, but now, past midnight, she was fading. Her sheer, dogged determination kept her poring over the paperwork. She took notes. She leaned back against the tall wooden chair and he could see the beautiful chest of Paolo's woman. Her graceful neck. Her blood would taste sweet, he thought.

Paolo, you are a lucky man.

Paolo was allowed a mortal bride, a pleasure partner. Lionel would have to defend her with his own life if need be. Yet Lionel would never be allowed to have this for himself. It wasn't fair, but it was the way of it. Lionel knew it didn't do anyone any good to dredge up those latent feelings that perhaps there could have been another future for him. If he'd taken another path.

He knew Paolo regretted his choice to become vampire. It had weighed on his mother heavily. She'd wanted to remain mortal, though her husband wanted the change. But Maria, beautiful, full of life Maria, didn't want to live forever. Lionel couldn't understand that. Who wouldn't want to live forever?

She bore all eight of her children as a mortal woman. Back in those days, women died in childbirth all the time, but Maria was blessed with a strong body and an even stronger will. Lionel had to admit, it was her will that he had loved, even as he lusted for her body. He could have gladly married her, even if he could never touch her, just to be close to her.

In the end, he had to be satisfied with being her personal body-guard and most trusted companion, and later most trusted advisor as her health deteriorated, as she was left alone, as the children she bore adopted the vampiric life and had children of their own if they met their fated mates. She didn't want to live to hear all the stories, she said. At the time of her death, Paolo, Laurel and Marcus were unmarried and had never felt the fating.

He wondered if there ever could be a fating between Golden and dark. Was that the secret she bore? Why she wouldn't take the turning, even when her children begged her? Perhaps as a mortal woman she could bear the children she would not be able to bear as a vampire lady. Perhaps she was not fated to her husband. Perhaps she was fated to—

Lionel heard a sound and shook the snoring form of the SEAL.

"We have company, I do believe," he whispered to Andrew.

"Roger that." The SEAL woke up ready, just as Lionel had expected. He radioed his counterpart on the other side of the building.

"They haven't seen anything," Andrew reported back.

"There's something out there. I can smell it," Lionel breathed He motioned a zipper to his lip, indicating they'd be doing hand signals from now on.

Andrew donned his night vision goggles and then switched to in-frared. He tapped a thumbs up and passed an extra pair to Lionel. A torch of deep orange was gliding, floating across the street and up towards the window of Cara's bedroom. It was the heat sig of a tracing vamp, but it was in slow motion, as if the individual wanted to be detected.

Curious, Lionel motioned for caution and continued to watch the torch blend through the walls and stand in the bedroom beyond. Lionel decided he didn't want to wait any longer to get between this creature and the woman he was hired to protect.

He motioned to the SEAL, who slipped an arm around Lionel's shoulder so he could trace them both to a spot in the hallway beyond. As they landed, a flash of light temporarily blinded them. The tracing vamp had been wired to explode, and if they had been in the same room, would have been killed. As it was, Andrew had suffered a head injury. He lay on his back, blood draining from both ears. Lionel examined himself and determined somehow he'd been unscathed. He heard Cara scream, and immediately he dashed for her home office.

Cara was wrestling with a dark vamp who turned and gave Lionel a bloody smile. He had taken a bite out of Cara's neck and was trying to wrench her head from her body.

Dag.

"Too late again for the party, Lionel. You can have seconds, if you like. I know you love mortal flesh."

Lionel's fury overtook him. He grappled with the coven leader, sure that others were going to follow. Andrew came to his feet, assisted by another SEAL teammate. Jeb and Hugh took hold of Cara.

"To the villa," was all Lionel could say before he was thrown against and through the wall of Cara's apartment. As he landed on the ground outside, he briefly saw his two brothers trace Cara away, hopefully to safety.

"Still doing the Monteleone's dirty work, Lionel? Can't seem to get a woman of your own, but you'll die defending theirs? That what your life's about?"

"What would you know about my life, you miserable creature? You've lived a third of my lifetime. I've killed more of you than I can remember."

"Your own kind. You've killed your own kin, for what? For them? You think they understand you? Care about you and your needs?" Dag was smirking, circling Lionel with lethal intent. Lionel realized he was waiting for something. He didn't have to wait long to find out what it was.

A silver net fell over Lionel's body, encapsulating the guardian and denying him the ability to do further harm.

Before they injected him with the sleeping serum, Lionel saw the face of Dag's new executioner, who was wearing heavy gloves to protect his hands from the silver netting. He aimed the pistol containing the tranquilizing agent at Lionel's heart, and laughed.

Chapter 36

CARA LOOKED AROUND her at the band of men who stood as if they were going to take orders from her. She was unclear what had just happened. But somehow she had been transported, *flown* here at a high rate of speed. She must have passed out, yet she had no sense of losing consciousness. Something about the two-second ride was familiar to her. It felt like her skin had tiny pinpricks all over it. And she *knew* that it wasn't the first time that had happened.

She looked from the face of one man to another, one by one. Until she found the man who had grabbed her by the waist and had done the flying—if that is what it could be called.

He was handsome, and huge. Sandy brown hair covered his camouflage-painted forehead. He didn't flinch as she stepped toward him. "What exactly just happened, you want to tell me what you just did to me?"

"Ma'am. You were in danger. We brought you here to safety." The giant then pointed to her neck, which suddenly hurt. She placed her fingers on the sore spot, and they came back bloody. Black spots began to form in front of her eyes, and even they seemed familiar, but she fought the urge to sink to the ground. One of the men stepped forward to help her steady herself and she pushed off the tattoo-covered arm.

"Just how did you do it? You grabbed me and the next thing I knew we were here. I want answers and I want them right now."

Several of the men began to smile, but others solemnly nodded their heads.

"And I want to go back to salvage what's left of my apartment."

"They've got Lionel, Huge," one of the men said to the gentleman who had carried her. The big man looked angry.

"You've been placed here in protective custody until the Monteleones can return home. Until then, you are to stay here with us," he said.

"Like hell I will. Monteleone? Did you say Monteleone? As in the head of security for the University?" she asked.

The band of men laughed. White teeth, dimples, bulging chests and war paint. They didn't look like killers from the way they laughed, but they were sure dressed for it.

"What's so funny? I'd be able to show you his card, except my apartment seems to have been blown up. This the security office?"

She realized how stupid she sounded. There was no mistaking the fact that the two-story room with carved ceilings was the great room of a grand estate, and not a security office.

"You'll want to freshen up until they return. It's been a long night, but you're safe here, honest." The big man held our his hand, "My name is Hugh Jett. This is my brother, Jeb, and these are our team members. We are the private security force of the Monteleone family, your hosts, and owner of this villa."

One by one the men peeled off from the circle, leaving Cara alone with Hugh and Jeb Jett. "This way, ma'am," Jeb pointed to the iron stairway leading to the second floor.

"Do I have a choice in the matter?" Cara asked.

"Not if you want to live." Hugh Jett answered her from behind. She hung onto the handrail and began the long climb. It began to be too much for her and she started to faint.

Hugh Jett was right there, as he had been before, with his arm around her waist. Before she could protest, he had lifted her and carried her up the stairs as easily as she might carry a pillow. He brought her to a set of double doors, which he opened, revealing a dark chamber with a roaring fireplace. A large bed with satin sheets stood against the wall opposite the fireplace. The room was warm. The bed looked inviting. Cara suddenly felt very, very tired.

"I will have one of the girls come get you ready for bed. We will provide some bedclothes for you, and some clothes for the morning. But tonight you must stay here, for your own protection, understand?" Hugh looked down on her like he was talking to a child. She felt like a child.

"Of course," was all she could think of to say. Although she wanted to take a shower and get clean, she desperately needed to sleep. There would be time enough tomorrow for fighting.

"Ma'am. I have some things for you, plus a nice bowl of warm soup." A young girl in maid uniform brought a tray with a soup bowl and glass of water. Tucked under her arm was a fluffy flannel nightie. "This is mine. I think it will fit." The girl set the tray down and whisked the two giants out of the room.

"Whose room is this?" Cara asked as she accompanied the girl to the light brown marble bathroom. A man's robe hung on a brass hook shaped like a palm. She noted a slight lemony scent to it.

"This is the guest room, currently occupied by Mr. Paolo Monteleone. His brother owns this villa, and the winery.

"Ah. He runs the security company that Sonoma State contracts with, is that right?"

"I'm not sure what the nature of Mr. Monteleone's business is here. He lives in Tuscany, ma'am."

"And where is he this evening?"

The girl blushed as she tested the shower water she'd just started. "He left for Tuscany this evening. You'll not be disturbed. Don't worry."

Cara looked in the mirror at her ruined clothes, the blood that had seeped down the side of her blouse. The skin around the wound was getting pink and swollen. "This is going to need some attention. Perhaps after my shower I should be taken to the Emergency Room."

"No, ma'am. You are safer here. We have a healing balm that will take care of most of the pain and the infection."

"You have no idea what just happened to me. I was bitten, by this man—"

"Yes, I understand. I can see as much. But, trust me, we have a very effective salve we use for all injuries around the estate. There will not be anyone available to take you to the hospital until tomorrow. But, we will see to whatever you need. Please?" she motioned for Cara to come toward the shower.

Cara allowed the girl to remove her blouse. She was becoming stiff. Her back ached from the jarring she took as she—

Flew?

Cara thought she was losing her mind. First Mr. Monteleone told her she'd forgotten about the death of her assistant, and that police had questioned her and she had no recollection of it. Now she was standing in a stranger's bedroom, about to disrobe, and be treated for a bite wound?

And what about the rare book? The book about—

Vampires. Ohmygod, this is all about vampires. Did one bite her?

"You have to get me out of here," she whispered to the young maid.

"No, ma'am. You must stay here. It is for your safety. Trust me when I tell you there is no safer place than this home. You are in danger. There has been already loss of life."

"Yes. My assistant was murdered."

"And Jeb and Hugh Jett lost their brother tonight as well. They lost him while rescuing you."

Cara could see the girl was speaking what she believed to be the truth. She wondered if the girl would answer her next question truthfully.

"I need to ask you something and I want you to be honest with me. Do vampires exist?"

The maid turned her gaze to the ground and nodded. "Under the Monteleone's care there is no greater protection."

"Are they—?"

"No more questions. Everything will be explained tomorrow. Tonight you must shower, I'll apply the healing salve and someone will discuss all these things with you in the morning. Fair enough?"

Cara stepped into the shower, which had filled with steam. The lemony soap was exhilarating on her skin, gave a little lift of hope to her insides, the feeling that perhaps the nightmare was about to end, that there was a new chapter beginning in her life.

And everything in her life was about to change forever.

Again.

Chapter 37

LIONEL WAS TRUSSED and hung from the rafters in the old warehouse Rubin the executioner used as his own private torture palace. A perimeter security current prevented him from tracing out to a safe place. His strength had waned. When the dark guards and soldiers went off for their daytime sleep, a mortal brute was brought in to continue waking Lionel up, whipping him, dousing him in vinegar, and making fun of how fast he healed from his injuries, which prompted spurts of more cruelty.

The senior Jett brother was growing weary of the game, and knew that unless a vital organ were hit, he could continue on this way for centuries. In fact, there were stories about this kind of sacrifice, a dark prisoner outliving several lifespans of his mortal torturers. Lionel wondered if he, too, would someday be looked upon as a fixture on the wall, no different than one of those ugly, buzzing fluorescent lamps no one ever looked at. His groans and moans would be background noise to an otherwise busy day, or lost in the dusty corners of the abandoned warehouse.

He actually liked it when someone was present, even if it meant torture. The boredom of hanging, reacting to every strange sound, the wind jangling the chains that held the doors shut or the scurrying of a tiny rodent was mind-numbing. But even if he wanted to, Lionel knew he could and would not end himself. As long as he was alive, his mission was still to live, protect and give witness to the mighty Monteleone clan.

The executioner had brought a couple of curious girls to the warehouse, no doubt to prove his manhood and cruelty, something Lionel thought Rubin felt a bit self-conscious about for some reason.

He talked them into the leather restraints. He whipped them with a crop, and if they didn't cry out enough, he'd whip Lionel, causing a ribbon of flesh to fly off his body. They'd scream just watching Lionel suffer.

Later on, Rubin brought someone else who definitely was not using drugs and was a whole octave higher on the intelligence scale. Lionel could sense she was a dark vamp, and a recent turning. Rubin's bloodstained fingers massaged the little tart's breasts from behind as she stood in front of Lionel, watching every ripple and movement of muscle his body made. She was naked and had nice skin. She revealed a sullen smile when his pecker rose for a salute, not that she deserved that. He just couldn't help it.

The executioner had seen her arousal at another man's dick and cried foul.

"Shut up, sweetheart," she replied to him. "I'm the one you're going to fuck. Let's do it right here, in front of him. Maybe he'll come in my face."

Rubin grunted and got to work, bending his knees to make up for their difference in height. He wasn't light on his feet and was having positional difficulties. The little vixen sighed, grabbed Lionel's thighs and bent herself forward, balancing on the bloody prisoner. This gave Rubin full access to either orifice and he got to work, until he noticed she had licked Lionel's cock and began licking the old sticky blood from his body.

"Hey. Not. Sure. I. Like. That," Rubin gasped between thrusts.

She wiggled her eyebrows up and down and mouthed *whatever,* then got back to work, teasing the prisoner to the point of making him pop.

Lionel had to admit he wanted to push her head into his groin and smother her, but his hands remained tied high above his head. He tried to focus on her face and where her tongue was going, rather than what was happening behind her. She had a nice touch. He could almost say she was gentle.

"I want your cum, lover boy," she whispered between licks. She took a couple of steps closer and enclosed him with her mouth, no longer teasing but working on him with in a very skilled and professional style.

Rubin didn't seem to notice. The executioner's eyes were squeezed shut as he grunted his release, probably thinking she was referring to him.

Lionel let her have it, all eight fuckin' ounces of it or however much it was. He'd never measured. She got most of it down, and her breasts were creamy and covered in his sticky seed that had leaked from her lips. He could tell she would be gagging soon, but instead, she rammed him deeper, all the way down her throat, which sent a new wave of cum from him in response.

Holy shit.

If he ever made it out of here, he'd have a hard time getting his brothers and the Monteleone boys to believe what had transpired.

Not that he had any choice in the matter than to relax and allow himself to become a tool.

Rubin was done and he began to wipe himself up with a dirty rag. The blonde righted herself and smeared the cum over her breasts. She was breathing hard as she studied Lionel. He saw a question there, but had no idea what she really had on her mind. Just that she was the most twisted lady he'd ever met. Her eyes had gone dark. Lionel could tell she was enjoying the pleasures of his preternatural sperm. She licked her lips and gave him a wicked smile. He knew he was in for more sex if he didn't get out of this warehouse. Maybe he could use her arousal to his advantage.

"I'll show you a real good time if you untie my hands."

"I don't need your hands. I need your cock."

"Hey, missy, you've had cock," Rubin objected. "Give me a little time and I'll be right back on your little ass so fast—"

She turned and cut him off with a slap across the face. Lionel was instantly alarmed. He didn't like to see a fight erupt when he was unable to do anything about it.

"Why you ungrateful little bitch," Rubin lunged after her, going for his preferred method of killing women: strangulation.

But she was fast, much faster than he was. Her lilting, teasing laugh echoed throughout the building, making a couple of trapped pigeons fly up and hit the metal ceiling. Rubin lost his balance and fell on his stomach.

She pulled a gun from her bag. Lionel judged the thing to be a Raptor II. He hoped to God she'd put silver bullets in it, or she was in for a nasty surprise when the executioner got up and continued chasing her.

Lionel watched her breasts bounce as she pranced around the room, brandishing the gun. The executioner was livid with rage. Lionel just hoped she'd get on with it, but no, she seemed to want to tease the fat vamp until he had to stop, bending over to brace himself on his knees, out of breath. He shook his head.

"Okay, okay, missy. You win this round. Come on, let's kiss and make up." He massaged his limp dick a few times and almost got it to salute for her when Lionel heard the gun go off. Sure as shit she'd shot the vamp and only a silver bullet in the middle of his chest could have stopped him clean like that.

She blew the barrel of the gun like a gunslinger from Hollywood. But she certainly didn't look like any gunslinger he'd ever seen before.

Forgive my evil thoughts. He'd never wanted a woman more in his life. He thought about begging her to get right to it, not even untying him first, he was so hot for her. But then reason came flooding into his brain, and he remembered the mission.

"Untie me."

"And you'll do what?"

"I said I'd make it up to you. And I will."

She cocked her head to the side. Her gaze dropped to his groin and, sure enough, he was ready to perform for hours on end. He was twice the size he had been when she had him in her mouth.

"How do you guys do that?"

"This?" he said, looking down. "I have no fuckin' clue. I just know that I like it."

"Aren't you afraid of me?"

"Should I be?"

She nodded very slowly. "I almost killed Dag."

That did earn a little respect from Lionel. "How the hell did you do that?"

"Tied him up with silver when he was sleeping. Your employer left him in a terrible shape. Disgusting burned flesh. I think that's why he came over and got you. After I healed him, of course."

"So why aren't you with him now? Why choose his man?"

"Because I wanted to see you. And besides, Dag wants to kill me now. So you see, we are a match made in heaven. He wants us both dead."

"Wanna celebrate?" Lionel was trying to sound casual, maybe a little sexy. He was starting to get alarmed that perhaps this little lady only liked to torture her conquests. That he had grossly misjudged her, as had Dag.

"Thought you'd never ask. Beg me."

"Please."

"Not good enough. I can wait all day, but you can't. You haven't much time. They'll be over here for Round Two."

"If you and I were alone together, and I had my hands, I'd first explore every inch of your body. I'd scrub your sex so hard you'd come in my shower. I'd remove any trace of that filthy disgusting slimeball excuse for a vamp, and then I'd replace it with some good clean cum and make you glow from the inside out. You'd want me so bad you'd keep me in a darkened room and fuck me 24/7. And I'd make you come, baby, every conceivable way possible. There. How's that?"

She jumped his bones, wrapping her legs around his waist, which pulled his restraints and hurt like hell. But he'd made a promise, and if she kept hers, he'd keep his. She whispered in his ear, "I can't wait."

She ran buck naked to search through Rubin's pants until she found the restraint keys, then ran back to unhook each wrist.

Lionel was grateful.

"Thanks, sweetheart. I can trace us somewhere for a quickie, but I got things I need to do, and I sure as hell have to get out of here, and I think you do, too."

She nodded her head. She was going to be putty in his hands.

"I keep my word. You let me go, and I promise to come back and send you to heaven a few dozen times, but not right now, honey. You understand?" He lifted her chin with his fingers and placed a sweet kiss on her lips.

She began to wrap her arms around his neck and he ducked out. "Nope. Sorry. Just hold that thought. If we both survive the next few days, I'll be back."

"Take me with you. I'm an ally now. I've fought your enemy. I've aided your cause."

"Doesn't work that way. I don't make the rules. You're going to have to fend for yourself for a bit until this is all over."

"Did I tell you I qualified expert?"

Lionel began taking Rubin's clothes. The pants he had to cinch up with the belt high above his waist. His shoes were about five sizes too small.

"I can believe that."

"Let me be a member of your team."

"I don't get to choose that."

"Let me try out."

He thought about it for a moment and then decided yes; he had room for one more, especially if she was a crack shot. "Okay, get your clothes. We gotta disappear right now or it will be too late."

She was quick. He took her hand and they opened a side door to the night. "Hang on, sweetheart," he whispered in her ear. Lionel traced them to the Monteleone villa, dead center in the living room, like he'd done dozens of time before. She stepped clear of Lionel and they both studied a cadre of muscled and well-armed men grinning from ear to ear. Some had been playing video games, some were lounging in front of a big screen TV. Pizza boxes and fast food wrappers were everywhere. Lionel knew the Monteleones would be royally pissed if they saw the scene in front of them.

"Holy cow. Lionel's brought the cavalry," someone said.

"That's right, boys," she said with a twinkle in her eye. "I'm the inspirational speaker for tonight's meeting."

Chapter 38

CARA AWOKE TO the sounds of cheering coming from down below. She slipped out of the luscious, buttery sheets and padded barefoot across the room to the double doors. She was pleased when she found them unlocked. On the landing she could hear lots of chatter and movement down below. Music was playing, and she could smell sweat and something else besides the left-over aromas of fast food. A glance to the corner by the front door explained it all. A small arsenal was leaning against the plaster walls of the grand house in case any intruders chose to come uninvited.

There was some raucous party happening in the living room. Waves of laughter erupted. Someone wearing a shirt and no pants disappeared into what looked like a hallway guest bath.

No pants?

The music sounded like a home Karaoke machine and the male singer was horrible, flat and off key. But a female singer took over to the whistles and catcalls of the audience. She was singing a song Cara had seen on old Marilyn Monroe films. But this singer was better than the great lady herself.

Cara retreated to the bedroom. Beside the door she spotted a wicker basket with a set of clean clothes and a pair of shoes. She quickly dressed. Grateful that the maid had provided tennis shoes, she tiptoed down the hallway and found a rear exit leading to the back yard of the house. She opened the back door and began to run like hell.

PAOLO DIDN'T LIKE airplanes. He usually traced. But the tracing always scared Lucius to death, so this time he sat back and allowed himself to be transported more slowly, enjoying quality time with his son, and politely fending off the attendant who kept inserting her body parts everywhere.

Lucius waved a generous goodbye to her as they were deplaning. "I think she liked, me, Father."

When Paolo turned to look back, she winked at him.

"You know, son, I think maybe you're right."

Paolo and Lucius were picked up at the airport by Marcus, who drove an armored Suburban. It surprised Paolo he was not taking more precautions.

"How was your flight, brother?"

"Long." It was morning in Italy, and Paolo wished he could go straight to bed.

"It was awesome, Marcus. I played video games, and we watched three movies."

"Oh, my." Marcus picked up Lucius' bag and slung it over his shoulder. "You get any rest, then?"

"Not a wink."

"Well, I'm afraid to say you'll not get any for a bit longer. I have to get over to the Council chambers within the hour. There's just time enough to drop Lucius off."

"Where's your driver, Marcus?"

"I needed to speak to you in private, if you know what I mean."

"Problems?"

"Complications. And I'm having trouble with some loyalty issues."

Paolo paused after he deposited Lucius in the second seat and made sure he was strapped in. "Not the Jett brothers?"

"No. God, no. They're golden."

Paolo looked back at his brother who chuckled, "Well, not Golden, but no, no problems there. Dag made a raid on Cara's apartment about an hour ago. She's safe; Jeb and Huge traced her to my house. But they captured Lionel."

"Not good."

They sped along the freeway, Lucius becoming engrossed in the movie playing behind the driver's seat on a portable screen. The countryside was greener than he remembered. The farms and olive orchards they passed, nestled amongst old stone ruins, looked smaller after living for a while California, where the scenery was similar, but with larger open spaces. But Tuscany was his home, and he was glad to be here at last. He wished Cara were at his side.

"I've alerted the local authorities," Marcus began. "The SEAL embedded with them said Cara was sorting through lots of papers last night. And she made a couple of calls. We're trying to track the numbers now."

"Surely you don't suspect Cara of—"

"No, brother. But I think she's beginning to piece together her last forty-eight hours, not that she remembers any of it, but she's retracing her steps."

They got behind a tractor pulling an enormous tiller. Marcus had to reduce speed. He checked the clock on the dash. "We have to hurry to make our allotted time slot."

"You should have brought the driver, Marcus," Paolo said.

"I can see that now. But, we need the privacy."

"So what else is going on?" Paolo asked.

"The Council is very concerned about the missing book. They hold the family partly responsible for its disappearance. Praetor says they have already had one meeting."

"No way we could have known. I think we told them as soon as we found out. It's not like we were hiding things from them."

"I agree. We have to make the Council understand. They can impose sanctions if they feel we have mismanaged things, brother."

"That would be so unfair. We have all risked much."

"And complacently underestimated the gathering forces of the dark coven leaders."

"Leaders?" Paolo knew about Dag. But the Monteleones had a long history of coexisting peacefully with the dark coven lords, helping them through tough times on occasion. They had been generous with their time and their money.

"The leaders are uniting. There is a scramble. Word is, the book contains something so powerful it could affect us all."

Paolo had felt such a shift in the temperature of their world.

"So I was right, she was looking for the book last night," he said to Marcus. "Perhaps it wasn't wise to erase her memory. We might have needed information she had stored in her head."

"I admit, perhaps I acted rashly."

The tractor pulled off on a dirt road and Marcus gunned the Suburban. They tore down the narrow country road until they saw the villa mounted high atop the hill, like a crowned jewel amongst the pale olive trees that had been in their family for nearly a thousand years. Was all this at stake, Paolo wondered?

"Whatever happens, I am with you till the very end. You will not have to suffer for any of my misdeeds, as has happened in the past."

"Love. Always complicated. Sometimes fleeting, and for us, usually dangerous."

"Very dangerous. I should have been more careful, Marcus. I have much to make up for. First Lucius, nearly costing you your life, and the life of your Anne. Now Lionel, who has been loyal to this family since before we were born. I pray to the God of vampires he will be returned to us safe."

They rounded a sharp corner and Marcus nearly lost control of the vehicle. Paolo held on to the handgrip bolted into the ceiling.

"In a sad way, your becoming involved with Cara has perhaps saved us. Had we not known about the book, the coven leader and his designs, we might not have been as prepared. So don't take that guilty tone with the Council. We have to convince them we have done all we could. I fear the day they would take the power away from us to act on the Council's behalf."

"If not us, who?"

"I don't know. I have been away this past year. Laurel doesn't involve herself in politics, so I have no clue, brother."

They drove up to the stone pillars that meant home. It was bittersweet—he was so grateful to see the apricot colored stucco of the family villa, but he faced the possibility it all could be confiscated, or worse yet, lost in a dark coven war that might claim them all.

As soon as the vehicle stopped, Paolo dashed out and ran around to unstrap Lucius, carrying him into the house. Marcus came behind with the luggage.

"There you are, young prince," Laurel said as she ran to her nephew and lifted him in her arms, twirling him around the kitchen. Laurel was wearing flowers woven into her hair, and her blouse was frilly, with a big collar that fluffed up in the breeze coming from the kitchen. "Let me look at you. Oh, so handsome." Lucius blushed and giggled under his aunt's affections.

Laurel addressed Paolo, giving him a hug. Paolo could feel her shaking. His sister was scared. So was he, for the first time in centuries.

"Marcus tells me there is a new love in your life. I am so happy for you." Laurel was Marcus and Paolo's unmarried sister. She had served as a link between Paolo and the rest of his family while he was living out his fantasy of a normal, mortal life in the States, as he said farewell and buried three wives.

Paolo had loved spending time at this house, where she had entertained him over the years, talking about Marcus and his investments and adventures. Laurel was the one who kept Paolo informed about family business, the marriages and births, and occasionally the tragedies, making sure he stayed loosely connected in case he ever wanted to return to the fold. And now perhaps it was too late. He could see it in her eyes.

It was in this house, Paolo remembered, that he learned the fragrance of the orchard as it bloomed in the spring months. As a young boy his mother had taken him through the warm sunny hillside, back when he was mortal. When everything was perfect. He still missed that idyllic life, even now.

"You are lovely, even more beautiful than before I left."

Laurel's caramel-colored hair and fair complexion were similar to his own. They'd been mistaken for twins growing up, and they were the closest in age. However, Laurel took the turning two years before Marcus and Paolo, anxious to be done with her mortal life and ready to begin a family.

But time had not been their friend, and so neither of them had married. Laurel had never met her fated mate, and Paolo hadn't wanted anything to do with his. Because they all believed Marcus had fathered the child, Laurel made it her job to look after young Lucius for her bachelor brother. "Laurel," Marcus said to her, "we have to trace to the Council immediately. You will see to it Lucius gets settled?"

"I will, certainly. Safe journeys."

Outside the villa, Paolo asked a question he'd been wondering about for the past half hour. "Any idea what number she called?" Paolo was curious to see if someone else had gotten close to Cara and was directing her actions.

"A number in Eastern Europe."

"Give me the number."

Marcus gave Paolo a slip of paper with the number written in Marcus' scrawl.

"We have no time for that. Let's meet with the Council, and then we'll make plans," Marcus said.

They both knew the way, having traveled to the little Council headquarters numerous times. Their tracing appeared with practiced precision at the steps to the chamber building. The brothers entered, and the tall copper doors with copper bas-relief designed by Michelangelo himself, shut behind them, sounding like the boom of a cannon.

In the anteroom, a robed novice greeted them. She was a beautiful girl, probably not quite twenty and not yet the age of choice, for she had porcelain features and appeared to be affected by the two handsome brothers. That was a mortal trait.

Paolo cursed under his breath when he saw her.

Careful, brother, Marcus mentally warned.

The Council, made up of aging Golden vamps of legendary lineage, always surrounded itself with younger girls, and it was well known that Council members occasionally bedded them.

Paolo checked his attitude, inhaled, and set his mind on the task at hand, not quite knowing if this would be the last day he would wander around Italy as a free man.

The lovely novice opened the doors to the inner chamber and they stood before the dais of the Council. Paolo recognized almost all of them. But a few newcomers were present who did not smile. Two members were hunched over in wheelchairs, red IVs dripping into their arms. He'd always thought it was odd some members would waste their lives on things that would make them weak and sick, and wondered why their advice could be valued considering their aged, addicted state.

In the center of the council sat Praetor Artemis. At last Paolo had something to feel grateful for. He knew the Golden vamp to be an honest man who had helped Marcus out of the predicament of the murder trial. But since most the Council were made up of men who were clinging to power, Paolo wondered how much of a tightrope his old friend had to walk to stay on as Chairman.

"Welcome back," Praetor began. "You've had some adventures out in the Wild West, I'm told." Someone at the end of the dais sniggered.

The brothers bowed in tandem, as they had done for decades. They both made sure the bow was long, and low.

"Thank you for agreeing to see us at such short notice, Council," Marcus began. "We have urgent news we felt the Council needed to hear from us directly, and in person."

One of the members Paolo did not recognize slammed his fist on the table and yelled, "Where is the book, Marcus? That is all that matters here."

"We are trying to locate it—"

"I'm told you had it in your possession, and yet you allowed a mortal woman to take it away with her? How can that be?" another member demanded.

"Not true, sire. We have never seen this book. Only heard about it. To my knowledge, no one has seen this book since it disappeared in the fire before we were born," Marcus replied calmly. "It could very well be destroyed, for all we know."

"Then why the hell are all the darks revving up for war over it?" another Council member asked.

"I don't have an answer for that." Marcus was running out of room to maneuver. Paolo could see his brother shaking slightly. So much was at stake. They'd had little time to plan for this. The sudden accusatory tone of the Council distressed him as much as it did his brother.

Paolo stepped in front of his brother. "Members of the Council. I am the one responsible for this series of events. I came to be acquainted with a young woman, a college professor in California, who is an expert on vampire mythology. During this casual conversation I discovered that, while she did not believe in vampires, she had followed a lead to a rare book on the subject that she was able to purchase from a bookseller in Prague."

Several members nodded. Two muttered something unflattering. Paolo paid little attention. He focused on Praetor Artemis as he completed his statement. "What happened next was a lapse in judgment, something you are all aware has happened to me before."

The room fell silent. Paolo knew no one could argue with the logic of his statement. "It was my error that I became too obviously curious about her studies. But, in the course of the conversation, I learned she had found this book, which claimed to have been written by a British explorer who studied early vampire legends. He traveled throughout India and wrote a book about the Temples of the Vampires in the Sind, dating back to a few hundred years after the death of Christ. She found references to a joining, an apex of races. I believe he may have discovered the book, or information about the origins of our species."

"This is blasphemy!" the member who had slammed his fist on the table. "There is no such history. There is no apex."

"Oh, but there is," a voice behind them said smugly. Paolo and Marcus turned to see Dag Nielsen standing just inside the doors. He was the first dark coven leader to ever be allowed entrance into the Council chamber.

Chapter 39

D AG SAUNTERED TO the front of the room, and began pacing in front of the dais. Paolo wanted to wipe the smirk off his face, but he struggled to tamp down his emotions so as not to give the dark leader something else to gloat about.

Marcus appeared to be in shock. Praetor was searching the table from side to side. "Who gave this man entry?"

"I did," the angry council member responded sweetly. "It seems we've been blinded by the legendary Monteleone family and their secrets. I call it a fatal case of hero worship." The robed member leaned back in his chair, studying the brothers, then abruptly turned and addressed Praetor. "And since you are friend to these two, I call for a vote of no confidence. I believe your judgment has been colored by your affection for this family."

"Nonsense. No dark coven leader has ever been granted admission to our halls. Never in thousands of years."

"But, with all due respect, you've never faced the extinction of your race," Dag inserted himself. Several on the Council gasped. Groups of two or three members whispered and muttered amongst themselves.

Paolo swallowed hard. His light-hearted thought about this being the last day of his freedom came back to haunt him, turning his stomach into a pit of oily black rage.

"As I see it, we have two items on the floor," one member spoke up from the opposite side of the table. "First we have a vote of no confidence which has been leveled at Praetor Artemis, a man I have found to be exceedingly fair and just in all the years I have known him. But it is Capuro's right to request a vote. The timing is what I find unclear."

Artemis leaned forward. "And since I am not yet the unseated Council member, the other item on this floor is the admittance of a dark coven leader to our halls. And for that, I do not give my permission at this time."

Capuro leaned back and stared at the ceiling, extending his hands out to the sides as if he'd tried his best and was giving up. Dag began to turn beet red at the attempt to muzzle him. Before he could spew out something venomous, Paolo stepped toward the dark leader and grabbed him by the elbow.

"This man is a traitor—not only to himself and his own family, but to the entire race of dark vampires. He is amassing an army. He is killing the Goldens' mortal children. I now formally accuse him of also planning the destruction of this great body. He is not your ally nor your friend. He does not seek peace. He cannot be trusted. He is dangerous, and he is my sworn enemy. As well as yours. If he remains here, then this body, this Council, will no longer speak for me."

The collective gasp that erupted from the dais surprised even Paolo. He continued to hold Dag by the elbow, taking care to make sure the dark leader remained in a small amount of pain.

"You would listen to the man who has ordered the killing of young Rory Monteleone and his younger brother, who was only a boy of ten?" Paolo shouted over the commotion.

Artemis stood. "And I have knowledge of three other children of this house who have perished at the hands of a dark guard. They were not accidents. There is a systematic attack going on, consuming the lives of some of our youngest and brightest children. This has never happened while I have been a member of this Council."

No one said a word. Dag had inhaled to shout something, but Paolo twisted his arm up at an angle and thought perhaps he felt a small bone break. The pain set Dag off, just as Paolo knew it would.

"You! You and your stuffed hedonistic bodies and your sanctimonious attitudes." Dag jerked himself free and swore as his arm hung at an unnatural angle. "Who are you to tell any of the dark covens they are not your equals? Just because you have the privilege of walking in daylight, doesn't mean you have the right to claim dominion over everyone and everything else. I'll personally watch each one of you burn in the fires of Hell. And I'll do it while fucking your wives, your girlfriends and your daughters. I will spread my seed and spawn throughout the Golden vampire race and will create a lineage that will last forever, the lineage originally denied me. I claim dominion! Mark my words. I will prevail."

Marcus and Paolo glanced at each other.

Guards traced to surround Dag as he struggled to free himself from their confinement. As quickly as it had begun, it was all over. Dag had traced himself away to a safe location.

Paolo cursed to himself, wishing he'd grabbed the man and traveled to the middle of the sun-baked deserts of Death Valley. He wanted to smell the burning flesh of this animal and watch until he had withered to nothing.

The guards were looking around for signs Dag was still in the room.

"You. You are a traitor," Artemis pointed to Capuro. "You allowed him entry without Council permission, nearly costing all of us our lives." Artemis gave the order and guards took the former Council member away in silver chains.

The whispering amongst Council members subsided. Praetor Artemis sat back down and straightened his red robe. He was not smiling. He showed Paolo and Marcus no friendship, no mercy. "This changes little. All the facts are still the same. The book must be found and if you can't do it, then we will and you will be stripped of your holdings, you will be denied the protection of the Council, and you will be left to your own devices."

Paolo and Marcus both bowed. He hadn't given them a time limit, which was good, Paolo thought.

"One more thing," Artemis said as he stood up. "You have twenty-four hours to produce the book. And bring the girl here."

"Cara? Here?" Paolo asked. "Why—"

"You wish to argue with my lenient proposal? In twenty-four hours the fates of everyone in this room will be sealed. If I thought I could do this any faster, I'd have you in chains and would go about it myself. But if you test me, if you fail, everyone you care about will pay dearly. Some with their lives." He sat down. Looking from side to side he came upon a sea of nodding heads and one who had fallen asleep in his wheelchair and was snoring.

Artemis leaned forward on one elbow, braced his chin on his arched fingers, and said with icy clarity, "I suggest you get going right away. You now have less than twenty-four hours left."

Marcus and Paolo didn't bother to take the time to bow. They looked into each other's faces and traced away. They had both been thinking about home, the villa in Imprunetta. That's where they went.

LUCIUS WAS GIGGLING in the yard outside the tall metal and glass doors to the kitchen. The kitchen smelled of freshly baking pies, which was a custom in the Monteleone household, since Lucius still ate as a mortal child. His favorite was blackberry.

Laurel was gathering flowers in the garden. Paolo sighed as he looked at them both. Marcus capped his shoulder with his palm. "They will be safe. Somehow, we've got to make this work."

"Brother, I—"

"Nonsense, Paolo. Your instincts were perfect. You assessed the situation far better than I could, and your actions probably saved our lives, possibly the life of Artemis as well. I'm beginning to believe in divine intervention. Your meeting her has turned out to be a godsend. Just think what would have happened if we'd had no warning? Lucky for us, we have her safely stowed away at the villa in California. Otherwise, I'd be willing to bet we'd be thoroughly screwed."

Chapter 40

Paolo wanted to trace to California to see her again, but the urgency of the mission to learn more about the bookseller in Prague eclipsed his desire. At least he felt it was desire that prompted his need to see her, and he was learning how to do the right thing, rather than the first thing that came into his head.

When he arrived in Prague, he was greeted by an early afternoon sun that warmed his otherwise cold flesh. He walked down the designated street and stopped in front of the bookstore, troubled to see that it was boarded up.

He looked at the slip of paper Marcus had given him and dialed the number. He was rewarded with the sound of a phone ringing inside the store. No one answered. He redialed and again got no response.

He tried calling the bookstore once more. This time an answering machine answered with a message in a heavily accented, guttural man's voice. He decided against leaving a message, and against calling the local police.

He scanned the area around the little shop, looking for someone on guard, and saw none. He stepped closer to the once hand-lettered windows of the bookstore and peered between the shards of broken glass and pieces of metal and scrap wood keeping out the public. He saw that some books remained, and that someone had been packing them into crates. He needed to investigate further. Checking to make sure there was a clear spot inside the store, he stepped into the alleyway and traced to inside without being noticed.

He was immediately assaulted by the smell of death and decay.

Saturated by the distinct iron smell of blood, he walked carefully around the concrete floor, which was littered with papers and remnants of books torn asunder. When he accidentally stepped into a nearly dry pool of blood, his boots almost stuck to the floor.

Paolo knew the police wouldn't be investigating this scene. There was no evidence on the outside that a crime had even been committed here. That was both good and bad. Good that he would be allowed to rummage through the contents of the store without being disturbed. Bad that he had little time in which to do it, and since he was alone, it would use up precious minutes they could ill afford to lose.

Where to begin?

He walked over to the crates. They were all being shipped to a bookstore in San Francisco. It was clearly Dag's handiwork. Paolo sniffed the air. No trace of the dark vamp remained, if he'd even done this himself. Probably Dag had assigned the executioner and the other dark guards he used to do his bidding.

Paolo's boots made crackling noises as he stepped on more broken glass. Protective bookcase doors had been shattered. Even reading lamps and tables had been upended. A cash register, the old fashioned kind without a digital anything, was yawning open. Its vacant drawer hung down like the tongue of an old prospector.

Towards the back of the store was a narrow stairway leading up. Paolo stepped quietly, but the boards underfoot groaned anyway due to his size. He wasn't sure what he'd find there, so, although he needed the element of surprise, his need for safety was primary, so he did not trace.

A few precious moments later, he found a young, pregnant woman lying dead, next to the bodies of a pudgy little boy and his dog. It was an execution killing, done several days ago, and the stench consumed the room. No trace of the bookseller, but from the size of the pool of dried blood below, Paolo didn't doubt he was dead as well.

He was sure the perpetrator had wanted information and didn't shrink from using innocents to obtain it. However, if they had found the information they sought, the place wouldn't have been ransacked. Cara's office had been similarly ransacked.

Holy God of vampires. They don't yet have the book!

Was it too much to hope?

He glanced around the little family living space. He was looking for the phone, so dialed the number again. It rang next to a bed that had been ripped apart, and the mattress stuffing strewn all over the room. Drawers were ripped from the dressers and their meager contents dumped on the floor. Under the phone sat a square device with a blinking light. Paolo pushed the red button and heard the familiar voice of the women he now knew he loved.

He listened to Cara's message. "You also said you were receiving another shipment. I would be most interested in what you found."

Another shipment?

Paolo was about to go downstairs when he heard the end of Cara's message, and another one left after it.

The man was speaking in broken English. Paolo could barely make out that the man was from a trucking company, and was asking for instructions for delivery of a crate of books from overseas. Paolo was ecstatic.

He ran back to the machine and replayed it again, jotting down the phone number and address. He hesitated, but then decided to erase the tape, just in case he was being followed.

Once outside the shop, he ran through several alleyways until he came to the dirty riverfront. He could see the name of the warehouse across a delicate metal span bridge. He ran across the metal planks on the walkway as little cars buzzed past him.

At the office of A. Novak & Company he spoke softly to the shipping clerk who sat behind metal bars, sending some glamour her way. Her eyes fluttered, crossed, and then she promptly fainted, her plump legs resting on the swivel chair cushion she had been sitting on.

Damn it.

He took a chance and traced into the little office. In the back he heard the sound of workers and machinery, including forklifts. He decided she would make a good front for him to gain entry.

"Scusi," he said, using his practiced pigeon English/Italian dialect. "The signora has fainted. Please. Come. You must help me. She is too heavy for me to carry." He pretended to nearly drop her and several workmen came running over to give him a hand.

A clerk with a clipboard and without a hard hat addressed him. "You see what happened?"

"I was jes talking to her. She fell over. I think she hit her head, maybe? I don't know. So sorry."

The man looked Paolo over carefully, ending with laser focus on his shoes. It occurred to Paolo he might recognize his $1000 leather pumps. "My brother-in-love is a shoemaker in Napoli. He gets me the very finest at a good price."

That seemed to satisfy the man.

"Scusi, but I am sent here to pick up a crate for a mister—" Paolo dug the slip of paper from his pocket. "Tomas Novotny." He showed Marcus's note to the man. "I was to be here yesterday, and I am so sorry. I have car trouble."

The man frowned. "Hope you have something bigger than a car. This crate is full of books."

"Perhaps I will find a truck for taking crate back to Napoli."

"Thought you said it was for Tomas Novotny."

"Yes, yes, it is. But I am to sell for him in Napoli at the book festival. You've heard of it perhaps?"

"All right. You can come this way."

Paolo walked behind the man just as he heard the woman beginning to talk. He was glad she had not been hurt by the fall.

The crate for Tomas Novotny was about four feet cubed.

"You want to inspect it?"

"Sure, sure. Yes, I can do that."

The workman pried open the top with a crowbar. He removed some shredded pine packing material to reveal several antique book covers.

"Ah! Molto bello. Can look for a moment or two?" Paolo asked. "Fine."

"I also call my friend and see if he has right truck."

The man walked away without saying a word.

Paolo took out his cell phone and dialed Marcus.

"I think I've found what they were looking for," he said.

"You found the book?"

"I found a crate that was destined for Novotny's bookstore. I don't think anyone else knows about it."

"You know what you're looking for?"

"Help me out a little bit, brother. Or, do you want to send a big truck and we'll take them all?"

"That would take too much time. It will be pretty damaged, probably flaking. I'm trying to remember what color the rest of the books were."

"You saw them?"

"Yes, when I was little. This was part of Grandfather's set, and he showed me the books before the war. I wish I'd paid more attention then. God, if only they were still alive."

"We are the old ones now, brother. Would you recognize the book if you saw it? Why don't you trace here and help me look?" Though Paolo was whispering, he felt his voice was carrying too loudly throughout the warehouse. Several of the men surrounding the woman had turned to look at him. And she was pointing right at him. "Um, I'm afraid I've run out of time. You best not do that—"

Marcus appeared right next to him and cleared his throat. Paolo darted a quick glance at the crowd of onlookers and several of them crossed themselves. Well, if they were afraid, that could give the brothers a few extra minutes. He'd have felt much better if they had one of the Jett brothers to help out. Marcus was doing a stare-down with the man Paolo thought was the foreman.

"Don't look at them. Let's get to work," Paolo said to his brother.

Incredibly, under the second layer of books was a light greenish-brown book that had been covered in green plastic archival wrap. There was no title on the outside, which Paolo thought was odd.

Marcus untaped the wrap and opened the interior of the book. There were diagrams and charts, sketches and celestial maps for navigating the oceans. A hole had been carved into the pages of the book without damaging the text. Inside the hollowed-out pages was a tiny skeleton key.

"What's this? Did grandfather ever speak of this?" Paolo asked.

"No. Never." Marcus put the key in his pocket and re-wrapped the book in the green plastic. The group of men began to descend upon them, but by the time they were close, Marcus and Paolo had traced back to the family villa in Imprunetta, taking the sacred text and the key with them.

Chapter 41

PAOLO AND MARCUS were ecstatic with their find until they got the call from Lionel Jett.

"Lionel! You escaped, thank the God of vampires. Good to hear your voice. We had feared the worst," Marcus said.

"Prepare yourself, Marcus. I have some bad news."

Paolo couldn't help but overhear the conversation. He instantly thought of Cara. He had not felt anything coming from her for some time. He'd thought perhaps her altered memory had made the physical distance between them more significant than it had been earlier.

"Cara is missing."

Paolo grabbed the phone. "Lionel, was she taken?"

"No, Paolo. I am sorry to say we misjudged her and she slipped right out, when we were distracted."

"Distracted?"

"It's a long story. I must bear the responsibility myself."

"When?"

"Sometime this evening. She had been put to bed. The maid brought her some fresh clothes and a nightgown, and watched her fall asleep. When she checked on her later, Cara was gone. Sometime between midnight and two."

"Who do you have looking for her?"

"Just about everyone."

"I'll be there shortly. Let me make arrangements and I'll come help out."

"Thank you. And Paolo?"

"Yes?"

"I am so sorry for my poor judgment. We were sort of celebrating. All my fault."

Paolo didn't want an apology. He wanted Cara back. She was at huge risk, being out there by herself. But he also knew Lionel would even lay down his life if necessary to save her.

"Let's concentrate, Lionel. We need to be sharp, or we won't find her."

"That's affirmative."

Paolo handed Marcus back his phone. "No matter what, you stay here with Anne and the baby until all this is over. Protect Lucius. I have to go find her. If you have to, go before the Council with the book and give it to them. Explain this to them. I wish I could stay and study it with you, but I think I can still feel her emotions, and that gives us an advantage."

"And you are also doing the Council's bidding. You forget that they want to see her tomorrow."

"No, Marcus. I haven't forgotten the stakes. I will not fail you again."

Paolo peeked outside the kitchen windows and saw Lucius and Laurel in serious conversation about something on the patio. He walked over to his son and hugged him, inhaling the boy's fresh scent one last time. This wasn't the kind of war he'd expected to wage, chasing after a mortal woman down a dark alley. Waiting for the dark forces to rain down their wrath on all their innocent women and children. On his son.

"Lucius, you mind Laurel. I have to go away for a little bit."

"How long?"

"I'll be back very soon. I promise." He hated to make a promise he wasn't sure he could keep, and a glance at Laurel told him he was a bad liar. She was fighting back tears.

"You are going alone?" she asked.

"We have all the guys back in California. Marcus will stay here with you, Anne, the baby and Lucius. Cara's escaped."

"Oh Paolo, I'm so sorry. Don't be foolish. We need you. If she has a death wish, don't let it cost—" she stopped because Lucius was hanging on every word. The boy's lower lip quivered.

"Be brave, Lucius. Can you do that for me, for auntie?" Paolo asked.

Lucius sullenly nodded his head.

Paolo picked up his duffel bag, gave the boy's hair a tussle, kissed Laurel on the cheek. As was his tracing routine, he inhaled, as if taking the last breath of the land he loved so much. He arrived a moment later in the living room of Marcus and Anne's house in Healdsburg.

Lionel Jett was waiting for him. Paolo noticed Lionel wouldn't look him in the eye. He could tell the man was filled with remorse.

"You've got to get a grip, Lionel. Things happen."

"But I let you and the family down, sir."

"No, you've been our loyal, trusted bodyguard for centuries. We owe you our lives from so many occasions in the past. This is a complicated mess. We must concentrate. Can you do that for me?"

"Affirmative."

"Where should we start? Know anything about what she was thinking before she left?"

"No. I didn't speak with her. I was otherwise occupied," Lionel blushed and squeezed his eyes shut. He briefly told him what had transpired in the warehouse.

"And she is with your men, looking?"

"Yessir."

"You trust her?"

Lionel was having difficulty answering. "I just don't know who to trust anymore, sir, and I needed the manpower. The woman is fearless, Paolo. I don't feel she means to do us any harm. She could have done that easily already." Lionel blushed again as he looked at his feet.

"Lionel, I thought you were smarter than that. For all we know, your little lapse in judgment wasn't that, but a carefully orchestrated plan to draw Cara out into the open so they could snag her."

"I've thought of that."

"Where is everyone else?"

"Where *aren't* they? We're in radio communication. Since Cara doesn't have a vehicle, we're all over Sonoma County."

"Do a check-in with everyone. See if there are any new leads," Paolo directed. He walked into the study, scanned the bookshelf and satisfied himself that the book was still where Marcus had placed it. He wanted to touch it, knowing it was something Cara had touched, but he didn't want to leave his scent anywhere it could be detected by a dark vamp.

CARA WAS FREEZING cold, which only added to her confusion. She was running away from a house full of armed guards into the night filled with who-knew-what crazies. What was she running from? But her instincts had demanded she get out of that house. Something else internally told her she didn't have much time to get her hands on that book before it fell into the wrong hands.

Though she had on a long-sleeved shirt and jeans, they had not provided her with a jacket. She was going to have to find an all-night restaurant that served hot coffee, and had a decent bathroom. Then she'd sit down and think about what her next step should be.

Over and over in her head she thought about the dark, handsome campus security staffer, Paolo Monteleone. Hadn't she seen something in that face she could trust? Why was she not surprised when she slid into that bed last night and felt his presence? Was that the room he stayed in? Surely the master of a house that size would have a lavish master suite. And the maid had said it was a *guest bedroom.* So Mr. Monteleone was a guest?

She scanned the pebbles along the dirt pathway that shone in the moonlight. It helped to keep moving. There was, thankfully, no wind. She would need some money in case she wound up on the road for a few days. She cursed the fact that she had no cell phone.

She remembered her old phone, which was in a box at the apartment. Perhaps it had survived the bomb. She had planned to give it to Johnny. She stopped, frozen in space.

Johnny. Suddenly she was filled with images of him lying in a pool of blood in her office, his head ripped almost completely off his body.

She remembered the police and rescue crews. She now remembered the questioning she had undergone.

So, Paolo Monteleone, whoever the hell he was, had been right. She had forgotten all these things, temporarily. Now they were coming back in layers.

Cara headed further down the dirt path along the country road she knew led to the square in downtown Healdsburg. There might be a coffee shop open somewhere nearby. Someone who might give her a free cup, since she had no money.

Paolo Monteleone. Something in her heart called out to him.

And she felt the warm response in return. *I am here, mi amore.*

Cara stopped and turned around. The street was deserted. An oncoming car's headlights, though distant, scared her. She jumped behind some hedges and waited for it to pass.

Her mind was racing as little pieces of memory began to stitch themselves together. She remembered the smell of the lemon shower gel, the way the robe in the bathroom had left a tingling sensation on her skin when she brushed against it. Sliding into the almond-colored satin sheets had been like sliding into—

Then she saw the lovemaking. Paolo leaning over her, kissing her, filling her with his love. Hot tears began to slip down her cheeks. How could she have forgotten so much? Or were all these just vivid dreams?

Are they dreams, or did I live them? What is happening to me?

She started to run, seeing lights of a gas station directly in front of her. Checking her surroundings, she saw a car full of men waiting in the shadows. Grateful they hadn't noticed her, she detoured around the bright lot, heading down Healdsburg Avenue toward the square.

The bar crowd was letting out, and several couples lingered under twinkle lights of the square, gazing into shop windows. She pretended she was one of them. A bar was still open on her right, so she entered.

Grateful for the darkly lit room, she motioned to the bartender she wanted to use the restroom and was granted a nod, as he pointed to the back. Locking the bathroom door behind her, she collapsed to fetal position, leaning against the wall covered in graffiti. The tears came. She felt hunted. Trapped in a strange bathroom. No money, no help. And there was something else; something dark and sinister had formed around her.

Her eyes had been shut. When she opened them, a man she recognized from her apartment, dressed in black, stood before her in the women's rest room.

It was not Paolo.

Instinctively she held her neck.

"That's right, little one. I nearly separated your pretty little head from your luscious body."

His hungry eyes perused her body like he owned her.

"Paolo should be shot for keeping you all to himself."

"But I am not with Paolo." She tried to sound brave. It didn't work.

"And good for me, then. Does this mean I won't have to beat you to submission?" Dag stepped closer and yanked her to her feet, gripping her by the upper arm. "Or, do you like it rough, my sweet?"

His foul breath sickened her. *Paolo. Help me. He is here.*

Dag cocked his head to the side. "How nice. You speak to each other non-verbally. I get to eavesdrop on the lovers. This is a most unexpected pleasure."

Cara was terrified she'd committed a fatal error. She was hoping the fact that Paolo wasn't answering her back meant that he was trying to locate her without being detected. She could tell he was close. God, she needed him and his strong arms.

"When you and I are having delicious sex, your lover boy will be able to enjoy the festivities as well. How nice for you both." Dag smiled and Cara could see the pink healing scar on his cheek from the wound Paolo had given him. Dag grabbed her by the hair and forced her face against his. His tongue plunged down her throat and made her gag.

"I'm going to enjoy this. I shall kill you slowly, as I fuck you to death, Cara. Or, excuse me if I call you by the very apt name he gave you, *mi amore.*"

Dag hauled her to the hallway and pulled her through the bar. She looked with alarm at the bartender, who frowned. He bent down and reached for something from under the bar. Dag turned on him before he could stand up.

"Not wise, unless you want to sacrifice your life for hers."

The bartender stood back and raised his hands in surrender. "No trouble, please, no trouble," he babbled nervously.

"That's what I thought. Good choice," Dag said and continued to haul Cara out onto the street. A black van pulled up with its rear doors flapping open. Dag threw Cara inside and into the arms of several men, then slammed the door shut.

She was assaulted by the rotten cabbage smell first. She tried to move and accidentally kneed someone's foot. That someone was huge. He howled like a wolf. As the van began to take off, in the streetlight glare she could see a large, protruding, festering toe and what looked like a thoroughly rotten toenail sticking out from a hole crudely cut into a boot. The toe began to bleed.

"Sorry," she said, out of reflex.

She was rewarded with a slap across the face that made the whole world go dark.

PAOLO LOST HER location just prior to arriving with Lionel at the square. The only opened structure on the block was a bar. He ran over to the bartender.

"Have you seen a brown-haired woman, about twenty-six—"

"Yes, she was just here. A guy dressed in black broke in the women's restroom and took her. They took her in a black van." He pointed outside. "They went down towards the freeway."

"Shit." To Lionel's wounded face he said, "They've got her. Damnit. Must have done something to her, because I can't get a read on her. We were that close," he held up his thumb and forefinger.

"I'm going to call on Huge and Jeb and some of the boys to meet us here. We can trace the SEALs anywhere you say.

"Come again?"

"They dig the ride. Again, Paolo, long story. We don't have time for this."

"Your little distraction will be among them?"

"Fuckin'-A, she will be."

"You be careful. She could turn on you. Or be a secret ally of Dag."

"Not likely. She's killed his executioner, just remember that."

Lionel radioed the rest of the teams, and a crowd of armed men in dark glasses traced, arms in arm, to the nearly abandoned streets of the square and quickly separated upon arrival. Paolo could hear a couple of *wa-HOOs* erupt from the crowd as he felt the sizzle of their energy, pumped and ready for war.

In the middle of the group was a stunningly beautiful blonde warrior woman, covered in camouflage face paint, wearing a skimpy top that showed her flat, muscled midriff. She also wore a pair of cutoff jeans revealing long, tanned thighs and muscular calves narrowing into steel-toed boots. Paolo was taken aback.

"I'm Shirley," she said, extending a leather-gloved hand. She wore an ammunition belt buckled over her shoulder, and gripped an H&K MP5 semiautomatic assault rifle like she was balancing a toddler on her hip. Paolo could feel Lionel's testosterone level spiking off the charts, as well as that of the rest of the team.

"Welcome to our war," Paolo said and was rewarded with huge grins all around the group.

Then he caught an internal image of a warehouse door being slid open. Cara's vision was blurry, but he saw what she saw. She was sending him the images with great detail.

He turned to Lionel. "Warehouse, greenish silver on the outside, near a chain link fence, like a school."

"I know right where it is," Lionel replied. "Men, we're rolling in, and hot. Shirley, you stick with me and Paolo."

"Yessir," came the group reply. Arms were clasped. Paolo found himself being hugged by a couple of really huge mortal guys with tattoos covering their forearms and necks. Linked together, they traced to the warehouse.

The team spread out. Lionel was whispering orders in his Invisio.

Paolo wondered where he had gotten the training, but he was also very grateful the men seemed to know what they were doing. Shirley stayed by his side the whole time. He made a point to stay out of her way, too.

He wondered if he should telegraph to Cara he was here. He decided it would be too dangerous for her. But the visions he got next speared him through his core. Cara was chained by the wrists. Her clothes were being stripped. She was standing naked in front of a room full of dark henchmen. Through Cara's terrified eyes, he saw the images of every one of their faces, and he counted the numbers, grateful she had her wits about her.

"I count fifteen at least," Paolo turned and told Lionel. Jeb and Hugh Jett each took five men and planted them outside the other two entrances.

"You stay back. You're a primary target," Lionel said.

"Nope. I'm going in with the rest of you."

"That's what they want. That's why they have her."

"Not an option."

Lionel sighed and spoke into his microphone. "On my mark."

Before he could give the order, Paolo heard Cara's scream and then the distinctive shrill voice of Dag Nielsen.

"Oh lover boyyyyy. She *needs* you. Come in and she won't be harmed, any further, that is. Your lovely beauty has just lost her right eye."

Paolo was furious and immediately traced to inside the warehouse. He saw Cara's face, with both her eyes intact. But her neck had been sliced open and her blood was spurting in a light fan spray all over the concrete floor. Dark vamps around the warehouse were smacking their lips.

"Oops. I lied," Dag said as a net of silver with a restraining charge fell over Paolo's body, immobilizing him.

The SEALs led by the Jett brothers traced inside and began engaging the dark guards.

"Stop!" screamed Dag. "I have Paolo and the girl. What are you fighting for?"

Dag was hit with automatic machine gun fire and he laughed as he saw smoke erupt from his chest. "Silver bullets? You found silver for those?" He was distracted momentarily by the fact that the person who had fired the shots was Shirley. "Well, I guess you didn't miss me, then."

Shirley fired off another set of rounds but Dag had traced to right next to her. This allowed Jeb to overcome the guard next to Dag and release Cara's bonds.

But Dag was not going to die. "You'll pay for that, and slowly," he said to her. Dag traced several feet away, dragging Shirley by the hair. He landed next to Paolo's net before any other rounds could hit him. Shirley was on him, was carving up his stomach with a KA-BAR knife she'd pulled from her boots.

"Fucking little twat," Dag said as he got hold of her neck. Shirley's arms and legs were flying around wildly, trying to find something to connect with. "Go ahead," Dag said calmly while he battled with Shirley with one arm. "You see, it isn't as easy as you thought to kill me. And if you do, you'll kill Paolo too, and this little lady, although I'm tiring of this game." Dag swung Shirley's body through the air, slamming her against the corrugated metal of the warehouse, where she lay motionless until Dag kicked her aside.

Lionel began to take a step toward him. "Oh please. You want the Council knowing you ended the life of the handsome Paolo Monteleone?" Dag smirked as he gave a signal that triggered the sounds of guns cocking and safeties being disengaged.

A forest of barrels pointed right at Paolo's head.

Dag was smug. He'd thought of everything, Paolo brooded. Though the silver netting was heavy, it didn't burn his skin like it would dark vamp's. It was the anti-tracing charge that was the problem. Paolo was powerless to do a thing.

"I can have him eliminated with a click of my fingers. You will please drop your weapons, and stand down," Dag said, especially to Lionel, who nodded, and the men lowered their weapons.

"No, I said Stand Down! That means you drop your fucking guns," Dag screamed.

The men complied as Paolo heard the crashes as weapons hit the concrete floor.

Cara hid behind Jeb's muscular frame. Paolo could see she hoped Dag would be so focused on the battle, he'd forget about her.

But Paolo's hopes were dashed when Dag strode over to Cara and pulled her by the hair into the center of the warehouse, several feet in front of the security webbing where Paolo was confined.

Blood had poured down her chest in thick, four-inch ribbons. Paolo could tell she might very easily bleed out if they didn't resolve things quickly. Even worse, Dag held her head back, throwing her slightly off balance, and increasing the flow of her blood. They were about out of time.

"Stop. I have what you want. I have the book," Paolo heard himself say. He couldn't believe he'd offered it.

"No, Paolo," Cara sobbed. "Don't believe him. He's lying to protect me."

Dag was interested and leaned closer to the netting. "Come again?"

Cara was starting to pass out. Paolo could see the Jett brothers were tensed and ready for action. Lionel was fixated on the little blonde's body near the dark corner. Then each of the brothers nodded almost imperceptibly, staring at each other. Paolo could tell they had formed an unwritten, unspoken pact.

"Please, don't interfere," Paolo said to Lionel. "Let me do this. I have the book, Dag. It's at the house, just down the road."

Cara was literally being held up by her hair, but her face had gone grey and her eyes were closed. Her mouth hung open and blood drooled slowly down her chin and breast. Paolo tried to revive her mentally, but he did not get a response.

Dag dropped Cara's torso and started over to the netting. "Good boy. Just what I wanted to know."

In a burst of speed, Jeb Jett grabbed Dag and tried to trace out of the warehouse, but the protection barrier held and they fell to the ground. One of the SEALs picked up a grenade launcher and blasted a hole the size of a truck in the wall of the warehouse before Dag could right himself. Jeb lunged at the dark coven leader again, and they disappeared out the opening into the night air.

The battle between the dark guards and the Team guys never began because their leader was gone. The dark coven guards faded away, some quickly, some walking backward, slowly.

And suddenly the room was full of sorrow. Lionel and Hugh hung their heads over their brother's sacrifice. Paolo was grief-stricken at the enormous sacrifice of life. Then he threw an anguished look at Cara, lying dead nearby, and wished with all his heart and soul that he could join her right now in eternal sleep.

Hugh and the others removed his netting while Lionel kneeled beside Shirley's crumpled body. "She still breathes!" he said triumphantly.

After extricating himself from the security webbing, Paolo ran to Cara's side. She had no pulse. He grabbed her body and held her tenderly, screaming his rage and despair. Cara remained limp in his arms. Everyone waited.

She continued to turn paler, and her skin began to feel clammy and cold. Her lips were turning deep purple. Paolo kissed those lips, tried to breathe life into them, but it was no use.

"You have a decision to make, Paolo," Hugh said as he put a hand on Paolo's shoulder.

"No. I cannot do that."

"She is gone to us now, Paolo. She is entering death's doorway. You would rob her of her immortal life because of your loathing for your choice? She cannot make a choice. You must make it for her."

"I cannot take her humanity away from her."

"It's done. Dag did that. Jeb sacrificed himself for you, and for her. Don't dishonor his gift."

"No, I am responsible. I killed her by loving her. I am her executioner as surely as if I'd carved open her neck myself." Paolo buried his head in Cara's chest. He knew he would not be able to endure a lifetime without her. He swore he'd take a tracing to Death Valley, where he assumed Jeb Jett had gone with Dag. He'd end himself before the next sunrise.

And then an image of his precious son intruded on his grief. The choice and the path became very clear.

"I am so sorry, Cara. Please forgive me." He bit his wrist and placed it over her lips. The blood from his vein ran down the side of her cheek. He opened her lips, kissed the little pillows of flesh he'd loved, tried to empty a few droplets onto her tongue.

Cara, please forgive me. Come back. Please, if you want a life with me, please come back. I promise to make the rest of your days filled with everything you desire.

The men began to fidget. Paolo knew they wouldn't let him sit there and grieve all night. At some point he'd have to stop working on her. Not every turning worked. Not every life could be saved. Only if they were compatible, but God of vampires, how Paolo wished they were compatible, how he believed—no, knew—they were.

And then Cara began to breathe. At her first raspy gasp her hand gripped her own throat, as if she was suffocating again. Paolo held his wrist to her lips and she finally bit down on him, and began to suck.

She fed ravenously as her cheeks turned pink, and her grip on his arm actually left welts on his flesh. Delicious welts. Welts he blessed and celebrated. The wound in her neck began to close, and all that remained were stains of red, which dried and began to flake off.

Cara looked up at Paolo and, yes, he could see that she was confused, but looking to him for guidance. She *trusted* him. He hoped in time she would forgive him for the choice he had made for her.

He bent down, pulling aside his wrist as she kissed him, almost as if by instinct, and closed his wound with her tongue. With his own blood still on her lips, he kissed her, feeling her little shaking body melt into his strength.

Inside him a bonfire began to burn. It wasn't the fating he'd experienced years ago, but it was something else. Something wonderful.

Chapter 42

PAOLO AND MARCUS entered the anteroom off the great hall of the Council chambers with Cara between them. They'd been told to wait for their summons. Marcus held the old book they'd found in Prague, and Cara held the book by Alasdair Fraser. Paolo had insisted she carry it, since she was the one who had discovered its existence.

She'd asked a lot of questions about her making while they prepared for this meeting. How her life would change. What would she eat? All the little basic things Paolo hadn't thought much about, since his routine had been established almost three hundred years ago.

Marcus had been so distracted over the upcoming meeting that he hadn't engaged in much conversation, certainly no small talk. Therefore, Paolo was as worried, but did his best to cover it up. There'd be time for celebration, he decided, once they fulfilled their duty to the ruling Council. He hoped there would be no surprises.

So, they waited in the anteroom. No one attended them. For all they knew, they awaited an execution, but Paolo was careful not to think about that for fear Cara would hear his thoughts. He tried to think about sunny days in the orchard in Tuscany, and picking apples with Lucius.

He decided suddenly that it was time to set aside his fears and focus instead on life's beauties. He'd begin by being more attentive to Cara as she snuggled against him, so he wrapped his arm around her shoulder and kissed the top of her head. Marcus watched the demonstration of affection, and smiled.

"It is good to see you happy, brother," he finally said.

More minutes passed. They were now beyond their time limit of twenty-four hours. The large, carved wooden doors opened with a sucking sound, and two novices in white robes emerged. They each linked elbows with Cara and asked that the men wait outside.

Cara turned to give the book to Paolo and one novice instructed her to keep it. At the last moment, she looked back over her shoulder at him, alarm filling her lovely countenance.

Love you, Paolo.

Love you, mi amore. All will be well. You'll see. Just answer their questions.

She bravely stood straight and focused ahead as she was led through the doors. With a heavy boom, Paolo and his brother were cut off from any hope of rescuing her. It was now in the hands of the gods.

"What do you think they will ask her?" Paolo muttered as he stared at the doors.

"Hard to say. What her background is. What she thinks of vampires. Does she bleed."

"Does she bleed?"

"They asked that of Anne."

"Why on earth for?"

"To see if she was fated."

"But Cara does not bleed, at least I don't think she—I have no idea. I have never asked her."

"You've not even known her for a full cycle, Paolo."

"True."

"Women's private things. They are so confusing. But the Council will focus on the blood, the blood lines, the possibility she could be useful in some way, like to bring offspring into their world."

"You say their world, like it isn't yours."

Marcus hesitated. "I read nearly this whole book while you were in California. I now know why the darks wanted it."

Paolo watched the hand of his brother as it smoothed over the blotchy and peeling surface of the old book with reverence. "This book has cost many, many lives of our kind. It will cost more."

"Tell me."

"The human condition? It was an experiment, brother."

"I don't understand."

"Someone had the bright idea to mess with God's handiwork. Perhaps it was devil-inspired. But the bible is correct. Humans were created, except they weren't created by God."

"Who created them?" Paolo asked.

"We did, brother. We are the original race."

"Not possible." Paolo's heart thumped loudly, seeming to echo in his chest cavity.

"I'm not sure the Council knows this fact, Paolo. I'm not sure they need to know."

"The book spells this out?"

"Yes. We were the result of natural selection, until a small group of our kind began to mess with our DNA. They created two sub-races. One was mortal but could live under the sun and the moon. The other was immortal, but could not go out in the sun. It was believed that because of humans' limitations, we could hold dominion over them. It was a failsafe mechanism built into their bloodlines."

"So how can a turning occur?"

"Our blood is stronger. Our blood will prevail. I think Dag was trying to eliminate as many of the Goldens as he could, and then would rule supreme over the whole world: human, dark vampire, Golden vampire. It's just a theory, but I think he wanted to force one of us to turn him so he was free from the limitations."

"Where did he learn of this?" Paolo asked.

"That's an excellent question, and one we must investigate."

"In secret."

"If we live long enough. If they let us live."

The doors opened. Marcus leaned to Paolo and whispered, "Continue thinking of Lucius picking apples, brother."

Paolo was heartened to see Praetor Artemis down on the main floor, smiling and discussing something with Cara, who sat in a carved chair, unharmed.

Thank the Gods.

She had been given one of Laurel's white fluffy blouses with the low-cut neckline, and he noticed Artemis was drawn to the way she looked. Paolo unconsciously made a fist, but Marcus placed his palm on his brother's forearm in warning.

Artemis greeted them warmly, winking at Paolo, which was something that had never happened before. "She's lovely," he whispered to him.

"Thank you."

"Distinguished members of the Council, I give you the two heroes of the day, Paolo and Marcus Monteleone."

The brothers bowed. Cara sat directly behind them.

I especially like the view, Paolo heard Cara say. Marcus winced like he'd been slapped.

Shhh.

Paolo experienced a flood of liquid dreams of them making love on the cream satin sheets. He was starting to get hard, and it couldn't be a more inappropriate moment for it to happen.

Marcus stepped on his foot. Hard. It jarred his attention back to the Council. He heard Artemis snigger.

Is my whole life an open book for anyone to read? Cara silently asked him.

He hears my thoughts only. But I'm sure that was enough, Bella.

"Excuse me, Council members. I must speak to Cara for just a moment." Paolo didn't wait for permission. He grabbed her elbow and led her to a corner. "You will stop this. Right now. It is not appropriate."

Cara looked back at him and swung her body from side to side, her sultry eyes at half-mast. "But I love the way my new body feels, and I'm anxious to try it out. Can you make it quick? I can be good for a few minutes, but only a few."

Paolo looked at his brother, who awkwardly tried to come to the rescue by inserting a comment. "Members of the Council. My brother is having trouble with his, his—"

"Fiancé," Cara shouted out. The Council went aghast. A gavel was pounded on the table. Paolo scowled and Praetor Artemis nearly doubled over with laughter.

"Well, that's what he promised me, anyway," she added with conspicuous innocence.

Paolo looked at Marcus, who shrugged. There was no help from any quarter, so Paolo began stuttering as if he'd been caught in a lie to gain sexual favors.

"You must forgive what I've said in the heat of passion," Paolo told the Council. Cara slapped him, but Paolo smiled, "I say many things, and I don't always agree with all of them, or remember what has been said, or promised."

Several members of the Council laughed. The oldest member woke up from his sleep and asked if the meeting was over.

Marcus tried to hide his giddiness at the brilliance of the deception. Even Praetor seemed anxious to keep things on a very light and celebratory note.

"Then let it be said, Paolo Monteleone," a gray-haired Council member stood and delivered, holding onto the tabletop, "you are to wed this woman within the next thirty days, as punishment for your insolence. The debt for your turning her will be satisfied if you make her an honest woman."

A cheer went up. Even some of the novices at the sides of the room clapped. "And you, Carabella Sampson, shall honor and obey your husband-to-be, and shall submit to him whenever and whatever he desires. Do you agree to this?"

Cara crossed her arms, feigning some slight disagreement, but then ran to Paolo, put her arms around his neck and said, "I will. Most certainly I accept your terms."

Congratulations were given generously. Within a matter of minutes, Praetor said he would accompany them home, in his private limo. As they left the chamber hall one member of the Council shouted out.

"The book! What about the book?"

Marcus turned and bowed. "I shall return it to my grandfather's study, from whence it came, for safekeeping, of course."

"Excellent," the member said. "Make it so."

Cara found it very hard to behave herself during the limo ride. Her hormones were raging. She wanted to strip off her blouse and skirt and ride Paolo's cock all the way home, with or without an audience. She slipped her hand around Paolo's side, and between the leather seat and his waistband, managed to slip a couple of fingers under the fabric, feeling a bit of flesh at the top of his thigh.

Marcus was engaging in conversation with Praetor, but Paolo's constant jumps and twitches whenever Cara tickled and stroked another inappropriate and extremely private body part finally elicited a comment from him.

"You two. There will be centuries for that. Trust me. It never gets old, Cara. No reason to rush into things."

"I am starved."

Praetor's eyes sparkled at the blush of her lust, which filled the whole vehicle.

"She is charming," Praetor had said to Paolo, but was staring right at Cara.

Her bra felt two sizes too small; her panties were wet with her juices. Crossing and uncrossing her legs only pressed her lips against her nub and made her shudder. It was an ache like she'd never experienced before. She had become a wanton woman, and not afraid to show it.

"Five minutes, Cara. We'll be home in only five minutes," Paolo said to her, but he too was grinning.

Cara feigned impatience and swiveled around, presenting the men with her back. Her arms were crossed and she looked out the side window at the cobblestoned streets of the village, gleaming wet with rain. Paolo found a way to move his palm up under her skirt. He slid two long fingers around and under her lace panties and found her core.

Cara hitched her breath as he sunk the fingers inside her. "Better?" he whispered in her ear.

She moved her pelvis against his palm, rubbing herself and pulling his fingers in deeper by way of an answer. She barely heard even dribbles of the conversation the three men were having.

"And so I want to spend some time studying every chapter in this tome. Just the three of us," Marcus said.

Praetor agreed. Paolo mumbled a "yes" into Cara's hair.

"Until we thoroughly analyze it, we say nothing to anyone else, can we all agree to that?" Praetor asked.

The plan was formed. Marcus and Praetor would begin work on the project in the morning. Paolo would begin work whenever he would manage to escape from the bedroom.

WITH THE DOORS closed behind them, the fireplace roaring, Cara felt a little timid, now that she was going to have her first encounter with the man she loved as a vampire female. A Golden vampire female. Though she'd studied the myths and legends in her teachings, she never in her wildest dreams thought she'd be preparing for a night like this.

Every minute she remained untouched by Paolo was painful to her. The desire to couple with him, to mate in the old, ritualistic way Alasdair Fraser described in his lovely book, was stronger than any other need. Stronger than breathing. She was burning up with lust. Her ears buzzed. Her neck pulsed and her breasts shook with the pounding of her heart.

He came up behind her and whispered, "You were very naughty today."

The feel of his warm breath on the side of her face and in her ear sent her spine tingling, and the little sparks of passion found their way all the way to her toes. "I hope I can make it up to you," she whispered in return. She helped his palms find her breasts and she moaned and rolled her head back on his shoulder when he squeezed them.

"I've been told I have to make you obey."

"Do you want me to fight?"

"I want to let you do whatever you want to do."

"I want to please you."

"But you do, my Carabella. You do."

He slid her blouse over her shoulders, undid the zipper at the back of her skirt and slid the fabric down over her thighs as he came to his knees behind her. She'd worn the black high-hip panties that showed off her full bottom and he hissed, and then kissed her flesh, one cheek at a time. He turned her around to face him, still on his knees.

A lazy forefinger traced down the crack between her buttocks while his hand palmed her mound from the front. He drew her to his mouth, slipped the lacy fabric to the side with his tongue and found her labial lips. She felt a nip as he bit he there and drew blood.

"So sweet, Carabella," he whispered. "I want more."

"Yes," she said as she looked over her shoulder at him. His tongue had found her folds, ridges, and then her insides. His saliva tingled on her skin, healing the first wound before he bit harder, creating another one.

She groaned and bent over, giving him better access. She entwined her fingers in his as he gripped her thighs, his face buried in her sex. From out of the corner of her eye she could see the growing tent in his pants.

"I want to taste you too," she whispered. "Show me how it is done."

"Very well."

He took her hand, led her to his bed and let her remove his shirt. She knelt before him and undid the old-fashioned silver clasps of his waistband and snaked her hand inside to feel his shaft and balls, giving them a gentle squeeze. Paolo arched into her hand. "Yes. That is how it is done."

"Can I bite you there?" She asked.

"Um. No. Well, I've not done—"

Before he could say anything further she had slipped his pants down over his hips and had bitten him on the upper thigh next to his balls. She sucked the wound and then sucked his cock, spreading his own blood all over the shaft. Paolo bent over her, smoothing his palms down her back, down over her buttocks, squeezing them.

He angled himself so she took him in her mouth and pressed her breasts into his thigh as she sucked, scraping a canine over the surface just enough to draw a little blood. The tiny droplets made the lips of her sex swell, made her nipples hard and knotted.

The bra was getting uncomfortable, so she stood and removed it. They were man to woman, completely naked, and hungry.

"I want to do it the first time the way your ancestors do it."

Paolo nodded. He pointed to the bed. She lay back and he covered her body, licking the side of her neck, kissing her from her earlobe to her shoulder.

"You do what I do. You follow me."

"Yes," she sighed. She licked and gave sucking kisses to the hard muscle running down the right side of his neck. She tasted the saltiness of the skin near his shoulders.

"Your tongue will soften the sting, like this." He traced a trail along her jugular. She could feel her body defer to him, as the vein pushed itself to the surface of her flesh for easy penetration.

Cara did the same to Paolo, and yes, his skin became soft under her tongue. She could smell the blood thumping there.

"We become one plus one." He kneed her legs apart and thrust inside her, making her arch back at the feel of his huge cock stretching and filling her. He stroked her insides with circular motions, coating her with fire, setting her aflame. Deep inside her, he stopped.

"And now we take the bite." Paolo cracked the skin of her neck and all she could do was push up against him, the need for him to take all of her was so strong. "Take me, Cara," he begged.

She found the warm flesh of his neck and pressed her teeth against it. Her new fangs slid into his skin without a sound. She tasted his elixir and instantly needed more.

She felt ancient. She felt powerful, stronger than ever before. He rocked her body with his powerful hips. She raised her knees folding her legs over his shoulders, and he took her deep.

When at last he shuddered his release, she began to explode as well. Her body glowed from the inside out. The delicious ripple of her orgasm traveled up and down her spine, sparking at every nerve ending. Her fingertips were covered in pinpricks. She moaned her pleasure into his hungry lips.

"Yes, I want all of you," he said. "Give me everything, Carabella.

Mi amore."

They stilled but he didn't pull out. Breathing heavily, he balanced part of his weight on one elbow. She loved the feel of him pressing on top of her, inside her. She traced along his hairline, gazing into the deep chocolate of his eyes. His full lips came down and planted a delicate kiss, and then deepened.

"Thank you," she said.

"For what? I thank you, mi amore. I have never felt such ecstasy."

"Thank you for showing me."

Paolo chuckled.

"What's so funny? Did I say something wrong?"

"Mi amore, I have only begun to teach you. This, my sweet Cara-bella, is only the beginning of your beautiful immortal life."

Christmas Bite

Golden Vampires of Tuscany
Book 3

S. Hamil

Chapter 1

LIONEL JETT HAD always thought Christmastime was more about angels, than celebrating vampires and their vampire society. But the emotional responses within his soul ticked like a timebomb. On the one hand, the beautiful candlelit services, held at night so he could attend, were striking and revived in him his higher calling to protect the innocent and all things good and pure. To eliminate evil.

Christmas celebrated the birth of an innocent, after all—a birth that would forever change humanity. Mortals believed that a woman conceived a child without having sex. Well, Lionel had seen many things in his three hundred years of life, and he couldn't rule out that this legend was actually fact. For if that occurred, then the possibility of redemption for himself, existed, as well as the chance for peace amongst the two vampire species.

His thick frame was forced to hunch a bit, his shoulders rounded so he could fit into the pews made for much smaller beings, mostly mortal. The wooden, hand-carved benches weren't constructed for huge, dark coven vampires, unless they were designed to say, "you are not welcome."

The Gregorian chants reverberated throughout the halls of the chapel where Marcus had first met his fated mate, Anne. Lionel watched a woman and her children light tiny, red votive candles in the alcove at the side. The light made their faces glow with that effect only mortals had. It was as if the goodness in them showed through their transparent skin, laced with the life-giving blood of their species, an elixir to some, and the highly prized substance others would die to protect.

Of all their traits, mortals' best gift to the world was that of love and innocence. Though some of their race claimed to be warriors, they would never be matches for the evil likes of the strongest dark covens.

But their God had told mortals they could achieve anything if they had faith. They had the gift of belief because their lives were so short. Of course, they believed in miracles. Unfortunately, they'd never live long enough to see true miracles or the way the world really was.

He could sign on to safeguard those ideas. It was something that spoke to him as a true warrior. He'd be able to defend those who had no clue they needed protecting. And he might die doing so, without any observance on their part.

Mortals were a strange combination of emotions and traits. They scared easily. They sometimes maintained bravado, like the David and Goliath story from their bible. They were underdogs, but like in the beloved story, they never stopped fighting though the odds were against them. They sometimes allowed anger to interrupt their lifeline or justified its benefits when it really never helped them.

But their most stunning quality was that of compassion. On that, they could teach the world. They had the gift of living a life untainted, if they so choose. Trusting in their God when, in actuality, their unseen vampire brethren were responsible for much of their safety. They believed in the laws of nature more than the laws of vampire. Lionel found this humorous.

The delicate children's choir made their way down the center aisle, each child holding an inverted paper cup with a white candle stuck into the base, so their little hands would be protected from any dripping wax. Their voices were soothing. He could make out every one of them, and it left him gentled, like listening to a babbling brook with water flowing over pebbles beneath the current. Each child had a distinctive series of tones, sometimes with thoughts laced in there, if the mind read was strong with them.

He remembered the night they said mass for Maria Monteleone, the only woman in Lionel's life he ever loved. He'd gladly foregone any chance at having a sexual relationship with her just to be in her presence and had begged her to live on after the death of her mortal husband, to take the turning late in her life. It was always a difficult decision for every Golden, all born as mortal children, and given the option to take the turning ceremony beyond after puberty. Most chose to live a life of immortality. But she, like her predeceased husband before her, refused, smiled, touched his cheek with her dainty lavender scented palm, and shared a tear with him.

"Lionel, my trusted protector, I know what's in your heart. I am given life enough with the knowledge that it's there. No need for us to speak of it or demonstrate it to anyone but ourselves. Our eternal secret."

He'd wanted to take her in his arms, but he would never shatter what they had. He was the only one she would take on as a protector, and the family knew Lionel would die doing so, if necessary. It was beautiful Maria who had saved his life by asking he and his two brothers be made vampire when she found all them left for dead after an attack by a dark coven lord who had obliterated their family.

The elder Monteleones had decided a trusted dark would do the turning, so that there would always be distance between Maria and her dear Lionel. He always wondered if she'd argued for another choice for him. Had she desired he be made in her own image or requested she be his maker? That question haunted Lionel for centuries.

He was there when she married Marcus and Paolo's father, was there as she bore him the dozen children, and as she continually turned down her husband's request to turn together. As a faithful husband, he dutifully remained at her side, mortal, sharing their short love and family.

Lionel was with her as her mortal life left her, on a starlit evening when the real stars were in her eyes, until they became fixed on him and then floated away. Like a piece of tissue paper, her spirit was gone, to become one with her God of Humans and her Mother Nature.

The hole in his heart was still the largest pain in his life. There wasn't a day that went by when he didn't wonder what would have happened if he'd chosen to take a more active role in that relationship with her or could have fought stronger for what he knew was something like an inter-species fating that never could be consummated.

He looked up at the bleeding figure of Christ nailed to a wooden cross, and he understood the man's pain, the regrets he might have had, his need to protect and love his flock, and to die for them. The miracle had been sent, only to have the evil factions of the mortal crowd kill him off. He walked amongst his people understanding this, all the while he remained on earth.

Lionel hoped that he still lived somewhere they called Heaven. For he and his vampire brothers and sisters, death was usually just the end of a long, long life. There was no Heaven. There was no happily ever after in the clouds that sent rain and wind and sometimes covered the sun and the moon. It was just death, with nothing beyond.

And yet, as he listened to the beautiful chanting and allowed the scents of mortals to envelop him, he felt the heat of their bodies, and some of their thoughts and worries. He'd like to pretend he believed in a time that would last, where everything would be perfect and not end. Where love, like the love he had for Maria, would reign eternal.

He was hopeful. It was a silly thought, but it was something that warmed him from the inside, as if he was a mortal again, as if he still held that innocent light inside.

THE WEDDING FEAST had begun. It was humorous that the Monteleones made a great show of eating to excess, though Lionel knew they'd be sick as dogs afterward. But they were stubborn about their secrecy, and as long as it was a mixed crowd of both trusted mortals and vampires of both species, the ruse would be continued. He stood with his arm around young Lucius while they watched his father, the handsome Paolo, and his new bride, Carabella, dance to the alluring viola music around a huge firepit stoked with logs the size of most humans. Paolo's face was filled with the mirth Lionel had always envied.

Out of the blue, Lucius asked his question. "Do you miss your brother?"

Jeb had traced the dark coven lord, Dag, to a desert somewhere on the other side of the globe, to end him, saving Lucius' father's life at the cost of his own.

"Of course, young prince. But his time had come. He'd had a wonderful and exciting life, keeping all you lot safe so your family can save the world. Don't you know that?"

Lucius thought about that for a short time. His six years was not commensurate with his knowledge of the ways of the world. He'd seen a lot in his brief time as son to one brother, only to find out he belonged to the other.

"Can I tell you something I've never told anyone?"

"Careful, young Lucius. I am bound to tell the truth, always."

"I know it. But I want to tell you anyway."

The boy's eyes followed his new stepmom and his father across the amphitheater. Lionel remembered days when there were dark coven sacrifices held in this space. He remembered the blood rituals of those difficult times, shortly before Maria's boys were grown. Although he was not sure, some of his relatives might have lost their lives in this very place. He shook off the vision and answered the boy. "You can certainly trust in my confidence."

"I don't miss my mother. I like that Cara is going to be my new mother. I think she'll bring me a little brother or sister."

Lionel was struck with this thought. Cara had been made, and the turning had taken place, which wasn't always successful, just before her mortal death. Paolo had given her his own blood. Even so, he wasn't sure Cara and Paolo could have offspring.

Lucius looked up at him. "Am I evil for saying this?"

Lionel knelt, placing his plate-sized hands on Lucius' forearms and elbows, his face eye-level with the boy. "You are very lucky, young princeling. Your mortal aunt was forgiven for your mother's demise because she protected all of you in that action. Maya would have not been the kind of mother you deserve. You deserve—"

He saw a group of young Goldens arrive, all of them in their teens and early twenties. Some had taken the turning, but several were clearly still mortal. He understood them to be friends since childhood.

As the group parted, some took to the dance floor. A tall dark-haired beauty swayed to the music, engaging the troupe of fiddlers who enjoyed her sultry dance moves. She was a curiously carefree mortal woman and Lionel couldn't take his eyes off her. She threw her head back, swung her hips from side to side and sent her light, peach-colored, mortal arms reaching out to the sky. She pulled up her long curls, holding them atop her head as she swiveled her hips and turned in his direction.

When their eyes met, her mouth dropped open and she became motionless, though the lively music continued behind her.

Lionel's heart leapt from his chest. Grateful she was not yet turned, he did not have to make some excuse if she heard the kettle-drum in his chest that pumped his life force into overdrive. He resisted the urge to run to her, pick her up and carry her away, where he could satisfy all his questions.

Was this woman Maria, come back to life after three hundred years? The Maria he first knew before her marriage, her family, and her death?

The woman who stood across the bonfire from him looked identical to Maria.

Lucius wiggled free as Lionel had gripped his arms and gave his young charge welts.

"I'm sorry, son. I just thought I saw something. Forgive me if I hurt you."

Lucius remained two steps away from him, watching, as Lionel rose to full height, slowly uncoiling his enormous body. His mouth dry, his fangs aching, his mind reeled from the erotic thoughts that came at him like a firehose.

All too suddenly, she was gone. She'd pulled a brightly colored shawl over her head and neck and ran into the heavy foliage at the edge of the clearing.

Lucius turned to see what he was focusing on.

"The young woman who was dancing over there, she should not have gone into the forest alone. I fear for her life," he told his charge.

Lucius nodded. "Then go get her. Protect her, Lionel—or—" he peered up at him with a question on his face—"don't you want to?"

"It isn't that, but I'm to stay and protect you."

This part was true. He caught the attention of his younger brother, Hugh—"huge" as he was known to the ladies he bedded—and angled his head towards the woods. Hugh had a lapse in judgment and traced, instead of running like a mortal. Lionel scanned the crowd, and no one seemed to have noticed.

What am I looking for, brother? Hugh asked telepathically from behind the wooded surround.

"The spitting image of Maria Monteleone. Tell me it isn't so, brother. I pray to god she's safe, but I also pray it isn't her," he whispered.

"What?" asked Lucius.

"Sorry, I was giving instructions to Hugh."

Seconds later, a group of the young Goldens came screaming from the woods, followed by a dark vamp dressed in black rags. He stopped at the site of the campfire. His flesh peeled, and part of his face had been scratched off. His tongue hung limply, dripping bloody saliva.

The fiddle music stopped as several males from the partygoers came within feet of his disgusting frame. Several in the crowd began to moan, and there were a few suppressed screams. Precious seconds passed while the dark vamp and his would-be attackers held the standoff. Lionel scanned the young Goldens and didn't see any sign of the young Maria look-alike.

The dark vamp began to grin, his chest heaving. He fingered something around his neck Lionel had missed. It was the colorful shawl the young Golden had been wearing just moments before.

Lionel didn't have time to look for his brother. He traced to the creature, hoisting him high up into the sky and tearing his head from his body out of eyesight of the crowd below. He threw the remnants of the vamp's torso into another bonfire he found several miles away, at a distant farm. Before he let the body loose, he removed the shawl and stuffed it into his shirt.

Damages, brother? Are you there?

All is well, Lionel. She is alive, and safe. He was a rogue no coven to back him up. But it has us all shook.

He won't be back, Lionel told his brother.

He traced to the edge of the celebration, then walked through dense foliage toward the circle of fire. They had brought the young Golden toward the heat, and a group of elder men surrounded her, so he could not see her face. As he pressed himself towards the center, he could see the ugly, bloody bite on her neck and the rivulets of dark ooze descending down her chest, meeting between her breasts. Her eyes were dazed as she rolled her head back and cried.

Paolo was there, giving her first aid. Lionel sat next to her mother, who brought warm compresses and was whispering questions.

"Will she be infected, Paolo? She is still mortal and a virgin. Will this affect—?"

"No, Freya. She's intact. He didn't do a blood rape. She's intact."

"Oh, thank God," the woman sighed, leaning into Lionel's chest. Paolo gave him a frown.

"I have Lucius," said Hugh from the back of the crowd.

Freya's daughter stubbornly righted herself and accepted the salve that was applied to her neck taken from the kit Paolo carried with him 24/7. Her eyes swung around, perusing the crowd until she saw Lionel again, and their stares locked.

Her gaze lowered slightly, looking at something on Lionel's chest.

"He's gone, Madame," he told her. "He will no longer trouble you, or any of us."

But she was still peering at his chest. Looking down, he saw the remnants of her flowered shawl sticking out from the buttons on his white shirt. He drew it out, damp from the mixture of sweat and bloody detritus. He extended his arm and handed it to her.

She didn't look at the shawl. As she grabbed the cloth, her eyes were fixed on Lionel like he was her lifeline, her future.

He was instantly hit with the cold facts of their state. She would most likely be not his lifeline, but a straight ticket to Hell itself.

Chapter 2

P HOEBE WAS PLACED in the second seat of a Mercedes stretch limo
for the trip back to her parents' villa. Paolo was with her. She was
also being given an IV with her father's blood, for healing and
strength. She'd heard the whispers over her near-sleeping body, about
how her turning should be guarded and done soon to prevent another
event like this one. It was felt she was now a target for the non-Golden
covens. She should avoid tracing with her parents, turned siblings, or
friends due to her condition. And no airline flights.

Since she was still pure and intact as a Golden virgin, it was
thought her father's blood was best, but no one really knew the
answers to these questions. Freya told them she'd have that talk with
Phoebe. All of them were sure it would help making a turning easier,
as she was now introduced to her father's Golden bloodlines. Acceptance of the new blood was always the trickiest part of the turning.

Her heart pounded fierce in her chest, and she felt like her breath
was sucking all the air out of the limo, then replacing it with her
exhale. It was like a body sat on her chest. But upon opening her eyes,
she noticed it was only the shawl, tucked up around her ears and
under her chin. It gave her courage, for some strange reason, and
hope. Her blouse had been removed earlier, she vaguely remembered,
so that the shawl was against her bare, mortal flesh.

A healing vape came over her, not from the salve or the blood being administered, but from the shawl itself. She detected gentle steam
pouring forth from it, coming directly toward her nose. She inhaled
deeply, taking it all in. With the exhale, she felt her limbs go light, her
head filled with twinkling stars that coursed throughout her body
from her spine, around to her frontside, descending down to her toes.

One of the passengers had tried to remove the shawl, but she clutched it fiercely and stared into the eyes of her distant cousin, the kind and gentle Paolo. The man looked stunned.

She stumbled for words, but then finally came out with, "Please, sir, my modesty."

That took the tension off, and immediately the nervous banter continued. Paolo slipped little peeks between comments, carefully monitoring her expressions and answers.

Before they arrived at the villa, Paolo removed the IV infusion catheter with the life-enhancing blood from her father. "Hold this down hard for a few seconds," he said as he pressed a gauze pad to the puncture. Her fingers applied pressure until he found a wrap material that held the gauze in place, so it wouldn't bleed or form a bruise beneath the surface of her skin.

He checked her eyes, smelled her breath, which seemed odd, checked the sides of her face, her wrists, both ankles and declared she should be seen by the family physician as soon as possible, but that she was healthy and fully recovered.

As they pulled up to the villa, Paolo recommended, "She shouldn't leave the house until she's been checked out, however."

"Can she wash up?" Freya asked. "Or does she need—"

"No, she should wash the wound with soap. Then we'll apply more salve. You'll see when she removes the cloth she will have started to heal."

"Excellent. Thank you, Paolo," her father whispered.

While the men stayed downstairs, two household helpers and her mother brought her to her bedroom on the second floor, helping her to climb the enormous darkly carved bannister that switched back and forth to all three levels.

When they opened her door, the warm fire was already burning. Her bed was prepared and drawn back, and the room smelled of roses and lavender, her favorite fragrances. Everything was as she'd left it earlier in the day. Her hairbrushes were all angled the same direction on her dressing table. Her old baby crib filled with well-worn stuffed toys from her childhood stood in the shadows at the corner. Moonlight shone on the heavily polished wooden floor, giving off a blue cast to any smooth surface.

"Phoebe, we're going to undress you and then help you to the shower. Do you think you can stand and wash off, or do you need help?" her mother purred to her ear, making them both buzz. She heard extra inflections, sounds of her mother's voice in octaves she'd never heard before.

"I'm okay. I can—"

But they'd already removed her skirt, and placed it on a side chair, along with the shawl. Fully naked, she removed her sandals and stared into the full-length mirror on the way to her private bath. Her nipples were engorged and bright red, as if they'd been rubbed raw, and her face was flushed. But looking down at her sex, she noticed her lips were swollen and a deep rose-red in color. The sensation as she walked to the shower wasn't unpleasant.

"You must be sure to wash your neck with soap, little one," the maid whispered, then attached a clip to hold her curls up. The sound of the young woman's voice was like the wind blowing through the trees at the forest.

She was not left alone in the shower, but she kept her back to her audience, taking the soap and rubbing across her chest and up and around her neck, which was tender and swollen, around her chin and down her arms. As she smoothed the bubbles over her tummy and lower, her breathing hitched. She'd touched one side of her netherlips, and she was filled with such exquisite pleasure, she felt afraid she might pass out. She grabbed the shower wand and forced water between her legs and felt a tightening of muscles inside her lower abdomen she didn't know existed before.

She was handed an oversized bath sheet as she emerged from the shower, wrapping it tightly around her. Her mother lovingly applied more salve to her neck. She removed the clip and shook her hair loose, staring into the mirror.

Her eyes confirmed what her feelings were telling her: she'd stepped through a doorway. It had nothing to do with the dark coven vamp who tried to take her life, but the vamp who stood in the crowd and took her breath away. Something that was ancient and buried in her heart had risen from a bloody grave and was running loose inside her.

She was filled with terror.

She was also filled with erotic fantasies of pure pleasure.

She knew there was nothing she could do to stop it.

Phoebe slipped on a white gown and allowed her hair to be combed by her mother, who sent the others away.

"Phoebe, I know you heard some of what's been discussed between your father, Paolo, and I," Freya began.

"Yes, Mother."

"I want you to just put all that out of your mind right now. We'll get your evaluation done and see to it that everything is on a firm footing before we make any decisions."

Freya slipped around the stool to face her seated form. Her warm, lined face showed centuries of compassion. She tenderly held Phoebe's cheeks in the palms of her hands as she kissed her forehead and sighed.

"Your face is hot. Are you hot all over?" Her eyes bore into Phoebe and would not be denied.

"Yes, Mother." She worked to make her voice sound compliant, but her heartbeat had not slowed. She asked the question that had been lingering. "What is this sensation?"

"Your father's blood is strong in your veins. As a fully turned male vampire, even though he's your father, it's bound to affect you in special ways."

Phoebe wrinkled her nose and turned away from her.

"Nothing to worry about, Daughter." Freya touched her chin and turned her, so they could see each other straight on. "You are mortal, but not quite human. Do you understand this?"

She nodded yes.

"Your bloodline is sensitive to the vampire side of you. It seeks it as a natural protection, since it would be normal for you to seek a male vampire to protect you and help you bring young into this world who would be healthy. It is part of the selection process."

"But he's my father!"

"I'm talking about your yearning. Perhaps you have come into close proximity with another—someone who could bring you into the circle of fating. He may be distant, not even in this town, but he could be close by, perhaps."

"I would be that sensitive to it?"

Freya bowed her head and then smiled at her daughter. "It happens differently for different people. If it is beginning, it will be glorious. The most magnificent thing you've ever experienced in your life."

Her eyes twinkled with the extra moisture lingering there.

"This conversation has to remain confidential, just between the two of us, Mother. I don't think father would understand."

"Nonsense, Phoebe. Men don't understand many things about women, but they do understand the fating."

"But you need to promise me."

"All right. Now, come. Time for bed, Phoebe."

"How did it start for you?" Phoebe asked as she sat on the edge of the bed.

"I had to wait nearly two hundred years for your father. I used to worry that my early turning, before I'd found my mate, interfered with the sensors, or the fating, in some way. I thought I'd be barren, childless. And then when I met him, everything exploded onto the scene, and our romance was such a whirlwind. All those years and years of waiting were over in mere seconds it seemed. We got to work and right away got pregnant with you, then your three brothers."

"Yes, Mama. I've heard the stories."

"We never had any time to just become friends together, he and I. We had to live our lives completely different. We had to spend all our waking hours protecting all of you." She glanced out the window, biting her lower lip.

"And I'm grateful for all you've done."

"This is such a special time for you." She grabbed Phoebe's two hands in hers. "It will be confusing, but it will be worth it. Now, with all these coven leaders fighting each other, the beautiful parties, dances, balls, and galas are problematic. I wish you could have lived in those days. Now, we have to be so careful."

"Yes, Mama. I understand."

"So what I'm saying is that it might take a hundred years of protection, or more, until you find The One. This could be just a close encounter, a whiff of someone drifting by—someone you will meet years from now. We never know."

Phoebe wanted to tell her mother she had felt some kind of a shift but wasn't sure she should. Instead, she asked, "Will it be very obvious when it happens? Will everything shift in an instant?"

"Yes, my dear. But what I want to guard you most about is getting your hopes up too high. It doesn't mean anything if it takes a century or two or a few hours. You have to be sort of 'on call,' and yet that could last centuries. And still, you have to be ready, emotionally and physically, for when it comes."

"Yes, I understand."

Freya looked down at their entwined fingers. "But have you thought about the turning, Phoebe? How it might make things easier for—for all of us?"

It wasn't what she was expecting.

"You mean I could defend myself better, mother?"

"Yes. Partly that. But don't you have a feeling, a knowledge deep inside of what form you wish to take? Do you want to be a mortal woman or a Golden Vampire? I mean, one is weak, the other, well, stronger. Capable of protecting herself. Do you want to spend your life worried about the dark? About strange people and not being able to defend yourself?"

She nodded. She was going to tell the truth. "I've thought about it some, but not deeply. Mama, I'm unsure what form I want. I haven't made up my mind."

"If you turn now, by the time you find your mate, you will still be young and able to have children. If you take the turning at an older age, that comes with a different set of rules. Do you understand this? You risk the possibility of some injury or disfigurement to your body. Right now, dear Phoebe, your body is perfect. You have unsullied

Golden bloodline in your veins. You'd remain this way forever."

"Yes, I see. And it would be more difficult to live alone, wouldn't it?"

"You want to leave the family?"

"I want to travel, Mother. I want to go to all sorts of places I've never seen. I'd like to live on the beach, in a cabin in the mountains, somewhere in the jungle—I want to explore so much."

"And you can do all that as a Golden. Your choices are so much more limited as a mortal. Not to mention how vulnerable you'd be."

"I know. But this is all I've known so far. I like who I am right now. Do mortals think about this? Worry about all this?"

Her mother chuckled, "All the time, my child. You know so little about them. Vain, doing all sorts of things to their bodies to cheat death. But luckily for their race, most of them are not like that. They accept that death is their partner. You, however, can control death. Send him elsewhere."

"Except I still will need protection when I have children."

"Yes. That's why we have the dark covens and others we hire to help with that. They live to take care of us, now, don't they?"

"Our protectors."

"Exactly."

"Like tonight."

"Well, yes. The dark security detail Paolo brought to watch over his son—he's the one who first noticed you and alerted others to get you to safety while he disposed of the garbage. He's a perfect example."

"So I would have a protector, like he is, then?"

"Yes."

"But what about one as a husband?"

Freya's head shot up, her eyes blazing. "Not as a *real* husband. Never that!" She softened a bit and then stroked the sides of her daughter's face. "Sweetheart, I can see I have not explained things to you properly. You can respect and even befriend them on a temporary basis before you are attached. But as far as a *life partner*, that is not allowed, my dear daughter. You will remain with your own kind, for the purity of the bloodline. We don't think a healthy child could ever come from such a union, even if it were possible, and the stories say it could never be."

"But what about Lucius?"

"He has no dark coven blood. Some witch and God knows other things, but no other coven blood. Paolo would never mate with a dark coven female." Then she added, "But Paolo was very lucky. His boy could have been deformed. We have seen some of these come into the world, recently. Horrible creatures."

She pulled the covers up.

"Come, you must rest. A good night's sleep will do you some good. Dream of a handsome Golden prince coming for you when you least expect it. It will be a glorious warm summer day, and you'll have flowers in your hair. You'll be partaking in the sacred ritual generations of Golden women have gone through. We don't wring our hands, complaining about our lives, our men, or our families. We embrace it with all the life and light we are given. It is our birthright, Phoebe. Yours too. Who knows? Perhaps you could have the double gift of having your fated mate turn you himself."

She hugged and kissed her, adjusting the cool sheets over her, touching her hair. As Phoebe lay back on the pillow and peered out at the stars from the open window, she watched her mother leave the room, closing the door behind her.

Then she remembered the shawl. Dashing out of bed, she searched the pile of clothes on the chair near the bathroom door and found it. She wrapped it around her neck and shoulders, dove back into the sheets and fingered the silky fabric as she watched the night sky again.

Her eyelids grew heavy. She heard music, saw bonfires and dancing maidens clutching maypole vines, lovers kissing in the shadows, and smelled cinnamon and other exotic spices, mixing with the strange vapor-like scent that refreshed her soul coming from the shawl.

She knew she was waiting. But for what? Her next adventure?

And with whom?

And would her family ever allow it?

Chapter 3

LIONEL PACED THE hallway outside the two-story walnut-paneled library at the great Monteleone estate. Hugh was at his side. He remembered how he'd paced the night Marcus and then Paolo came into the world, when Maria was in labor upstairs, screaming her lungs out. Half the men that night begged her husband to turn her during the birth to take the pain away from her mortal body, but she wouldn't have anything to do with it. Her husband defended her wishes.

It had been centuries since he'd felt so out of sorts, nervous. Filled with something he couldn't put his finger on. They'd both been summoned, *officially* summoned. He had a hard time wondering if, somehow, his employers sensed what was growing inside him, something he wished he could control and obliterate.

"I don't understand the summons, brother," Hugh whispered to him. "Is there anything wrong? Something I have missed?"

Lionel was pressing his fingernails into his own palms, barely listening to his brother.

"Yes," he began tentatively. "Something—but I can't make it out. I'm confused." He stared at his younger brother and shared the man's compassion.

"Not like you, Lionel. What confuses you? Or are they visions, signals from beyond—?"

Lionel clutched at the curly locks above his ears and pulled, as if the pain of nearly pulling them out by the roots would right his thinking. His heart was beating with adrenaline as if he'd been tracing all night long. He was filled with foreboding, and something else he couldn't identify.

Hugh tried to stop him, pulling his hands from his scalp. "Stop it, brother. You need a drink," he said, and he ran to the bar well-stocked with wines, elixirs, and spirits. Hugh poured a large tumbler for his brother and presented the crystal goblet to his lips. "Take it all down, Lionel. Calm yourself. Or do you want a meditation incantation? I can get one of the—"

"No! No witches. I've had it with witches."

Hugh accepted back the empty goblet thrust into his chest with a twinkle in his eye. "On the contrary, brother, when you need to forget everything, witches are exactly the right tonic for an overly developed and frustrated male of our species. You know this to be true."

"Not now. I have to keep my wits about me."

"But why?" Hugh replaced the liquid with more dark amber whisky, pouring a shot glass of Absinthe for himself. "Another. Together. Always together," he said as he handed the goblet back to Lionel.

"Always together," Lionel echoed and threw back the drink. He kept his eyes closed, searching his brain for something to focus on. Through the vague mist of the whiskey, he saw a huge bed with a woman sleeping there. He tried to study the environs but found it unfamiliar. He watched as her hands covered her breasts, rubbing flowery material over her ripe red nipples. He felt his tongue curl and his lips pucker as if he were suckling those nipples like juicy red cherries. The scent of her neck overwhelmed him as she turned and angled herself. His nose dove into the small hairs beneath and behind her pink ears. His wet lips drew across her cheek until they mated with her soft pillows, sucking them into submission. When she moaned into his mouth, he immediately opened his eyes in horror.

Phoebe! She feels me!

He worked to mask his errant thoughts just as he saw the back of Hugh's frame quickly turn to greet the crack in the library door as it opened to the warm, golden light inside.

"Hugh," acknowledged Marcus. His cousin's dark, kind eyes scanned Lionel's face. Out of centuries of instinct, Lionel lowered his and nodded to his master.

They were shown into the library, to a gathering of a handful of chairs in a semicircle, filled with Goldens of the Monteleone clan. Paolo carefully studied Lionel and Hugh as they were guided to chairs, completing the circle. The eyes continued to bore in, and Lionel worked a smile and nod to everyone else in the group, landing at last on Paolo's face.

"Sir."

The gesture was returned with formality.

Marcus began the discussion after a male servant brought a silver tray of spirits into the room, including two chilled glasses of blood for those who needed nourishment. Lionel took one of those and noticed the effects of pure Golden elixir as it coursed throughout his bloodstream. His stomach stopped churning, but his heartbeat remained rapid, though no longer labored.

"This meeting is called in an effort to discuss measures that are deemed urgent and necessary." Marcus remained standing and touched Lionel's shoulder. "These two brothers are a part of this family in every way but one. And if I could change that, I would."

Lionel darted a look to his employer.

"Yes, you're surprised at this, old friend?"

"I am," Lionel said with gravel in his throat nearly cutting off his wind. Marcus had never called him "old friend" before.

Lionel searched Hugh's face and got a reactive shrug.

"The brothers have sacrificed much—their own brother, in fact—to protect this family. They have spilled their dark blood to save ours. I trust them more than members of my own family," Marcus continued.

Lionel watched Paolo squirm. His son, Lucius, was the offspring of a union between he and a Golden part-witch female, luckily now dead. But Maya's family was a constant sore subject in the Monteleone discussions of bloodlines and family. His brother, Jeb, had given his life for this mixed-race boy and his father.

"Paolo and I have some things to share with you. But I must first tell all of you, this meeting is being done in complete secrecy. No others outside our immediate family are to hear what I have to tell you. And if anyone repeats any of this to persons—no matter who they are—outside this room, it is not only grounds for dismissal from this little council. It would mean your own death."

Several of the men shifted themselves. Someone swore in Italian. Paolo stared at his boots, his shoulders hanging down limply at his sides as he took a huge sigh. Whatever it was had been weighing on both of them heavily.

Marcus went to the library shelves and drew out a book. "This, gentlemen, is the missing book to my grandfather's collection." He placed the book on a table at the edge of the circle. "It is the history of our family. There are many things in here that give us clues to what is going on right now between the two vampire covens."

Marcus studied his brother and then continued.

"It refers to another book, The Book of Spawn, which we have yet to find." He glanced again at Paolo, who nodded in agreement.

"But we are doing ongoing research. We'll find it, eventually," said Paolo, making eye contact with the rest of his family. He gave quick nods to Hugh and Lionel and then looked back down at his boots.

"Yes, Paolo's Carabella is the one who discovered this book." Marcus pointed to the family tome. "She's since turned it over to us so that the library is complete and under guard."

"This is information we're allowed to read?" said one of the members of the group.

"As a Monteleone, yes. No other Golden is allowed," answered Marcus, gruffly. "And you are commanded not to discuss it with any of your wives, your offspring, your parents, or other relatives. No one outside of this room will be allowed access to these books, or to this library as of tonight."

"So why is all this being shared, and why with them?" one of the other members asked, pointing to the two Jett brothers.

"Because their trust and loyalty are without question," whispered Marcus. "They are mistaken as outsiders to some of our family, but mostly to the dark hordes with whom they share a bloodline, and I'm choosing to leave it that way, for now. We are going to need their access to some of the other coven leaders, any of the ones who are not at war with the Monteleones."

"But won't their loyalties lie with the dark covens?" asked an aging member of the audience. His worried brow was duplicated by several of the other elders present.

"Yes, how can you be sure, Marcus?" added one of the others. "And hear me, no offense intended, Hugh and Lionel. I mean you no disrespect, but our rules are based on natural selection. *Our* blood never lies. But, there are things beyond even *our* control," the other elder continued. "How would they be expected to share this to those of us outside their species?"

Marcus seemed unfazed. "I have asked myself this question, and I have looked inside their hearts. I see only loyalty and service there." Marcus gripped Lionel's shoulder again, squeezing it to the point of pain.

Lionel remained motionless, like a rock, envisioning slugs and cold slimy things in the earth so as to mask any emotions or fears. He understood the questions about his loyalty, but it didn't set well with him.

"You think this is just against the Monteleones?" asked Hugh, breaking the awkward silence.

"Gentlemen," Marcus began, "We think it's coordinated to take us out first. Then they'll work on some of the other families, who have allowed others infiltrating their bloodlines. For some reason, our fated lines have remained nearly pure." He glanced quickly at Paolo, who winced but didn't look back at his brother.

Lionel's stomach began to gurgle, which started Hugh in a chuckle that soon spread to all the other members.

"Apparently, my wife's blood cocktail doesn't agree with you," Marcus said with a smirk.

"Pardon me, but no. That's not it. That could never be it." Lionel snuck short glances at several of the other members to make sure his point was made. Hugh continued to chuckle until Lionel hit him on the bicep and nearly toppled the huge vamp.

"Okay. It's late, and we're tired. There will be more coming, which will mean more meetings. But not tonight. It's been a big weekend and the young bride and groom are safely on their way sailing around the world. The party was saved by the heroics of these two." Marcus grabbed Lionel's shoulder again and held it like the top of a staff. The rest of the room clapped. "So now it's time for some of us to travel, some of us to visit and vacation, and some of us to go back to bed."

Everyone stood in a circle, arms around each other's shoulders. Paolo led the circle chant, which everyone said in unison. Lionel had learned it many decades ago, but had never been part of the circle, until this evening.

"We are one family, one people, one blood. We eternally stand for what is precious and good, what is innocent and pure. We pass the flame of eternal life on to the worthy."

THE CONCLAVE BROKE. Both Jett brothers shook hands with most the other members and took their exit. Lionel felt the eyes of the two Monteleone brothers on his back as he and Hugh walked across the crushed granite driveway to their motorcycles.

"You game for some recreation, brother?" Hugh asked. It meant he wanted to share a female. The need for blood was equally as important as his lust for sex.

"No, Huge. I don't trust myself tonight." He stared up at the moon, remarking how many stars were out tonight in the clear midnight sky. The other Monteleones left, piling into two vehicles. The orange square of the front door closed, and the brothers were alone at last under the dome of nature, staring up through old gnarled olive trees.

"Trust yourself? Your mood is curious tonight, Lionel. Where is your mind?"

"As I mentioned, all these changes, even tonight's meeting, has me uneasy. For some reason, I'm feeling the need to remain vigilant. It's like there's a fight about to break out any second. Don't you feel it?"

Hugh shrugged, turning with is arms outstretched as if willing all the dark forces of the universe to hit him square in the solar plexus. "I feel nothing, except a need to feed and spawn."

"Nights like this I miss Jeb," Lionel whispered to the moon.

Something rustling in the bushes made them both jump. A huge dark cat ran across the driveway and scampered around the stone foundation of the enormous villa.

"I thought I heard him yesterday," Hugh sighed. "Even smelled those disgusting little things he liked to suck on."

"Sardines." It made Lionel begin a rumbling chuckle that soon was uncontrollable.

"Yuck." Hugh shook his head and shoulders in a shiver of movement. "What was it about them he liked?"

"The salt. He had a salt tooth."

"I could never understand—" Hugh began.

Still smiling, Lionel jumped on his kick starter and allowed his motorcycle to roar to life. He looked behind him as Hugh did the same.

The two brothers followed the road which bordered the river, using moonlight and their preternatural vision to guide them. Night creatures cavorted in the woods and fields as they passed. Owls swung low searching for prey. Several families of tree bats hovered above the water's edge. Lionel loved the simplicity of nighttime. Movements were efficient, intentional, with life or death consequences. All creatures of the night hunted.

At last, they came upon their bungalow, buried behind rows of thick berry vines. Nestled amongst the vines was an automatic gate behind a well-traveled path just wide enough to allow them and their bikes through. Lionel swished over the tire tracks outside with a broken oak tree branch full of dead leaves to hide their entrance to mortal interference.

Inside, the little home was cozy and warm. Their part-time daytime staff, hired by Marcus himself, had long since retired, but left behind a roaring fire and a hearty beef stew simmering on the stove they would dispose of when they retired for their daytime sleep. The windows had been shuttered and draped over. Each brother retired to his own bedroom, leaving Jeb's room door wide open, but paying respects to him first before retiring. A red candle was lit beside Jeb's bed, as if to leave a light on for his safe return, which would never occur.

Lionel locked his door and placed the iron key beneath his pillow. He wished he could sleep with the windows open, so he could watch the stars all night until the sky pinkened like the bottom of a cherub, but that was too dangerous in these times. He'd awaken to save himself from the dawn, but it was the other night creatures, the other dark coven members he feared most. Safety precautions were taken with the perimeter walls.

Removing all his clothes, he decided to sleep naked. The clean white sheets felt like a mortal woman's backside tonight as he snuggled to find a comfortable position. He knew it might take him a few hours to drop off. He placed his arms beneath his pillow, rested his head, and waited, thinking.

He too had picked up a sensation of Jeb, but not in the same way Hugh had. His aura traveled on a dry wind from the south. He'd been in the old Souks in Marrakesh and Casablanca, where they sold colorful spices in huge reed jars as tall as a man and oils infused with every kind of scent imaginable. He wondered if his strong sense of smell was picking up something from across the Mediterranean, something from North Africa. But he felt Jeb was calling to him in a message from that parched, scented wind.

He traced the roughhewn timbers that held his ceiling in place, noticing the lattice pattern and circular indentations of a skilled artisan's blade. His eyelids felt heavy, and he let them fall.

He drifted off to a gentle sleep, hearing sounds of the ocean lap upon a sandy shore, but as he became more discerning, he determined the rhythm of the sea was really the sounds of heavy breathing. He was back in the room with the golden fireplace illuminating the mounds and valleys of the mortal woman's body.

He knew he could turn her over with a suggestion she'd not recall but was afraid to try at first and then gave in to the urge to see her writhing in her bed. Her shoulder turned, then came her arm, and, at last her torso lay back into the bed, as her hands pushed back the covers. Her body had produced delicate beads of sweat like tiny diamonds that shimmered in the light of the flames. Around her neck was draped the shawl that he'd held inside his shirt as he traveled to her, his heart ardently striking its dull cord like a homing beacon.

He dared not speak her name, or even think it. She was agitated, flailing back and forth, eventually turning back to her stomach. One thigh and butt cheek were exposed to the flickering light in the otherwise silent room. He could almost feel the firm flesh beneath his fingertips as he smoothed over her, searched for the crevice between her cheeks. His mouth watered.

I can taste you, Phoebe.

He'd said it in his mind before he could stop himself. He should open his eyes and begin reading a book, or watching some television, but he couldn't stop the dream.

She rotated her body again, laying on her back and pushing the covers down over her chest. It moved beyond her waist, and she raised her nightgown and then exposed the juncture between her legs. With her chin extended toward the ceiling, she raised her knees, touched herself with one hand, and whispered, "Taste me."

Lionel sat up immediately. He scrambled to his feet, examining the bed as if it was to blame for his erotic thoughts, and then noticed his hard-on. He swore, storming off to the shower, and stood beneath the cold spring water spray until his teeth began to chatter. He lathered his body with the heavy clove and cinnamon-scented soap he'd bought in the village. He rinsed his mouth out, even adding soap to his tongue to interfere with the pheromones he'd inhaled in his dream.

Exhausted, he sat dripping wet, shivering in the dark room, alone. He couldn't afford to sleep until he was sure the vision he'd had was completely severed from his psyche.

Minutes turned into three hours. He allowed the cold to chill his soul even as he heard sounds from the outside that indicated dawn was approaching. Any hint of emotion or warmth, he stomped out until sleep began to overtake him.

He stumbled to his cold bed, wishing for oblivion, death. Seeking a grave somewhere. Dirt. Worms, stones, and carcasses of dead animals. Bones staring back at him. Just before he plunged deep into the midnight sea of sleep that was his legacy, he heard her once more.

"Taste me."

Chapter 4

PHOEBE WAS STARTLED when her attendant awakened her. Her gown was twisted about her waist and upper chest, the covers nearly ripped from her bed.

"Goodness, Princess, you've had an awful night," Selena said to her charge.

Phoebe went back into her memory and couldn't recall anything, except the warm glow deep inside her soul. She'd been drifting in an erotic wind where fabric, and coarse skin of a mysterious male's cheek pressed against her breasts and made her rise up to present herself. It was unlike anything she'd ever felt before.

"Is there anyone else in the household?" she asked.

"No, miss. Your mother and father are downstairs in the garden room. But they are expecting visitors this morning. They asked me to get you ready to receive them."

"Who?" Phoebe asked.

"Don't know, sweet child. A delegation of some kind, I think."

Just then, they heard an automobile pull up to the front. They both watched as an elderly priest extracted himself from the back seat then placed his cap firmly atop his bald head. With the help of an accolade and two other younger priests in black robes, he was ushered to the entrance of the villa.

"Come, Phoebe, we must prepare quickly. Your mother will be angry with me if we don't get down there soon."

"I'm starving," Phoebe moaned, holding her stomach.

"She's prepared a full breakfast for our visitors, it seems. Can't you smell it?"

She could. Satisfied with the clothes laid out, she sent Selena away to announce her imminent arrival. She jumped into the shower, again feeling the sensitive and blooming parts of her body. Fear had left her. Her mood turned happy now that the effects of the bite and the dreams it had caused last night were distanced.

She did her hair up in a bright red ribbon and wore the deep red garnet necklace her mother had given her last year, with the matching heart-shaped earrings that had belonged to her distant great-grandmother. She wore a dark burgundy frock over flowing black leggings, slipped on her black leather pumps, and examined herself in the mirror after applying red lipstick.

The raw marks on her neck were still present, but the healing had nearly completed. The remaining tissue was swollen and as bright red as her lips. She used some of the salve left behind, dabbing the green substance over her scarring flesh, and noticed how it made her surface skin tingle then numb.

Not knowing who her visitors were, she decided it would be prudent to drape a clean shawl around her shoulders to cover up the mark, in case the event wasn't known to the audience downstairs. Taking the ends of the material and tossing them behind her, she straightened her bedding, and skipped her way downstairs to the waiting crowd.

Father Domenico Flavius regarded her from his sitting position in the garden room like a cherub. His round face and pink shiny cheeks resembled a baby's bottom.

"Ah, Freya, how lovely she has grown!" He set his plate of sweets down and stood, outstretching his arms. "Child of God in Heaven! The Lord looks down upon you with favor!"

She ran toward him, remembering him from her brother's birthday party some years ago when he took a vow as a youngster to help in the church—a vow which was quickly expunged by the family. Her brother was a kind and helpful soul who wished to live a life of service to his community.

"Brother Domenico! I'm surprised you remember me. I have all my teeth at last! See?" She gave him a wide smile showing her mouthful of perfect white teeth. Then she hugged the rotund gentleman. She noticed the black-robed younger priests fidget, switching their weight from leg to leg while they presented brittle smiles. Her father was frowning but her mother clasped her hands together and beamed.

"Look at you, my dear," Father Domenico said as he held her at arm's length. "As beautiful as your mother, as all the women of your family." His hand cupped her cheek.

Phoebe felt her cheeks blush from all the attention. She recognized one of the young priests.

"Mario! You've taken the cloth."

"I have, dear Phoebe. Although looking at you now, I'm seriously reconsidering that option. Was I premature?" he said as he winked at her. His stiff blond-colored hair appeared not to have been combed for several days and stood out at his sides like straw.

Phoebe had played with Mario and his brothers all during her childhood, until his parents intervened over two years ago as Phoebe blossomed from child to young woman. It was explained that it would be improper for her to be alone with him, unless accompanied by members of her family and the security detail employed to watch over the children.

"You have a good heart, like Damian."

Phoebe's mother put her palm to her mouth at the mention of Phoebe's brother, who was away at a camp for the young Goldens going into family winery businesses.

Mario glanced at Father Domenico nervously and then gave Phoebe a chaste kiss on her cheek. "Bless you, Phoebe. You always see the good in everyone. That's a gift," he whispered, with his eyes downturned.

Her father cleared his throat and extended his arm around Father Domenico. "Phoebe, your mother and I are making plans for your coming of age party."

His smile was plastered to his face, but his eyes were deadly serious. Phoebe knew well there was another meaning to them. Her mood darkened at the reminder of the decisions she was being pressured to make. But it was awkward to discuss it with members of the clergy, as well as childhood friends, who were all mortal, with no vampiric bloodlines. It felt like a betrayal of her friends that they were excluded.

"Yes, Father. That would be lovely." She worked to make her voice sound compliant, as she always did around him. But she clearly saw the strain in his face, the wrinkle between his eyes he could not mask. And her mother had stopped smiling.

Even the older priest seemed a bit ill at ease.

"Is there a special someone who could also be part of this celebration, my dear family?"

He looked from Salvatore Dominichelli, to his wife, Freya, and then back to Phoebe without getting a nod or answer of any kind. His fingers started flickering beneath his robes, which extended past his first two knuckles.

At last Phoebe burst out into laughter to break the tension. "Father! You rascal! Of course not. I'm way too young."

Her mother angled her head and sweetly smiled. Her father ground his teeth and held his jaw firm.

She twirled, her eyes dancing over all the faces in her presence. She hugged herself, pulling the shawl tight across her chest for comfort. She didn't want to show the bite mark. The older priest would certainly be able to recognize it. Nor did she want to show the goosebumps on her arms and chest. She sashayed towards the kitchen fireplace, hugging their cook along the way.

"I'm starved! Can I join you in breakfast?" she finally asked the nonplussed crowd.

"Yes, yes. Forgive me, Father. Where are my manners?" Freya said as she flitted over to the kitchen, lifting trays of breakfast breads, jams, and several fancy egg dishes.

Phoebe sank into the chair at the head of the table without waiting for anyone else to join her and dove into the food. It was a welcome distraction.

AFTER THE ENTOURAGE left, Phoebe turned from the closed front door and addressed her parents.

"And what was *that*?"

"Phoebe, you remember—?" Her mother began.

"It's been decided you need to either take seriously your choices or take a husband. Your mother and I are beside ourselves with worry, now that you've come to the attention of the dark covens."

"That might not be true," Phoebe protested.

"Oh, for Heaven's sake, Phoebe, look around you," her mother added. "You have to be able to feel all this change going on. Your father and I do. You told me last night—"

"In confidence, Mother. Does half the village know about all this, this decision made without consulting me?"

"No final decision has been made, Daughter," her mother whispered, then searched her husband's face for help.

Her father stepped closer and took both her hands in his. "You must know how much I love you, Phoebe. I just wouldn't be able to live with myself if anything happened. I could drop everything else and guard you every waking minute myself, but that's not realistic. We are worried. And we don't think history is lining up very favorably for our family, for any of the Golden families. Even the Monteleones are worried."

"I'm sorry, Father." She searched his face, noticing his lack of aging, the familiar lines that remained ever since she was old enough to remember him. The older she got, the closer in physical age to both he and her mother she was becoming. She knew the mortal population would notice it sooner or later. It meant that some children who elected not to turn had to leave their homes to live elsewhere.

He drew his large arms around her and kissed the top of her head. "Phoebe, I'm not sure why I am so protective of you. You are smart, capable, and beautiful. You've been a wonderful, obedient daughter, accepting of all that is about this family. Not rebellious like some of the other families. You are a model for all young Golden virgins. A father couldn't ask for anything more."

His hand rested at the back of her head and lazily rubbed her curls. The heat from his body felt reassuring to her, even though there was going to be a large "but" in his conversation soon.

She decided to take a chance he might understand her. "I honestly haven't decided, Father," she said to his chest.

"Could you—?" His breath hitched as the emotions overtook the normally cool and logical family icon. "Could you consider speeding up your choice? Or could it be possible you could take a husband, even if he wasn't fated to be yours? Not a mate, but a protector."

She withdrew from him, scanning their faces back and forth.

"A marriage without love? Just a protection? That would be a lie."

"An arrangement," said her mother.

"But I thought you said—"

"Your father and I have discussed it at length after we spoke. It would be *with* the understanding when the fating came, you'd be free to go. That you'd remain unsullied, a virgin, until that time."

"But you said this was never allowed."

"In special circumstances," said her father.

"With a non-Golden husband? A protector?"

Both her parents nodded. "It's allowed and done. Especially now that these wars are beginning, Phoebe. We are having to resort to desperate ways to protect our young. You are the future of this family. You and your siblings," said Dominichelli.

"How would this be arranged?"

"We would pair you with someone we *trust*. You'd have no obligation. In fact, you'd be requested *not* to consummate the marriage. It wouldn't be a *real* marriage. But it will protect your place in our bloodline. And your womanhood."

"But who?"

Chapter 5

THE MESSAGE STARTED as a shrill whistle, coming from the south. Lionel had been polishing an old knife his grandfather had given him when he was a boy of not more than ten. He'd been waiting until Hugh rose from his slumber.

As he angled his head, the whistle became louder. He shook his head and then tapped his ears as if to allow bugs to fall from his brain. Nothing stopped the noise.

Hugh swung open his door and stood naked, holding an axe.

"Hold there, brother. I mean you no harm," shouted Lionel.

"One thing to be rousted up from a wonderful wet dream and quite another to hear a banshee—it is from a creature, not a man-made instrument," Hugh spat. "The bastard who dares do this will pay for it by giving me his dick."

"What if that whistle is a woman?"

Hugh tossed his head from side to side. "Damn! It's incessant. I hope she's an ugly witch or she-banshee, a female troll with warts and green skin. Would be a shame to behead a beauty, now, wouldn't it?"

The sound stopped abruptly. The two brothers waited several seconds before relaxing. Lionel spat on the metal blade he was polishing, rubbing it against the sharpening stone by candlelight. Hugh laid the axe into the doorway and removed blood from the refrigerator, adding it to a protein shaker and topping it off with whiskey. After giving the mixture several vigorous shakes, he drank the contents down and let out a gut-wrenching burp.

"You'll never marry, Hugh. I think that alone could undo any fating coming your way."

"Nah, I don't believe in it any longer. It would have happened by now, with all the sampling we've done."

"We've been tethered to one family, one employer. We've not traveled much for the past century. Who knows what's out there?" Lionel had pondered it for decades.

Hugh rinsed his shaker. "You want me to make a concoction for you, Brother?"

"Nope. I'm not hungry at the moment."

Hugh collapsed into the heavy wooden chair and sat across the table from Lionel's finishing cloths, oils and polishing pastes. "You seem calmer today. You thinking more clearly?"

He nodded. "I am. I'm of a good frame of mind tonight. My rest was restorative. You?"

Hugh got up and suddenly discovered he was still naked. "Now I'm the one distracted. But, unlike you, I'm going to go hunting. I can see you won't join me."

Lionel's cell rang. Both brothers noted the screen read *Marcus M.*

"Sir?" he answered.

"I have some news you'll want to hear. Jeb has been found. Alive."

Lionel stood. Even Hugh had heard the scratchy voice of their employer from the cell phone and scrambled to his feet, tracing through the table to put his ear against the little device.

"H-How is that possible?" Lionel asked. His heart was racing. He'd hoped the signals were not just his over-active imagination.

"He was rescued by a Bedouin tribe in the Sahara, near death. He was clutching to the charred, dead remains of Dag, who is confirmed truly dead. Good and dead, thank God."

Lionel was almost giddy. It had always struck him so odd that Goldens liked to swear and thank God for things he had nothing to do with, if he even existed.

"Where is he?" Hugh blurted out.

Marcus chuckled. "Right now, he's wrapped like a mummy in a very thick carpet, and stored in a cool, dark place, so that he doesn't lose any more flesh before he can regenerate."

"He needs a host. Are they feeding him, Sir?" Lionel asked.

"Apparently, they know all about your kind. And they recognized the vamp who perished at his hands, which is why he was spared, I'm told. Dag was an enemy of those people."

"So they are a dark coven, then?" Lionel asked.

"I don't think so. In fact, I think they may become mortal allies."

"When will he return?"

"Lionel, I'm sending you to go bring him back. I can't spare the both of you, so Hugh, you'll stay here."

"Very good, sir. How will I find him? You have the location?"

"They will be sending you a signal to guide you. It's a frequency only your species can hear."

"We've had it! I woke up to it this morning," gasped Hugh.

"Good. I will let Paolo know, then. You can leave whenever you are ready, Lionel. But don't linger there. Use your mental gifts to alert Hugh to anything dangerous. And be careful. It could be a trap."

Lionel considered his options before he committed to the mission. His mind wandered to the bedroom of a certain mortal woman again. Hugh felt it, staring back in horror at him, and shook his head.

His duty and honor to the Monteleone family was his primary directive, and at last he sighed, resolute with his decision. "I'll leave within the hour. I'll make sure Hugh is fully made aware of my progress." He hesitated and then added. "Marcus, promise me you'll add extra detail to your family and that of the young Dominichelli woman. I have reason to feel you are all in danger, and if I am gone, it will seem like an opportunity to some."

Hugh frowned now, his hands on his hips, his legendary cock swinging almost to his knees.

"I'll take your advice and act on it, Lionel. Thank you for the protection of my family. Please keep yourself out of danger. If it wasn't Jeb, I'd not send you. But I couldn't let you sacrifice your brother. I couldn't ask that of you."

"I understand. I will return intact and with Jeb, in whatever form he remains."

After the call was ended, Hugh punched him in the stomach, sending him rolling backwards, upturning a lamp and small chair. His anger roared, and his fists sought to smash his own flesh and blood, but he stopped short.

"What are you thinking? What were those visions?" Hugh demanded.

"I'm dealing with it." Lionel turned to begin gathering things for his trip. He was looking for the healing bag they carried with them everywhere. Hugh blocked the doorway.

"Was that what I felt it was?"

Lionel looked up to him, feeling guilty and unable to mask his shame.

"I am unable to control it, brother. It's like a—"

Hugh was on him, covering his mouth. "Do not speak of it, brother! It's blasphemy to say it."

"I'm going to find a way to set it aside. Perhaps not eliminate it, but set it aside, to the back of my mind, where it can't hurt me, or—" He stopped, unable to speak her name for fear the dragon of lust building inside him would get loose and wreak havoc with his soul and the souls of both his brothers.

Hugh stepped away and watched him glumly gather things. He only needed a small backpack, enough to bring a cloaking cape in an emergency, some implements like silver handcuffs he had to gingerly handle with heavy work gloves he stuck in there as well. He used a dirty shirt to pick up a string of small silver chain, along with the herbal salve and the healing bag. He fingered over the lavender drawstring pouch with the distinctive letter M embroidered on the top, done by the nimble and impossibly tiny pink fingers of Maria Monteleone herself.

"It is not her, brother," Hugh said, watching Lionel's preoccupation with the stitching.

"You are right. It is not her." He knew Maria Monteleone was dust and bones over two hundred years ago. "But the girl is of her bloodline, I can tell. And you know what we say in Marcus' house."

"Yes. *Blood never lies*," Hugh whispered. "But, what is the *truth*?"

Lionel reached, gripping his brother's shoulder. "Two days ago, I could have told you. Two days ago, I didn't see these things or feel the burning in my gut. Two days ago, Jeb was dead and buried. We were attending that wedding, and the world was dangerous, but manageable." He paused, squeezing the muscles on his brother's upper arm, feeling the strength and power of this magnificent creature he was lucky to call brother. "But today my truth is a journey, a dangerous one, and something I hope I survive. Whether I go or stay behind, it is just as dangerous, Hugh. I can only tackle one mystery at a time. If I survive the first, I'll come back to attend to the other one. In the meantime, keep the ones we love safe from harm."

Hugh embraced him timidly, due to his state of undress. "Consider it done."

Chapter 6

PHOEBE FELT ILL as the first light of morning broke into her room. Her legs became heavy, like made of concrete, causing her to stumble out of bed and barely make it to the bathroom. Her attendant found her with her head in the toilet bowl.

"Oh, little one. I should get your mother. Are you ill?"

"I'm just sick. I have the flu or something."

The room was spinning in all directions. The taste of her vomit was especially bitter, reflecting the deep brownish red contents lying in the bottom of the toilet bowl.

Her mother rushed to her side with a warm towel.

"Phoebe, oh honey. Let's get you up and back to bed."

She brushed her face with the warm towel, but Phoebe's thirst drove her to the sink where she cupped her hands and drank water from the tap. She noticed her throat was raw and sore.

"You are warm again. Do you have a fever?"

She felt her forehead and confirmed what her mother deduced. "I have a sore throat too, and yes, I think I have a fever." She examined herself in the mirror. Her eyes were rimmed in red, her nose was running. The acrid taste was still lingering in her mouth, so she brushed her teeth and began to feel better.

Her mother was fussing to pin her hair up and she stopped her.

"Quit. Just leave it. I need to rest."

"Yes, I think that's best. I'm going to call for the doctor. Here, let's get you back and covered, but first a fresh nightgown." she said, helping Phoebe remove the wet gown and replacing it with a freshly laundered one. She climbed back into her soaking sheets.

Under the circumstances, the coolness of the damp sheets was welcome, and while she listened to her mother and the attendant make plans to remake the bed, she drifted off.

IT WAS LATER in the day when she awoke at last. She could hear voices coming from downstairs, and then the door opened to her room. Dr. Luciano entered, his hat in hand, clutching his black physician's bag. He'd always reminded her of a little mouse, with his small spectacles, grey frizzy hair, and long sideburns. Like a character from a Dicken's novel.

"Bella, Phoebe. Your mother tells me you are unwell," he said as he approached the bed. "May I?" he gestured toward the edge.

"Please."

He sat, repositioning his glasses and taking her pulse. He examined her eyes, frowning, which made his glasses slip so he had to reset them across the bridge of his nose. "Is there any pain here?" he asked as he took her wrist and pressed the veins there.

"No."

"Here?" he asked as he pressed the side of her neck under her ear.

She shrank away from his touch, uneasy to let him see the old bite mark there. "No," she whined and moved away. "It's my stomach."

He turned to ask for help from Freya. He carefully lifted her nightgown to just below her breasts, adjusting the covers down so he could examine her midriff above her navel. He pressed two cold fingers down into her stomach cavity and she felt a sharp pain, followed by a gagging reflex. He listened with a stethoscope to the right of her belly button and then through her nightgown at her upper chest. He pressed his fingers again on the right, and again, she felt pain.

"So you are tender there? What kind of a pain is it? Sharp? Or dull?"

"Sort of in-between. Like I have gas. I feel bloated."

"Ah, yes."

"Dr. Luciano, you should examine the wound. It's nearly healed, but perhaps this is related to some resulting infection?" Freya asked.

"May I, please?"

Phoebe turned her face and pulled down the eyelet lace around her neck to expose the old wound. She felt his cold fingers manipulating the puckered pink flesh of her neck beneath her left ear. He felt for a pulse and nodded.

"I'd like to see the cream you've been using," he asked.

Freya returned from the bathroom and showed him the green vial of salve. He sniffed it and felt it between his two fingers and his thumb, sniffing it again.

"Is there something wrong, doctor?"

"No. Everything seems normal. The healing is remarkable, and there's no issue of infection at the wound site, but something has gotten into her bloodstream and is making her sick. She was given an infusion?"

"Yes, her father's blood."

"Well, that would explain the quick healing. Did she receive more than one feeding?"

"Doctor, she is unturned, so we gave her only one."

"I realize, Freya." He replaced her nightie and drew the covers up to her chin. "I think there is a chance that it was too much for her system. Perhaps she's more delicate than we often see."

Phoebe was concerned. "I've been having strange dreams, too, and my—" She felt her breasts and discovered the swelling had reduced and beneath the cotton fabric of her nightgown her skin didn't feel as tender. "I had other skin irritations, but they seem to be gone now."

"Well, my dear, you're a strong young lady, but not quite strong enough for your father's pure bloodline, at least at this time. I think you overdosed a bit on your family's love." He stood, chuckling, and then addressed Freya. "I wish I could say the same of some others of your clan. Things are so watered down these days."

"You wish to see the contents of what she threw up?" Freya asked him.

When he returned from the bathroom, he smiled. "I think my diagnosis earlier is spot on. You did the right thing by giving her a feeding, but I'd limit this if the need should arise again. I think she took on too much."

Freya was distracted with some distant thought.

"I think you'll be better tomorrow. I'd stay in bed and drink lots of liquids. You're thirsty?"

"Yes, very."

"All normal. Drink broth or something very bland. Herbal tea, if you like. Jell-O?" He grinned. "All the things you liked as a child, my dear."

Phoebe smiled back at him. He'd remembered her favorite was lime Jell-O.

He handed the salve back to Freya. "And let's hold off on this for a day or two until she feels more herself. It's closed the wound and fought infection. Now we let the body do its natural thing."

Her mother tucked the salve into her skirt pocket and nodded her agreement.

He turned to go, giving Phoebe a wink.

"Thank you, doctor."

"Rest, my dear. Rest is your friend. Forget the strange dreams and just rest. That's what you need."

AROUND DUSK, PHOEBE awoke again. The fire had been stoked while she was sleeping and now felt oppressively warm. She pulled back the sheets to air them out and found a small spot of fresh blood on the bottom sheet no larger than the size of a silver dollar. She was frozen in place. As was common with Goldens, she hadn't begun to menstruate since that was a symptom of fating and not usually a natural event for young Golden girls.

She tore the sheets from her bed and scrubbed the remnants of the bloody stain on her feather mattress. But she couldn't remove it entirely, so she flipped the mattress over, pulled fresh sheets from her closet, and remade the bed quickly. She scrubbed the dirty sheet with her hairbrush and got most of it out with soap and cold water, leaving them in a pile in the corner of her bedroom.

She added her soaked nightgown to the pile and stepped into the shower. The warm water soothed her nerves and took the chill from her soul. She scrubbed everywhere, including between her legs, relieved to find no further evidence of bleeding.

She put on her favorite pair of sloppy jeans and an oversized sweatshirt. She pulled her wet hair up on top of her head in a clip, applied some lip gloss and moisturizer, and decided to head downstairs to spend time with the rest of the family. Her brother was due to come home soon, possibly today, and she didn't want to sleep through the homecoming.

At the bathroom doorway, she nearly tripped on the flowered shawl that had comforted her and even protected her two days prior. She drew it to her nose and sniffed, detecting the pungent musky smell of the dark vamp who had saved her life. The hair at the back of her neck stood to attention as the familiar scent continued to bring her comfort.

But she decided to take another action. She threw the shawl on top of the pile of dirty sheets and exited the room, closing the door on that chapter from the wedding.

She was feeling like her old self. It was time to move on with the rest of her life.

Chapter 7

LIONEL TRACED ALONG the whistle sound, bouncing off the edges of the sonar vibration. He found if he stayed just slightly outside the strongest signal he was more conscious of his surroundings. At times, it was difficult to hold back his desire to make the trip at full tracing speed, but managed to slow down, since he wasn't sure what he'd find when he showed up. If it weren't for the fact that his brother's health was at stake, he'd have taken the even more prudent route to go on foot and be preceded by an advanced guard. He wished he'd been able to bring some of the former SEALs his brother had trained.

He'd judged correctly that the night would be in full bloom once he arrived in the desert, where he traced between campsites, clumps of trees, and ancient ruins for cover. He was careful to watch the moon's arc, so he would have time to find a dark space for his sleep requirements. He could push the envelope and go without sleep for one day, provided he didn't use the extra energy to fend off light. But two days could leave him too weakened to make the return trip home.

He scouted caves in stony outcroppings along his journey. But judging from the quality of the beacon tone, he would be traveling across smooth sand, with nothing but man-made temporary shelters to protect him. That was an unacceptable risk under most circumstances. It required he calculate the distance and time factor to Jeb's location first and then await a full dusk to dawn timeframe for his extraction and trip home.

At last, he came upon a cluster of brightly-colored tents lit by campfires. Herds of camel moved restlessly between a watering hole and the vicinity of their keepers. Though it was midnight, Lionel observed the crowd of strangers who moved slowly across sandy peaks and valleys, ducking under layers of heavy carpet. It was obvious they were getting ready to move while the night was still upon them.

He sent out a mental signal to Jeb and didn't get a response. He was going to wait until the next moon when something wafted past him and caught his keen sense of smell. The hair on his arms began to stiffen, his preternatural warning sign. Again, he called to his brother with a low frequency, mental message, and this time heard a faint squeak that was familiar. The signal duplicated the length of his, but the sound was undefined in terms of words.

He drew closer to the source, which led him to a large red tent surrounded by bright orange and yellow flags and long purple streamers. A dozen dark horses nervously whinnied and pulled against their tethers nearby.

He cloaked himself and traced through the fabric, finding an outer tent housing several smaller animals tied to stakes driven in the ground. Wind moaned through the tunnels of the large tent and made his bones chill. He smelled blood—a mixture of vampire as well as mortal blood. He also smelled death.

Lionel was at a crossroads. He was concerned that the element of surprise was not on his side, so it felt dangerous to remain. But he knew Jeb was close by. The air was pregnant with a pattern he heard between the whistling of the winds over the sand as it splashed up against the walls. He risked sending a message to Hugh, with a warning he feared he'd fallen into a trap.

He listened, tuning carefully to the vibration while keeping his cloaking device from scaring the small animals. At last, he heard the plea for help from Jeb, coming like air through a small reed. It was mostly the sound of breathing but laced between were definitely vocal sounds. And then he felt the mind pattern, and his heart warmed to the knowledge that Jeb was indeed alive. But very weak and broken.

"Come in, traveler," came the clipped voice of a stranger behind him. Lionel was sure the cloaking was still functioning, so he turned to find a giant of a dark man smiling down on him. His robed arm lifted a carpeted curtain, revealing a golden glow and warmth inside.

Lionel remained frozen in place. He tapped down his apprehension and tried not to react to the invitation given him. He could not afford to trust the man, even with Jeb nearby. Until he could make communication with him, he wasn't going to move.

The giant began to laugh. "You think I talk to myself?"

Lionel traced to a space behind the dark shadow, who didn't turn in response, seemingly unable to adjust to his movement.

He sent out another message to Jeb and recognized the answering silent scream.

"*Run!*"

Lionel immediately traced to the opposite side of the tent and stopped, controlling his breathing, his thoughts and even the speed at which his preternatural blood was flowing. He pressed out any of the images of his journey, images of his recent past. Instead, he concentrated on scenes from his childhood, visions of him and his brothers playing as mortal children before their turning.

He heard his brother sob as the visions reached him. That gave Lionel the coordinates he needed. He traced and found Jeb lying in a heap of bloody rags. Just as Marcus had told, Jeb had been draped in bandages, which were seeping with some mixture that included blood. The smell was foul.

Jeb was missing one lower arm, which was wrapped as far as his elbow joint, which appeared in working order. But his arms were thin, and several places revealed raw bone the bandages failed to cover. Both his legs were there, but cast at odd angles, and obviously not useable in their present state. Like leaves scattered in the fall, pieces of blackened flaky skin littered the ground all around him.

Lionel knew it was Jeb, because he felt his lifeforce, but the skull that angled up toward him was unrecognizable. He was missing eyes, the dark caverns hollowly staring up at him as if he could still see.

"No," Jeb began to whisper. "Go away. Save yourself." His lips could barely form words, and his speech was more slurred than spoken. But the danger in those words was impossible to miss.

Suddenly, a large silver cage dropped from the ceiling and trapped both brothers inside. While hearing the sound of evil laughter echoing throughout his cell, Lionel took stock of the room by dim torchlight and noted the source of the awful smell. Rotting corpses lay strewn about, most of them shriveled and burned to a crisp. Various metal implements and spears with silver tips eerily reflected the dancing flames.

Knowing the silver would prevent him from any type of action, Lionel stared down at the frame of his brother shivering at his feet. The trap had been sprung, and now the rescuer was the prey in need of saving. He could not help but feel his heart breaking at what could become of them both.

HE CALMLY ASSESSED his status. If he was lured to Jeb's side to be executed, it would have happened by now. No, Lionel thought, he was being caught alive, not because of *who* he was but *what* he was.

He held Jeb's face up off the bloody rags, sliced one of his own wrists open with his teeth, and dropped some of his blood inside his brother's gaping mouth, rubbing it over Jeb's gums and lips. Instantly, Jeb's skin began to change color and then shape. Under the golden light of the torch, he watched as portions of Jeb's bones were covered in muscle, veins, arteries, and then pink flesh protecting the network of nutrient delivery. His arm healed, restoring some of his muscle tissue, all the way to the elbow, and then ended in a puckering stump that broke free of the bandages.

Lionel knew time was not on his side, but he was hoping that just enough of it would help bring Jeb to a form able to help in his own escape, if the opportunity arrived.

Jeb's thoughts were streaming past him. Lionel saw visions of the bonfire of Jeb's entwined body, clutching Dag's crispy form, even grappling with the mere skeleton of Dag as it tried to slither across the sand in the hot noon sun. He saw Jeb awaken, felt the terror and the pain that he was on fire. Later, he saw Jeb being tended to, huddled at the bottom of an ornate cage as if made for a large pet bird or monkey.

Or a pet vampire.

He sent out a healing message as the blood from his wrist dribbled down over his brother's lips and onto his chest.

I've seen it, Jeb. Now drink. Be whole. I am here, Brother.

Eyelids formed, covering the vacant caverns where his tender brown eyes had once been. And when they opened, he saw that Jeb's sight had been restored. The twisted smile from thin lips that barely covered his teeth and gums was one of the most beautiful things Lionel had ever seen.

The heavy laughter coming from overhead turned his veins ice cold. Jeb coughed up and attempted to right himself to sitting position, using his arm stump. Lionel left his wrist against his brother's mouth but looked up at the evil face of his captor.

"Welcome, Lionel Jett. I am so happy to see you earning your keep. It's been expensive keeping your brother alive. He has a strong will to live."

"As do I," Lionel challenged him.

"I can see that."

"State your purpose." Lionel reverted to his warrior frame of mind.

"To make a trade."

"But I have nothing to offer," Lionel barked.

"Oh, but you do," the large man laughed. Gold in his teeth glistened, and a large ring hung from one torn earlobe. A scar slashed across his otherwise smooth and weathered face creating a permanent scowl of his upper lip. His gnarled fingers were adorned with shiny jeweled rings, and his wrists were encrusted in dozens of gold bands, which jingled as he pointed to Lionel's wrist at Jeb's mouth.

Lionel knew this man was mortal, but under the weight of the silver bars, even the strength of both he and his brother combined, if they were both healthy, would be no match for the mortal enemy. It would mean a waiting game of opportunity before he was reduced to flakes and charred bones like that which now surrounded him.

He was hoping, even incanting a small prayer, to be underestimated. He wondered how much of the night he had left. He wondered if any of his mental messages to Hugh had gotten through. With the silver in place, this would no longer be possible.

"So name your terms, captor."

"You act like you have some say in the matter." He chuckled while pulling up a stool and stared down at the two of them. "I am Salaman, and I control everything in this place you can see with your eyes. I'll show you when it's light. From one horizon, to the other, all mine."

Lionel couldn't help but flinch.

Salaman continued. "Yes, I know you fear the sun. So perhaps that won't be possible, but never mind. As I was saying, I am looking for a trade. And you, Lionel Jett, are part of the bargain, not a party to the negotiations. You are a valuable commodity."

Lionel could only imagine several parties who might be interested in negotiating for their release. Certainly, the Monteleones would pay handsomely, or he hoped they would. If the price wasn't too dear.

"I have spoken to your employer. He is aware you have arrived. He is also aware of the condition of your brother."

Jeb began to sit upright, pushing away Lionel's wrist. His ears were growing back before Lionel's eyes, his breathing deepened, but his legs were still emaciated and not able to hold his weight. His mind, though, was returning. Lionel could see Jeb was interested in the conversation now, just as much as he was.

Salaman smiled, revealing his golden canines. His gaze was hungry, as if what he was about to say was so delicious he nearly drooled. He leaned forward, placing his weight on his oversized forearms piled atop his tree stump knees covered in heavy robes.

"What I want is what has been stolen from me. I have studied your kind for a very long time. I have imprisoned hundreds, enjoyed, well—" He waved over the detritus that rotted around them all. "I have a taste for your kind. But I crave the Golden bloodlines even more. I've had difficulty obtaining them."

He leaned back on his stool and crossed his arms with a smug tight-lipped smile.

"He will not give you what you want," Lionel spat back.

"Oh, I think he will."

"You know he would never sacrifice a Golden for one of us, and I would never stand for it, either."

"You're the bait. The bargain. You have no say."

"No, I'm a living being who will fight you till the death. And then what will you have?"

"So I find another. Eventually, I will find a nice, ripe Golden. Perhaps a virgin? Would he not sacrifice one to save the family? You are an important part of his protection, even his family."

Lionel was struck with the realization that some of the confidential information they'd discussed in the Monteleone library was now privy to Salaman. There was a betrayal within the family, and Marcus was unaware of this.

He could feel Jeb's thoughts. He was searching the perimeter of the cage, inspecting for some weak spot. Some way out.

Quiet, brother.

But I'm nearly thin enough to get through these bars.

No.

Their private conversation didn't appear to faze Salaman in any fashion. That told Lionel that they now had a good weapon to use, once Jeb was fully restored. He reached over and righted first one leg and then the other, squeezing to feel evidence of some healing, and did sense a tiny vibration beginning to build.

"I understand your desire for a Golden," Lionel began.

"*Unsullied* Golden."

"As you say," Lionel repeated and extended his wrist to Jeb again. "But surely you have a second request, perhaps a compromise."

Salaman laughed and stood, kicking the stool to the corner. "Right you are, vampire! But what I haven't told you is that a virgin Golden female *is* my second choice." He waited.

Lionel was full of dread.

"I want the book your employer has. I desire to own the book that was destined to become mine. I think you know it. It's called *The Book of Spawn.*"

Chapter 8

PHOEBE WAS JOINED by several men from Marcus' protective detail. Her cousin, Paolo, was there to introduce them to her, one by one.

"Your mother has asked me to acquaint you with some young gentlemen we employ. Marcus and I have decided you should be able to choose your protection."

She darted a look to her mother, who remained stoic. Phoebe could tell she'd been crying.

"My protection? Not—?"

"Not yet, Daughter," her father interrupted. He turned his attention to Paolo. "Phoebe and her mother have discussed many options with me for her protection."

She held her breath, hoping her father wouldn't betray much of their personal conversation. She was relieved when he stopped.

Paolo continued. "As you know, we've trained these gentlemen, who were former Special Forces Operators, mostly former SEALs."

Phoebe watched as several of the men inhaled, extending their chests out. They were well-built, clean shaven, and none of them gave off any sort of disrespect to her, even accounting for her lack of experience or age. They stared straight ahead. All but one.

The only man in the lineup who looked at her was the dark vamp she'd seen the day of the wedding, the one who shared the protection of Paolo's son, Lucius. As soon as their eyes met, he averted his gaze away.

Phoebe stared longingly at her mother for direction. "How many do I choose? I don't know how to make the selection. Mother—" She ran to her mother's side, whispering, "I wasn't prepared to do this tonight. How am I supposed to do this?"

"No cause for alarm, Phoebe." Freya nodded to the line of men and, without asking for input from her husband, said, "Please pick three."

Paolo gasped.

Her husband added, "Wait, Freya. I don't think Marcus expected—"

But Paolo whisked her away into the garden room off the kitchen where Phoebe could hear their argument. She examined each of the men, noticing tattoos and scars, the size of their muscled arms, how they nervously swallowed or moved their fingers. Though she was very close as she passed by each of them, none made eye contact. She was fascinated with little variations in their form, the fullness of their lips, the color of their eyes, and their scent. Some wore cologne and others smelled of soap and shave cream. One of them had cut himself doing so. Another had a band aid over his third finger knuckle.

She wondered if any of them danced, what they looked like when they played a game of catch or rode a bicycle. She wondered if her mother would ever let her kiss one of them, or perhaps two.

If I had to choose a husband, which one would it be? How could I ever tell? I don't feel the pulling in my gut or my breath getting heavy. The hairs at the back of my neck and my upper arms don't stand out. My mouth isn't parched nor is it overly wet. My heartbeat isn't rapid, and I am not sweating. None of the things that happened before are happening now.

Why?

As she ended her slow perusal of the line of men, she stood before the large dark vamp who was with her that day at the wedding. Noticing she also didn't have a physical reaction to his presence, she asked him,

"And you are Hugh Jett."

"Yes, Miss," he returned softly. He did not meet her gaze.

"But your brother calls you something else."

"Yes, Miss. He often calls me Brother."

"Not that," she said carefully. "He has another first name he calls you. I've heard it."

Some of the men began to snicker and one coughed into his fist.

"Yes, Miss. He sometimes calls me—Huge."

Now three men stepped out of line and coughed, each taking a second to compose themselves before returning to the column. Hugh's eyelids were halfway closed, and Phoebe could see he didn't like being toyed with and was masking being annoyed.

Her father stepped beside her. "Phoebe, this is no game. We are serious about your welfare."

Just as her mother and Paolo returned, Phoebe reached for the hand of the former military man who had the tattoo of a mermaid on his forearm. "I chose you." Then she walked to Hugh and also took his hand. "And I pick Huge."

She turned and surveyed the shocked expression on her mother's face.

"Only two. This mortal for daytime, and one for night."

ARRANGEMENTS WERE MADE for the two of them to report to the villa tomorrow evening, where Samuel would be given a room on the second floor across from Phoebe's, since Hugh had quarters he shared with his brother off site. It would also serve as their base of operation.

They'd be given a tour of the grounds and all the rooms, even the private rooms of the Dominichelli family only servants were allowed in. Preparations were made to go over house security, the necessary vetting of all the household staff, some of their intimate family rules and customs and their upcoming travel plans, including when Phoebe's two brothers would return home.

Before they could complete the instructions, Paolo received a call from his brother and had to return home with his men.

Phoebe didn't miss the whisper her cousin gave to Hugh, which set his face ashen. As he tore from the room, he neglected to say goodbye.

She walked behind her parents as they entered the warm kitchen area. Their cook gave Phoebe another bowl of chicken broth, and she was grateful for her kindness.

"You are better?" her mother asked, sifting her fingers through Phoebe's long hair and attempting to re-tie her ribbon.

She nodded. "No more stomachache. I felt well enough to change my own sheets."

"Wonderful." Freya said as she hugged her. Feeling her forehead, she remarked, "And your fever is down. I think Dr. Luciano was correct in his diagnosis."

Phoebe's father rolled his eyes and then his shoulders.

"What was all that with Marcus? Did you hear?" Freya asked him.

"I wasn't given that information. A family matter. I think it had to do with Hugh's brother."

"That's Lionel. His name is Lionel," whispered Phoebe.

The sound of his name spoken left a pleasant taste in her mouth.

SHE STAYED UP with her mother, working together on hand top-stitching a quilt that was to be presented to another marrying couple. A wedding band quilt, the pattern was that of many concentric and interloping circles. Phoebe preferred square, more balanced patterns of color, but the design was a tradition in her family and would be displayed proudly for generations to come.

"So, just to be clear, I am not picking a husband."

"Correct. Although you could always change your mind."

"I feel nothing for any of them. I don't even know them."

"Friendships between male and female are difficult and sometimes strange. They take years to develop properly sometimes. Best to become friends now, then companions later."

"So you had friends? You know they now call them friends with benefits?" Phoebe felt wicked for making her mother throw down her needlework.

"Honestly, Phoebe. There is a streak in you I'm not pleased to see develop."

"But you've told me I have to remain strong, to learn to defend myself. I don't want to leave my future in someone else's hands, even if it is yours and Father's. Maybe I'm just beginning to experiment with taking over the reins I'll have to wield."

"I accept your apology," Freya retorted with a huff.

Phoebe sighed and squinted to see the edges of fabric she was supposed to follow. Within seconds, her eyes filled with tears.

Though the effects of the attack and her father's infusion were gone, the lingering apprehension remained in her chest that the world had tilted three days ago, and her life would forever be altered. New things would be expected of her—things she'd never encountered. And her family support network was also changing. She began to feel it drifting away. Her place safely embedded between her parents, their only daughter and the special one of the family, was somehow being dislodged.

It was a bit like playing hide-and-seek with the blindfold on. Except this wasn't a child's game any longer. There were life and death consequences to winning or losing.

Over the silence that spread past several minutes, she wondered how it would feel to have a male protector outside her bedroom door. It had always been her father, and now it was going to gradually become some stranger. And both these new protectors were of different species, with backgrounds different than her own. Would they understand her? Or, could she learn from them?

She told her mother she was tired and retreated upstairs. Before entering her bedroom, she opened the small guest room that would be soon occupied. In the daytime, it had a glorious view of her mother's gardens and the rolling vineyards beyond. A writing desk stood in front of the window, with one of the hand-made journals her father liked to make and an antique fountain pen with the Dominichelli crest on the side in gold. She fingered the book, loving the smooth texture of the imported paper her father used.

To her right was the enormous four-poster bed that she'd always coveted, but her mother saved for only special guests.

"It's not a proper bed for a young lady, Phoebe," her mother had said.

The opulent designs over the headboard and the vines carved in relief along the four heavy columns that held the burgundy tapestry canopy had always been a curiosity to her. Even as a small child, she'd loved to trace the figurines and make up stories of what could have been or what might have happened centuries ago.

Some nights, she snuck into the room and slept there, returning to her own chamber before daylight. She dreamt she was the queen of a kingdom that adored her.

Phoebe tore herself away from her childhood fantasies and returned to her room, to the warmth of the well-provisioned fire, the glowing bright white sheets lovingly laid back for her, and the pillows plumped and ready for her head.

The dirty pile of sheets in the corner was gone, but the shawl was laid across an iron grate and was drying by the fireplace, having been washed by hand.

As she scanned the room, she noticed the window had been barred shut, and knew this was intentional. Gone would be her nights staring at the stars or dreaming in the moonlight. These were dangerous days ahead. She'd need a good dose of courage, as well as logic, to figure out the maze that was coming upon her. It was a race that didn't leave her much time to win. Perhaps not nearly enough time.

She slipped into the covers and fell back on the pillows, waiting. She wanted to remember the tranquility of this night, the way it felt to know what she knew, just before she began her next adventure. It was the calm before the storm.

Just as she drifted off to sleep, she touched her lips and felt the word spoken into the warm night air as she uttered it.

"Lionel."

Chapter 9

"Even if he had it, and he's claimed he doesn't, Marcus would never trade that book for us, brother." Lionel had paced for an hour after Salaman left. During that time, Jeb had inspected each rung of the silver bars, top to bottom, still looking for a weakness.

"You're going to worry yourself to death, Lionel. Stop with the pacing. Rest. Save your strength for some useful mental exercise."

"I should have foreseen this, Jeb. I blame myself. And now we have almost no time left. It must be close to dawn. I've failed Marcus, Paolo—all of them."

"Marcus has resources, brother. And he has friends. Look at me." He spread his arms to the side, displaying his stub on one side and his outstretched hand on the other. With difficulty, he stood without using the silver bars for balance, which would have caused another burn he didn't need. He hopped, favoring his left leg, until he could put half his weight on it. "See?"

"You are far from being able to save us, Jeb. You need more time to heal."

"But look at me, Brother. I had given up all hope. I never thought I'd see your face again. Yet here we are. Not like it used to be, but much has changed since you arrived. I can risk feeling hopeful again. You've brought that to me." He lowered his head and wiggled his eyebrows. "I might even hope to find some sardines!"

"God in Heaven, Jeb. We're in the middle of the desert. The Sahara Desert."

"Hope springs eternal. What I'm saying, Brother, is that you've given me hope for a future I'd completely given up on."

"Yes, by placing myself on the altar as a sacrificial lamb."

"No, not sacrificial. You are the object of desire, brother. You were meant to be desired. If it is your last thought, remember that."

Lionel didn't like the direction of the conversation. "I desire to escape, brother. That is all I desire."

"Not that kind of desire, Lionel. I've seen her."

Lionel shot his brother a dangerous look.

"You've met the new Maria. The one you never thought you could have," Jeb whispered, trying to smile. His lips still looked shriveled and taught.

Lionel saw the angelic face of young Maria Monteleone, unchanged by years of mortal decay. He could almost taste her.

"*That* one, Brother. The one you denied yourself once. Who is she?"

"I won't speak of it."

"*Tell* me. If I can feel it in my weakened condition, something is important there."

Finally, Lionel resigned himself to divulge his secret. "She's a Dominichelli, but Maria's a many times great grandmother, so she has Monteleone blood in her veins on her mother's side. I think it's her appearance that has me so haunted."

"Haunted? No, Brother. It isn't a haunting you feel."

"Stop it, Jeb. I've put it out of my mind."

"Like Hell you have. I can feel her all over your insides, Lionel. You carry her scent. Any preternatural being could feel it as well."

Lionel hadn't thought he was thinking that transparently.

"Are you going to allow this evil salesman to steal your right to a life of devoted love?"

"It's blasphemy. We won't discuss it any longer."

"No. Make it the *reason* to survive, Lionel. You'd die to protect Marcus, and Paolo and the wives and children—Lucius and his progeny to come. But her? She is your *reason to live*."

The words hit Lionel in the gut and forced him to sit down hard. He'd been steeling his chest, holding back any emotion, but now the full import of his regret, the years of mourning one woman only to be given a chance with another, became too heavy to bear. He'd only shed tears twice in his life. The first time was when young Maria told him she was going to remain mortal, but that she wanted him as her protector. She had said she did not have any right to ask it of him. He'd cried that night.

The second time was as the seconds of her life slipped away under the stars as he held her frail body before it left on its journey to her Heaven. If she'd but asked him, he'd have given her immortality, but that wasn't her wish. She chose to spend eternity with her husband who had gone before her. Lionel remembered the shock and pain of understanding he had not been chosen.

The hot tears that coursed down his cheeks were heavy, but they fell silently like snow.

Jeb's face appeared in front of him, waking him from his morose dreams. "I said live, Lionel. Think—no, *feel*—the will to live. To find her and to protect her."

As Lionel studied his brother's eyes, he understood that love was stronger than duty or honor. Or sacrifice. He no longer felt it was a betrayal he'd feel guilty over.

As if they'd together conjured it from thin air, several young women covered from head to toe in traditional nomadic garb appeared. Between them there were whispers of an unfamiliar language using a series of tongue clicks. A brown bony hand extended through the bars, dropping several large pieces of cloth at their feet. Jeb sniffed the fabric, wrapping it around his arm, then covering his head. He began swathing his body with more fabric given by other hands.

"Do it, brother," Jeb whispered. "Cover yourself."

One of the women demonstrated the wrapping, extending her arms through the silver to adjust and secure fabric covering their faces everywhere except for their eyes. They were encouraged to stand. Lionel held Jeb's waist, looking above his head and hearing a metal clanging sound as the cage was lifted several feet, enough so that he could bend and get free, pulling Jeb behind him across the floor.

The women whispered and motioned for them to follow.

An opening was made to the outside. Lionel could see the pink dawn fast approaching, and he shook his head. Jeb's body had already tensed up, his new skin becoming sensitive to the light penetrating the fabric. Lionel also felt burning begin at the edges of his eyes where there was no protection.

A cloth was placed over his head, but the pain seemed to come from his insides out as his flesh simmered, sending smoke to his nostrils and making him cough dizzyingly. He felt the press of a woman's body against his and then another, clawing and clutching at him, constricting his movements.

"Jeb," he whispered, unable to see.

"You must trace us home. I will help all I can. I'm—" Jeb's voice ended in a deep muffled moan sounding like he was biting his own arm to keep from screaming.

Lionel again felt the press of bodies and then the firm hand of his brother. He mentally reached low into his own chest and felt his heart muscle expand to near bursting, matching his conscious intention and an inner resolve he'd never felt before. The strength and power of his ancient species filled him.

He bit his lip, tasting blood, and held his breath as young Phoebe's face came to him. He knew he'd be losing consciousness within seconds but concentrated on getting as close to her as possible. If he could build momentum, this force might complete his journey home while unconscious.

In a ball of fire, while encumbered by all the attachments of those who clung to him, he hurled through the sky like a comet.

His strength gave out mere seconds later as he fell into a pool of water, which turned to steam all around him. The weight of the fabric pulled him down as he desperately struggled for air. He began shedding the arms and legs that had hold of him, removing everything that was an impediment. Beneath the water, he could hear his brother scream. He rolled over, dragging Jeb with him until he felt land beneath his feet.

The pink sky was now turning brighter and becoming blue as his skin continued to combust where it came in contact with the light. Olive branches overhead still smoldered with fire. Jeb was dead weight to him. In his weakened condition he could not drag his brother out of the bright light and into shade. He felt skin slough off and burn his palms as he tried.

Dark splotches formed in front of his eyes just before he felt arms pull him under the shoulders and then lift him into a dark box smelling of diesel. He suddenly realized he was in a lorry or van of some kind. The gracious metal clanging doors at last put him into complete darkness.

He hung onto his consciousness long enough to hear someone make the comment, "It's Jeb. He's brought Jeb back from the dead."

LIONEL WOKE TO the awful acrid smell of burning flesh. His flesh. He opened his eyes and could not see a thing. His fingers explored his face and confirmed he'd not lost his eyes. His skin was slippery, covered in salve, which stung and made him tear up.

Carefully, he inhaled as deeply as he could, then let the air out slowly. Judging how much control he had with his own breathing, he was satisfied he was going to survive.

His preternatural sight was coming back, and he discovered he was in his own room, on the Monteleone estate in Tuscany. He could not remember exactly how he'd gotten there, but he was grateful for the first aid he'd received by loving hands.

He swung his legs off the platform bed and felt the cool wooden floor on his bare feet. One arm and shoulder were wrapped in a tight bandage steeped in something that smelled as terrible as the burning flesh. As he stood, his balance returned, and his thigh muscles began to work holding up his solid frame. However long he'd spent in the early morning light had apparently not burned him all the way to the bone. But he still hurt all over.

Hearing coughing in the next room, he pushed aside his bedroom door and entered their tiny living room. Jeb's room was occupied at last. He saw light from under the door and burst through.

Paolo and Marcus were shaken at the sudden action and stood at once. By the light of the single candle flame he could see his brother's frail frame. The bones of his chest rose and fell as Jeb was taking air on his own. His face was a bloody mess of bandages and peeling skin. All the hair had been burned off his head.

Lionel began to sway as the room spun out of control. Darkness overtook him as he felt himself fall to the floor.

Because the back of his head hurt, he knew he was not yet dead.

Chapter 10

THE ENTIRE VILLAGE was abuzz with news that Lionel had returned and brought Jeb with him. Like Lazarus being raised from the dead, the next several days were filled with stories of Lionel's heroics.

Phoebe sat with Hugh in the kitchen while she ate her late supper. He'd been talking non-stop. He was so proud of his brother. It was as if the family had needed some good news and clung to every detail.

"So when will he be fully recovered?" she asked.

"He's recovered now! He's tending to Jeb, but my brothers are starting to argue, which is always a good sign."

Phoebe wondered why, if he was well, Lionel didn't come by the house or check in with Hugh at the little room prepared for her protectors. She hoped she wasn't mistaken. She was sure he'd want to see her.

"Maybe I'll bring him some flowers," she whispered, drifting off into a dreamlike state.

Hugh scrunched up his face like a prune. "Lionel? Flowers?"

"For good health. For speedy recovery."

"If you want that, bring him salve."

"Chicken soup?"

"Phoebe, what's gotten into you? There is nothing you can do. He'll be going back to California with Marcus and Paolo soon, anyway. I'm sure they'll have him busy getting ready for the trip."

She decided she'd waited too long. "Take me there, tonight."

"I'm not allowed. Your parents would never permit that."

"I want to thank him. I never got to properly thank him for my rescue."

"No." Hugh was hugging himself as if cold. "That's a very bad idea. Besides, he was protecting Lucius. Disposing of wayward dark coven vamps, well, we do that all the time. Happening more and more these days."

"Hugh, trace me there."

"That's also forbidden. You heard the doctor's orders. You're not even allowed outside."

"But I'm completely well. I'm eating solid food. I feel—" She suddenly realized her cheeks were flushed and her nipples were once again tender. "I won't be outside. You'll trace me from inside this kitchen to inside your home."

"Not our home."

"The home you were given for your stay."

Hugh cracked his neck and looked upstairs. "Your parents are asleep?"

"They've retired, but I have no idea. We won't be long. Just a quick trip there, and a quick trip back again before anyone misses us."

Hugh was still wrestling with his conscience. Phoebe grabbed his upper arms and pleaded. "Please. A favor for me. One little favor." She held up her thumb and forefinger to demonstrate just how little the favor was. Her smile was warming Hugh's expression.

"I'm going to regret this. I know it for certain."

"Take me," Phoebe sighed, closing her eyes and holding out her arms. She heard Hugh's laughter and spared a glance through her squint.

"Not that way. Here, put your arms around me like we were dancing."

"Which reminds me. Samuel and I are taking dancing lessons. I want you to come as well."

"No. Absolutely not. That's out of the question. As a matter of fact—"

"Okay, okay, no dancing lessons. Let's go."

She wrapped her arms around Hugh's waist and closed her eyes, leaning her head against his chest just beneath his jawline.

The sensation was not unlike being in an elevator. When she opened her eyes, the room was so dark she stumbled into Hugh, who had taken her hand and was leading her into Jeb's bedroom.

Lionel was seated on the bed, placing bandages against Jeb's naked body. His fingers were covered in the greenish salve that had worked so well on her wound. He turned to face her, and she saw him tense, slamming his mouth shut.

"Get her out of here," Lionel shouted. "Right now."

"I know, I know. But the woman is damned convincing. Sorry, I'll just—"

"I came to say thank you to my protector. To the one who helped save my life."

Everyone was stunned until Jeb swore and threw a blanket over his hard-on. "Dammit. I don't want anyone seeing me until I stop looking like a freak!"

Phoebe dropped Hugh's hand and put a palm to her mouth. Tufts of hair were struggling to regrow in patches all over Jeb's scalp. His left arm was missing a forearm and one of his bloody toes was missing.

Something smelled awful, a new sensation for her. She wrinkled up her nose. "Your flesh. When it burns, it smells like fish!"

Jeb began swearing.

Lionel was on her in a flash, closing the door behind him to give his brother privacy. He grabbed her arm and shook her. The pain he'd inflicted was sudden and it scared her. She reflexively slapped him across the face and watched as his eyes flared in anger.

She was angry too. She defiantly yanked herself free from his grip. "You're hurting me. Stop it and let me talk to you."

Lionel turned his back to her. Hugh shrugged, unable to find words.

Phoebe found the courage to step closer to the hulking dark protector and placed her hand on his shoulder blade through the material of his shirt. "Lionel, I mean you no harm. I only wanted to say thank you. I'm happy that your family is reunited." She paused, her hand still rubbing his back. "F-For some reason, I was *called* to see you."

Lionel whipped around, and her hand was left in midair. Until Lionel clasped it in both of his.

"Thank you, dear lady." His eyes were kind, like melted pools of chocolate. She felt the pulse of his heartbeat strong and increasing in speed. She tried to place her palm up to his cheek, but he stopped her.

"It is enough that you come here in person to say thank you."

"Phoebe. Say my name. Phoebe."

He stumbled, at first scanning the ground. "Phoebe," he whispered.

"Lionel," she returned. "Will you come visit with me tomorrow night?"

"I'm not sure that's wise."

"But will you anyway?" She was transfixed by his gentle aura enveloping her like a protective shield. Their fingers had become entwined. As she drank from his eyes, she heard Hugh swear out of the shadows in the corner.

"I-I…"

"Just say yes. Just come for a visit. It's all I'll ask of you tonight. Promise me." She brought his palm to her cheek and drew the answer from him.

"Yes. I'll be there at seven."

HUGH TRACED THEM back to the warm kitchen. "I need a drink."

Phoebe smiled, enjoying the way her skin tingled where Lionel had touched her. She retrieved two goblets from the dining room and poured Hugh a whiskey from her father's rare reserve collection. Then she poured another one for herself.

Hugh downed the liquid and carefully set the crystal glass on the counter. "Not a word. Not to anyone. Not your brothers, your mother or father, not the priest, or to Samuel."

Phoebe was enjoying his squirming. Her heart was filled with joy.

"No worries, Hugh," she said as she touched his cheek.

"Don't." Hugh batted her hand down. "I don't want to be seen anywhere when you touch me, unless I'm lifting you out of a wagon or carriage, or—" He began pacing. "I will rot in Hell for this. I can feel it as sure as I'm standing here."

"Hugh, you only did what I requested. And see, I'm safe. You got me back home safe and sound. No worries. All is forgotten, and no one needs to know."

"But *I'll* know. And Jeb knows what I did as well. I'm going to be discharged from all my duties. I've betrayed the family trust."

"Don't be silly." She ran to the dining room and came back with the whiskey carafe. "More?"

"No. And you shouldn't, either."

"I have to, or I won't sleep."

"Phoebe," Hugh blurted out as he watched her pour another full glass of spirit. "You have to get to bed before anyone in the house discovers you're up. If they ask questions, I won't be able to lie. You know this."

"I do, and I love you for it," she said over her shoulder, feeling the warm glow of the whiskey in her stomach.

"Don't say that. This is no joke."

"Hugh, nothing you can tell me tonight will dampen my mood. I feel positively ancient. I'm the happiest I've ever been." She ran towards him, and he shrank away, pushing his hands out in front for protection.

"Don't *touch* me, Phoebe. I mean it." She could see that Hugh was at a near-panic state.

With her hands on her hips she gave him a stern warning. "I need to talk to him about a couple of things, Hugh. It would have been a tragedy if he left for California without that discussion. That was the urgency. I had to speak to him before he left. That's not so unusual, is it?"

Hugh didn't want to look at her, but he acknowledged her words and even nodded his agreement. "That's the way we'll leave it. God-dammit, you're stubborn!"

His face was lined with worry. She wished she could convince him that all would be well. Now that she'd confirmed some of her deepest secrets, all *would* be well.

It was going to be a bumpy ride, but it wasn't going to take a hundred years, or more, either.

"I'll leave you the bottle while I get to bed. Up to you what happens next. But, from the bottom of my heart, thank you, Hugh." She pressed her palms together as if in prayer, backed out of the room, then danced up the stairs, and shut her door.

Chapter 11

LIONEL HAD TAKEN his shirt off and changed it three times before he removed the tie he had intended to wear and threw it on his bed, leaving his collar open, unbuttoned at the top. He already felt like he had a garrote around his neck.

Jeb leaned against his doorway, stabilizing his frame on a metal crutch.

"Kinda helps you appreciate what Paolo and Marcus went through when they did their ceremony," Jeb whispered.

Lionel turned on him. "There's no fuckin' ceremony. And in about two seconds there will be no meet and greet, either."

Jeb was having trouble keeping a straight face. "What men go through to torture themselves for the women in their lives."

"Stop it, Jeb. Not. Helping."

Lionel asked himself if she was indeed the woman in his life, and the conclusion was a puddle of question marks. The possible fating would have to remain a secret, forever. He thought it prudent to remind his younger brother.

"While I appreciate the pep talk you gave me in North Africa, which also happened to save your backside, I'm not sure I can call her the woman in my life. For me, and you know this,"—He'd pointed to Jeb with two fingers—"there has never been more than one woman in my life. Phoebe is not *her*."

"Go ahead and convince yourself if it makes it easier, Lionel, but I'm not believing a word of it. And for the record, I'll not be speaking about it until it becomes something we can. That I'll give you. But know the truth. You have the fate, which is the joy and the curse of our species, all over you. It's like your head has been reattached to your body, backwards."

Lionel sat on his bed, studying things in his room he'd cherished—things no female had ever seen. Next to his pillow was a miniature painting of the young and healthy Maria Monteleone. It was the first thing he packed when he traveled privately, and the last thing he looked at in the early morning before he turned in for the restorative sleep.

"I am more fearful of today than I was tracing to your location in the Sahara."

"I can see that."

"I harbor a crime deep within my heart. And the repercussions, if it were made public, could also affect you and Hugh."

They shared the private gaze that was so common when one of them or all of them were going off to war or on some dangerous mission. When it was acknowledged that one of them might not survive.

"I don't hold you responsible for things you cannot control. I only hope it happens to me that way."

"It's against everything I've trained for," Lionel stopped him.

"And it's everything a healthy male yearns for. We stand beside you. You'd do it for either of us, Lionel."

He knew his brother was right.

The two brothers embraced and then separated. Lionel kick-started his motorcycle and tore off into the mild, Fall night.

A shopkeeper was doing some nighttime cleanup as he rounded the curve, slowing down to cruise through the back way to the Dominichelli estate. Her colorful roses were still in their stands. He chose yellow ones, hoping they'd be considered safe, allowed the old woman to wrap them in green waxed paper, and stuck them inside his jacket, unzipping the leather just enough to keep the flowers from becoming smashed.

The Dominichelli long, crushed granite driveway filed through groves of olives, bordered by tall Cypress trees in clumps of three every few meters. In the starlit night, the tall silent beings stood witness to the gauntlet he was about to walk. Like judges or executioners, they showed no emotion as he passed on the most important mission of his lifetime. His last mission, if he'd misjudged.

The heavy carved door with the Dominichelli crest swung inside before he appeared on the stoop. He recognized his brother's bike and a couple of vehicles parked in the yard on the right.

He'd met her mother, Freya, for the first time at the wedding that day. She studied him carefully, blocking the doorway. He knew she couldn't hear his thoughts, so he decided to reassure her to ease the pulsing vein at her temple.

"She has called for me. I hope that you were made aware, Madam Dominichelli," he said as he bowed to her, sending the yellow roses up and into his nostrils.

She held her head at a strange angle and was waiting for him to notice she'd extended her hand for him to kiss. He did so with chaste speed.

He retrieved the roses from his jacket and handed them to the beautiful woman, who smiled at the gesture.

"Lovely. Phoebe will love them. Yellow is one of her favorite colors." She delicately pushed them back to his chest. "Come, protector. Or, can I call you Lionel?"

"What do you call Hugh?"

She threw her head back as he followed her through the anteroom and into a small hallway leading to the kitchen, which was their traditional gathering place. She smelled wonderful.

"We call him Huge, but I'm not quite sure he's comfortable with it yet. My daughter said she heard you call him that, and somehow, it just stuck."

Lionel cursed under his breath. His voice broke as he spoke. "Then I suppose you could call me Lionel, ma'am."

"Phoebe, my love, your guest is here," Freya announced.

With the fireplace warming her backside, Phoebe stood in a burgundy frock, wearing a necklace and heart-shaped earrings he recognized immediately as belonging to Maria Monteleone. Hugh stood beside her and gave a nervous grin. He frowned when he noted the roses.

"Miss Phoebe, these are for you."

She was in front of him in a flash, her pink nose buried in the velvet petals. The color reflected in her face and made it seem golden. The tiny earrings on charm hooks sizzled to the rhythm of her heartbeat. She was nervous too.

"Thank you. And here it should be I presenting you a gift, not the other way around. But you are a true hero, aren't you, Lionel? Never seeking anything for himself."

Phoebe's father entered behind him and gave him a slap on the back. "If thanks are being had, please allow me to join the receiving line. You have done this family a great service, and for that we are eternally in your debt."

"I wasn't acting alone. Hugh also—" he began.

"Nonsense," Hugh objected. "You were the one who took notice and disposed of the garbage. All I did was return her to the safety of her family."

Phoebe had placed the flowers in a crystal vase, spreading and tending to them like Maria used to arrange her flowers. Lionel closed his eyes for a second and willed the past to leave him.

Phoebe stood so close to him that the muscles in his thighs began to expand, not to mention another body part that was complaining about being restricted. She began addressing her parents.

"I have something to share." Her hands were clasped inside themselves at her waist as if she was giving a music recital.

The brothers shared the warning gaze that sent both their blood pressures rising and widened their eyes. Hugh looked like he was about to pass out, but very slightly shrugged, telling Lionel he had no idea what was to come.

"I was resistant to it at first," Phoebe continued. "But I've decided to make a change to my security detail. I've taken the trouble to consult Marcus on this just this morning."

Lionel swallowed. Hard. He widened his stance.

"Hugh and I have discussed this as well."

This brought a scowl to Hugh's brows and lips. He avoided Lionel's eyes.

"With Marcus and Hugh's permission, I've decided to switch my detail. I'm inviting Lionel to become my personal protector."

She could not know how much pain he was in. He wanted to shake her as he had last night at the bungalow, to make her come to her senses. In no way was this a safe thing to do.

As she smiled up at him, she took his hand. He took a step back. She giggled softly and grabbed his hand again.

"My mother has advised me it would be prudent to take a husband, until such time as I have found my fated mate," she whispered, lying through her teeth and making him want to put a paw over her mouth to stop her. But he was unable to say or do anything. Her fingers entwined with his in an intimate familiarity that was dangerous to both of them.

"Lionel, if you will allow my request, I am asking you to become my husband until that day comes. To protect me and act on my behalf, not as a paid employee, but as a husband would care for his wife."

This isn't wise, he found himself messaging her, though he knew she couldn't hear him. There was no way that the two species could hear each other.

But will you do it? came her answer. It completely immobilized him.

He looked at the little group, watching the way her chest heaved, breaking free from the low-cut frock she wore. Her hand was moist, and from it came a soothing glow that soon traveled all over his body. Her father's mouth hung open. His eyes were difficult to read. But Freya had clasped her breast and was smiling, tears streaming down her cheeks.

"Well done, Daughter. And look how shy he is. He is the perfect choice."

Lionel could tell Hugh was calculating and re-calculating in his head all the possible scenarios as if he'd arrived at the party late.

"Do you always make your ladies wait, Lionel?" Phoebe purred, pushing the envelope into dangerous territory.

"My ladies? I-I have never been asked to perform this task."

She'd stepped so close that now he could feel the heat of her body. Phoebe was hanging on every word.

"A husband? In name only, of course," Lionel continued.

"Yes, of course!" Salvatore Dominichelli blurted out nervously. "Phoebe is to remain virgin. There will be no consummation of this marriage. You have that correct, my man."

But her eyes challenged him as he saw the battle lines being drawn. He was torn between being the person her parents thought he was, the person Marcus and Paolo and the whole Monteleone clan thought he was, and the male she was becoming to know. The man who was feeding and tending a growing fate that would certainly complicate all their lives. And yet, he found strength in her face.

He suddenly didn't want to share her with the rest of the world.

Her blush told him he'd not been smart and had let his thoughts roam freely between them.

Is this a mistake, dear Phoebe?

All I want to know—and I won't ever be able to sleep again until I do—is, will you do it?

He knew there was only one answer, God help him. He decided it would be good form to call up the God of mortals for extra strength. He went down on one knee.

"With God's help, I will serve you faithfully, will honor your womanhood, and protect you from harm. And I'll perform any and all the tasks that you require with a willing heart."

Out of the corner of his eye, he could see that even Hugh was calling on the God of mortals. His brother closed his eyes, bowed his head, and crossed himself, even though there was no one now who could save them.

Chapter 12

PLANS BEGAN WITHIN hours after it was confirmed by her father that, indeed, Marcus and the rest of his family had approved of the choice to take Lionel as her husband. Most of her friends and family were delighted. Those of the household staff were guarded and shared a level of enthusiasm that seemed tepid at best. Phoebe believed it to be because they still worried for her safety and expected she'd save herself and everyone around her by taking to the turning soon and *then* marry.

The subject had been brought up several times by her mother, and on each occasion, she fended off the arguments with the same resolve she'd had the day she made her decision.

"*After*, Mother. After some time, if I feel a calling to that part of my life, I will do so. In the meantime, could you just tolerate a mere mortal in your household for a bit longer?"

Freya always broke down and agreed with her each time they had the discussion. Phoebe was careful to thank her mother and her father and especially the household staff, on whom the burden of cooking, cleaning and protecting her mortal world fell. It was a world closer to them than that of her parents.

She decided to celebrate her new engagement at her dance studio, where she and Samuel had been learning ballroom and jazz couples dancing. She wanted to bring Lionel as her special guest of honor, but he refused. She had not seen him for two days after the announcement, and she was disappointed. But tonight would be his first night at the villa with them all.

"He's been preparing his things for the move tonight, Phoebe. I've helped Samuel take a room downstairs by the kitchen, since you are now an engaged young woman. Lionel will be here later on. You'll see. My duties are complete, and it's *adios* soon."

"I shall miss you, Huge."

He gave her a careful hug. "We've enjoyed our brief tryst, madam. Haven't we?" he said with a deep bow. He zipped his lips. "It will be our secret."

She was filled with giggles. "Have you ever been in love, Hugh?"

"I don't think there is love for most dark coven members. Not like what you feel, for instance. Most of us submit to a life of service, and there's meaning in that. Love is not a luxury we can afford."

"How sad," she said, touching his cheek.

"You have to stop touching me, lovely Phoebe. We can't be seen as too familiar. Only with your husband."

She thought the comment odd, but let it stand. "So fating would be how it works, then?" she pried.

Hugh turned his head from side to side as if he were helping the pieces of his brain to fit together, to give him a complete picture and a coherent answer. "I think that's mostly true. I'm sure the evil ones have just an animalistic blood lust. They'd eat their wives if it was necessary. Perhaps their children as well."

He shook all over.

"Would it be odd if a dark vamp did fall in love? Or felt the fating?"

"Ah, how clever of you." Hugh ticked his finger at her face. "I'm not going to willingly fall into that silver trap. You'll have to ask him yourself."

"Ask whom?" came the voice of Lionel behind her.

Phoebe ran to Lionel's arms, hitching skirts and wrapping her legs around his hips.

You shouldn't be doing this, Phoebe.

She noted the gruffness in his tone and met it with defiance of her own.

Stop me.

The picture he sent her made her drop to her knees, panting. In the vision, he'd removed her petticoats, slid down her panties, turned her over his knees, and was slapping her bare bottom so hard there were red welts the size of his enormous hands on each cheek.

She pulled herself up and frowned like a spoiled child, rubbing her backside.

"Ow."

Lionel sighed and faced the ceiling. Hugh was nearly doubling over with laughter. "Promise me, brother, you will take your fake honeymoon in a screened and protective space. I don't want to see any of it or know anything about it."

"There will be no honeymoon, Brother. She takes liberties at her home she will regret doing some day." Facing her, he repeated himself. "You should not get comfortable with these games, Phoebe. It's dangerous."

"See? I told you exactly the same," added Hugh.

"Very well." Vowing to get even, she demanded, "When you finish getting situated, there are a few items that require your attention."

Lionel turned his head, but she'd masked everything she could. "I'll be upstairs when you feel in the mood to serve."

As she left the room, she brushed against his thigh with one of her own. When the electricity sparked the inside of her entire right leg, she hitched her breath and gave him a subtle moan.

All she heard at her back was some swearing. She thought Italian was much more pleasing to the ear, told him so telepathically, giggling all the way to the top of the second-floor landing and her bedroom beyond.

She heard cars on the driveway and then happy voices of her brothers returning with her parents. Phoebe ran to overlook downstairs and waved at Rodrigo and Santos. Their return had been delayed due to an emergency at the camp.

Little Santos was only eight and rattled stories to his mother in Italian. Rodrigo stood tall, then ran up to his sister.

"You were missed, Brother," she said as she hugged his bony frame.

His handsome face was partially covered by hair that had grown too long.

"Look at this!" she said, extending his curls out five inches from the sides of his head.

"Mama has already told me I'm to report to cook so I'm not mistaken for one of the coven ruffians." He pondered his well-worn canvas slip-ons. "They came, you know."

"I heard. Did they take anyone?"

He sadly nodded. "Two boys from families in Washington State who had apparently gotten lost in the forest. They found the bloody tracking devices stuffed in their backpacks with their cell phones."

The realities of being mortal were growing heavier with each passing week. Phoebe knew the wedding would be a welcome distraction for the entire Tuscan clans, as well as others from abroad.

"You heard my news, then?"

"Phoebe, I can't believe it. But a dark lord? How could you agree to obey and be companion to anyone but a Golden?"

"You see any eligible Goldens who want me?"

"He *wants* you? They are *allowing* you to do this?"

"No, silly. It's a marriage for protection and convenience. He's allowed certain liberties he wouldn't have as an employee. But the marriage is still for my protection. That's all you have to know."

"I couldn't do it, Phoebe. I just couldn't."

She pulled him to her again and, stroking the top of his head, whispered, "You're only fifteen, Rodrigo. Wait until you turn nineteen. You'll see things differently. Trust me on that."

She followed his skipping form upstairs to the third floor where her parents had their bedchamber. When she peered below, Lionel had just started the ascent with a cardboard box filled with several items. She waited until he passed her on the way to the room across from hers. He stopped in the hallway beyond, turned, and asked for directions. She pointed to the right.

At his doorway, she watched his massive back and upper arms from behind as he bent over the box laid tenderly on the bed, pulling several things out. She knew he sensed her.

"I'm supposed to be keeping an eye on you, not the other way around," he mumbled to his box.

"I find you fun to watch."

"Fun? What is that?" he said, holding an electronic piece of equipment with the cord dangling.

"The opposite of obligation. A freebie."

He had his room set up in less than five minutes.

"You always travel light?" she asked.

He stoked the fireplace with several new pieces of split oak. He washed his hands and then laid his canvas satchel next to the sink. He slowly approached with his head bowed. "I have very few things in this world that I care about. I require little in the way of comforts. I don't like jewelry or adornments. I am a simple man, Phoebe. You'll learn that about me in time."

"Am I—?" She was going to touch his cheek again, but he caught her wrist in mid-air.

"You make it difficult. Please, let me get my bearings first. My primary job is to keep you safe. I can't do that if I don't concentrate."

Her eyes teared up. Perhaps she'd been wrong, and what she was feeling wasn't matched on his side. Or maybe it was her mortality that caused her to be needy. He was warning her, and all she wanted to do was run into the danger of his arms.

It took courage to turn away from him and walk toward her doorway without looking back, until she heard the warm whisky of his voice.

"But the answer to your question, dear Phoebe, is yes. You are one of the things that I care about, a dangerous and pleasurable joy."

When she looked over her shoulder he didn't hide the deep studying perusal, drinking in every contour and feature of her body as if it was the last time he'd see her.

There. You feel how I want you, see you, Phoebe? Is it enough for now?

She knew he was hoping for a de-escalation between them, but her heart wouldn't let that happen. She dropped her arms by her sides.

It is not enough, Lionel. It will never be enough for me.

He reacted like he'd been slapped. He gulped in air and squeezed his hands into fists. She knew he was at the same edge she was, and it took her breath away.

They heard her mother and father were making their way upstairs. She waited for him to break eye contact first, and then swung herself over to the landing, embraced her mother, and kissed her good night. Her parents retired up the stairs, holding hands. Her mother was babbling about something she'd seen today at the market and was not paying attention to her, or to the dark man at her back whose eyes Phoebe could feel, whose hot breath warmed her from ten feet away where he stood at his own doorway, ready to fall into Hell with her, or anything else she might command.

Chapter 13

FEELING HER THOUGHTS was like watching a woman undress behind a frosted glass curtain. Occasionally, he'd catch a tinge of red or a fold of flesh with a charcoal grey shadow separating a smooth surface from a mysterious cavern.

The scent of her arousal seared his nostrils and made him bite his own tongue. He licked his lips and extended his hand so that his fingertips rested on the white flesh of her delicate shoulder. Pinching an errant curl from the back of her neck, he tucked it into the crystal-studded clip clasped there. His palm widened as he traveled the arch of her neck from the top of her blouse until his fingers dove into her hairline.

Phoebe leaned her head back, and he angled forward where he could place his cheek against hers. He inhaled her perfume, dabbed beneath her ear in the fine, delicate hairs. His lips parted as he ran his tongue along the jugular vein and felt the movement of attracted tissue below the surface.

She grabbed his hand and placed it to her breast, mating with his fingers and squeezing her flesh.

"I have never tasted anything so exquisite, Phoebe."

She slid in his arms to press her gentle body against his, pressing her mounds of flesh against his knotted nipples reaching out to her through the cotton of his shirt.

"I have need, Lionel. I can't think."

He held her head, his hands sliding to the graceful arch of her neck to clutch and pull her face to him.

"It is wrong, Phoebe. You know this is wrong." He marveled in the smooth marble of her skin, planting little kisses and hearing his love purring in her ear.

Having charmed her, he was going to pull away and flee to the safety of a locked oak door, but she lowered her chin, placed her fingers at his lips, and whispered, "Then kiss me like an appropriate arranged marriage partner would. Teach me how to be obedient to your will, my future consort, so that I can bloom alongside of you and give you comfort as a good wife should."

The prospect of teaching her about sex, being her first experience, patterning kisses over her body with the ancient mating knowledge, and filling her every orifice with his seed brought down his canines. As their lips met, she opened to him, sucking his tongue deep inside the warm cavern of her mouth. He repeated the kiss, curling to cover her tongue, caressing it under his sharp incisor and pricking the surface to taste her sweet elixir.

Her fingers covered his lips, her hot breath and mouth feeding from him. He clipped his own tongue and spread his blood over her teeth and gums, which made her shudder.

"Too much?" he whispered, running his fingers over the blue vein in her neck, admiring it like the wonder that was her body.

"No. Never too much. I. Need. This." She grabbed his head, deepening her kiss until he could barely breathe.

She pulled him backwards into her room and closed the door behind him. Then she began to disrobe.

"No."

She didn't pay attention and removed her blouse and a lacy undergarment.

"No, Phoebe. I won't be able to stop. We cannot do this."

Her fingers gripped the fabric of his shirt and jerked, popping the buttons all over the floor.

"Phoebe, your desire for me is flattering, but it's dangerous."

"Then do what you can. Do everything you can. Everything a husband is legally required and commanded to do. Serve me, Lionel. Make me whole. Change me forever."

He was losing the will to think. If he did not figure out something and quick, they'd not live to have another encounter.

He lifted her, draping her gently over her bed. By the light of the fireplace, he watched her peach body wracked with need. Her bare breasts stood in stiff peaks, her nipples bright red and bursting with the blood he'd summoned in her body. Seeing the power he had over her emboldened him further. His cock ardently sought redemption, but he denied himself, instead pulling up her skirts and exposing her sex to him.

He slid to the bed with his knees bent, supporting her buttocks in his lap, steadying her hips in an angle for his hungry tongue. He licked the gash between her legs, rubbing his sharp canines over her little bud, nicking it.

Her eyes flew open, and her hands clutched his thighs. Even through his trousers, she'd drawn blood. Her petals fell back on themselves as he pressed his thumb into her opening, then pinched and bled her nub, bringing the blood of her sex to his mouth.

"Yes. Taste me, Lionel."

He bent down, curling his tongue, before sliding it in and around the fleshy plug that held her virginity safely in place. He sucked at the young girl she was, begging her to become his woman with every stroke lovingly delivered.

He righted himself slowly, noticing the pain and satisfaction crossing her face and her desperate need for more. He considered the gray area in which he tread. Pleasuring her orally, he could make her come for him over and over again. Of that he was certain. He could fill her body with such exquisite pleasure she'd never want to be without him. He could give her all that.

But he could not give her the blood bite ritual that would forever alter her trajectory and rob her of her mortal life. He could lead her up to the precipice and then let her fall back into his arms over and over again until she had no strength left, until there was no breath in her body. She was not Maria. She was the woman Maria primed him for, the one he'd waited centuries to claim as his own.

But he'd have to wait a bit longer. He had no right to claim her fully. Not yet.

"Taste me," she moaned.

With hot tears in his eyes, he cried for the fourth time. He licked the delicate, engorged lips of her sex, applied his spittle to the soft bowl between those golden folds and the top of her thigh, then bit deep and hard, robbing her of her blood, but not her virginity nor her mortal life. As her warm elixir traveled over his tongue and down his throat, everything became very clear.

They were indeed a fated pair, but they'd have to wait to assuage what he really needed most, and until he got permission, he'd have to remain unsatisfied.

Someday, he'd claim her for all eternity, for his own.

And nothing would be able to stop him.

Chapter 14

PHOEBE AWOKE ALONE, the sheets of her bed twisted and torn from the mattress. The taste of his sweet kisses still lingered in her mouth. She inhaled, stretching, feeling the power of the fire growing in her soul. She was going to find it difficult to spend the many daylight hours until they could physically be together again.

Selena arrived and put her hand to her mouth at the shocking sight of her ravished bed.

"Miss Phoebe. You had a difficult night?"

Phoebe rolled her head slowly in a careful circle, allowing her hair to hang and cover her laughing face. "Dreams. I had so many wild dreams."

"Your illness has returned then? Are you with fever again?" The young woman felt her forehead and shook her head, no. "Your stomach?" The attendant began to lift her nightgown, and Phoebe pressed it back down.

She didn't even remember putting on the gown, or what time it was when Lionel left her bed. Her petticoats and frock were thrown in a bundle in the corner.

Her bed was re-made, and she was ushered to the shower. "Your mother is waiting for you downstairs. Your future husband has locked himself in his room, but Samuel is awake and taking breakfast with your brothers."

"Thank you. I'll be down shortly."

The soapy bubbles were soothing, until she felt the dull ache at the top of her leg next to her sex. Her fingers traveled over two swollen bumps, once deep puncture wounds now healed but still evident. Her fingers came back without blood. She pressed the delicate tissue, and the pain made her cry out.

She quickly washed her hair, combing it out with the rare oil her father had brought back from one of his visits to North Africa. Her favorite pair of sloppy jeans slipped easily up to her hips and didn't disturb her wounds.

With her light pink lipstick applied to cover the raw red color her lips had become, she tied her hair back in a ponytail, and danced her way downstairs barefoot.

Her brothers were eating waffles and orange juice, as was Samuel, who sat across from them. She joined her family and took a fresh-squeezed glass for herself. Her parents sipped their daily cappuccino and shared a handful of grapes.

Freya was studying her carefully, her eyes boring into her flesh. Phoebe pretended not to notice by changing the subject.

"Samuel, tonight is the dance celebration. Perhaps we could go over to the hall and practice before nightfall?"

"Nothing would please me more," he said with a smile and toasted her with his orange juice.

Salvatore Dominichelli studied a paper in German, one of seven he read each day. Phoebe and her mother's eyes finally met. "Mother, would you like to attend the party this evening?"

"No. Our dancing days are over for right now. But we are going to the Monteleones', to listen to some new recordings Marcus has obtained. Very old and very rare." She lowered her lashes and smiled to her cappuccino. "And I'm going to discuss some arrangements for the wedding with Anne."

Of course, Phoebe thought. Lionel was not a man of means, and he only had bachelor brothers without wives, so there was no one on his side to help with the preparations.

"He likes things simple. Not fancy or ornate."

"Well then," she cleared her throat and returned with, "When he finds a fated female and has daughters of his own, he will understand that the groom has very little say about it. Everything is about the bride."

Samuel gave a puzzled expression, but her brothers kept eating.

PHOEBE AND SAMUEL rode their bicycles over to the studio. A car with two additional protectors followed a distance behind. The fall colors were ripe with oranges and deep burgundy, leaves skittling over the narrow cobblestoned streets.

The dance hall had been an assembly hall during World War II, a place for political speeches and protests, even some bloodshed, or so she was told. Her father confided to her about the olive oil and money he donated to the Italian armies, especially when they returned from losing campaigns. The family had considered moving to the States, but Salvatore was certain the winery and olive groves would be confiscated and never returned to them. They stayed to defend their lands, while appearing to defend the armies of their country and whatever politician they could befriend and trust.

But now the wooden building had been renovated and painted a soft peach. The wood floors inside were sanded and re-finished, making them perfect for dancing. The huge windows let in the most beautiful sunlight by day, showing full moon and stars at night.

A ballet class currently practiced, with youngsters of preschool age, dressed in pink tutus, taught by a skinny nun in a black modern habit. She and Samuel sat quietly and watched their attempts at running, leaping, and assuming various positions. The sister's exacting fingers, tried to make them do what their little limbs could not yet achieve.

The pianist was also the woman who occasionally drove several of the parish priests on their errands. She was a full-time resident at the Catholic school Phoebe had attended.

At last, she smiled in their direction, collected her music, waddled across the floor in lace-up shoes that squeaked. The bevy of young dancers disappeared like petals in the wind as their parents stopped by to pick them up.

Samuel took her hand and pulled her around the dance floor. She threw her head back and allowed the centrifugal force to pull her body, making it feel like she was flying. He broke his hold to turn on the music, and they cavorted back and forth in an Argentinian Tango. He held her close, then pushed her hip away with the palm of his other hand until she ran out of tether and came back to him. He spun her, slid on his knees to her feet, and even worked a cartwheel into the routine.

Phoebe was filled with delight.

"Where did you learn this?"

"I watch television, but my mother had always wanted me to be a dancer," he said, breathing heavily. "She took me everywhere to live shows. I loved them."

"But I can see you took it up. You're a natural."

"Never took lessons until recently, with you. But gymnastics was my gig. And then there was soccer—football as you call it here."

She followed his lead through several other sets and knew that, had she never met Lionel, she could convince herself to want to spend time with a man like this. He was handsome, athletic, and he liked to move and to laugh. He enjoyed exploring, and he smiled often. Life would be uncomplicated with someone like him.

But there would be no passion, no fire. No danger. She wanted to be stalked, hunted, and claimed. If she closed her eyes, she could imagine she was dancing in Lionel's arms.

As the next piece came on, Phoebe recognized the rhythm of a waltz. She assumed her square box arms position and allowed him to glide her across the floor, twirling, leaning back as she did so.

The two American protectors from the car showed up in the doorway.

Samuel shrugged. "I think this means we have to go home."

THE AFTERNOON HOURS dragged on. She attempted to read a book. Then she took a nap by the fireplace downstairs. Samuel studied some maps, then grabbed his computer to order several items online. He called one of the other team members who were readying a trip back to California with Marcus and Paolo and the family.

Phoebe's mother and father left with her brothers for the evening with the Monteleones as the sun was setting. Her heart began to race the deeper blue it got outside, until she heard the distinctive turn of the lock and the heavy iron hinges squeak, indicating Lionel was now awake.

"He's up," she whispered to Samuel. "I'm going to try one more time to get him to come with us."

"Good luck with that. I'm going to shower, so I'll be ready whenever you are."

"Thank you for today. I had a wonderful time."

"Me too." He embraced her, giving her a quick kiss on her cheek.

Phoebe felt the hot eyes of her future husband burning a hole in the back of her neck and what sounded like a growl. She was not surprised to see Lionel standing at the foot of the stairway with his hands made into fists.

"Oh, I'm glad you're awake." She walked carefully towards him, slightly embarrassed by the fantasies dancing in her head she was trying desperately to mask. "Remember about the dance at the hall, Lionel? Samuel and I are going to go this evening. I know you've said no before, but could you please find it in your heart to accompany me—us?"

Samuel was motionless, waiting for Lionel's response.

"How long?" he asked.

Samuel spoke first before Phoebe could. "Not long. An hour, two at the most. She'd like to show you the routines we've worked out."

She heard his soft growl again.

Fingering a buttonhole in his shirt, she whispered, "And I wanted to formally introduce you to the other couples. It's not a large crowd. Why don't you come? I think you'd like it."

Please, Lionel. I would like you there, and I also think it would be smart.

"Okay, but I have no other help tonight, and your parents are gone. Hugh is with Jeb."

"Thank you." Phoebe turned to Samuel. "Go, off with you. Get your shower in, quick!" She clapped her hands, and Samuel shot to the back of the kitchen and disappeared.

She returned to the buttonhole, but he caught her hand before she could slither her errant finger through to touch him.

Phoebe closed her eyes and angled her mouth up towards him. "Give me one of those appropriate, arranged marriage kisses that makes me loose my mind." Her lips created a generous pucker for effect.

He covered her mouth and gave her a taste of his blood, which sent an electric shot down her spine that made her tingle all over.

"You must promise me you'll be careful tonight," he whispered, stroking her cheek with the back of his hand.

"At the dance?"

"Yes, of course, at the dance. Be aware of everything. I don't know these people."

"But I do. Some of them are my turned cousins."

"All the more reason to be careful. No messages, Phoebe. We cannot take any chances we could be overheard."

"I'll try."

He gripped her arm and pulled it harshly to his side. "No. You won't *try*. You will behave."

"I promise I won't make a fool out of either one of us. I'll be your most compliant future wife. I'll do anything you ask me to do, Lionel. Anything."

IT WAS DELICIOUS being next to him in the back seat as Samuel drove her mother's car to the dance hall. She matched the rhythm of his breathing until he whispered, "Stop it."

Dancers had already taken their spots on the floor while several young women set out cookies and a Sangria-like punch based on an old, mulled wine recipe. She presented a cup to Lionel, and he declined.

She finished the warm liquid just in time for a young man to ask her to dance. He was new to the group, an American university student, he said. He held her loosely, not forcing himself at her while they waltzed. Every time he turned her, she saw Lionel's measured stare, noticing everything around her.

Samuel cut in, and they danced their West Coast Swing routine.

One time during the dance, she swung close, barely grazing against Lionel's chest, and heard Lionel growl again. She tossed her head from side to side, rocked her hips to the rhythm of the lively music, and spun beneath Samuel's guidance.

They both clapped, and she scanned the room. Lionel had retreated to a dark corner until a woman dressed in a red poodle skirt pulled up a chair, and sat too close. He backed up discretely, but the woman leaned toward him, talking to him with her chin placed into the palm of her hand, her elbow on the table.

Phoebe decided to join the pair until a firm arm grabbed her around the waist and spun her tight against his muscled frame. Next to her cousin Daniel stood another newcomer. She smelled the distinctive vape of a dark vamp. She shot a worried look at Daniel as the dark vamp spoke.

"My lucky day. The legendary virgin Golden daughter without her protectors." His smile was disingenuous. Phoebe didn't trust him.

Daniel was trying to separate the two of them, but the vamp was much stronger.

"Get off me, boy. When you turn, you will become a man. This beauty desires a real man, don't you, dear Phoebe?"

She was shocked he knew her name, which again indicated Daniel had not been discrete with their family information. The newcomer squeezed her waist between his thumb and fingers, as if he was going to crush her ribs.

In a flutter of wind and dark cloth, Lionel was there. He'd inserted himself hard against the dark vamp, towering above him by several inches as he stepped on the man's foot. Phoebe could hear the crunch of bone and noted the slight sweat forming at the forehead of the newcomer, but he did not scream.

"You have an impending appointment with a physician and a cast maker, my young traveler. You are not welcome here." Lionel took back his foot and scanned the crowd.

"He came with me. We came alone," stuttered Daniel.

"He's my cousin. Daniel," Phoebe hurried.

"You make unwise choices, young Daniel."

"Who—?" Her cousin pointed to Lionel as a crowd began to form around the little circle.

Phoebe inhaled and took Lionel's hand. "He is my husband-to-be, Daniel. This was to be the night I was going to introduce you all to him."

Frowns turned into smiles as the room erupted in spontaneous clapping. Out of the corner of her eye, she noticed the dark guest limp toward the doorway and slither away into the night. She looked up at Lionel, who was following the same line of sight.

Lionel was asked to dance, and he declined repeatedly. Instead, he stood in the middle of the floor, watching Phoebe take partner after partner. He was never more than a handful of feet from her side, which became quite the topic of whispers and tittering laughter. But he remained motionless except for the small steps he needed to take to get closer to her. Occasionally, he glanced out the windows and doorway, but for most of the remaining minutes, he was transfixed watching her and every movement she made.

The trip home was silent. Samuel gave up making small talk and resigned himself to being just the driver.

Inside the kitchen, she gave the young protector a hug and then watched him retire to his room, closing the door behind.

Lionel had checked the doors and windows. She knew they were now alone. What she'd been dreaming of all day was suddenly here.

"Lionel, thank you. I—"

But his lips covered her mouth, then hoisted her in his arms and traced upstairs to his bedroom. The strong scent of his sleep still drifted past her, making her ears buzz and her heart pound. At his back she saw the dark carved four-poster bed that had been in her family for generations.

"Your parents will return soon," he whispered to her. His fingers slipped her blouse over her shoulder, and he kissed her there. Her lips grazed past his rough cheek. She pressed her forehead to the side of his face.

"What are we to do? This is driving me mad."

"I can relieve the pressure, give us both a temporary reprieve until we are assured of being alone again, but there is a limit to my will power, and if I should fail—"

She sucked his lower lip, pressing her mound to his groin. "Then you will take me with you to Hell and back. I want an unbridled kiss with your full heart."

He looked upon her in the firelight. "I promised your mother. I will not break that vow, but understand if I could, I'd fill you with my seed, and I'd demand every ounce of your soul."

"When? Lionel, when? Will it ever happen?"

"On my life, I will find a way to love you to eternity."

"And if I remain human?"

"Eternity for me is the same whether you are turned or human, sweet Phoebe. I've done it once. But this will be the last time."

"Take my wrist and give me yours."

He sliced a thin line of red across his left wrist and placed it to her lips. She drew hard, attempting to increase the size of the wound.

"No. There is much to teach you first. Just enough to start the burn in your belly. Do you feel it? If we are fated, you will burn. And you will bleed."

"I already have, Lionel." She lapped the remaining lifeblood from her lips. "Now, take from me."

She held out her wrist, but he fell to his knees, smoothing both hands up her leg beneath her skirts, and discovered she'd worn no panties. He spread her thighs, then dipped his head beneath the layers of petticoat fabric, laving her swollen bud and drawing her lips under the tip of his canine. He nipped her, which made her shiver from the surprise and the pleasure of it. His thick tongue pressed against the little bumps where he'd wounded her last night. He inhaled and breached her flesh again.

She knew the more their blood mixed, the more she'd demand from him. She hoped they'd create a solution to their mating issue before it was too late.

Minutes later, he was carrying her to her own bed.

This will have to be enough for tonight, my bride.

It will never be enough for me, she told him just before she fell into a deep sleep.

Chapter 15

MARCUS WELCOMED LIONEL to the library for the requested audience.

"What brings you to my home, Lionel? Everything progressing with your plans for the wedding? Any second thoughts or regrets?"

"No, sir. I am good with my decision."

"And my cousin Phoebe, is she doing any better with the manners?"

Lionel smiled to the floor. "That's going to always be a problem."

Marcus laughed. He handed Lionel a tumbler containing legendary whiskey from his extensive collection. The drink was smooth and helped to settle his nerves.

"Then is that why you've come?"

"I fear I need marital advice," Lionel blurted out before he lost his courage altogether.

Marcus uncrossed his legs, set his drink down, and leaned forward in his leather rocker. "You surprise me. Isn't this soon to have marital discord? The wedding is tomorrow."

"She desires that I—do things to her of a sexual nature. I am her husband, but in name only. I understand this. But she is bending the boundaries—and I don't mean to blame her for this, as I feel a strong attraction myself. But I wouldn't be the man you can count on if I didn't inform you of this."

There. It was said. He'd tossed all day and most of his waking time the night before rehearsing over and over what he wanted to tell Marcus.

"I see."

Lionel finished his drink but was not offered another. He didn't want to impose so set the empty goblet down. He'd made another miscalculation. Perhaps this wasn't news Marcus could receive.

"Is it like a fating, then?"

"Well, it couldn't be, could it? I mean, all my life I've been told that's impossible between the species."

"But you feel something? The same as she?"

"I don't think so, no. Could it be that she has what mortals call love? Could it be a real love and not an animalistic fating? Perhaps something purer?"

Marcus paced across the heavily carpeted floor.

"I'm looking first for an explanation before I can decide what to do," Lionel admitted.

"You aren't considering calling everything off, are you?"

"Should I? Tell me honestly, Marcus."

"You would have shamed her. Does her family know of this?"

"We've not violated anything for which we should feel guilty. Perhaps stretched the boundaries a bit. I call it healthy experimentation."

"With a Golden female."

Lionel was disappointed to discover now he was feeling shame for his lack of restraint. "I have not penetrated her. She is and will always be virgin while I'm alive to protect her. No worries there. I haven't broken my vow to her family or to her."

"Who is responsible for instigating the advances?"

Lionel didn't want to answer, so he lied. "I guess that would be me."

Marcus began to laugh again. "Lionel, you are the last of the honest men on this planet. Are you sure a Golden is not in your bloodline?"

"I'm not understanding, sir."

"You just lied to me. I don't believe for a minute you forced her or glammed her or, in any way, began this relationship." He grabbed Lionel's goblet and headed for the minibar. "She's done to you what my mother couldn't bring herself to do."

He didn't think he'd heard Marcus correctly. Did Marcus know of his love for his mother?

"I've never spoken of my feelings for your mother. I assure you, Marcus, nothing inappropriate happened there. I knew my place then, and I know my place now."

"I've not told you everything I know, Lionel. I think both Paolo and I have noticed the chemistry between the two of you. I was not aware of the fondness you and my mother had for each other until I was told at a much older age. When I first saw the now-grown Phoebe, the first person I thought of was you and how it would affect you to meet her."

"Of course. I understand all this."

"But the distance between our species is of great interest to me. And I've done some research."

"I *knew* you'd found the book!" he said as he stood.

"Sit." Marcus handed him the goblet. "You and Paolo are the only people who know, other than Ann and Paolo's wife, Carabella, who led us to the book."

"The Book of Spawn."

"The very one."

He pressed a panel of walnut on the wall, revealing a safe. Marcus dialed the combination and unlocked the dark compartment. He removed a large, ragged book several inches thick and laid it on the table next to Lionel.

"It's an odd book. It doesn't read from front to back, but from the middle to the front, with another story from the middle to the back. It's written in multiple languages, and the passages contain riddles and clues to other passages so that it's nearly impossible to follow sequentially. I've merely scratched the surface, and it reveals more questions than it does answers."

"May I?"

Marcus nodded, allowing Lionel to pick up the book and examine the front and back covers. The canvas was worn along the spine; gold lettering was partially rubbed off. As Lionel held it, he felt a faint heartbeat coming from the pages inside. He looked up at his employer.

"You feel it too?"

Lionel nodded.

"Then this confirms what I'd suspected all along. There is a connection between our families. Your story, our story, stories that are not yet lived are written in this book, I think."

"Why would the evil ones want such a storybook? If it isn't written for them, why value it so highly, or is it just because it's of value to you that they want to possess it?"

"It explains the origins of our species. Ours, yours, and human mortals."

Lionel was confused.

"We share a common bloodline, Lionel. We are branches of the same tree. The tree of life."

Lionel handed the book back to Marcus. "Put it away. I am not to be trusted with this relic. You must never let it leave your side."

Marcus placed the tome back in the safe, turned the knob, then closed the secret door. He dragged a chair so that he could sit knee-to-knee with his employee. Or was he now considered family?

"When I told you at the conclave that you were family, I'd gained this knowledge from the book. I don't know who I can trust. I may not be able to trust members of my own Golden clan. I may need someone who is seemingly on the outside, like you."

"I sensed the pirate had knowledge of our meeting already, Marcus. I told you so when I returned."

"Indeed. But I don't know who. One thing is certain. It isn't you, or Paolo."

"And I don't think it could be Hugh, or Jeb. Jeb was gone when the meeting took place, already the man's prisoner."

"Yes. But for the time being, only the three of us will know a very important secret. If I didn't trust you with the lives of my children, nieces, nephews, my wife, my siblings, and their wives and children, I would keep this from you."

"Keep what?"

"It tells of a people who lived for centuries, and as their culture evolved, they created rules and mores. Subsets of people. Some were satisfied, and some were bored with their lineage. Many no longer thought it was a higher form to live immortally."

"They had perfection, and they rejected it?" Lionel found this hard to believe.

"No, they didn't reject it. They *altered* it."

Lionel sat up straight and finished his drink. He examined the colorful chards cut into the crystal, sending tiny pieces of a rainbow onto the wall and ceiling above. "They created the separation of the species?"

"Yes."

"So who came first?"

"Think about it. They lived forever but wanted to make a finite choice, so they created the dark creatures of your line. To control the new breed, they imposed limitations, so they would be easier to track and to regulate."

"Go on."

"And then they created a species that would never be immortal. Fearing these would take over the earth, they built into their DNA a failsafe date. They would die. They were stripped of their ability to choose between a mortal life and that of our lineage. The Goldens were the ones who messed it all up for everyone."

"They messed with the creation of the perfect being." The logic was undeniable and explained so many things which Lionel had pondered for years.

Marcus scooted his chair closer and grabbed Lionel's hand. "We are distant cousins. All of us. And what that means is there could be intermingling of the species. And perhaps what was done could be undone."

"What do we do with this information, Marcus?"

"For now, we keep it from everyone, especially the evil ones. They must never learn what we three now know. Until we are armed with some kind of way we can find a solution. For everyone."

Chapter 16

PHOEBE'S WEDDING DAY was beginning. Unlike most blushing brides, she could not see her husband until he emerged from his locked room. There would be no wedding in the sunshine with flower petals falling from baskets held by little angels.

But for a man who loved simple things, Lionel's request to be married in the chapel was an odd one. It was the chapel where Marcus had wed Anne, where he had first met his fated female in her mortal form, and first began his long journey to follow her, protect her, and eventually claim her for his own.

She was aware he'd spent some time in the chapel in quiet reflection last night, that he'd started to become interested in her stories about the family she was raised in.

Over the years, it had been said that the dark vamps had no soul, or were prone to evil, yet she had found in Lionel one of the most tender men she'd ever met. His depth of understanding of her kind wasn't as matched to her understanding of him. He dismissed his history as unimportant, and that surprised her.

So the evening wedding was to be a church service, with children's choirs and a chorus of nuns from the local school. There was to be a processional of accolades swinging incense like was done centuries ago. It was an ornate service, with lots of detail. Far from being simple, he had embraced this wedding as if a miracle were to be performed before their eyes.

He'd talked her into traveling back to California soon, so they could live on the Healdsburg Monteleone estate with Marcus and Anne. Phoebe was anxious to live where things were new and not centuries old. And although Lionel would never be able to enjoy it, she looked forward to the California sun.

For now, her mother and father were told none of their plans. The antique vestments were brought out, linens hundreds of years old and only worn on high holy days. Her dress was once worn by Marcus' mother. Her necklace complimented the intricate lace at her bodice. Lionel had insisted he place the heart-shaped earrings on her ears himself and told her he was ready to trace them some place private, so he could have her all to himself. He didn't believe in the superstition about seeing the bride before the wedding.

Nothing was going to dampen her desire for the perfect wedding, or how she was going to demonstrate her love for this man.

The service moved her to tears. By candlelight, he removed her veil and tenderly tucked his fingers beneath her jawline, placing a blood-stained kiss there that she would remember the rest of her days.

The audience was so quiet. The mixture of mortals, dark, and Golden vamps dotted the pews and shed tears together, some with hands entwined.

As they made their exit, he lifted her like he'd done several times in secret, carried her down the aisle. She felt like she was the prize of his life.

As the weeks turned to Christmas, her mother stopped correcting her when she touched his lips in front of the family, and when she smiled at his strong embrace. The marriage between them was turning into something more than an arrangement, and everyone knew it.

She began to believe in miracles.

Afterword

CARMINE MONTELEONE WAITED at the little espresso stand and watched mortals rush children to school as well as scurry to their employers. Mixed in with them were a scattering of pigeons, harvesting crumbs along the cobblestone streets and walkways, dodging pedestrians and cars.

The traveler was larger than he'd imagined, and the gash running diagonally across his face was an unpleasant sight. He was unaccustomed to seeing disfigurement, especially on the face. But mortals could not help their lot in life. Their flesh did not heal fully, replenish itself, nor was it free from the aging process.

The rest of him looked healthy. Carmine would even say glowing. He'd been told of this mortal's appetites, which probably contributed to his robust build and sharp eyes. He was the most dangerous mortal he'd ever met.

"Espresso?" he asked, trying to appear casual.

"Nah."

As the young waitress arrived he ordered a Campari soda over ice. Carmine never understood the fascination with watered down sweet drinks, though this wasn't as sweet as some that mortals craved. The fruit didn't taste real, but then he was not a big fan of the food anyway. He preferred aged heavy spirits that took centuries to ripen in casks as old as he was. But he hid his second disgust of the day.

"I take it your trip was uneventful?" he asked the big man. That's when he noticed his deformed ear, like part of it had been bitten or torn off with teeth that definitely were not mortal.

"Delightful, as a matter of fact. You ever travel on those beautiful planes? They do everything for you except suck your cock. I slept like a baby."

Carmine nodded. He'd never ridden in a plane. When he was a child, before his turning, they hadn't been invented yet.

"What's it like for you?"

Carmine wasn't sure what the question was. "Excuse me?"

"Flying. Or are you lot all about tracing, moving across the globe in seconds or minutes without enjoying any of it? Not like you don't have the time to spare."

The elder Monteleone returned a brittle smile. "It isn't the flying. It's putting my life in the hands of the mortal flying the plane."

"Ah." When his drink was served, he guzzled it halfway down, spilling several pinkish drops on his tunic. "Well, perhaps that will change. I can see your dark brethren becoming pilots."

Carmine could imagine the scene. Pilot and co-pilot who were dark coven vamps, taking turns harvesting the four hundred or so unlucky passengers. It would be messy, he thought.

"You could always trace," the traveler said.

"Not from a pressurized environment. I might turn up melded into a window or an engine blade."

"That's funny. I like your sense of humor, Monteleone. You think on your feet."

Carmine had been merely telling the truth.

"Have you found the girls?" the big man asked.

"Disappeared into thin air. No one has seen any of them."

"Well, there will be time enough for that. After. It will take years to extract my revenge once I do."

Carmine decided to change the subject because he wasn't liking the string of disgusting things he'd been imagining so early in the morning. He'd been in a good mood when he left his villa. Now he felt as wet and helpless as the pigeons at his feet who couldn't find enough food.

"So what's next, Salaman?"

"You get me the book."

"But like I've been telling you, I'm not sure where it is."

The mortal leaned across the table and was not smiling. "I've traveled a fair distance and foregone some more pleasurable pastimes to come here. I expect that you will fulfill your end of the bargain. Otherwise, we have nothing to discuss."

Carmine nearly peed his pants. Although Salaman's promise of riches was a motivating factor for him, his primary motive was to secure the safety of his family, especially his wife and three children and their offspring. He'd grown tired waiting for the Monteleone heads to come up with a foolproof plan to assure everyone's safety. And while most of his relatives were wealthy, his lineage had squandered their wealth, making poor investments. He'd married into his wife's money. So, even though he was a Monteleone, his wife controlled what money they had.

He had to beg for every Euro of spending money.

"I will find it," he said at last, his voice changing an octave.

"And tell me again why you are certain of this?" the traveler demanded.

"Because I've asked Marcus three times, and all three times, I'm sure he's lied to me. He tells me they are working on some leads but won't tell me what they are. He's an honest man, and honest men don't make very good liars."

"We agree on that. That's why I chose you."

Carmine squirmed in his seat, re-crossed his trousers, and took another sip of coffee. His hand shook as he brought the little white porcelain teacup down onto the saucer with a rattle.

Hoping to deflect another unpleasant image, Carmine blurted out, "Have you heard the news about the female you seek?"

Salaman finished his drink. His expression was a challenge. "Humor me."

Carmine was going to enjoy the next few seconds, which might be the only happy ones he'd ever have with this man again. He slowly emptied his little espresso cup and smiled.

"She's taken a husband." He savored the look of shock on the traveler's face.

"And she's—"

"Yes, yes. No fear there. It's a marriage of convenience. It is not a fating, and she's supposed to still be a virgin. She's married him for protection and nothing more, although there are rumors of—"

Salaman grabbed Carmine by the collar and yanked him across the table, oblivious to the passers-by, who shied away and whispered amongst themselves.

"Tell me the name of this unfortunate gentleman who is about to find himself disemboweled."

Carmine removed Salaman's hands like they were dirty rags, straightened up his jacket and shirt underneath, and sat tall. "You know this man."

"Who, dammit?" the traveler demanded, pounding the table and sending silverware to the sidewalk.

"Lionel Jett."

Midnight Bite

Golden Vampires of Tuscany
Book 4

S. Hamil

Chapter 1

L IONEL AWOKE TO the gentle breathing of his new bride, smelling of roses and lavender. His internal clock had roused him. It was dusk and all light from the sun had probably dissipated by now. His world of night, the beginning of his new day, was upon him.

He savored this part of his dark morning. Phoebe's nude body had been restless due to her trying to adjust to his nighttime schedule.

Bless her beautiful mortal heart.

She was trying to be a dutiful, good wife. She'd told him she wanted to live in his world. He wished he could live in hers. He'd give up immortality to stay with her, protect and be a regular husband to her if he could, but the laws of nature wouldn't allow that.

Lionel made the commitment to the Monteleone family centuries ago. He'd also recently made the promise to her parents that he'd not violate her and that he'd use his awesome dark powers to keep their daughter safe from the other dark coven vamps that preyed on the fragile mortal offspring of the Golden Clan. And he also promised to deliver her still a virgin if and when her Golden Vampire fated mate should arrive.

It was an impossible place to be, he thought. Totally impossible. On one hand he had his honor and promise as a dedicated warrior, and on the other, he had his heart. But not only that, he had her heart to think of. And he knew she loved him. She loved him as a mortal, like Maria Monteleone, Marcus' mother, had loved him.

Now he was in between making the same mistake again, to go on loving someone for centuries perhaps, a person he would be happy with for eternity, but someone who was forbidden to him. He'd not experienced a blood mating, but he knew there was that bond there, as sure as he knew that if he stood in the sun, he'd burn up in flames until his life would travel across the land like a delicate piece of black ash. He'd be reduced to that. That same sun that could cause his death was the same sun Phoebe loved and which gave her inspiration. The same sun she was trying to live without.

Her struggle to live in his timetable, his world, was keeping her from her family. It was every bit as hard on her as it was on him.

He'd spent centuries sleeping alone in the middle of the day or sleeping with another hot witch or other dark coven vamp, one of his many paramours. As a newly made dark, he'd enjoyed getting drunk and filled with lust with those of his own kind, seeing most mortal women as if they were a piece of wilted lettuce. None of them, until Maria, appealed to him in any shape or form. He'd always viewed this as a safety feature built into his breed by his maker.

But his unsatisfied experimentation with his new bride he could pleasure, but never mate fully with, and her desire to match his ministrations with those of her own, tendered his heart. The desire to not only love, but protect this fragile creature was overwhelming. If this was some form of fating, well, so be it. If not, he had enough within him forged out of three centuries of control, to be able to stop them both before her hands, her lips and her soft body drove him crazy.

He watched her nestle beside him, cleave to him already in her sleep. Phoebe knew so little about it, yet she was very clearly blooming under the proximity he had to her. His flesh ignited hers. His touch made her shudder in pleasure. His kiss made her lose all sense of who she was or what time she was living in. His vampiric pride took stock of this. His chest grew and his groin came to life. Again.

"Husband, I awaken to the hardness of your member. May I pleasure you?" she whispered.

Lionel had hoped to remain in the middle of this new day erotic fantasy—perhaps for a few minutes longer until she awoke, but that was not to be. Now he had to keep his wits about him, for both of their sakes.

"Phoebe, you wear me out." But as he was waking, she was moving her nude body over him, climbing his hips and purring her sex against his in a dangerous dance. Her nipples were bruised where he'd kissed them so roughly before they'd retired.

"But—" she pulled her hair up to the top of her head. "What can I do? I am drunk with the smell of your body, husband. I feel everything."

Her hand drifted to between them as she wrapped her fingers around his shaft.

He gently pulled her to the side. She turned her back to him and curled in a ball, beginning to cry. His heart broke. He wanted to spoon to her backside but knew that this was only a temporary cruel pleasure and not fair to her.

There were two sides to this situation. As a male vampire he took pride in how overcome she was with the touch and smell of him. As her protector, he was tormented that his desire could send her straight into a fiery early grave. Again, he paused, allowing both sensations to wash over him, stuck in the inaction of indecision, both loving and hating the position they were suffering under. The suffering that was their pleasure.

He lay his palm against the top of her shoulders, extending his fingers into her hair. He clutched her head, demonstrating his strength, while she moaned, attempted to turn to him, yet he held her still.

"If I were to jam your mouth over my cock you would be repulsed. But yes, I desire it."

"I want you to be rough with me, Lionel. Do it. Force me. Please, I want to bring you pleasure."

He allowed his fingers to massage her scalp as he watched her undulating on herself, her hands busy between her legs. He could pretend, yes, he could even smell what it would be like to ram himself into her core and be the only man to taste her virgin blood.

She broke free, her lips wet and plump, wanting him.

"Lionel, I want to taste you again."

He sighed as she attempted to mount him for the second time. He held her above his body, her hair falling down between them. "By all the vampire gods, if there are any, I will bed you, sweet Phoebe, if only in our dreams."

"Take me, husband," she whispered again.

It was so unfair and yet it was so exquisite, her struggle in his arms, this yearning between them.

"Patience, little one," he whispered, kissing her hard.

She moaned and pulled away after he presented her a tiny taste of his blood. "I don't want your patience. I want your cock."

He chuckled. It was everything he'd ever wanted, this fantasy playing out in real time. But it was still a nightmare.

As Phoebe resigned herself and settled back into a deep sleep, he pondered about the days that had recently passed. They'd managed to have some privacy in the locked guest bedroom of her parent's house, but Lionel knew this could not be a permanent solution. Phoebe was not to leave the house, so it meant that all their intimate interactions happened when the family was asleep, and the house was quiet. They had limited communication with her mother, father and brothers, usually during the dinner hour, after dark.

Before the wedding, he'd convinced her to move to California, where they could stay in the Monteleone estate with Marcus and Anne and their toddler, Ian. But Phoebe had been hesitant to just up and leave Tuscany, and her loved ones. She'd never lived anywhere else.

Until now.

He knew that without the added burden of her parents perhaps listening through walls that it might be easier for them to bend or blend the rules between them. This excited as well as worried Lionel. Phoebe's quest for his body had turned into nighttime forages into the war zone of their growing fate. He knew they needed distance, and true privacy. He had the family's trust, but for how much longer, he wasn't certain. Phoebe was growing less and less shy about demonstrating her affection for him in public, and he could feel the eyes on his back.

Tonight, he was going to broach the subject with her parents, over dinner. A small gathering of the clan had been arranged as a going away celebration since Marcus and Anne were leaving the next day.

But for now, he waited, resting with the sounds of his mortal wife breathing next to him, cloaking his naked body with her own sweet-scented flesh. He pretended to feel like the luckiest man in the world: married to the most beautiful Golden female in all of Tuscany, a lineage he honored and had already devoted his life to. A woman who was growing in her desire for him with every kiss, every passing hour of the day or night. He just couldn't imagine that the mortal God in their heaven wouldn't grant him one slice of the happiness he so richly deserved. Hadn't he been a warrior for good? Wasn't this his reward for all his decades of faithful service? Wasn't this what their mortal Bible talked about?

Perhaps Marcus and he could research the Book of Spawn together and find a solution for all of them.

He'd never had hope before. But he knew what love was, and he knew that love was the most healing elixir in the universe. And that held true for all the species.

Inhaling her body-scent one last time, he closed his eyes and willed himself into an erotic dream—something he hoped would be in their future.

Chapter 2

P HOEBE TOOK EXTRA time allowing Lionel to dress her. She loved the feel of his fingers on the back of her neck as he buttoned her 27-button bodice top and applied the layers of gold chain jewelry she'd collected over her young lifespan. It was a tradition in her family to give her one gold chain each birthday, as opposed to a silver chain she wouldn't be able to wear once she turned.

Her mother was slightly irritated with how long it was taking them to dress and had knocked on their bedroom door several times, her displeasure rising.

"Phoebe," her mother barked through the heavy wooden door, "everyone's waiting downstairs. Whatever are you two doing in there?"

Phoebe's willful and happy mood was going to cause an eruption of giggles, but Lionel quickly covered her mouth with his hand, pulling her backwards into his chest. With one arm around her waist and the other clutching her fingers, constraining her from twisting loose, he whispered, "If you wish to be my dessert after dinner then you must behave, young bride."

She stilled to hear the rest of his message, delivered in that grumbly deliverance only he could produce. It was as if her skin desired to mate with his lips and prevent his speech.

"We do not want to upset your mother now do we?"

The rumble of his words sent a sizzle down her spine and quickened her heartbeat and the veins in her upper thigh.

With her new keen sense of hearing, brought on by all the exposure to her new husband and the small tastes of his blood, Phoebe heard her mother sigh. She'd forgotten the woman was still standing there, waiting for an answer that wasn't going to come. Then she heard creaking in the oak flooring as the matriarch of the Dominicelli household descended down the stairway. Phoebe knew her mother was near the breaking point.

All that remained was Lionel's coarse breathing and his muscled frame, warming her from behind, making her ears buzz. Her fingers found his cuff and smoothed over his wrist to touch him flesh on flesh. She felt the thumping of his accelerating pulse.

Lionel's freehand made it up to her chest where he massaged her breasts one at a time, groaning into her ear as he did so. She undulated her backside into his groin area, then slowly turned to face him. The lines of age barely showed on his face though he was centuries older than she. His eyes had always been bright and mischievous, smiling at her, even showing a bit of his sharp canines. But his lips didn't. She knew she could coax a kiss from him and wetted her lips, staring up to him in mock defiance. She reveled in a deep inhale, allowing him to feel the shudder overtaking her entire body at the mere proximity to her fated mate.

"But husband," she whispered. "It is so exciting and reckless to have your hands on me when you dress me. It will be so painful for me to sit there over dinner and talk chitchat about little things—things that don't mean anything at all to me—all the time dreaming of having you unbutton all those 27 buttons, lift my petticoats and drive me insane with your kisses, your tongue and the incantations you speak to me so sweetly. Dinner is a long foreplay to what I hope will be an even longer and deeper sexual encounter."

She was delighted she had flustered him again. She confirmed it by placing her right palm against his growing package and staring deep into his warm brown eyes. She did not fear the pulsing power beneath her hand, nor the forever alteration he could cause. On the contrary, she desired his random acts of abandon and surprise.

He stepped back, and held her at arm's length, growling. Phoebe always thought Lionel was his handsomest when he growled. She felt it all the way to her womb.

"You must stop. This cannot go on," he said through clenched teeth.

"Is it so wrong that I desire you 24/7?"

"Is it wrong to want you so badly I would go to hell shortly for even attempting it? Is it wrong we would be doomed to a life forever in pain and sadness?" His breathing became ragged.

His eyes searched hers back and forth, his hands still on her shoulders holding her at bay. It last, his grip softened, and he allowed her to lean into him and then against his chest. She twined her arms up, her hands slipped around his neck to pull his face to hers, his lips to her mouth as she hungrily kissed him. Her tongue had already started seeking the sharpness of one canine to show surrender in all ways possible.

He suddenly threw her over his shoulder and ran to the bed where he tossed her down. Pressing his body against hers he separated her thighs with his knees. Lifting her petticoats, he began unclasping his britches, and then suddenly stopped.

He traced from her body to the furthest corner of the bedroom, and she felt instantly cold and needy. She could barely see the arch of his back and shoulders as his enormous frame stood in the shadows, bowing, nodding to some god or goddess lurking there. He was in quiet contemplation, one palm to his mouth, fingers lacing over his bottom lip ever so slightly.

At last he turned, and she could see he was near collapse, his face was streaked with grief.

"Dearest Phoebe, must I change my mind and take back my vow? Is this what you want for me? To live in agony?"

"No, husband." Phoebe was beside yourself knowing she caused him real pain. "I feel in my bones and every cell of my body that's the reason there is a path, husband. But as you say the god of vampires or humans or whomever is in control this feeling between us would have mercy on us. We are one in every way except one. And I feel our bond growing stronger every hour every minute of every day."

He dove for the foot of the bed, knelt in front of her, placing his forearms and hands together in prayer. "Please, dear precious wife. Please help me to serve you."

She slid down to straddle his shoulders and arms, her fingers sifting through his hair. She smoothed over his lower lip with her thumbs and once again followed this gesture up with a deepening kiss.

"You do serve me, husband, by bringing me life, the full beating of my heart and the warmth in my womb. It's everything I've always dreamed of. You do serve without any satisfaction for yourself. I want to give you some tiny token of what you give me every day. I want to return the favor. I beg you to let me give myself to you in the one way only a wife can. Your fated mate, Lionel. You know I am this woman. For all eternity I shall be your woman."

He fingered her breast, twisting and pinching her engorged nipple. Moistening his lips, he opened his mouth and moved toward her chest.

She held her breath, in rapt anticipation.

A hard knock at the wooden door interrupted the moment.

"Phoebe!" her father shouted. "This is unacceptable. Come down here at once. And Lionel if you are in there with her you will fulfill your duty and bring my daughter down to dinner and to our guests."

Lionel was at the door, opening it fully to allow Phoebe's father to see that they were indeed dressed and ready to come join the party.

"It is entirely my fault sir. We will be down in seconds."

"Very well."

Lionel didn't bother to close the door but reached for her hand which she took and hung onto until they began their ascent down stairwell. Her father had disappeared into the drawing room amid titters and soft conversation.

She wouldn't let go of Lionel's hand as he attempted to escort her. She protested so loudly that in the end Lionel gave up and traced them both to the foyer. Tracing with her new husband was one of the most exciting things in her daily ritual and she tried to do it repeatedly.

"Phoebe, your mother must wonder why you make me trace from one room to the next," her husband whispered. "It is a small travel. Is it really necessary?"

"It is and I must. I love the feel my arms wrapped around your hard body my husband."

She knew Lionel stifled a sigh when they entered the great room lit by candlelight and filled with a dozen or more house guests. The Monteleones were in their best finery. Marcus and Anne and their baby were in the middle. Paulo and Cara Bella stood to the side as Lucius advanced upon them.

"Great to see you cousin. And Lionel, I hope we get to see each other again soon. I sure will miss you in California."

Phoebe clutched Lionel's hand tightly understanding that they had yet to broach the subject of their leaving for California with her parents.

"That's very kind Lucius," said Lionel. "I too look forward to spending more time with you."

Marcus had a special gleam in his eye as he approached Lionel. "My man, how is married life today?" Her cousin's lopsided grin and wink of the eye lead Phoebe to believe they had had some private conversation about their sexual struggles. She took it as a compliment that Lionel had mentioned this to Marcus. With this small triumph in her belly she extended her hand for Marcus to place a kiss at her fingers.

"No fears cousin. Lionel has been a perfect gentleman in all re-spects. Isn't that correct?" Phoebe teased.

Lionel's brittle smile and sharp eyes told her he was struggling with his answer. She sensed he was about to make a comment when his nostrils flared as he took a deep breath. Before he could speak, she dashed off in search of her mother, leaving Lionel alone with Marcus Monteleone.

"You are finally here Phoebe," her mother mused. Taking stock of her daughter, Mrs. Dominicelli's eyes wandered up and down. She smiled warmly. "I was beginning to think you might be taking dinner in your bedroom—that you were ill."

"I am not, but my stomach is churning. I'm simply starved!" Phoebe quickly shot back. Then she turned to greet the couple standing nearby. "Nice to see you both tonight." Although elder Monteleones well into their second century together, Phoebe was always amazed at how young Athena appeared. She could easily pass for Phoebe's older sister. Carmine had taken the turn much older in life and appeared with a bit of white beard and a middle-aged paunch.

They bowed slightly. "You look ravishing, Phoebe. I have never seen you prettier," gushed Athena. Carmine nodded and grumbled agreement.

Mrs. Dominicelli pulled at Phoebe's arm. "Excuse me, but I must whisk my blushing young bride-daughter away."

As the mother-daughter duo drifted away to a quiet corner, Phoebe could hear her mother's cousin whisper to her husband, "I believe someone else has already done this, if I'm not mistaken."

Phoebe felt tension flare in her mother's body. She didn't let on about her keen hearing, which would have brought on the discussion of boundaries being dangerously crossed with Lionel.

"Stop it, mother. Not such a bad thing that they all know how Lionel and I feel about each other. I do believe it is natural for husband and wife to feel some affection, even in an arranged marriage of convenience."

Her mother whirled around and faced her. With her forehead creased, she spoke in a low grumble. "Phoebe. Why must you make things so difficult? I don't want you to give off the impression that your arrangement boundaries are being breached—that Lionel is violating his obligation to our family."

"But what about me, mother? What about *my* needs?"

Her mother scanned the room behind Phoebe's shoulder looking for someone in particular. She tried but could not feel a telepathic request coming from the woman.

Drilling a look that nearly implanted on the back of Phoebe's skull, matriarch Dominicelli whispered, "Although there have been some who have experimented with the other covens until the time their fated mates arrived, none have done so before the turning." As an afterthought, she added, "And I have never done so, but I have known others who have."

Phoebe could see the graveness of her mother's warning.

"Experimentation is one thing. But I was thinking of your welfare when we agreed to the marriage with Lionel, and, well, we were pleased that he was so sweet with you. His honor has never been questioned. I mean, why share a marriage with someone you can't stand, right?"

"I agree. But that's not—"

"You will know the true difference between a sexual dalliance, a playful romp with someone so attractive as Lionel, and your one true fated mate someday. You would not be able to keep your hands from him. Most newly fated and properly mated couples stay secluded 24/7 for their first years, practically not going out—"

"Mother, listen to me."

"I'm not going to let you tell me you know anything about this, because, dear Phoebe, it hasn't happened yet. You have years and years, and perhaps centuries to learn about all that. Your father and I like that he is pleasing to you. It makes us happy that you are enjoying your duty-bound husband. And you tease him so—" she allowed her palm to swish through the air as if picking up the thought with her fingers and bringing it back down to her chest. "So convincingly, like a sister, or a dear friend. And a dear friend he will always be. He will always look after your children, perhaps. The Monteleones have seen this. They might be agreed to allow him to be in your service once your offspring are born."

"You don't understand—"

Her mother's eyes raged. "Don't test me, Phoebe. I understand perfectly well. You shouldn't underestimate the lengths I will go to keep you safe."

"Caged."

"Unfair. Have you no inkling of the danger you place not only yourself but your brothers in? Other members of the non-turned family? You are connected by a strong bloodline. Don't make the mistake of thinking your life can exist without the protection our entire family can give you. Lionel is there to make sure all the bases are covered."

She wanted to message Lionel, but still was keeping this method of communication secret from her parents, as well as any other eaves-droppers.

But her mother had scared her, fracturing her fragile happy mood.

Chapter 3

LIONEL WATCHED THE interaction between Phoebe and her mother with rapt attention. For a moment, he forgot he'd been carrying on a conversation with Marcus Monteleone and had stopped mid-sentence.

Marcus shuffled his feet, cleared his throat and asked, "Is there something wrong, my friend?"

It was reassuring to hear the helpful tone in Marcus' voice. "I don't believe so. But I really don't understand women and have never found it to be one of my strongest skills." He switched his gaze back to Phoebe, who had turned, giving him a sweet smile. He sensed she wanted to communicate with their telepathy. His slight shake of the head would not be perceptible to Marcus, but he hoped Phoebe would get the message.

"Women," Marcus began. "Life's greatest and most beautiful mysteries. How simple things would be without them. But boring, really." Marcus was careful not to expose his words to general scrutiny as he examined the crowd of partygoers. He added, "You know, Lionel, that if there is ever anything, I can do to help you and your young Phoebe out, all you need do is ask. Even from California, there is much we can do on a moment's notice."

Lionel understood perhaps now was the proper time for his request.

"Marcus, I have a question for you."

"Ask away."

"I am thinking it would be good, and perhaps safer for Phoebe and I to move to California, if it could be arranged. Would this be something you could agree to?"

"Have her parents agreed?"

"Not her parents, no. But Phoebe very much would like to move outside the walls of the family compound, and I personally think it would be healthy for her."

"You think you can protect her just as well in California, then?"

"Yes. Well, you'll have Jeb and Hugh. After almost losing Jeb, I yearn to be close by his side. And there would be safety in numbers. Our bond as made brothers is a strong symbiotic one. It could help with the security of your family as well. But what I'm also asking is that we be under your roof, for a time. Until—"

"You mean until such time as she finds her fated—"

"Yes, or until she takes the turn." Lionel didn't want to mislead Marcus, so he decided not to go further, unless asked.

"I must admit, I was loathe to lose you, friend. I think accommodations can be made within our main home, similar to what you have here. I will discuss it with Anne. But I do agree that it would be best for Phoebe to be under the safety of our secure walls."

"Definitely."

"We can study the great book together, as well, Marcus."

"That I would look forward to."

"But you'd have to convince Freya and her father. I'm not sure they'll agree."

"I believe her mother already suspects something. But having your support might be the exact thing that would make a decision in our favor more likely. I doubt they'd agree to us setting up a household separate from the confines of your villa."

"Consider my support a done deal."

"And you are sure this isn't asking too much, with the new baby?"

"I think Anne would love the company. Perhaps she can help with the other decision as well."

"What decision is that, sir?"

"Convincing Phoebe to take the turning. You know it is the one way she'd truly be protected best."

"She doesn't desire it. But I completely agree, Marcus."

"What is her hesitation then?"

"She fears that she will not like her new situation. I think she's conflicted about joining the Golden vampire dynasty and I think she also has a concern that perhaps it would interfere with—well, the only way to say this Marcus is to tell you."

"Tell me what?"

He realized they'd reached that threshold once crossed before. "She believes she is fated to me or developing a fating toward me."

"And you?"

"Marcus, I have to tell you I do feel there is something between us perhaps a strong mortal sense of what I can only describe as love—I mean, is this mortal love—can this cause such a reaction between us?"

"What are her symptoms?"

He understood that, as part of the vampire breed, she'd not just have her mortal desires, but deep-seated urges she wouldn't understand until her turning. "She feels a fullness in her chest and in her womb." Lionel looked to the floor as if some answers were written there. "I have to say it is exactly as some have described to me as a fating. I have heard your species women discuss it—overheard actually, because no one has ever come to me and said they feel what Phoebe feels. And although I loved your mother, Marcus, I loved her from a mortal state. I don't believe it was a true fating. But Phoebe causes in me—something miraculous. I cannot describe it fully."

Lionel waited for his employer to react, allowing him to study the way his hands tucked in his pockets and his bowing to the floor. He owed Marcus and his family his life as well as the lives of his brothers. Yet, he owed them so much more. He had to ask the question that had been burning in his soul.

"Marcus, I consider you more than my employer and you know this. Does this mean that perhaps I am unqualified to be Phoebe's husband? Will you tell me true?"

"Lionel, if I felt you were unqualified, I never would've allowed the marriage. It is what Phoebe has requested, what she wants, and I do believe what she needs. But be careful. There are dark forces out there who would undo our family's generations and centuries of history. Young Phoebe is right in the middle of it. You are best suited to protect her and that's why nothing you could tell me would make me think you were *un*qualified. You are the one best equipped to see to her safety. And although I hesitate to say this to you, I do believe it is your destiny."

AT LAST, THE partygoers left and while the staff finished cleaning up, Lionel and Phoebe sat with her parents in the living room. The younger children had all been put to bed over two hours ago. Salvatore Dominicelli poured him an aged brandy, offering a tumbler to his wife, but not to Phoebe. She was seated next to her mother, while her father sat in an overstuffed chair adjacent Lionel.

"We shall miss them, just as I'm sure you'll miss your brothers, Lionel," whispered Mr. Dominicelli to his glass. He appeared tired, as did his wife. "We thank you for your sacrifice."

That gave Lionel the opening he needed. He noted it was as if it had been orchestrated for the opportunity. He glanced at Phoebe, who was stifling some telepathic message he was glad she had control over. Such misbehavior would complicate the request he had to make of her parents. He inhaled and decided the time had come.

"Sir, I won't lie. It will indeed be difficult to be without my brothers. And I have always had a keen fondness for Marcus and Paolo, developed over these past centuries, as you know. They have become family to me and have treated me as one of their own. As you both have," he said.

"Thank you, Lionel," gushed Freya.

Phoebe's chest was heaving, red blotches mottling her skin, enhanced by the low-cut bodice with the twenty-seven buttons down her back holding everything deliciously in place. He cursed to himself at his thoughts.

Which made Phoebe smile.

As their mortal staff left the compound, the four were at last truly alone. The family's other protector was outside the building with several other mortal security personnel. All four of them could hear the squawking of their radios. At no time was the entire household asleep. Several security members were always vigilant 24/7.

"Phoebe and I have talked at length, and I have spoken to Marcus this evening. We both agree it might be in Phoebe's best interest if she were to accompany the Monteleones to California."

"What?" her father gasped. "Surely you are not asking that she be sent away?"

"If you will hear me out, sir, I hope you will see the logic of my argument. I understand this is perhaps sudden, but it is something Phoebe and I have discussed for several weeks."

Freya Dominicelli grabbed Phoebe's hand and stared into her eyes, worry lines crossing her forehead and her lips turned down in a sad frown.

"Listen to him, mother," said Phoebe, her voice soft and lilting.

"First, from a purely risk-averse standpoint, it isn't wise for all your offspring to remain in the same household. If the staff were overcome, the dark covens could wipe out your entire lineage, as they have done to several other families here in Tuscany, and elsewhere. And Marcus agrees with me that there is a much smaller concentration of these dark lords in the United States than in Italy, where they seem to be multiplying daily. They are *making* their own kind. I believe they are making armies of their coven."

"We've heard such talk, but I have to say, Lionel, Freya and I have dismissed it as fear mongering," barked Salvatore Dominicelli.

"Well, here's perhaps something else to consider. Marcus agrees with me that it would be good for Phoebe to be in the company of Anne, who was once herself human, and has taken the change, and borne a child to Marcus. The experience of the turning, accepting her new lifestyle, is fresh in Anne's history. She could be the perfect teacher—to prepare Phoebe for her new duties, some day." Lionel's voice trailed off at the suggestion that perhaps she'd find another to become her fated husband, someone of the Golden clan.

He could feel his bride's defiance, prickling the hairs on his forearms and thighs, making his mouth parched. He had to force himself not to look at her. He knew the only instruction Phoebe wanted was something only he could satisfy.

"You'd agree to the turning, daughter?" asked her father.

"No, I haven't agreed. I'm still obtaining information about what is involved in maintaining a true vampire wife's lifestyle."

Her eyes were half-lidded but showed fire inside which spurred Lionel's libido. He needed to get this negotiation concluded quickly as his urge to be alone again with Phoebe was eclipsing his decorum.

"But you will consider it?" her father persisted.

Lionel wanted to whisk her away in his arms when his bride demurely whispered, "Yes, father. It is a decision I'm becoming more and more warmed to. I understand my capacity to love will be greatly enhanced by the turning. I want to live my life to the fullest, and I no longer want to be a burden to you, or to my husband here."

His burden was bulging between his legs as he fully understood her double meaning. He could smell her arousal and it was driving him insane.

Freya Dominicelli lifted her hand from Phoebe's lap and sat erect. "Well, I'd like a few days to get used to the idea of my daughter being gone from my household. And I'd like to make sure with Marcus that this is indeed a welcomed invitation."

"Of course, dear lady," Lionel mused.

"What's to consider? You can go with them as they travel, or you can visit very soon. We could both go," said her father.

"And leave the boys unprotected?" she asked.

"They were at camp. We let them go places with their protection nearly every week."

"Not across the ocean, where tracing is problematic these days, husband."

"If it makes the decision any clearer for you, Mrs. Dominicelli, we would be residing inside the Monteleone compound, inside Marcus and Anne's villa, not in a separate dwelling, much the same as the arrangement here," informed Lionel. He waited for what he'd hoped would be open permission.

He didn't have to wait long.

"Let them go, Freya. You have to let her go some day. The older she becomes, the more and more dangerous it is for her to remain here. This is, I think, the perfect solution. It would give her space to make this decision without our meddling. And under Marcus' protection, as well as with the loving devotion we have here with Lionel, she is far better off than here with us and the boys." He turned to face Lionel straight on. "I give my permission."

All eyes were on Freya, who had begun to cry. Phoebe embraced her.

"No one could keep me safer than Lionel, and with Marcus and his family, and the Jett brothers, surely you see it's the perfect solution." She kissed her mother on the cheek. "And, it's what I want."

Chapter 4

PHOEBE FELT LIKE she nearly had the powers of tracing as she flew up the stairway with urgency to the privacy of their bedroom. The deep musky blast of scent coming from her husband's bed made her dizzy, all while every cell in her body soaked in the lovely aura. She heard his heavy footsteps behind her, heard the door close and the lock turn with delicious metal on metal scraping.

Then she felt his warm body standing still behind her. She turned toward him.

His eyes were warm pools of molten chocolate framed between lines on his flesh that would never form into deep creases as most men aged. He'd remain just the same as he appeared today, no matter the centuries.

His breathing was deep, and his head slightly turned to one side. His lips formed a smirk, the end on his right side turning upward as if protecting a deep scar resident there.

He was in every way the lover, the husband, the boyfriend and the dark man she dreamed about all throughout her young years. And now in the flesh, his body dangerously close to hers, she understood the full meaning of adulthood, of her responsibilities to her family. She understood the power of his desire to not only love her and protect her but to save her in every way possible.

Lionel's raspy voice barely whispered a question. "Say something Phoebe. Say anything." He stepped toward her, their torsos touching, pressing against one another, feeling the rhythm of their steady breathing.

"I know what love is Lionel and I know that I now share the heritage of generations of mortal vampire maidens still unturned but willing to accept the bed of their husbands for all eternity. I cannot understand the decision anyone would make to not turn to be with their true mate at night. You know this is what I desire, Lionel."

He placed his hands beneath her jaw and kissed her. Her attempts to deepen the kiss were rebuffed. He held her head steady, not allowing her to approach further.

"I know. I feel it too Phoebe. God help me, I feel it too."

He caught several strands of hair covering her forehead and eyes and tucked them in gently behind her ears. His four fingers traced the line around her lips he studied as if knowing their future.

"Phoebe, it is a miracle your parents have agreed to your request. But there's one thing I need to express to you, my sweetheart. We cannot consummate this marriage no matter how this feeling grows. If we do, it will muck up all of the research I must perform to find a way for us to be together… it will make it impossible for that to occur. Do you understand this?"

"I do. But I'm not sure I can do what you request."

She allowed her arms to come up to his neck tugging on the curls at the back of his skull, sifting and searching, her spirit full of hope, and letting him feel the heavy thump of her heart. She wished she could give him so much more.

His quick growl surprised her. Then his enormous hands grabbed and pressed her buttocks into his groin lifting her from the ground. As she entangled her legs around his hips her arms rose up to the ceiling. He buried his mouth in the side of her neck.

She angled her head to the side, luxuriating in the feel of this course beard as he opened his mouth, his tongue grazing over her vein as her pulse quickened. Instead of plunging to drink from her he applied gentle suction, making her ears buzz and her sex quiver. It left her breathless.

His nibbling kisses traced upward until he bit her earlobe, coaxing and playing with it with his tongue. She heard the familiar words expressed that were centuries old, the ancient incantations in Latin. Then came something in Italian and something otherworldly. The clicks of this tongue made her shudder. Raspy and sounding like the wind in some lonely desert that lasted for a thousand years and didn't understand his words.

But her body understood their meaning.

"I desire you more Phoebe than all the universe. Just know that I will have you some day. Please understand it is something I need and shall have before I die."

She arched back to stare at him. "Die?" She was not sure where this was coming from. "Lionel, what are you saying?"

He focused on her lips as she covered his to stop him from speaking further as if it was blasphemy for him to do so. She demanded an answer. Her fingertips felt him smile beneath their touch as if he was soaking up every cell of her body. Pressing and kneading her rear again, his powerful hands undulated her up and down over his package.

His eyes became mischievous. "I love to see you lust for me my sweet. It is exquisite."

"But it's unfair it's—it's so unfair Lionel."

"You forget that I have lived for over 300 years my dear. What is waiting for one more day, one night or one month?"

"But I don't want to wait. Don't you understand? I need to be mated to you."

"And you are, little one. Very nearly in every way, except one."

A hush fell between them. The world was completely silent.

"You know what I mean. Don't play with me. Be my teacher, my lover, my husband."

His gentle laughter both soothed and aggravated her mood at the same time. She wanted to shout, to slap him or do something to shake the current impasse between them. She was about to launch into another protest when he interrupted her gently, his voice wooing and glamming her into submission. She felt her will soften as she fell against him.

"Phoebe, my princess. Understand that if Marcus and I are successful in our research we could have centuries together. We will be loving for perhaps thousands of years. Why risk it all for our impatience? For just one night together? That is why I enjoy your desire for me. I know even if there isn't a God of vampires that your God—your mortal God—your Golden clan God of love—whatever I am to call him, will grant me—will grant *us* his favor someday. I know it just as certain as I know I live now and will live forever."

"Hold me tight tonight Lionel. And then peel these layers between our bodies off me. Love me as if I were your fated vampire female. Perhaps take me to the edge right up to the very edge when I can take no more. Will you take me there, husband? Make it almost too close? Make it dangerous please?"

"I will my lady. I will do my very best to do your bidding tonight. And tomorrow we will fly to California with the Monteleones if we can. We must wait until the evening, but we will go with them. And we shall start our new adventure together and build our lives of forever in California, my sweet."

He let go of her rear allowing her to slide down the front of him, her arms still entwined about his neck. Then he abruptly picked her up, crossed the room in one long stride and gently lay her back on the large carved bed. All the stories, the visions and dreams of her childhood were carved into the relief of that four-poster bed. She saw the ceiling fabric stretched across the arch of the woodwork come alive with village scenes of people moving about town as if it was a home movie.

He slipped her bodice over her shoulders, pulling it down onto her forearms. Meticulously, he pulled the fabric down further uncovering her breasts. With her arms bound to her sides by her own clothing, he bent his head and encircled her aching nipples with his tongue, rubbing his sharp incisor across the deep pink of her areolas. Her fingers and hands could do nothing but clutch the sides of her skirts as he tenderly kissed between her breasts, then beneath them, and slowly covered her upper body with them. He savored her flesh, moving up to her neck again, and under her chin before he claimed her mouth again. She gave herself in tender submission begging him for more with her kisses in response. She answered his deep-seated growls with her own desperate moans.

His knees straddled the sides of her hips as he pulled her up to sitting position and fingered the twenty-seven buttons of her bodice top releasing her to the coldness of the night. He tossed it to the ground, then unbuttoned her skirt and slid it down her thighs. As he arched up to look down upon her, she was left helpless and wanting, aching for his touch, with only red panties to defend her womanhood.

She covered her breasts with her hands and slid up to the top of the massive bed, burying her head in the pillows. His muscled body worked to disrobe quickly, until he was fully naked.

Distracted by something, he looked up to the window, traced across the room and closed the massive shutters, locking them in safely, barricading whatever was in the night from their private, intimate space. At last he came to her.

She slipped beneath the coverlet and he joined her there. His hands roamed her body, kissing her navel, nibbling the sides of her hips and then raising her knee up over his shoulder. He kissed her sex, his tongue plunging in deep. The gentle undulation pleasured her. She felt the wave of his glam as she watched him feed between her legs. Her fingers sorted through the top of his head.

Slowly, he pressed her right thigh to the side placing his fingers at her opening and pressed her bud with his thumb. She arched up, calling his name, her fingers covering his hand, and then reaching out to him, begging for his tongue inside her again. His canine pricked the soft tissues there. She felt the gentle tug on her labia as he sucked and repaired his tender violation, his tongue massaging her stiff little pulsing bud.

She never wanted it to end.

He was a careful lover, his ministrations growing stronger with the pressure applied. With his fingers and expert mouth, he would take her just to the threshold of orgasm and then gently allow her to cool. Each time she got closer and closer to her peak, until finally she exploded, feeling the fire of his love deep within her body.

As her body shuddered its final release, he drew from her everything she had until at last she was fully drained. Her limp sweating body felt like a rag doll. She was unable to even move her arms. She wrapped her legs around his and, safely tucked in his arms, gently drifted off to a place she'd never been.

And that's the last she remembered of that evening—the evening before he would take her to California. She had a fleeting thought just before she dozed off, wondering if the vineyards in the hills in California would smell like the beloved hills and valleys of Tuscany where she'd spent her entire life. She wondered if in the blushing grapes and green vineyards of Sonoma County that there would be a place for this almost vampire mortal woman who wanted nothing more than to take her place and be his woman in every way possible. Would they find a new life there? Would she be able to withstand the days or weeks or months of waiting? And was their fating foretold in the famous documents Lionel said he was researching with Marcus?

There was so much to understand, so much to know. They had, as Lionel had reminded her, centuries to do so. But only if she took the turning.

She knew that decision was coming upon her quickly as she heard the morning birds chirping in the beginning of the new morning. She saw Lionel walking with her and the full light of day, hand in hand, strolling through the bucolic valley floor of her new home. She hoped the dreams ruminating in her heart and in her head where half as good as what her future would look like in real time.

Chapter 5

LIONEL KNEW DUSK was upon them but allowed Phoebe to continue to sleep. He remembered that she'd tossed and turned, and he wondered if she'd gotten up to wander the house, since it was her last few hours there.

Her pink aura was nestled amongst the untucked and strangely positioned comforters from their limited and one-sided lovemaking in the early morning hours before sunrise. With the evening fast approaching, he also recalled being awakened during his sleep by sounds of the household staff moving things inside the large villa. There was a part of him that wanted to help the preparations.

He was careful not to disturb Phoebe while he dressed and went downstairs in search of her parents.

Mr. Dominicelli was drinking a brandy in his office and offered him one.

"I thank you sir. But no. My day is just beginning."

"Understood. Well I'm afraid Freya has not slept last night after you retired and today has been napping off and on."

"Is your wife ill, sir?"

"No. Just impossible to satisfy. Fidgeting with everything. Speaking in sentences she doesn't finish. That sort of thing. Distracted."

"Phoebe has been restless as well. Perhaps they talked some when I was sleeping?"

"Doubt it. Freya would have told me." Mr. Dominicelli finished his Brandy and poured himself another. "You sure?" he said as he held the decanter up.

"Thank you, sir. I'm fine."

Phoebe's father watched the last of the servants leave through the front door, each carrying cardboard packing boxes. "This has been quite a day. She's exhausted. She's anxious."

"I understand. Only natural. I think we all are on edge a bit. What about you?"

The Golden lord leaned toward him, staring straight with his dark eyes looking for something deep within his heart. "I am really of no consequence these days, Lionel. I live to protect her, and the boys, now that you are here. But this is so important to Freya. I know you understand that she loves her daughter dearly. I fear she would no longer want to remain alive if anything were to happen to dear Phoebe."

"I feel for her. Of course I do."

"I apologize if this is adding a burden on you, Lionel, but I must request that Phoebe check in with Freya. Every day, if she can."

"You can count on it, sir. I will see to it that she does this. And thank you again sir for your trust and faith in me."

Dominicelli put his arm on Lionel's shoulder. "It is getting to be so dangerous everywhere. Such strange times."

"Sir? Has there been something new that I am not aware of?"

"I have received information from one of our family protectors that there is a new stranger in Tuscany who has traveled far and is keenly interested in our particular branch of the family. I'm told he has a fondness for young Golden females."

"A dark vampire?"

"We believe he could be, or he could be mortal. We understand that he has been living off the Golden blood of young virgins."

Lionel stiffened with this new knowledge that perhaps the evil one he left in the desert might have somehow survived and come to do harm. Perhaps get even.

"This disturbs me as well. He walks in the light of day?"

"Yes. We believe he does. I have asked for more information. It could be mortal gossip, so I hesitate to question too sharply for fear I will attract attention. But we intend to discover further what his intentions are after you and Phoebe leave Tuscany and are safely ensconced in California. But just know this. I have been warned."

"Warned? And by whom?"

"Our staff discusses things with those working for other families. It seems he is someone known to those of our kind who live in tribes in the deserts of North Africa. I'm sure you've heard the rumors and who knows whether any of this is true."

"Yes. When I was learning about The Family ways, Maria Monteleone used to tell me the stories coming from India and elsewhere. Before I knew my place, they frightened me. She told me of sultans and great kings who kept vampires as pets in silver cages and harvested their blood."

"Yes. Sickening creatures, although I have never met them. We used to tell the children those gothic tales so they would not wander without their protection details. I must admit, Phoebe and her brothers spent some sleepless nights awakening from nightmares."

Dominicelli then went into detail explaining to Lionel everything that had taken place that day. He showed him the trunks and boxes being prepared and loaded for shipping. The staff had packed up all of Phoebe's personal things, including furniture and personal items that they knew as a family she would want to take with them to California. It was all arranged to be shipped in the huge steel shipping container and would take approximately two weeks to arrive.

"We have left certain items that Phoebe may want to take with her on the airplane. Have you traveled by plane before, Lionel?" Her father squinted, looking up to him.

"Yes. I have accompanied Monteleone children ever since airplanes were invented, though it was always the family's preference that we traced the children to places they were traveling when young Marcus and Paolo were growing up, as was the only option available at that time. But I've flown with Lucius many times. Now that things are more complicated, airline travel is their new preference."

"You encounter other species on those flights?"

"Indeed, I did. The dark coven lords actually enjoy traveling in large groups with mortals. Unfortunately, that's how they meet women, find their prey. Disgusting."

"I am not so sure I could have your stomach for the plane rides.

Frankly, I'm more afraid of mortals, with all the problems they've been having on planes. Who knows whom one can trust?"

"I see your point. However, Marcus has secured the entire manifest, so there won't be anyone traveling he has not approved, sir."

Mr. Dominicelli went on as if he'd not heard Lionel. "Knowing what I know of mortals, as well as all the crazy dark covens out there, I'm just not convinced it's safe. I mean, can you imagine someone wanting to end themselves by driving a plane into a building? And they are *young* mortals." He shuddered.

Lionel agreed that he greatly preferred the company of other Goldens, even some other dark covens, covens created by birth and not turned, like he and his brothers, than he did to large groups of mortals.

"Very good. At least this way you will travel with Marcus and Paolo and Anne and the baby, as well as the rest of the family and loyal staff on a secure plane. And that I think is smart. But be aware, Phoebe may be completely frightened of the experience."

Lionel had a private chuckle. If only her father knew how fearless his daughter was in the bedroom, perhaps he'd be less concerned. But of course, this would have to remain private.

Lionel left her father, and returned to his chambers, finding Phoebe in the shower. He spoke to her through the glass door even though she begged him to join her. Her soapy breasts pressed against the glass and made him instantly hard. He changed the subject to get his mind off those orbs, or they'd miss their flight tonight.

"Your father has given me all the travel arrangements. You have about two hours to gather your things. They've left you several items in your room to search through and pack—items they thought perhaps you'd like on the airplane and others to send along later."

"Just a quick shower. A little tease? Some good clean fun?"

She hadn't heard a word he'd said.

"As much as I'd like to, my love, I cannot dally. There is still much to do."

She rinsed quickly and then stepped out of the shower dripping wet, luscious in her fresh lavender soap scent, making her young mortal body as soft as the finest silk. Her exquisite form pulsed with passion and promise. It made him feel right as a new day. He handed her a towel reluctantly and she pressed it to her flesh her eyes dancing and teasing him, waiting for him to regret his abstention.

He placed a kiss on her cheek and growled when she dropped the towel to the floor.

"Don't tempt me Phoebe." His voice strained, images of the two of them fucking like rabbits difficult to remove from his head.

"Oh, naughty, husband!" she blushed.

He cursed under his breath and tried to think of worms and dirt, which didn't help this time. He saw himself fucking her in the garden, covered in the black loamy soil of their future home in California.

By way of sweet reprimand, she stepped on his feet and wrapped her arms around his neck. "I live to tempt you, dear husband. I hope to do it the rest of our lives. It is simply the most joyful thing of my day. My really pretty place."

And she was certainly his. How far he'd come, from dark brooding coven vampire to thinking about pretty things and what he could do to make her scream his name and want to dig her nails in his backside.

"You know this." She continued her insufferable penetration of his mind space. It was almost cruel, all the ways he wanted to get even with her. He knew what he could shove in her mouth to make her stop wiggling and talking, urging him on so.

Her eyes flashed, eyebrows raised. "Yes! We can do that. I'll swallow you whole," she said between her fresh rosy lips, her tiny pink tongue darting around her white teeth, looking for a playmate.

"Dammit," he said to himself and traced to the hallway.

LIONEL CHECKED TRUNKS that had been stowed in a large shipping container that had been delivered to the front yard. He even helped to lift crates with some of the gloved helpers. He checked the manifest, noting that over half of the trunks contained Phoebe's clothing and toiletry items as well as small lamps and tables from her bedroom. He could smell her scent everywhere in the container.

He also noted that a trunk of items were packed for a household staff who was planning to travel with them. He wanted to check this out further with her father.

He caught the elder Dominicelli as he was headed toward his rooms.

"Excuse me sir. It appears there is a household staff who will be accompanying us?"

"Yes, Lionel. Elena has decided to join you in California. She's known Phoebe since she was a young girl. I think it will help with the transition."

"Very well. And when will she join us, or shall we pick her up on the way to the airport?"

"She is at the Monteleone's right now and will be traveling with them to the airport. Her younger sister will be tending to Anne and the new baby and has just been chosen for that service. You and Phoebe will meet up with them at the airport."

"Very well sir. I think we are nearly ready. I've checked everything. My own needs can be stowed in a small satchel I can take on the plane."

"Nothing more? After all these decades you've not accumulated anything for yourself?"

"I've been given many wonderful things in my lifetime of service, but none of them are material. My job and my life have never been about *things*, but people, duty and protection."

"Honorable. My only regret that you're leaving is that I've so much to learn about you, Lionel."

"I'm not going anywhere, sir. We have centuries to catch up." Then he remembered one of Phoebe's requests. "Your daughter has told me she wishes that I trace, but if she's bringing too much on her person, I'm not sure it's a wise decision."

The elder Monteleone he chuckled. "The women in this family are fabulous, Lionel. But they are far too attached to their clothing and jewelry. It seems that as the centuries go, they collect more and more stuff. I don't have to tell you that there is protocol. You are staying in someone else's home. I am not entirely sure that Marcus and Anne will appreciate all the items Phoebe wishes to send. But you have my permission to trace with her, if you desire it."

"Thank you. And, I understand. I believe my first test as protector-husband might be to part Phoebe from some of her things. We will make sure anything of long-standing family heirloom quality will be returned to you here in Tuscany, sir."

"Very well." Dominicelli frowned and looked both ways up and down the hallway. "Freya has decided not to say goodbye," he whispered. "She's already gone to bed. I hope you will let Phoebe know?"

Lionel shook her father's hand, placing his other hand on top "You have been a wonderful father. I continue your legacy, in quite the same vein." Lionel hoped Mr. Dominicelli didn't pick up on his little lie. "I also promise that I will not rest until Phoebe has traveled safely into the arms of her fated mate and future husband. As much as it may pain me to say it, what I do will be a labor of love. I love your daughter sir. You and Freya understand this, I'm sure. But I will willingly send her on to her true destiny when the time comes. Rest assured, this will happen."

Lionel witnessed her father tear up just before he closed the door behind him. He knew that if the roles were reversed, Lionel would never be able to give his daughter up. Possibly ever.

He'd been telling the truth about finding Phoebe's fated mate because he felt certain somehow that would mean he would be the chosen one.

THE AIRPORT WAS a busy scene. Lionel escorted Phoebe to the terminal desk where they presented their oversized bags to the attendant. Marcus stepped forward when a minor kerfuffle arose with the airline employee. He paid the overage in cash generously. He justified this and argued with the employee that since so many of their family didn't have baggage, and since they'd secured the entire plane, that Lionel and Phoebe's baggage should be disregarded. With an added glamming for good measure, all was made well.

At last they all made their way on board the plane. The entire First Class section was taken up with the Monteleone family and a few trusted staff. Everyone else sat in the rear of the plane. Hugh had offered his seat to someone else so he could sit in the middle of several of the young household mortal women. He settled in with a drink and began using his powers to line up future liaisons. Jeb was seated behind Lionel and Phoebe and rolled his eyes each time he turned to watch the smooth moves of his brother. Peals of laughter filled the rear of the plane. Hugh was going to be the flight entertainment, nestled in the middle of nearly twenty young women, from kitchen staff to housemaids. He was getting drunk and dosing them with glam.

"So, are you excited, brother?" Jeb asked over the back of the leather seat.

Lionel wasn't sure whether he would call it excitement or apprehension. Phoebe was watching his face as well as watching through the window at all the activity below. Before he could answer, the flight attendant announced the plane was ready for takeoff.

She leaned into him and whispered, "So, if something goes wrong, would you have time to rescue me? I mean, have you ever traced from an airplane before, Lionel?" Her eyes were wide, innocent, and he just wanted to watch her think.

"We've speculated that it could be done. But I wouldn't call it recreational, like the times I trace us downstairs, or out into the middle of the forest, Phoebe. With all the moving parts of the plane," he continued as the jet engines kicked in and at last the plane darted forward down the runway, "we've sometimes speculated that upon landing we might take with us a piece of the plane, perhaps embedded in an inconvenient spot."

"Really?"

He couldn't hold back the laughter that was making him feel like he'd explode. "I have no idea, sweetheart. You wanna do it just for fun? Is that what you're saying?" He grabbed her wrist. "Come on, let's do it!"

She balked, deep worry lines forming at the top of her nose, as the force of the plane pressed her back against the seat. She clutched his hand, her fingers threading between his. "I'm scared."

He knew exactly what to do, and it didn't involve giving her some erotic fantasy that would eliminate her fear state of mind. Turning to face her head-on, he blew into her nose, sending wisps of hair up off her forehead as her eyes grew heavy and she fell into a deep sleep. He gazed upon her young face for several minutes before he sent a message to Jeb. He was confident none of the Monteleones would be able to hear him.

'I sincerely hope this will happen to you some day, Jeb.'

'Not a chance. I've already experienced enough of the things you two do in the shower, and in that upper room at her parent's house to know that it's just not my thing. Right now, I am rather enjoying being a spectator.'

'You scoundrel. Have you no shame?'

'Better than Netflix. Less expensive, too. A little too much pink for my tastes, though.'

'Now I'm seriously considering how unwise it was to save your sorry ass.'

He decided to will himself to sleep as well, thinking of all the wonderful things he could show his new bride in California. He would need to arrange a protector to show her the area during daylight hours. He knew from pictures he'd seen, that she'd love it. He wanted to show her everything he and his brothers loved about living there.

The flight was long and as they headed into New York and approached the eastern seaboard, the sun was just beginning to cross over the horizon. The brothers and several other protectors of the dark clan were housed in a hotel suite to sleep the day. The nonstop flight from New York to San Francisco would commence at dusk that evening.

When the final leg of the trip was completed, a long line of black limousines were waiting for them at the arrival gate. Although he showed Phoebe the lights of San Francisco and the Golden Gate bridge, he knew that somehow he would manage to get her an escort so she could see the beauty of the bridge and the sailboats on the bay during the light of day.

The two-hour limo ride was unremarkable, and she slept resting against him.

At last they traveled through the trendy town of Healdsburg in the early morning hours before sunrise. Lionel remembered well their evenings of partying and chasing mortal women when he and his brothers got an infrequent evening off. No doubt Jeb and Hugh would enjoy those times again.

Several new buildings had been built and the town was preparing for some kind of a festival with colorful banners that arched across the Square. Phoebe's face had been plastered to the window asking questions about various things she saw as the limo sped up along its way through the Dry Creek Valley. Meandering up through legendary vineyards, at last the massive Monteleone estate could be seen. It was flooded with light, like a castle perched on the hill, a crowning jewel at the top of the moon-lit vineyards and valley floor below.

"Oh my God I can't believe I'm in California. Look at this place Lionel. It's amazing!" Phoebe was like a little girl again, trying to take it all in.

"Yes sweetheart. It does rival anything you've ever seen in Tuscany. I think it is the most beautiful villa in the whole world. I've spent centuries studying places and I have to tell you that I think you will be very very happy here."

The bags and trunks were unloaded by the staff who greeted Marcus at his own doorway. He hugged and spoke to each of them, one by one. Several of them fawned over the sleeping toddler in Anne's arms. At last, Marcus greeted his new visitors and welcomed them inside.

"Phoebe, I want you to understand that this home is now your home. You may stay here as long as you wish. With the extra protections we have within these walls you should feel quite safe and comfortable. We have lined the entire property with special electronica, and we have a full-time staff that does nothing but see to it that all of our mortal family is protected."

Phoebe ran into the foyer, twirled like a schoolgirl, and shouted her expression of joy. She turned to Marcus.

"Where is our room?" she asked.

"Upstairs." Marcus pointed, and gave Lionel a wink.

Anne stepped forward, holding baby Ian. "Sweet cousin let me show you. It's on the second floor. And you have the entire wing to yourselves. There is a kitchen staff who can serve you day or night. You have your own living room. You may entertain as you wish. And your bedroom is twice the size of the room you had in your mother's home."

Phoebe turned to Lionel, putting her hands on his shoulders. "Trace me there immediately please, husband."

Jeb and Hugh behind him chuckled. Marcus shrugged his shoulders. Anne smiled, jostling the baby. Lionel stepped back, bowed to Phoebe, and then stepped into her embrace. He traced the two of them to the landing above.

Looking down upon the family who had begun congregating in the foyer, he reveled in their laughter.

Phoebe tore down the hallway, and Lionel ran behind her to catch up. "This is so cool!" she said as she grabbed Lionel's hand.

He wanted to trace her to the bedroom where he could strip the clothes off her body. The urge had gotten stronger over the past 24 hours. But he was also enjoying her total mirth at being in California, sharing part of his intimate history with him at the beautiful estate.

The large oak doors opened almost on command. Lionel remembered that there were sensors on every doorway which could be turned off and on manually. This was to ensure that whomever stayed there, if they had a mortal companion, wouldn't be compromised in the middle of a restorative sleep.

The windows had remained open, but Lionel knew they'd be automatically closed at the full of nighttime to give the occupants full protection. A large bed in the center of the room was covered with a gold tapestry fabric which matched the fabric on the settee placed in front of the window ledge and the adjacent one that was its mate. There was a walk-in closet that was nearly as large as the old bedroom in the Dominicelli estate. Phoebe turned around in circles looking at the size and scope of it, preening in front of the floor-to-ceiling mirror.

"Do you think your clothes will fit here, or do you think we'll have to rent a storage facility?" he asked. Phoebe ran to him and again wrapped her arms around his torso and squeezed.

"Oh my God Lionel this is just amazing. I have never dreamed I would live in such a space. Who was this created for?"

"At the time this villa was built, Marcus had not met Anne. This wing was added so that they could entertain Anne's mortal family who would come to visit. Our species and your Golden species mingle with mortals frequently as you know. Precautions have to be taken. This is a special wing designated for special guests."

Lionel walked to the window and heard the mechanism begin to warm up. Soon they would be protected from the rest of the world so he could have his required sleep. As the shutters closed and Phoebe joined him at his side, he kissed the top of her head.

"Time for bed my love. I am actually feeling rather weary from the long trip, which is unusual for me. But let's retire. Tomorrow, I'm going to arrange for your protection so Marcus can give you a tour of the winery during the light of day. It's beautiful from what I've seen from moving pictures. I've only seen it by moonlight, of course. But I'd like you to know what it looks like as I cannot join you.

"I wish you could join us."

"No fears, Phoebe. My life is shielded in darkness. You are my princess of the night."

He tenderly touched her cheek and planted a kiss there.

"What's your first priority?"

"After you are settled, I hope to schedule some study sessions with Marcus. The two of us have much to discuss. As soon as he's available, of course. We are guests, Phoebe. But I hope to discover things which will be illuminating for our situation."

He took his new bride in his arms and together they snuggled into bed. The sheets were scented with lavender. Or maybe it was the lavender that he tasted and smelled in the ridges and folds a Phoebe's young moist skin. She thanked him with her body and kissed him every place she explored.

"I've listened to my heart Lionel. And I can be patient. I will be patient for you. For us. For the life we have together. I want this life now. I want you to explore how we can be together. I think it's time for me to take my turning."

He was tired but not too tired to pleasure her several times, leaving her damp, wrung out and lifeless in his arms, knowing that she'd been fully satisfied. He knew he could continue this with the alternative means available to him for some time. But he dreamt of the days he could take that bite and join her. Until then, he felt loved. He knew it was something more than what he had experienced with Maria Monteleone.

And that it was growing, entangling him further through a one-way portal he hoped would lead to centuries of love and rearing a family. And even if it didn't lead there, it was the path he would willingly take, couldn't help but take.

There *had* to be a God of Vampires out there somewhere who would protect him and his Golden bride.

Chapter 6

THE HEAVYSET PRIEST traveled down the gravel driveway, his leather sandals crunching over the delicious pale peach-colored crushed stones. Stopping at the gate with the enormous scripted M for Monteleone, the family crest of all the Goldens in this region, he was surprised to find it unlocked.

The hinges on the twenty-foot high iron gate squeaked like the sounds of a cat in heat. The Villa appeared quiet. One garden worker was trimming hedges to the right and didn't look up as the priest passed him.

The priest exchanged the wicker basket from his right to his left arm. Inside, it contained white envelopes with notes on their outside scrolled in Latin. The basket was flat on the bottom and sprinkled amongst the contents were several petals from camellias and roses he had collected on his short journey from town.

He came upon the stone stoop, grasping one heavy metal ring that hung from a carved lion's head on each door. He banged it loudly against the metal plate beneath it. Stepping back several paces, he waited.

Inside the house he could hear footsteps and muffled voices, including several children. He smiled. He'd waited to greet the family he thought about all evening.

As the door opened, he was presented with the face of a perfect cherub. She would've made the perfect angel model Michelangelo would have enjoyed painting. She must've been no more than five years old. Her hair was mussed, with its unruliness confined to a long braid in delicious colors of caramel floating down her back.

"May I help you, sir?" the cherub asked of him.

The priest was delighted. Inspired. In spite of his dark soul, he actually felt pleasure, mirth, and expectation of something special. He knew he had found pay dirt.

"And you must be Isabella is that correct?" he asked the child.

"Yes, sir I am," the child answered.

From the distance he could hear someone yelling, "Isabella!"

"I'm here mummy. I'm at the door. There is a priest here who wants to speak to us."

"A priest?"

In the next instant, the priest laid eyes on one of the most beautiful women he had ever seen. Her brown chestnut hair fell around her shoulders and upper arms, cascading in the shimmering sunlight. Her lips were full and painted bright red. Her dark eyes were enhanced by thick brows. With her porcelain skin and plump lips, she was not in need of any makeup to be one of the most stunning women in the world.

Carmine's beauty.

This was the woman the elder Monteleone had chased halfway around the world for until she agreed to marry him. Carmine had taken the turning late, never meeting his fated mate, and then found the lovely young Athena. As her namesake hinted, she was thought to be descended from a Greek goddess of an ancient lineage. The priest remembered the story. It was emblazoned on his soul. And, just as he suspected, this woman would bear many beautiful children. Virgin females. A bountiful harvest for one so dark as he.

"Priest, what is your mission?" The lovely lady asked him.

He could feel effects of her spice perfume burning the insides of his nostrils. A fully actualized Golden vampire female was too powerful for him. But just as little dogs often fight great Danes, it didn't lessen his ardor or his desire to compete with a man who had claimed this woman for his bed. Carmine might have to pay an awful price. This woman would have to be caged, since she would never submit willingly. Or perhaps she would give herself up to him to save her daughters. The priest was calculating all of this. He was getting more and more excited by the minute.

"I am father Luigi Salvatore, Madame." The priest bowed as low as his mortal knees and hips would lower. He was feeling his age, and the length between his last Golden feeding. As he raised his torso, he allowed his eyes to wander from the soft fleshy cheeks of the cherub up behind her to the luscious mother draped in red and purple silks. She had a small waist, demurely disguised behind layers of fabric, a large bust and an upper chest that was heaving, making the red garnet and gold necklace undulate deliciously. The large stone's facets gleamed in the morning sun.

"Yes, father. What can I do for you?"

If he hadn't already selected a target, she would have made the perfect mate/sex slave.

"I am here collecting contributions for the poor, Madame. In these envelopes I have names of certain families who have sick or missing children. They are not of your cast Madame. They are poor, paupers in our congregation."

The priest held the basket high in front of her face showing the white envelopes.

"Would you do me the honor of picking one to become your charity?"

She examined the basket and then her eyes returned to the priest's face. She squinted. "I see, but father Salvatore, I do not recognize you from our parish."

"Ah, yes, yes. Madame, I am on a special mission to visit all of the great families in Tuscany, especially those in the Monteleone dynasty. We have come to understand in our order that the Monteleones are very generous with the poor mortals that live among them."

At the word *mortal* Mrs. Monteleone's eyebrows raised. She put her hand in front of her daughter's eyes and with the other pushed the basket back into the priest's chest. She whisked little Isabella behind, calling to someone from the inside remove the child.

She closed the door behind her as she stepped out onto the stoop, dangerously close to the priest's protruding gut.

"I have sensed your aura sir. I do not believe you are a priest. Before I get my protectors to throw you out, I would ask that you leave our premises. And please consider yourself dis-invited."

"Tell your husband the traveler has returned to pick up the item your husband has secured for me."

With that, he turned, carrying his basket over his right arm, his fingers laced together as if in prayer or contemplation. Whistling, he walked through the metal gate, slowly closing it behind him and peered back through the black iron bars at the woman standing in her doorway. Did she know that she had just had an encounter with her dark future?

IT DIDN'T TAKE Carmine Monteleone long to find the traveler. He sat at the same little table and sipped his espresso carefully as the Golden Lord approached him. His lips were tightened into a thin line. His gait was determined. His jaw set. The look in his eyes to anyone else on the planet would be worrisome. But the traveler was used to anger, especially fits of anger from Golden males. And he had an ace up his sleeve that Carmine Monteleone would soon discover.

"Just what was this personal visit to my home all about, traveler? I am furious with this display. We never agreed it would be this way. Your lack of decorum will never be tolerated."

"I'm sorry Carmine. You seem to misunderstand the fact that I am avidly seeking the *Book of Spawn*. I have talked about it for years now. I have discussed it with you every single time we've gotten together."

"But this is irresponsible, appearing before my wife and my child. I never gave approval for this."

"I never gave you permission to take so long to find this book. I understand that you may perhaps have conflicted loyalties. I'm here to merely remind you that you have an obligation to me from which you cannot retreat." He leaned forward for emphasis. "Let's put it this way, if you retreat it will be terrible for you and bloody for your family. I have run across people of your ilk over the past several years. I have learned to be ruthless. And I have learned that I always get my way, given that I apply the correct pressure in the correct locations."

Carmen looked like his eyes were going to explode from his skull.

His already round face was bulbous. The blue vein at the side of his neck pulsed dangerously. The priest didn't want to make a comment of it because it was actually something he liked watching. It could make his forward motion less impeded if Carmen were out of the way. Especially if it were a natural death. And if he continued to scare and put pressure on poor old Carmine Monteleone, he would certainly not come under scrutiny at the old vamp's passing.

The man was breathing hard and doing a decent job of calming himself down. "I apologize."

The traveler could see it was one of the most difficult things Carmine had ever said in his life. He noted that the elder man was just as soft in his resolve as he was in his belly.

"That's a good start Carmine. You have my attention."

Monteleone studied the pigeons, the people passing by, the traffic on the tiny village road. He was assessing his location, his vulnerability, the time of day, and the traveler knew he was examining his insides as well. He sensed the gentleman would soon have to use the potty.

The traveler sat back, crossed his arms and watched him squirm.

"My family is all that I live far. As you know, since you've probably studied me for years before approaching me about the book, I am not in a very strong position to negotiate."

"Duly noted. And thank you for being bright about it. There's nothing worse than negotiating with someone who doesn't understand they don't have a freaking leg to stand on."

Carmine's face sported a sarcastic grin as his right eye twitched. He blinked several times and then focused back on the traveler's hands folded at the table in front of him. Then the man spoke.

"As I have said before, my life is rather precarious. Our wealth is gone. I wish no pleasures for myself, although in younger years I strayed from our vampire ways, and that's how you found me no doubt. But I love my wife and my children. My daughters."

"Yes. Your daughters. That is also noted. You have exceptionally beautiful daughters. You have an exceptionally beautiful wife. And it would be a shame if some harm were to come to any of them." The traveler placed his palm against his heart and continued, "I certainly do not desire to cause you pain. But if I don't get my way Carmine, trust me, you will feel it, perhaps not as strongly as the females in your family would, but you would feel it in your heart. I do not wish to cause you that pain. Trust me."

Carmine's smirk was dangerous, but the traveler knew he was subdued and would do his bidding. The problem was he wasn't sure if he could accomplish the goals he had set for the man. Other things were at play and he was uncomfortable, almost angry about the situation they were now facing. His streak of defiance made him unreliable. There were others who had congregated interest in the book. If Salaman did not get it in time, his position would be vulnerable. And he didn't like being vulnerable.

"So, the news of the book then?"

Carmine examined his lap, grumbled, and then looked back up and tried to act brave. The traveler had never liked weak men and now he was beginning to see some of the legendary Monteleone bravery even though the man's lower lip was quivering, and a tear shed down one cheek.

"I'm afraid I have some bad news, traveler. I am informed that instead of waiting, the entire Monteleone clan has left for America. More specifically, California. Lionel Jett and his new bride Phoebe Dominicelli are with the group now. I have not heard yet, but I believe they traveled by plane. And they should be there now."

"So, what you were saying Carmine is that the book is with them?"

"Oh, I would guess so. Unfortunately, yes."

It didn't make sense to the traveler that Marcus and Paulo would leave the precious documents behind. And he knew that the plans had been to move back to California all along. And, in a way, it made his plans easier with the mere fact that Phoebe had gone with them. There were two things in the world he lusted for and he would die trying to obtain either one. Of first importance was the *Book of Spawn*. But the other, nearly as important to him, was capturing Phoebe.

"This doesn't have to be a problem, Carmine. You can perhaps go follow them to California and retrieve the book for me."

"But I am not sure I will be welcomed."

"I don't think that should be a sufficient impediment. Do I have to remind you for the third time today that the health and safety of your wife and daughters is dependent on this mission?"

The two men stared back at each other. The traveler's skin was beginning to itch, indicating he needed to feed. As a mortal, if he didn't feed soon, he would start aging dramatically. And even if he were to be replenished, he would never reverse the aging process. He was going to need to find a host very soon.

"I need a favor first. I desire a meal. I do desire female Goldens. Do you know of such a person right now who is unaccompanied by a protector?"

Carmine reared back, his face filled with fright. "You cannot make me do this. I will not sacrifice anyone I know. I will not sacrifice my family. Surely you are not thinking along those lines?" Deep worry had created gashes in the bridge above his nose.

"Calm down please. I'm not asking to host half your family. Surely you have enemies. Surely your wife has someone she would like to get rid of? A rival of yours in business? Someone who has a luscious Golden daughter? All I require is one for today. And then if I can be on my way, if I have a direct contact with the book, I shall return to North Africa."

Carmine was shaking his head as he leaned over the table, bracing himself against what he knew he could not face. The traveler saw that he was very close to a full mental collapse, and if this occurred, he'd be no further use.

His captive pleaded, "Why can't you host off of a mortal woman? I can think of several that would be available. Do you have to murder them, or can they be willing subjects for a time perhaps two? That I can arrange."

"A prostitute? No, Carmine, only an unturned virgin female will give me the blood power I require. Otherwise the nourishment is adequate but won't sustain me for more than a few hours—perhaps minutes even. I will have to feed less if I can feed on quality. That way,

I don't have to feed with quantity."

The traveler didn't want to mention the aging process or what would happen if he didn't find a Golden female. He decided his accomplice didn't need to have that information at the present time.

"But if you insist on not choosing one then perhaps I'll choose for myself."

"You stay away from my family, traveler. I have no reason to live if anyone in my family is harmed."

"This I understand fully, and I will abide, for now." A new idea came into his head. "Carmine, wasn't there a banker you especially disliked, I believe he was your cousin, and he threatened to take away the estate if the arrearages were not paid? Does the gentleman have any daughters?"

Carmine angled his head, thinking about this. "He has four. Four girls, and one son."

"Then he has several spares. And he owes you a favor. If it weren't for him, you might never have met me. Surely that deserves a good turn?"

The traveler watched the older Monteleone Golden vampire retreat. He'd given the man two days to get an invite to the Monteleones in California. That would give him enough time to follow-up on the name he'd been provided, obtain nourishment, and then catch up on his sleep.

He wondered what would happen if some day mortals reigned supreme over their vampire brethren. He knew that the *Book of Spawn* was his ticket to not only immortality but a way of controlling the most powerful families in the world. He knew that if he could eradicate them the world might be a safer place for people like him. And he knew the world would be doomed for the dark coven lords. As long as enough of them were allowed to remain, mortals like himself could rule the world.

Carmine Monteleone was a useful idiot in that plan. He didn't know that he was contributing to the assured destruction of all the Golden vampires. It wasn't important that he see the train coming. It was just important that the train came at all, and that he lived to see the balance of power shift.

He held his palm on the table, fingers splayed to the sides. It was time for the immortals of the world to understand their days were numbered. It was time for the *mortals* of the world to embrace their immortality.

Chapter 7

PHOEBE HAD GOTTEN acquainted with Marcus and Anne's staff and the new young attendant who would be taking care of her. As promised, she toured the vineyards with Marcus one afternoon. It brought up lots of questions.

"Cousin Marcus, so Lionel has never seen your estate in the daytime?" she asked.

Phoebe could see he was pensive. He parked the SUV and then shut off the motor. Their windows were left open. A large hawk was calling in the distance while smaller birds chirped together socially in oak trees that lined the working line road.

She could smell the dirt, the budding vines and even the mustard flowers with their sour scent, growing between the rows. The blue sky against the dark earth and green grasses was a stunning contrast and was every bit as beautiful as the pictures and paintings she'd seen. It did look like Tuscany, but with more light. And it was bigger.

Marcus slowly turned in the seat and regarded her carefully. "Lionel is a rare breed, Phoebe, as I'm sure you've discovered. I often think to myself how sad it is that the brothers have never seen this magnificent property in the full light of day. But they do remember what it was like to be mortal as they were before their turning. I'm not sure if that's good or bad. But I have never heard them complain. Not once. I wonder, if, given the same situation, I wouldn't pine for those warm summer afternoons that I remember as a mortal child."

"But if I turned—if I turned dark, would I be able to see daytime still?"

"No, dear Phoebe. If you were turned dark, then you would have all the traits that Lionel possesses. You would forever remain a creature of the night, cousin. I'm not sure that is even a choice for you, thankfully."

"My understanding is from my parents that Lionel and Hugh and Jeb were all turned by a dark coven Lord that your family trusted. Why weren't they turned by a Golden?"

"That was my mother's and father's decision to make. It was a very difficult situation. All three brothers were left for dead. It was hoped that they would serve the Monteleone family in exchange for their gift of immortality. But they were never asked for the choice."

"I understand the elders in Tuscany were consulted?"

"Well, they tried, from what my mother tells me, but, frankly, there was no time to really sort it out. Without the Council's approval, and it was deemed likely they wouldn't approve, the family could save their lives, but only if they were made dark."

"And they've given their lives to the Family."

"Without a whimper. I like to think our family has treated them well."

She knew Lionel felt like one of the family himself, but she wanted to hear it from Marcus. "You've treated them as any other family member. For, are they not family, in your opinion?"

"By blood, no. But by their duty and honor, their loyalty, yes. I have always felt a kinship with the Jett brothers. I have trusted my own offspring to their care, stemming back to the days when I was made to believe I'd fathered Lucius."

"Which is why you were keen to the idea of allowing Lionel to marry me, to be my protector."

Marcus looked thoughtful before he answered. "Yes, I suppose that is part of it. We have a peculiar hierarchy, this symbiotic relationship between the brothers and ourselves."

"You and Lionel are going to do some research, he's told me."

"Yes. I've recently acquired a body of work that has left me with more questions than answers. I've asked Lionel to help me with my study, and he's agreed."

"Has your family turned others?"

"The answer to that is I don't know, but probably. I've only turned one. I am Anne's maker and in doing so, I violated several rules."

"Rules?" She asked.

"We are to obtain permission before we can add additional Goldens to our bloodline. We also need permission before we turn Goldens who come of age. It is usually performed by a member of the Directorate. We don't turn children, we don't turn young people until they are at or past puberty. We give them the decision, the choice. Anne was not given that choice. I made it for her, and I nearly paid for it with my life."

"Yes, my mother told me you had risked much. But I didn't understand it was because of Anne's origins. But it all makes sense now, cousin." She paused, ready to get to the crux of her question. "So, about my marriage, my relationship with Lionel—and he has shared this with you I believe, is that correct?"

"Yes, Phoebe he has."

"This relationship with him I feel is some natural selection process. It may not be the same kind of fating as you had with Anne, but I feel it is something growing—something like a fating. Could it be that something about either myself or Lionel is incomplete and if it were completed, we would experience a true bond?"

"The bond happens during the blood mating ritual. The fating is what makes the bond possible. It attracts the male and female together with such a strong desire that one cannot live without the other. It takes over one's entire life. It becomes air and water and food to the Golden who is part of this ritual. I am told it is the same for those of Lionel's clan."

"Marcus, did you ever have strong feelings for anyone else other than Anne?"

Marcus tapped on the steering wheel with his fingers and searched through the windshield as if looking for a face in a crowd somewhere. "In three hundred years, Phoebe, I never met my fated mate until I met Anne. I had dalliances, I had affairs and I enjoyed my mortal years as a young man in society way back then, but I was always searching for that special woman, and I never sensed her presence, until I met Anne that night in the chapel in Tuscany."

"The chapel where we wed, correct?"

"That very one."

"So how do you explain this experience that Lionel and I have?"

Marcus shook his head and then smiled at her. He was such a kind, understanding man, Phoebe thought, so honorable, handsome, and always wise. She knew he would always tell her the truth.

"I can't. I wish I had answers for you, Phoebe, but I can't. I just don't know how to explain it at all."

Phoebe thought long and hard about what it must be like to never see the sun or lie in the early morning hours and allow the warm air to caress her flesh. If she turned to the dark side and joined Lionel, if that was even possible, or allowed, would she regret the life she could've lived as a Golden vampire? She tried to live by evening and sleep by day as was Lionel's routine, just to be supportive of him, but would she in time tire of this?

And though they were married, if she took a dark turn, would she be able to bear him children? These were things that weighed heavily on her mind.

She would keep asking questions until she got answers that resonated with her. Until then, she knew, no matter what she felt, that she would have to wait. She knew she could count on Lionel to be discreet, but she did not know if she could count on herself. It was the only thing she worried about now.

ARRANGEMENTS WERE MADE for a large party at the Monteleone estate as they received news that several of their Tuscan relatives were to be arriving in California for a visit. Her parents were among the guests. She worked with Anne to create a menu that would not make her turned relatives sick but would also please the younger unturned members who were coming.

"They practically live on macaroni and cheese," she said to her cousin. Phoebe had been discussing her brothers.

"I still sneak a taste now and then, remembering how I loved it so. We'll make sure there is enough so they can consume it for breakfast, lunch and dinner!" said Anne.

"How do you nourish yourself?" Phoebe asked her.

"Bone broth is my favorite, though I sometimes have lean, raw beef."

"Bone broth?" Phoebe scrunched up her nose. "That sounds disgusting. You do mean raw, is that right?"

"Not at all. It's warm and extremely nutritious for us. Made from the bones of large cattle." She paused. "But fated mates can give each other nourishment which can last them for centuries. You'll find one day when you turn, after the initial period, your need for sustenance dwindles greatly."

Ian was playing in the corner of the dining room, where the two women sat. They continued searching through recipes and making seating plans. The baby had become fascinated with pots and pans, or anything that made noise from the kitchen.

One of the sisters, Amalia, appeared as soon as Ian began to fuss.

"Ma'am, let me give him a bath and feed him, yes?"

"Thank you, sweetie. Phoebe and I are nearly finished, but that would be a great help." She smiled across the table. "I never thought I'd get used to having servants. Now I can't understand how I ever lived without them."

Phoebe had never known a time when the house didn't employ servants. "What was it like, Anne, growing up?"

She rolled her eyes. "I worked hard. I had a job I loved. I was responsible. I got up early. I often worked all day without a break. I went to bed late. I took care of everything. I didn't have anyone to cook or clean or do laundry. Honestly, as a mortal woman I understand how difficult it can be. How people age. We are so lucky you and I."

"What was it like, your turning?"

"Well I didn't know what had happened to me. I was one day at my wedding—"

Phoebe leaned forward, shocked. "Your wedding?"

"Yes. I'm not exactly proud of it, but I did get engaged to a mortal man who would've made and actually did make a terrible husband.

Honestly, the guy couldn't keep his pants on. I caught him in the bathroom with my maid of honor at our reception. After the reception, I took my trip, which was to have been our honeymoon, in Tuscany. Since I paid for it with my own money, I decided to go anyway without Robert, my husband. I intended to divorce him as soon as I came home."

"I never knew you were married once before. Once to a moral man and now to Marcus?"

"There's absolutely no comparison. Marcus was always the man I was destined to marry. He saved me from a life of hell. He saved me in every way possible Phoebe."

She was touched with Anne's story. "And so how did you eventually meet Marcus?"

Anne stood, pacing the floor back-and-forth, and then continued. "I stumbled upon the little chapel where you and Lionel were married. I decided to say a prayer, to forgive my husband and to beg for a miracle. I hardly noticed the three people sitting in the front of the church discussing something. I would find out later that it was Marcus consulting a priest with a woman he was being forced to marry."

"I can't see Marcus doing anything he didn't have to."

"She'd told him Lucius was his, when in reality, Paulo was the real father. I left the chapel thinking that I did all I could. I prayed about it, I made a donation and lit a red candle. I'd sent my wish up to Heaven. And within minutes, as I was trying to find my way back to my hotel, this vampire female attacked me and I felt my life's blood drain out on the cobblestone streets. I died that evening, Phoebe. She stole my mortal life from me."

Anne sat back down at the table and grabbed Phoebe's hands in both of hers. "For you, the path is different. You were always destined to be who you are, a Golden female. I, on the other hand, had a different destiny. It was *altered*. I didn't recognize the fating nor did I even know about vampires or vampire society or the two species of vampires. I knew absolutely nothing of this world."

"So, how did you deal with all this?"

"I didn't know what had happened to me. I wandered along the South of France, into Spain. I knew that something had changed, but I didn't know what. I thought I was losing my mind. I felt so helpless and confused."

"How horrifying!"

"It was. I can see why they make so many rules about this. I was very vulnerable, or at least felt vulnerable. But in reality, I had Marcus there, invisibly guiding me the whole way. After we met, I fell in love with him and in the beginning, it was Marcus who helped me bridge the gap. They have this rule that if a new Golden being is created that the maker cannot contact that person for thirty days. Marcus abided by it carefully, but he followed me. He protected me, as it turned out. And on the 30th day he appeared to me, finally."

"Would you let me ask you a question?"

"Ask away."

"Did you feel *fated* to Marcus?"

"There was something there Phoebe. Yes. It took me awhile to understand what was going on, but I have to say, yes, I knew immediately that whomever he was, this dark male nearly stalking me, was my ticket out. I felt the intensity of his love right away. I trusted him. For the first time in my life, I belonged somewhere, and that was right at his side. Do you understand?"

"Yes. I think I do."

"It was dangerous. But he made me feel like I've never felt before. And it didn't take long before in his presence I completely changed. My whole outlook changed. I embraced it, Phoebe. I brought Marcus into my life and I've never regretted it."

Phoebe knew Lionel would be awakening soon. She slipped inside the bedroom and nestled next to him, watching him sleep. When he reached for her, she allowed his fingers to undress her carefully, peeling her free from the bonds of her clothes so that her flesh could awaken to his touch. She allowed his lips to trace and bless all her private parts.

She remembered Anne's words that had been spoken to her just minutes before. And she knew, just as strongly as she felt the way her body responded to her husband, that Anne had felt the fating, and that it grew within her just like it was growing within Phoebe tonight.

Each time he showered her with kisses and spoke to her inner soul with those Latin incantations, she was molded into his woman step by glorious step, along with that tug on her womb that wanted to bear him a child. It was more than passion. It was a persistent pull to be consumed in the flames of his love. She was submitting to his will, transforming, just like a real turning.

But it wasn't a dark future she saw. She saw bright sunshine, and light filtering through his hair as he leaned down and kissed her. She saw herself giving Lionel her whole body in the middle of a sunny day, his shaft entering her needy sex, spilling seed and lining her insides with a pleasure so exquisite, she burst into tears. In her fantasy, they lay in plain view, under the Heavens, a picnic in a vineyard. Their love making was long and arduous, tender and fierce. When at last she was fully spent, she lay her head against his chest and they watched the clouds drift through the bright blue sky together.

Lionel arched up, interrupting her pleasant vision.

"What are you showing me?" He had stopped, demanding an answer.

"I see our future."

Chapter 8

MARCUS' STUDY WAS quiet except for the crackling fire in the fireplace. He shared his reading table with Lionel. The *Book of Spawn* was opened to a section in the first third of the tome. They'd been pouring over a particular passage.

"So, it says there was a disturbance amongst the population during the time of Vinkus." Marcus looked up at him. "I'm not exactly sure what year that is but if I'm not mistaken the Vinkus dynasties began in the second and third centuries in India. A great king came into power, and he led the people on a crusade to populate. It's even written in history books I've studied from England and France," said Marcus.

"I think they refer to it sometimes as the second coming?" added Lionel.

"Exactly. It was an Age of Enlightenment for India and the surrounding Hindu areas. In the West we don't study this but explorers in the seventeenth and eighteenth centuries uncovered temples long buried under jungle foliage that depict sexual acts of every form. I guess it was considered a variation of the Christian theme of a God of love."

Lionel leaned back in the leather armchair and tapped his fingers to his lips. "So you are thinking that this great ruler during the dynasty of Vinkus was actually a vampire?"

"The book is unclear. See what it says here, '*and the God of Vinkus gave onto his people the art of love.*' What they are saying here is that this particular ruler lead them on a sexual journey I guess is the best way to put it." Marcus grinned. "It refers to the years preceding the emergence of this ruler is the years of despair."

Lionel leaned over and read for himself a passage that directed the reader to another passage in the book of sorrows. "Where is this book of sorrows?"

Marcus examined the script. "I've never seen that before. Good job, Lionel. Let me see, because I wasn't aware there was a Book of Sorrows, but you're right." He flipped from the index and re-opened the book to nearly the end.

"It's here in the back." Marcus turned several pages forward and then back and came to a chapter in the last third. "Here it is."

Lionel looked over the page and realized it was written in a script he could not understand. "I cannot read it."

"I think it's Aramaic or perhaps some lost language. I'm not sure. It isn't Latin. I don't recognize all of the characters. See these S shapes and some of the crosses here? It looks like it's almost a combination hieroglyphics and phonetics but to my knowledge there is no language that exists matching this."

"We'll have to consult a Greek or Jewish scholar to see if we can find someone who can read a portion of this text." Lionel turned the book around and noted the characters looked more familiar by reading them upside down.

Marcus chuckled, watching him move the book back and forth. "Now you see the problem I've been having reading this? Just when you think you're getting to something you can understand it goes all crazy. It's like the messages are hidden within the book itself."

"I wonder if there is a key somewhere. Is there any mention of this?" Lionel asked.

Marcus showed him what appeared to be a table of contents, but the order of the chapters didn't match the order of the chapters in the book.

"There is mention of a great civilization surrounded by ocean which disappeared or was destroyed. It gives no clue as to where this land exists today," added Marcus.

"Do you have any idea the time span under which this book was written?" Lionel asked.

"Not really. It refers to a lost civilization, but it isn't clear whether it occurred before or after the time of Vinkus. But this time is very significant. I find references to it all throughout the book."

Marcus rose and poured them each a brandy. The aged liquid burned all the way down Lionel's throat and was oddly soothing.

"You know it appears to me," Marcus began, "that this great king or ruler, led his people on some sort of sexual expedition or journey."

Lionel agreed. "Whatever caused the affliction or illness during the age of sorrows the cure seems to be the sexual act itself." Lionel considered what he just said and added, "The opposite of sorrow is joy. Or could this mean that he was leading them to a journey of self-discovery and sexual pleasures that brought joy to a population that no longer had it? Could that be the affliction or the disease?" Lionel wondered.

"I think the chapter containing the book of sorrows is one of the keys here. I'm going to see if I can find amongst some of my Jewish friends, a rabbi who might be able to help decipher parts of this chapter. I'll start there, at least."

"That's an excellent idea Marcus."

They studied the book until the early hours of the morning shortly before Lionel would need to take his restorative sleep. Marcus had been yawning and as the Brandy continued to flow, at one point he fell asleep in his chair.

Lionel made some notes as he flipped through the pages. He examined sketches and pictures of pyramids, temples with rounded corners and archways. He knew the development of the arch was something that hadn't occurred until much later in time, yet these temples clearly had them.

As Marcus continued in his slumber, Lionel leafed through pages, discovering a chapter written in Arabic. He also discovered several pages written in what appeared to be an Egyptian hieroglyphic text. He wondered where he and Marcus would find such a learned scholar to be able to translate the book since it would require somebody with knowledge of ancient texts from several parts of the world.

At last Lionel saw the pink light of sunrise peering through the large windows in Marcus' study. He gently tapped his host on the shoulder.

"Marcus, I need to retire. I also suggest that you put this book away, and perhaps we can do further study tomorrow."

"Very well. I can't say that we've discovered anything, but I suspect it will take us quite a while to find the correct path. We've made a good beginning."

"I agree. Perhaps amongst your circle of friends or family you can find scholars who can assist us."

"But I'm not going to show them the book. Only a handful of us are allowed to know about its very existence," Marcus said as he closed the thick leather binding and placed it back in his wall safe. He then slid a bookshelf across it which was built to hide the safe from public view.

"I agree. Until tomorrow then. And thank you for the Brandy."

The house was coming alive as Lionel made his way to their chambers. Several gardeners had pulled up in two separate trucks, unloading equipment in the predawn minutes before their day would begin. Two cooks also arrived, unloading shopping bags from the back of their car.

The rest of the house as well as their mortal protectors were still in bed. Phoebe had spent the night sleeping all during the time Marcus and Lionel were researching, plowing through the great book. She was still in bed and smiled as he arrived.

"I am so sorry husband. I guess I needed the rest. Was your session with Marcus productive?"

"It was." Lionel shed his shoes, shirt and his jeans. He left his boxers on and climbed into bed, wrapping his arms around his wife. She nestled her head just beneath his chin. "The more time I spend with Marcus the more I appreciate him as head of the household. We are learning together about the history of your species. These are things I didn't know existed."

"You say my species but what about yours?" she asked him.

"We can't be certain, my love. But I am tired. I've had too much Brandy. And I need my restorative sleep. Are you going to join me or are you off today?"

Phoebe sat up and looked down upon him, her dark caramel-colored hair cascading around her shoulders and demurely covering up her chest. "I think I am off to Healdsburg today. The town. Lucius wants to show me some stores. Is there anything you desire?"

Lionel grinned. He played for Phoebe several erotic scenes in his own mind and watched her face blush.

"I like that we have this feature. It's so efficient. And so completely yummy." She bent down and gave him a kiss. Then his lovely wife dashed off to the bathroom while he snuggled in his bed and prepared to fall asleep.

Several hours later he awoke, showered, then prepared to dress for the party. He looked for Phoebe upstairs and then searched the kitchen and library downstairs as well as Marcus' office. She was nowhere to be found.

Marcus entered through the kitchen door carrying a load of fire-wood which he placed in the living room on their stone hearth. "I see you are up, Lionel. Where is your better half?"

"I was hoping you could tell me. I've not seen her since early this morning. She said she was going shopping, getting some last-minute things for the event."

Marcus stood, checked his watch and frowned. "Anne is upstairs with the baby. I did not hear the car, so I presume they have not returned. I honestly thought she was with you Lionel."

"Who was her protection detail?" he asked.

"Now you have me worried." Marcus picked up his cell phone which had been clipped to his belt and placed a call. "Ransom? This is Marcus. Do you know where Lucius, Phoebe and the others are at this moment?" He listened while being given information. "Well I want someone to find them immediately. And I want to know on who's authorization it was that they would remain on an errand when nightfall has hit. That is not what we set up. I'm not happy about this at all." He listened briefly and then hung up.

"So there is a problem, is that what you're saying?" Lionel was be-ginning to become agitated. He reached out to Phoebe sending her a message. "Where are you?"

Marcus placed another call when Lionel received back the message from his wife, '*I have met my parents in downtown Healdsburg. I have just been visiting them and should return soon. It was quite by accident. I'm sorry I didn't let you know.*'

Lionel held his hand up. Marcus stopped his phone call mid-sentence.

"She's in town with her parents."

"That is not the arrangement," Marcus shouted. "You need to explain to Phoebe that she is not to alter the plan. Her protection detail is supposed to follow certain protocols. They are supposed to contact me if things are not followed according to that protocol."

"I will have that conversation sir."

At last they heard the car arrive, and Phoebe, Lucius, one of the wait staff and the two protectors entered the foyer. Marcus rushed to intercept them.

"You had us worried and you put Miss Phoebe and Lucius in danger!" Marcus screamed at the two mid twenty-year-old protectors who had escorted Phoebe and Lucius. He threatened to fire all three of them, even the kitchen helper.

When Phoebe came to their defense, Marcus turned on her, his face bright red in anger.

"I have made a solemn vow to your parents Phoebe that you are to be protected. I cannot do this if you do not abide by my rules. If you find that this is too restrictive then perhaps you should go back to Tuscany and live with your parents. I will not be responsible for something happening to you unless you follow our instructions and guidance. That doesn't mean the rules you fancy, it means *all* the rules. Do you understand me? You *have* to take this seriously, child."

Phoebe began to cry. She buried her face in her palms. Though it saddened him, Lionel knew it would be a mistake to comfort her. He also agreed with Marcus that Phoebe's lack of attention, while it may not lead to her own peril, could endanger the lives of Lucius or any of the other people in her detail. He sent her a stern warning telepathically. She looked over her shoulder at him and glared.

"You too? For goodness sake, Lionel, I was with my *parents!*" She pleaded with Marcus. "The very people you have sworn your vow to. Honestly, you expect me to tell my own parents that I can't see them because the Lord of this house has set in place the rules for how I am to engage?"

Marcus tried to sound calm, but Lionel could see he was way beyond boiling. He spoke through clenched teeth. "It is a strange world, Phoebe, and getting stranger by the minute. There are lots of creatures out there, with new hybrids coming out every day, it seems. Some you can see and some you cannot see. Phoebe, in your vast experience, your nineteen years of living, have you ever seen a shifter? Have you seen a body thief?"

Phoebe's cheeks blushed red as her eyes continued to shed tears. She began to shake. Slowly, she turned to Lionel. *'What are these creatures, husband?'* She asked telepathically.

Lionel answered her verbally coming to her side and placing his palms at the sides of her face. He spoke to her softly so as not to scare her further. "Our world is not nearly as safe as it appears, my wife. These creatures are very devious and extremely dangerous. And they only prey after sunset. So we would have given you a different detail. These men understand this and disobeyed Marcus."

Phoebe fell into his arms.

The two former special ops protectors apologized for their mishandling of the situation. Marcus elected to give them one additional chance but warned them.

"This is how it happens," Marcus began. "Just like when you were serving in the military. It is quiet for long stretches of time, almost boring, right? We forget to be careful. Somebody does something unexpected, and all of a sudden, we have a problem. A *big* problem. Or, one of us is lost. It happens in the blink of an eye, gentlemen. It happens so fast, your life or someone you care about can just be *gone!*"

Lionel spoke over Phoebe's shoulder. "My wife is never to be escorted after sunset by anyone but myself or one of my two brothers, is that understood?"

"Yes sir," the two protectors said in unison.

"And where are the other Jett brothers?" Marcus wanted to know.

Lionel could tell that unless Jeb and Hugh appeared soon, they'd catch a bit of Marcus' wrath.

"We were to meet here, at the house." The protector looked down and shrugged his shoulders. "But we were to meet them before dark."

Just then the front door burst open. Both Hugh and Jeb were covered in dark brownish-red blood. Sweat stained their shirts. Jeb's hair was littered with twigs and dried leaves like they'd been wrestling in an alleyway.

"You had five," Hugh held up his fingers to show the number, "dark coven teenagers following after all of you. They were in the bookstore. One of them served you coffee, Rory," he said as he addressed one of the protectors, "and they were delighted to have discovered two Golden mortals they were about to make a meal of."

"Fucking slimy bastards," the other protector spat. "I knew there was something wrong with that kid, that barista with the green hair. I just knew it."

"Well there you have it. You boys owe your life to these two brothers. You very nearly sacrificed Phoebe out of your own ignorance. Consider yourselves lucky to even be in my employ. But don't expect I will trust you with this much responsibility again." Marcus then ordered them out.

Lionel followed Phoebe up to the bedroom. He locked the bedroom door for good measure but didn't expect anyone to interrupt them. Phoebe was throwing her clothes in the corner whispering and mumbling. Lionel was beside himself not knowing exactly what to do. He was so relieved with Phoebe's current safety, he found it difficult to be mad. But his agitation was still boiling. He held back, due to Phoebe's lack of worldly experience. He didn't want to be disconnected to her and her thoughts, which were confusing him.

"Phoebe, if you're going to be upset just come out with it. Just swear. Let me hear it!"

"Because I don't want to swear at my husband. How could you do this to me?"

"Do what?" He tried to read her mind and found she'd blocked him.

"You didn't back me up."

Lionel was stunned. "Did you hear nothing of the conversation? Did you not see Hugh and Jeb covered with some dark coven vampire's blood? Do you realize what it takes to do battle with—with—" He was momentarily left speechless by the realization that Hugh and Jeb had actually battled members of his own race. They had killed their own kind, and Phoebe seemed to not have an opinion or consideration about it.

"Yes. I understand and I appreciate their sacrifice. But the sun was only down for less than a half an hour. It's not like we were wandering around the community. We sat in the lobby of the old hotel there. My parents and several of the other Monteleones were having cocktails. I chanced walking by when it was still light. I went inside and had a drink *with them* that's all Lionel. That's all!"

He had to make her understand. "So where is it written that these nasty teenagers won't attack you if you were merely visiting your parents or getting a cup of coffee?"

She ran straight for him and drew her hand back to slap him across the face, but he grabbed her wrist and held her. His beautiful wife was but a child. He could see in her eyes the anger she had not learned to control. He worked to sound reasonable, even though he was holding the wrist of the woman he loved, who wanted to strike him for it.

"Think. Calm down and think, Phoebe." He could feel her pulse quickening. His own breathing was deep and ragged. He had never before encountered a woman, vampire or mortal, or otherwise, who attempted to cause him physical pain. It was as though they had crossed a new threshold.

Lionel saw in her face the rigid determination of her ancestors. He saw Maria's face, stubborn, racked with pain as she lay dying on the bed and later in his arms as he held her at the beach under the stars, watching her lifeforce slip away. He saw the stubbornness of Phoebe's soul which was identical to Maria's. He had lost Maria because their two worlds did not mix. Now he was staring back into the face of his beloved and realized for the first time that perhaps once again he was in a different world than the woman he loved.

Perhaps there was no way out.

He released her wrist and turned his back to her. He did not want her to see that his eyes had filled with water. Even without the slap, her wounding was deep, and he understood how vulnerable he was.

She took two steps and then touched his shoulder. He shrugged her off and moved away, mumbling, "Don't touch me."

THE PARTY WAS a welcome distraction to the frostiness between Lionel and his wife. They tried not to look at each other. But he snuck several sideways glances her way, until he felt her turn toward him. It felt like the evening was all about showing each other how cold they could be to one another. He had no appetite for the bone broth that was served at dinner, or for the home-baked bread. He drank four glasses of Claret, while she had nearly an entire bottle of champagne.

Lionel endured the stares and whispers they incurred by the other party goers. The conversation was muted. It was not a festive occasion. Even Marcus seemed to be mentally off on some distant planet. The celebration to welcome family members from Tuscany was anything but a pleasant affair.

Thankfully, the entire event was over in less than two hours. He gave a chaste kiss to Phoebe's mother and shook her father's hand without making eye contact. His stomach was churning, and he felt he might even be sick. But he did not allow Phoebe to be unprotected, and as she moved from room to room, was always nearby, although never at her side.

With most the partygoers gone, she announced that she was tired and wanted to turn in. He followed her silently upstairs. He opened the bedroom door and then dutifully closed it behind him. But instead of readying himself for bed, he collapsed onto the gold-colored settee, crossed his legs and stared at the floor. Phoebe soon took up the seat across from him.

"So is this what married life with you is going to be like?" she huffed.

"It will be if you don't behave, Phoebe."

"Do you understand how disgusting that makes me feel? To *behave*? To follow your prescribed rules?

"They are not *my* rules Phoebe, they are Marcus' rules."

"But you agree with them. You just told me that I must obey."

He flashed her and angry sneer. "There was a time you used to fantasize about obeying my every command."

"Unfair. I call foul, husband."

"You don't understand how dangerous it is and what kind of peril it puts us all in when you do not abide by practices and protocols that have been put in place for your own protection. What about that don't you understand? You not only risked your own life, but that of Lucius' as well."

Her stubbornness wouldn't let her admit what he knew she felt in her heart. He could feel the layers of attraction pulling at him through her anger. He was ashamed of himself for finding her stubbornness strangely alluring. And in spite of all, as he looked upon his wife's face, he understood full well how dangerous he was to her.

They were dancing on the ledge and if either of them fell, they would both go. One side of the ledge would lead to unspeakable and exquisite passion. The other side would lead to horror and death. He wondered what he would've done if his hand had not stopped her slap.

His heart was aching with the knowledge that he shouldn't back down, that he shouldn't submit to her. But something else inside him brewed a tender thread. He leaned forward, extending his hand, and instead of taking it, she threw herself into his arms.

Chapter 9

PHOEBE LAY AWAKE. Her husband's sweat and arousal was still mingling with her own as her breathing slowed. Lionel slept in that deep place he always went for his restorative time. She loved him so much her heart was growing jealous of those hours he could only spend alone. These were times and places he had to go without her. And she wanted every part of him.

He lived, he loved, and he made love just as deeply and passionately as he slept. How she wished she could delve into that cavern, that bad night of his soul. She knew this place was what was separating them. It broke her heart to know this. It was everything she could do to stop herself from making him cross that barrier into the unknown. The end of the story was unknown, but the happily ever after they sought would be dashed forever if they went too far with their lovemaking.

But as he worked her body last night, as he pleasured her, as he needed her, every cell jumped and screamed out for him. He was drawing from her every last ounce of her resistance. All she could give him was everything she had, and that was to meet somewhere in the middle. She wanted his child, even though that would be impossible under their present condition. But even though it was wrong, she wanted it more than anything else in the world.

It just didn't seem logical that the God who made her, the God of vampires as he often laughed, would have created the two of them, with this strong attraction, without some way to solve the problem that attraction caused. There had to be a solution.

His lips and his tongue did everything they could to squeeze and control her body into thinking she was being fully pleasured as a true vampire wife would be. But that little dark space in the back of her mind knew there was a locked cabinet and he had the key. With each stroke of his tongue, with each small taste of his blood and with each kiss, he was dangling the key in front of her.

"Sweet Lionel," she whispered, "You have no idea how much I wish I could join you in every way possible."

She knew he couldn't hear her. But she stroked the side of his face and laced her fingers through his hair, dreaming about the day they would walk in the sunshine together. Or, maybe it was the day they would walk into the fire of their demise?

Inhaling deeply, she slipped her body beneath his and allowed the heavy weight of his chest and upper torso fall upon hers as she cradled him in his deep sleep. Her hands moved down his back to his waist. Her fingers barely grazed over the enormous mounds of his buttocks, stroking him, feeling the pleasure of the bundles of muscles from his waist up to his shoulders again.

He was a strong, complicated man. Her passion in life was to fall into his arms and give him back something close to what he gave her. It was so unfair for him to be so unfulfilled. It was so unfair for him to see her being so unfulfilled, although she tried to pretend that she was receiving everything she needed to make her happy. But he knew.

Phoebe thought about the *Book of Spawn* and wondered. Maybe if she looked at the book or read the pages perhaps, she could help them discover something that could solve this problem between them. She smiled to herself. It wasn't a real problem of course. It was the most wonderful thing that had happened to her, falling in love with Lionel. It was everything she dreamt of as a young teen growing up. And she knew that if she took the turning her strong love for Lionel would only increase.

Her mother and some of her friends had warned her that if she turned, perhaps her attraction to her husband would wane. Phoebe wasn't worried about this at all. She knew it wasn't true. There was too much love she was experiencing as a human woman not to carry forward as she turned.

Although she had intended to spend the whole day sheltering Lionel's body, watching him sleep and being the first person he saw when he awoke in the dusk of day, she needed to speak with Marcus.

It bothered Phoebe that Marcus was so angry with her. She understood why, even though she didn't want to accept it. Marcus was an honorable man. He made the vow to her parents, and he'd offered her the sanctuary of his home. She'd be ungrateful if she matched his kindness with her own lack of appreciation. It was important that she made it right.

Carefully leaving the warmth of her husband's bed, she tiptoed across the room. In minutes she was dressed, closed the huge bedroom door behind her and scampered downstairs to find Marcus or Anne.

She found them outside on the patio overlooking the gardens and vineyards below.

"Oh, so there you are." She leaned over Marcus's frame giving him a shoulder hug and a peck on his cheek. Anne looked up from rocking little Ian and gave her a smile. The toddler stirred, breaking loose from his mother to peer up at the newcomer. Phoebe held her arms out as Anne placed him in her grasp. She jostled the beautiful brown curly haired child with the huge chocolate brown eyes the same color as Marcus'.

"You are so lucky, Anne." She rocked the little one back-and-forth and made faces at his enchanted, smiling expression.

"He likes you, Phoebe," Anne whispered. "I think mothering will come naturally to you. You enjoy children, don't you?" she asked.

"I adore them. And I plan to have dozens. Just like my famous ancestor, Maria Monteleone." She made another surprise expression to Ian, which drew a giggle, then she gave a sly wink to Anne. "Who knew?"

"I knew it the first time I saw you, dear," Anne replied. "All of this is so fascinating to me, since my growing up was so different than yours. Now that I am turned, I have a great deal of appreciation, and I admit, some envy, of the woman you are becoming, Phoebe."

Marcus had been sipping his coffee quietly staring off into the distance. But he quickly glanced up at her as Phoebe handed the child back to his mother.

"You should consider a turning, Phoebe," he said coldly.

Phoebe's heart raced. "I'm not sure that would be a good idea, until you learn more—"

"More?" Marcus angled his head and frowned.

"Lionel says you are studying the book. I know about this book. And Marcus, I'd actually like to read it, if I could."

"Absolutely not. And you should not speak of it either, Phoebe."

Marcus' his jaw was set, his lips in a thin line pursed together. Anne looked upon him skeptically. The baby began to fuss.

"Marcus are you absolutely sure that that's the only way?" his wife asked.

Marcus stared down at his coffee again and without saying a word nodded solemnly. Then he spoke to both Phoebe and his wife. "It puts us all in danger the more people learn of this book. It's too easy to forget and mention something that we shouldn't. I don't want some kind of a random mind-reading to extract information from you, Phoebe should we run across a family member or a creature who could do this without you even being aware. It's just too risky, and there is so much at stake."

"But isn't it my heritage as well as yours, Marcus?" Phoebe felt her blood pressure rise. "Why is it the women of this family can't take part in running it?"

"Because that's just not the way it's done."

She could see that far from straightening things out with Marcus she had picked a scab. But Phoebe's concern was stronger than her need to be proper with her cousin. "Then maybe it's time for things to change. Maybe women should have more of a say in running the family. Maybe—"

"Stop it!" Marcus stood, pacing back-and-forth. He squeezed his hands into fists, then opened them again, took a deep breath and then stopped "It's an argument I've heard before." His brief glance at his wife told Phoebe they had already engaged in some stern discussions. She didn't want to cause further friction.

"Phoebe," Anne started, "I understand completely how you feel. I consider myself somewhat of an ally. But like you, my experience with Golden vampires is limited. The family has always done things a certain way, even though we've had very strong women leaders. I think what Marcus is saying is that his experience trumps ours. Not that he needs to be in control, but that he has centuries of experience. Centuries of history, stories told to him ever since childhood. He has seen civilizations come and go, wars fought, men die, and vampires sacrificed. Family fortunes have been squandered, and he's seen these struggles in his lifetime that you and I can only imagine."

"It isn't fair." Phoebes frustration rose to a dangerous level. She knew Lionel would be displeased with her. But she was angry with Marcus concerning his earlier comment about her turning.

"So, when will someone tell me what my future is?" Phoebe blurted out, following her comment by drilling a glare at him.

"Your future is very much in your control, within certain rules. Just like we breathe the air. Just like we cannot fly in outer space. My family existed before the modern age. We didn't know anything about flight or rockets to the moon or anything having to do with the speed of light or cosmic forces. We have learned all these things just as humans have learned these things. They've learned them together. They've discovered them together. But, within the laws of this universe there are certain rules of nature. Regardless of how much I'd like to, I cannot travel or trace to the moon. That's not possible. It's also not possible right now for your husband to mate with you."

"But he can. I know he can." Phoebe saw the shocked expression on both Marcus and Ann's faces.

"You have consummated your marriage, Phoebe?" Anne had placed her hand up to her mouth while Marcus demanded his answer.

"No. Of course not. But we could." Phoebe thought carefully about what she was going to say next. Marcus and Anne watched her pace back and forth until she was calm enough to deliver. "And we want to. One day, we will."

Marcus had dropped to his chest and he shook back-and-forth denying internally what he'd heard. She knew this message was not going to be delivered well to her husband. She knew her parents would be furious with her as well. But it was her future that she craved and wanted to have some control over the big decisions needing to be made. It seemed so wrong to be told all she could do was wait for someone else.

"I mean you no disrespect cousin. I swear on my life's blood I sincerely thank you for all of the opportunity that you have given Lionel for his service to you, for your family's commitment to my safety. I sincerely appreciate all that you have done for all of the Golden families over the years. This is not disrespecting you in anyway. But I have briefly tasted something that is so miraculous that surely both of you could understand why I want more."

She looked from Marcus to Anne and back to Marcus again. She could see Anne's tears streaming down her cheeks. The baby had gracefully and thankfully fallen asleep against her chest. Marcus leaned back, scanning the heavens.

"I have thought about this myself many times, Phoebe." Marcus whispered after a long silence. "I have discussed it with Lionel, and he has told me of your strong attraction to each other. I don't believe I'm violating any confidence to tell you this."

"No that sounds exactly like him," Phoebe confirmed. She waited.

"Lionel is more like a brother to me than an employee. I do consider him family. Our histories are connected by our duty and are oaths. But there is something more, I know there is. I just don't have the answers, right now."

"Marcus—"

He cut Anne off, holding up his palm. "Just let me handle this and say to you both that I promise we will find an answer eventually. But until that happens, we must keep to the plan. I know from the many many military man I have met in my lifetime—people who have served in and run battle commands—that it is folly to jump in to a theater without knowing the script, without knowing where all the players are and what could happen. Without a plan. This is dangerous territory, Phoebe. You have to understand that the fear of the unknown, or the fear of making a terrible mistake, is something that is holding me back. I want to be sure before we take action."

He walked toward her placing his enormous hands on her shoulders, gripping her, shaking her very gently. He smiled, looking down upon her as her father had done many many times during her growing up. "You bring great challenge to this house, Phoebe. But you also bring tremendous joy to your husband, my most loyal and trusted brother. In fact, Lionel and I have spent many more days and nights together, than I have my own brother, Paolo. Your husband is the finest of his clan. This joy that you bring him gives me so much satisfaction, as I'm sure it does him. He deserves you. He deserves to be happy. He's earned it. I promise—" he placed his hand over his heart—"I promise that I will work tirelessly to research some solution to your relationship. And, if possible, I will bring you choices. Wouldn't that be a miracle, Phoebe?"

She placed her palms over his, and nodded, unable to look into his eyes. A shudder rippled through her body at the glimpse of her visions in that other life with Lionel. She was already walking on the beach at sunset. Being able to love him in every way, and it was worth the hole in her heart it would create if such a vision were deemed impossible.

"I will wait, cousin Marcus. I trust you. I trust our family. I want a life like you have. I didn't know this until a year ago. I want a family I want to create a dynasty like Maria did. I think I was given this opportunity and I'm not afraid."

SEVERAL DAYS PASSED. Phoebe knew that she would remember this conversation for the rest of her life. She knew that somehow; she must have a hand in her own destiny. And like learning about traveling to the moon or the stars beyond as Golden vampires had done alongside their human brothers, times had changed. It was time for the Monteleones to embrace the fact that from now on women would be more prominent in making family decisions. And on route to finding her own happiness, perhaps she would also be forging a path for all the future young Golden women just like her herself. Perhaps she'd be that trailblazer, and through her love of her husband, she should be able to show them the way, and help the men in her family overcome their tradition.

She mused at the thought it was something they would never be able to hold back anyway.

She knew there was a war coming. She knew the dark covens and the Goldens as well as the human races were all tied together in some fashion through history. Because it would require everyone's help in the cause of peace. Marcus perhaps wasn't aware of it, but he'd need the women of his family if he was going to be successful.

She knew Anne could be her ally, having lived in the human world until recently. She knew that and would help her and understood her plight. But Phoebe also understood that she was in love with a dark coven Lord who was more than three centuries old, and change might prove difficult for him. It was more important to Phoebe that he try to change, or show her that he wanted to, more than it was important that he do so.

Afterall, when the day was done and when she lay in her bed and listened to his incantations and felt his ministrations and the outpouring of love for her, she had to admit, she liked living with a man of honor, even if he was a bit of a Neanderthal.

Chapter 10

N EWS OF THE death of two Golden females in Tuscany followed the day after the Italian contingent of families arrived in California. It hit them like an ill wind, the portent of something sinister, darker, looming on the horizon that would affect them all. Lionel felt like the two were connected.

The meeting was called, and elders who were present gathered at the Monteleone home. Phoebe's father was among the guests as were several of the other clan family elder statesman. Lionel knew most of them, however several families were introduced to him as family from other parts of California.

Since this meeting was not a celebratory one, no one spoke in anything but a whisper. There were many frowns, many people examining their feet, pacing back-and-forth. They were a nervous group, Lionel observed. There was a younger member of the grieving family present but the elder leaders, two brothers, both prominent bankers in Italy, remained at home to attend to the funeral of their daughters.

Lionel could feel Phoebe's questions just as if she was standing behind him whispering in his ear. He tried to block her thoughts from him but was only successful in causing them to fade slightly, not disappear entirely. She was fighting him, protesting that he was locking her out of this important meeting.

'Phoebe, it is for your own protection. There is much for me to concentrate on, and I can't be having you piggyback.'

'Husband, whatever it is involves me as well. Or do you not think this is true?'

'I do. You know I do.'

'Then let me stay. I promise I will be silent.'

Lionel inhaled, found strength in the gentle California night air filling his lungs, sending fresh oxygen to his brain as if he'd done a timed run. He told her telepathically that he'd try.

Marcus stood in the middle of the group and began.

"So, we are gathered here today for a very solemn meeting. Tragic news from Italy has ruined this Family reunion."

Lionel observed how the rest of the body paid attention to Marcus. He was the rock. They drew strength from him. Lionel was proud to be in Marcus' confidence and looked forward to supporting whatever his plans were. They were overdue for another session with the book, but that would have to come later.

"We have two more members of our family who have perished at the hands of a dark coven Lord. We are not exactly sure who has done this, but it does follow a familiar pattern."

"My father thinks whomever this person is he's human. He cages and lives off of the blood of our Golden virgins. I'm surprised your contacts have not revealed this, Marcus." Alexi Vitoli was the older brother sent to represent the family of the fallen girls.

Lionel knew it was obvious to the group that Alexi's family was far from satisfied with the lack of previous protection measures. He gave the young Golden Lord, not older than twenty, a wide berth and made excuses due to his young age. He had only turned this past summer, and was a friend growing up, a playmate, of Phoebe's.

"Alexi," Marcus continued, "my heart aches with regret and sadness. In no way could I begin to understand the pain that your family must be going through. We are so very sorry for this situation and I am pledged..." He glanced around the room his arms in a big sweeping motion, addressing all the other visitors... "We all are committed to finding out who has done this."

Alexi sneered back at the elder Monteleone. There were several in the group who could not hide their shocked expressions. Someone even gasped. Lionel found himself grinding his molars and clenching his fists, quickly hiding them behind his back. Although he was fully in charge of Phoebe, he still owed loyalty to Marcus, and would protect him to the end. He knew Marcus was doing all he could.

"Again, Alexi, I am so sorry. If there was any way I could have stopped this I would." Marcos followed this statement with a deep, graceful bow to the newly minted young Golden vampire.

"My father and my uncle believe your family is not wholly innocent," Alexi shot back and looked to the audience for approval but received none.

"Is this a conversation we should have in private then my friend?" Marcus asked with caution.

"I have nothing to say that I cannot say to the entire congregation gathered here this evening. It's just a coincidence, that while we are preparing and coming over to America to visit that our family has been attacked."

"What are you saying boy?" Asked Phoebe's father. "You surely don't think Marcus had anything to do with this, do you?"

The young Vitoli was wise to stay silent. Lionel noticed both Jeb and Hugh were about ready to dismember the boy, an act that would truly cause their end.

'Don't do a thing brothers.'

Hugh shrugged his shoulders, feigning surprise. Jeb refused to look him in the eyes, but Lionel noticed he was nibbling on his lower lip. Outside the living room window he could see other security searching the perimeter of the estate, flashlights beaming in the night, disturbing the peace. The whole situation made Lionel nervous.

"I would say it's more likely young Vitoli that it was an opportunity," said another gentleman Lionel didn't recognize. "We all have left family behind. We all are vulnerable at this point. I will be returning home as soon as I can arrange it."

Several others in the group agreed with this comment. The consensus was that the Italian families would be returning to Tuscany very soon.

"I understand completely. I would do the same," said Marcus. "So, let's sort out whatever disagreements we have between us. Let's air them all," he said as he nodded to the Vitoli youth. "I don't want to prepare a plan before I hear everyone's thoughts on the matter. This is to be something we can all easily agree to. That is my goal, at least."

Lionel observed one member of the family appeared to be in some sort of discomfort. His face was bright pink, and Lionel noticed that he had consumed a large amount of Marcus' prized Brandy. Lionel stepped behind another member of the family so he could watch the man from the safety of the shadows without detection.

Carmine Monteleone looked like he was on the verge of collapse. His eyes were bulging from his skull. He loosened his shirt, squirming as if hanging from a noose. He was also sweating profusely, and Lionel noted the top of his collar was completely drenched. Unlike many of the other members of the elder conclave, Carmine brought his wife with him. Athena was fussing over him, making the elder Monteleone further agitated. She was one of only four women in the group. Phoebe's mother was one of the others.

Lionel had been avoiding her all evening.

He always considered it a breach of security to have a woman present at the important meetings but since Marcus hadn't objected, he went along with it. Perhaps Carmine was in some form of medical distress. This was very uncommon in their Golden clan. Diseases were rare, but occasionally some affliction would befall one of the members, and they would be forced to live with it. Generally, bedrest was recommended in these cases, much the same as it was for the human population. But since it usually took an act of violence to terminate their lives, getting well wasn't about surviving, but surviving with a quality of life they could live with. Afterall, they wouldn't die, they'd just suffer for hundreds of years.

But Lionel surmised this wasn't a medical situation. He saw in the man's eyes—even his face—the soul and the heart of a coward. He wondered if perhaps there was an element to the recent murders that troubled old Carmine. He decided to bring it up with Marcus later when they were alone.

Marcus asked Alexi about what he knew of his sister's kidnap and murder. The group surrounding him leaned forward in rapt attention. They stopped sipping wine or Brandy. Athena Monteleone put down her champagne flute, turned her back on her husband, and peered through the outside window.

Alexi laced his fingers together as if he were in prayer. He took several seconds gathering his thoughts. "My two sisters were at home. Apparently, somebody came to the front door who bypassed our security detail. Or, they were not paying attention. In any event, they were caught off guard and paid for it with their lives. When my parents came home, they found the front door wide open and both of their rooms empty. But the place looked like a crime scene. There was blood all over my older sister's room with a large pool of it soaking into her mattress. There were sprays of blood on the hallway walls along with handprints. It appears they tried to fight off their attackers."

Marcus spoke up. "Attackers? You said attackers not one single attacker?"

Alexi shook his head and then shrugged. "We really don't know sir. From the amount of damage the house sustained it looked like a band of marauders had come through there my mother said. I wasn't allowed to go home. I'm glad I didn't see it. They just put me on a plane for California with my protector."

"We're glad you arrived safely. You're welcome to stay at my villa…"

"I have already made accommodations, sir. But thank you," Alexi answered tersely.

"So, have they found your sisters?" Marcus asked.

"They found parts."

The room gave out a collective gasp. Lionel could only imagine what the scene was like. He'd observed far too many of these situations firsthand and remembered well the night a dark coven Lord came for him and his brothers.

"I might have been included in the carnage except for the fact that I was not yet home from a meeting." Alexi added.

Lionel and Jeb exchanged glances. Jeb's thoughts were filled with a replay of screams and sounds of carnage he had suffered while being held captive in the desert.

'It sounds awfully like the same person, Lionel.'

'I agree.'

When Lionel looked up, Marcus had laid a stare on him so fierce he felt he'd been tied to a stake with silver chains. He nodded slightly just to confirm what he knew Marcus had suspected.

"Thank you, Alexi."

Marcus placed his hand over his mouth as he paced, his forehead creased with worry. And then he stopped. When their eyes met, Lionel knew he would have to say something about Jeb's experience, and what they knew of the creature who had stolen Jeb's blood and kept him alive, albeit just barely.

Lionel didn't want to share with the crowd, because he knew some family members present didn't approve of how closely he was aligned with the Monteleones. It was one thing to be a protector, but it was another to have married a Golden female, a virgin female, who should have been saved for another Golden lord to further her family's dynasty. He also knew that there were many in the group who didn't trust him, just because he was a dark coven vamp. It mattered little to somehow devoted he was to Marcus and his clan, or how much he loved Phoebe.

"Sir, I really have no desire to speak. Perhaps you could share what you see fit?" Lionel pleaded with his employer.

"Very well. Many of you know that Jeb here, Lionel's brother, was held captive for some months after Jeb had traced the vile dark coven Lord, Dag, to the middle of the Sahara. This act of heroism we all thought had resulted in Jeb's death. But we were wrong. As you know, Jeb was found by a Bedouin tribe, who was proficient in restoring creatures, dark coven creatures, back to health. They thought perhaps Jeb could help them or, perhaps he would be worth some reward, coming from my household. So, just as he was ready and well enough to transport and send a communication home, he was captured by this despicable creature we now know as Salaman. This mortal man used Jeb's blood to obtain powers he would not normally have obtained on his own. He used Jeb as a beacon, a way to lure members of my household to his location to rescue Jeb. And it worked. Except he was not quite prepared for Lionel."

One of the members spoke up. "Alexi how is it that your parents thought your sisters' murderer was human?"

"Because, our house is literally made with a silver netting behind the walls. There is no way a dark vamp could've entered."

"So why did he wish to attract Lionel or someone from the Monteleone family? Why didn't he just hold Jeb for ransom, that you surely would have paid, Marcus, correct?"

"Indeed, I would."

Lionel felt he had to speak up finally. "No, he wasn't interested in money. He was interested in attracting a Golden female. In particular, he was looking for Phoebe. He knew all about her. I mistakenly fell into his trap. I'm afraid I'm responsible for leading him to Tuscany."

The room became agitated. The crosstalk continued even though Marcus tried to calm everyone. Lionel knew the families would have a horrible time with his confession. He wished he'd been stronger and resisted his employer's urge to tell the story. But Lionel also understood that it was important to tell the truth, so they all could plan for the coming weeks, months and years ahead. In fact, Lionel thought it was possible these family members would be battling the dark coven lords for centuries.

Lionel shot a quick glance at Carmine Monteleone and noticed that the pink-faced elder was frozen in place. He had the suspicion that Carmine knew something about Salaman. It was time to reveal his suspicion.

"Carmine?" Lionel's booming voice cut through the room like a sword. He dialed his intensity back. "I think you know something about this man. You need to tell us right now. I for one deserve it because I am Phoebe's husband."

He heard the gasps again and the scowls that came his way.

"This is blasphemy! I will not listen to a dark coven Lord challenge my husband, in my family's presence," shrieked Athena Monteleone. "Marcus, what kind of a household are you running?"

Before Marcus could answer Lionel stepped forward and barked in return, "I am pledged to protect Phoebe with my life until she finds her fated mate. That is all, no more, and no less." Lionel felt the hot blood of his anger turning his skin to metal, readying himself to take on the whole pack if he had to. His brothers drew up to fighting stance.

"But that is only *one* reason," he continued. "Your husband has valuable information about someone who puts us all in peril. I do not judge him, but I am certain he knows something he's not telling us."

Members of the family parted as Lionel stepped backwards and into the shadows again.

Athena was going to lash out at Marcus, at Lionel, or anyone else she felt could be opposed to her. But before she could begin, Marcus commanded, "Stop, woman!"

He grabbed Carmine by the shirt collar and yanked him to the center of the floor nearly toppling him. "You will tell me now, or I will take you back to Tuscany and have you tried or judged by the Council."

Athena was going to interrupt again, but this time her husband stopped her. "Shut up. Marcus is correct. I have met this man Salaman." He angled his head until he could make eye contact with Lionel. "And yes, he wants Phoebe. But I think I know something he wants even more."

Lionel wanted to trace to this man's side, cover up his mouth and take him out into the woods and give him a beating. He knew what Carmine was going to say, but unfortunately, Marcus did not.

"Go ahead man. Tell me. Perhaps there is some way I can pay him off." Marcus had resumed his logical demeanor, his anger having subsided.

Carmine's sickly smile revealed further proof that the man, although he was of the mighty Golden vampire clan, was really a reptile, with the heart and soul of a creature somewhere between an alligator and a snake with fangs. He was disgusting. If it wasn't for the danger it would create for Phoebe and the rest of the family, he would have removed Carmine from the universe right then and there. But he had to let Marcus make the mistake. He was just the man who was supposed to fix those mistakes for him.

"He wants the *Book of Spawn*. He told me himself that if he could have that book Phoebe's life, in fact all of our lives, would be spared. Don't you accuse me of something perhaps I never did, or you'll have to explain to this body the fact that you have the secret book, and that the world is beginning to understand and demand access. You cannot hostage your entire family just so you can keep this book for yourself."

He faced his wife, who was sobbing, and then added, "Before any of you judge me, I have lived with this terrible burden for several weeks now. I'm the victim here, being used, prodded and poked, riding in some cage in the middle of the desert. I have lived under and accepted the rules of this family." He glared at his wife again. "I have begged for every penny I've had to spend. I have watched as my beautiful wife has dalliances with younger men, and even dark coven men, and I've said nothing!"

Athena slapped him across the face. "You dog!"

The crowd began to close in on the couple. For a second, Lionel thought perhaps both Carmine and his wife would be torn to shreds. But instead, each family member screamed their disapproval, and several threatened to take Carmine before the council.

"I gladly yield the floor," Carmine sputtered above the fray, obviously afraid for his life. Raising his chin to the ceiling, he proclaimed, "In fact, if anyone of you wants to negotiate with this animal, I will help put you two together. He's done his research. He knows things."

Then Carmine was allowed to stand in front of Marcus, as he barked, "He knows more about that book than I do. Now, Marcus, do you want to explain that to the council in Tuscany, or should I?"

Chapter 11

PHOEBE WAS ANXIOUS to find out about the meeting last night. She tried to stay awake for Lionel's return but was having difficulty shifting back-and-forth between daytime and nighttime routines, wanting to spend quality time with Anne and Marcus, while keeping up with Lionel and his routine of sleeping by day and living at night.

She slipped out of the room and scampered downstairs finding Cara and Lucius sitting in the kitchen. Lucius was eating cold cereal, one of those colorful fruity kinds with a pour over of his favorite, chocolate milk. Cara noticed the smirk on her face and shrugged.

"I can't do anything about it. He likes his sugar, chocolate, sugary cereal, energy bars. I hope he doesn't decide not to take the turning when he reaches puberty, if his teeth will last that long."

Phoebe giggled. "Can I ask you a question?"

"Of course."

"If he had to have a filling, would that be something that he'd have the rest of his life, I mean for centuries then?"

"Yes, and he'd probably have to have that filling replaced hundreds of times, although, I think in the next hundred years they might perfect a way that he could re-grow it. But that's just a guess."

"New teeth for a vampire?"

"Oh yes. As you know I was not raised that way. I was raised as a human and turned as an adult."

"Yes, I knew that."

"But Paolo has told me of someone who had such a disfigurement in his youth, knocking out half his teeth. It was a problem for him since one of those teeth was his upper canine." Cara shook her head from side to side. "And before you go asking, yes, we have a great dentist."

The ladies shared a laugh.

Lucius got up, deposited his bowl in the sink and rinsed it. "I'm going upstairs to do some homework. Don't forget, I have a game later this afternoon," he reminded his stepmom.

Cara nodded. "Absolutely, Lucius. We'll both be there."

As Lucas' footsteps shook the staircase, Cara returned to her laptop, which had been left open on the counter. Phoebe helped herself to some coffee. She watched Cara mumble and frown at her screen, click several keys, hit a final return, and then close the laptop lid down with a slap.

"I'm trying to set up a vacation. We'd like to go to Europe this summer, but, with all of this other stuff going on, Paolo doesn't think it safe. So, I'm trying to find an Airbnb someplace pretty that we could stay for a month."

This was a complete surprise for Phoebe. "Where are you thinking of going?"

"The south of France, or somewhere overlooking the Mediterranean. I like Capri or at least the pictures I've seen of it. Paolo thinks it's too close to Tuscany."

"Gosh, Lionel and I have never talked about vacations. I guess between the wedding and all the events both here and back home there just doesn't seem to be any time."

"Yes, and it's especially difficult now with a child. They are so precious. So vulnerable. Everywhere we go we are bringing with us armed guards. For Lucius' soccer game this afternoon I have to make sure the security detail doesn't look like Secret Service. He hates the attention, and the boys sometimes tease him about getting rides with big men in dark glasses and suits driving dark Suburbans. They think he's a little rich kid. I'm just glad he enjoys soccer and is a damn good player. Otherwise, his world would be so small. And I worry about that."

Phoebe's heart lurched, understanding how difficult it must be for a parent to raise a Golden child these days.

"I suppose staying in one place for a longer period of time, where you can set up your protective detail, is the only way, really."

Cara nodded, yes.

Phoebe approached Cara softly, beginning her real fact-finding mission. "You've always been so nice to me, Cara. You and Anne both have been so incredibly understanding. And your families have been so generous with their properties, their protection and everything else. I have some questions which I hope you can answer for me."

"Of course."

"You said I could ask you a question anytime, so I'm hoping this isn't an imposition."

Cara deposited herself in a chair at the kitchen table and pointed across the Formica to an empty chair. "Sit, and let's hear it."

"Can you explain to me about the fating process?"

"I wasn't built that way. As you know, my DNA is considerably different. But I wouldn't call our early relationship a fated relationship, because I didn't have the capacity for it, like I do now as a turned female."

"But would you have chosen it?"

"Not if I hadn't met Paolo. But I fell in love. You know how that goes, Phoebe." Cara winked at her.

Phoebe blushed. "I do indeed. Did you worry that some of your feelings toward him would change once you went through the journey?"

Cara nodded, smiling, and then breaking out into a giggle. "Well you see, I wasn't present for my own turning, due to the fact that I was unconscious. Nearly dead. I just remember waking up and there he was. Everything was made right. Things were done and I was saved. I've never thought about it, to be honest."

Cara's answer disturbed Phoebe. "But when you've talked to other women who've gone through the turning—other women such as myself who accept the turning, did anybody tell you that it changed them in some way?"

Cara leaned forward on the table placing her hands clasped together in front of her. "Well, the answer to that question is it depends. I think some young lady such as yourself, in love when they do the turning, I would guess that attraction wouldn't diminish. Sometimes they are lucky enough to have their husbands turn them when they get married. It's all arranged you know. The families arrange it."

"And if they are in love before and think they have chosen someone because they feel they could be fated then does it ever happen that they won't feel as strong toward their lover or their chosen partner as they did before the turning?"

Cara angled her head and then squinted. "Why so many questions?"

"I just wanted to know."

"I think that's pretty impossible. What would make you think love is an automatic thing, having to do with just species, biology, and scientific hocus pocus. It's love, Phoebe. Your heart does all the heavy lifting."

"But Rory, and some of the boys told me—"

"Well if it's *you* we're discussing, Phoebe of course Rory and several of those boys might be considered suitors. They're going to say something like that to you to eliminate the competition. And just for the record, we *are* talking about you and Lionel, correct?"

Phoebe felt embarrassed.

"Phoebe?"

"Yes. And before we go much further, I need to reveal something to you, Cara. I'm falling in love with Lionel."

"You think?"

"Excuse me?"

"Do you think that any of us in this household are so thick-headed that we wouldn't have noticed the attraction between you two?"

Phoebe blushed again.

"Honestly, child, what kind of a rock did your parents raise you under. Did they not explain anything to you about all this? No mother-daughter talks?"

"I wasn't ready."

"I can't believe I'm hearing this. My mother sat me down when I was twelve and gave me an explanation about everything, and what she expected of me. From then on, I was pretty clear where I stood.

Your parents sound like they have no common sense. Like royalty. Everything was handed to them. Am I correct?"

"They've lived in the past, yes. Our rules have always kept us safe."

"Except when they don't." Cara patted her arm and started to chuckle. "Lionel must really have his hands full."

Phoebe wondered if she'd revealed too much. "Please don't—"

"Oh, for Heaven's sakes, stop asking that. We're real world here. Maybe sometimes too real, or too frank. But that's the way things work here. You must be frustrated as Hell."

Phoebe knew she was right.

"You learn to take your shots, Phoebe. Go for it. Grab what you can."

"So that's why I've not gotten the lecture, then?"

"What lecture?"

"The one about saving myself for my true fated Golden male."

"Oh Jeez. You're all in with the questions today, aren't you? So, here's my answer on that one. It's a matter between you and your parents and Lionel, although God help you figure all that out. But generally, I don't think there's anyone in this household who would disagree. You make a suitable match for each other. Perhaps not in the classic sense of it, but these are strange times. For instance, my husband had three mortal wives before he chose me. And he swears that we are fated. It wasn't like some bolt of lightning thing for me. I just loved him, and I feel a much stronger attraction for him now than I did before. That's why I said I think it's impossible for that not to happen. But I didn't grow up vampire, did I?"

"And here I thought Lionel and I were being so discreet." Phoebe was irritated with herself for being so blind. But after she thought about it, she was happy that the burden of her feelings was now lifted.

"You do have the issue of the promise that Lionel has made to your parents. Everyone in the community has heard him take that oath. So, you must be careful, Phoebe, not to do anything that would jeopardize his position. I think it's awkward. But all I can say is, please be careful, but go for it with all you've got. We don't get a lot of second chances."

"We will. And in case you're wondering, he has kept his word." Despite her will she be felt the hot tears trickle down her cheeks. Cara reached over and grabbed one hand.

"Sweetie. How difficult this must be for you. Caught between two worlds, aren't you? And all these men telling you what to do? I'd go out of my mind."

Phoebe looked up at her cousin and saw the true face of a friend. Another ally. "Thank you, Cara. Please just keep this between the two of us?"

"You didn't even have to ask. This family has a lot of bottled-up drama. I've managed to stay pretty much clear of all that. That's good advice for you, too, dear."

At that moment Anne entered the kitchen. "Have you seen any of them yet?"

"Them, as in the men," Cara barked. She stole a wink at Phoebe.

"A fire could go off in our room and Lionel would not awaken. He got in very late last night," Phoebe answered. "But you know that's the way he is."

Cara glanced up at Anne. "Is Marcus gone already?"

"Yes. I don't think he went to bed at all last night."

"Oh dear. Do you think he's OK?" Cara pressed.

"He left me a note, and said he needed to do some inspections in the Vineyard. He has a new crew coming in to do trimming. I know that working in the vineyard is good for him because it helps him think. I'm also sure he didn't want to be pestered with my questions. But I heard last night's meeting was very contentious and didn't exactly go the way he wanted it to."

With her disheveled auburn hair cascading down around her shoulders, and even with the lack of makeup, barefoot and padding about the kitchen in her nighty and robe, she was still one of the most beautiful women Phoebe had ever seen. Her brilliance and elegance shone through, in spite of her lack of preparation.

Cara quipped, "Paulo told me there were demands made by Carmine. Things about the Book. I know we're not supposed to talk about it, but there it is. He begged off any further questions."

"I did hear Marcus on the phone with the Council. Carmine is being watched very closely, and he might be stripped of his voting rights. Marcus may have to produce the book for the elders, but they're still making up their minds. Things take forever," Anne said, sighing.

Phoebe inhaled and tried to inch closer to her real question, her *burning* question, which now was more appropriate than ever. "So, this brings me to another query, if you two don't mind."

"You *still* have questions?"

Anne whipped around to face her as she added cream to her coffee. Her forehead sported a slight crease of worry. "You know you can ask me anything, Phoebe. You must consider me your sister, not a stranger. You can trust me with all your questions."

Cara chuckled and crossed her arms. "You may regret being so generous, Anne. Phoebe and I have had quite a little discussion already." Cara's face lit up in a wide smile. "About love!" she said as she wiggled her eyebrows up and down.

"Oh, that," whispered Anne. She brought her coffee to the table and joined the other two. "Have you told your parents?"

"I'm trying to figure it all out," said Phoebe. "I don't know where I stand right now. I feel like I want to be in one place and yet I find myself behind locked doors in another. I hate waiting. I don't want to seem ungrateful but there is a part of my situation that surely I must be able to control. And yet, I'm told that I must wait—wait for answers I fear might never come."

"Well it won't be for lack of trying. You should hear her questions, Anne."

In spite of Cara's comment, Phoebe could tell that Anne understood what she was talking about. She was considering an answer, when Phoebe's impatience burst forth.

"Here it is. Cara and I have just been discussing this, too. Don't the women in this family make any decisions at all?" she asked.

Nobody moved at first. Then, Anne and Cara exchanged a long glance, before Anne began her answer.

"I'm not sure what I'm able to tell you, Phoebe. But I will say that the Monteleone brothers, my husband probably being the instigator of this, are very set in their ways."

"Stubborn," added Cara.

"Rigid." Anne covered her mouth and rolled her eyes at Cara. "And I don't mean that to be a sexual term. Sorry, Phoebe."

Phoebe blushed in spite of herself. "I think some rigidity is a sign of a healthy marriage, Anne. Not that I would know, of course." She felt her cheeks burn.

All three women burst out laughing.

"Honest to God, there are days, Phoebe, when I want to run Paulo over with his own tractor," said Cara.

"Trace him to the bottom of the ocean," said Anne.

"Stick them in the fermentation tank and throw away the key!" added Cara.

Phoebe giggled so hard she nearly wet her pants. "So, I guess my observation is accurate, then."

"We love them, but sometimes we hate them," moaned Anne. "I mean I really do get angry with them. They can be so pig-headed sometimes, when a little softness or kindness would do. They love to be in control."

Cara piped up, "Always. Even when they're wrong, too."

"So how do you handle it?" asked Phoebe.

"Honestly, I go have my nails done. Or I go work in the garden—I just need some alone time."

"That's more difficult with a little one." said Cara. "I try to help out, when we're in California."

Anne nodded, scanning the large picture window in the kitchen overlooking the vineyard. "I think every woman finds certain aspects of her society difficult from time to time. The men, they mean well. They love passionately. They are hard on themselves in their devotion, their dedication to family and to their businesses. At least the Monteleones are. Not all the families work that hard or take on such a heavy burden. But then they are leaders."

"So, if they could share the burden, perhaps some other responsibilities with their wives, wouldn't that make things easier?" Phoebe asked what she hoped would be the obvious.

Anne's eyes grew near the size of hard-boiled eggs. "Are you kidding?"

"Think about it, Anne. It's difficult for us to see them struggle so much, when some of the help could come from us, the people they love and trust." Phoebe was adamant the two women would see her point.

Cara grinned. "That would be the day. I had difficulty just keeping my teaching position when I married Paolo. He didn't want me going anywhere, he was so protective."

Phoebe smiled. "It just seems like women are doing so much now. There are heads of large corporations, and leaders in business, careers, positions in government, leading scientists and experts in all fields. We see this in the human world, but I don't see any of this in our families—our families plural." Phoebe searched both Cara and Ann's faces for a trace of recognition, or agreement.

"You have a point," sighed Anne." Let me think about this a bit," she added.

It was Phoebe's turn to lean into the table. "So, here's another thing I've thought of. It concerns the Book of Spawn."

"If you bring up that book, that's a sure-fire way to get your cousin Marcus on your bad side, Phoebe," said Anne sternly. Her eyebrows were still raised when Phoebe gave her an answer.

"But this is not for the general public. This is just between us, the women who live in this house, and who love the men in it. It's not for anyone outside the small group."

"So, what's your question about the book?" asked Cara.

Phoebe knew she had to be careful when she said the words. "I was thinking that we all should attempt to read it, as well as the men. I was thinking that with your studies, Cara, your experiences being once mortal women, new to the clan, that you could see the Book with a set of fresh eyes. And I want to explore it as well. Like I said earlier I'm frustrated with the waiting. I want answers. I want to know why it is I feel something more than just some kind of mortal love for my husband. Although he says he's satisfied with this, I want to know if it ever would be possible for us to be a true partnership. And I think the book will help tell me this."

"Boy, Phoebe, this is dangerous territory," Anne whispered. "I'm not sure this is a good idea. Don't get your hopes up."

"But you've seen the book right, Anne?" Phoebe asked.

"I have. I've seen Marcus hold it open, and I've seen him put it away in his safe. It travels with us wherever we go, so I know it is of great importance. But as far as allowing me to read it, I have asked, but he's never been willing."

Cara tapped her fingers on the table "Well, I have read parts of the book. And I think Phoebe is right."

Ann's head shot up, listening to Cara's reveal.

"You don't mean that, surely."

"I most certainly do."

"What's it like?" Phoebe asked. "I mean the parts that you've read, what did they say?"

"They talk about histories of people, and then there are pages and pages of rules. But mostly it's a story told by multiple people, points of view."

Cara studied Ann's face and then gave Phoebe a gentle wink.

"What?" Phoebe asked.

"The book is not like any other I've ever seen," said Cara. "It is a database, a pool of knowledge, but unlike an ordinary book, this book controls the reading experience."

"That doesn't make any sense," said Anne.

"It's like the book gets to decide what information it releases, depending on the reader. So you might read it for instance, Phoebe, and come away with different information than if Lionel or Marcus read it."

Both Phoebe and Anne waited for her to continue. She wondered if Cara had ever divulged any of this information to her husband, and Phoebe presumed that she hadn't.

"That's why it would do no good to copy the book," Cara told them. "I don't even know if the pages *would* copy. Some of the words appear when the reader puts their eyes on them. So you are quite correct Phoebe. Depending on who is doing the study, the information in the book will be different."

Anne put her hand to her mouth. "Oh my God. They could be leading us right off a cliff."

The three women looked at each other. Phoebe knew they had come to an important milestone. And, unlike what they'd been told, their input was not only important, it might spell the difference between success and failure in preserving the lives of their families.

Before Phoebe went upstairs, Cara pulled her aside.

"Hey, I just want to say welcome to the family, such as it is."

"Thanks."

"You follow your intuition, Phoebe. That's the way out. Remember what I said, grab what you can. Don't wait for your happiness, and for God's sake, get rid of all the questions!"

Phoebe chuckled. "Yes, ma'am."

She leaned closer and whispered. "Does Lionel know what he's in for?"

"I don't think so, Cara."

"Oh, what a lucky boy. I can hardly wait to see the fireworks."

Chapter 12

WHEN LIONEL USUALLY awoke, the bedroom would be completely dark. But today there was a golden light in the air that shown through his closed eyelids, making him wonder if he was still dreaming.

As he continued to awaken, he began inhaling some kind of scent he found familiar and pleasing, a mixture of lavender, vanilla and cinnamon. He was conscious his restorative sleep was over, yet he chose to linger a bit in bed and enjoy the sensuous warm glow and the aromas he could almost taste now.

When he heard rustling in the distance, he became certain he was no longer dreaming.

He opened his eyes.

Phoebe's pink nude body slipped gently beside him. Her legs wrapped around his thighs as his arms encircled her waist. He sifted his fingers through her wild auburn hair and uncovered the face of his beloved. She fit nicely in his arms, tightening the grip on his thigh with hers as she pressed her mound back-and-forth against him.

At last her lips were on his. Their tongues mated in gentle play until his arousal became so strong, he quickly rolled her body beneath him and kissed her deep.

She arched up to receive him spreading her legs and bending her knees in that submissive position that was so dangerous for him.

He reared back to look down on her. Two soft fingers traced the outlines of his lips. He wanted her more this morning than ever before.

Her forefinger was pressed against his upper right canine and drew blood. The pupils of her eyes dilated when he sucked her finger and took the precious drops she offered him.

When he released her hand, he felt her fingers crawl and snake between them until at last she found his member. Her eyes closed slowly as she moved, stroking him up and down, her fingers squeezing him firmly. She rubbed the pre-cum that had formed all over his crown.

Her fingers rimmed her own opening. He could feel her gentle shudder, her body's natural reaction to his stimulating fluid meant to prepare her for sex that wouldn't be coming today. She arched back again, moaning, gently rocking as she tried to guide the tip of his member to her opening.

He quickly stopped her. His hand gripped her wrist and drew her arm up from under the covers, laying it gently above her head on the pillow. But that did not stop the undulation between her legs or the tender stroking her thighs made over his, over his hip and over the back of his buttocks.

"Phoebe, sweetheart," he said as he attempted to request her attention. "Look at me, sweetheart."

A thin frown line appeared in the middle of her flawless forehead just before she opened her eyes and took every part of him inside her with that sensual gaze. Her need and will was growing. His resistance was crumbling.

While her eyes fixated on his mouth she undulated again, attempting to hook her sex on him. His cock was rock hard, nearly bursting with desire for her. But he still found the strength to hold back.

"Love me. Make me your woman. I need this," her sultry voice called out.

He touched her cheek with his palm. "I do love you Phoebe. And someday, we will mate. I promise."

She covered his mouth with three fingers and shushed him. "No. The time is right. I am ripe with love for you. You are my one true love."

He started to plead his case, but again she covered his mouth with her fingers.

It pleased him how much she wanted him. He could never be angry with her for acting on her desires, because she was young, impulsive, and so damn magical! He felt like he was the luckiest man alive.

Her hand found his member again. "Please," she pleaded as she stroked him. "Take me Lionel. Take me now."

He felt moisture form in his eyes. His heart ached to fully pleasure her, to give her what she needed. "Not just yet. Soon, my love."

"Can you tell the future?" She asked. Before he could answer she interrupted him again. "Can you tell me with one hundred percent certainty that I'll live long enough until it's time?"

This was new, and it alarmed him. He could see her frustration brewing. She did not like to be told no. It didn't matter whether it was an extra helping of ice cream, a few extra strawberries, or the times when she demanded he trace to the store to buy whipped cream for the sole purpose of obeying her command to lick it off her tender flesh. He loved caving into her demands because she was so strong, so relentless. But this was deeper. This was far more serious.

"What has happened?" he asked.

"Are you oblivious to these times we live in?"

"Of course not."

"What if something were to happen to one of us? What if eternity is not in our future? What if one of us perishes, and the other has to go on living for centuries without the other?"

"You're not making any sense, sweetheart. What is this new dark notion infecting your spirit? Do you not trust that I shall be able to protect you?"

"That's not it, Lionel. Of course I believe you. But, the women in this family are waiting. We're waiting for some kind of a plan."

"But we are trying to locate this devil who has caused so much harm to the family. He was probably the same creature who held Jeb captive. He is mortal, Phoebe. He can be destroyed, and we intend to do so."

"Why must we wait when you know this is right? We were meant for each other. Why restrict our love when you know that I'm telling you the truth? Or, are you merely humoring me? Pretending. I'm beginning to think you're waiting for me to meet someone else. Could that be what's going on? Because there is no reason to wait. No one will know."

"But I gave my promise." Lionel felt his sexual buzz waning, being quickly replaced by anger. He needed to be careful or he'd say something he would later regret. "How can you possibly think I would allow anything to happen to you? It just is not possible."

"But that's exactly what I'm talking about, Lionel. How do you know for certain what our future is?"

"No one knows that," he shot back, and then regretted his tone.

"Then, if you are certain, husband, take me now. Prove to me that you are absolutely going to find this nemesis and remove him from the planet. Swear to me that you will be my husband in *all* ways possible."

He was going to interrupt again, but she quickly covered his mouth.

"Swear it, husband. And then prove it. Take me across the threshold from girl to woman. Make me yours. I'm not asking for us to declare it publicly. I'm asking that you trust me with our secret."

He didn't like being challenged. If he said he was certain of the outcome, he meant it. But while he didn't need the proof, Phoebe did. He began to understand her frustration. She wanted more than words from him. And he could give her that. But the cost, or the risk, could be great.

Was the risk worth it? Her logic was valid. What if Phoebe was right, and they were forever separated, and they had to walk alone in this cold and lonely world without each other? He knew if that were the case, he'd just end his life. But what about Phoebe?

She was telling him that she wanted to be an equal partner in their sexual relationship. That she no longer wanted him to make the decision about going forward. Lionel saw for the first time, that perhaps his judgment had been clouded.

Looking down upon her, he wondered if it were possible that their secret would hold, or did this no longer matter?

She was waiting for his answer. She'd also been waiting all these weeks, and he knew they were no closer to finding a real solution then they were the day he married her. But what was changing every single day is that their love was growing. It was vibrant and gave him an even greater purpose in life.

He'd even told Marcus that he couldn't conceive of the fact that their attraction to one another wasn't blessed. It was more than animal lust. It was a fating.

They'd reached the point of no return.

He smiled down upon her. His thumb traced the dark vein at the side of her neck all the way down until it was buried in the top of her shoulder. The familiar thirst for her fluids made his mouth feel parched. She watched him lick his lips. He didn't hold back showing her his desire. She watched as his tongue rubbed over one of his canines, leaving a wound, preparing to give her a taste.

Her eyes were hopeful. He saw her astonishment as he pulled back the covers, knelt in front of her and bowed his head. He grabbed a pillow from the top of the bed and gently placed it under her rear. He saw red blotchy marks on her chest, and the way she struggled for air. It excited him to see her so nervous.

He needed to ask one question with three very important words.

"Are you sure?" he whispered.

She rose up, throwing her arms around his neck, kissing him, taking the red elixir he'd prepared for her. She inhaled and squeezed his torso as hard as she could.

"I have never been surer, husband. I knew it from the first day I saw you. I knew we were destined in this way. It means so much to me that you honor my request. That you trust me to handle whatever consequence this brings us. I promise that I will never regret our decision to be made one." Brave tears framed her eyes and he was filled with tenderness.

He lifted her chin with his thumb and forefinger. "It's going to be a bumpy ride, Phoebe. Always know that I do this out of my love for you."

"And my love for you, husband."

He grinned.

"What?"

"I used to secretly dream about having you call my name as I pleasured you in my arms." He pressed his thumb from the top of her forehead down her nose and then back-and-forth across her lips. "You are my wife, but you are *Phoebe* to me. Humor me, call me by my name, my *Christian* name."

Her eyes opened wide at first and then she caught the joke. "If I have my wits about me, Lionel, I promise."

He gently lay her back on the bed, admiring her perfect form. Her breasts were ripe and fully round, her nipples swollen and bright red like succulent cherries. He knew what most of her body felt like under his tongue. He also knew how it tasted. He could feel the little pulsing veins and capillaries as she nourished herself with the tiny droplets of his blood he'd shared with her before in their almost-lovemaking. But this was going to be different. He was going to savor every minute and remember every element as her body responded to him. And he prayed it would be as pleasurable for her as well.

He read her mind as she wondered if there was going to be any pain.

"I'm going to be very gentle," he answered to her musing, leaning over. He whispered in her ear, "Just relax, and give yourself to me."

She blushed that her inner thoughts had been discovered.

'You can't hide from me,' he said to her telepathically. *'In time, you'll bare it all without hesitation.'*

Lionel once more appreciated the beautiful curve of her neck and the bluish vein he felt pulsing beneath his fingers. He sent a series of nibbling kisses up and down, from her left ear to her clavicle, and then whispered again to her, "Now, does that hurt?"

Phoebe giggled.

His fingers massaged her opening just as she had done a few minutes before, and placed himself, ready to enter her. He twisted her bud between his thumb and third finger, which made her jump.

And then slowly he breached the walls of her virginity.

Her fingers were flailing at the sides of her face until he took one hand and gently placed it around his member so she could feel where they joined. Together, they traced where her tissues stretched to accept him until at last, he was fully inside.

He began the incantations of love, the words spoken by vampire men to their fated mates for centuries. The words made her skin begin to glow, as if a light inside had suddenly been lit. He knew once she turned, this would be even more pronounced. But there was no mistaking the stunning and beautiful evidence displayed before him.

He felt her soften, relax, and accept him fully as he penetrated deeper. The expression on her face was one of surprise as he withdrew slightly and then filled her all the way to his hilt.

Lionel caressed Phoebe's neck again with his tongue. Her head rushed to the side, fully exposing her vein to him. He let her fingers explore his mouth, touching his engorged fangs ready to take her.

"Yes, oh please, Lionel. Please take me as your woman." she whispered.

He allowed the words to wash over him, satisfying his strong, protective maleness.

He drew in air and then plunged deep into her neck, as she moaned and quivered beneath him, making mewling sounds while squeezing and scratching his back.

Phoebe's elixir made him ravenous for her. The long-dormant animal spirits in him rose and roared to the universe as he claimed her while he fucked her hard. His hips begin working furiously, and the harder he entered the softer and more pliable she became. She clutched his neck, pressing his face into her harder and deeper to take more.

As he came up for air he blew into her face, pulling her torso up onto him. Adjusting his knees, he raised her to balance on his groin, holding her by the hips and moving her gently back and forth in a rocking motion as her sex began to quiver and then spasm.

Her hair was drenched around the sides of her face and beads of sweat had collected on her upper lip and forehead. He smelled her arousal under her ear and even tasted remnants of it as he seared the tiny wound in her neck with his saliva. His fingers stroked her one more time appreciatively. He buried his nose between her breasts and lapped droplets of her essence.

Lionel helped her peak in her arousal, and then cool off several times. She began to take charge, initiating intimate touches and changing angles as she rode him aggressively.

He decided it was time for one more experience.

"Now you will drink from me. Not too much, or it could make you sick. You will not have fangs of course until you turn." He smiled as he continued to rock her up and down on his cock. She was so light he could hold her with one arm. He looked down at the place where they joined and invited her to feel him inside her. Her fingers reached for his balls and she squeezed.

With one arm still around her waist, he leaned back to allow her to sit atop him. She hesitated as he lifted her up and then back down grinding her so that his cock met resistance deep inside her.

She frowned.

"Did I hurt you?"

"Oh, Lionel I love this," she said. Her eyes were unfocused. She pushed herself by her arms against his chest and he removed his hands letting her move herself up and down his shaft. Her body once again begin to shudder.

He made a small slit over his right wrist and presented it to his wife. With both hands she gripped his forearm and sucked.

He knew it would make her come instantly and was glad he hadn't told her beforehand, so it came as a complete, pleasurable surprise. Dropping his arm, she arched, undulated, held her hair atop her head, squeezed her breasts, and allowed the long unforgiving orgasm to completely wash over her, filling her body with waves of pleasure he could feel as well.

Lionel's body responded in kind, as he filled her.

He wasn't sure she noticed. But he was determined to repeat the scene as many times as it took until she did.

Chapter 13

PHOEBE KNEW SOMEONE in the family would figure out what they'd done if she didn't stop dropping things and bumping into people. She and Lionel were playing it risky several times a day with little antics like having quickies in the kitchen pantry or asking Marcus if they could ride the little Kubota lawnmower around the front yard in the moonlight, all the time with Lionel's cock firmly planted between her legs as she sat on his lap.

She knew someone would eventually notice. And that could interfere with her plans to get hold of the book.

She began to understand why Lionel was so good at being a bodyguard. He could keep a straight face, control his breathing. He could even stop his ejaculations and then turn them back on for her, which had been a bet she'd lost.

The golden hue of her skin tone did concern her, however, because she knew, even if Anne and Cara didn't know to notice it, Marcus or Paolo or one of the other men would definitely catch on. Lionel told her she'd have to stop giving him orals or she'd start torching like a firecracker and might even glow in the dark. She returned a smart retort, telling him she had no intention of cutting back and that now she wanted to watch them fuck in front of a mirror so she could experience all of it. She knew he was playing a joke on her, but it mattered not.

He was losing arguments every day to her, or perhaps pretending to. At any rate, it was fun, and the games continued.

"Are you sure I won't get pregnant?" she asked Lionel one night.

He was furiously pumping her from behind and gasped at her question. Out of breath, and more than a little irritated, he hissed,

"Ask me in about five, no ten minutes. I need to fuck."

She liked that he talked dirty to her more now that they'd been so familiar.

The memory of the dark murders had nearly been erased, even though it had been less than a week. When they were told that the man known as Salaman had returned to the desert, the whole family breathed a collective sigh of relief.

Trying to redeem himself, Carmine broke the news to Marcus over the phone after they returned to their home in Tuscany. The council wanted him to be given a second chance, and the order for Marcus to appear was rescinded.

That started the agreement with Marcus to allow Anne, Cara and Phoebe access to the book. Phoebe was thrilled to learn more about the world she had now officially joined.

Cara, Anne, and Phoebe sat together on the long leather couch in Marcus' study. Paolo stood in the corner, his legs and arms crossed, leaning against the bookcase. Lionel had not yet begun his day and was upstairs in their room.

"I have agreed to allow the three of you to study on one condition. You must promise not to reveal its contents to anyone else. Obviously, I cannot stop you from discussing it amongst yourselves, but I ask you to do so privately, when you are certain you won't be overheard."

"I'd like to insert something please." Paolo walked over to the large library table that held the book and lightly traced his fingers over the ridges of the intricate gold tooling on the cover. "For the record, I'm not sure I approve. And I think Lionel agrees with me. Cara has discussed with me some of the properties of this book, and I'm not entirely sure it's healthy. I've learned to be skeptical of things I don't fully understand."

Cara lowered her head, and whispered, "Like love?"

Paulo threw his arms out to the side, clutching the book in one hand, addressing Marcus. "I can see I'm going to lose that argument."

"Paolo, "Cara cooed. "We are going to be extremely careful. All I meant to say with my comment was that we deal with things every day we don't understand."

Paolo returned the book to the table and went back to his corner.

Anne leaned forward, her elbows on her knees, and asked, "Marcus, why don't you begin by telling us what you've discovered so far? And we agree to share with you everything we find. One of the things that Cara has told us is that perhaps your reading of the book would be different than our reading of the book. And that could be very significant. All we want is more information."

"Lionel and I have probably poured 20 or 30 hours over it so far. We found passages in Greek, Aramaic, which is the ancient language spoken at the time of Christ." Marcus crossed the room, leaned over and picked up the heavy tome, clutching it between his enormous fingers.

"We read a story in French. Actually, it was an early ancestor of the French language, and the story told of a people who overthrew their king. It seemed to go on and on until toward the end it referred to another chapter toward the back of the book. That chapter contains graphs and lists of things and what look like hieroglyphics."

Marcus continued, "It's almost like whomever wrote this book— or maybe it was written by multiple people, I don't know. But it does appear that whomever wrote it never intended that the reader start from the beginning and follow all the way to the end. It seems like there are multiple stories. There are at least three which are the biggest ones. One of them starts in the middle and yet we find pieces of the same story in the beginning of the book and in the end."

Cara asked him if they had employed a rabbi or someone schooled in early Egyptian writings done on papyrus, or early Sanskrit texts. "I believe Muslim scholars might be able to shed some light," she said. "From what I've read, there are pages in this book written in Arabic."

Marcus set the book down and took a chair across from the ladies now seated before him. "I have not been able to find anyone who can translate any of these writings that appear to be in Arabic. I have received some minor success with the Aramaic and Hebrew translations, but Aramaic was not always a written language, and yet phonetically, we have some here."

Marcus told them that on one occasion, in one of his earliest sessions, he found reference to "Men of The Eternal Order", which he took to mean descendants of the Golden Vampire clans.

"It recounted a sort of Sodom and Gomorrah tale of boredom and debauchery. They had developed a great civilization, with ambassadors exploring every corner of the globe. They traveled through the sky, the story tells us, much like how we trace today. But their culture lost its way. It seems the population rebelled against the rule of law, overthrew their elders, and started on some form of creation study. It was very strange."

"Creation, you mean like creating them through turning?" asked Phoebe.

"Yes, I think that was it exactly. Something happened to their children. So, they created children of their own, in their own image. Not by procreation either."

"Where is this passage?" asked Anne.

"That is what is so strange. I cannot find it again. It's like it's just disappeared from the book."

"Which is consistent with what Cara told us. The book shows the reader what it wants the reader to see," added Phoebe.

"So, Marcus, you told me that story. You repeated it to Lionel. Maybe that's all that was supposed to happen," added Paolo.

"May I see the book, Marcus?" Phoebe asked.

Her cousin quickly retrieved it, placing it on her lap. With Anne on one side, and Cara on the other, she carefully opened it, trying to get to the center section. The pages were stiff and bulky, their edges dipped in red liquid, inconsistently applied. In the very center of the page was a sketch depicting a woman with long hair, lying prostrate in front of a large cage which contained a lion.

Her fingers touched the drawing and immediately gold letters, looking like writing in fire, became visible. She couldn't recognize any of the characters.

When she removed her hand, the words quickly faded.

"This is amazing," said Anne. "Marcus, Cara is right. I touch this page and no such writing appears. See?"

Her hand swept across the page and then scrolled down the opposite page. Nothing was altered. Nothing changed colors. Anne's touch caused no affect whatsoever.

"Could it be because she is not a native-born Golden woman?" asked Paolo.

"I have no idea," answered Marcus. "I have touched these pages many times, as have you Paulo."

"Yes. So has Lionel. We've never seen this."

"But I did," interrupted Cara. "I saw passages appear that I swear weren't there before."

"Is it random, then?" asked Anne.

"No," Marcus said as he stared down into Phoebe's face, just as her father had done over the years. His eyes were gentle and loving. "Not random."

She couldn't help but wonder if he suspected what she and Lionel had done, or if the letters her fingers generated were some kind of message about their transgressions. She struggled to push all the thoughts and images of her past few days of dalliances out of her mind.

Marcus held out his hand to her. "It appears the book has also affected you, my child." As he took both Phoebe's hands in his, he rubbed his thumb across the knuckles on her right. "Even your hands are Golden."

Chapter 14

S ALAMAN WAS FURIOUS. He couldn't wait to get his claws into the neck of that treacherous coward, Carmine Monteleone, and his witch of a wife. He'd dismember her and her two daughters in little chunks and feed them to the ducks on the pond where he was staying. He had rented a cottage behind one of the wineries in Healdsburg, hoping to use it as his base of operation.

But all that had suddenly changed.

Now, he didn't know exactly what he was going to do. He *was* going to kill that family, that was for sure. But now that the whole family was privy to his presence, he wasn't quite sure he could get to all of them in time. It was an incredible amount of work to wipe out a whole clan all by himself.

And he wasn't that hungry, either.

As for his methods, he'd exact his revenge painfully, slowly, even if robbed of the element of surprise. They would know who he was, and how ruthless he was. Maybe it would be worth it to watch terror bloom in their eyes as he eliminated them from the face of the earth one by one, and then eliminating their progeny.

However, he did have one concern. The only people he was worried about coming up against were the three Jett brothers. He regretted that they had history, but there wasn't anything he could do now about that.

What bothered him was their strength, their stealth, the telepathy that they had between them, and their loyalty and honor. They were very experienced warriors, familiar with methods and devices. It made them formidable enemies.

Monteleone attack dogs.

Unlike Carmine, these men would not be cowards. They would die defending the Monteleones, and by extension, their beautiful cousin, Phoebe.

It was such a joke that she would choose a dark coven Lord to be her husband... even if it was her pretend husband. The whole fucking clan was crazy. They didn't know the first thing about protecting their women, really. Without the Jett brothers, it was like taking candy from a baby. But with them, he'd have to be more careful. With their preternatural sense of smell and abilities to trace, he could find himself suddenly orbiting the moon if he wasn't careful.

He told himself that if he could just get the book, then he might consider leaving the family alone, unless he was bored. But he really needed to make a statement to avenge for the disrespect Carmine had shown him so publicly. Sparing the family was totally out of the question. He'd make it bloody and loud.

He mentally ticked off everything he needed to complete before he could leave California. Three days. It was too cold and damp here. He much preferred the desert. And in the desert, he had a distinct advantage over the dark vampire lords, who were really his only enemy. He also had lots of allies in the desert—people who were terrified of him and would stay in his good graces by offering protection. The hot desert sun was also his formidable ally against the dark Lords.

The traveler also didn't care for the California scenery, the brown scorched earth, the little rows of twigs that covered the hills, looking like baby dreadlocks on a fat Martian's behind. The whole place was overrated. He'd tasted food all over the world, and here, people ate cold cheeses and green lettuce as if they had goat DNA. Goats were disgusting creatures.

Now the wine, that was another story. But he'd raided wine caves all over Europe and he found them unremarkable. Besides, the musty fermentation smell of the young grape juice seeping into concrete floors or oozing out through the cracks in those oak barrels made him sneeze. He did like to drink the finished product, as long as it was sanitary and wouldn't get him sick, but he didn't care much for the process.

Joel, the traveler's Uber driver who had transported him all the way from San Francisco airport, was still in the passenger side of his black Lexus SUV. His face was growing paler by the minute, even beginning to develop a gray-bluish tint, due to the lack of blood in his body. The traveler was going to have to dispose of him somehow so he could use the vehicle. He'd already given Joel's phone with the Uber tracking device to a kid panhandling outside a grocery store.

"Hey, thanks man," The kids said as he loped away.

The traveler hoped the young man took a long journey with the phone, perhaps even selling it to someone else. It would make locating the former owner more difficult.

Since it was time for him to make an appearance, he walked outside, opened the passenger door, and captured Joel's body under the armpits, dragging him into the pond. He found a dry tree branch to give him a little send off, tapping him in the belly to expel some air. He was hoping this would make him sink. The traveler watched the young man's body float to the center of the pond, become the object of curiosity for several large geese and a bevy of much smaller ducks, before it silently disappeared under water.

By the time they knew Joel was missing, he'd be back in North Africa, with his prize, of course.

Looking down at his feet, he noticed that his shoes were encrusted in gooey mud. He wished he didn't have to purchase another pair. He didn't want to be seen disposing of this one, so he stood at the edge of the pond on dry ground, took his shoes off and tossed them one by one into the water. In his stocking feet, he made it back to the SUV.

The traveler tore out of the gravel road, sending a spray of rocks to the side like he was water skiing. Healdsburg was a quick ten-minute ride.

Carmine told him the Tuscan relatives were staying in the old Healdsburg Hotel, having booked the top two floors. He parked the Lexus across the Square and hiked over the grassy knoll, making a detour around a large white gazebo. An electric guitarist was playing music to a small crowd of wine tasters. Two hippie chicks were dancing.

Suddenly self-conscious of his stocking feet, he purchased a pair of shoes from a gentlemen's store on the Square, and then headed toward the old hotel.

He didn't expect to find all of the family members there, but he was surprised when he discovered that none of them had prolonged their stay. He rubbed his fingers to the sides of his face at his temples, trying to press the pounding headache in his brain outward so that he could concentrate. Things were slipping through his fingers. He didn't have the luxury of wreaking havoc on the entire clan all in one place. Eliminating them one by one back in Tuscany or wherever the heck they landed, was now going to be an even bigger job.

"Is there anything else I can do for you, sir?" The pretty receptionist asked him.

"I'm looking for the Monteleone Estate. I understand they have very good wine there. Can you direct me?"

"Of course. The family comes to town quite often. I'm sorry you missed them. But if you follow the map here—" she ripped a piece of paper from a tablet on the desk, circling the hotel's location on the town square. Then she drew a line following a winding country road bordered by numerous wineries. At last, she circled the Monteleone Estate. "It's right here. Only take you about twenty minutes I believe."

"Thank you."

Salaman pulled into the driveway of an adjacent winery and found a parking space near the back of the tasting room. He calculated it would be a brisk ten-minute walk to reach the Monteleone Estate.

He stepped over a small wooden fence and began walking through the freshly tilled dark brown soil of the adjacent family vineyard. He was glad he'd purchased new shoes. As he approached the enormous structure sitting atop the tallest hill, he began to hear voices. At first, he thought he was imagining them. But as he stopped to listen, he could tell the language was Spanish, and that's when he came upon the group of farmworkers pruning young vines and tying them to metal strings. He waved and couldn't remember the Spanish phrase greeting, so he continued on his track.

As he got closer to the large tasting room area the whole place appeared abandoned. There was an old pick-up truck parked in front of a large set of doors that had been chained shut. No large lights came from the inside. He appeared through the window to confirm that everything was dark and no one was present.

There was a slender dirt path leading to steps that approached a flower garden at the side of the large Victorian-style home. The plants began to make him sneeze, so he pulled a tissue from his pocket and held his nose. There were stubby plants with red flowers bordering along the walkway. Around several olive trees benches had been built adorned with lacey blue and white flowers.

He was about to just walk in the back door, which he presumed to lead to the kitchen, when he nearly bumped into Phoebe, of all people. He was quite taken aback with her beauty.

"Oh!"

"I'm sorry, did I startle you?" Salaman quickly made up a story. "I was looking for Mr. Lionel Jett? He lives at this address I believe?" He observed her studying his face. With the slash across one eye and his torn earlobe, he knew he didn't look quite presentable enough as a stranger. Salaman also knew that Lionel would be sleeping during the day, so he ran no risk of actually running into the man.

"He's busy. I'm his wife, may I help you?"

"Well I came from the tasting room and Lionel had asked me to bring a used car he wanted to take a look at it."

Salaman could see Phoebe was hesitant and didn't quite trust him yet. She was looking around for someone else, probably one of her protectors.

"Forgive my appearance, Mrs. Jett. I must give you a bit of a fright. You see, I'm a wounded veteran, in case you were wondering. This job is very important to me."

"I see."

He decided he might not have the opportunity he needed, and so determined that he probably would not be able to take her today. But he still had to try.

"I'm Bryce Conley, ma'am. I sell cars at the dealership downtown, um, my re-entry job. I should've introduced myself; I apologize."

"I'm fairly sure he would've told me if he was looking for a car. We've been so busy—"

"Oh dear. I think I've done it. I believe this was to be a belated wedding present?" He squinted feigning a request to be forgiven. "I'm afraid I've blown it completely here. Again, I'm so sorry."

Phoebe hesitated, then grinned. "Well, where is this car then?"

Salaman could not believe his luck. He pointed back to the tasting room. If you will accompany me, I'd be happy to show you. You can even take a test drive if you like."

Phoebe started to follow him down the path but suddenly stopped.

"I think I need to go home. Mr....?"

"Connally Bryce Connally."

"I'm sorry, but I just remembered I have left something back in the house. And I don't have my purse so I wouldn't be able to test drive it. I don't have a California license."

"I'm not a stickler for details, ma'am. You do drive, don't you?"

"A little."

"Well, you can just drive around the parking lot a bit. You should probably wait until your husband comes but I brought the car today and, well, I just thought I could surprise him. And now I see I have completely blown his secret. I'll come back later, and I'll give him a call first to make sure he's home."

The traveler turned, praying that he could lure Phoebe just a few steps more. If she were out of eyesight from any of the windows of the house, he could immobilize her quickly and then carry her to the car. Just in case, he fingered the little bottle in his pocket and felt the small square of flannel material he brought with it.

Just as he hoped, she called out to his back, "Mr. Connally, I think I'd like to take a look at the car. But I have to get back right away."

Salaman turned, showing his mirth. It wasn't an act. She was completely charming, as she made her way down the steps of the garden and headed right for him. In just a few seconds, he was looking into the soft face of beautiful Phoebe Jett. She was every bit as lovely as everyone said she was. The glow of her virgin womanhood was almost blinding him, as his pulse quickened. He understood immediately why Lionel was so much in love with her. She was graceful and innocent.

Her lack of fear would be her undoing.

He whispered so as not to spoil the moment. "Excellent. It would be my pleasure."

Chapter 15

THE HOUSE WAS in panic mode. Hugh was the first to burst into Lionel's bedroom, awakening him just before dusk. No one could remember seeing Phoebe since mid-day, and she had been outside, wandering in the garden, picking flowers. Her plastic bucket still sat on one of the cobblestone walls. The water was warm, so they deduced it had been there for several hours.

"Where was her detail?" asked Lionel.

Marcus had been on the phone, checking with everyone he could. "They were inside. There is no way to explain it. It is entirely my fault Lionel and I am horrified this is happened."

"Let's just focus on where she is."

It was difficult for Lionel to keep the horror of thoughts that kept creeping through his brain, especially knowing Phoebe may be able to hear them or feel them. But after he tried several times, unsuccessfully, to reach her, he knew that she was either immobilized, meaning unconscious, or worse yet, dead.

The thought that Salaman would have his hands on her, might touch her, or feed from her, sent rage into every cell of his body. Everything, including all of the promises he had made to her parents and to the Monteleones, was secondary. He'd eventually sort out everything, make amends, fix the whole rest of the damn world, but he had to find Phoebe. And he had to put an end to this devil's stranglehold on the family.

HE LOOKED AT the face of his employer, heavily lined, appearing to age decades in front of him. But Lionel couldn't focus on that. Just like he couldn't focus on what he would do if they be were suddenly permanently gone. Everything had to go into a rescue plan.

He closed his eyes and called out to her one more time, straining to feel if there was any disturbance anywhere, anything that came back to him, even a weakened signal from her. But absolutely nothing came back to him.

Jeb and Hugh were at his side. They knew, because they felt his frantic message to her, and they waited for further instructions.

Anne approached. "I should call her parents Lionel. It might be better if I did it. But of course they're going to want to hear from you."

"Of course." He knew he couldn't speak to them right now. It wasn't cowardice, because when the time came, he could have that conversation. He just didn't want to speak to them until he knew something further.

"I'll get on the phone as well," said Marcus, who followed his wife inside.

Jeb gave him a pat on the back. "What do you want us to do? Should we go through the day's events again? Do you want to speak to the detail? The staff, anyone who was not asleep during the afternoon?"

"Yes. Let's ask everybody again." He sat next to the pink bucket on the patio as Jeb left to arrange the interviews. As an afterthought, he shouted to Jeb's back, "No police, unless Marcus insists."

"You got it."

Cara approached, handing him a tumbler of brandy. "Take this Lionel. Time to go inside. You can't see anything out here."

He looked up at her face and although she was a respected family member, he was angry with her suggestion. The gap between their two worlds had never seemed wider.

"This *is* my world. Darkness is where I live. I see in the darkness. I feel things when I'm out here." He put his hand on the paint bucket. "This is as close to her as I can be right now."

Cara's outstretched hand still held the Tumblr. "Then take this from me, and I'll send the men out to see you here."

Lionel grabbed the Crystal and drank the Brandy in one gulp.

He was informed that there were staff members who had already gone home, and Marcus requested that everyone return. Several of the household staff lived on the property, so it would not be difficult to get them. But he was told the new vineyard crew lived wherever they could, all over the county.

"I want every single one of them. I don't want a single person not reached and brought here right now." Lionel demanded.

"We'll keep trying until we get them all," Marcus assured him.

The process took nearly an hour, and not everyone was able to be contacted, but Marcus told him that every group had at least one person to represent them. Also, during that period of time, he was told Phoebe's parents had been informed as were some of the family members in Tuscany. Marcus had placed a call to Carmine, just in case.

"I'm not sure he's been honest with us, again," said Marcus. "I will personally see to it that he pays for any involvement he has in this situation."

"At this point Marcus I don't care, but I look forward to handing out whatever justice he deserves."

A parade of men and household staff represented to Lionel. The patio lights were turned on, chairs were brought out to accommodate the group.

"So, we're going to start this all over again. I know Marcus and other members of the family have asked you questions. But I am convinced there's something we're not paying attention to. I want to hear from everybody when I ask you, a full and complete description of everybody you saw on this estate today."

He scanned the faces of the three former military men, three house staff, two men dressed in khaki uniforms, who appeared to be gardeners, and a young woman caring a child in a sarong about her chest.

"Does everybody speak English?"

Everybody nodded their heads with the exception of three individuals at the back of the group. Lionel motioned for them to come forward. "Do you speak English?"

The woman with a baby and the two men in khaki uniform looked between themselves and then turned for guidance to some of the group who stood behind them.

Lionel heard Hugh swear under his breath.

"Español." The woman with the baby said. "Only Espanol."

"Someone help her, please." Demanded Lionel. One of Marcus' house staff stepped up and agreed to help.

After a brief back-and-forth, the three Latino workers nodded their heads in agreement with their new translator.

"OK. So, has anyone today seen any strangers, someone new they haven't seen before? "Lionel waited for the translator, and then he watched the crowd's faces. No one's hand raised.

"Are you absolutely sure?"

THE THREE FORMER military men shook their heads quickly, several of the staff spoke softly amongst themselves and also indicated no. Lionel was about to ask another question when the translator pointed to the woman with the baby.

"Señor, she says that they saw a man and a woman. He was walking through the vineyard by himself, but then he comes back sometime later, with a woman."

"When did this occur?"

After checking, the translator responded, "She says it was about 2 o'clock. It was before and after they take a bathroom break."

"She was willingly walking with him?" Lionel asked.

"No, senior. She tells me that this man is carrying her like a child. She is sleeping."

"Did anyone else see this man?" Lionel asked. "Anyone?"

Again, the answer was no.

"Jeb go with this woman and have her show you where this occurred. I want to know what direction they went, and then check to see if there are any buildings around who might have security footage."

"I'm on it now."

Although the news wasn't good, he was grateful that the mystery was beginning to lift. The fog of uncertainty that was clouding his mind had started to dissipate.

Further questioning didn't give them any more information, so Lionel had the group dismissed.

"I'm going to call Carmine," said Lionel.

Marcus pulled out his telephone and dialed the Monteleones in Tuscany, then handed the phone to Lionel. "Tell him he has to make this right. I'm sure we don't have to tell him what the Council will do with him."

Lionel spoke into the phone. "No, it's me Lionel, but Marcus is here. You've heard?"

"I have. We are armed to the teeth here. So this means he is still in California?"

"Why did you tell us he had left?"

"After he told me what he was going to do to me and my family, he let it slip. He said he had wasted a good deal of time and that he'd come back later to finish the job when he could have the element of surprise. I thought he called to make sure I understood that everybody in my family was under threat of death."

"Do you have any way to reach him?"

"No. He always contacts me. He likes to just show up and insert himself into my life."

"Yes." Lionel hesitated, and then added, "I don't think I have to tell you that if he tries to contact you again, I want to know about it immediately, understood?"

"If I hear from him again, there's a high likelihood that I won't survive the meeting. But I'll try to find some way to get you a message. He never lets people who cross him get away with it."

"What was to be your job, Carmine?"

"My job?"

"What did he want you to do?"

"Originally, I was to get invited to Marcus' estate, and report back about the location of the book. Possibly help him get it. Lionel, you know that's what he really wants."

"I'm not so sure."

"If you ask me, he's going to use her so he can get that book. You, Marcus, everybody needs to be prepared for that request. I don't think he would just take her and disappear. What he really wants is the *Book of Spawn*."

Inside, Lionel sat with Hugh and Marcus. Anne and Cara tended to the children, putting them to bed and then later joined them. As the three men talked, the wives turned pages of the ancient text, studying several maps and pictures.

"When he requests the exchange," Marcus started, "I want you to do it Lionel, if you would. And I think you should take your brothers with you." He looked down at his empty brandy and then shook his head. "I'm giving you full authorization to terminate him if you can. I'm not asking for permission, I don't want any Council interference."

"You could not have stopped me, Marcus. If there is any certainty out of this situation, I believe in my heart that he will not kill or even damage her, until he has the opportunity to get the text. We have leverage, and it's huge."

"And so is the risk, Lionel. But that's why you should be the only one to handle it."

Jeb returned with a thumb drive which he placed in Anne's computer. They all watched the video clip of Salaman loading Phoebe into the back of the SUV like a piece of luggage. And then he drove away.

Upon closer examination, they were able to get an enhanced picture of the license plate and its number. They also identified the vehicle as a black Lexus SUV.

It was now time to involve the local Healdsburg police and the Sonoma County Sheriff.

Chapter 16

THE TRAVELER DROVE past a local hardware store, where he had previously seen groups of would-be workers standing in one corner of the parking lot, waiting to be picked up for day jobs. Although it was dark, he found a group of nearly a dozen sitting by a fire made from a metal drum. Usually undocumented workers, they did cash jobs, and not too many questions were asked or answered.

Salaman didn't even care if they spoke English or not. They did hard manual work and wouldn't complain. Most of all, they were not connected to any form of law-enforcement, so using them was less of a risk.

He slowed as he entered the parking lot, kept the engine running, stepped out of the driver seat and motioned, holding two fingers up, indicating he needed two workers. A third man offered his services and Salaman sent him away.

"Get in."

One worker was gray-haired and wore a straw cowboy hat, which he removed before he sat down. The other worker appeared to be about in his mid-twenties. Without saying a word, they strapped themselves in and Salaman brought his little crew to the winery and then parked in the rear where the cabin was.

Next door was a large warehouse where several pieces of farm equipment were stored, as well as the remnants of a large truck. The vineyard manager stored several cases of weed killer and insecticide in a locked room with steel bars. He found tools, mainly shovels and rakes, along with some gloves and wire cutters.

He brought them inside, had them get the shovels and gloves, and showed them a place just off of the gravel driveway in the middle between two rows of vines, a place that had been freshly tilled. He held up his fingers again.

"Two."

He took a metal stake and drew large squares in the soft soil, indicating where he wanted them to dig. He held his hands proximately 4 feet apart to indicate how deep he wanted them to go. Both men removed their jackets, took the shovels and gloves from him and began to work.

Whenever he traveled, he brought a suitcase full of pieces of equipment that were coated in silver. He whistled, asking the men to follow him to the cabin where he had them bring a mattress he found, while he lugged the large suitcase with his equipment in it.

He ordered them to go back to work after the mattress and suitcase were placed on one long wall without windows. It was approximately twenty feet from the locked storage area.

Opening his suitcase, he laid aside the lightweight metal fabric, his invention, manufactured with threads of silver woven in into the material. Beneath the folded material was a set of bolt cutters which he used to snap open the padlock on the door and have access to the poison room. He took out one of several silver coated chains with a padlock and looped it around the opened door.

Searching for other items he could use, he found a red gasoline can, a cooler containing an unopened case of water bottles, several garbage cans filled with machine parts, and trash. He also located a rusted-out Skill saw which he doubted would work. He found three packages of nails and screws, several hammers as well as two screw guns that hadn't yet lost their battery power.

Next to a pile of six well-worn heavy equipment tires, he located a sheet of corrugated metal flashing and an old bench seat from a pickup truck. He almost toppled the ashtrays, overflowing with cigarette butts. At last, he was delighted to find a book of matches. He had everything he needed to create a huge bonfire that would attract attention for miles.

After moving everything but the tires, and even dragging the bench seat, everything he planned on needing was located in one spot close to the mattress.

With all of the items organized, he was pleased with what he'd found.

He needed to check on Phoebe's condition and bring her into the warehouse without his helpers seeing her. He repositioned the car just outside the sliding barn door at the back. Opening the hatch, he lifted her up and inside, carrying her to the mattress on the floor. The trunk of Joel's SUV contained an old quilt which he retrieved and placed over Phoebe's body. He checked her pulse, and her eyes. He moved her head back-and-forth lightly slapping her cheek to see if he could rouse her and found that she was still unconscious. But her pulse was weaker than he wanted, her body heat was low, so he knew he had to be careful with future injections.

He sat on the truck bench and walked through what he had to do before he made the call.

He brought two bottles of water out to the men who had nearly finished their trenches. He held up two thumbs, indicating he was pleased with their work.

Salaman did not have a soft spot in his heart, but he did feel like rewarding good behavior with another good deed, so he decided to spare their lives. He brought the SUV around and asked them to get in, explaining that he was going to take them back to the hardware store. One of the men took both shovels and headed for the door of the barn and Salaman stopped him immediately.

"Not necessary. Leave them there," he pointed. Again, motioning to the car, he had them get in and he began the short drive back to the hardware store. The sun was beginning to set, and that meant the Brothers would be out and about soon. He was running out of time.

He wondered if the workers had any idea how close to death they'd been. If they'd put up some kind of a fight, it might have been fun to spar with them a bit. But they did perform work he would have wrenched his back over, so they were useful. Besides, there was no sport in people who were cooperative. And their deaths wouldn't make the kind of statement he wanted to make.

Just as they turned inside the parking lot, he stopped, got out his wallet, and paid them each forty dollars.

He considered buying some sort of snack food inside the hardware store but vetoed it, because he was impatient to get his plan going. On the way back to the warehouse he also considered calling Carmine and getting him involved again. But he ruled it out, guessing that by now, the Golden clans would be checking his every movement. He couldn't afford to be traced. Not until he wanted them to.

The sky was now fully darkened. About halfway to the warehouse and cabin, he noticed he'd picked up a local sheriff. The car had two occupants and lingered back far enough so as not to appear ready to pounce. No doubt they were calling in their sighting. So Salaman knew he had to lead them away from where he had Phoebe stored. The inconvenience irritated him.

Instead of turning down the winery road he kept going straight, the road winding along the banks of the Russian River, heading into dense clumps of redwood trees here and there. Summer cabins dotted the roadway. He was looking for a driveway with multiple mailboxes, hoping to find something private and difficult to describe.

He located the perfect narrow gravel road, marked with a hand-made sign, framed by a dozen mailboxes lined up in a row. By moonlight, he could barely make out the hill above. It appeared to be steep with deep canyons, covered in fir and redwood trees. Just after he turned, he saw the patrol car give him distance, but make the same turn, which confirmed the jig was up and they were onto him. It was time to act fast.

Pulling into a random driveway, he parked his car in front of an opened garage packed to the gills with junk, and waited, leaving the engine running and his lights on.

The patrol car blocked his retreat. One officer on the passenger side approached while the other stayed behind the wheel.

The traveler rolled down his window, peering up at the beefy officer, who had one hand on the service weapon he'd just unsnapped from his belt, and the other holding a flashlight he shone in his eyes.

Salaman knew what was coming next, so, before the uniform could ask the appropriate question, he plunged a six-inch blade right into the middle of his gut. Out of control now, the officer couldn't help but pitch forward, bumping his head on the roof of the SUV. That gave Salaman just enough time to retrieve his knife and slit his jugular, which dropped him to the ground.

In his rearview mirror, Salaman observed the driver on the radio. Putting the Lexus in reverse, he rammed the patrol car, pushing it off the narrow driveway and down into the ravine, where it tumbled, overturning several times, until it reached the bottom.

He knew his chances for escape were predicated on his leaving the scene quickly or he'd get ensnared in a multiple call event, which would certainly result in his capture. He raced back to the main road leading to the winery, back down in the valley floor, rounding the corner just before he heard sirens arriving in the distance.

He left the Lexus at the back of the warehouse and ran through the sliding door.

Just as he'd feared, he saw Phoebe beginning to stir. He quickly took out the drug kit from his tool bag and administered the tranquilizer, which stopped her movement.

Her forehead was getting cold, and Salaman began to worry. He needed to speed up the process. He had no choice but to call Carmine Monteleone.

"Shut up and if you value the lives of your family you'll do exactly as I say," The traveler commanded.

He heard Carmine's gasp of fear.

"I just talked to them about an hour ago. They know about you, Traveler. I think you're fucked."

"Yeah? Seems to me I do hold some pretty important cards. But never mind. I could care less what you think about it. You're in no position to negotiate."

"I can't help you. I promised. They're watching me."

"I'll bet they are. I'm counting on it."

"I—I can't travel. I'm not going there anymore."

"I don't want you to. And since when is your word worth anything? Remember, I chose you because you're a good liar. But don't you dare lie to me."

"I can't help you."

"You're going to have to. I want you to call Marcus Monteleone and arrange for a trade. I have Phoebe, and I want to exchange her for the Book of Spawn," he said.

"That's what I told them. I told them you would trade."

"That's very good, Carmine. I'm actually pleased you said that. So, you have Marcus come all by himself. Not with any of his attack dogs. And he's to bring the book. Once I have it, I'll release Phoebe."

"Where?" Carmine asked.

Salaman gave the address of the cottage. "Tell him I'll be waiting there. Once I have the book, I'll let him know where he can pick up Phoebe."

"After this, I'm done. No more of this. As it is, I'll be lucky if they don't strip me of all my land holdings. I'll be begging on the streets."

"You'll be done when I say you'll be done." The groan he heard on the other end of the line was satisfying. "I'm going to call you in five minutes, and you can report back that he's agreed to come."

Chapter 17

LIONEL RECEIVED A very weak message from Phoebe lasting less than thirty seconds. She was confused, her head hurt, and she was trying to recount what had happened, but the link kept going in and out, from a jumble of emotions to blankness. He immediately reached out, trying to strengthen the connection, repeating his question over and over again to find out her location. He hoped that he could then follow, trace to her side.

Everyone in the house held their breath as he repeated and then awaited her instructions.

But before Phoebe could answer, their link completely disappeared. No matter how intensely he tried, he just couldn't reach her. A wave of sadness washed over him as he wondered if he'd lost her.

Jeb and Hugh were at his side, consoling him. "Have I failed to get there in time?" he sobbed. Nothing the brothers could say would remove his total sense of dread. Marcus had an explanation.

"I think she's being drugged. I think that perhaps she started to come to and then was drugged again," he whispered. "That's the only explanation for this."

"Unless she's gone. Oh, the God of Vampires has failed me!" Lionel shouted, making the windows in the entire estate rattle. He tore himself loose from his brothers' embrace and began to pace the room. Every object he looked at he wanted to destroy, and he had the strength to do it, too. His fingernails dug into his palms while he clutched and scratched at the very air he breathed, trying to hold on to some trace of her.

Just then, Marcus received a call from the Sonoma County Sheriff. He put it to speaker phone so everyone could hear.

"We had a car following a Lexus of that description. They've not been able to verify the plate, but it appears to have a single occupant."

"Where? I need an address," Lionel barked.

"The vehicle is moving, but as soon as our deputy checks in, we'll get that for you."

Marcus interrupted. "Can you give us some street coordinates? Perhaps we could send someone to assist in the search."

"We generally don't want civilian population involved—"

"This is an extremely special case," Marcus returned. "We have assets—"

"As soon as they check in. They were headed out River Road, away from town, and that's all I'm going to be able to give you, Marcus."

Lionel looked up and saw the raw pain and determination of his two brothers. "Do you think—?"

"On it," Hugh said. The two conferred, picking a location they were familiar with and were gone within seconds.

Lionel tried to reach Phoebe, but still the connection was silent.

Anne and Cara appeared at the doorway to Marcus' library, Paolo trailing a short distance behind. Cara held the Book in her hands. "We've found something, Marcus." She brought the heavy tome over to where Lionel had seated himself, laying it on his lap and turning it around.

"We started looking for the plate Phoebe accessed yesterday," Anne began. "And we've found it."

She fingered a piece of paper used to save a location, opening it on Lionel's lap. Everyone saw the drawing with the cage and the lion.

"Look at what's in the cage," Cara pointed.

Lionel focused on the drawing, seeing objects he'd not recalled before. The lion looked the same, in stylized, seated form, like a statue on a pyramid or temple, proudly looking down on the woman lying on the ground before his feet. Beside him lay a book, a very thick book, like the one that was on his lap.

"Oh my God!" he gasped. "What does this mean?"

Cara answered first. "We don't know, but I have a hunch. Touch it, Lionel. Run your fingers over it just like Phoebe did yesterday."

As he did so, letters appeared at the side. Anne and Cara smiled to each other.

"Marcus, can you read this? I believe it's Latin," Lionel asked.

He knelt to get a better view. Lionel took his fingers off the page and the letters disappeared.

"No, keep touching it, don't stop," said Paolo.

Marcus craned his neck and mumbled something, testing out a meaning, and then stopped. "It doesn't make sense."

"Tell me, dammit," Lionel demanded.

"Bonds of the heart are stronger than blood," or something to that effect."

"Do you suppose the words are different for Phoebe?" Paolo asked.

"Could be. But my sense is this is you, Lionel. This lion is you."

"And the woman must be Phoebe. Where, where is this cage?"

"But don't you see?" said Cara. "This shows you together, Lionel. You've found her. And these words are the key."

"Try sending something to her from your heart. Don't think about it. Feel your message coming to her from your heart. It's a healing message, not a request for information," explained Anne.

Her comment sent Marcus on his rear. "I wonder—"

Lionel closed his eyes and let the warmth in his chest expand until he could feel the heavy thumping of his heart muscle throughout his body. He didn't use words, but searched for her not in a place, but by searching for a match to the vibrations of his heart.

And he found her. He even saw her moving.

A shadow crossed his vision and he retreated to a corner to remain undetected. He was vaguely aware someone had tucked the folded book under his arm and as he held it securely, he traced to the room where Phoebe lay on a dirty mattress.

But she was not alone. Salaman had just injected her with a yellowish liquid. He tried to scream but found he had no voice.

He reached out again from his heart, sending healing her way in a vapor Salaman apparently couldn't detect. But Phoebe stopped moaning and lay perfectly still.

A cell phone rang and in the distance. He heard Marcus answer it.

"Tell me again," he heard Marcus say as the response was played on speaker.

"I'm on my way," Marcus whispered. Lionel said the same, which drew the attention of Salaman.

The tracing was complete. Lionel stood in the middle of a locked compartment. A few feet away, Phoebe's lifeless body lay on the mattress he'd visualized before. Salaman was headed right for him, and then he noticed the silver chains wound around the closure.

He kicked the door grate wide open before the chains could be wrapped around the bars, but Salaman still stood in front of him holding the shiny links. He threw them at Lionel, catching him on the left arm and causing him to drop the book. The echo of the heavy text hitting the concrete floor sounded like canon fire.

Silver burns began to send Lionel's shirt into flames. He quickly shed the white fabric and threw it on the ground. It landed on top of the book.

Salaman screamed, running to protect the precious ancient pages. Lionel traced beyond the storage room to the other side, next to Anne, picking her up, prepared to trace.

Marcus suddenly appeared and began kicking Salaman hard as he bent over the floor stamping out flames of a rapidly spreading fire. Part of the cover was already burning. He kicked the mortal devil again and then yanked him up by his arms, shaking him until he could hear the crunch of bone. The man's scream was cut short when Marcus twisted his head around, breaking his neck.

Flames were spreading when the fire hit the gasoline canister and exploded.

"Go!" Marcus yelled.

Lionel had already begun to trace the two of them back to the Monteleone estate.

The last he saw of Marcus was as he pulled the burning book from the floor and tucked it to his chest.

Lionel and Phoebe appeared on the patio near Anne's flower garden. He heard faint sirens in the distance, and ran inside, laying the lifeless Phoebe down on the couch just as Marcus arrived. Deep red and black burn marks scarred his skin. His hands were black, but they still held the smoldering book, which he dropped to the floor.

"Is she alive?" he wanted to know.

Lionel checked her pulse and felt her cool, clammy skin. His heart sank. He knew the lifeforce was leaving her, her heartbeat was slowing down and soon would stop.

"He's overdosed her," Lionel gasped. "I'm losing her."

All four people in the room knew the choices that had to be made. Even if it meant breaking all the taboos, Phoebe's life came first.

Lionel only had seconds. He began to open his wrist.

"Wait!" Cara screamed. "Trace to the chapel, the place you were married. Or, Marcus you will have to do it. Otherwise, she'll be dark."

"We have no more time." Marcus' calm demeanor helped Lionel think.

The words. What are the words?

"The heart is stronger than the blood," Lionel recited. "I'm going to try."

"Wait," Marcus interrupted him. "It's nearly sunrise there. Will you make it before it turns day?"

"I must," Lionel said as he grabbed Phoebe and traced to the chapel. He pushed out of his mind all the concerns about it being full of worshipers, or that he'd land in the narthex by open doors and would end up in a fireball, killing the woman he loved. But he shut everything off, opened his eyes and was blissfully engulfed in cool darkness.

He'd heard about these turnings, supposed to be done by a priest, but also could be done by a fated mate, and Lionel was certain they were. He only hoped he hadn't gotten there too late.

He lay her down on the cool marble slab of the altar, brushing aside the crosses and gold implements of their service. Her beautiful lips were turning blue, just like dying looked on the mortals he'd seen.

With tears streaming down his cheeks, he spoke the words again. And again. He cut his wrist and applied his blood to her mouth, puckering her a bit so it would fall on her tongue.

She didn't move.

He deepened the cut, applying it again to her mouth, and was about to slice deeper when her upper torso arched up and she gasped for breath. She was still limp, but she was breathing, craving the blood of his body, and her color was pinking up.

Both Marcus and Paolo suddenly appeared, running down the center aisle toward them both.

"She's breathing!" he shouted.

Phoebe's hands came up to his forearm and she grabbed him tight, taking in more of Lionel's blood. At last, she opened her eyes.

She saw his tears, and worry overtook her expression. Marcus and Paolo stood beside him as she asked, "What have you done?"

Lionel was relieved he'd saved her life, but suddenly ashamed he'd not turned her as he'd wanted.

"Forgive me, my beloved. Please forgive me. I have forever taken away your mortal life. I will leave you, if you desire, but you are safe now. I would not be able to live with myself if I didn't do this."

He couldn't stop the visions of their lovemaking and how he ached for her. His chest was warmed by the memories of exploration that had grown what he was sure was their destiny. He was grateful they'd had those days, and wondered if her recall would do the same, softening her heart. But she did not smile. She sat, stunned.

And then she began speaking the words he'd spoken to her, "The bonds of the heart are stronger than blood. You said that to me."

"Yes."

He watched her examine her hands and rub her tongue over her teeth. She closed her eyes and when she opened them, she finally smiled. Lionel's heart leapt.

Two small fangs protruded beneath her upper lip.

"I am alive. I felt myself die, my spirit left my body."

"But you came back. Our love brought you back." He embraced her tenderly, careful not to hurt her fragile body.

Marcus cleared his throat, attempting to get their attention. Lionel turned to him, but Phoebe remained fixated on her husband.

"I've seen it done, some of these ceremonies," he said softly. "Go ahead and complete the cycle. You should drink from her, let her body give you back the life that you've given her, and perhaps you will be turned as well with her Golden blood."

"I already have," Lionel whispered. "And we are not only a fated pair, but we are a mated pair as well."

"I'm going to let you explain all this to her parents, then." Marcus and Paolo took several steps back and disappeared into the ether.

"No more secrets?" she asked, her forefinger rubbing against his lower lip. She was continuing to warm up to him, her cheeks now flushed and healthy.

"None. Everything I have is yours, Phoebe. It always will be." His doubts crept in again. "Do you suppose we are the same, or different?"

"Does it matter?"

"No, sweet Phoebe, because the heart is stronger. What I have inside is stronger than how I was made."

"Can I try?" she asked, rolling up her lip to show her fangs.

"With pleasure. And may I?"

"With wild abandon."

"Should we trace home, do it there?" he asked.

"Why take chances with our eternity? Take from me now, while I do the same. We'll add all the rest when we're back in California, unless you want to join me in Hell."

Phoebe's smile was wide. She was self-conscious of how it exposed her new identity, and Lionel knew she'd make the adjustment in time, like he had. She brushed her hair from her neck and shoulder as he kissed the side of her cheek and nibbled kisses under her ear. He heard her moan as he dug deep, tasting the sweet elixir of his beloved.

There was no doubt in Lionel's mind that she'd changed. He thanked the God of Vampires for giving him the chance to have eternity with the one he loved.

'Teach me, Phoebe. Help me become your perfect mate.'

'You already are, Lionel.'

Her hot breath made the hairs on the back of his neck stand to attention. As he had instructed, she kissed a line from his ear down to his clavicle, coating it with her tongue. She bit down, breeching his skin, completing the eternal cycle.

Chapter 18

SHE WOULD REMEMBER that day in Tuscany, so different than the last time she was in that chapel. That had been her wedding day. This had been the first day of her real life. She trusted the words Lionel had whispered to her, the words he'd read in the *Book of Spawn*. If it was really true, and not some gothic fairytale, he'd be able to take those first steps out of the chapel, and walk with her through the busy streets, losing himself in the crowd of shoppers.

As the large carved oak doors creaked open, sunlight flooded the foyer, casting bright streaks across the black and cream tiled room. It illuminated the white marble holy water font and the tips of his shoes. They held hands, side by side. He paused.

"Are you sure you're ready?" she asked. "Remember, you asked me that a few days ago, remember?"

Lionel was in deep contemplation, but that generated a smile on his lips. "I remember every detail of that evening." He squeezed her hand, but still stared down at his feet.

"Do you feel anything through your shoes?"

"It's warm. The sun is warm."

"Lionel, look at me," she teased. "You'll remind me if you're about to turn into a human candle, right?"

Their eyes locked. "You don't want to die with me today?" After first being expressionless, his warm brown eyes smiled before his lips did.

She was bathed in sunlight. He was still in the shadows. He bent forward. She hadn't realized the real color of his hair, or the fact that his eyelashes were extremely long, and dark. His flawless handsomeness was even more attractive in the pink early morning sun. He licked his lips, and then caressed a kiss from hers. She wrapped her arms around him and twirled slowly, dancing with him, bringing him out of the shadows and fully into the light. He held her face between his enormous palms and kissed her again.

Her heart was ready to burst from her chest. Taking his hand in hers, she led him down the stone steps of the chapel to the busy street corner, where he viewed the landscape in front of him.

"I'd forgotten," he whispered.

"Forgotten what?"

"How bright it was. You have to remember, it's been over three hundred years, Phoebe. The first thing I'm going to do is buy some sunglasses."

She laughed and hugged him again. "Now I know you're going to be okay."

THEY STROLLED THE farmer's market after being unsuccessful in the shopping district finding a baseball cap large enough to fit on Lionel's large head. He picked up a pair of glasses with the side sunshields on them, and Lionel was finally happy. He refused to wear anything like a floppy straw hat she'd offered him. She suggested they visit her parents and he quickly declined.

Phoebe noticed he was moving slower and slower, so she asked what was wrong, wondering if something about the turning had not completed.

"There's too much distraction. Too much noise. I can't think."

"You want to sit down somewhere? We can have a coffee," she offered.

He cupped her jaw with one palm. "I want to go back. I belong in California with the family, Phoebe. I don't want to be here anymore. I'd like to see my brothers."

They returned to the little chapel, which was hosting mass. Lionel drew her into a dark corner in the foyer, away from any curious eyes, wrapped his arms around her and traced them back to Healdsburg.

Their bed was freshly made. A huge bouquet of Anne's flowers sat on the small table between the two golden settees. The windows were drawn closed.

"Wait until you see the view. It's the most spectacular in all the world, Lionel."

"Everything turns," he whispered in her ear.

"That's a nice thought," she said as she leaned against him, enjoying the sound of his breathing and the feel of his arms around her waist.

"Marcus told me that was one of the first things he showed Anne. It's a balance, a cycle in nature. We are all part of it, not separate from it. I think that's part of the story of the Book."

"You're right. It sort of makes me wonder about all the rules that were imposed on all of us for centuries, when the answer was simple, right there in front of everyone all along."

"The council, the hierarchy, dark covens and Goldens fighting over control. It didn't have to happen. None of it did."

They heard sounds of Jeb and Hugh shouting, running up the stairway, which caused the whole house to shake.

"It shouldn't be kept a secret, Phoebe. No one owns it. It belongs to everybody."

Their kiss was interrupted with the brothers, separating them, raising Lionel up into the air and carrying him downstairs. Left alone, she was suddenly tired.

Anne and Cara were at her doorway.

"Is it true?" Cara asked. "Are you both turned?" Both women ran to her.

"Give me a few days to make sure I don't start losing body parts, but I think everything went okay. I am getting stronger by the hour. And Lionel has spent time in the sun without problem."

"What a miracle!" said Anne.

The family celebrated until dawn, when at last Jeb and Hugh returned to their cottage. Phoebe was exhausted, so Lionel traced her to the upper landing outside their bedroom door.

In the quiet of their little sanctuary, the lovemaking once again filled her heart with flame. As she lay in Lionel's arms, she understood the true depth of being a fated mate.

PHOEBE AWOKE LATE, pushing open the windows so she could see the vineyards below. Lionel joined her, still naked. "Come back to bed."

"But look. This is the view you always imagined. See how everything grows? Just like you said last night."

She watched the sun brighten his face. Unless she was mistaken, water had collected in the corners of his eyes. He was taking it all in.

"I have a request, husband."

"Oh yes? Can I afford it?"

"If you'll give me the gift of your time."

"All of it is yours, you know that, Phoebe."

She allowed her forefinger to outline his lips. He moved closer to her and she could feel his arousal growing. Their thighs touched slightly. Her breath hitched as his fingers traveled down her arms and then to her waist as he pulled her into his groin.

"Tell me what it is you want, and it's yours, Phoebe. But do it quick, or I'll not let you loose for another several hours. You'll be my captive."

She leaned into him, pressing her chest against his, pulled his head down and kissed him. "As wonderful as that sounds, I'm taking you into my dreams."

"You already have done that," he said as he pulled her toward the bed.

"I want to take a picnic."

He was kissing her neck, then lifted her gently onto the bedcovers. "Tell me more," he whispered as he kissed her belly button, and then lower.

The feel of his tongue on her sex made her quiver with pleasure. She couldn't speak.

"You were telling me about a picnic, Phoebe."

"I can't think—"

He kissed her again, and then layered the kisses all the way up her side until he was covering her body once again. "A picnic, you said?"

he whispered in her ear.

"Yes."

"In the sunshine? We'll make love in the vineyard?"

"Yes. Oh yes."

"I'd like that, Phoebe, very much," he said as he entered her deep.

"Can we do that?"

"Will there be whipped cream?" he asked.

"I promise."

She gasped as he began moving back and forth inside her, sending chills down her spine. Finally, he said, "How about tomorrow?"

About the Author

S. HAMIL, Sharon Hamilton's twisted sister, writes paranormal romance with a central theme of the healing power of true love. Her characters from multiple worlds including Heaven and the Underworld are angels, dark angels, vampires and some who are not quite sure what they are. They follow a bumpy path to redemption, but not exactly what they taught you in Sunday School!

She loves hearing from her fans:
Sharonhamilton2001@gmail.com

Her website is:
sharonhamiltonauthor.com

Find out more about S. Hamil, her upcoming releases, appearances and news when you sign up for S. Hamil's newsletter.

Facebook:
facebook.com/SharonHamiltonAuthor

Twitter:
twitter.com/sharonlhamilton

Pinterest:
pinterest.com/AuthorSharonH

Amazon:
amazon.com/Sharon-Hamilton/e/B004FQQMAC

BookBub:
bookbub.com/authors/sharon-hamilton

Youtube:
youtube.com/channel/UCDInkxXFpXp_4Vnq08ZxMBQ

Soundcloud:
soundcloud.com/sharon-hamilton-1

S. Hamil's Rockin' Romance Readers:
facebook.com/groups/sealteamromance

S. Hamil's Goodreads Group:
goodreads.com/group/show/199125-sharon-hamilton-readers-group

Visit S. Hamil's Online Store:
sharon-hamilton-author.myshopify.com

Join S. Hamil's Review Teams:

eBook Reviews:
sharonhamiltonassistant@gmail.com

Audio Reviews:
sharonhamiltonassistant@gmail.com

Life is one fool thing after another.
Love is two fool things after each other.

Reviews

"Well to say the least I was thoroughly surprise. I have read many Vampire books, from Ann Rice to Kym Grosso and few other Authors, so yes I do like Vampires, not the super scary ones from the old days, but the new ones are far more interesting far more human than one can remember. I found Honeymoon Bite a totally engrossing book, I was not able to put it down, page after page I found delight, love, understanding, well that is until the bad bad Vamp started being really bad. But seeing someone love another person so much that they would do anything to protect them, well that had me going, then well there was more and for a while I thought it was the end of a beautiful love story that spanned not only time but, spanned Italy and California. Won't divulge how it ended, but I did shed a few tears after screaming but Sharon Hamilton did not let me down, she took me on amazing trip that I loved, look forward to reading another Vampire book of hers."

"An excellent paranormal romance that was exciting, romantic, entertaining and very satisfying to read. It had me anticipating what would happen next many times over, so much so I could not put it down and even finished it up in a day. The vampires in this book were different from your average vampire, but I enjoy different variations and changes to the same old stuff. It made for a more unpredictable read and more adventurous to explore! Vampire lovers, any paranormal readers and even those who love the romance genre will enjoy Honeymoon Bite."

"This is the first non-Seal book of this author's I have read and I loved it. There is a cast-like hierarchy in this vampire community with humans at the very bottom and Golden vampires at the top. Lionel is a dark vampire who are servants of the Goldens. Phoebe is a Golden who has not decided if she will remain human or accept the turning to become a vampire. Either way she and Lionel can never be together since it is forbidden.

I enjoyed this story and I am looking forward to the next installment."

"A hauntingly romantic read. Old love lost and new love found. Family, heart, intrigue and vampires. Grabbed my attention and couldn't put down. Would definitely recommend."

PRAISE FOR THE
SEAL BROTHERHOOD SERIES

"Fans of Navy SEAL romance, I found a new author to feed your addiction. Finely written and loaded delicious with moments, Sharon Hamilton's storytelling satisfies like a thick bar of chocolate." — Marliss Melton, bestselling author of the *Team Twelve* Navy SEALs series

"Sharon Hamilton does an EXCELLENT job of fitting all the characters into a brotherhood of SEALS that may not be real but sure makes you feel that you have entered the circle and security of their world. The stories intertwine with each book before...and each book after and THAT is what makes Sharon Hamilton's SEAL Brotherhood Series so very interesting. You won't want to put down ANY of her books and they will keep you reading into the night when you should be sleeping. Start with this book...and you will not want to stop until you've read the whole series and then...you will be waiting for Sharon to write the next one." (5 Star Review)

"Kyle and Christy explode all over the pages in this first book, *[Accidental SEAL]*, in a whole new series of SEALs. If the twist and turns don't get your heart jumping, then maybe the suspense will. This is a must read for those that are looking for love and adventure with a little sloppy love thrown in for good measure." (5 Star Review)

PRAISE FOR THE
BAD BOYS OF SEAL TEAM 3 SERIES

"I love reading this series! Once you start these books, you can hardly put them down. The mix of romance and suspense keeps you turning the pages one right after another! Can't wait until the next book!" (5 Star Review)

"I love all of Sharon's Seal books, but [SEAL's Code] may just be her best to date. Danny and Luci's journey is filled with a wonderful insight into the Native American life. It is a love story that will fill you with warmth and contentment. You will enjoy Danny's journey to become a SEAL and his reasons for it. Good job Sharon!" (5 Star Review)

PRAISE FOR THE
BAND OF BACHELORS SERIES

"[Lucas] was the first book in the Band of Bachelors series and it was a phenomenal start. I loved how we got to see the other SEALs we all love and we got a look at Lucas and Marcy. They had an instant attraction, and their love was very intense. This book had it all, suspense, steamy romance, humor, everything you want in a riveting, outstanding read. I can't wait to read the next book in this series." (5 Star Review)

PRAISE FOR THE
TRUE BLUE SEALS SERIES

"Keep the tissues box nearby as you read *True Blue SEALs: Zak* by Sharon Hamilton. I imagine more than I wish to that the circumstances surrounding Zak and Amy are all too real for returning military personnel and their families. Ms. Hamilton has put us right in the middle of struggles and successes that these two high school sweethearts endure. I have read several of Sharon Hamilton's military romances but will say this is the most emotionally intense of the ones that I have read. This is a well-written, realistic story with authentic characters that will have you rooting for them and proud of those who serve to keep us safe. This is an author who writes amazing stories that you love and cry with the characters. Fans of Jessica Scott and Marliss Melton will want to add Sharon Hamilton to their list of realistic military romance writers." (5 Star Review)